THRONES OF SHADOWS & FLAMES

The Five Realms   Book Three

JENESSA REN

Olymazi
Vitour
Galdr
Molsi

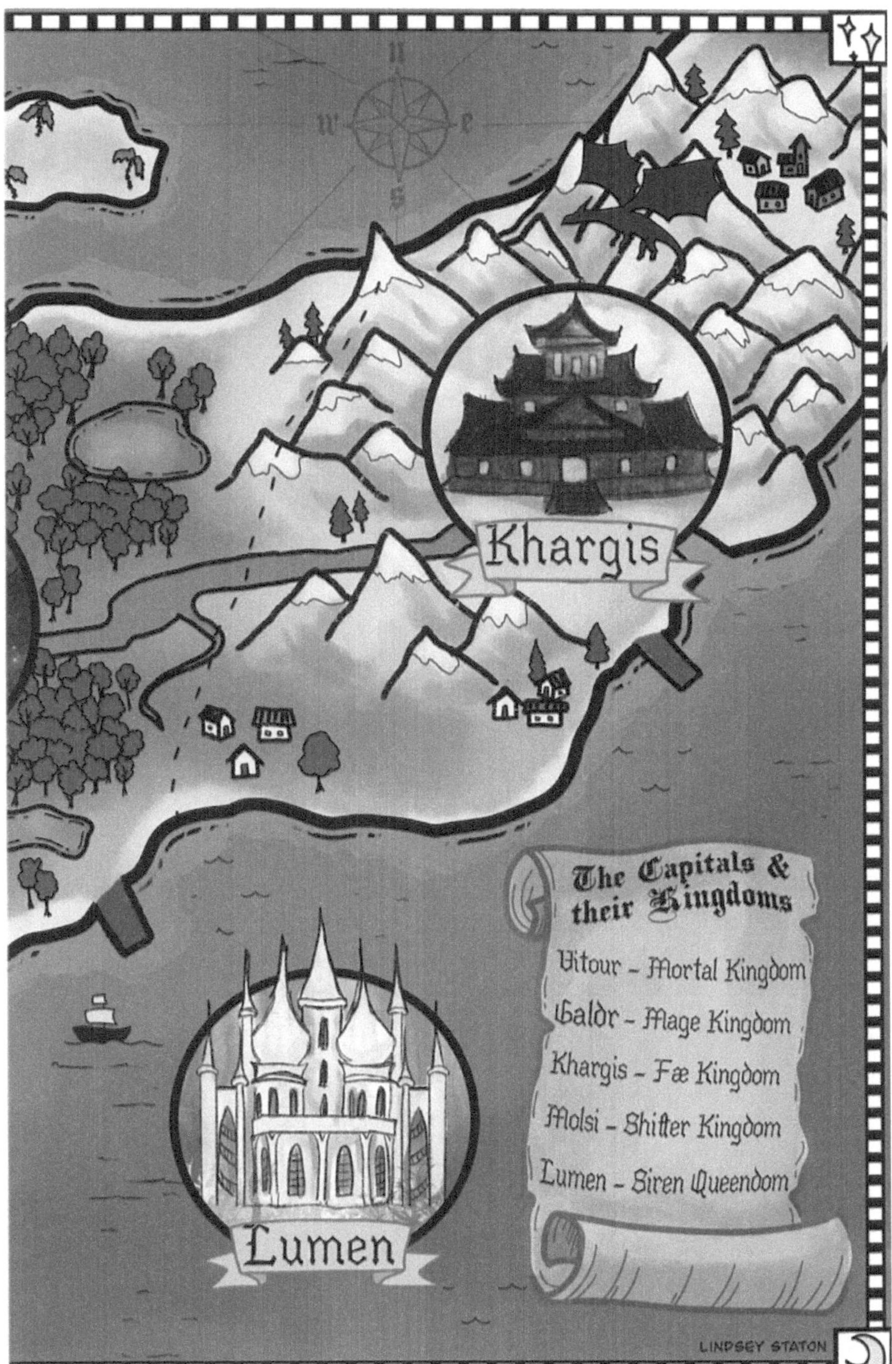

Khargis
Lumen
The Capitals &
their Kingdoms
Vitour – Mortal Kingdom
Galdr – Mage Kingdom
Khargis – Fæ Kingdom
Molsi – Shifter Kingdom
Lumen – Siren Queendom
LINDSEY STATON

Content Warnings

This story contains depictions of:
    Suicide ideation and attempted suicide
    Physchological and physical torture
    Mental, verbal, emotional, and psychological abuse and manipulation
    Sexual assault and sexual coercion
    Gore, murder, and death, including that of a pregnant being (off page)
    Depression, anxiety, and depictions of grief
    Religious trauma and manipulation
    Sexually explicit scenes
    Adult content
    Incest ideation

Each topic has been approached sensitively and written with the utmost respect and care, but should any of these topics be triggering for you, please do not read.
Your mental health matters.
-Jenessa

For every woman who has smiled through pain. Who has screamed in heartache.
Who stood up for herself.
And for every woman who couldn't.
For every woman who held on to her softness, despite how the world tried to take
it, and for every one who let rage fuel her. Sharpen her.
This book is for you.

Prologue

SUMMER SOLSTICE

Twenty-two years prior...

She came when the sun was at its highest in the sky.

I woke and marveled at the beautiful summer day, at how the sky seemed more blue, the meadows just past the castle more green as pops of purple, red, yellow, and white dotted the landscape. Drinking tea from my balcony, the warm air brushing against my cheek, I had thought to myself that it was a lovely day for this baby to arrive. And maybe it was luck or something more serendipitous, but the moment the thought flitted from my mind, the first pains of labor began.

The midwives warn me that it will be difficult as they prepare the bed for me to lay in, explaining that a baby's preference is to stay in the womb. They make it sound violent, like each push by my body is the equivalent of yanking my baby away from the only comfort and safety she has known for months and months. In truth, it terrifies me to know that her first moments after crossing the veil from womb to world will be filled with pain. But the birth is gentle. As if she knows it is her time to come. Between one breath and the next, she is born. *She.* I collapse back onto the bed, eyes shutting as joy suffuses me.

"She's silent," Conrad whispers to the head midwife, Lilah, from where he is sitting by my side, a hand gently brushing hair from my face.

I lift my head, looking down to where they are cleaning her, my heart thundering at the fact that he is right—it is quiet, and quiet only ushers in fear and sadness and longing. Lilah doesn't answer, her face pinched in concentration while Conrad's turns red, a sign of his frustration building. I lace my fingers with his, tugging on his hand until his gaze falls to my own.

"How are you feeling?" he asks, a slight edge to his voice that tells me he is asking beyond just the physical.

My eyes dart to the midwives, but they are focused on the baby, so I speak only loud enough for us to hear. "Good. The tinctures seem to be working, if only temporarily. I have not felt my magic once." He tips my chin up to kiss me, the movement of his lips gentle. "Have you decided on a name?" I ask, smiling when his hazel eyes soften. They have always been the most expressive part of him, a fact I know he hates because it always gives his intention away before he means to. In our early days together, I had used the ability to read him as a weapon. Something to poke and prod and taunt. Now, however, I stare at my husband and see the fear and uncertainty in his eyes, and I simply want to take the burden for myself.

"You gave me two lovely options. Perhaps we should go with—"

"Here she is," Lilah interrupts, carrying a bundle that appears to be only blankets until I see the curl of tiny fingers reaching up past the layers.

"Healthy?" Conrad asks, taking his daughter into his arms.

Lilah grins fondly, having been the one who helped Conrad's mother deliver him. "She is *perfect.*"

His smile is wide as he returns his gaze to our baby girl, and I have the midwives help me sit up. He drinks in every detail of her that I cannot yet see, and when his eyes lift to meet mine, tears line them. "She's perfect," he repeats, finally leaning down so that I can see her. I thought I might know what to expect. That after nine months of carrying her, half of those spent feeling her move in the womb, I would know with certainty *how* to be a mother. As if the knowledge would rush in suddenly, leaving no room for doubt.

And, maybe, to a small degree that happens. When I look at her, fear still lingers beneath my skin, an incessant hum that reminds me I am now in charge of this brand-new life. But stronger than that, coursing through my veins with relentless undeniability, is love. A love unlike the one I feel with Conrad. With my parents or my friends or any other being in these realms.

Taking her into my arms, I lean down and brush my lips against her head, the golden fuzz of hair tickling my nose. Conrad's arm wraps around my shoulders, his other finger tracing over our daughter's cheek right where a stream of golden sunlight shines. "My little ray of sunshine," he whispers, and I marvel at the awe in his voice. At how such a small being could soften such a powerful man—a king. "Rhea."

"You're sure?"

A tear slips free, painting his skin as nods. "Yes."

My gut warms as a rightness coils through me. "Rhea," I repeat, smiling as her eyes flutter open, like she's answering the call of her name. I bring her closer, every part of me settling with her cradled in my arms. *Rhea,* I whisper in my mind. "My little sun."

Night comes quickly, as do the return of Conrad's duties. "My brother says it's urgent," he says while kissing my cheek, his fingers tucking an errant strand of honey-blonde hair behind my ear. "I will come back as soon as I can."

I swallow as I reach for his wrist, halting his steps away from me. "I love you." The words are foreign on my tongue, and for a moment panic surges that I shouldn't have said them. But then Conrad's shoulders relax—an invisible tension releasing—and the look he's giving me prompts the words to lay on my tongue again.

"You are my everything, Luna." He leans over to press his forehead against mine. "And this is only the beginning of the rest of our lives." My eyes shut at the promise of his words, and then I'm left alone with Rhea for the first time.

I ensure she is asleep in her cot next to the window before I bathe, taking my time as if I'm washing away who I was *before*. Then again, perhaps it's not a matter of stepping into something new so much as it is finally feeling like I'm where I'm meant to be. *The beginning of the rest of our lives* Conrad had said. I smile as I trace over my lips with my fingers, his kiss still lingering on them. I liked the sound of that.

Once I'm dressed, I check on Rhea again and then move to the sitting room, grateful for the food and tea left there by the servants. Moving carefully, I carry the tray of food to the couch, setting it down on the table in front of it before slowly taking my seat. I manage a few bites before I rush to check on Rhea, sure I've heard her cry. But she sleeps peacefully, so I return to the sitting room and sit again, eager to eat a little more. The door to the space opens just as I pop a grape into my mouth. "How did it go?" I ask as I chew, turning to look over my shoulder just as the door closes.

But it isn't Conrad who stares back at me.

"I hear she looks like you."

"Dolian." I use the armrest of the couch to push myself up again as I stare at Conrad's younger brother. "What are you doing here?"

His lips quirk as he tilts his head and takes a step towards me, his hands clasped behind his back. "Can I not come to congratulate my queen on the birth of my niece?"

I stiffen at his use of the words *my queen*, the connotation undeniable.

"Of course you can," I reply, moving to put myself between Dolian and the door that leads to Rhea. I can't say why I do it—he has never hurt me beyond the use of words—and yet, as I stare into the same hazel eyes that Conrad has, I can't read his intentions. All emotion is stricken from his face except for the air of superiority he wears like a mask. So different from the man I used to know. "I just thought you were with Conrad."

At his brother's name, Dolian frowns, and I fight back the urge to shout at him for it. It has been *years* since he and I were anything more than just friends, and even *that* was fleeting. Conrad may have been the catalyst for the termination of whatever relationship we could have had, but in the end, it was the right decision. Dolian and I were never compatible in the way I yearned for. In the way he *deserved*. "You don't have to be with him."

I rock back a step at the desperation in his voice, the eager way his eyes gleam as he stares at me. Panic tightens like a vice around my throat when he steps nearer, a hand reaching out to grab one of mine. "What do you mean?"

"I've figured out a way for us to be together. Free of Conrad's rule." Though his grip on me remains soft, it is unrelenting. At the look on my face, he steps close enough for his chest to brush against mine, his breath stirring the hairs along my temples.

"Stop," I rasp, attempting to put space between us only for him to immediately fill it.

"Do you want me to beg, Luna? Is that what you need for me to prove myself to you?" He drops down onto his knees, his grip on my hand tightening as he looks up at me with pleading eyes. Behind me, I think I hear Rhea stir, but my heart beats so loudly in my ears that I can't be sure. "We can still have everything we dreamed about. All those conversations about freedom and desire—it can all be ours."

My heart clenches at the desperation in his tone, even as warning bells ring in my head. "Dolian, that was a different time. *We* were different. You and I can never be."

"But we can. I know that what we had was short, but you are the only person who I've ever felt completely *safe* with. And I have had to watch for years as Conrad cocooned you away from everyone else just so *he* could have you!"

"Is that what you think?" I snap, tugging on his hand to get him to stand. He does, but he sticks close enough for me to see the faint freckles that dot his cheeks. "Conrad and I may have had a rough beginning, but I *chose* him."

"No—"

"*Yes!*" I hiss, just as a fussy cry sounds through the open door. Inhaling a deep breath, I slowly release it through my nose. "I love Conrad. We have a daughter together and—"

"You love him?" he interrupts, the air growing thick. At my nod, a breath shudders from him, and finally the mask drops, revealing a flash of regret followed by one of unrelenting fury. "You could have been *my* queen," he says raggedly, a hand diving into his hair as stares at me. "You could have been *mine!*" His shout reverberates, making Rhea cry louder as every instinct within me begs to go to her.

I retreat a step, bringing my hands out in front of me as I call on my magic for the first time in *years*. I feel it stir somewhere distantly, as if it has been placed behind a hundred locked doors. *The tincture*. I had taken it so I wouldn't accidentally draw on my power while giving birth. Pain flares behind my ribs as my heart pounds, my mouth growing dry. And Dolian... he knows about my magic. About the curse I viewed it as. He sees the way I try to draw on it now, and I watch as he strengthens his defenses behind that building rage. And for the first time since I met him, I'm *terrified* by what I see.

"Guards!" I scream, and take another step back.

"You would have them apprehend me? Simply for *loving you*?"

"This is not love. This is something else—something *twisted*." Though my voice shakes, I keep my hands drawn out in front of me. "Go. Before Conrad returns. He will punish you for being here not as your brother but as your *king*."

Dolian blinks, and then he's impossible to read again, his steps sure as he marches towards me. "I'm afraid Conrad's been relieved of those duties."

My back hits the frame of the door, and I don't give myself time to register what Dolian has said before I turn and sprint into the bedroom.

"Luna!" he shouts, his steps vibrating over the floor as he runs after me. The room feels too big, and each step is like trudging through honey, my body still recovering from birth. Dolian's hand closes around my arm, and something sharp pierces my lower back, pain flaring and making me scream. I stumble into him as the pressure surrounding the pain releases, something wet and warm coating my back. Dolian's hand tightens on my arm.

"What are you doing?" I ask, calling on my magic again only to have a hollow silence answer. Dolian flashes a knife in front of me, my blood coating it as my knees wobble beneath my weight. I try to tug out of his hold, my gaze shifting to Rhea, her small hands reaching above the edge of the cot, fingers curling open then closed as she cries.

"It didn't have to be this way," he growls, and a scream tears up my throat when he plunges the blade into my shoulder. Once, then twice. I collapse to the ground, blood already dripping down my arm as I begin to crawl.

Gods, do not harm her. Please, help me. I had never imagined what I might look like as a mother before becoming pregnant. My spirit was a wild one—one that called for adventure and freedom. Children had always been the symbol of a slower life, of surrendering to someone else's schedule. But, as I stared into my daughter's eyes after her birth, a knowing filled me. Being a mother could be whatever *I* defined it as. Whatever Rhea needed me to be. I would do *anything* to protect her. To make her happy. To see her *live*.

My head slams against the ground as Dolian flips me over, his knees bracketing my hips. Silver moonlight paints his face in a horrifying glow, my blood speckled over his skin like a macabre collection of new freckles.

"Don't hurt her," I wheeze between gurgled breaths, the taste of iron blooming over my tongue. "Rhea is—" He drives the blade down into my stomach. *Protect her. Protect her. Protect her.* My hands catch his wrists, his silhouette blurring as he bares his teeth at me.

"It didn't have to be this way! You made *this* the only option!"

The ceiling above him spins, shadows swirling in from the edges of my vision, and still, I grip his wrists. I dig my nails into his flesh. *If there are any gods listening, please help me.* Dolian shakes free of my hold, my fingers and toes tingling as my arms fall lifelessly to my sides.

The darkness above grows, sweeping in as Dolian raises his hands again, the dagger glinting against the night stars behind him. "I love you, Luna, and because of that love, I will make this next part quick." His scream echoes out as his arms begin to descend, Rhea's cries drawing my head in her direction, a whisper of her name passing my lips. *Protect her.* In my ear, someone whispers, their voice deep and resonant as warmth presses at my chest and white light flares behind my lids.

Protect her. Protect her. Protect her.

Part One

Naivety might have been a cloak which I could hide beneath before, but I refuse to let it be one now.

Chapter One

RHEA

YOU ARE TO DO *as I command. You are free to explore the castle, but you are forbidden from leaving it without me. You are never to take off that ring.*

I squeeze my eyes shut and draw my bottom lip between my teeth to stop its trembling. The short list of demands King Dolian had given me before he left for the night repeat in my head. After revealing that we were not at the castle near Vitour but instead at a secret royal residence in a small seaside town called Windseren, my captor announced that I was to bathe and then rest. I protested the maid that he sent in, a young woman with hair a shade lighter than my own and beautiful blue eyes that fell somewhere between Cass's and Daje's. The last person to help me bathe had been Nox, and the memory of his fingers massaging my scalp and sliding over my slick body was not one I wanted replaced. No matter how benign. The king had merely smiled and tilted his head, as if he were somehow contemplating my thoughts. He then *commanded* that I let her help me bathe, and I was powerless to stop it, trapped words of anger and frustration building behind my teeth. I could do nothing as she gently scrubbed at my skin and cleaned my hair. The tears that stained my cheeks mocked me. I had the agency to *cry* but not to move my own body.

Moonlight pools onto the cover of my bed, pouring in through the large window in front of me. How reminiscent it is of all those nights in the tower; only this time, my confinement is truly solitary. There is no Bella snoring softly at my side, no guard I want to visit me. Sitting up, I stare at my hand, the soft pearl of the new ring adorning my finger stark against the night. I spent a good portion of the evening studying the jewelry that looked forged by the sea itself. I had tried—*gods, how I tried*—to pull it off. Going so far as to saw first at the gold coral-like band with my dinner knife and then my own finger, to no avail. A tender spot right below the ring now stings as I poke it with my thumb—evidence of my failed attempt. Perhaps cutting an appendage off might have been too desperate an act, but I am not above exploring any option at my disposal. I have to try.

Which is why tonight, I'm going to escape.

I have no idea where I am in respect to the front entrance of this *residence*. I nearly asked the handmaiden who tended to me for information until I caught a glimpse of the scar marring her palm. It could have been something other than a blood oath, but its resemblance to the crescent-shaped one Alexi carried was enough for me to swallow my need for knowledge back down. I couldn't risk her getting suspicious and going to the king, and she had offered nothing in the way of conversation to make me think she was someone to be trusted.

Naivety might have been a cloak which I could hide beneath before, but I refuse to let it be one now.

Letting my determination steady me, I open the door to the room slowly and peer out into the softly lit hall. There are no guards visible—a fact that I'm surprised by, but one that I intend to capitalize on. My toes stretch out over the firm rug lining the floor of the hallway, its pattern like blooming flowers colored crimson and gold under the light of flaming sconces on the wall. Drawing my gaze down over myself, I resist smacking my forehead at my idiotic choice to almost leave *barefoot* in my nightgown.

"Come on, Rhea. Be smarter than this." Rushing back into the room, I grab a pair of black hard-soled flats that the maid left in the flower-painted armoire as well as the first dress my hands can reach. Throwing the lavender fabric over my chemise, I slip on the flats and then dash out into the hall. My pace is quick but quiet, and a chill works along my spine as my nerves ignite within me the farther I move away from the bedroom.

My hand instinctively goes to where the dragon pendant should have been hanging around my neck, only to remember that I don't have it. In fact, none of the jewelry I had been wearing the night of the ball is with me.

Get her ring. Someone had yelled that while Daje and I were attacked, and though I replayed the voice in my head over and over again, I couldn't pinpoint who it was. Then again, was I expecting to *know* the people that attacked us? Beyond the *who*, there was the burning question of *how* those in the Mage Kingdom were connected with my uncle. No one but Nox, Cass, Daje, and Elora knew I was from the Mortal Kingdom, and only Nox and Cass had known I was its princess. I didn't want to think there was a world in which any of them would betray Nox. Betray *me*.

I come to a split in the hallway, the option to go left or right. My heart races as I look each direction, knowing that every second I delay could be the one that someone finds me. But choosing the wrong direction could be just as equally perilous. "Damn it," I mutter, glancing one more time each way before choosing to go right. I run from one shadow cast by the sconces to the next, continuing down the hallway as double doors come into view on my left. *Don't stop.* The eerie sensation of being watched raises the hairs on the back of my neck, but I push forward, unsure whether I'm going in any direction but circles when the hall *finally* gives way to a large space that might be a foyer.

Slowing down, I lean against the cool stone wall and rest my hand on my chest as I work to catch my breath. Though blood rushes past my ears, I listen for a hint of anyone else nearby. But it's still unnervingly quiet, and a part of me wonders if my uncle would be so bold as to not have anyone guarding me. Perhaps there are *no* guards here at all—a thought which makes another terrified shiver work down my spine. Then again, why would he need them? At least with respect to me, I have no choice but to follow his commands because of the ring on my finger. He had already hinted that the place we are at isn't one widely known, certainly not one Nox would think to go to first if he were on his way.

Shaking out my hands, I peek around the corner of the hall, my clammy fingers curling over the stone. Silver light from the moon shines in from windows set high above me on the opposite wall. Beneath them, elegant stone arches indicate more unknown corridors, ones I *hope* are currently empty. I lean out a little more, my hair gliding over my shoulder and hanging away from my body as I look to my left. More light from above pours into the space, but I can't make out anything beyond the continuing foyer.

But when I look to the right, my heart leaps into my throat, and it's hard not to let a smile unfurl on my lips. Centered between two pillars of stone, elegant lines carved into each one, is a curved door made of wood and accented with metal. I don't need to know the intricacies of this new-to-me residence to recognize a front door when I see one. And it's completely *unguarded.*

The discordant rhythm of my heart beats loudly in my ears as I leave the relative protection of the hallway and enter the open space. I half expect someone to leap from the shadows or for the king himself to descend upon me like a wild summer storm, but despite the way my mind is *convinced* someone is watching, no one appears.

The door looms over me as I tilt my head back to take in the carved design on its front: A roaring lion made of gold sits at its center, while looping golden vines with small flowers frame the door's border. Swallowing down my nausea at the sight of the Mortal Kingdom's sigil—at the reminder of where I am—I reach for the long handle, the cold metal biting into my palm. Breathing in sharply, I brace myself to move as quickly as possible once the door opens. Regardless of what awaits me on the other side. With a final glance over my shoulder, I tug on the door. And tug. *And tug.* But it doesn't open. I take a step back, my eyes scouring over the wood until I spot the black metal plate with a small hole at its center placed over the handle.

"Oh no," I whisper, my fear rising as my mind begins to churn. *I need a key.*

As I contemplate what options, if any, I have, a man's voice from the darkness behind me rings out. "His Majesty will *not* be too pleased to see this."

Chapter Two

RHEA

MY SURPRISED YELP ECHOES out as I spin around to find a stout older man standing in the center of the foyer. The moon highlights his short hair, the strands a blend of black and gray. He pulls his lips to the right, clasping his hands behind him as he takes a measured step towards me.

My back hits the door, the urge to call my magic met with a frustrating sense of hollowness.

"This door requires a key," the man drawls slowly, reaching into his pocket. My next inhale stays frozen in my chest, my body bracing for an attack, but when he removes his hand from his trousers and holds it out to me, a metal key gleams in his palm. "Take it." At my stunned silence, he widens his grin and takes another step towards me, dark eyes glittering with an emotion I can't quite place.

My eyes dart away and look for another way out that I might have missed from before. I can either sprint down one of the unknown hallways carved out on either side of me, *or* I can see what awaits on the other side of the foyer, deeper into the darkness. None of them are guaranteed to lead anywhere better than where I currently stand.

"I understand your trepidation, so let me make it easier for you." He tosses the key to the stone floor, and I cringe at the high-pitched noise it makes, sure everyone in this place will hear it. Terrified that *one* of those people will be the king. "Go on, Lady Rhea. Take it."

He knows my name, and this is a trap. It is most definitely and *decidedly* a trap. *But what if it isn't?*

I grip on to that tiny seedling of hope as I lean forward. I am no stranger to the way hope can flare in desperate times. It can be as strong as a hug from a lover, but it can fray as easily as a torn thread. Yet it's the space in the middle, the one that sits between confidence and desperation, that I currently find myself in. I'm inclined to hope that this stranger genuinely wants to help me. That his intentions are *good*. So, despite my reservations, I dash for the key, picking it up and quickly turning to slide it into the lock.

A *click* rings out, the hope within me bursting at the seams when I tug again on the handle and the door moves. Cool late night air caresses my face, rustling the strands of my hair that frame it. The hinges of the door groan quietly as I pull it only wide enough for me to squeeze through the opening. I don't spare the man a second glance as I step over the threshold, my gaze tracking over the star-filled night sky and the lapping waves of the ocean in the distance.

Hope lets tears crest when I take another step, taking note of the staircase in front of me. Gripping my dress in my hands, I lift my foot to descend the stairs, only to find I can't move any farther. I tilt my weight forward, content to tumble down the stairs if that's what it takes, but as if there is an invisible wall blocking me, I go absolutely *nowhere*.

"*No.*" The single word slips out, blending into the sound of the water just ahead as I push myself forward again. And again. My stomach churns as I heave out a cry, the word repeating while I slam my shoulder into what looks like nothing but air.

It's when I hear *his* horrific voice that that fragile hope officially frays. It's when *he* wraps his arms around my body and hauls me to his chest that it disintegrates completely. And as something is placed over my mouth, its acrid taste flooding my tongue, I understand why hope is such a fickle thing. Then everything goes black.

⁂

"Rhea." Selene's voice, normally dulcet, calls out to me with an edge of panic, barely detectable over the riotous beating of my heart. An ominous sensation hovers over me, my body acutely aware even if I can't see it or give it a name. "Rhea," she calls again.

"What is happening?" I ask aloud. Her voice isn't the only one painted in anxiousness. Whispers answer in return, too faint for me to understand. I try to sit up, but beyond being able to tilt my head to either side, I am immobile. It's as if I'm pinned in place, shackled in a space between worlds.

"We don't have much time," she whispers. Or perhaps her voice is already fading away. "With your magic blocked, I cannot speak with you as easily. Or for as long."

"How did he get the power to block my magic?"

"It is something ancient and familiar, but right now, you need to remember that you aren't alone." The memory of my last visit with Selene surfaces, those exact words a vow I had given her. The promise feels hollow now. *"No,"* she says, her voice even quieter than before. A deeper sound skates over me, goosebumps rising on my skin as a foreign touch follows. *"You are* not *alone. I am always here with you, Rhea. Always."*

My eyes flutter open, a bright light above me immediately making me squint. I wait for the prickling sensation that happens from a return from the Middle, but it never comes. "Ah, my darling, you're finally awake. I was about to reprimand Simon for using too much of that *potion* on you."

Groaning, I let my head fall to the side. Colors whirl together, my surroundings blurry as my vision struggles to adjust.

"Have faith in me, Your Majesty. Potions of this nature have been a specialty of mine for a long, long time." The two men continue talking, the sound discordant in my ears as a wave of dizziness consumes me. Eventually, my vision adjusts, and with a deep breath, I take stock of the room I'm in. It's a small space, walls of stone brick in varying shades of gray sending a familiar pang of disquiet through me. Brown shelves hold glass jars full of different colored liquids, their tops sealed with light brown corks. Hanging on the wall nearest to my feet are chains and weapons, though the latter look like no instruments I've ever seen before. Silver blades that curve like crescent moons and wooden paddles with gleaming spikes catch my attention first, but there is every manner of dagger and sword competing for it as I push a rough swallow down my throat.

"Rhea, look at me," my uncle says, his fingers gripping my chin as he turns my head, afternoon sunlight streaming in through a window above him. His appearance is as pristine and coiffed as always. A trimmed chestnut beard frames a malevolent smirk while his hazel eyes glow as they stare down into mine. "You had an eventful evening."

I attempt to jerk away from him and realize that I'm bound to a table, leather straps holding my limbs in place at my wrists and ankles. King Dolian's gaze shreds me apart as it roams over my cheeks and then to my lips, where it lingers. "So much more defiant." He trails the backs of his fingers over my arm, the action making me involuntarily shiver. Disgusted fury rages within me, my chest heaving as I snarl at him. When his eyes meet mine again, a sinister edge hardens his jaw. "You're thinking of *him*, aren't you?" I tense at the question but refrain from answering. *Nox.* His name is a soothing balm, even in the chaos of my internal thoughts and turbulent fear. The king nods his head. "Yes, I can see it in your eyes. They gleam for him in a way I've never seen from you before."

Warm air rushes past me, too hot to be from outside, the scent of *burning* accompanying it.

"I wonder who felt your story was more fairytale-esque, you or the mage prince? In your quiet moments together, did you both revel in the idea that your clandestine meetings and subsequent escape from me was meant to be?" Leaning farther down so that his breath brushes my temple, he whispers, "Tell me this, even if I were to hand you back to him on a silver platter, would he want you knowing you've been tainted? That you've been *marked* by me?"

"He *loves* me." Though my voice is merely a rasp, it still rings out loudly in the room. My very soul is entwined with Nox's. Our love is cosmic. It is limitless and *powerful* and tethers us to each other in ways that seem unfathomable without divine intervention. But we *had* continually chosen each other. Through each trial and obstacle thrown before us, those invisible strings bound us even closer together. "And I will *never* love you. No matter what you do or how you try to control me, you will have to live with the fact that there is *nothing* you can do to change that."

King Dolian's expression falters, and though I didn't believe him to be capable of having the emotion, I swear sadness crosses his features briefly. "We'll see." Straightening, he releases my chin and the man he's been speaking with steps closer. *Simon.* If his white-streaked dark hair didn't give him away, his serpentine smirk certainly would. He's the stranger from last night, the one who preyed on my foolish hope. "Consider what is about to happen next as my assurance that you will always belong to *me*." Grabbing the hem of my dress between his hands, King Dolian grunts as he pulls the fabric apart. The sound of it ripping turns my stomach to lead. My heart ricochets painfully in my chest, robbing me of the breath I desperately try to draw in.

"Don't *touch* me!" I growl, jerking against my restraints.

"Stop fighting me, Rhea," he responds smoothly, exposing all of my left leg to him.

"I will *never* stop fighting you!" I heave, but even as I speak, the power of his command washes the fight from my body like the tide returning to the ocean.

"Then I suppose it's a good thing the ring you are wearing prevents you from doing so." With a final tear, my hip becomes exposed to him. Dread uncoils into absolute *horror*. Splaying the two lower halves of my dress open, King Dolian holds his hand out above my body. From where he stands to my right, Simon hands the king a thick glove that matches the one he is wearing, but it's the long metal rod he's holding that grabs my attention fully.

"What are you—" The question dies as I study the item more intently. My eyes flick to the raging fire I can just barely make out in a hearth above my shoulder, a terrible understanding dawning on me. I know pain intimately. My entire life has been building up a tolerance to it, especially the kind the monster at my side specializes in. I often wondered if his abuse, and the subsequent years of my own mental torment, would leave a brand upon me that was irreversible. Something that couldn't be seen by others but that *I* undoubtedly knew was there. Yet as I stare at that menacing glowing metal, I realize King Dolian aims to make his mark on me visible by all. It will no longer be something hidden in the shadows of my mind but something undeniable. Something *permanent*.

King Dolian's eyes drop to mine as he takes hold of the branding iron and spins it around until its burning end is hovering a few inches over me. "What have I always told you, darling? You *are* mine. You have *always* been mine. And after this? I am the only one who will want you. Now, *don't* move." My quick intake of air is cut short when he plunges the end of the iron down onto my hip, stilling the world for a single second. A buzzing in my ears temporarily drowns everything out before it all comes rushing back to me in an avalanche of white-hot, *fiery* pain.

The scent of burnt flesh mingles with the crackling of the brand melting my skin as smoke wafts into the air, and every nerve ending alights with the agony of it. My eyes slam shut, and though I can't actively move my body, tremors still wrack through it while a blood-curdling scream is ripped from my throat. He finally lifts the iron and I suck in an unobstructed breath, the pressure and pain lancing through my skin horrific and unyielding. It permeates out from my hip and down my legs, my toes spasming as the muscles contract. I hate the way that I cry out, that it's my body's natural reaction to what's just happened. To how I've been *marked*.

Tears blur my eyes as I watch King Dolian hand the iron back to Simon, taking off the glove and moving to cup my face in his hands. "Hush. The sooner you accept that this is your new reality, the better it will be for you. I will make you my queen. You will have more freedom than you ever did in that tower." He brushes his thumbs over my cheekbones, wiping at the tears while my rapid breaths make my consciousness grow hazy. "Simon, give her something to help her sleep."

The next moments pass by in a blur as something floral-scented is swiped beneath my nose. I glare at my uncle, hatred seeping from me as my lips lift in the briefest of sneers before I pass out.

Chapter Three

BAHIRA

MY FINGERS TIGHTEN AROUND the railing of the ship as the Mage Kingdom's coast comes into view. The cobalt ocean water batters the sides of the vessel, mirroring that uneasy feeling that has taken root in my gut. It's not something easily explained, not beyond the fact that every day and night spent sailing here has been filled with thoughts of Kai and Jahlee. Of Rhea and Nox and my parents, and of what may be going on that would make them not answer Kai's summons through the Mirror. I half expected that, as the ship neared my homeland's beaches, smoke and fire would pour from the trees—a telltale sign that something is wrong. Instead, the dread that's buried itself in me seems to be of the invisible nature. Hopefully nothing more than my imagination gone wild.

"We will be at the dock within half an hour." I look over my shoulder and nod my head in acknowledgement to Akamu, one of three shifter males that volunteered to sail to the Mage Kingdom with me when his king had asked. When he retreats, I turn my attention back in the direction the palace of Galdr lies, tucking a wild strand of hair loosened from my ponytail behind my ear.

I had gotten to know the males on this ship in the small amounts of downtime where I couldn't sleep and they weren't shifted into their animal forms. Akamu and Vetu are twin brothers, their broad bodies and short black hair identical. If not for their tattoos—Akamu's only inked on his left arm and leg, while the black lines and swirls mark nearly all of Vetu's torso—it would be impossible to tell them apart. Laki was the third, a male in his fifth decade whose reasoning for volunteering left me speechless when he confessed it. His brother is Adrian, the male whose son had become a horrific casualty in the pillaging of Kai sympathizers—a movement led by Kai's uncle and closest advisor, Tua. Laki

11

knew I had been helping Kai with the blight but, more importantly, he knew that Kai had frequented Adrian's business. That he had taken me there the day the rebels attacked. I wasn't sure what to expect from him, but I wouldn't have been surprised if it were anger and resentment. My presence along with the king's had led to his nephew's death. Despite that, Laki has only regarded me with an open, if a bit curious, expression. He drank in the retelling of my time in the dungeon—all three males did.

Kai had not told me to keep what happened with the rebels a secret, and I figured if anyone should know, it should be a male whose life was directly altered by what those rebels had done. I didn't want to complicate things for Kai in any way, but I also wanted him to know who his supporters were. The nobles of the palace and inhabitants of Molsi needed to be thoroughly vetted, and an easy way to do that was for these three males to return home with the story of what had happened to me. To share and gauge the reactions of those who heard the tale. I just had to hope Kai agreed.

I close my eyes, letting the breeze billowing off the ocean slide along my skin. Kai's parting words float through my mind as I recall his scent. His touch. The way he felt beneath my hands. *Be my ruin. Be my poison. Be the reason I question just who the fuck I am and what I'm doing. The reason I give a shit at all. Be all those things and whatever else you want to, Bahira.*

My chin drops to my chest as I force a rough exhale out. It was an apology, and it wasn't. He had given me more than anyone else, and he had also hurt me with a fervor that rivaled Daje's ultimatum. I had been comparing the two since the moment I saved Kai from the rebels that night in the jungle, but the one factor that had driven them both to a breaking point was *me*. My inability to speak with Daje about how our relationship had changed created a rift between us that I suspect will never be filled, even if I *had* married him. My deception with Kai had tarnished something before it ever truly had the ability to shine. Maybe that was the way it would always be with me—a woman whose selfish desires would always consume those closest to her.

I was both too much and not enough, and the only way I could ever hope to achieve balance would be to finally claim the one thing that I placed above all else—my magic.

I had learned that magic and blood were connected, both through my own experiments and what Tua had hinted at concerning Kai's father and mother. How I yearned to be able to spend more time in the Shifter Kingdom and find those notes he mentioned. The journals that King Noa kept supposedly explained *exactly* what he had learned and how he used that knowledge to somehow alter Kai. Had I been able to reach my parents through the Mirror, had a shifter named Siyala not strode into the throne room with a worried frown for the woman my brother returned from the Mortal Kingdom with, I would have stayed. Because I have never been that close to an answer before. Upon reflection, my previous experiments not only just barely touched the surface of a solution, but they were scratching the wrong one.

If I had stayed, perhaps Kai and I might have found a way to move past the mistakes that plagued us both. That cycle of "what ifs" has played in my mind far too many times on this voyage. Though it's foolish to push the thoughts away after already reconciling with the fact that *ignoring* my problems only makes them worse, I do so in favor of the newest *potential* discovery. The Spell *has* to be connected to the siphoning of magic in my own kingdom and the blight in Kai's. As eager as I am to make sure everything is alright with my family, I'm just as anxious to dig deeper into knowledge about the Spell.

Sandy tan beaches and the Mage Kingdom's dock loom closer. The sun is warm on the crown of my head as I steel my spine and lift my chin. Though the sight of my people and the other boats docked is a welcome familiarity, something still prickles like an itch I cannot scratch. Surely, if there was something wrong with the king and queen, or the crown prince, these people would not be carrying on with life as if there wasn't, right?

I bid farewell to Akamu and Vetu when we dock, Laki carrying my trunk, while I hoist my pack—my spear slid into its loops—onto my back. We walk the length of the pier, this space a concoction of mostly mages but also a few fae unloading goods on one side and mortals doing the same on the other. It has been over two centuries since the Spell went up, plenty of time for each kingdom to figure out the most efficient way to drop goods off and then leave. Our trades have certainly diminished over time, whittled down to only the most basic essentials for each kingdom that couldn't be grown, produced, or unearthed on their lands or by their people.

The salt air mixes with the pungent odors of sweaty bodies and produce and meat, and by the time I descend the small wooden flight of stairs to the soft sand below, my nose is stuck in a crinkle. The wall of the Spell shimmers in front of me, and Laki places my trunk gently at his feet before shifting his stance, glowering at a few mages who stare in his direction.

"Thank you, Laki, for offering to sail the ship and for carrying my luggage." I extend my hand out to him, watching his apprehension give way to appreciation as he clasps his hand around mine. Those gazes feel weightier now, the people—*my* people—staring with unabashed interest. Releasing his hand, I turn and scan those on the other side of the Spell, calling a man over.

"Yes, Princess Bahira?" he rushes out, his steps skidding to a stop and sending sand gliding over my boots. *Princess.* I hear the title in my ear said by a smokier voice, one deep and harsh. One that could carve between valleys as easily as it slid over my skin, leaving me wanton and wanting.

Swallowing down thoughts of the shifter king, I address the man. "Can you please arrange for a carriage to come pick me up?" He rushes out an "of course" before bolting towards where the trees grow thick just beyond the beach. I turn to Laki who dips his chin, a small grin curling his lips.

"Until next time, Bahira."

I fight back the strange woven thicket of emotions that scratch at my throat and repeat, "Until next time." As he returns to the ship with the others, their orders not to linger long, I silently hope that the journey back home for them is uneventful. Then I face forward and heft up my trunk, walking through the Spell. The unease I had hoped would be squashed upon setting foot in my kingdom still writhing within.

It's a short trip to the palace, and I watch the trees as they pass through the window with that uncomfortable tightness growing larger in my chest. It's strange to return to the only home I have ever known and feel like things aren't quite right anymore. Is it because I am worried for my family? Or is it that for the first time in my life, my heart feels split between two places. *Gods, this is going to be a fucking terrible next few weeks if I can't get my emotions under control.*

When the carriage slows and turns, and the front of the palace comes into view, I scoot as close as I can to the window. While nothing is on fire, that worry thankfully proven false, palace guards *are* stationed both at the top of the white stone steps that lead to the front doors and spread around the grounds in both directions. My brows furrow, and as my ride comes to a stop and the guard operating as my driver opens the door, I ask, "What is going on?"

"I do not know, Your Highness," he answers, clearing his throat. "The king and queen requested extra guards at all entrances to the palace the morning after the Autumnal Ball, but they have not yet given an explanation as to why. Though it may have something to do with the body—" My eyes snap to his as he halts his words, his lips pinching together while pink tints his cheeks. "Sorry, Your Highness. I am not supposed to speak of it."

"Please ensure my trunk is brought to my room." I don't wait for him to agree before I dart past him and down the walkway, right to where three guards wait, blocking the stairs. All of them do a double take before recognition dawns on their faces. They let me pass easily, my feet taking the steps two at time as one of them shouts up to the men guarding the landing. "Make way for the Princess!"

My breaths seize in my chest as I climb, a million scenarios playing in my mind. *The body.* Whose? Surely, it cannot be Nox or Daje. I would know. *I would know.*

The double doors to the palace are pulled open, the detailed celestial carvings on their fronts catching a trickle of golden sunlight cutting through the canopy above. My boots beat against the glittering black stone floors of the foyer as

I pivot and turn directly towards my father's office. The presence of guards is overwhelming, some simply walking the perimeter and halls, while another small group stands at the base of the stairs that lead up to the higher levels. A frantic whimper lodges itself in my throat, but I force it to stay there, unwilling to give in to my fear. My arms pump at my sides as I run down the corridor, blood rushing in my ears. I can't sense magic, not like a *normal* mage, but I still try to feel *something*. Anything to indicate my family is okay.

A door creaks down the hall before a figure steps from a room and blocks my path. I suck in an inhale, slowing my speed as my attention devolves from the chaos churning through my mind to the man standing in front of me. He runs a hand over the top of his bowed head, his shoulders drooped in defeat. Upon hearing my steps, his gaze snaps up and his hand falls abruptly to his side as he gapes at me. *Short brown hair. Tawny brown skin. Piercing blue eyes.* We stare at each other, mirrors of the same shock expressed on both of our faces.

"Daje," I whisper.

"Bahira," he rasps back.

Chapter Four

BAHIRA

Hⁱˢ ꜱʜᴏᴄᴋ ᴏɴʟʏ ꜱᴇɪᴢᴇꜱ him for a few seconds before he eats up the remaining distance between us in just a few strides. His hands frame my face, my own clutching his wrists.

"Are you okay? You're home earlier than expected. Did you— Was it because—" He swallows, his eyes searching mine for answers to the questions that dangle perilously between us.

Did I come home early for him? Does this mean I will marry him? Fucking gods, I hate that my gut response is to get angry with him. Not because I actually *am*, but because this seems unimportant compared to *whatever* else is wrong here.

"Please tell me what is going on with the guards? Is my family well?"

Daje's thumbs slide over my cheekbones, his touch on me gentle as if he's holding something delicate. We both know I'm anything but. Slowly, I draw his hands away, and something flashes in his expression that's there and gone in the length of a blink. "A lot has happened in the past few days," he answers, his voice lowering while his attention focuses on something behind me. "It's best to hear it directly from your father. Come on, he and your mother are in the council room." He takes my hand, his fingers trembling in mine.

"Daje, you did not answer my question. Is my family *alright*?" In the silence that grows, I bounce my focus from Daje to the hallway and back again. Nothing *looks* out of place, but everything *feels* wrong. As we near the door to the council room, he finally answers me.

"I honestly don't know." Then he tugs on the door, and I step into chaos.

Each of the council members is standing around the ancient wooden table, their cheeks stained red as eyes of gray, blue, and brown bore into each other with ferocity. My father *glowers* from the head of the table, his gaze firmly fixed on Daje's father as the men speak through gritted teeth. The other council members argue around them, Borris and Osiris's voices the loudest amongst the group. My focus shifts from the table to the startling cracks that trickle up the large wall to the right of the table and up to the ceiling, where one of the chandeliers hangs crookedly. The jagged cuts into the stone spread like a spiderweb down the length of the room and to the adjacent wall, right to where a woman with familiar curly brown hair is standing and staring out one of the windows to the forest beyond, her hand cradling the side of her face. I let go of Daje, tension bracketing my shoulders as I make my way to my mother, ignoring the council as my boots crunch over loose debris.

Whipping her head around, her deep gray eyes meet mine, a glassy sheen covering them. Dressed in a short-sleeved mauve day dress, a belt of gold leaves cinching her waist, she would appear as regal and steadfast as she always did to anyone who only knew her queenly façade. But I know her as my *mother*, and as I close the gap between us, I see what she tries to conceal from everyone else. The furrow of her brows and the pursing of her lips. Instead of a healthy glow to her brown skin, it's paled to the point that the dark circles cresting beneath her eyes stand out viciously.

"Bahira," she rasps, reaching out for me just as I curl into her embrace. She smells like the flowers of this kingdom, like the earth after it's been freshly tilled. Robust and delicate, all at once. "Thank the gods you are here." Her hand rests on the back of my head, holding me to her as her body quakes in mine.

"What is going on," I whisper into her hair, my eyes once more drawn to the damage that's evident around the room.

"Something has happened, and your brother—"

"Bahira." My father's voice ricochets through my chest as I watch him approach. His black wavy hair hangs freely, the ends scraping his shoulders. He wears a tunic of black, an intricate silver design threaded along the collar. Yet it's his face that stalls my next inhale. He looks older than he did mere months ago. Deep lines brace his mouth and dig into his forehead, his warm gray eyes lined with red that usually accompanies sleepless nights or boundless worry. "You're home."

Mother carefully unwraps her arms from around me, just in time for my father to replace them with his. Neither of us speaks, the embrace saying more than words could ever allow. I am home, and something is wrong. I am home. *And something is wrong.*

Unnerving silence settles into the room, and after a moment, my father releases me, and together with my mother, we walk to the table, the gazes of the council heavy upon us.

"Princess Bahira, it is good to see you back in your own kingdom," Councilman Arav says, his light blue eyes assessing as he smirks. I glance over his appearance, everything about him disheveled from his blonde hair to the gray tunic he wears. I scan the other councilmen, finding the state of their clothing to be in a similar disarray.

"It is good to be home, though I would be remiss if I did not point out that tensions seem to be rather *high*." At this, Councilman Kallin's jaw clenches and Borris snickers under his breath. "Would someone please catch me up on what is happening?"

The sound of my father's finger gently tapping the table top is the only sound in the room as seconds pass before *finally* Councilman Hadrik answers. "Prince Nox's fiancée, Lady Rhea, was taken."

I try to temper my reaction as Kallin watches me closely, but my heart fucking skips a beat at the news. Siyala was right to fear for Rhea's safety, it seems. I measure my words carefully. "Taken? How can that be?"

"My fellow councilman is leaving out a crucial detail," Kallin answers for Hadrik, sliding a piece of parchment across the table to me. It's a letter, one addressed to Nox from Rhea. My gaze flicks to my father's, then my mother's, both of them torn between looks of pity and ones of deep concern. "This letter, along with the engagement ring His Highness gave to Lady Rhea, were left in the prince's room. Not something someone who was *taken* abruptly would have the forethought to leave behind."

Hadrik narrows his eyes at Kallin, but I turn my attention back to the letter as I open it. Rhea's handwriting—loopy but elegant—details her fears of becoming queen and her subsequent decision that Nox deserved someone at his side who was better fit to rule. She claims she cannot in good conscience marry him despite loving him because of the tension their marriage would cause in the kingdom. Added at the bottom of the page is a warning not to go after her.

I lay the letter back on the table as I reconcile its words with the woman who I did not know but had seen glimpses of. The one I met on the beach who was timid and frightened. The one I later saw in the Mirror who appeared shy but loyal. She clung to my brother, and he to her, as if they were each a pillar made to support the other. *That* Rhea didn't match the one that would leave my brother with only a note. Siyala had been *so* worried about her friend. *So* sure that the mortal king would do something, even if she didn't have proof of *how* he could.

"Where is Nox?" I ask, folding my arms over my chest.

"We found him passed out at the beach. He is in the healers' wing," Councilman Borris quips, making my eyes narrow as he adds, "The prince has all but denounced his claim to the throne over this gi—" His words sputter, his fingers tracing over his neck as if something is bothering him there. I glance out of the corner of my eye to my father, watching as his lips twitch just once before he evens out his expression. "Over Lady Rhea," he finally spits out.

"Nox wouldn't do that," I say, earning a noise of derision from Councilman Osiris, his forehead wrinkled in disdain. I give him a look that silences whatever stupid retort tries to bubble up his throat as I add, "My brother loves his kingdom."

"Love and duty to one's kingdom can be two separate things," Kallin retorts, his dark gray eyes latching on to mine. "The council's role is to aid the king in ensuring that this kingdom is protected and secure. While I have no doubts that your brother would never let an enemy take over these lands without a fight, his loyalty to the kingdom and this council has been tested in a rather unfavorable light for him."

"Let us not forget that you placed an impossible choice at his feet. One that should have been denounced *years* ago," my mother *snarls* at the head councilman.

Charged silence thickens the air, making the hair on the back of my neck rise. "What does she mean?"

Kallin sighs, the sound heavy with barely tempered defiance. "We informed Prince Nox that while he has the ability to choose a consort, it is up to the council to vote on whether or not we believe the match to be a good fit for the kingdom. It appears neither he, nor His Majesty, were aware the council possessed that power."

"Of course I wasn't aware," my father grits out, light purple flaring around him as his magic seeps from his profile. "I had no reason to question what I was *led to believe* was already true."

"An unfortunate lesson, indeed," Kallin responds. It's an effort not to let my jaw unhinge at the blatant disrespect. "Regardless, the next matter at hand is to make sure our borders are secure. There is no telling where Lady Rhea might go—who she might let whispers spill to of what she's learned while wooing the prince and—"

"You cannot be serious," my father interrupts.

Kallin has the gall to look *upset*. "Unfortunately, I am. We have proof that Lady Rhea left of her own volition with that note. What we do not know is if everything she wrote in it was true. If those things were her only motivation. Preparing for possible threats should be our first priority."

"What about what happened to your *son*?" my mother snaps, her hand gesturing to where Daje has pulled an extra chair to the other end of the table. "He came to us beaten and bloody, with no memory of what happened. What proof does that sound like to you?"

He had been beaten? *Bloody*?

"Perhaps it is proof of Lady Rhea's intentions," Councilman Arav offers, his light blue magic twirling over his knuckles as he plays with it. "All we know is that she and Daje were last seen together before the latter was knocked out and the former is now gone."

"And what of his claim that a guard retrieved them?" my father asks, his tenor as foreboding as the sliding of a sword from its sheath.

Councilman Kallin regards his son. "Perhaps he only *thinks* that is what happened. Such a nasty hit as the one he received could have altered his memory of what actually occurred."

Daje glares in his father's direction. "I am *sure* there was a guard," he growls, leaning so far forward that the edge of the table digs into his torso as anger contorts his features. "I am *sure* that they beckoned Rhea and I towards the beach under the guise that Nox wanted to speak with us. I am *sure* that I spoke to Rhea as we walked under the night sky. And I am *sure* that I awoke to blood tainting the pathway, *both mine and hers.*"

My stomach drops as I shake my head. "You were ambushed by someone?"

Daje's eyes snare mine, their hue the brightest I've ever seen them. "Yes."

The councilmen begin chattering over each other as I sit back against my chair. It is only now clicking in my head that in order for all of this to have happened, it means there are mages working with King Dolian. What would motivate them to do that?

"What is more likely, Son? That you and the lady were attacked out of the blue the same night she pens a goodbye letter? Or that perhaps, with your guard lowered around her, she took advantage of you to aid in her own escape?"

"She wouldn't have done that—"

"And you know her?" his father cuts in, spearing Daje with a menacing scowl. "Well enough to predict her actions? Her whims and desires?"

"She was my friend!" Daje shouts, slamming a fist on the table and lurching from his chair. "And Nox entrusted me to keep her safe, and I—" He stumbles backwards, a hand running over his head and then down his face. He stares at his father, unspoken fury floating between them before he spins on his heel and marches out of the room.

My father stands from his chair and reaches a hand out towards my mother. "I think this council needs a break. We should adjourn for now."

Surprisingly, Kallin agrees. "Our job, first and foremost, is the protection of this kingdom and the people that reside within it. If that expectation cannot be met under the current state of affairs, then we will act as we need to in accordance with the rules that are laid out for our kingdom."

The threat pierces my father's chest, but he does a good job of hiding his reaction. Our laws are written to retain a balance of power between sovereign and council *except* in moments when the council feels their ruler is not acting in the kingdom's best interest. If the majority votes to remove my father as king, there is nothing he can do to stop it.

I stand from my chair and move to join my parents when Kallin speaks at my back. "Princess Bahira, I understand you have only just returned, but we expect a full report of what you have learned in the Shifter Kingdom. As well as if relations with them are still on *friendly* terms should this event with Lady Rhea turn into something more." Trepidation slithers down my spine, and I don't spare the councilman a glance before exiting the council room with my parents.

I follow them down the hall, heading deeper into the palace and ignoring the way our presence—or more accurately, *my* presence—draws the gazes of those we pass. "Where are we going?"

My father waits until a pair of guards walks past us to answer. "To see your brother."

Chapter Five

BAHIRA

I RUN MY FINGERS through Nox's hair, pulling the wavy strands away from his forehead. It had apparently only been a day since the guards found him on the beach after the ball, passed out in what my parents had described to me as a crater in the sand, its diameter at least ten feet wide.

"Wake up, idiot," I whisper, earning a snort from Cass who leans against the wall next to the door, officially off duty but standing in as Nox's personal guard anyway.

"I'm sure being called that will coax him right awake," he drawls, though his levity is only a fraction of what I'm used to.

I snort before I sit back in the chair propped at the side of the bed. "Tell me again what happened." Cass has already run through the events of the ball and what happened after, when Nox learned Rhea was missing. It explains the state of the council room and the destruction of the Mirror, the latter a piece of information that gutted me to learn. I knew I had to tell Kai—or more specifically, Siyala—about Rhea. Anything beyond that, however, I hadn't decided on. With the possibility of talking to the shifters now gone, it's suddenly all I can think about. Would Kai try to reach out through the Mirror when a week or two or three went by without word from me? Would he even *care* beyond needing the information for Siyala? Or would my silence encourage him to move on, if there *is* even anything about us to move on from? I ignore the way the thought slices through my gut.

Cass clears his throat when he finishes his full recap of events again, and when I shoot him a glance, he's a few feet closer than he was before. "You alright?" he asks, a single brow drawing up. "You looked as if you were in a daydream."

"Sorry. There's just a lot on my mind." Tilting my head back, I look up at the ceiling, tracing the long wooden beams that cross the room. The astringent scent of the healing wing is layered in every breath, this part of the palace one I grew familiar with as a child but had never seen Nox step foot in. Perks of him having strong magic and all.

"He'll be okay," Cass says softly. "Galen thinks he just expended too much magic."

At the uncertainty of his tone, I ask, "And what do *you* think?"

"I don't know. A part of me has always thought of Nox's magic as infinite. Something ever present. To assume that he reached an otherwise unknown limit, enough so that he needs to fall into a deep sleep in order to repair himself, isn't exactly a comforting thought."

I hum in agreement, closing my eyes as I draw in a deep breath.

When Nox first began training with his magic as a child, he was reckless with it. He'd draw it out and toss it around as if it was a toy. When the council suggested he train more extensively, trading in classroom time for more hands-on manipulation practice, he had eagerly agreed. The lessons seemed excruciating, Nox often gone for the entirety of the day, but he learned to control it far beyond most could at his age. When his shadows were discovered, the council then *insisted* he dedicate even more time to controlling it. So the idea that he somehow slipped and drained his body of power is unsettling indeed.

"There's also the fact that I can't sense his magical signature."

At that, I open my eyes and lift my head to look at Cass, growing wary at the tight lines that bracket his mouth. "At all?"

"Well, I can if I'm right at his side, but it's like there's something *wrong* with it. I didn't think anything of it at first, but for an entire day to pass and have it still be off..." He gives his head a shake. "Perhaps he just needs more time to rest, like Rhea did when she first came here."

That *had* been an interesting fact to learn. Something about how Cass described her magic had tugged at my mind, but I couldn't quite place why it sounded so familiar other than the fact that it is akin to Nox's.

"What do you think will happen when he wakes up?" I murmur. *When he remembers that Rhea is gone* goes unsaid. Daje's recollection of events, as well as Siyala's worry for her, cast the supposed goodbye letter left by Rhea in doubt despite the council's protests that she left of her own free will. Normally, I would never question the intentions of a woman who had gone through as much as I was led to believe Rhea had, yet so much of this entire situation felt like reading a book with missing pages. In any case, Daje was hurt, Rhea is still missing, and Nox is otherwise incapacitated.

And I would eventually have to answer to the council about what I saw and learned in the Shifter Kingdom.

Cass draws his white-blond hair back into a ponytail, the strands draping over the hilt of his sword and the sun and moon insignia there that peeks up just past his shoulder. "I don't know," he says after a moment, the rawness of his voice forming a knot in my throat. "I know you didn't really see them together, but he *loves* her, Bahira. And she loves him. There is no scenario where she just left of her own accord." His eyes meet mine with uncharacteristic seriousness blazing within them. "And there is no chance Nox won't do everything necessary to find her."

Exhaustion catches up to me quickly, and I don't realize I have fallen asleep until the door opens with a creak, jerking me awake as my mother and Galen step inside. The palace healer goes straight to Nox, his hands hovering over Nox's body as his green magic pulses from his palms. I watch his expression tighten, his arms shaking as he makes his way from Nox's head to his chest.

"Go, my rose. I will make sure you are told immediately if he wakes." My mother joins me, and I take in her gaunt expression, her own fatigue evident. Her normally tamed curls are piled on her head in a messy array, as if she couldn't waste a single moment to do them.

"I can stay—"

"No," she interrupts, gripping my hand in hers. "Things are precarious right now, Bahira. Your father's focus is needed on the council, and yours, I know, is needed everywhere else. Now go. Should Nox wake, I will send someone to get you."

Sighing, I grab my pack from the floor and secure it on my back, my mother giving me a reassuring grin. I spare Nox one more glance before hugging Cass, and once the door is shut behind me, I take a moment to drag in a breath before heading back down the corridor to the foyer. In the silence, without Nox or my work to focus on, my thoughts drift back to Kai.

Not once before has anyone taken up so much space in my head like he has. I want to ignore the reasons as to why, but even I cannot pretend that I don't see the facts for what they are. Kai had shown me what it was to have someone relish in all the imperfect edges that lined me. However brief it had been, what I always longed for was suddenly within my hands. *And over my body and inside of me.* While Daje wanted a past version of me, I had made Kai crave a woman who simply didn't exist. I had lied, knowing the whole time that my deception would ruin everything. I packaged myself up as one thing, and when I pulled on the string that held me together, revealing what was actually underneath, he had deemed me *worthless*.

He was right when he said he couldn't take the words back, but he was wrong when he assumed I was strong enough to handle them. And fucking stars above, I *hate* that all I can think about is reaching out to him again and asking if he really did see *me*. Not the magicless princess or the mage or the warrior, but the woman who was melded between those things. If his hurt had found comfort with mine like I felt mine had with him. But I suppose the answers to those questions remain to be seen, at least until the Mirror is repaired. Blinking away the uncomfortable feeling that rises, I continue down the hall until I see the wooden door to the council room. Slowing my steps, I listen to hear if anyone is in there before taking the silence as a sign of its emptiness and reaching for the door handle.

The space is dotted in amber light from the setting sun that streams in through the windows. Nox's magic had almost obliterated this room—could likely have toppled this entire wing of the palace if he had tried hard enough. Perhaps that is the most unnerving part about all of this; not that Nox's magic has the potential to destroy something to this magnitude. It is that *he* has the capability to do this without even realizing it.

All because he is in love with someone.

Is that the other side to love? Not the sweet and enduring tenderness of my parents, but something wilder. Something that consumes every part of you until you are inexplicably out of control. Kai's throne room flashes in my mind, the memory making me shiver as I recall how he so effortlessly killed his uncle when the guard had overpowered me and held a knife to my throat. *That's different, isn't it?* It was a necessity, a foreign king protecting the asset of another kingdom. The lie doesn't make me feel any better, so I turn back to inspecting the council room.

I had missed what remains of the Mirror on my earlier visit, but I inspect the shards of the glass still stuck to the wooden frame tilted against a wall now. It is said that the Mirrors were formed at the very beginning of life on Olymazi—one given to each kingdom by the gods so that the rulers could communicate with each other. It had been full of ancient magic for so long, and now it just looks ordinary. Lifeless. No longer showing evidence that it had held such power.

"One thing at a time," I murmur to myself as I turn for the exit. Fixing the Mirror just became my first priority, followed by somehow testing my theory on the Spell *and* figuring out how to get my magic. *Simple.* I nearly snort out loud.

I pass a plethora of guards on my way to my room, including a new one who is posted where Barron should be. We exchange quick pleasantries before I continue on towards my room, only to find Daje sitting on the ground in front of my door.

"Hey, Bahira," he says, a morose kind of pain hidden behind a forced grin.

I return one just as pitiful. "Hey, Daje." We stare in silence at each other, and though there is likely not a worse time to have this conversation, I know it is one that can no longer be avoided. "Let's talk."

Chapter Six

BAHIRA

DROPPING MY PACK DOWN in the center of the room, I pull out one of the chairs at the small table off to the side for Daje before sinking down into my own. "How are you?" I ask, brushing my curls off of my shoulders.

"Do you want the expected answer or the truth?"

"I always want the truth from you."

His silence lingers a heartbeat too long. "Do you?"

The corner of my mouth lifts in an apathetic smirk. "I deserved that—and likely much more."

He breathes out a short laugh, slouching back against his chair. "I suppose I should say that I'm fine. My wounds have healed, and I can go back to whatever my life was before the ball. Before you left." He crosses his arms over the wrinkled green tunic he wears as his brows draw down. "But the truth is, nothing has felt right since the day I watched you walk away with the shifter king."

I force myself to hold his stare, my throat working a rough swallow as guilt simmers in my veins. With the sun having fully set now, Daje ignites new spelled flames in the glass orbs around my room. It sends light flooding over the space and right onto me, making me feel as if I'm put on display and there is nowhere to hide. *Pathetic*, I chide myself, sitting up taller in the chair. I have avoided this conversation for far too long, and I owe it to us both to be nothing but honest with him. Like I had told myself after the rebel attack in the woods with Kai, if the consequences of Daje's terms come to pass, *he* will have to bear the weight of that choice. Not me. Still, my heart beats furiously in my chest.

"You didn't come home with any intention of marrying me, did you?"

"No." My answer is immediate.

"Did you at least *leave* here with it as a possibility?"

Even at my lowest moment, before I had found any hint of progress in my experiments, considering a betrothal to Daje had always felt like a finality I didn't want to acknowledge. A line I couldn't cross. I hated that this would hurt him, but I hated even more that he put us in this position to begin with.

"You know I care about you." He shifts uncomfortably in his chair, his eyes like polished sapphires as they study me. "But who I am and who you *believe* me to be are not the same person, Daje. A part of me wishes they could be, that I could fit into the mold you so clearly want me to, but I can't."

"I just want you to be yourself," he counters.

"Do you?" I volley back with soft accusation.

His jaw clenches as he glances away, staring at the wall. "When you were gone, I spent some time with Rhea. I found her to be somewhat of an anomaly at first. She was quiet yet vibrant, shy yet subconsciously commanded the attention of whoever was near her. She moved through this kingdom as if she wasn't aware of the presence she held, and it reminded me of your brother." His gaze shifts back to mine as he runs a hand over his head. "Nox has always been the most powerful among us, but his command is a quiet lethality that only just tempts you to pull it out of him. Yet when they were together? There was no clashing of verbal swords. I don't doubt they argued, but they made being in love look so *easy*. I couldn't help but think that *nothing* with you has ever been that way."

I can tell by the gentleness of his voice—the way it rasps and nearly cracks at the end—that he doesn't mean it as an insult. Still, claws of irritation sink deeply into me. It shouldn't hurt to realize that perhaps our friendship wasn't as I made it out to be in my mind. At least not to him. Wasn't that the crux of it? How many times would I find out that my selfish desires and the pursuit of them had blinded me so?

"And even with that realization, I still want what we *could* be together. I still want *you*," he continues.

A yawning pit opens within me. How easy it was to be steadfast in my decision to break his heart while I was in the Shifter Kingdom, and how naïve I am to think it would be anything other than awful. "I *can't*."

His hands come to rest on the table, the shadows of the nearby flames dancing across his face as he lifts a brow. "I've never known you to back down from a challenge, and I don't understand why you are doing so now."

"Daje, listen to what you're saying. I'm telling you I cannot be with you in the way you want, and you're telling me to *work harder* at trying to be? Who does that benefit? Who wins in that scenario?"

"We do!" he snaps, his fingers stretching out towards me. "What you feel for me, it can be enough—"

"I don't want to just feel *enough*!" I shout, standing so abruptly my chair falls behind me. "I want to be consumed. I—" My chest heaves, the sound of my heart beating like an angry drum through my skull. "I want to feel like I'm so overcome with what it means to *be* in your presence that I can think of nothing else. I want to feel your absence like a stake to the chest!"

He shakes out his head, standing to lean over the table. "That's not love, Bahira; that's *obsession*."

"Can't they be the same?" I hate the way he looks at me, as if I'm nothing more than a child attempting to speak about something I have no knowledge on. Maybe I am. But what I experienced with Kai and my past with Daje clash together in my head and in my heart, clearly pointing out the differences between the two in a way that I can't deny.

"*No*. Love is tender and soft. It's caring for someone even when it's hard."

"Oh, please," I snarl, narrowing my eyes. "That is what *your* love looks like, not mine."

"And how would you know what yours looks like?"

"Because I have felt it!" Like a death knell, the words ring out and hit their mark. The stunned quiet that follows grows taut between us, an arrow pulled on a string just waiting to be released. Except I am not sure who is holding the bow.

"Not with anyone here, which means—" His expression shifts as he looks at me. *Fuck.* I swallow any kind of retort down, pushing it into that deep chasm within me, but it's too late. Whatever look is on my face makes Daje solemnly chuckle, his hand forming a fist and pounding into the table three times to the cadence of his words. "Of-fucking-*course*. You've fallen in love."

"I'm not in love," I argue defensively, the retort weak even to my own ears. *No, I can't be in love.* Hadn't I just analyzed what love looks like moments ago in the council room? It was not love with Kai—it *can't* be. Regret winds with my own indignation down my spine at how the conversation has so clearly gone in the wrong direction. "Daje, I'm sorry—"

"It's fine, Bahira. Really," he interrupts, dropping his gaze to the table. "Though it might not have always been done in the right way, all I've ever wanted is for you to see just how fucking perfect you are *as is*. If you've found someone who makes you feel that way..." His eyes lift up to meet mine while he stands. "Then what do I have to be upset about?"

Silence is all I can manage as I watch him leave. The room grows colder in his absence, his words leaving their mark on me as stark as the tattoos that are drawn on Kai's skin. It isn't just what Daje said but what I unconsciously confessed to us both. Infatuation with the shifter king is one thing, and even I, in all my stunted emotional availability, can recognize that I care for him beyond what I ever thought I would. *But love*? I can't admit to that, because doing so means that I have sacrificed so much more than I ever intended to, and if that is true, how am I supposed to move forward?

"Are you alright, Bahi?" my father asks from his place across the table the next day, weariness evident in the lilt of his voice. I lift my eyes from where I've been staring at my plate of food, the steam once wafting from it now gone. The queen's dining room seems bigger than it did before, full of empty seats at the table and shadows that linger menacingly in the corners.

"Yes."

Reeling in the aftermath of my conversation with Daje, I had done the only thing that seemed logical and dived right back into my work. I didn't want to remain in my room, not with the condemnation of his words still echoing within it. How the revelation of my own screamed with them. I checked in on Nox, who remains slumbering in an eerily still manner, Cass returning from the break my mother forced him to take as I was leaving. We all wore varying degrees of exhaustion on our faces, even if Cass tried to hide it beneath a terrible joke or two.

Then I made my way to the library, returning the journals I had taken with me to the Shifter Kingdom—much to Elisha's relief—before asking her to point me to any text that might speak of two things: the creation of the Spell and the ancient mages who experimented with blood. While researching the Spell certainly wasn't out of the ordinary, asking for information on the latter was. It had practically been a scary bedtime story, the tale of mages who mixed blood and magic with devastating results. But I imagined, like most stories, there was a bit of truth woven into the tales. Elisha had only stared at me, her eyes growing wide for a brief moment before she tucked a graying strand of hair back into the bun on the top of her head.

Leaning in close, she kept her voice low. "Those texts would likely be kept in the palace archives, Your Highness. You'll need permission from a council member to enter there."

My answering grimace made her chuckle, though she couldn't know it was because asking the council to help with *anything* right now seemed a perilous task. She at least guided me towards a section of text that she claimed spoke of life in the Mage Kingdom through the millennia.

"Perhaps there is something to go off of in one of these," she said, gesturing with a wrinkled hand before returning back to her desk.

After spending some time perusing, I grabbed a few titles of interest, intent on reading the rest of the morning when my return to the palace was interrupted by a run-in with my father. It was easy to say yes when he asked me to join him for a meal. I had missed my family while I was gone and with the worry that had captured me on the journey back, the urge to spend time with them pressed on me.

"The council has once more asked for a debriefing from you," my father says, his finger tapping on the table. "Have you decided what you are going to divulge?" I had given my father a small recap of the more important things that had happened during my time on the island. It felt nice, getting to talk with him about Kai in even the barest sense.

I purse my lips as I use my fork to toy with the food on my plate. My own fatigue thins out my armor, the weight of all that has come to pass and the uncertainty of the future heavier than it ever has been. So much has changed in the past few months, and yet it simply feels as if I am back to square one again. A pattern, it seems, that I'm destined to repeat. "I don't know. The Shifter Kingdom is in upheaval, and though the king did not ask me to keep the details of their current state of affairs or of the magical blight a secret, a part of me wonders what information is safe with the council." I level my gaze back on his. "And that concern feels nearly as dangerous as knowing there were rebels who outwardly opposed King Kai in his own court."

My father nods. "One never expects to question the integrity of the men they have chosen to be their sounding boards. I'm realizing that I've made an error in that way. One that Nox is now going to pay the price for, because even if there is a *small* chance that Rhea left on her own accord, the council's vehement disapproval of her as Nox's choice of partner drove her to that decision."

"You didn't know," I reply. He had told me of what the council revealed. That they had twisted his request that his children and future generations be given the choice to pick whomever they marry into something that still required their approval. Their betrayal of his trust causes me to wince, like someone has pressed on a fresh bruise.

"No, but I've grown too complacent. I've forgotten one of the most common lessons that is taught throughout history."

"And what is that?" I ask, sitting up taller and leaning my elbows on the table.

"That men can grow fickle, none more so than those with something to lose." A chill works its way down my spine as I draw in a slow breath. "We must balance keeping the council happy while also figuring out who betrayed us in the first place. All while hoping that we can convince your brother to act rationally when he recovers."

I tilt my head to the side, my meal officially abandoned as I think over my father's words. "In other words, we must pretend to give them what they want." He nods in agreement.

"When Nox wakes, he will want to go find Rhea, and I don't think he will *care* for the chaos doing so will cause. The council has already shown us what they are willing to do and threaten in the name of safety, and I highly doubt they will appease Nox's urge to go searching for the woman they already didn't like," he continues, his voice low. "Our next steps must be made carefully. Until we can figure out who is on our side. Tell the council whatever you deem safe for them to know and nothing else."

I nod as my father stares in the direction of the portraits of our family that line the wall behind me.

"And, *by the gods*, may your brother not take down the entire palace when he wakes."

Chapter Seven

ARIA

D AYS HAVE PASSED SINCE we handed over the mage woman to the ship in the middle of the ocean, and my unease regarding the entire situation has only grown. I have kept to my room as much as possible, a decision that certainly isn't wise considering I have orders from Nia, the queen, and a meeting with a fae to prepare for. I just can't bring myself to care about those things yet, not when acknowledging them means accepting what had come to pass.

Mashaka is gone, my cave is no longer a secret place of refuge, and I'm being watched more than ever before. And now there is this.

I stare at my entwined fingers in my lap, filtered sunlight from my window reflecting red flares from the scales near my stomach onto my dark brown skin.

"Aria, did you hear me?" Lyre's voice is soft from where she sits on my bed behind me, the silky kelp stuffing it shifting as she slides closer.

"Yes," I answer, though I can't bring myself to look at her yet. I had a sinking feeling when she showed up at my door this morning, her lavender eyes holding mine with something that resembled pity. *Pregnant.* It isn't the first time Lyre has become so, the nature of our lives as sirens giving us frequent *opportunities* to grow our bellies with offspring. Still, this reveal by my older sister is yet another sickening twist of the imaginary blade that has taken residence in my gut lately.

Her being pregnant changes *everything.*

"Does Mother know?" I ask, finally looking over my shoulder to meet her eyes. They droop in sadness, the corners of her full mouth resting in a tight line. She gives me a single nod that makes me squeeze my hands more tightly together. "She must be happy."

"I could no longer hide it," Lyre says, gesturing to her already growing belly. It isn't an obvious thing, something only noticeable when specifically looking.

Siren pregnancies are short, only lasting four months. For her to already be showing even a little, she must be close to her second month. "I know this is *less* than ideal, Aria, but we will figure it out. Perhaps, I can convince Mother to let me continue going on hunts for a while longer with you."

I shake my head, swimming off of the bed as I begin to pace my room. "That's wishful thinking, Lyre. You know that she will make you stay within the walls of the palace until you give birth to ensure you stay protected." Chewing on my lower lip, I let my talons dig into my arm to help ground me. "There will be no hiding my lack of magic now."

The last time Lyre was pregnant, I was too young to go out on hunts. I haven't yet had to navigate around my secret without her help. With our mother insisting she stay within the palace—as she has done for every other sister to get pregnant—I'll be *alone* at the whim of Allegra and all the other sirens present on those hunts.

The magic that flows in my veins is confusing. *Uncharted.* I am meant to lure *males* under my spell, but I recently learned that the opposite is true. My song only affects *females*, and without Lyre's help during hunts, without her singing next to me to make it seem like my magic is working as it is supposed to, it is only a matter of time until someone finds out the truth.

Lyre's silence only adds to the anxiousness swirling within me. She leaves the bed, swimming until she is floating next to me. Her finger curls beneath my chin, tilting my head up until my gaze meets hers. "What if this pregnancy marks a different change?"

"What do you mean?"

Her voice drops to a whisper as her eyes scan my face before she releases her hold on me. "What if we don't follow the rules this time? What if we decide that enough is enough and just *leave*?" My heart beats at my ribs as I watch Lyre gently rest her hands on her belly, the tender display lodging a rock in my throat. Her eyes turn wistful as she rubs at the skin above her womb. "Last time, I tried to detach myself from the babe that was growing within me," she starts softly, referencing her first pregnancy. "I focused as much of my attention as I could on you while also busying myself around the palace under the guise of trying to impress our mother. But I was only fooling myself."

"What happened?" I had assumed that Lyre actually wasn't attached to her pregnancy. That it, like everything else, was just another part of our life beneath our mother's rule that held no emotional value. By the devastation on her face, I can see just how wrong I was.

"It's hard to ignore when you feel that fluttering of movement for the first time. When it grows as the weeks pass into something that demands attention. By the time I was far enough along to give birth, I became accustomed to the movement. I expected it, longed for it in a way that terrified me because I knew then, as I know now, what our mother insists become of our offspring. How we are separated from them, made strangers until they are adults."

It had been that way for as long as records were kept. All sirens born within the royal line were raised by others, and only those born to the currently ruling queen got recognized as official princesses. There were babies born to my mother before she took rule of our queendom, sisters by blood that I had never met and likely never would. Ones that perhaps didn't even know that the queen was their mother.

"When she was born, I didn't get more than a glimpse at her," she whispers, and the ache in her voice forces my hand to reach out to her. Gripping her fingers between mine, I watch as Lyre's eyes close and her head hangs low. "It all happened so quickly. Mother was there through it all, watching as I pretended to not care that there was suddenly an emptiness where there had been life. Ensuring that I felt the same detachment about my child that she feels about us. But I was *dying*, Aria."

That imaginary dagger within me twists deeper. To know that my sister was suffering, that for *years* she had held on to this pain and endured it all alone sends regret slinking through me. "Lyre, I had no idea."

"I didn't want you to know," she answers simply, and if I thought it wasn't possible to love my sister more, I'm proven wrong right then. Giving my hand a squeeze, she releases it to cradle her belly once more. "But I will not go through that again. I will not give our mother the satisfaction of knowing that she has once more successfully torn a piece of us away in her attempt to make us more like *her*. I haven't done enough to protect us, Aria, but that is going to change."

My brows draw together, the determination in her words sending a jolt of fear through me. "Lyre—"

"After she is born, I'm taking her and leaving Lumen."

"*What?*"

"I have scoped out a route I don't think could be easily tracked, not even by Sade or Allegra. It will take weeks to get far enough away, and carrying my daughter with me will make the journey hard, but I'm going to do it." Her eyes shine bright as the fingers cradling her belly tighten a little more. "And I want you to come with me."

Too many emotions battle for attention as my stomach twists in on itself. Terror and uncertainty predominantly shout in my mind, screaming that this is madness. *No one* escapes the wrath of the siren queen. Yet something else whispers from a lone corner, a voice that sounds like excitement, like *hope*. *This could work*, it says.

But the fear of what could happen is too much to ignore. "Lyre, there *is* no escaping from this." No matter the outpost or town—whatever the distance away from Lumen—it isn't far enough. It won't ever be.

"We could do this, Aria. Together. We can protect each other—"

"I can't even protect myself!" I shout, my arms flaring wide. "I couldn't protect Mashaka. I—" Shaking my head, I back away from her attempt to reach me. "This is a death sentence."

"Isn't our life already one as it is? You think our mother won't sacrifice us the moment it becomes convenient? How much longer do you think you can go without getting pregnant before she decides your life holds no value and she lets Allegra have her way with you?" Her voice carries in my room, as powerful as the current that surrounds us. Her amethyst scales glint in the sunlight as she swims towards me. "You deserve a life outside of this. *We both do.* I have had a long time to plan this, and I have no intention of failing. Just as I have no intention of leaving you behind. So, please, if you cannot trust in yourself to do this, then trust in *me.*"

"What if I can't help protect you? Protect your daughter? I'm not a warrior, Lyre. I'm not strong or clever or valuable. My own magic doesn't even work!"

Though Lyre's gaze widens at first, she immediately softens it, resting her hands on my shoulders. "What you have endured is no small feat. Sometimes, fighting back is as simple as existing in a world that believes you are weak for doing just that. I do not see someone who is feeble when I look at you, Sister. You are brave and caring and smarter than any—including yourself—give you credit for. After all"—a small smile tilts her lips—"you would have to be those things in order to have a secret cave full of treasures."

I nearly choke on the water surrounding us. "You—you *know* about that?" In all the years I had been visiting my secret spot, not once had Lyre ever given a hint that she was aware of it.

My sister nods, the ends of her braids tickling her shoulders with the movement. "You aren't the best at making sure you aren't being followed." At that, I can't help but chuckle. I nearly tell Lyre of Nia and the deal I've been forced into with her. Of my bargain with the fae, Myla, and what I asked for following Mashaka's death, but I keep those truths held in. If this is something Lyre really wants to do, I can't have her aware of things that may derail her one opportunity at the life she deserves to live. If our mother finds out about any of it, we're as good as dead, and though Queen Amari is already holding my love for Lyre over my head to help her find the missing sirens of the seamounts, I wouldn't give her any more ammunition.

The consequences of those choices are mine alone to bear. My heart thrums, that small whisper gaining against the trepidation within me.

But the reminder of Myla sparks a different thought. I had made that bargain with her to learn how to fight, hadn't I? I couldn't have known that Lyre would present me with a *real* chance to escape, but I would be a fool to let both opportunities slip through my fingers because this life—this all-consuming *fear*—is all I know.

I may not trust myself, but I do trust Lyre. And after all she's sacrificed for me, how could I not take a leap of faith with her? I often thought there wasn't anyone willing to stick their neck out for me, but Lyre had continued to do so, and though I was terrified I would fail her, something in me sparked at the chance to do *something good*.

"Okay," I rasp, unable to stop the smile that tugs on my mouth. Lyre's mirroring one brings a warmth to my chest that is foreign and unfamiliar, but I grasp on to it as hard as I can.

"We can do this. We *will* do this. Together." We linger, and though my mind threatens to race back into panic mode, I force myself to enjoy the feeling of hope. "There is one more thing." She reaches around her back, tugging on a braided cord that is secured around her waist until a small pouch comes into view. Untying it from the cord, she places the pouch gently in my hand, closing my fingers around it until I feel the small round objects that are inside. "I will not need these for a while, so I want you to have them. Add them to your stash, and there should be enough to protect you for a while yet."

Opening the pouch, I peer inside. *Golina berries*. They are rare, only found growing in small pockets of sea that the queen hasn't yet destroyed in her search for the plant. The tiny bitter fruit, when taken within the correct time frame, can stop a pregnancy from taking root. Lyre had been sneaking the berries to me since my very first hunt.

"Thank you," I rasp, taking the pouch from her and placing it in the only other hiding spot I have now that my cave is no longer my own. Lifting a bundle of the sea kelp in my bed, I tuck it into the sliver of empty space there before smoothing the kelp back over.

"Mother will be announcing my pregnancy this afternoon at the queen's address."

That small bit of warmth in my chest ices over as I nod my head.

⚘ ⚘

The yellow sea glass door to the throne room opens, and my mother, flanked by legionaries, enters, swimming down the center aisle with a powerful and raw elegance. The light from the open waters above gets lost in the fathomless black of her braids and the cold darkness of her deep purple eyes. Unlike those who inhabit the pit past Tula Ledge, *she* is the only creature here that induces fear.

"My subjects, welcome!" Her greeting quiets the murmurings of the sirens present, all of their attention focusing intently on their queen as she moves up the dais and lowers herself gracefully into her throne. "Thank you all for joining me today. We have something lovely to celebrate." She taps her trident against the stone once, and the noise beckons Lyre to swim to the front. "It is my absolute pleasure to announce that my daughter, your princess, Lyre is pregnant." A single moment of utter shock ripples over the room before claps and cheers of congratulations ring out, the chattering of the females in front of us full of excitement as their eyes eagerly devour my sister.

I glance back to my mother, her smile sharp and eyes keen as she looks down at the sirens filling the room. She taps her trident again, ushering in silence as Lyre bows and then returns to her spot next to me.

"But this is not all we have to rejoice over." I catch the quick line that forms between Lyre's brows before she smooths it back out. Allegra's deep blue tail flashes before us as she makes her way to the front.

Part of the reason I've taken to hiding in my room is to also avoid seeing *her*. The memory of Mashaka—his dying wails and bloody body—skewers me all over again every time Allegra is present. She doesn't even care that he's gone. A creature that she had captured and formed *some* kind of bond with over years is dead, *murdered*, and Allegra behaves like nothing of value has been lost. I know better than to be so affected by her callousness, yet I still can't fathom how she can be so *cold*.

"The goddesses have blessed us with not one pregnant princess but two. Allegra is with offspring as well!"

More cheering. More clapping. More tiny white bubbles lifting to the surface from the chaotic delight of the sirens below us as my heart seizes in my chest. Lyre's arm brushes against my own as she claps. I can't move, can hardly hear my own thoughts above the discordant celebration. She does it again, roughly enough to draw my attention.

"*Clap*," she whispers from the corner of her mouth. I immediately begin doing so, scanning the throne room in a haze. It isn't that I am necessarily surprised; Allegra has been pregnant many times before. Her pregnancy has the opposite effect on me that Lyre's does. In the same way that Lyre is now bound to the palace, so too is our eldest sister.

My mother addresses the crowd with the rest of her announcements, cryptically citing the dawning of a new era, which causes even more excitement than the pregnancy reveals did. I stay tucked into the possibilities of my mind, wondering if I've *finally* been given reprieve from the constant dread that has settled into its corners. If Allegra can no longer lead the hunts I'm forced to go on, will *anyone* else watch me as closely as she did?

When the address is over and I attempt to leave, my mother's smooth voice halts my retreat. "We have more matters to discuss, Daughter." *Jaw and shoulders relaxed, lips flat, spine straight, and attitude vicious.* I silently repeat my mantra as I turn around and force my gaze to hers. "We must prepare to leave and meet with the king of the Mortal Realm."

"*Why?*" Allegra hisses from her place at the queen's side.

"Has your pregnancy turned you into an imbecile, or are you simply choosing to not understand?" My mother's brashness makes something flash in Allegra's eyes before she bows her head and drops her gaze.

"What do we need to know before we go to the surface?" Sade cuts in, her conch shell helmet held against the orange scales at her side. She wears no other armor and clutches the smaller trident that mirrors our mother's in her other hand. Her façade is steady, calm, a lethal brutality lingering beneath it.

"Sade, Aria, and Dyanna, you will accompany me to speak to King Dolian. The mortal king is in my debt, and I want to ensure my plans do not falter. We cannot give him the opportunity to do something foolish, as his kind is prone to." Queen Amari lifts her hand up in front of her, her dark eyes studying the pearl ring that adorns her finger. Softly, as if the words are only meant for her, she adds, "I will not make the same mistakes as before the war."

"And what about me?" Allegra asks.

My mother drops her hand back to her lap. "You and Lyre are to remain here, both to enforce my rule with me gone and to stay protected."

Allegra's blue eyes widen, her lips lifting into a snarl. "You want me to *stay here*? I am one of your fiercest warriors—"

"You are not," she cuts in smoothly, sliding a talon down one of the diamond-inlaid prongs of her trident. "Sade, as the commander of the legion, is."

Allegra snarls in response but doesn't speak another word.

"Was the king on that ship?" Sade asks, earning our mother's nod.

"And who was the mage we handed over to them?" The question slips unbidden from me, from the place it has rattled since that night.

My mother's attention falls to me, her full lips twisting with something too ghastly to be called a grin. "She may just be the key to finally getting *everything* we are owed. In due time, we will show the beings of Olymazi what happens when they try to contain us. We will show the males of these lands the reckoning that has been brewing beneath their shores. Until then, you will continue to serve me as I command and without question." She looks around at my sisters as she leans back on her throne. "Tell me what progress you've made in finding the traitors of the seamounts?"

The question locks my shoulders and careens my heart against my ribcage. "I—I don't know where to start looking for them."

Tilting her head, her eyelids lower in displeasure. "Disappointing, but unsurprising. Sade will aid you in your search for them once we return from our visit with the king."

What? I look to Sade, surprised to find the same confusion hinted at in her sunset eyes. "Your Majesty, you know I am but a servant to your will, but working with Aria will be a waste of my valuable time."

"You will help her form a plan to find the traitors and then report the progress she has made to me. I hardly think that will interfere with your normal duties, Daughter."

"And if she has nothing to report?" Sade questions, her eyes snapping to mine.

"The next few months will be crucial in solidifying our plans and reclaiming what is *ours*. I cannot have a group of traitors plotting against the queendom while I try to raise us from the sea. They *will* be taken care of, or I shall show our people just how little I care for blood when it comes to extending my mercy."

Sade's talons scrape against her helmet as she curls her fingers inward. "As you wish, Your Majesty."

Satisfied, my mother tilts her head back and closes her eyes. "Prepare what is needed for our departure. I would like to leave within the hour."

It isn't until I'm finished packing my own small woven eelgrass satchel that I realize that traveling with my mother to the Mortal Kingdom means I'm going to miss my first meeting with the fae female.

Shit.

Chapter Eight

MYLA

THE DRAGON FIELDS SMELL of sulfur and death. Piles of charred remains litter the lush emerald-green grass, and I have no idea if they are animals unlucky enough to be caught in a dragons' quarrel or the remnants of fae ordered to their deaths by my father. Some of those fae undoubtedly deserved their fiery end—there is no shortage of vile beings in this kingdom. Yet some I knew had committed the most minor of infractions, stealing food to feed their families or medicine to rid a persistent sickness. Because those things took money from vendors which in turn took money from the king, all who were caught received the maximum punishment: death by dragon fire.

Scorched earth surrounds the bundles of singed bones, some of them still lit with lingering embers. I keep to the outskirts of the fields, hidden within the treeline as I dart around the evergreens and pines. I'm under no illusion that I'm invisible to the dragons, my scent is one they can smell on the wind. Still, walking out into the open field is not only the equivalent of asking a dragon to burn me to ash but also stupid, as a dragon rider might spot me from above. Bonding a dragon is essential to my plan, and it would be a real fucking shame to die before that happens.

My palms slide against the rough bark of a pine tree, dirt from traversing the mountain tunnels to get here caked over them along with the dried blood of the male I *visited* prior. Looking to the east, I blow out a startled breath at the small sliver of sun already rising over the horizon. I swear it hadn't taken long for Dagan, my poor subject of the evening, to drunkenly stumble from the tavern he loved to frequent. He was as most of the males of this city are—power hungry, angry, and stupid. Instead of channeling that energy into anything productive, he took his aggressions out on his wife. Nightly, and often to the point of knocking her unconscious. Or so my informant told me.

Moving into a run, I finally reach the mountainous edge of the dragon fields, a burning pile of *something* nearby casting a golden glow over the rocky cave in front of me.

The Fae Kingdom is built in and surrounded by mountains, the horizon littered with black peaks and hazy mist. One might think us vulnerable in such open terrain. What is mist compared to the cover of thickly woven trees or miles of ocean? The mist isn't meant to protect us, however. The dragons are, and no other kingdom can lay claim to the beasts but the fae.

I let out a low whistle in warning, prowling forward towards the mountain front. The ends of my hair brush against my shoulders at the *hot* breeze that blows from the opening, the smell of burnt carrion making my nose crinkle. Just one of her luminous yellow eyes is visible at first against the impossible darkness behind her. Then her head swivels, hard black scales glistening as she emerges from the mouth of the cave, shrewd gaze landing on me. The ground beneath my boots rumbles with the impact of her steps, her massive size blocking my field of vision entirely. With a head larger than my own body and a wingspan that would stretch past ten lengths of me, Bali is the largest of her dragonkind, as those of the Khar line are. Her tail—the end tipped in a trio of spikes the size of my forearm—lifts high behind her while she lowers her head down, the serpentine movements of her neck making my stomach hollow as she assesses whether she's in the mood to humor or cook me.

"Bali," I offer by way of greeting, forcing my voice to be loud but steady while I straighten my spine a little more. The fine hairs on my arms lift as she emits a noise that sounds like rolling thunder, the vibration of it rattling my skull. Behind her, a slightly higher-pitched growl answers as it reverberates off the surrounding rock. Bali snarls at me, her four canines showcasing the blood that still stains them from her last meal.

The tip of her snout skims over me as she blows out through her nostrils, ruffling her leathery wings in tandem at her sides. The blood from Dagan is still speckled over my clothing, likely what draws the dragon's attention. A deeper sound rumbles from her as she lifts her head and opens her mouth wide, revealing the molten dragon flame balled at the base of her throat. It churns in a beautiful display of vivid red, orange, and golden yellow, the colors as hypnotizing as they are fear inducing. She blows out a singeing breath that forces me to close my eyes and turn my head. Sweat glides down my body beneath my black leathers, but I keep my feet rooted to the ground as I endure her display of dominance. Or rather, her test of my own.

Dragons are loyal creatures by nature, and bonding them to a rider only magnifies that loyalty. Before The War Of Five Kingdoms, a bond between dragon and rider was only severed when the rider died, as a fae's lifespan is less than half of a dragon's, or when a dragon willfully ended it. However, in the centuries that have passed, the connection between these ferocious beasts and the fae have faltered. Growing more common are instances of bonds nearly as old as the war itself fading away until there is nothing that remains.

When a rider loses their bond, it's devastating. When a dragon loses a bond and the severing *isn't* enacted by them, it can drive the beast mad. Most will choose a new rider to bond with because of it.

Bali finally extinguishes the swirling flame and closes her mouth. I observe her as she stares at me, seeing just enough of her outline in the growing early morning light to make out the massive pointed horns on the top of her head. They're surrounded by smaller ones of different heights and thicknesses, the diamond-shaped scales covering her iridescently black. The Khar line possesses a fearsome blend of brute strength and cocky bravery. The color and shape of their scales are unique to this line, and while most dragons tend to be a mix of two different lines, Bali remains one of only a few dragons alive whose line is completely pure.

I glance to the east again, my heart rate kicking up at how little time I have left to spend here. *Fuck.* I should already be home. But if I, a female, want to bond with a dragon—a feat that has never been accomplished in our history—then I *have* to spend as much time here as I can. Especially as my bargain with the siren begins this week. Annoyance is a tight knot in my throat, but I force it down roughly. There is no time to ruminate on that now.

Bali turns to stalk away, her tail swinging harshly enough behind her to send a small gust of air towards me in a warning. With my view of the cave once more unobstructed, I focus in on the second set of glowing eyes that appear in the opening.

It has taken *years* of coming here for Bali to only threaten me partially—though I wonder if that is a courtesy she extends to me simply because of who I am related to. Her former rider, my older brother, Shah, was murdered in the war, and though Bali could have no way of knowing I am his younger sister, I sometimes wonder if she can sense it. Whether through the scent of my blood or some other mystical means, she hasn't acted nearly as aggressive with me as she has with anyone else who happens to wander into the dragon fields.

My brother was the kingdom's darling, a crown prince everyone was honored to have and proud to know. My parents still celebrate his birthday every year as if he hasn't missed the past two hundred of them. His death did more than just devastate our parents; it changed the course of the kingdom nearly more than the war had. A century later and against all odds, my mother became pregnant, and there was reason to celebrate again. Until my birth was deemed not a blessing by the gods but an omen. *A punishment*, the brethren of the church declared.

The sound of rustling leather wings echoes as the smaller black dragon, Bali's spitting image in every way but size for now, steps out onto the rocky ground. She flares her wings out, a satisfied whine pushing past her sharp teeth at the stretch before they snap back in. I take a step closer to her, those brilliant eyes looking at me curiously. The horns that adorn her scales are only barely starting to sharpen, but despite her young age, she is just as deadly as her mother to a fae.

Sunis is still a fucking dragon, after all.

To name her already without a bond between us is foolish. Despite how my father and the brethren of the church might disagree, I try very hard to be anything *but* foolish. I had chosen Bali's offspring to attempt bonding with purely because it seemed like the most practical choice. Shah had bonded with Bali, and Bali didn't incinerate me the moment I stood outside of her home for the first time. As far as naming her, well, I thought I might try being optimistic about something in my gods-cursed life. So far, that optimism has gotten me nowhere.

She lowers her head until my hand meets the smooth scales on her nose. Hot air blasts past me through her nostrils as one of her green-tinged eyes meets mine. The bonding process with a dragon is kept secret, not spoken about outside of the circles of males who are already bound. From my brother, Navin—a male who enjoys breaking from tradition and, above all, *gossiping*—I've learned that bonding doesn't necessarily give dragons the ability to *speak* to their rider. Instead, it builds a mental pathway between them so that they can understand each other's emotions and intentions. Staring at Sunis now, I wonder if my time spent coming here almost daily for the past few years is *finally* beginning to pay off.

Grinding my teeth together, I drag my hand up the side of her face, searching for what Navin had annoyingly called the bonding *tingle*. "Let today be the day." I close my eyes and steady my hand, my heart thundering in my chest.

Sunis chuffs before bumping her enormous head into me and knocking me to the ground. I let out a growl as my eyes open, the fucking dragon answering it with a much louder one of her own before she turns and trots onto the dragon field. With a groan, I roll onto my stomach and push up to stand, brushing myself off. Lifting the hood attached to my cloak, I fix it over my head and then tug my mask up to cover the bottom half of my face. I wait until Sunis and Bali take flight, likely off to go hunt, before I turn, and race home against the incoming daylight.

Chapter Nine

MYLA

THE GLASS SLIDER SHAKES as I knock on it again, my annoyance with my brother making me contemplate if wrapping my cloak around my hand and punching through the glass might be a better option. My muscles ache, the adrenaline from sprinting through the forest and then the rocky tunnels connecting the palace to the mountain beginning to wear off. They were thought to be sealed off, used long ago as a way for the palace inhabitants to escape should there be a siege, yet with the Spell now in place, the fear of an attack from other kingdoms is long over. While all the passageways within the palace that lead to the tunnels are indeed blocked, there's one exterior entrance near Navin's bedroom balcony that remains untouched. Likely due to the fact that it's also near a ramp for dragons to land, giving a fae rider much quicker and easier access to mount.

Another minute passes, and I kick the slider hard enough that the glass rattles. Navin finally appears on the other side, grumbling as he runs a hand through his rumpled hair. The raven locks hang tangled past his shoulders, covering some of the colorful ink that adorns his muscular frame.

"Good morning, *princess*," I tease, pushing past him once the slider is open wide enough.

"I hate you," he grumbles, his voice still groggy with sleep. I make my way to his bathroom, unclasping the cloak and leather vest that's strapped to me as I do. Though barely conscious, Navin doesn't let the silence linger. "Long night?"

"Yes." I ignore the weight of his gaze on me as he checks me for injuries, something he's done since he inconveniently caught me sneaking in from a visit to Khargis one night.

My vest hits the floor of his bathroom, the hilts of my daggers tucked into the sheaths that line my ribs clanging on the stone. I pull my weapons from the vest and grab the final two daggers from the straps at my thighs, piling them on top of a towel. Navin tosses one of the spare nightgowns I keep hidden in his room in my direction before giving me the privacy to undress completely.

Once I'm changed, I gather up my blood and dirt-covered clothes and toss them into the wicker basket on the other side of the bathroom before carefully rolling up the towel and padding barefoot out into his room, my boots also in hand. "Thank you."

He grunts, pulling a white tunic over his head. "I can't decide if I should be offended that *none* of the staff have questioned why flying leathers that are clearly too small for me end up in my laundry so frequently."

"Perhaps you aren't as large as your ego would have you believe," I counter, entering the sitting space that adjoins our bedrooms. Though he has the option to move to the heir's wing of the palace—a wing much nicer and larger than this one—he's opted to stay here. The common area we share is large enough to fit a collection of sofas and reading chairs as well as a dining table set up at the center. Bookcases filled with tomes on the history of the kingdom line most of the walls, only broken up by hanging tapestries and paintings.

"You're unusually cruel this morning." Following behind, he leans his hip against the back of a ruby-red chair, its gold stitching shining in the pale sunlight that pours in through another glass slider.

"Blame it on the fact that I'm not much of a morning person."

"And yet here you are. Awake after a night risking your life for the scum of Khargis."

"You act as if you did not train me yourself," I counter, raising a brow as I mirror his position, leaning against a black velvet couch. That gets him to smirk, though it quickly falls.

"I could help you—"

"No."

"Myla—"

"Enough, Navin," I cut in, letting my voice drop as I glare at him. I know he means well; he always does when it comes to me. There's a reason he took on training me, and he knows better than anyone else roaming this palace that sneaking into the city and finding those who deserve the end of my blade isn't about feeding some aching thirst for blood.

At least it didn't start that way.

It is a way to gain control. To help females and children who are already considered second-class citizens amongst males and free them from a hell that they have never deserved. It's the only form of vengeance I can claim, so I hold onto it with a white-knuckled grip. It's a version of freedom for *me*, and though

Navin's intentions are honorable and born purely out of the need to make sure I am alright, what I do in Khargis is mine and mine alone.

I watch as his words pile up behind his pursed lips, his hand twitching at his side while he bites his tongue. Voices sound in the hall beyond our room, and with a sigh, Navin jumps over the back of the chair he was leaning against and transforms into the arrogant but aloof prince that he plays well. "I'll buy you some time."

I rush to my room, slipping past the door and shutting it just as I hear Leesi's voice filter in. "You're up early, Your Highness," she trills. I'm too far away to hear Navin's answer, but based on her high-pitched laugh, it was probably something flirtatious. Though we grew up together, Navin is over a hundred years older than I am. He was born just before the Spell was cast, his parents—my aunt and uncle—dying on the same day Shah did during the war. My own parents made sure he was taken care of, a royal though not a prince by blood. They officially claimed him as their heir the day after I was born. It's a role he's never wanted, one that he knows should be mine. But until I bond a dragon, I cannot attempt to claim it.

Crossing my bedroom, I pull open the double doors to a large wooden wardrobe, the front covered with an intricately carved dragon in mid-flight. Pushing a divider that separates the hanging clothes from the cubbies below, metal clicks, and it pulls open to reveal a hollowed-out space. Unrolling the towel on my bed, I gather the daggers and methodically lay them into the small hidden niche, pushing the façade back before shutting the wardrobe, shoving my boots under the bed, and heading to the bathroom.

I undress as the shower warms, tossing the towel and my nightgown into my own laundry basket before stepping beneath the water just as Leesi enters my room.

"Good morning."

I don't respond to her curt tone, dragging my soapy hands over my face and hoping that any lingering blood or dirt will be washed away before she sees it.

"You're once again curiously up before the sun. I know that you stay up too late to warrant such early rising." Rinsing my face beneath the water spraying from above, I work to quiet my thoughts. *She can't know where I've been or what I've done. She has no way of knowing.* I'd prefer not to kill her, as hiding a body in the palace is a much more difficult task than doing so in Khargis. "Perhaps you need more devotional time." Blinking the water from my lashes, I turn to look at her. She holds a bundle of towels, her slender face showing only a small hint at her age with the short wrinkles that surround her currently squinted eyes. "As a proper princess would do. Not spend her evenings with her nose stuck in a book," she continues, shaking her head.

Years ago, when the urge to venture outside the palace walls first struck, I knew I needed to come up with an alibi should anyone try to enter my room in the middle of the night. Locking my door was the easiest solution, but it took a while to convince the head maid that it was simply because I didn't want to be disturbed while reading. It was a pathetic excuse, one that likely should have caused me embarrassment, but my reputation was already tarnished with rumors that were far worse than being a female who *reads*.

Reaching for a washcloth and the bar of soap, I turn away from Leesi's glare as I begin to clean the rest of my body.

"It's a busy day. Your mother hasn't forgotten that you missed your last tea date with her."

Unsurprising. My mother and I are not close, the fundamental differences in our ideologies of what females should be subjected to in our kingdom makes it difficult to connect as a daughter should to her mother. She wishes for a daughter who is content milling about the palace and gossiping with nobles similar in age about the flowers or handsome nobles or whatever the fuck it is they talk about. Instead, she is stuck with me and the taste of shame that my name leaves on her tongue.

Though the mention of the missed tea date reminds me of my upcoming meeting with the siren. To have survived an attack by the foul creatures was, in and of itself, some sort of miracle. But to then owe a life debt to one? *Unfathomable*. Gaps in my memory when I fell from the sinking ship to when I woke up on the beach make my chest tighten in anger. The wide-eyed stare of that red-headed siren, her freckled nose crinkling in confusion at my mention of the life debt oath I now owed her almost made me believe she genuinely had no idea what I was talking about. But their kind is manipulative, just as their magic would suggest. *And now I owed a fucking life debt to one.*

"You're as clean as you're going to get," Leesi says from outside my shower, the steam doing nothing to hide her judgmental glare. "Out."

My skin crawls with the urge to defy her, but I know from experience that it won't give me anything but temporary triumph now and more attention I do not want later. Turning the water off, I step out of the shower and stand in the cold room as she runs a towel over my body, the rough strokes of her hands leaving my normally pale skin red. Once I'm dry, I follow her back into the bedroom, where my clothing is already laid out. "Before tea, you have a meeting with the Divine Father in his office."

My chest tightens at the mention of Father Yamin. So much for avoiding unwanted attention.

Leesi waits for me to stand in front of her, my arms spread out wide. Today's gown is a satin pink monstrosity, the wide sleeves hanging past my fingers as she slips it over my arms. I keep my gaze on the wall across from me, above the standing mirror and in between two portraits of some goddesses I am sure I'm supposed to know the name of, as she cinches the wrap gown around my waist, tugging on its straps until a burst of breath is forced from me. Panic flares briefly, my nails digging into my palms and vision blurring before I force myself to calm as she reaches for my headdress. Tiny pearls on transparent strings tickle my forehead where they dangle, a veil in matching pink draping over my shoulders to hide most of my hair. She connects the piece that covers the lower half of my face with small clips, only my eyes and the bridge of my nose fully unobstructed. As she works her way around to my back, ensuring no thread is out of place on my gown, I stare at my reflection in the mirror. Lightless eyes glare back, the dark depths of them as empty as the space between my ribs.

Visiting Father Yamin is nothing new. It has been encouraged by the king since the moment I was born. *The gods so hated that we put our faith in our neighbors to the west that they cursed us with a princess instead of a prince. And they gave her the spirit of the traitors who tricked us. There is only one way to fix what has been done. We must pray, and we must show the gods that no matter how far a fae has strayed from their teachings, we can bring them back. Our faith in the gods must be strengthened, and all those who oppose their reign must bear the consequences of their actions.*

I had spent a lifetime hearing that prophecy. My skin bears the scars of those consequences, to the point that not even fae healing abilities could rid me of the evidence of them. Of the pain that still flares from time to time.

"You are set. Now go before Father Yamin is kept waiting too long."

❧ ❧ ❧

Incense is heavy in the air, the cloying scent churning my stomach as I continue deeper into the bowels of the inner sanctum wing of the palace. I pass framed pictures of moments in our history meant to inspire piety. A hand wreathed in light reaching down from the heavens to pour liquid gold onto a dying field—the ground coming to life where the light touches it. Another shows a woman, her dark skin and curvy figure glowing against the white sash that is wrapped around her body, concealing it all except for the swell of her belly. White light glows in the background of another, a trio of fae females staring longingly at the goddess dressed in black and white in front of them. The farther I continue down the corridor, the cooler the air gets and the more that the natural light is replaced by flames flickering in sconces on the black stone walls.

I have dragged my knife across the throats of countless fae in the past five years, all without hesitation. Yet as I near a familiar black metal and wood door, my steps nearly falter. *Get it the fuck together.* I have already been through the worst that the father and his brethren can do. I have experienced their wrath—anger and power disguised as righteous indignation under the council of gods that are supposed to protect us. But there is no protection here, only the will of the males who have always viewed themselves above everyone else.

The guards that follow me—two males dressed head to toe in burnished silver, their swords peeking up over both shoulders—come to a halt, metal creaking from the weight of their steps. My knocking is loud in the cavernous space, making my ears ring.

A rush of thicker incensed air billows out when the door creaks open, a male who can't be much older than I am pushing his head past the threshold. "Ah, Princess, we've been expecting you." Despite his relaxed tone, his black brows draw down towards the center of his nose, like he isn't sure if my arrival was indeed expected or not. I walk past him, careful not to let my garments brush against the dark brown robe he wears, a silver chain belt holding it closed.

Once I'm past the door, he lets it shut, and the space plunges into silence. I wait until he walks past me, keeping a *respectful* distance between us. Visions of what it would feel like to plunge a blade into his shoulder works to calm my heart rate, and by the time I've been guided to the main prayer room, everything I feel about this impending meeting is hidden behind a mental shield.

"He will join you here in a moment." The brother leaves through a small side door, a whisper of air sounding as it seals me in the room. I turn my attention to the dais at the front, each step lined with a bundle of thick pillar candles, their flames casting small shadows on the pulpit that sits centered at the top.

I interlace my fingers together in front of me, the pulsing of my blood somehow louder in this space—a place so devoid of anything *good*. Not that I deserve such a thing. There was a time in my life, long ago, when I thought I might. When I strived to be devoted to the teachings. To be as *obedient* as possible. It took far too long to realize that was a futile effort, that the nature of having a womb would automatically make me a target for things far more sinister than praying away the evil they claim I have within me.

The door behind me opens, but I stay facing the dais, staring at a painting of a god that takes up the entirety of the wall there. His dark hair is cropped close to his head while his golden eyes glow in sharp contrast to the dark pigment of his skin. He is a beautiful male, his pointed ears marking him as fae. The gods and goddesses are always depicted as some version of fae or mortal, a fact I find heinously ironic. If one were truly all powerful and all knowing, why would they dress themselves up as their more common parishioners? I don't adhere to the belief that there are gods—benevolent or otherwise—watching over us, but I do believe in the power of a different source. *Dragons.* I will not cower before an invisible deity based on the rantings of supposed holy males, but I will bend the knee in honor of a different beast. One that rules over sky and flame. Freedom is a luxury granted not to those who are worthy of it but to those willing to fight for it. And only dragons have the power to *take* it.

"It seems you can't go more than a few weeks without earning a reprimand," Father Yamin says as he steps up to my side, the sneer on his face evidenced by the disdain in his voice. As if he hasn't looked forward to another *disciplining* session with me. When I don't respond, he blows a heavy breath past his thin lips, and I know a cruel smile shapes them without having to look. "Why must you rebel against those who want only the best for us?" Again, I say nothing. "Your father, our great and magnificent king, has spent *centuries* trying to rectify the consequences of the war. Our dragons are being turned against us, the gods so displeased with the faithless in this land that they are taking away that which is most precious to us. And you act as nothing more than a petulant child. One who digs her heels in to the destruction that she's brought upon the land."

Destruction. His dramatics, as they usually do, draw a smirk to my lips. The action is hidden by my veil and mask, but Father Yamin must sense it in his ancient bones because he abruptly grabs my arm and yanks me forward towards the first step of the dais.

"Repentance is the only way forward for someone like *you*," he snarls. I let him push me down onto my knees, my bones slamming into the stone with a deafening crack. "You will repent until your sins no longer stain this kingdom." His hand lands on the middle of my back, and I go willingly as he forces my upper body to bow. "You will pray until your knees bleed and I no longer sense such unholy defiance within you."

Seconds drip into minutes that burn into hours, the pain in my body nothing compared to the fantasies that drift in my mind. There is no praying anymore. There is no begging to be something other than what I am. There is only the vision of my knife in my hand, the blood that it spills for those who deserve it. My piety now starts and ends at the altar of my blade, and I vow to myself as the father's hand grips on to my shoulder roughly that I will one day sacrifice the entirety of the church to that altar.

Chapter Ten

RHEA

I WAKE FROM A *night of dreamless sleep, stretching my arms overhead before turning onto my side and finding Nox still asleep. Tucking my hands beneath my pillow, I let my gaze roam over the perfect lines of his face, his expression soft and relaxed in a way he rarely lets anyone else see. I smile at how his onyx waves tumble over his forehead, the ends pointing in every direction as if they can't decide which way to settle. It's the only part of him that has always shown up as less than composed, a small detail that is just so entirely him.*

My eyes work their way down his throat to his bare chest, the memory of the taste of his skin an unexpected pleasure I never even considered experiencing before. In truth, every part of him was both unexpected and immensely pleasurable. Tugging my bottom lip in between my teeth, I replay our joining from the night before in my mind. I didn't know what to expect when it came to physical intimacy. I suppose, in some small way, I thought that it might not ever compare to the way my heart leaps at the sound of Nox's voice or how he continually finds pieces of my soul that are rough to smooth out with his words and his actions. How can anything compare? How can it be any better?

And yet there was capacity for more.

Nox's attentiveness while pleasuring me went beyond anything I could have imagined. I didn't just feel loved when he moved inside me—when his mouth and fingers did things I had only ever read about before. I felt worshipped. *Every time we came together, he looked at me with the same momentous awe that I felt deep inside. And I wonder, studying him now, if losing myself in him is both the smartest and the most reckless thing I have ever done. I love him, so much that I would sacrifice myself a hundred times over for him. But in that love—that all-consuming, impossible love—was there anything I wasn't willing to do? If it meant keeping him just like this? Safe and at my side and filled with my devotion? I had read enough to know that love like that could be as devastating as it was beautiful, and hadn't I begun to see that play out with Nox and his struggles with the council? Their insistence that he marry Haylee instead of someone without a title and with no claim to anything other than his heart?*

Nox left no doubt to where I stood when compared to his priorities, and I have no doubts about where he stands within my own. I would move worlds to be with him. But I can admit to myself here, in the quiet early morning, that a part of me is terrified by that notion.

Reaching my hand out, I brush his hair away from his forehead, my smile growing when his waves just tumble back.

"You're beautiful when you smile."

My fingers curl back, a laugh spilling out of me. "You can't even see me." His eyes are still closed.

"I don't have to see you to know you're happy, Sunshine," he says, blindly reaching for my hand and bringing it to his mouth. He plants a kiss on my palm, his own lips curling up. "I can feel it. I can feel you."

I can't explain why that makes a knot form in my throat or why it also makes my thighs clench together. A confusing juxtaposition if there ever was one. "I am happy," I whisper, earning the cracking open of one eyelid followed by the other.

His hand releases mine only to cup the side of my face, letting his thumb trace along my lower lip while his eyes watch the movement. "Tell me that you love me," he says, his voice hoarse in a way that isn't due to him just waking up.

Laying my hand over his, I wait until he meets my gaze, his star-flecked eyes focused so intensely that for a moment, I forget how to breathe. "I love you." As if someone's tugged on the invisible string connecting us, Nox and I both move towards each other, and before long, I'm lost once more in his body and his breath. In the way his lips pray against my own—worshipping.

I'm lost in him, and I never want to be found.

⁕⁕⁕⁕⁕

"Rhea." My name is called gruffly while cool fingertips drag along my jawline. "It's time to wake up." The sweet memory immediately gives way to terror as my eyes flare open and I suck in a short breath. "There you are."

Jerking upright, I push his hand away from me only to be met with a sickening wave of unrelenting *agony* that sends me right back down on the bed. *Everything* hurts. The muscles of my feet and legs feel as if I have been flexing them the entirety of my time asleep. My back and chest throb to the beat of my heart, the ache that radiates through them enough to cut each inhale short. But, gods, my *hip*. It is as if the flesh is being pulled back layer by individual layer, followed by someone lighting a match and holding the open flame to the exposed nerves. It is a misery I've *never* felt before and one that sends panic flitting through me, quick as a lightning strike.

"Careful," King Dolian says, drawing the word out. "I need to check your wound."

I heave my breaths through gritted teeth, my head too clouded with the pain of the brand to verbalize a retort. *Brand*. He *branded* me.

"Did you hear me?" The bed dips under his weight, his knee driving into the mattress while his hand reaches out to touch the side of my face. In my shocked stupor, I don't fight against his hold, even as he guides my gaze to his. His thumb traces a nauseating line beneath my trembling lower lip as he looks me over. "Gods, you are beautiful," he rasps, the words rough.

I don't want compliments from him. I don't want him to look at me like he's unearthed buried treasure. And I *certainly* don't want the feel of his touch on *any* part of my body. But the misery that cascades through me at the memory that I've been *branded* overshadows any of those thoughts.

He moves to pull the rest of the blanket off of me from where it's gathered at my hips, and I gather enough awareness together to clutch it tightly before he can. His hazel eyes narrow. "Show me what I want to see, *Rhea*."

"No," I growl through my teeth. "Don't *touch* me."

His sigh is long as he stands before stalking to the foot of the bed. The king is not a man I would call strong and neither is he built that way. Where Nox's arms and legs show carved muscle due to a lifetime of training, King Dolian's frame is more slender. I know he can wield a sword—I saw as much the night I escaped from the tower—but his profile bears no evidence of being a warrior. "I can command you to show me, and you know that I will," he says smoothly, sliding a single hand into the pocket of his navy trousers. "But I'd like for you to choose to do as I ask."

I can't help the shocked noise that leaves me as I look down and realize I'm wearing nothing but a satin white chemise. I pull the blanket up higher to cover my body. "You do realize the irony in that, don't you? I have *no* choice here. There has *never* been a choice when it comes to you."

"I agree with the fact that you had less *options* in your tower, which is why I aim to rectify that now. You can wander this residence at your leisure. Did you know there is a library? A solarium filled with the most vibrant and decadent plants you can imagine? While the staff is only what is necessary, there are still enough servants to tend to your every want and desire." His blade-like grin grows into a full smile. "And the ones they can't tend to, *I* can. You have a multitude of choices now, Rhea."

"Stuffing me into a cage and then asking me to choose between the bread-crumbs you toss into it isn't autonomy. It's merely the illusion of it. You may enjoy pretending that you're offering me something better than my life in that tower, but I *know* who you truly are, *Your Majesty*, and because of my time with—" I stumble over my words, Nox's name still trapped behind the magic command he gave me on the first day. "Because I experienced true freedom, I now have the clarity to see through your lies, to see through your attempted manipulation. You think me to be weak and pliable, but I will *never* stop fighting you. I will *never* bend to your will. I would rather die attempting to escape you a hundred times over than *ever* do a single thing you bid."

Charged silence settles between us, pulsing like the angry burn from my hip, as the king's artificial smile slowly fades until his own contempt and rage seeps out in his expression. "You wanted to speak *his* name right then, didn't you?" he snarls. I say nothing in response, my bravery teetering beneath his malicious stare. "Lay down."

The feeling of being dragged beneath water washes over me, my ears ringing with the heavy thumping of my heart as I recline back against my will until my head meets the pillow again. *No.* King Dolian's steps are measured as he prowls closer.

"You make me do this, my darling," he says softly, the hand that was in his pocket comes out to yank the blanket from my grasp. "I want us to be able to move on with *some* level of understanding. But I fear that may never happen as long as you keep holding on to *him.* As long as you believe the prince to be a possibility, you will never even give us a chance."

"You're my *uncle*! What you want with me is not something that can *ever* be! You—"

"I am your future!" he interrupts with a harrowing bellow, my eyes snapping shut as he leans over me. The weight of his hip brushes against mine, and I cry out at the pressure he places on the tender flesh of the brand. "Look at me."

At the rush of power that barrels into me, my eyes are forced open. That precarious bravery within me falters. I know I'm a different woman than the one who cowered beneath his touch before. That I'm *stronger.* But what does it matter if he can so easily strip me of that strength? Reaching over my body, he plants his hand next to my head while the one gripping the comforter pulls it completely off. My fingers curl around the hemline of the chemise, holding it down at my thighs as I attempt to keep as much of myself covered as I can. But his gaze leaves an oily trail as it roams over me, making me feel even more exposed.

Terror slices through me when he reaches out to drag his fingers up the outside of my thigh, unbidden tears springing to my eyes. "Stop," I breathe through quivering lips to no avail. His movements slow when he reaches the chemise, and he toys with the ribbon lining the hem as he inhales deeply through his nose.

"Do you tremble because of my touch? Because of what I might see or do?" he asks without looking at me, a disturbing amount of awe woven into his voice. "I tremble for the same. Let go of the nightgown, Rhea."

My body obeys, my eyes flicking to the ceiling as he lifts the fabric higher. I try to sink back into that numb place—the one that was so easily tucked into the dark corners of my mind. But it had been so long since I had any need to, and I am petrified to discover I can't quite reach it anymore.

The pad of his finger presses lightly on the brand, drawing a shaky cry from me. I suppose I never thought that facing this monster again would be harder the second time around. That the armor I thought I had expertly crafted in my time away from him so that I would never again be vulnerable had somehow only made me weaker. Because it is at this moment, as my uncle's unwanted touch invades my body, that I realize I haven't exactly dealt with everything that plagued me before. I have simply replaced pain with pleasure, anger with love. I have built armor, yes, but it is the *wrong* kind, and now water is seeping in at all the misaligned spots. Threatening to pull me under. Try as I might to pretend otherwise, I feel every brush of his skin against mine as it irritates the flesh of my wound. Every waft of his warm breath against my cheek as he leans in closer.

"Did he touch you like this? Reverently and with purpose? Did you let him?" My eyes begin to sting from how wide I hold them open, tears falling onto my cheeks. Time passes slowly, like watching individual grains of sand tumble down an hourglass. King Dolian murmurs something as he drags the edges of my chemise back down, his hand pausing on my thigh before he stands from the bed. My eyes don't move from their focus on the ceiling, not even when the king leaves and I'm alone with nothing but my fear, anger, guilt, and shame.

Chapter Eleven

RHEA

Tʜᴇ sᴏᴜɴᴅ ᴏꜰ ᴛʜᴇ waves breaking against the shoreline ahead spikes fear within me as I stand at my window, looking down at the slight drop to the fine sand below. Whatever this magic is that binds me to the king's will, it makes me feel like I'm drowning. Like my head is pushed beneath the surface the moment a command leaves his lips. I suck in a harsh breath at the thought, gasping for air even though I'm out in the open. My skin stretches and pulls at the brand with the movement, and just as quickly, that breath is pushed out of me at the fiery pain that erupts at my hip, forcing my hands to brace the windowsill as I lean into the cooler breeze blowing in from the water.

King Dolian hadn't come back to visit me the rest of the day. Instead, he sent the assigned handmaiden. I was still in bed when she came with lunch on a silver tray, her blue eyes rounding when they had met mine. After setting the tray down on one of the tables by the bed, she pulled a linen pouch from her white apron and told me the king said she was to clean an abrasion. Panic curdled my stomach at the thought of another's touch on me again, and I tried to tell her that her assistance wasn't necessary. But the handmaiden gave me a small smile and relayed that the king had commanded it of her, and I understood what she couldn't say then. She had a blood oath with the king and, much like myself, had little choice in what he demanded she do.

"It is on your hip, correct?" At my reluctant nod, she moved to the side of the bed and slowly lifted my chemise up, the blanket still discarded on the floor where the king had thrown it earlier. Her shocked inhale echoed out in the room, and the curse she let slip after had our eyes meeting in unspoken horror. Clearly this wasn't just an abrasion, and if any part of me thought that perhaps my reaction to the pain—to the *idea* that I was marked with a branding iron—was overly dramatic, the color that leached from the handmaiden's face when she looked back down at my hip confirmed that it wasn't. She worked in silence, her touch gentle but diligent. The ointment she slathered over the aching flesh soothed it a little before she covered it with a bandage. When she was done, she grabbed the blanket and laid over my legs, making sure I could reach it should I want it pulled up again. Then she hurried out of the room like she might be sick. I stared out the window across from me until day bled to night, and she returned again, this time with a dinner tray.

Now I look back out to the starry night sky, my dinner still sitting where the handmaiden left it. Every shift of the small residence and noise outside the hall sends my pulse racing, my eyes darting over my shoulder to watch the door should King Dolian enter my room again. He hadn't touched me beyond where the brand was and my thigh, but he had seen my undergarments. Seen more of me than he ever should have been allowed. Would he stop next time? Or would he let his fingers explore other parts of me, let them undress me just as eagerly as his gaze did. I swallow at the thought and reach out to grip either side of the window, its height low enough that I can, with a little maneuvering, step onto the ledge in front of it.

I cry out as I'm forced into a crouch, my heartbeat pulsing over my tender flesh, every nerve ending singing its displeasure at my position. I blink through the tears that form in my eyes, gritting my teeth as I clench my jaw and focus on the ground below. I had been in too much pain to care about changing out my chemise, instead grabbing a velvet cloak from the wooden armoire in the room and securing it around my neck.

The king's command said I couldn't leave the residence without him being at my side, but surely the magic of it couldn't know what I was doing at every minute. My own power works off of intention; is it the same for this ring? Can I trick it if I tell myself I'm just going for a stroll? Hissing through my teeth, I lean forward and prepare to jump, only to be met with resistance. That invisible barrier of magic preventing me from going farther. "No," I growl, abandoning my hold on the window to push with both hands. But the unseen obstacle holds firm.

I adjust my stance, a groan of pain rumbling up my throat as I move onto the balls of my feet, only to lose my balance. My back crashes into the floor behind me, the reverberation of the impact sending a blinding wave of pain through me. My hands shake as they hover over my hip, but there is nothing I can do. I can't call up my magic. I can't soothe it. I can only endure, calling out to Selene as I do. "Please, help me," I say between broken sobs, my vision blurring and throat growing raw. When she doesn't answer, I call out to Nox. To Bella. To Alexi. But the night continues without so much as a whisper of their presence, only the unfathomable pain of a mark I'll never be able to get rid of keeping me company.

The handmaiden comes the next morning and helps me shower. The water hitting my singed skin is no relief, and though I try to keep myself composed in front of her, I completely fall apart at the white-hot stinging that lances through me. Afterwards, she dresses me in a gown of soft satin, though I still smart when it grazes my hip, fighting back nausea that travels its way up my throat. She does my hair, braiding it away from my face and down my back, and the moment she ties it off, someone knocks on the door.

I tense at the sound, my eyes clashing with hers in the reflection of the vanity mirror in front of me. I stand as she strides to the door, my heart sinking when she opens it and reveals who is on the other side. *Xander.*

"The king has called for you to meet with him this morning." The sound of his voice draws up memories of Alexi's death, of his harsh tone whenever he spoke to me in the tower. I swallow as I take a step, and my knees falter as my head begins to swim. *Perhaps I should have eaten something yesterday.*

"Lady Rhea, are you alright?" the handmaiden asks, taking a step towards me. Concern lines her face, but I shake it off as I force my chin to lift, blinking away the haziness from my vision.

"I'm fine." Xander's attention stays fixed on me as he steps to the side to let me pass, those dark eyes of his briefly meeting mine. He's not dressed in full armor, instead wearing the same chest and back piece over a black tunic and pants that Alexi and Nox wore. His black hair is tied back, a few shorter strands escaping and framing his face. At his hip is a golden sword, a small dagger also strapped to his thigh. He's larger up close than I remember, though I suppose the interactions I've had with him have been ones that I'd like to forget.

Xander walks behind me as we move down the corridor, my memories once more faulty as I can't recall exactly how long it has been since I tried to escape. Was it two days ago? Three? How much time had I lost between when I was knocked unconscious at the front door and again after I was branded? When we reach the split in the hallway, I pause.

"Right," he practically barks out as he passes me, and I would scowl if it weren't for the fact that I'm just trying to keep myself upright with every step I take. The front foyer comes into view, daylight now giving sight to details that were previously hidden in the shadows, and I follow Xander as he turns left, knowing the front door is behind me but avoiding the urge to look over my shoulder. The sun plays off of the gold that covers his back, the ends of his hair brushing against the top of it. His skin color is a little darker than Nox's, more rich in its olive pigment. I can't begin to guess his height, but I imagine it is somewhat close to Nox's as well. In fact, the more I study the bulkiness of Xander's frame, the more I find physical similarities between the two.

"The kitchens are right up here. Should you find yourself hungry outside of meal hours, there will always be someone on staff there to help you," Xander informs me, his voice monotone like he's given a hundred tours of this place and is now *bored* of it. Arched corridors line either side of us, a few of the aforementioned maids and servants popping in and out of them. Their eyes grow wide as they meet mine, and I can't tell if it's shock or something more that lines their faces, but they don't linger long enough for me to decipher it.

Straight ahead, double doors loom tall, reaching the dark gray stone ceiling above. The kingdom's sigil is brandished in gold on the front of both, that *horrific* roaring lion inescapable. In my glaring at the doors, I don't see the small rumple in the rug ahead of me and trip on it. I recover quickly, but catching my balance sends a sharp bite of pain flaring down my leg. I stop short, gasping for air as I breathe through it.

"Are you okay?" Xander asks, drawing my eyes towards his. Despite the question, his face remains unbothered, as if he's speaking not to a person but the wall. Pushing the pain as far down as I can, I swallow and right myself, heat flaring up my neck and to my cheeks. His jaw works, the only sign of his annoyance at me ignoring him, before he turns and continues past the doors and to the left, down a new corridor. There, he stops abruptly and turns to face me. "Do you think he will come for you?"

My gaze snaps to his, and my voice echoes in the hall when I sharply ask, "Excuse me?"

Xander brings his finger to his lips, taking a step towards me that I counter with one backwards, my nostrils flaring at the ache that pulses over me. "Flynn or Nox. Whatever name you call him. Will he come for you?"

I shake my head, ignoring the little bit of concern that I swear leaks past his otherwise stony façade in favor of the voice in my head that screams it's a trap. Had I not *just* told myself that naivety was something I couldn't afford anymore? Rolling my shoulders back, I lift my chin, anger clashing with something grittier—something that's sat inside of me for a long, long while, that I hadn't realized was there until now.

"I remember, you know," I start, dropping my voice low. Xander's brows furrow as he watches me. "I remember you being there for *all* of it. The way your eyes met mine as the king hit me. How you held Alexi's hair in your grasp as he was killed. I—" I draw in a deep breath, Xander mirroring it as his hands curl tightly at his sides. "I remember the way you so *cruelly* returned me to that tower when I tried to escape. *I remember.*"

His expression settles into the same one as the day Alexi died, and it takes *everything* in me not to scream my frustration over it. He didn't *care*. He never had, and I won't let myself lose anything else to someone like *him*.

"What is going on here?" King Dolian's voice pierces the tension between Xander and I as he strides out from beneath an arched doorway, one hand slid into his pocket. He comes to stand next to Xander, but his eyes spear mine before they roam down my body.

"Your Majesty, I was escorting Lady Rhea to you."

The king tilts his head, chestnut-brown hair staying in place as he does. "Were you? Because it almost looks like the two of you were talking with each other." Unease slides down my spine, locking my body in place as I glare at my uncle.

Xander says nothing, instead clasping his hands behind himself as he rolls his shoulders back. "My allegiance is always to you, Your Majesty. If you question it, ask the lady herself."

The ire that raged for the guard burns brighter, but I know better than to look away from King Dolian. He closes the distance between us in two easy strides, the scent of him washing over me with my next breath. Cedar and something sickly sweet. I'm forced to arch my neck, my head tilting back as I dig my nails into my palm. I let every ounce of that anger for Xander and my *hatred* of him seep to the surface of my green eyes, my breaths so choppy that my chest heaves with each one.

"Tell me what you two were talking about." Magic infiltrates every corner of my mind, pushing the words to my mouth before I can even think around them.

"I told him that I remember him," I say, pain flaring up my temples at how tightly my jaw is clenched. "He helped you kill Alexi."

King Dolian *smirks.* "Ah, yes. The lowly guard who sought to take what is *mine.*"

I reach for my magic, invisible fingers stretching towards that ancient cold. That deadly power within me. I have *never* wanted to use it as badly as I do now. But just like when I had tried to escape from this place, I'm met with resistance. Something cutting me off from my magic in a way that I can't see. So instead, I reach for my anger. "I am *not* yours! And Alexi was one hundred times the man you—"

His hand snaps out to grip my upper arm before he pulls me towards him, the front of my body crashing into his. My ears ring as I cry out in pain, my chest tightening with the air trapped in my lungs. I expect him to berate me, to wield his words as viciously as he does his hands on my body. Instead, he leans in close enough for the short bristles of his beard to scrape against my cheek, his breath hot on my ear. "My, my, Rhea. The fire in you is so much brighter than I ever realized. But flames need to be tended to or they grow too big. They turn from beacons of light to bearers of destruction. I can see that being around the mage prince has left you flaring too brightly, made you too reckless. It's not something we can't rectify before the wedding, however."

My heart momentarily drops to my stomach, terror attempting to take root before I grip it tightly. I force a laugh up my throat, the sound jarring and unnatural. It causes the king to pull back to look at me, his brows dropping low over his eyes. "You actually think there is a scenario where we get married, don't you?" I ask, my confidence bolstered by the way his cheeks start to pinken. "You really think he won't rescue me? That he won't come? That he won't destroy everyone who stands in his way with hardly a second thought?" I relish in the way King Dolian's eyes search mine, and I hope he can see the rage that binds my words as truth.

He exhales roughly, leaning back as he looks down his nose at me, his hands smoothing out his navy and gold vest. "Commander, ensure Rhea has something to eat before bringing her to the throne room. I want to show her something there."

"I'm not hun—"

"You *will* eat," he snaps, and I startle at his voice. The magic of his command or the ring or *whatever* it is that binds me to him washes over me, and I know I do not have a choice in this. Then he takes a step to the left and walks past me, leaving Xander to stare at me. But my gaze is on the man who was hidden by King Dolian's frame. Simon *glares,* his lips in a flat line while his arms are folded over his chest. It feels like minutes pass, but eventually Xander jerks his head towards Simon. I only make it a step before the older man speaks.

"You take advantage of the king's affection for you. Of his generosity."

My lip peels back over my teeth as I prepare to bark something back because how *dare* he suggest that I'm doing anything of the sort, but Xander steps in front of me and blocks my view.

"I'm sure you are needed elsewhere, Simon," he says, and I don't think I'm imagining the wrath in his tenor.

"I'm needed wherever the king tells me to be," he retorts but moves away from the door as I pass. Though I feel his gaze on my back like the scraping of nails.

Only when I'm sure he's actually gone, the space outside the doorway empty, do I risk asking Xander, "Who was that?"

Xander looks momentarily stunned that I've not only engaged in conversation but initiated it, but he quickly hides his surprise under his icy mask. "Simon. The king's head advisor." His dark eyes snap to mine from where he stands near the door. "And one of the worst men in the king's employ. Including the king himself."

Chapter Twelve

RHEA

MY EYES LINGER ON the gold roaring lions in front of me, the sharp sting of shame curling between my ribs. I hate the sigil. Hate the man waiting on the other side of the doors that forced it onto my skin. Xander had given me a few minutes to heed the king's command in what appeared to be a small dining room, and I was able to take a few bites of an egg and vegetable dish before the magic subsided and my body became my own again. I should have kept going, but the moment I had my autonomy back, all I wanted to do was push away from the table and get whatever cruel thing the king had planned next over with. That, and it was *impossible* to eat when I could still smell the burning of my flesh in my nose. When each breath and small movement stung in a way that was hard to describe.

"You shouldn't taunt him." Xander keeps his voice only loud enough for me to hear, but my steps falter as I give him a sidelong glance. I don't know what to say, afraid of somehow revealing too much about myself or getting tricked into talking about Nox. So I keep quiet as Xander forces our steps to slow and those lions loom closer. "He'll only make things worse for you."

I pinch my lips to keep from responding, even as the dread of knowing that the king absolutely *could* do that pricks at the back of my neck.

Xander's hand presses to the side of his thigh, right over the blade strapped there. "I remember it, too," he says softly. The gentlest he's ever spoken to me. "And you will never know how much I wish there had been a different way."

At that, I look at him fully, turning my head as I acknowledge the way a little emotion seeps through his mask. Not enough to warrant believing him, but just enough that for a moment, I consider it. But then my eyes catch on the front of his armor and the way his sword hangs so frivolously at his hip. A weapon that I know he can wield there to remind me that he had and that a man I loved dearly had been skewered on its end. I wobble in place but turn back to the doors and stride towards them. Xander moves fast enough that he gets to them before I do, his fingers curling around one of the golden handles. I swallow back the fear that makes my heart race faster, the commander's gaze heavy on the side of my face.

"I'll wait out here." He says it like it's supposed to mean something to me. Like there's comfort in knowing that.

"And I'll endure in there." His body stiffens before he pulls the door open on silent hinges, and a room far grander than any I had been shown so far appears. Polished cream tile glistens under the sunlight streaming in from the four large rectangular windows in front of me, and my steps click loudly over it as I enter, searching for the king.

"How are you feeling after eating?" he asks, and I find him sitting on a throne centered on a dais only a few steps high. The throne, like the rest of the room, is beautiful in the way all opulent things are. The ornate details—the obvious display of wealth—it all speaks loudly of trying to cover something hideous with something that sparkles. It's a distraction, and one I refuse to fall for.

I stop a healthy distance away from him, clutching on to any defiance that I can. Even as simple as keeping space between us when I know he wishes there were none. "Is a throne room necessary in a secondary, *hidden* residence?"

He props his jaw on his hand, the laziest I've ever seen his posture. "Necessary? No. But a king must always be prepared in case he needs to flaunt his power."

"And you believe sitting in that chair does that?"

"No," he answers, dropping his arm to the armrest as he straightens. "But having you at my side will." He stands and steps down the dais, gesturing to his right. "I want to show you something." When I hesitate to follow, he pivots and marches towards me, gripping my arm and all but dragging me to where a mirror stands tall. "You know I don't mind reminding you of your place. Of the title you have *yet* to earn." Jerking me to a stop, he reaches for the braid hanging down my back and tugs on it until my back arches. I grunt out at the movement, searing pain traveling in waves out from my hip. "I want your hair unrestrained for me from now on," he growls, trailing his knuckles down my cheek.

When he finally lets me go, I blink away the pressure building behind my eyes as I stare at him, forcing a rough exhale from my mouth. "I *hate* you."

"For now," he responds, his voice hard with resolve. "But you'll see soon enough. That ring on your finger may not have been the one I chose for you, but it is a symbol of my love for you nonetheless. You just have to stop fighting me."

I scoff, my brows raising incredulously. "*Love* is not something you can force upon someone. It is not some weapon you can wield to get what you want."

"And what would you know of it?" he counters, eyes bright with challenge. "What would a woman who spent her life protected in a tower know of the intricacies of the emotion or, better yet, the true intentions of the men around her? Did you know that *Flynn* was actually the mage prince? Or did you trust him to be honest with you?"

I ignore his use of the word *protected*, of the way he tries to tarnish Nox's reputation. Yes, he had lied, but so had I. And I knew that since we had promised to be honest with each other, we both had. "And what would *you* know of it? What would a man who thinks marrying his niece—"

The action happens so abruptly. Between one word and the next, Dolian rises and slaps me, my head jerking to the side as tears immediately spring to my eyes. I gasp a breath as I steady myself, my hand cupping my cheek tenderly. "You may doubt my feelings for you, but I have never lied about them, Rhea. I have always shown you exactly who I am. Did it ever occur to you that if he'd lie once, it would be easy for him to do it again? Did you ever *think* that your inexperience made you an easy target?"

"I think that not everyone approaches relationships and love as if they need to control every facet of it. I think people make mistakes, but it's how they prove themselves in their actions after those mistakes that defines who they are."

"If that's the case, let's test the loyalty of such a worthy prince now." King Dolian takes a few steps forward and the glass of the mirror in front of us begins to *ripple*. Gods above, it isn't just any mirror but *the* Mirror. Air rushes from me as I let my lips part, surprise mingling with dread until they are crawling up my throat. "Let's see what happens when we call upon the Mage Kingdom." I step closer, my eyes locked on the Mirror as the glass moves like a current of water. He wraps an arm around my back, his fingers perilously close to the brand. "King Sadryn *or* Prince Nox of the Mage Kingdom."

My heart stutters in its beats at Nox's name, and I don't need to look at my reflection in the Mirror to know that there is an eagerness in my eyes that I should be doing a better job at hiding. The glass fogs over, a silver haziness that mimics storm clouds blurring out my face and that of the king next to me as the magic reaches out to the Mage Kingdom. For a moment, the pain of my hip is lost to the desperate hope that spears me at the thought of seeing Nox. But then I realize that I'd more than likely see Sadryn, especially if Nox has already left. The fogginess of the Mirror dissipates, my brows furrowing when it returns back to a liquid state. King Dolian calls out again, but the minutes pass and no one appears on the other side.

"Curious, isn't it?" he asks, voice low as he turns to face me.

"What is?"

"The lack of response. It makes one wonder why there is no urgency to answer another king."

I try to swallow, but a lump sits heavily in my throat. "Perhaps there is no one near the Mirror at this exact moment."

"That could be true." His fingers grip my chin as he tugs me head to the right, my gaze clashing with his. "But it doesn't explain the lack of answering yesterday. Or the day before."

My blood runs cold as I draw in a breath. "You've been trying to reach them since—"

"Since you've come home, yes. I wanted to let them know you were safe here." The devious smile that parts his lips says otherwise and I jerk my head out of his hold.

"You wanted to *gloat*."

His laugh is hollow. "A little of that too, yes. But they never answered those other times, either, Rhea. I'm afraid we are left to wonder if either the entire royal family is missing from the palace or, the more likely scenario, they just aren't missing *you*."

It is an impossible notion. I know that. It is just King Dolian's brand of torture—adding to my physical afflictions by turning this into mental warfare. I know that too. I keep my disdain for the king plastered on my face throughout the rest of the day. As he walks me from room to room in the residence, my arm forcibly linked with his, I ignore the worm he's so carelessly dropped in the garden of my mind. At least there is enjoyment to be had in the mounting frustration I sense from him when he expects me to react as if this grand tour is something I'm excited about. As if I should be. But later, when I'm once more alone in my room and staring out at the ocean blanketed in orange and pink light from sunset, I can't help but let my thoughts wander back to the Mage Kingdom. No part of me worries that I am not missed, but what if Dolian is right and something else is wrong?

The council had been so insistent on Nox not marrying me that if they knew the lengths he'd go to get me back, would they retaliate against Sadryn and Alexandria? Despite the impossibility of it all, *someone* from the Mage Kingdom is working with King Dolian, as if evidenced by me being *here*. Perhaps they are still there, intent on hurting Nox and his family in other ways now that I'm gone.

Chewing my bottom lip raw, I lean down on the window sill and close my eyes against the waning sunlight. I hate that King Dolian thinks so little of Nox—that he doubted our love for each other. But even more, I *hate* the tiny seedling of doubt that rises to the surface and asks, *what if he's right*? That isn't Nox speaking. That isn't even my own conscience. It's simply my fears being molded by the king's words.

I blow out a frustrated breath and wince, my fingers tightening on the windowsill. Nox and I aren't the only players in this game amongst powerful men, and I can't be foolish enough to assume that it starts and ends with only us.

Autumn woods and a hint of spice linger in the air, a smile curling at my lips because of who that scent belongs to. "Nox," I whisper. Warmth cradles me from all sides, the weight of his arm draping over my body a comfort. The urge to open my eyes tugs at my lids, but I fight it off, instead settling into the way I feel safe here. I know that this is only a dream, but I'll take any connection to Nox that I can feel and so for a long while, I don't try to call out again or move or do anything that might disrupt this perfect place where there is no pain or anxiousness or heartbreak. There is only him.

The weight of his arm on top of me grows heavier and as I take my next inhale, a stabbing pain flares to life over my left hip. It's brief, there and gone within the length of a breath, but I part my lips to call his name again, hoping it will tether me here. Except that the word is thick on my tongue. Sadness flares when I try and fail again to call for him, the command to not speak Nox's name suddenly affecting me in the dream. My heartbeat kicks up its rhythm, but even with the way it beats in my chest, something weaves around the sound to my ears. Something that sounds like humming. *I strain my ears to hear it, even as I fight to cling on to this dream for a little longer. But Nox's warmth begins to seep away and though I can only form his name in my mind, I call out for him. Again and again, to no avail. When reality begins to creep in, I squeeze my eyes shut and search for those old pockets of numbness. But I can't find them.*

My head throbs, the pulsing of my heart a steady rhythm in both temples while an acidic taste taunts the back of my throat. My eyelids are heavy as I pry them open, surprised to find that it is still nighttime, the stars sparkling brightly outside the window across from the foot of my bed. My heart sinks at the recognition of the room.

I shift my gaze to the ceiling above, blowing out a shaky breath as I try to gain some sense of equilibrium. Goosebumps bloom over my arms and legs, the sensation of static electricity—like that of an impending storm—washing over me and making me shiver. Or maybe it's the chill in the air and the realization that I must have kicked my comforter off at some point in the night. Groaning at my disorientation, I attempt to roll onto my side only to find that I can't.

"You'll find that moving will be quite difficult." I gasp at the unknown voice, cold dread settling over me as my eyes dart to every shadowy corner in the room. Through the small bit of silver moonlight, a figure emerges and stalks to the side of the bed, his menacing glare sending a shot of fear directly into my stomach. Simon.

I wait for the king to show himself, angry that my sweet dream was taken over by yet another nightmare. But the reveal never comes, and I can't decide if that is better or worse as I stare at his advisor. My fingers twitch at my side, something dark and oppressive pressing at my chest and placing an invisible hand over my lips, sealing in the questions that bubble up to the surface. I'm paralyzed in the dark, and based on the look Simon wears, he knows it.

Simon smirks and walks to the corner of the bed, lifting some sort of tray that rattles with items. "You know, when His Majesty told me that you escaped from your tower with a guard, I must admit a part of me was relieved." Setting the tray on the night table to my right, he picks up a small bottle, the room too dark for me to make it out. "You see, King Dolian has many strengths. He is willing to do the things that others won't to ensure that his kingdom stays safe. Compromise is a weakness, Lady Rhea, and one that the king does not possess. Except"—he lifts his gaze from the bottle between his thumb and pointer finger—"when it comes to you. Despite your abhorrent distaste for our great king, he keeps giving you grace."

Breath rushes in and out of me as I try to move myself out of my prone position. But the heaviness of my limbs remains, and my struggling attempts do nothing but tug on the tender flesh at my hip.

"King Dolian was so distraught after your departure. I have known him for a long time, and not since the night you were born had I seen him so upset. I take my role as his advisor very seriously, and so, though it went against my better judgement, I helped him formulate a plan to get you back." Our gazes hold. "And this *is how you repay him for wanting to make you his queen?" Simon lets out an indignant huff. "I won't tolerate you taking advantage of his generosity."*

I'm still dreaming. I have to be because surely, Simon is not talking about the same king I've come to know. The same king who would willfully beat me until I passed out from the abuse. The same one who looked at me not as his flesh and blood but as something to be conquered. Something to own.

"Magic is a powerful tool, but it is not the only one that the Continent has provided us. Herbs and plants can be just as valuable and more easily available to those not born of mage blood. Take, for example, the gelsemium plant. By appearance, it looks like nothing more than a beautiful, delicate flower. But when you break it down, crushing the petals and stem, it becomes something more. Something better. That is what we are going to do with you, Lady Rhea. As you are now, you are nothing but a liability to His Majesty. His love for you prevents him from doing what is necessary. So the task falls to me. I will break you—forge you into something better—so that you can serve him in the way a good queen should."

The threat settles between my ribs, a dagger of intention that stings as if it were real.

"You are under the influence of a gelsemium serum. A little swipe in your mouth while you slept is all it took to make you agreeable." I recoil at the idea of him sticking his finger in my mouth. "I can see your indignation, and rest assured, I took no pleasure in touching you. What's about to come next, however, well…" He lets his words linger ominously between us as he sets the bottle back down.

I watch from the corner of my eye as he uses one finger to caress whatever is on the tray next to the bottle. I can see glints of metal objects, but from my vantage point, I can't make out what exactly they are.

Simon continues his perusing until something in his expression shifts, and he plucks an object off the tray. "While the gelsemium temporarily paralyzes the body, it doesn't take away any of the senses. You can still experience them all." The object in his hand glints in the moonlight, and a desperate noise gurgles in my throat at the sight of it. It's a thin blade, unlike any I have ever seen before. He moves his hand down, wrist flicking with quick movement over my bare arm not covered by my nightgown. I yelp at the stinging slice of pain, glancing down to see an angry split to my skin as blood begins to well from the opening.

Wake up.

The king's advisor smiles, tilting his head to the side as his gaze assesses me in a way that has me begging to crawl out of my own skin.

"I've a bit of a reputation in our kingdom, you know."

There's another flash of silver, and a second cut opens beneath the first. My hand twitches with the pain, and though, in my mind, I'm screaming, nothing but a cracked bit of noise actually moves past my lips.

"His Majesty trusts me to get information for him, and I am quite good at what I do."

Slice. My vision goes hazy. Wake up.

"There is a certain kind of pleasure that can be found when someone is completely at my mercy. Though it's been a long while since a mage was the one beneath my knife." My cheeks grow wet as tears fall, the terror of being trapped here releasing itself by any means necessary. Simon takes no mercy, the drag of his blade becomes longer and more languid, the intensity of his focus on me growing as he watches blood pool and spill.

Wake up. Wake up. Wake up.

With a long, exaggerated inhale—as if he can taste the iron scent that taints the air—Simon moves to the other side of the bed. "Now, Lady Rhea, let our evening together serve as a reminder that I am always watching you, and if you refuse to treat your king with the respect that is owed, then I will keep slicing you apart until you're unrecognizable. Only then can you be remade."

With my heart in my throat, its beat a riotous chorus that blends into my broken pleas, I endure Simon's ministrations. Each cut is only on the surface of my skin, yet I feel the echo of them down to my bones. Time slips by in moments of conscious clarity in which agony wraps itself around me and in small seconds of reprieve when Simon moves to grab a different instrument. I had never realized just how many versions of torture there were to weather, and I wonder if perhaps that is what the summation of my life will be: How much can I endure? What is the imaginary line at which I claw until my nails break in order to escape it?

Darkness creeps in on my already cloudy vision, and though I can feel my blood cooling beneath my body, I make the choice to focus on the memories of the people I love instead. Though the voice of misery screams that there is no one coming for me, hope's quieter song reminds me that I am no longer alone.

And so I endure.

Chapter Thirteen

RHEA

I LIE AWAKE IN bed the next morning, anxiousness swimming through my veins. When I first opened my eyes, I tried wiggling my fingers and toes, relief sweeping through me when I found that they moved with ease. Then I attempted to sit up, only for my head to fall right back to the pillow. Between the aching sting of the brand and the throbbing tempo pounding in my skull, it takes me a few deep breaths before the dizziness subsides and I try again, this time *slowly*.

Running my hands over my arms, I take solace in the fact that my skin is smooth and unmarked. Despite how *visceral* the dream with the king's advisor had felt. I shiver at the memory of his instruments splitting my skin, of the sick way he took pleasure in hurting me. All in the name of the king. For a moment, I question if he really *had* been here. My nightmares always felt real in the moment, inescapable until my eyes fluttered open. But even in the morning light, my palms are still clammy and my heart beats too fast. As if my body is also remembering what Simon had done. I let loose a heavy sigh. It was only a dream, a strange conjuring of my mind.

I can't shake the unease settling within me despite how I repeat those words. Pushing the comforter off of me, I carefully lift my nightgown to inspect the brand. It looks worse than it did the day before, the skin surrounding it still hot to the touch. The grotesque lines and curves of the roaring lion are raised, blisters pulling the skin taut from the gathered fluid. Feeling ill, I tug the nightgown back down, only to pause. My breath catches at the light pink color of the satin, my fingers rustling it. *Light pink*? Hadn't I gone to bed in blue?

Heart in my throat, I peer over the edge of the bed, thinking perhaps I simply changed at some point and forgot. But there is no clothing on the floor. Nothing to indicate that I went to sleep in anything other than what I am wearing. And when I glance down at the sheets beneath me, they are the ones the handmaiden put on my bed yesterday morning.

It was only a dream.

Gingerly, I make my way to the washroom, starting the shower as I try to push down that lingering disquiet. The warm water at the very least works to lessen the headache pounding at my temples, even if it exacerbates the gnawing pain at my hip. I stay there for a long while before turning the water off and grabbing a white cotton towel that hangs on a nearby hook, wrapping it around myself as carefully as possible. It's a silly feat because the cotton strands still brush against the mark, forcing a hissed breath out through my clenched teeth.

Bracing my hands on the stone counter, I meet my own gaze in the bathroom mirror. How many times had I studied myself in a similar manner in the tower and found what I saw lacking? Not necessarily in my appearance—though there were often times I felt I looked more dead than alive—but intrinsically. In the things I so innately craved but that I was so desperately deprived of. And then in the Mage Kingdom, I had begun to see myself in a different light. I was stronger. More resilient. A tapestry of hurts and wants and lingering grief, yes, but I had started to believe that I was so much *more* than those things.

And now?

My gaze drops to the counter. Like smoke curling up from a fire, another emotion braids itself into my mind. *Fear.* The truth is, I'm beyond terrified by what might happen before I figure out how to get this ring off of me. While I wait for Nox to come. I'm scared of what's already occurred, of how many more concealed marks have been added to my soul. Of the one that's not so invisible on my body. And I wonder, not for the first time, if it's okay to be so afraid. If feeling this way undoes *everything* I thought I worked so hard for the past few months.

Does it make me as weak as I was when I lived secluded and beaten and so desperately *sad* in that tower? So many "should haves" and "could haves" bounce around in my head, the result of too much time spent looking at my past with newly critical eyes. Because it is so much easier now to pinpoint all the ways I've messed up.

Sighing, I push away from the counter and open the door to the bathroom, nearly running right into the handmaiden. "Gods!" I shout, stumbling backwards and then grimacing at the pain that radiates down my thigh.

"I'm so sorry!" she counters, tucking a strand of her blonde hair behind her ear, the rest of it pulled into a tight bun that rests at the nape of her neck. "I didn't mean to frighten you! I had knocked on the door to let you know I was here, but you must not have heard it."

I hadn't, and I nod as I grip the top edge of the towel wrapped around me. Awkward silence falls upon us, the handmaiden clutching the white apron that is tied around her gray dress as her eyes dart everywhere else in the room but to me.

"The king has asked that I ready you for the day," she says finally, forcing a small smile to her face. "He'd like to have breakfast with you."

I nearly grumble an "of course, he would" but manage to keep the words from leaving my mouth. Based on the small quirk of the handmaiden's lips, I'm less successful at keeping the emotion from my face.

"I would like to *ready* myself," I tell her, lifting my chin in a move I hope displays more confidence than I actually feel.

She cradles one hand in the other, her thumb rubbing at a spot on her palm. "I have been instructed to do as he asks." Our stares hold, blue eyes like the waters of the lake outside my tower meeting my meadow green ones. Is it that scar indicating a blood oath that gives her gaze an edge of desperation? From what I remember Alexi telling me about blood oaths, the king's command is as woven into the handmaiden's blood as it is in the ring suppressing my magic. She couldn't fight against it, even if she wanted to, or else she risked death. I just wish I knew whether she actually wanted to or not.

Intentions of the handmaiden aside, I still don't want anyone else's hands on my body, even for something as innocuous as getting dressed. I feel as raw and tender and exposed as the brand on my hip, and if I can control even this *small* facet, it's worth clinging on to. "What *exactly* did he say?" I ask her.

She cants her head to the side, eyebrows pulling together. "He said that I had to ready you. For the day," she answers slowly, working to clear her throat. "Because he'd like to meet you for breakfast."

"I want to dress myself," I say, reaching around to grab my damp hair and pull it over my shoulder. I can already see the protest forming in her mouth, so I add, "But I've always been awful at doing my hair. Perhaps you can help with that?" It's certainly not a lie. I hadn't taken Nox up on the offer he made in the woods of learning how to braid my hair. It was purposeful, of course. There was something intimate about him doing my hair, and I know that he enjoyed it too. I watch the handmaiden shift her weight, her eyes cast up to the ceiling in thought.

After a few more moments, her gaze meets mine again. "Alright," she says, before spinning on her heel and walking to the bathroom. "I'll give you time to dress while I clean up the bathroom. Just yell when you're done."

I wait until she is behind a closed door to exhale my relief. So there *is* some leeway with the commands of the blood oath. I ponder over the meaning of that as I reach the closet and look through my choices for dresses absentmindedly. Selecting a lavender one with a loose-fitting bodice and a skirt made of silk, I lay the dress on the made bed before going to the armoire to gather my chemise and undergarments. Dressing is again an arduous task, one that reminds me with every movement just how horrific the brand is. I can't help the way insidious thoughts crowd the edges of my mind like a black fog rolling in. *This will always be on me. I will never be free from it. Will Nox's hands avoid touching it? Will he avoid touching me? Will this irrevocably change things? Why does it feel as if it already has?*

Eventually, I manage to push everything down enough to sit through the handmaiden's gentle touch while cleaning and changing the bandage on my brand before she moves on to my hair. The distraction is welcome, and I watch as she gracefully braids small sections and then gathers them all into a twisted updo that I find beautiful.

You will leave your hair unbound. I immediately scowl at the memory of the king's words.

"Is everything alright?" she asks, sincerity carved on her expression.

It's a silly thing, to want to cling on to any small rebellion that I can. King Dolian may demand control over most of my being, but I'd be damned if I let him do it without a fight.

Meeting her gaze in the reflection of the mirror, I nod.

Xander is standing outside of my room when the handmaiden opens the door, a silent look passing between them as she walks past. His eyes might soften just the smallest amount when he dips his chin, but when he looks back to me, that gentleness is nowhere to be found. He motions for me to walk in front of him, shutting my door behind me before easily matching my stride.

"So you found out the Mage Kingdom isn't answering the Mirror." He keeps his voice low and face impassive as I glance at him from the corner of my eye. I shouldn't be surprised he knows what went on in the throne room yesterday, he was one of the king's Trusted for a reason. When I don't respond, his jaw flexes and he slows his pace. Inadvertently, I match it. "Listen, I know I've given you zero reason to trust me. To look at me as if I'm anything more than the king's pawn—"

"Aren't you?" I ask, no shortage of bitterness in my cadence.

"No. In fact, I might be the *only* person who can help you."

At that, I stop, the main entrance to this residence in sight ahead of us. "Whatever this is, you can *stop* it. I've already tested my luck trusting Simon's *good intentions*; your fake words will not work on me."

His eyes narrow as they grow darker, and he leans in a little closer, even though he speaks barely above a whisper. "What did Simon do to you?" It isn't just anger that glares back at me but a note of panic as well.

"Nothing," I answer, a bit hoarsely. "He just tricked me into believing he was going to help me escape. And then he—" I choke off my next words with a clearing of my throat, fighting the urge to lay my hand over my hip.

Xander's eyes assess me, but whatever conclusion he comes to in the growing silence between us, he doesn't share, instead straightening and casting his eyes out to the foyer behind me. "You are right to be wary of everyone here, none more than Simon and the other guards. But there are a select few who want to help, myself included."

I don't know what to respond, so I say nothing, and we continue walking again, Xander two steps ahead of me now. I wonder if the distance is so the king doesn't think anything is happening beyond him escorting me. That is the *last* thing I need. King Dolian is already so paranoid about everything when it comes to me. I am surprised he allows a guard to be alone with me in *any* capacity. It only gives me the bolstering I need to remind myself that I can't trust Xander, despite his words. If King Dolian gives him so much freedom with me, it is for a reason.

I enter the same dining room from the day before, the king and Simon already seated at the long table centered in the space. The king's head turns, and his eyes sweep over me slowly as I grit my teeth together under his inspection. He stands and moves to pull out the chair to his right. "You look beautiful, my darling." I take a seat and begin to reach for the food in front of me when he leans down, breath warm on my cheek. "And I *swear* that I told you to leave your hair unbound."

Keeping my chin lifted, I keep my gaze forward as I respond, "And I don't listen to *you*."

I brace for backlash of some kind. Words or fists or something else. But it doesn't come. Instead, King Dolian chuckles softly, pushing my chair in and then striding over to talk to Xander, his voice hushed.

"Good morning, Lady Rhea," Simon says, bringing a bronze chalice up to his lips. His black and white hair is pushed away from his face in a style that emulates the king's. His white button-up shirt is crisp and clean, the sleeves rolled up his forearms. Something about the way he looks so put together and unruffled makes me want to curl my shoulders in, but instead, I ignore him and reach for the serving spoon for the platter of chopped fruit in front of me.

King Dolian returns to the table, reaching over and smacking the spoon from my hand. Wide-eyed, I look at him only to find something cold and devious staring back at me. "Those of a higher status do not *serve* themselves." With a snap of his fingers, a woman I hadn't noticed tucked into the far corner of the room quickly approaches the king's side, her head ducked low.

"Yes, Your Majesty?"

"Serve my betrothed." The woman jumps into action, rounding behind the king's chair to come to my side, her gaze still downcast. She reaches a hand out for the serving spoon in front of me, but mine is already lifting to gently stop her.

"Thank you, but I can serve mys—"

"If you do not let her do the job she was *born* to do, Rhea, then there is no reason for her to be here." King Dolian's voice is as cruel as the look on his face, and the woman wilts further beneath his tone. My fingers curl into my palms, anger nipping at my heart as a rebuttal builds on my tongue. But then I look back at the woman, at the way her hands are shaking in front of her, and I realize that any fight I put up in this instance will not benefit me and will possibly *hurt* her.

Nodding, I let her serve me a few different foods in front of me, saying my thanks when my plate is full. She quickly retreats back to her corner, her head hanging low as she does. I stab at the strawberry on my plate, exhaling a rough breath through my nose. I don't like this, and I suppose I have been privileged in a way to never really think about the fact that there are servants in palaces. In the Mage Kingdom, I had never gotten the feeling that Nox or his parents felt they were *better* than those they employed to help.

The tension in the room is awkward as I force myself to eat a few bites, the weight of the king and Simon's glares heavy upon me. Even though I shouldn't, I feel relieved when Xander's steps sound as he re-enters the dining space. It dissipates, however, when my handmaiden follows behind, her brow crinkled in confusion.

"You called for me, Your Majesty?" she says.

"Come forward, Eve." She obeys, and my stomach grows tight with knots when the king rises from his seat and appraises her, one hand slipped into his pocket. Eve visibly shrinks when he steps closer, and then his free hand is gripping the back of her head, her body pliant as he shoves her down towards the table until her cheek hits the white cloth covering it. I startle, pushing back and standing, my hip throbbing from the abrupt movement.

"What are you doing?"

Eve is silent, though her breaths are loud between us.

"You test me, Rhea," King Dolian says, his voice calm, despite how his knuckles are white from how tightly he grips Eve's hair. "Come here."

I gasp as magic floods me, my feet moving before I command them to. When I reach the king's side, he takes his hand off of Eve's head, only to force me to replace it with my own, magic once more powering his words.

"Stop this," I rasp as I struggle to straighten my fingers, but my hold is just as harsh as his was, my heart fracturing when Eve whimpers beneath my touch. "Stop!"

"You may release her," he says, and I do so, immediately taking a large step back. Eve doesn't move, nothing beyond the quick movements of her breath. "Eve, return to Lady Rhea's room and clean it until no surface remains untouched." Eve rises and laces her fingers in front of her. She bows to the king, the sight of it churning my stomach further, and then she leaves on quick feet. The king moves behind me, and without warning, he closes his hand over the brand, the pressure *blinding*. I shout at the pain that explodes beneath his hand as it travels throughout my entire body as if I've been struck by lightning.

"Rhea, I warned you. You're burning too brightly for your own good." His cheek scrapes against mine, and my lip quivers as a tear slips from the corner of my eye. "You think I want to constantly punish you? That I relish hurting you?" *Yes!* I want to shout it. To scream it until everyone in this godsdamn palace hears me.

But the pain swallows me whole. I'm free falling into an open pit of fiery agony. He shakes me, my head lolling to the side. "Answer me."

Despite the dominance of his words, no magic pushes at me to answer him. My eyes lift to just over his shoulder, right where Xander is standing. The guard's words from earlier break through my torture in a single moment of clarity. *You shouldn't taunt him. He'll only make things worse for you.* King Dolian presses his thumb to my mouth, and I jerk my gaze back to meet his, his face blurry to my watery eyes. Showing him compliance—*submission*—is something I don't think I can do. Something that I don't *want* to do. But if he aims to hurt others in *my* place— Another squeeze of his hand at my hip has my knees weakening, my hands landing against his chest to catch myself.

"I'm sorry," I croak out, *hating* that I've said it. I reach desperately for my magic, mentally screaming at it to answer the call. But it doesn't. So I claw for that darkness in my mind. For that numbness to sink into. But it too doesn't lend itself to me. "I'm sorry," I say again, hot tears rolling down my cheeks.

King Dolian loosens his grip on the brand but tightens the hand holding my chin. I don't struggle when he turns his head enough for his lips to graze my cheek. "You will earn your title, Rhea. I will make sure of it." He leaves a ghost of a kiss on my skin and then releases me completely, returning to my chair and gesturing for me to sit. He takes his own seat after, and begins talking with Simon, as if nothing that has past was noteworthy. The numbness I begged for earlier finally makes itself present. At different points, I feel the gazes of everyone in the room on me, but I ignore them all in favor of staring at a strawberry on my plate.

The king says something about having the rest of the day to myself, and I nod as he and Simon leave before getting up from the table to join Xander where he waits. We walk in stilted silence, though I'm not sure I could say anything if he did try to speak with me. It's when we are halfway to my room that he stops, and after another step, I do too, looking back at him.

"This way." He doesn't add anything else, doesn't even wait for me to follow before he's walking down a corridor to our left.

I swallow, my eyes darting in both directions. A few guards stand post here and there, maids and male servants entering and exiting the corridors around us. I could go back to my room—and in all likelihood, I should—but everything in that space feels suffocating. It already holds too many bad memories, and the thought of being stuck there for an entire day alone... I hurry after Xander.

"Where are we going?" I ask, entirely too shaky.

Xander doesn't answer at first, not until a semi-familiar glass door is in front of us. I remember it from the brief tour the king took me on.

"The library?"

He nods, his lips in a flat line as he stares at the space through the glass on the door. "I figured you might want to be distracted for a bit," he answers, something uncharacteristically tender in his voice. I stare at him, bemused, and he tucks his hair behind his ear. "If the library doesn't sound appealing, there is an old aviary in the west wing that might be more in—"

"This is perfect," I interrupt, swallowing roughly. "Thank you."

"King Dolian will be occupied for most of the day."

I nod, hearing his unspoken words. *He won't bother you.* I take a step forward—eager for that distraction, to lose myself between the pages of someone else's world for a bit—before I pause and look over my shoulder. I open my mouth to say *something,* though I'm unsure what. It doesn't matter, however, because Xander is already retreating down the hall.

I follow the king's command the next morning when he sends Eve in to dress me and tell her to leave my hair down. I expect to be told to meet him for breakfast, but she surprises me when she says, "You're to accompany the king to a meeting."

Chapter Fourteen

ARIA

Thunder rolls overhead as I break the surface of the water, Dyanna's pink braids stark against the gray clouds from where she floats in the water in front of me. Ahead of us, Queen Amari and Sade stare at the shore and the line of golden guards standing behind the Spell, the top of a small castle poking up in the distance behind them.

"Is the king expecting you to attack him?" Dyanna asks.

"He's simply showing off as males do," our mother answers, her head tilting to the side. "Stay close to me and do not hesitate to sing should he decide to try something." She sinks beneath the surface, and my sisters and I follow. The tear in my fin from the rogue siren attack is still tender, made more so after days of travel, and the ever-present nervousness within me intensifies as we near shallow waters. Throughout our journey, my thoughts drifted briefly to the fae—*Myla*. What will she think when I'm absent for our first meeting? Would there be ramifications because I didn't show up when I said I would?

Queen Amari lifts her trident, bringing us to a stop. She transforms, legs and feet replacing her tail while her scales recede into her skin, only a faint shimmer remaining. My leg muscles shake as I push myself up through the thick layer of the Spell to stand, my head lifting above the water while my lungs draw in a breath of the salty air. The tightly woven ruby-red braids around my head loosen into ringlet curls, their length cascading over my shoulders and down my breasts, the tips brushing against my hips.

I adjust the strap of my satchel so it crosses over my chest, the bag covering the juncture of my thighs. Dyanna does the same, though her shorter pink curls don't cover much of anything on top. Our mother's black hair cascades all the way down her torso to the tops of her thighs, and she lifts her chin proudly as she approaches the shore with a confidence that can only come from knowing you are the most powerful creature attending this meeting. A crown of shining silver embellished with rare teal seashells, oval-cut diamonds, and delicate strands of blue eelgrass woven within it sits perfectly centered on her head, this piece of jewelry one I have never seen before.

Dyanna and Sade stand together at her right, leaving me alone on the queen's left while we approach the shore. As I look at the guards lined up across from us—their visibly wide eyes easy to see even through the Spell—I wonder if they realize just how much danger they're in.

"King Dolian, surely you don't intend for us to conduct our business separated by the very thing that has left my kind secluded for so long?" my mother says, her voice magically carrying over the roaring of the waves behind us.

Despite the swollen dark storm clouds above, the unmistakable gleam of a gold crown catches my eye, its wearer centered amongst the thirty or so guards. He's finely dressed, his clothing dark except for golden thread forming intricate patterns on the vest he wears. His trousers are tucked into shiny tall leather boots. A woman stands at his side, her lavender dress fluttering at her ankles in the wind. She has no crown upon her head, but the king reaches a hand out to her as he moves to take a step forward. When she hesitates, he leans over and says something to her that makes her stiffen before she concedes and lays her fingers into his waiting palm.

One of the guards nearest to the king moves with them, taking his helmet off to reveal dark shoulder-length hair, discontent painted all over his expression. Together, the three of them walk through the Spell, stopping only a few steps past it.

"I am nothing if not always agreeable to your terms, Queen Amari. You should know that by now," the king says, his voice holding a higher-pitched tenor than I would have presumed.

The woman at his side draws her brows together at his response, but her attention stays pointed in my mother's direction. I study her features—the healthy glow of her skin and the honey color of her hair—and recognition of where I've seen her before causes my lips to part on a quick inhale. The reaction turns her gaze to me, her lovely green eyes meeting mine with open curiosity.

"And we will ensure it stays that way," my mother responds. The guards remaining behind the Spell shift their stances, some even partially drawing their swords as if sensing the threat of my mother and sisters from just her words alone. The lone guard at the king's side raises his hand, steadying their movements. The siren queen turns her dark eyes to the woman we captured from the Mage Kingdom. "I was half afraid you would not bring her. You were rather *passionate* about getting her back in one piece."

"I thought about keeping her hidden, to be sure, but the allure of learning more about her magic was simply too strong to resist," he says, looking over to the woman as he brings their joined hands to his lips.

"Such a lovely little thing you are," my mother purrs. Lightning flashes in the distance, followed by a crack of thunder that makes the woman jump. The king's fingers grow tighter around her hand, and she grimaces at the contact.

"Whatever it is you would like her to show you, now might be the time, as I'd prefer *not* to get rained on," the king chides, his dark hazel eyes narrowing.

My mother hums as she takes a step forward. "What is your name?"

"Rhea," the woman offers quickly. "My name is Rhea, Your Majesty."

Queen Amari snaps her hand out and grabs Rhea's wrist, bringing it up higher as she inspects her fingers—and the ring that sits atop it. "Such a pretty ring," she says, angling Rhea's hand towards the king. "How have you enjoyed its benefits, King Dolian?"

"It works exactly as you said it would, and I find it is quite *useful* in helping Lady Rhea adjust to her new life." My blood runs cold at the insinuation—at how Rhea's attention drops to the tops of her feet. I take a glance at the ring and find it's matching one on my mother's finger. The king wearing the third piece of jewelry I brought back from the Northern Island.

"I'm not in the business of lying. Something your kind cannot claim."

To my utter surprise, the king heaves a long sigh before leveling his gaze at my mother. "I have earned your favor twice, Your Majesty, yet you still group me in with ancestors I have never met. I cannot control what the men of my lineage did centuries ago. I can only give you my word now. Show me what Rhea's magic can do and how I can wield it, and I will give you what I promised."

Queen Amari laughs, and my throat narrows at the sound—at the warning laced within. The guard next to Rhea slides his hand to the outside of his thigh where a dagger is strapped, only for Sade to snarl at him, her black talons growing from her fingers. "I need more than just a promise, Young King. I need proof that what happened in this spot two hundred years ago won't be repeated."

The king's brows lift towards his hairline as he gives my mother an incredulous look. "And how in the world do you want me to do that?"

"Your guards," she says, gesturing with her trident to the men waiting behind the Spell. "Your ancestors used their guards to act against my kind. Prove your loyalty by commanding Rhea to kill them."

My heart leaps up to my throat, while Rhea, the king, and even the *guard* all wear varying shades of shock on their faces. "Surely, you don't expect Rhea's magic to do such a thing?"

"If you want to know the true power the girl holds, if you want to ensure that our tentative alliance remains intact without the *threat* of interruption, you will do it." I watch as my mother's lips quirk into a smile she reserves for only the most heinous acts, my mind immediately tumbling into my past and making my entire body begin to tremble. When neither the king nor Rhea move, her eyes narrow and her voice deepens. "*Do it.*"

King Dolian looks to Rhea, something desperate flashing in his eyes as he meets hers. She shakes her head in anticipation of his command, but he doesn't hesitate. "Kill them with your magic." Each word is a struggle for the king to grit out, his hand shaking as it points to the men on the other side of the Spell.

Rhea's eyes widen, the horror in them making the emotion spike in me before she turns to face the Spell, her movements stiff as her chest heaves with labored breaths. A whimper leaves her as her arms lock straight out in front of her. Electricity sits heavily in the air, so much so that I draw my gaze from her to the clouds momentarily, waiting for the lightning that I can feel building to strike. But it never comes.

"Pl—please," she gasps, the tendons in her hands pulled taut from how widely her fingers are spread. Her begging is cut short by a harrowing scream. The sound alone would get me to stumble away from her, but then there is what comes out of Rhea's hands. Glittering black *shadows* gather at her palms, growing in size until they wrap around her hands completely. Like arrows fired from their bows, the dark magic then shoots forward and pierces through the Spell with startling ease before unfurling over the stunned guards like an inky, fathomless fog. Darkness completely eclipses them, smothering their golden armor as a suffocating silence blankets the beach.

The first scream that breaks it draws my shoulders up towards my ears. Then another joins. And another. No one moves as magic continues to pour from Rhea, the opaqueness of her shadows clashing with the sparkling veil of the Spell. The point of contact between them *flickers*, and my mother takes a step forward as if she aims to touch it before Dyanna plants a hand on her arm. Thunder cracks from the darkened sky above, blending with the cries of anguish of those trapped within Rhea's magic. She joins them as she screams, her spine uncomfortably straight while veins begin to bulge in her arms.

"Incredible," my mother whispers, and when I look her way, it isn't smug satisfaction on her face but pure *awe.*

As abruptly as it began, it ends. Rhea's magic retreating back to her. The other side of the Spell is eerily silent, and when the last wisp of black disappears, Rhea collapses onto her knees.

"I killed them," she cries into her hands, repeating the heartbroken admission over and over again. My eyes sting as I take in what remains on the other side. Heaps of golden armor lay not on top of sand but on mounds of black ash.

"Oh my gods," I whisper, my fingers going to my lips as I wrap my other arm around my torso.

"Did she just *incinerate* them?" Dyanna asks on a breath.

King Dolian pulls Rhea up by her arm until she is standing next to him.

"King Dolian, you can see that I've helped you attain more than just a future bride," my mother declares.

"I can," he grits out, turning Rhea to face the queen. Rain begins to fall, the thick drops mixing with the tears that line Rhea's cheeks. "I might ask that, in the future, you refrain from making your point at the expense of my men."

My mother simply laughs, pointing her trident in his direction. "You *will* continue to meet me when I call you through the Mirror. Our exploration of Rhea's magic has only just begun." The king stares at my mother as his shoulders stiffen, but he only nods in agreement before he drags Rhea back through the Spell, the guard following behind. Her movements are sluggish, causing her to stumble, and my heart clenches as I watch her, guilt weaving through me like a poison.

"A wedding is a lovely time to announce the unity of our two realms, King Dolian," the siren queen shouts after them, chuckling when he doesn't bother turning around.

"What the hell was *that*?" Sade asks, her wet tangerine curls sticking to her torso.

"Mage magic. It has been a while since I've seen it with my own eyes, and it is much more powerful than I remember. But it is how we will get what we are owed."

I force a deep inhale through my nose, my mind trying to reconcile what I just witnessed with what I know my mother wants. Movement nearer to me refocuses my gaze on the Spell where the black ash begins to pool in the sand as it mixes with the rain. Squinting my eyes, I notice the beach on the other side is easier to see, like the Spell has become more transparent in the spot where Rhea's magic pierced it. Blinking quickly, I look away, only to find my mother staring at it as well—her head tilted in contemplation before a smile breaks over her face, wide enough to show her canines.

Chapter Fifteen

ARIA

W E RETURN TO LUMEN two days later, swimming low to avoid the swells created by the storm that batters the sea.

The legionaries guarding the palace entrance bow before my mother as she leads our group past the sea glass door. "Dyanna, join me in the library. I want every piece of literature we can find about mage magic," Queen Amari orders from ahead.

Dyanna nods from her place at my side. "Yes, Your Majesty."

"Sade, you and Aria will converse on what should be done to catch the traitorous sirens of the seamounts. I don't want to waste a second more than necessary finding them."

I look to my older sister, her tangerine braids tied back behind her. Her jaw clenches tightly before she forces it to relax, her gaze then falling to me. "It will be done."

The queen and Dyanna depart for the library, leaving Sade and I to float in place in awkward silence. Did she remember how she held a male in her thrall until our mother brought me to him to fulfill my *duty*?

Sade's expression is placid, though her eyes remain keenly on me before she sighs. "Come. We will discuss this away from any prying ears." Shaking my hands out, I follow behind her until we come to a door, a citrine-colored jewel set at its center.

"Your bedroom?" I ask, lifting my brows in surprise. I have never been in any of my sister's rooms except Lyre's.

"Do you know anywhere else that we won't be overheard?"

I suppose she has a point.

"I'm hardly ever here anyways." As the commander of the Queen's Legion, Sade spends most of her time where they are stationed near the palace. I take in her room as we enter, the colors a bright combination of yellow and orange. A red clamshell bed, its pearlescent finish gleaming beneath glowing white crystals, is centered in the space though not much else decorates it. "What do you know about these sirens?" she asks, swimming to the bed and collapsing onto it.

"I'm afraid I don't know much."

"You visited them frequently, did you not?"

"You knew?"

She snorts, rolling onto her back and staring up at the ceiling. "Everyone did, Aria."

My shoulders round. "I did visit them, but I mostly played with the offspring. Or gave them spare coi—" *Shit.* Though I interrupt myself with a clearing of my throat, Sade sends a flat look my way.

"You needn't censor yourself for me. I only care about finding the traitors now, not what you did with them in the past."

Surprised, I can't help but ask, "You're not going to berate me for helping them?"

Sade sits up and runs her fingers through her braids. Where my features are softer—fuller lips and freckles lining my cheeks and nose—her chin is sharper. Her jawline more defined. Though her arms and stomach are toned with muscle, there's no shortage of curves to her physique. She's beautiful, as all sirens are, but that beauty doesn't hide her strength. Rather, it accentuates it. "What good does that do? You've already committed the act. As I said, I just want to find the traitors."

I nod, but dread sits heavy in my stomach. Finding them means betraying them, and while I may hold no love for Nia, I *do* care about the youngest sirens. My mind spins while I try to find a way to appease both Sade and Nia. I might not be able to stop my sister from her attempts to find them, but I could distract her. Perhaps misguide her even. Just long enough to get the weapons back to Nia and ensure they've found somewhere safe to hide.

"The ocean is vast, but a group that large cannot stay hidden for long. They moved with haste when they were tipped off about the legion coming for them," Sade says, her orange-tinted brows drawn low. "They must have had a preplanned place to meet."

"Do you have any leads on who tipped them off?"

She gives a curt shake of her head. "Nothing yet. As you can imagine, the queen is not pleased by this. Thankfully, her attention is forcibly split between the treasonous sirens and her new deal with the mortal king, or we might feel the brunt of her wrath over it."

"What that woman, Rhea, can do..." A shiver works through me.

"I have never seen anything like that. I suppose we should be grateful that our queen is able to control her, for a being that powerful is one that can't be trusted."

Grateful. As if there is joy to be found in robbing someone of their free will. Rhea's screams—and the pain that was laced within them—is a sound I won't ever forget. My guilt is thick, and it burns the back of my throat. If it were not for my retrieval of the rings, she would not be under my mother's control. How fitting a punishment to know that someone else is suffering a similar torment to the horrors that plague me, and *I* am one of the reasons why.

"In any case, we must find the traitors before they have time to plot anything else against the queen. I'm tempted to use the legion if only to help us scan the surrounding area more quickly," she says, tapping her fingers on the orange scales at the front of her tail.

No. While the seamount sirens are no strangers to keeping a low profile, it would be nearly impossible for them to stay hidden from Sade *and* her army. And I know they must be close by, if Nia's presence and insistence that I get their confiscated weapons back are any indication. "Surely, involving the legion now is not necessary?" I ask. Sade lifts a questioning brow. "I just mean, that between the two of us—"

"And what experience do you have tracking, Aria?" she interrupts, swimming languidly from the bed in my direction. "Unless you've got a secret set of skills no one knows about?"

The awkward laugh that tumbles out of me couldn't be more poorly timed. "Of course not."

"I don't know," she muses, her gaze searching mine in a way that makes me want to squirm. "It would certainly be easy for you to slip under the radar. You already defied the queen once by helping the seamount sirens, who's to say you aren't doing so again? That your intent isn't to lead *me* astray so that I do not find them?"

"I wouldn't do that," I lie, my back hitting the wall as she forces me to retreat.

"I think you would, but if there is anything I love, Little Sister, it is pursuing the hunt. Finding a weakness and exploiting it." The tips of her canines gleam as she smiles at me before she backs away and folds her arms over her chest. "We will start our search alone for now. I'll come by tomorrow morning with the details of the radius we will cover." Feeling my heart settle in my chest, I give her a quick nod and attempt to dart for the door. Her fingers—icy cold against the warmth of my skin—wrap around my arm, stopping my retreat as she leans in close to my ear. "Make no mistake, it is only a matter of time before I discover whatever it is you're hiding. And when I do, I am not the one you will need to answer to."

Lying in bed later that night, I toss and turn as Myla's face drifts into my mind. I asked her to teach me how to fight, but something tells me that my request was too vague and that the fae will capitalize on such a misstep. At least I will be able to venture to her without raising suspicions under the guise of searching for the seamount sirens. Throwing an arm over my eyes, I purse my lips. I am not delusional enough to think I can balance working both sides of this fight without getting caught. Add in my mother controlling someone like Rhea? A part of me that wonders if I'll even make it out alive at all.

Chapter Sixteen

MYLA

WARM BLOOD SPILLS DOWN the back of my hand, its rich iron scent heavy in the air around us. The male before me thrashes against his restraints, panic widening the pupils of his dark eyes before they roll towards the back of his head. I release a long exhale, the exaggerated sound erasing some of my tension as I pull my dagger away from his body.

"Please," he rasps, drawing in a heaving breath that tugs on the carved lines I've made in his chest. "I don't know what—"

"Malorie Stones, age thirteen," I begin in a deep voice, pacing behind him and using the tattered remains of his tunic to wipe his blood from my hand and dagger. Once the weapon is clean, I slide it back into the sheath at my thigh and then grip the hilt of the curved blade that rests on the opposite leg. The male stiffens for a second before sagging once more, his arms straining from the weight of his body. His hands are bound above his head, looped around a metal hook hanging from a chain attached to the ceiling. I keep my voice low as I continue. "Erina Calo, age twelve. Anya Fang, age *nine*." Each name strikes another match to the inferno within me, my fingers trembling in anticipation as the rage I just released upon his body is renewed.

I adjust my grip on the frayed leather wrapped around the hilt, my grandfather's initials carved into the black metal there. I had stolen it from one of the relic rooms in the palace, the urge to *sully* something as valuable as this with my touch too strong to ignore. Of course, no one except Navin knows I have it, and he had laughed as I presented the uniquely shaped weapon to him. It was the day after I had bested my brother in our secret training sessions for the first time. I wanted something to not only remember that moment but to remind me why

I was doing *this*. Why I traded in nights of rest in my gilded cage for the risk of getting caught outside the palace. I am needed, here, in the forgotten spaces of Khargis. *Vigilante. Assassin. Devil. Shadow.* I've heard the rumors of what I'm called, and I have far more respect for those titles than I do for any given to me by my royal status.

"I didn't know they were children. I swear—"

"Spare me your bullshit, Taran," I drawl, sliding the sharp dagger along his back and shredding what remains of his clothing until the expanse of his skin is before me. He whimpers, and a part of me wonders if I should be concerned by how much joy the sound brings me—though I've already accepted that my conscience is too twisted and gnarled to be a guiding voice anymore. "You are going to die tonight. It is going to be at *my* hands, and I am going to take my time hurting you. As you took your time hurting those young ones."

"As if you're"—he coughs, sending droplets of blood splattering onto the damp ground—"any better."

I smile beneath the black mask covering most of my face, a matching hood draped over my head. I don't *need* to hide any part of my identity as only a few in the palace know what I look like, and I doubt any of them will ever venture into the pits of the capital. Even if they did, the warehouse I secretly bought is hidden well. To the outside, it appears as any abandoned building might: boarded-up windows and dilapidated stone and wood sides. If someone decided to break in, all they would see is a large room empty of everything but cobwebs. They'd have to search for the trap door hidden within the westernmost wall. Then they'd have to descend a staircase that leads to a soundproof basement.

No one will ever see the horrors I inflict on my subjects here unless I want them to. "If you think we are similar, then you're as stupid as you are revolting." I dig the tip of the dagger into his back, twisting it slowly as he begins to scream.

"I'll give you—you anything you want. *Anything*. I have—I have money. Lots of it," he sputters.

I give another sharp twist of the dagger, waiting until his answering bellow ends before I ask, "How much?"

"Enough that you will not have to work again for a long while." His tone grows light with hope, and he releases a shuddering breath when I pull my weapon back and walk around to his front. There is no amount of money in the world I would take to stop doing this work, but the fact that *he* has enough of that money at all gives me pause. I don't discriminate when hunting for a predator—rich or poor, noble or without a title. If they partake in the same depravities, I do not hesitate to be their executioner. Though it is much more rare to find someone higher up on the social food chain, as they have the means to hide the evidence of what they do.

"How much do you think your life is worth? How much is *freedom* worth to you?" I ask softly, toying with that desperate hope flashing in his eyes. When he doesn't answer, I click my tongue and set my blade beneath his quivering chin. "Your chance at me letting you go is dwindling, Taran. I could happily spend another few hours just slicing you up until you're nothing but ribbons, and I can make sure you live through it all. That you *feel* it all." I tilt the blade, nicking the skin beneath his chin. "So answer the question."

His gulp is audible as his eyes search mine before he finally gives in. "I keep a large sum of money and gold hidden in the wall of a shed at the back of my property. Only my wife is home right now. She won't be able to stop you if you go."

I take a step back, dropping my hand to my side. "You would let someone that so easily caught and harmed *you* near your wife?"

He attempts a shrug and clears his throat, his cheeks stained with tears as he leans his head against one of his upraised arms. "You'd be doing me a favor."

Rage, hot and insistent, burns up my torso. It ignites my blood and tightens my grip so harshly that the already worn leather around the hilt creaks just slightly. There is no morality in males like him. I could cut at every inch of him in search of it and find nothing but iniquity and rancid blood. He smiles, letting his guard down as if he's won. It takes no effort to slide my blade down the center of his chest, just enough to split the skin.

"You asked if I wanted my freedom," he howls, his body jerking in the chains as he thrashes. "You fucking—"

"I asked if you wanted your freedom, yes. But, Taran, I don't give a shit if you do. I'm going to do exactly what I told you I would, and as I slice skin from your muscles and drain your blood slowly, I want you to remember that there is no mercy for those who take without permission. There will always be a reckoning."

"People will know if you kill me. They'll—they'll notice my absence. You *can't* do this!"

I hum, stepping up to him and pushing the tip of the dagger into the space between two of his ribs. "But will they care that you're gone?" I ask, dropping the modification on my voice. The higher pitch draws his brows together comically. Once the realization settles that I'm a *female*, I pull down my mask with my free hand, plunging the dagger deeper into his torso with the other. As he screams, I methodically—*cruelly*—carve my resentment and hatred for all those like him into his body until there is nothing left but blood and bone.

After disposing of Taran's body and paying a visit to my informant, I stop by the dragon fields again, only to find a sleeping Bali and Sunis in their cave. Despite the anxiousness to bond a dragon driving me, I'm not stupid enough to wake a slumbering beast for my own gain. Sneaking back into the palace, the adrenaline of the kill slowly wears off until I'm left hunched over myself in the shower. Flashes of Father Yamin and his torment take root in my mind—as they always do after a night such as this—and it isn't until I collapse onto my bed, not even bothering to get dressed in my nightgown, that the memories finally die down.

In just a few hours, I will head to the beach for my next meeting with the siren. One I hope the wretch will actually show up to. The sooner our deal is fulfilled, the sooner I can rid myself of yet another problem.

Sleep claims me swiftly, and in its darkness, I dream of nothing.

Chapter Seventeen

MYLA

L AN'S IRIDESCENT BLUE SCALES shimmer in the early morning light as his wings beat hard against a gust of wind. Navin's *amusement* over my meeting with the siren was almost enough to ensure that I walked the entire way here, if only to ignore him.

We soar over the black mountains that form our kingdom and through the cool mist rising from them. The meeting spot I suggested to the siren is a well-known fae landmark, its spearhead-shaped tip and jagged sides easily visible from the ocean and even some of the highest mountain peaks. What makes it more unique is that the rocky spectacle has a cavern accessible at its front. The coverage should prevent the siren and I from being spotted.

"There she is," he shouts, pointing to where a ruby-red head sticks out of the water. Lan begins his descent, crossing through the Spell and circling over the beach to land. Gripping the leather strap that holds me to the dragon, I brace for the impact, shutting my eyes against the sand that flies in all directions when we hit it. Lan's wings flare out for balance before he gives them a shake and tucks them in at his sides.

"Stay here for a moment," I tell Navin as I untangle my hand from the strap and climb down the dragon's extended front leg. Lan growls, his hot breath blasting my side and earning him a scowl in return. My brother chuckles, patting his dragon's head fondly.

Planting my boots in the sand, I watch as the siren shifts into her mortal form, the action more fluid than I would have thought. Within a few steps she stands in front of me, her eyes glowing more orange than hazel, and a hand gripping the strap of the bag across her bare chest. The wind stirs her ruby-red hair, but most of it hangs damp over her shoulders, covering a decent portion of the front of her body.

"Hello, beautiful!" Navin yells, a ridiculous amount of amusement in his voice. The siren's gaze lingers on him for a few seconds before it makes its way back to me. She swallows roughly.

"Where were you last week?"

"I couldn't—" She sighs and drops her gaze to the sand. "I will not miss another meeting."

Despite my annoyance, curiosity flickers at what might have kept her before I push the thought away. It isn't important, only fulfilling this oath as quickly as possible is. Turning, I shout over my shoulder to Navin. "Come back in an hour."

"I was thinking Lan and I could watch you two—" He stops at the look I send him, rolling his eyes before winking at the siren. "Fine. Play nice, Sister." It takes no time at all for Lan to leap into the air, wings beating against the wind as he and Navin soar high into the sky before crossing the Spell and heading back towards home.

I catch the awe on the siren's face before she notices my stare and abruptly flattens her features. The sea sprays water around her ankles, and upon a closer look, I make out the faint green scales there. They shimmer in the sunlight as they rise to her knees and the outsides of her thighs, the green slowly transitioning to golden yellow and then orange. A patch of scales graces her hips and peeks out from in between the strands of her hair, the orange changing to the same ruby red as her hair. She shifts her weight onto one leg, her expression unsure as she takes in my own appearance.

"Let's get this over with." The sun is warm on my back, penetrating through my black cloak and the flying leathers I wear beneath them. Because the days are still warm, I've chosen a lace-up flight vest, black fingerless leather gloves covering my forearms. It's much easier to hide blood against dark colors than it is on my own pale skin. The sand of this beach is softer than the ones that line the Continent to the east, and the finer granules make trudging through them annoying as I lead us beneath the cover of the cavern. The stone that juts out above us is dark, only broken by the holes that let the sunlight in and the occasional striation of white. "We'll meet here next time to ensure we avoid being spotted from above," I tell her, the shimmer of the Spell painting the farthest back wall in iridescent white. We come to a stop in front of some large boulders, and I lead the way, climbing up to where the stone is smooth, a natural platform. Behind it, a pool of water made from underground channels connecting to the ocean ripples, and surrounding us dark green vines creep up the walls, small flowers in tight buds clinging to them.

Going to the far wall, I turn and lean my back against the rock, folding my arms over my chest. The siren climbs up a few seconds later, hissing a breath when she bears weight on one of her legs. She takes in our surroundings, noting the thick green vines that climb the stone towards the ceiling and then the dark water that waits beyond the platform.

"I may not know much about training," she starts after an uncomfortable silence stretches between us, "but I'm pretty sure we should be doing more than just standing here."

I drag the tip of my boot along the ground, tracing a line of light that pours in from a crack in the ceiling. "If I'm being honest, Little Siren, I'm trying to figure out how I am supposed to teach you to defend yourself when my gut instinct is screaming for me to cut you open and see what color you bleed." Tipping my head up, I watch her work to swallow, her fingers intertwining in front of her nervously.

"How would killing me affect the life debt?" she rasps.

"There would be adverse effects—ones I'm not too keen on exploring." The magic that bound us together when the siren saved my life is sentient in a way I've never understood but that our history gives lengthy warnings on. If I act in bad faith with the siren, including harming her or not ensuring her safety in our time together, the magic will respond in equal measure and retaliate by mirroring those actions against *me*. "You are safe from that brand of torture." My eyes meet hers, and her chest rises with a quick inhale. "At least for now." Once I fulfill the terms of the deal and my life is once again my own, then what I do to the siren will be of no consequence.

Quiet settles around us once more, the sounds of wind and water only broken up by my booted steps as I begin to pace around the length of the platform. The siren keeps her eyes pinned to my movements, turning her body to follow me. "If our paths had crossed and you weren't bound by the life debt, would you have killed me that day?"

"Yes," I answer without hesitation, noting the way her shoulders flinch towards her ears. "I would say it isn't personal, but that's not exactly true."

"Seems unfair for it to be personal, considering we've never met before this."

I stop in front of her, my fingers idly dancing over the hilt of the blade strapped to my thigh. "You know the history of your own kind. The *brutality*. The feral way you all behave." I expect her to balk at that—to attempt to defend, if not her people, at least herself—but instead, her chin dips as her gaze falls. "Why do you want me to teach you how to fight?"

Looking up through her dark lashes, she releases a rough breath. "Does it matter why?"

"No, though it might help me gauge the style of training. Are you needing to learn how to defend yourself? How to fight off an enemy? Perhaps you're planning to lead a revolution within your queendom." At that, her eyes widen. "Though I'm less confident about that one."

She runs her fingers through her hair, brushing the tightly curled strands away from her face as her eyes fall closed. "Has there ever been a moment where you wanted something but you knew that you couldn't claim it as you were? That you weren't quite yet strong enough, bold enough, just *enough*, to have it?"

I don't respond, even as her question tugs roughly at my chest. I know, more than she will ever understand, what that feeling is like. My very existence is tied to accomplishing something that seems undoubtedly impossible, no matter how hard I try. But I keep my stare unforgiving, and eventually, the siren gives a shake of her head as she looks away from me.

"Exactly. *You* have never felt that, so you would never understand my reasoning." Clearing her throat, she lifts her bag over her shoulder and sets it at her feet, something clinking against the rock as she does. "Now, please, I know we would both rather be anywhere else with *anyone* else, but since we are stuck here, we might as well begin."

I smirk but she isn't wrong. So I push my feelings down until they're buried with every other part of myself I don't care to deal with and instruct her to stand with her feet shoulder width apart as I appraise her.

"Why are you just staring at me?"

"I'm not staring; I'm assessing. Your balance is horrible, and you keep shifting weight onto your right foot. Does that injury bother you?" I ask, pointing with my chin to the jagged scar that cuts deeply into the top of her foot, the edges of it still swollen.

"It aches from time to time," she answers after a moment, flexing her toes before relaxing them.

The scar is a different texture, its pigment lighter than the skin that surrounds it. *What sort of weapon would cause a mark like that?* In any case, it's hindering her ability to form a solid stance, which is essential to her learning how to fight at all.

"You need to build your strength up, especially those muscles. Right now, you are too weak to learn useful moves. Everything requires balance, and you have none."

Parallel lines form on her brow. "How do I do that?"

I lead her through some basic exercises—ones that, when done frequently enough, will work to build up her strength. When we finish with the first round, the siren looks underwhelmed. "This isn't what I had in mind when I asked you to teach me how to fight." Her chest heaves, her words taking on a desperate edge. "I think you're trying to get out of teaching me anything useful."

Folding my arms over my chest, I glare at her as I grind my teeth. "Foundations are essential if we are to be successful with this training. If you can't balance, you won't have proper leverage when it comes time to learn how to punch. How to wield a weapon or deliver a powerful kick. You won't be able to dodge an attack coming towards you without falling on your ass." I stretch my neck as I move my head from side to side, eager to mark this lesson as done. "Now, run through the exercises again. And when you're finished, do them once more." She presses her lips together, fingers curling in towards her palms but her tantrum lasts for all of a few seconds before she obeys.

The sounds of her breaths fill the space, and I use the opportunity to map out my next visit to Khargis, excitement brewing at the new target I've acquired.

A shadow blocks the sunlight temporarily from above, and I tense at the sound of wingbeats, crouching low enough to look out through the arched opening in the rock below us. From this vantage point, I can only see the dark blue feet and legs of the dragon, its tail swinging behind it as sand goes flying from its rough landing.

"Sister, I've come to save you from your plight!" Navin's voice carries into the cavern, and I contemplate the merits of punching him briefly when the soft laugh of the siren behind me draws my gaze her way.

"Who is he?" she asks, sitting on her knees as she leans forward to take in Navin and Lan. My skin prickles as I look at her, the notion that I am *so* close to a creature like her and can do nothing but bend to the will of the life debt only stokes my ire further. Sirens are greedy and malicious. They care for nothing and no one save themselves, and *this one* is no different. Despite how she might pretend to be.

Her eyes glow a bright hazel when they meet mine, and I snarl at them. At *her*. "You should bring clothes to change into during our meetings. Training a naked siren is not something I want to subject myself to. Life debt or not." Standing, I tug my hood back over my head and then climb down to the sand below, heading towards the opening where I can now see Navin atop his dragon.

"I don't own any clothing," she shouts back, drawing a curious look from Navin that I ignore. Lan lowers the front of his body and extends his left leg, allowing me to climb up until I'm balancing between the ridges on the back of his neck and taking a seat behind Navin.

"So," he drawls once we're past the Spell and the outskirts of Khargis come into view, "how did it go?"

"Fine." His answering chuckle has me contemplating testing out how quickly he would heal from a stab wound. "I'm so glad you find the fact that my life is tied to a *siren* so amusing."

"You're being dramatic, Myla," he says over his shoulder, our bodies tilting to the right as Lan adjusts to the air current. "This could be a good opportunity for you, you know? Maybe a chance to befriend someone without holding a knife to their throat."

I grip the strap holding me to the dragon more tightly, looking down over Khargis as we soar above it. "This isn't a fucking play date, Navin."

"I know, I'm just *saying*, it wouldn't be the worst thing for you to have someone to talk to who can't use that information against you. She'll never be able to tell another fae."

"Do you not remember what she is?" I growl, squeezing my thighs around Lan more tightly. "Do the details of our own history escape your memory, or are you simply *choosing* to be ignorant?" When Navin doesn't answer beyond a simple shake of his head, I bite down on the side of my cheek until I taste blood.

My hatred of the sirens goes beyond the fact that their actions led to the deaths of Shah and Navin's parents. The continental war they started set off a chain of events that led to my father believing that my very existence was proof that the gods were angry with him. For a century, I have been forced to live cognizant of the fact that my own father believes me to be a fucking punishment from the gods. As dragon bonds begin to fail, that only solidifies that belief to be true. It's made the king and brethren that work closely with him desperate.

Desperate males have only ever cared about two things: power and doing whatever it takes to maintain it.

"You need someone to talk to," Navin says finally as Lan begins to slow his speed down. "And since you refuse to talk to me, then I just thought—"

"I appreciate the concern, but this kingdom will freeze over before I *ever* confide in a siren."

Chapter Eighteen

NOX

SCREAMS ECHO AROUND ME *as the sensation of falling tugs on my stomach harshly. Despite a phantom wind tousling my hair, I feel weightless—like I'm floating on water. My chest aches with a hollowness I can't define, and I don't think I'm breathing, unsure my heart is even beating, as the space that houses my normally writhing power sits empty. Unused. Desolate in a way I haven't felt in a long time.*

A sharp awareness drags over my spine, stiffening it vertebrae by vertebrae as my consciousness tries to narrow in on where I am. Minutes or hours, perhaps even days, pass, and I still continue on in the same manner. My mind wanders to something that might ground me, might pull me out of this terrible existence, and I inevitably land on the image of Rhea. I picture her honey-blonde hair and the way it rests down her back. I feel the warmth of her body against mine, how we fit together so seamlessly. Our connection is one that was formed the day I walked into her tower for the first time, and since then, there has been a constant tether between us.

Except for now.

Threads, golden and blazing brightly as they flutter in the space around me, draw my attention. I know where they lead—where they should lead—yet when I try to tug on them, they don't bring her to me.

A voice sounds in the distance, light and silvery, comparable to the soft chiming of bells. I pull again on those threads, watching with growing horror as their light begins to flicker. Shadows move in from all sides, smothering them until they go out completely, and I'm left alone, once more plunging through darkness.

Nothing but an empty vessel without the presence of her.

Stillness. There is a heavy stillness around me, one made more obvious by the way it pushes on my chest. My heart beats rhythmically behind my ribs, the sound of blood rushing in my ears intensifying the pain throbbing between them.

"How is he here?*" The question is asked by a soft voice.*

"It should be fairly obvious," someone else answers, his words melodic and deep—laden with power that somehow rattles my bones. The woman growls, and he laughs. "Where she is filled with the sun and moon, he carries the stars. But it is all made of the same energy. All of the same cosmic origin."

"What the fuck."

It isn't until an uncomfortable silence lingers, feeling as if the eyes of thousands are upon me, that I realize I spoke the words aloud. The male chuckles, and I pry my eyes open. The sky above me is filled with a smattering of bright stars, their silver light flaring. It isn't just stars but swirls of other things *that dot the sky in colors of purple, green, blue, and red.*

"Seriously, what the fuck?" Turning my head, I find that the scenery above is the same all around, my body somehow floating in the middle of this fathomless space. The Middle... Rhea's description of where her magic sometimes pulled her to and the name of the woman who resides here—one who acts almost as a seer of sorts, though that word isn't one that is common in our vocabulary anymore—pushes to the forefront of my memory.

"It is an old word indeed, not one used for centuries but one that fits. In a roundabout way."

Blinking, I look around for the owner of the voice that I know to be Selene as the scent of something flowery suddenly punctuates the air. Cold trepidation spikes when I realize I hadn't spoken the seer comment aloud. Shit, hadn't Rhea also told me Selene could hear thoughts?

"Welcome, Nox Flynn Daxel, Crown Prince of the Mage Kingdom, Prince of Stars, and Protector of the True Queen. I am Selene, and it is an honor to finally meet you."

It takes a monumental amount of effort to bring myself up to a sitting position, as if there is a disconnect in the command from my mind to my body. Once I'm finally up, I draw a leg in and rest my elbow on it, cradling my aching head in my hand. "Just Nox is fine. That many titles is entirely ostentatious. And also incorrect." Her laugh is gentler than the male's was, and I swallow against the knot that forms in my throat at how much it reminds me of Rhea's. "Should I be concerned that I'm here?"

"No."

"Really? Because you certainly seemed concerned speaking to whoever that guy was," I counter.

"It is unusual *that you are here. He was correct when he said your magic is made of the same celestial power that Rhea's is, but I never thought..." She clears her throat multiple times. "It is just unusual," she repeats.*

"And who was that male?"

"Another who resides here."

An unhelpful answer, but one I choose to ignore in favor of a different question. "Where is Rhea?" I can't imagine that if I am here, she wouldn't be as well.

Selene is unnervingly quiet for so long that I wonder if she has left me, but eventually, she says, "I'm afraid I cannot tell you."

Unsurprising. Rhea had complained about how the woman in the Middle often provided more questions than answers. Still, in this instance, it only grows my frustration. "It is easier for her to access this place while she is sleeping," I muse, lifting my head from my hand and gazing at a particularly brightly burning star. "So if she isn't here and I am, what does that mean?"

"What is your last memory?"

I lift a brow. "In general?"

Amusement seeps into her tone. "With Rhea," she clarifies.

I open my mouth, prepared to pull from what should be a flood of memories, only to find that they are fragmented. "I can't remember. Why can't I remember?"

"It could be the magic that holds you here. Or it could be something else. Go further back until you can draw up a moment of the two of you that is unobstructed."

Following her instructions, I finally land on a full memory. "The ball," I murmur, furrowing my brows. "No, wait, it was just before that. When she said 'yes.'" Yes to marrying me. Yes to a lifetime of her at my side, as my queen. Another memory flashes. The temple covered in flowers—a cobalt blue flame. "Not just my queen, but the queen."

"Yes," Selene says softly, the scent of jasmine thick in the air around me. "Her reign will be one of heart and of blood." I don't know what to make of that. "What else?"

"We told my parents and the council about the engagement. The latter had summoned me and my father for a meeting on the matter. I found her after the meeting adjourned, and we danced." I tilt my head to the side, trying to recount what happened next as a haze begins to creep in on the edges of my mind. Fuck, why is this so difficult?

"What else?" Selene prods gently. "Take the memory one frame at a time."

It takes a stubborn amount of time, the throbbing between my temples growing the deeper I pull the memory free.

Dancing at the ball.

My tongue giving her pleasure.

Cass interrupting us.

Tienne—*an involuntary growl leaps from my mouth at the death of a woman I knew to be good. At the perpetrator I knew was responsible.*

And then...

As if I've tossed a spool of thread, the rest of the evening unravels piece by horrifying piece. I watch in stunned silence at the signs I missed—at how easily I allowed myself to be distracted. I can feel the salty air of the beach and sand beneath my knees as I collapsed onto it, a harrowing cry bellowing from some broken place deep within me.

Then there is only darkness. "Where is the rest?" I ask in a panicked rush. Selene doesn't answer right away. "Selene! What happens next? Where is Rhea?"

The stars flash—white, then gray, then black—and I slowly push to stand, preparing for a threat that I fear has already passed.

Selene confirms it when she answers, "With him."

"No." The single word is wrapped in both command and plea. "She can't be."

"I'm sorry," she says solemnly, but the tone of her words isn't so much laden in regret as it is resignation.

"You knew. You fucking knew *this would happen." I run a hand through my hair, tugging on the strands as I try once more to draw my power up. I need to get back to consciousness—to my real body—so that I can get to her. It has only been, what, a day? Two at most? I can make up that ground easily if I leave now. I can—*

"Nox."

I ignore Selene, just as my magic seems to be ignoring me. A dull ache flares across my back, followed by a prickling sensation that sends breath hissing through my teeth. Fine. *Perhaps I can't access it here like Rhea can. All the more reason to leave.*

"Nox, listen to me."

Closing my eyes, I focus on the mental picture I have in my mind of home, hoping that I can just will *myself there. It starts with the shape of the palace and morphs into something more detailed—my room and then the bed within it. And then her, always her. Her knees drawn up as she reads, early morning light playing against the crown of her head. Her eyes lifting from the pages to meet mine, joy and longing and love all expressed in one quick glance.*

Gods, I love her. I fucking love *her.*

"You cannot get to her." Like a blade slicing through flesh, the image splits, and I'm once more plunged back into the Middle when I open my eyes.

"Of course I can—"

"No," she says, a finality to her voice that I don't at all like. "Your magic has weakened, Prince, and your kingdom is in turmoil."

"I don't fucking care.*"*

"You should. She would." Some distant part of me knows she's right, but my anger—my guilt and sorrow and utter, absolute rage—doesn't care. She is gone, and I will sacrifice anything, stop at nothing, to get her back. "I don't blame you for your anger, but you must not let it blind you. Rhea would not want you to ruin many just to save one."

"Fuck you, and fuck that." Selene may be a goddess or whatever, but she doesn't know the way Rhea's eyes sparkle when she's learned something new. Selene doesn't know that when Rhea is nervous, she chews on her bottom lip. Sometimes to the point

that it brings her pain. She doesn't know that inside the woman who has only just begun to build herself up from the horrors that she has endured is a heart so perfect and precious that no one deserves to have it, least of all me. But it is mine, she is mine, and I will damn this entire continent before I let her uncle take anything more from her. There is no other choice. It is lunacy to believe otherwise.

I teeter on my feet, my balance faltering before outright failing and sending me to my hands and knees. Those wisps of my magic within me began to tug, invisible tethers pulling on me.

"Fate can be fickle and cruel, but it is not set in stone. You may feel like little more than a pawn, Prince of Stars, but you hold within you the power to bring about change. You are not made of shadows and darkness but of starlight. Remember that."

The world tilts, and what once felt solid beneath me disappears until I'm careening down. Stars whiz past my face at startling speeds, my stomach unsure of which way is up or down. Rhea's name leaves my lips—a whisper or a scream, I don't know—but I want to believe that she can hear it, wherever she is. That maybe it can be a sign that lets her know I am coming.

Darkness swallows me whole, and in its infinite embrace, there is only silence.

Chapter Nineteen

BAHIRA

MY STEPS ARE SOFT as I pace my room, frustration a gnawing headache that pounds at my head.

"Fucking useless books," I growl, immediately regretting my words as if the tomes stacked on my nightstand can hear them. Sighing, I pause at the center of my room. Between Nox *still* stuck in this "deep sleep" as the healers have called it, Councilman Kallin cornering me the day before and all but demanding that I come in to brief them on my time in the Shifter Kingdom, my rampant thoughts on the blood and magic and the Spell, and the incessant memories of Kai that only want to reveal themselves when I'm at my most exhausted and can't fight them off, I feel as if I'm not just stretched too thin but like I'm being pulled apart.

And the aforementioned books aren't helping matters.

They are the ones that Elisha thought might be helpful regarding the relationship between blood and magic. While there technically *are* mentions of the two, it is just more of the same warning I had heard repeated growing up. Elisha was right. I am going to have to request access to our kingdom's archives. It is a place that houses ancient artifacts, some dating back many millennia. While I can't be *positive* there will be enough information hidden within the restricted space to help me bridge the connection between magic and blood, what I *do* know is that any time a portion of the history is restricted, it's likely that the people in power are not giving the *full* truth as to why. Death may very well be the outcome when tampering with these two things, but something deep in my gut tells me that there is more to the story.

Tilting my head back, I let out a ragged sigh. The only way I will know for sure is to access the archives. And the only way I will be able to do *that* is by way of a councilman.

At least on that front, I do have *one* person on my side.

I shower and quickly dress, and with the beginnings of a plan formulating in my head, I start downstairs to make my first stop of the day. Palace guards are still crawling around the foyer and halls, groups of them clustered at the few entrances on the first level. I walk with my head held high, my eyes meeting those who pass. Some of them dip their chins in greeting, others regard me with a glance that I swear borders on wary.

I know I've entered the healers' wing when I'm hit with the bitter scent of cleaning alcohol and the air chills to a temperature that rivals an autumn evening. My fingers flex instinctively at my sides as I near the room holding Nox, the door opening as a man in a deep brown robe exits.

"Galen!" I call out, quickening my steps to meet the older mage, his eyes widening in surprise when they meet mine.

"Princess Bahira, it is lovely to see you." He hides his trembling hands within the sleeves of his robes as he brings them together in front of him, his gray eyes glassy from age.

"How is he?"

The palace healer smiles sadly at me, and my heart dips. "No different, I'm afraid," he says with a sigh, shaking his head. I swallow back my disappointment and fear as my gaze moves to the door. "Even the most powerful have weaknesses. I suppose it was only a matter of time before we found the prince's. But don't worry, we've got the best of the best looking out for him."

He pats my shoulder before ambling away, and I blink back the pressure building behind my eyes as I reach for the handle to the door. I spot Cass first, his white-blond hair pulled up into a ponytail while a few loose tendrils frame his face. He offers me a tired grin, one that I mirror as I shut the door behind me and walk to the foot of the bed. "How is he?"

"Did you see Galen leave?"

"I did," I respond, looking Nox over where he lies in perfect stillness. "But I want to hear it from you."

Cass releases a breath, his shoulders slumped beneath an invisible weight. "Nothing has changed. Not physically or magically, and I can't help—" His mouth closes abruptly, but not before I catch the tremor in his voice. The uncertainty in it.

"Can't help what?"

He looks over at Nox from where he sits at the side of the bed, his elbows resting on his knees. I give him the time to formulate his thoughts as I watch the steady rise and fall of Nox's chest.

"I can't help but wonder if this is more than just him overexerting his magic," he finally says, the words hardly louder than a whisper.

"In what way?" I ask, just as quietly.

"I have seen your brother in nearly every setting but war. True war. And I *thought* I had also seen him use his magic to near capacity." I raise my brow in question, folding my arms over my chest. Cass huffs out a small laugh, the smile on his face good to see, even though it only lasts for a few seconds. "He practiced a lot with it—"

"I'm aware," I drawl, tilting my head.

He smirks. "Well, what you might *not* know is that sometimes he and I would walk deep into the forest. I'm talking the kind of deep where the treetops aren't just woven together but the trunks right beneath them are too. Where light is scant and the air is silent of all noise except what the forest wants you to hear." He slips into the voice he uses when telling a story, its lilt just a bit lower. "And we went there because, occasionally, Nox would have this *urge* to use his magic in a way that he didn't normally."

"What do you mean?" Growing up, it was hardly uncommon for Nox and Cass to venture out together for days at a time, but I had never assumed it was for anything other than a need to explore.

"He said it felt like his magic was suffocating and that if he didn't heed its call to be used in the way *it* wanted to, he would go mad. We trekked to secluded spots where he wouldn't be spotted, and it was..." He shakes his head in near disbelief. "Incredible. His power would flow out of him, swaths of dark purple and black magic blanketing the forest for what felt like miles. Stars above, maybe it *was* for miles. Sometimes, he'd simply blanket the earth with his power for minutes, and other times, he would mold it. Morph it to mimic the trees and animals." His icy blue eyes hold mine, awe shining in them. "He created a world based entirely in shadows. His magic has always been something otherworldly, Bahira, but this was on a different scale. I'm struggling with the idea that the magic he released at the beach put him in such a state. Not when I've seen what he can *really* do."

I take in his story about my brother, turning the information over in my head. "I think we have to approach it from a different place of understanding his magic," I muse, rounding the opposite side of the bed from Cass and placing my hand over my brother's. His skin is cool beneath my touch, and he doesn't stir at all. "From what I gathered, Nox fled the palace in search of Rhea the moment he realized she was gone. He wasn't in his right mind. He was in a place of desperation. Perhaps, that is the difference."

Cass gives a noncommittal nod, and my heart falters a beat at the devastation on his face.

"He'll be okay." Looking down at Nox, I give his fingers a squeeze as I release a shaky breath. "He has to be."

Leaving is hard, but Cass promises to send for me the moment Nox wakes up. I shiver as I descend the palace stairs, the temperature pleasant but the coating of unease that follows me not so easily dispersed. The guards at the bottom of the steps separate to let me pass, dappled light from above dotting the white stone path as I make my way to my workshop.

I think of Cass's story and internally grimace that I had *no* idea my brother's magic affected him that way. I had read past recollections of the balance of magic—back when it was more robust amongst our people and not dwindling away year after year—that spoke to the effect of not using your magic for a long time. To curb that, most mages used small magic on a daily basis. Though I didn't take the courses myself for obvious reasons, early education teaches of the dangers of going long periods of time without using your magic. I had always assumed that the talk of someone going mad was a bit facetious. It doesn't seem so out of the realm of possibility now.

Walking up to the door of my workshop evokes a feeling of coming home all its own. This place where so many failures and so few victories are kept has always been a refuge for me. Despite the less-than-stellar progress I've made on my own inquiries, I still feel like a weight has been lifted off my chest when I step across the threshold. It smells the same as it always has, like the forest and something metallic.

I haven't spent time here since returning, nothing beyond quickly putting away my magnifier and some of the glass jars of experiments from the shifter isle. Dragging my fingers along the scarred wooden tabletop, I take inventory of everything that remains. In a corner on the countertop rests the glass jars filled with dead and decaying leaves, remnants of the last experiment I had done with magic. Cobwebs are tucked into the corners of the ceiling, perhaps a realistic representation of how little advancement I have made with finding my magic. A thin layer of dust coats every surface, prompting me to open one of the windows and grab a cloth to begin cleaning everything off.

I'm a few minutes into the process, focused on how I might organize my next test, when a small voice interrupts the silence, and I let loose a surprised yelp, my cloth flying from my hand as I come face to face with Starla.

Her dark eyebrow arches, a disappointed look crossing her face. "I would have thought that you of all people, Bahira, would know when someone is behind you."

I scoff, folding my arms over my chest. "I don't expect to be ambushed in my own shop."

She has the audacity to shrug, sliding one of her pointer fingers over the dust covering the table and scrunching her brows in response. "Well, you did offer me a job before you left. I wanted to make sure you made good on it."

"I—" *Shit.* The memory of me doing just that jumps to the forefront of my mind. I look over the little girl as I rest my hip against the edge of the table. Her hair has grown longer in the months since I've seen her, the little brown ringlets now dangling down to her midback. She's dressed in dark trousers and boots, her top a size too big in a light green color that hangs down to her hips. The orphanage must be low on clothing for girls her age, so I make a mental note to speak with my father and make sure we get them everything they need.

She mirrors my stance, her mannerisms making her appear so much older than she is.

"When I offered you that job, I hadn't known I was going to be leaving for the Shifter Kingdom. Things have changed a bit since then."

Her face falls for only a second before she fixes it into an impressive one of indignance. "So what? Are you saying that you don't want me to work with you anymore?"

"*No.* I'm saying, I don't know what kind of job I can give you." Then, more to myself than her, I add quietly, "I'm not even sure what *I'm* doing here."

"Well," she says, pausing as she tilts her head up towards the ceiling. A few moments pass as she thinks. "What's a problem you still need to solve?"

I can't help but chuckle, turning to grab my thrown cloth. "I have more problems than you can possibly imagine. I'm just... *stuck.*"

Starla nods, as if she completely understands. Fuck, maybe she does. I remember how cruel the other kids were to her when I found them fighting outside of my workshop. No matter how tough she pretends to be, their words will linger like thorns beneath the skin. I would know.

"Well I'm not much of a scientist like you, but sometimes, when I'm stuck on a problem in school, I like to remind myself that just because I don't know the answer *right now*, doesn't mean I'm not smart enough to find it. The answer is there; I just have to try harder."

I cock my head to the side, a grin tugging on the corner of my mouth. "That's true. Unknowns are just the things we haven't yet explored."

"Exactly. You're the smartest person in this kingdom and the only one who does experiments. So if anyone can figure out what you need to figure out, I know it will be you."

I clear my throat and turn to walk to the back of the room, pulling a drawer open and grabbing a second cloth from it. Starla's belief in me is sweet, even though I might wonder if it's misplaced. But she showed up here ready to work, and I'll be damned if I turn away a girl who's interested in learning.

"Here," I say, tossing the towel her way. She catches it, eyes growing wide. "While we finish cleaning this place up, you can tell me how you happened upon my workshop at the *exact* moment I got here. And then we are going to test a few things."

Chapter Twenty

BAHIRA

COUNCILMAN KALLIN'S BEADY EYES stare me down a few days later, an unrelenting challenge in them that makes my jaw clench.

Nox is still asleep with, according to everyone who could sense such things, a magical signature so weak it borders on nonexistent. What they *can* sense from him is... different. Changed in a way that they can't explain.

And yet I had been summoned no less than three times to give a briefing on the Shifter Kingdom. To supposedly *help* the council that so callously treated their crown prince's absence as if it was nothing of significance. Surrounded by them now, I swallow down the fury that stirs in my chest as I return Kallin's glare.

"Your reluctance to answer such basic questions is alarming, Princess Bahira," Councilman Borris states, Osiris adding an eager nod of his head. It takes everything in me not to roll my eyes.

"I've told you everything that is important to know. The magical blight affecting them was not something I could fix. That was the focus of my time there, and when it became obvious there was nothing more I could do, I came home." It is a partial truth, certainly not fully a lie, but it is all I feel comfortable telling them. Revealing that the kingdom was undergoing a rebuild of sorts, that Kai's own people had plotted against him and were intent on *killing* him doesn't just seem unnecessary for the council to know. It feels *wrong*.

"And what if what *you* deem important is different from our own thoughts?" Kallin asks, interlacing his fingers on the table in front of him. When I simply shrug my shoulders, folding my arms over my chest, he sighs, tipping his head towards the ceiling. "Why do the Daxel siblings insist on making things so difficult?"

I narrow my eyes, confident no such words would have left his mouth were my father or mother here. The latter I insisted stay at Nox's side—I didn't want my brother to wake up alone or to find only healers in the room with him. My father had been asked to lead this month's public forum day. But dealing with men who consistently underestimate me is not anything new, and so I plaster a docile smile on my face and tilt my head.

"It is only difficult because you feel as if you are at *my* mercy, right? You want to know everything that I do so that you can come to the same conclusions I have but call the decision *yours*." His expression grows tight. "But I promise you, Councilman, that there is nothing I haven't told you that is at all a threat to this kingdom or the people in it."

Someone—Councilman Arav, I think—lets out a poorly stifled snort before a glare from Kallin has him falling silent once more. I look around the table, meeting the eyes of those who surround it, and wonder at what point their perception of our family changed. It would be easy to point to Rhea as a catalyst, but I remember the tense meetings before I left for the Shifter Kingdom. The low-spoken, barely disguised threats while Nox was still in the Mortal Kingdom. Perhaps there wasn't a single major event but a series of smaller ones, and in our contentment with the way things were, we had gone blind to the direction we were heading. Or maybe, it is simply the aging of men and the way they themselves perceive the things that matter, like safety and keeping the status quo.

Clearing my throat, I push up from my chair, clasping my hands behind my back. "If that is all, I do have a brother to check in on." I make it four steps to the door before he calls out my name.

"Bahira, just one more question."

I bite back a groan and look over my shoulder, I answer, "Yes?"

"Who is Jahlee?"

My breath halts in my chest, a tendril of unease slithering down my spine as I fight to keep my face neutral. Kallin reaches into the pocket of his tunic and tosses a folded piece of parchment onto the table, its wax seal recognizable to me immediately. *A wolf with horns.* Fuck.

A few different answers fire off in my head, but I'm unsure of what direction to take. Especially without knowing what is in the letter. If it's from Jahlee, there is no telling if it spills Shifter Kingdom secrets or is just her rambling on about who is fucking who in the palace. A fist squeezes my heart at the thought of her, her missing presence one I never expected to feel so acutely. The silence builds while the council waits for me to answer, and when I finally do, I opt for being as vague as possible while I turn to face them. "She is a shifter female I met while working for the king."

Kallin reaches for the letter, my blood growing cold when I realize the seal is broken. "Shall I read it aloud? Jahlee is quite... *colorful* in her language."

There had been many times growing up that I had seriously contemplated punching Daje's father. The way he constantly looked at me like he could see the magicless parts of my soul—gaps of darkness where there should have been colorful light—and he hated it. How he always had this little sneer pulling on his lips, as if the sight of a magicless mage was one thing, but to know she was his princess? *Unfathomable.* Yet it is hearing him say Jahlee's name with that hint of superiority, like reading a single letter truly gives him enough information to judge her, that actually brings me the closest I've ever been to sending my fist into his face. I bite down on my tongue, hard enough to taste iron, and only when I feel more in control of my body, do I step towards the table and pick the letter up.

Dear Badass Bahira,

It has been over a week since you left, and we haven't heard from you through the Mirror. While things are going fine here, there's still an uneasy tension in the air. It's like waiting for the other shoe to drop only to realize that no one is wearing shoes and so it must be something even worse coming. Or whatever the metaphor is, but what I'm trying to say is that I know Kai hurt you, but he could really use your particular brand of encouragement and advice. You know what he's been through, and even with all of that, I've never seen him so... lost. Maybe that is manipulative of me to say. He can be an asshole with a rock for a brain sometimes, but I do know that he cares deeply for you. That he wishes he could take back the things he said (and yes, I did smack him upside the head when he told me how he reacted to you not having magic). Selfishly, there is a part of me that is hoping that the friendship you and I share isn't just something I made up in my head. That we actually did bond—just two extremely beautiful females who happen to have no magic.

So for the sake of my brother—and if not for him, then for me—can you please reach out to us? Siyala is unnerved that she has not received word on Rhea, and for all I'm talking you up to her, she gets less and less convinced that you're someone who is trustworthy the more time that passes. Remember, you have a home here too, Bahira.

I hope your experiments are going well.

Love,

Your Most Favorite Shifter Without A Penis,

Jahlee

I don't realize how tightly I'm holding the letter until I notice the small rip that's branched out from my grip. "Care to explain to me why my personal letter has been opened and read?"

"It has shown to be imperative with your family that we check the messages received from foreign kingdoms," Kallin answers, steepling his hands beneath his chin. "Though I'm curious to know how someone in the Shifter Kingdom is aware of the woman who was inadvisably engaged to your brother."

I slowly fold the letter back up and tuck it into my pocket, ignoring the dirty look Osiris sends me as I try to buy myself some time. "And how many messages are you receiving from foreign kingdoms?" Gods, if they are monitoring letters *into* the kingdom, certainly they are tracking the ones that leave too. And without knowing who will report back to the council, I can't risk responding to Jahlee's letter. Or sending one to Kai himself.

He smirks, leaning back in his chair. "Don't deflect, Princess Bahira. Part of your mission was to find out how the shifters knew that we could pass through the Spell, and you *apparently* failed to do so. The bargain we made with them specified your help, as chosen by the magic of the Continent, in exchange for their protection should we need it. You returned home early, and by your own accounts, were unsuccessful in that regard as well. But are we surprised considering your success here at home has been so mottled with disappointment?"

"I fulfilled my end of the bargain. The magic of the deal would not have allowed me to leave if I hadn't. With Nox home and the magical item no longer a threat, we have no need for the safety the shifters were providing."

Borris jumps in, his eyes locked on the door as if he can see through it and to some unnamed threat in the hall, "That remains to be seen."

A line forms between my brows at that.

"And now this letter reveals that they might know about *our* own weaknesses, fed to them by a member of the royal family."

Fury rises, giving birth to a tingling warmth that expands across my chest at his cadence. "What are you insinuating, Councilman Kallin?"

"Treason, Princess Bahira."

Words tangle in my throat as I glare at him. With the Mirror broken, there is no way for the council to confirm what Kai knows about our kingdom, not that I had even told him *anything* regarding our own plights. But just as *they* can't contact him, neither can *he* assure them that I'm speaking the truth.

A biting retort sits on my tongue, pushing at my teeth and lips to try to break free, but before it can, the door to the council room opens, one of the palace aides breathing heavily as he pokes his face through the opening.

"Your Highness. Councilmen." His wide eyes hold mine as he draws in a deep inhale. "Prince Nox has woken."

My feet pound over the glittering black stone floors, all thoughts of the council and their accusations pushed to the back of my mind as I run. The guards' presence hasn't lessened in the time since I've returned, and as I round the final corner and continue forward, I spot a cluster of them gathered in front of Nox's door. Their weapons glint where they are sheathed behind their backs, and they stand at attention, their faces serious even as a few cast curious glances as I bound towards them. But my surprise at the number of guards is quickly overshadowed by the familiar head of dark blonde hair that paces in front of them, her arms folded over her chest.

"Bahira!" Haylee shouts, throwing her arms out wide before drawing me in for a hug. I'm so stunned by the gesture that I stand there awkwardly, my breaths panting near her ear. *When was the last time we hugged each other?* I genuinely can't recall if we ever had.

"Haylee, what are you doing here?"

"I've been trying to visit Nox since the ball, but"—she shakes her head, her eyes darting to the closed door—"Cass has been strict about who he allows in. Which I suppose I understand. With everything going on..." She grows quiet, her eyes coming back to mine. "And I know I haven't sought you out yet; it's just my uncle has kept me so *busy*, and I—"

"Haylee, it's fine. We can catch up later, but right now, I need to see my brother." Letting her go, I step back and turn on my heel, my hand reaching for the door handle.

"Of course. I hope he's alright."

"I told you, no one is coming in here until the king himself—"

"It's me, Cass." Three clicks ring out before the door opens and Cass leans across the threshold, eyes assessing as they look back to Haylee.

"Sorry, Bahira," he says quietly, allowing me to pass. He shuts the door and locks it again, despite hearing Haylee's protest on the other side.

The air is still tainted with the astringent scent of medical supplies, but something else now lingers there too. Something that smells of metal—*of blood*.

My eyes go straight to where my brother is still laying in the bed, but the sight of him halts my steps. His clothing is rumpled and his hair is in disarray, but it's what swirls in the normally charcoal color of his irises that has my throat working hard to swallow. They've taken on a misty ink color and flecks of bright white dot them like stars in a night sky. "What's wrong with his eyes?" I ask, looking first to my mother and then to Cass from where they stand on either side of his bed. At my question, his head snaps towards me, a feral look the likes of which I have *never* seen on Nox sending my pulse through the roof.

"We do not know," my mother answers, her hand gently resting on top of Nox's head. Those eyes—somehow Nox's and not—narrow, and an eerie chill creeps over me as I near the bed. The rest of his body comes into view, and a rush of air is squeezed from my chest as I take in what is attached to his wrists and ankles. *Shackles.*

"What is the meaning of this?" My trembling voice comes out far too high.

This time, it's Cass who answers. "We had to." He doesn't meet my gaze, instead staring at where his fingers flex at the edge of the bed.

"Why?"

My mother runs the back of her hand over cheeks, gathering the tears that have fallen. Nox arches his back in an unnatural way, straining against the shackles as he grunts through clenched teeth.

"Since he woke, he's been disoriented. He did not understand that he was in the healers' wing, and—" She hushes him gently, attempting to calm him like one would a child who's just been injured.

"And what?" I whisper.

"He tried to kill three healers."

Chapter Twenty-One

BAHIRA

MY BALANCE SWAYS AS I cock my head, sure I must have misheard. "Did you just say he tried to *kill* them?"

Cass nods in answer, his sullen expression further bottoming out my stomach. "I had just stepped outside to use the bathroom as the next round of healers came in to try waking him again."

"It isn't your fault," my mother says, leaning forward until she draws Cass's attention to her. "Do you understand?" But he doesn't respond, only lays a hand over Nox's arm. My brother jerks at the contact, those strange eyes flicking to his best friend with zero recognition in them. "He was furious when he woke, and his eyes were just as they are now. Two healers approached him, and without warning, he attacked them. Caught off guard, they took some serious hits before the third healer and I were able to subdue him with our magic."

"Did he hurt you?"

"No," she says quickly, shaking her head. "It took everything I had just to hold him there until Cass returned, but he didn't hurt anyone else."

"I put the shackles on him." He says it like a shameful confession, and my heart lurches as his shoulders droop.

I blow out a shaky breath, watching my brother fight against his restraints. When the council learns of this, there is no telling how they will react. I might have been able to guess three months ago, but now it is almost as if they are looking for reasons to criminalize our family.

Perhaps to remove us from the throne.

"Is his magical signature still off?" I ask.

The look that Cass and my mother exchange is brief, but I catch the uncertainty on both of their faces. "Yes," Cass says, pinching his eyebrows together. "I can sense him in it, the usual *feel* of his power, but there is something else there too. Like..." He tilts his head back and forth, as if he can shake the words he's looking for free.

My mother offers her insight. "I, like Cassius, can sense him, but it's almost as if it is buried beneath *more*." She reaches out to cup Nox's face, the touch working to calm him. His muscles relax as he falls flat against the bed, his eyes fluttering shut.

The handle to the door jostles, startling the three of us, while Nox seems to have already fallen back into the deep sleep. My father's voice calls out through the wood, prompting Cass to rush over and let him in.

"Bahi," he says in greeting, kissing the top of my head. His affection works to ground me.

With a gentle squeeze of my shoulder, he turns and looks to Nox, sadness overtaking him. "Are they true?" he asks, looking to my mother. "The murmurs I heard on my way here?"

My eyes fall shut, a sinking feeling sending my heart crashing to the floor. To already have word spread of what Nox had done—no matter how accidental or unaware he was—is not going to bode well.

"He attacked the healers," she confirms, her voice laced with sadness. My father says nothing as he joins my mother at her side, his arm wrapping around his shoulders. "And his magic is still not *his*. At least, not fully."

My father nods, sitting on the bed's edge as his light purple magic glows from his palm and he extends his hand over Nox's body. "It's chaos," he mumbles quietly, drawing a confused look from the rest of us. My father's magic is stronger than most of those in our kingdom, and that makes his sensitivity to other's magical presence higher—more attuned. As he moves his hand farther up, it stops abruptly over Nox's chest. "Here," he says, tilting his head to the side, his brows drawn low in concentration. "It feels... *tangled*." Nox stirs, almost as if he's sensitive to the brush of our father's magic against him.

Tangled. But magic is supposed to be a fluid thing. It has always surrendered to the intentions of the mage it comes from, has always been molded and shaped into whatever the wielder asks.

"How do we *untangle* it, then?" Cass asks. No one answers, the silence taut as if balancing on a knife's edge. One wrong move will result in split skin and spilled blood, something our family cannot afford any more of.

Hours later, after the sun has set and the warm glow of the spelled flames lining the walls overtakes the room, Nox's eyes open again. This time, the man looking back at us is one I recognize.

"He's awake," my mother rasps, exhaustion pulling at every word. We had undone the restraints as soon as he calmed earlier, but no one had wanted to leave the room as he slept. Kallin had come to the door, eagerly trying to see my brother until my father was able to coax him away. There is a silent understanding that we can only deter the council for so long before their curiosity becomes more demanding, especially as the rumor of how Nox had attacked the healers spreads. But we need time to assess Nox. To bring him up to speed on what is happening, and what *had* happened, before any of us would dare leave him to the council's interrogation.

Cass leans forward in his chair next to me, his gaze assessing Nox.

"I must look like shit if you guys are fawning over me like this," Nox says, running a hand down his face before taking stock of everyone in the room. He does a double take when his eyes meet mine. "When did you get home?"

"Not long ago," I answer, avoiding the urge to shift in my chair beneath his gaze. Nox's ability to tell when I'm lying is something I don't know if I should find endearing or annoying. More often than not, I lean towards the latter.

My mother rises from the chair she's sitting in and walks over to a small side table where a silver pitcher of water and a few cups are stationed on top. Nox drains the cup she gives him, setting it on the end table next to the bed with a grimace. A labored breath hisses between his teeth when he attempts to sit up fully. "I feel as if I've been tossed off a mountain and hit every ledge on the way down."

"You look it too," I tease, earning his flat glare. His eyes shift then to his surroundings, a line forming between his brows.

"Where am I?"

"The healers' wing," my mother answers, her hand reaching out to hold his.

My father approaches from where he was sitting on the other side of the room, his outward demeanor calm, even as a finger lightly taps the side of his thigh. "What do you remember?" he asks, and Nox stiffens at the question. His eyes move side to side as he tilts his head, as if the question has triggered a series of thoughts.

It takes him a moment to work through them but when he does, his expression shifts and his hands fist the comforter on either side of his hips. "Tell me it was just a nightmare," he says, voice rough as his eyes scan the room. Looking for Rhea, I realize. "Tell me that she's still *here.*"

"I'm sorry, my star. I'm afraid it was no nightmare." My mother tells Nox of how long he's been asleep, of what has taken place here in that time, including both my arrival home and the breaking of the Mirror and the council's theory on

Rhea and where she might have gone. She also tells him about the healers, which he has no recollection of.

"I *know* where she is," Nox seethes when she's finished, his hands cradling either side of his head. "King Dolian is the only one stupid enough to risk my wrath. He's the only one who would spend the entirety of her freedom plotting a way to get her back. You shouldn't be asking *where* she is and instead asking who the fuck in our kingdom helped *him* get to her."

A heavy weight settles in the room, one that carries with it truths that haven't yet been spoken.

"I'm going to ask you something, Son, that I *need* to, even though I don't *want* to," our father says, looking at Nox. "Is there *any* chance Rhea left of her own accord? That the pressure would have gotten to her? Been too much? Did Rhea have any reservations at all about marrying you? About becoming our queen?"

He looks down at his lap, where his hands are resting. "We talked, of course, about everything a marriage to me would entail. What it would mean when it was time to step into a role that she had never considered for herself. Rhea is many incredible and wonderful and complicated things, but a willful liar has *never* been one of them. She wanted this, wanted *me*—" He stops abruptly to draw a deep inhale, roughly swallowing before lifting his gaze. "There is no doubt in my mind that Rhea's absence is *not* her choice."

"The council is convinced the opposite is true, and unfortunately, with the letter Rhea left—"

"Letter?" Nox interrupts Cass, jerking his body forward. The movement causes him to groan out in pain, his weight tipping forward before Cass and my father help to steady him. "I'm fine," he grunts out, turning to look at his friend. "What letter?"

Cass reaches for a leather pouch attached at his belt, uncinching its ties and pulling from it two items: a familiar folded letter on cream parchment and a ring. *The* ring, I realize as he holds it out to Nox. My parents had told me that Nox had proposed, and while a small part of me had felt a pang of sadness at not being here for the engagement—and the celebration after—a larger part still finds it a bit bewildering that he is engaged at all.

Nox turns the ring in his hand, the diamond and surrounding colorful gems glistening beneath the amber light. "Where did you get this?"

"Both items were found on the landing where Barron usually stands guard. Though"—Cass stretches his neck from side to side—"he has been noticeably absent since the night of the ball."

Nox takes in that piece of information with a frown, his attention then going to the letter. We fall silent as we watch him read, his eyes skimming it from top to bottom three times before he tosses it onto the bed ahead of him.

"She didn't write that."

Chapter Twenty-Two

BAHIRA

No one asks Nox to explain how he's so sure the letter isn't Rhea's. It's unnecessary. I might have wondered, briefly, if Rhea could have possibly left of her own accord before, but I watched the tenderness on Nox's face as Cass handed him another piece of jewelry from his small pouch, a locket that appeared broken, and I just *knew* that what he and Rhea had wasn't fleeting. It wasn't something you ran from, but to. The kind of love that Daje might have described, perhaps.

"I want to speak to the council about taking a small group of our army to the Mortal Kingdom."

All of the softness of Nox's expression dissipates, leaving only hardened resolve in its place.

"That's likely going to be an issue, Son. The council is viewing Rhea's actions as questionable. They've insinuated that she might have been working to get close to you in order to gain access to our secrets."

Nox blinks, a dark strand of wavy hair sliding over his forehead as he tilts his head. "I'm not even going to dignify that with a response," he says, making Cass chuckle. "If I can't count on them to help, then I'll just have to go alone."

"Excluding the fact that your magic is depleted—"

"It'll come back."

"And that you're weakened"—he sends a look of annoyance my way—"leaving right now might be the worst thing you can do."

"I don't care."

"The council has already threatened to dethrone our family," I say slowly, holding his gaze. "They suspect *me* of doing something treasonous in the Shifter Kingdom."

"They *what*?" My father's brows lower, the shadows cast from the spelled flames cutting sharp angles over his cheeks. "Did they say this today at your debriefing?"

I nod, joining my father in standing. "A letter was sent by King Kai's sister, and Kallin intercepted it. He's taken what he's read as evidence of me sharing our secrets with the shifter king. Which, just to be clear, I did not."

My mother sighs, shaking her head as she tucks pieces of her hair that have escaped back into the pile of curls on the top of her head. "We do not doubt your integrity, Bahira, and the council should know better than to do that as well."

"None of this has any bearing on me getting Rhea," Nox growls, bending a knee to rest his arm on it.

"Brother, I know you want to get to her. I do too. I may not have known her in the tower, but I got to know her the past few months. She is important to me, both as a friend and as my future queen." Cass's words soften Nox's exterior, and he clasps Nox on the shoulder before he continues. "But I think waiting until you're feeling your strongest, until we can figure out who the mole in our kingdom is *and* appease the council long enough to not retaliate when we *do* leave will be our best option."

"You cannot expect me to stay here while she is *there*, with him, being forced to do gods knows what." Nox's voice carries in the room, and he sags beneath the sound of it.

A sad smile tugs on the corners of Cass's mouth. "I expect you to help us make this place safe for Rhea to come back to."

"It is safe—"

"Nox, think this through. We have someone—perhaps *many* some-ones—who actively worked against you and your family to lure Rhea and Daje into a trap. To return her to King Dolian. Why would they do that? And who's to say they aren't planning something much worse? That they aren't counting on you acting brashly?"

"Then let them come for me! It won't stop me."

"Won't it?" I jump in, forcing my brother's gaze to mine. "When it comes to you versus other mages, it's nearly fair play right now. And yes, before you get snarky, I said *nearly*. You're still an amazing warrior, Nox, no one is doubting that part. But you're weakened, and while you could likely sneak out of here, do you think the mortal king will be dumb enough to leave Rhea in a vulnerable position? Do you think, now that she's once more in his grasp, that he will make it easy for her to escape again?"

"Bahira, I don't think this is helping," Cass drawls, gesturing to Nox, whose expression is entirely *murderous*.

I wave my hand idly in front of me. "I'm not wrong, and you know it. Is Rhea so weak that she cannot survive without you?"

"*Watch it*," he snarls.

My stomach twists in on itself at the anguish on his face, but I persist. "Is she truly a damsel that needs you—even weakened and powerless as you are—to rescue her?"

"Of course she isn't."

"Then be *smart*, Nox. Think this through. Because barreling out of here might get you to her sooner, but it will cause a destructive chain reaction in your wake."

He is quiet in response, and eventually, my father guides our conversation to trying to figure out who lured Daje and Rhea out of the room. "Daje didn't recognize him, but there are so many members in our guard that it isn't strange he didn't," Cass muses from where he's now laying at the foot of the bed, throwing a dagger hilt over tip above him and impressively catching at the hilt every time.

"No, it isn't. What *is* strange is that Barron is missing."

"He has been a guard close to our family since Nox was a child," my mother says softly, running her fingers through our father's hair where he sits in a chair in front of her, his eyes closed while he listens. "Can we believe he is capable of betraying us?"

"No one should be ruled out," Nox chimes in, his first words spoken since the shift in conversation. "*No one.*"

"We've already got men out looking for Barron. His partner raised the red flag on the second night that he didn't return home," my father says, his eyes opening. "He's never abandoned a post before."

I purse my lips as an insidious thought takes root. If Barron wasn't a participant in Rhea's abduction, was he a victim of it? Someone who happened to be in the way of those who wanted to harm her?

"I can ask around, talk with the guards who were present in the palace the night of the ball. See if they had anyone noticeably missing for a time," Cass says, catching his dagger and holding it above him.

"We have to be careful how we phrase our questions and who we ask. Prying too deeply might make its way back to the council before we have solid evidence to bring them."

Cass looks at my father. "You would think it would be in their best interest to help us. A mole in the kingdom is the same as a leak in a ship. They will sink both."

"But they believe Rhea left of her own accord," I counter, leaning my elbows on my knees. "Us questioning that outwardly only feeds into their fears that perhaps we don't have the kingdom's best interests at heart." Which is a conclusion I still don't understand the basis for. In any case, the process of weeding out just who all was involved is likely going to be a slow one. I glance in Nox's direction, watching as he methodically runs his thumb over the band of Rhea's engagement ring.

"What if we leave Rhea out of it, then?" Cass suggests, sitting up and sheathing his weapon. "We pose the question as if we are investigating the truth of Daje's story. Everyone in that council room saw his injuries. Even if they are likely to believe Rhea caused them, it would not be out of the norm for the king to put an inquiry out for those who might have seen or heard anything. To question the guards that were working."

My father gives Cass a firm nod. "Excellent idea. We can start there."

"What about the Mirror?" I ask.

"A harder conundrum to solve," he muses. "Gut instinct says we need to start researching books that might mention the creation of our kingdom and hope that knowledge of the Mirror is mixed up within that as well."

"That will take forever." Cass sighs before looking to me. "Unless *you* know somewhere to start?"

I shake my head and cross one ankle in front of the other. "Not off the top of my head. I'll have to search the library—"

"Elora." All heads swing towards Nox, his gaze still fastened on the ring. He curls his fingers around it, encasing it in his palm before letting his hand fall to his lap. "Elora has worked in the palace library for years next to Rayna. She knows that place inside and out. At the very least, she can point us in the right direction."

"And you trust her with all of this?" I ask, gesturing broadly. I have heard the name and, if memory serves me correctly, believe it to be attached to a woman with bright red hair and a voice entirely too loud for a library setting, but I haven't interacted with her enough to know if she is someone we can rely on to keep information quiet.

Nox answers without hesitation. "Rhea does."

I suppose that has to be reason enough. The rest of our plans come together quickly. While Cass and my father work to unsuspectingly weed out whoever hurt Daje and Rhea in our guard, Nox and I will partner with Elora to try and uncover any information we can about repairing the Mirror. I've also been tasked with tapping into the gossip network through Haylee, something I find mildly abhorrent.

"No one is more in tune to the workings of the court than she is," Cass says in response to my frown. "The woman always knows what's going on and with who."

"Fine." While I'd rather spend my time with my experiments or getting nicked relentlessly from a dull blade than speak about the whispers amongst my peers, I understand that—given the circumstances—it's necessary.

"We work quietly and check in weekly. The council will have to know that we are actively seeking information on how to repair the Mirror, but anything else *must* be kept secret for as long as possible. Only when we have the information we need do we approach them about bringing Rhea home." Everyone nods in agreement at my father.

Nox is practically hunched over himself by the end of our conversation, so we all begin to file out of the room in favor of letting him rest. I'm nearly across the threshold when my brother calls my name. Looking at him over my shoulder, I take in the hard planes of his face. "Yes?"

"I know you don't know Rhea and that you are only doing what you always do—objectively looking at things to find the truth." He lifts his chin slightly, his gaze boring into mine. "As my sister, you will always receive grace that I would never allow anyone else. But"—he drops his voice to something darker and more serious—"don't ever question her strength or the magnitude of her love for me or mine for her again. She has been through more than anyone has ever given her credit for, and I will be damned if my own family looks upon her with anything other than the respect she duly deserves."

Silence stretches thick and awkward between us, a million sharp retorts battling for the chance to be released behind my teeth. I let none of them slip through, instead giving my brother a small smile. "Don't do anything stupid." Shutting the door between us, I can only hope that the dread I feel is temporary.

I had expected to be summoned by the council to continue their inquisition, but as the evening bled away to morning—my steps pacing restlessly in my room—no such call arrived. I wondered if they were already speaking with Nox, if he was adhering to our plan of making the council believe he wasn't suspicious of them. Or mourning Rhea's absence. I thought of his parting words, of the look that transformed his face from one that I knew to a version that I didn't. Part of me was curious to know if he also saw someone different when he looked at me. If I wanted that to be true for myself.

After spending entirely too much time stuck in a loop of hypotheticals, I managed to get some sleep, only to be awoken by a nightmare of dark dungeons and rattling chains, warm blood coating my skin and golden eyes piercing me down to my very soul. I needed a distraction, so after showering and dressing and checking on Nox—who was thankfully still in his room asleep—I headed towards the palace library to speak with Elora.

It's quiet as I enter, a comfort in the lack of noise that only a place filled with books can provide. While I spent my early childhood hiding within the labyrinth of shelves here, as I grew older, I came to prefer the Galdr library instead. I think it had to do with its size—the way it was so easy for me to slip into any obscure aisle and lose myself in whatever story or history I was reading. Perhaps it went even deeper, like being able to physically remove myself from the palace that represented my family. Their magical strength the antithesis to my own.

Muffled voices draw me out of my annoyingly introspective thoughts, and as I round a corner, I find their owners. The aisle is long in front of me, an ornate rug centered on it with windows on one side and a maze of books on the other. At its end are the librarian desks, and perched in front of one of them, her hip leaning against its edge is Elora. Her hair is pulled into a braid that lays over one shoulder while her glasses catch the light of the morning sun that filters in through the treetops, occasionally causing a little flare to dance on the rug in front of her. But it's who she is speaking to that momentarily halts my steps. He stands with his feet hip width apart, his body partially turned so that I see more of his back than his front. But I'd recognize him anywhere.

I can't say why I just stand there and watch them talk, Elora speaking with more animation than Daje. He runs a hand over his head, letting it linger there before it falls abruptly to his side. She reaches out—tentatively, gently—and curls her fingers around his arm, leaning in a little closer to say something. It occurs to me then that perhaps this is something private or intimate or, at the very least, worthy of not having someone *watching* over, but as I pivot, intent on hiding within the bookcases for a few moments before making myself known, my name is called out, title included.

"Princess Bahira! What a lovely surprise."

Fuck. Plastering a smile on my face, I straighten myself out and force one foot in front of the other as I head towards them. I look at Daje for a moment, only to find that his eyes are on the ground in front of him. Elora's smile is bright, however.

"I hope I'm not interrupting," I say by way of greeting.

"No, not at all! Welcome home, Your Highness!"

"Just Bahira is fine. And thank you."

She nods, her gaze swinging from mine to Daje's. At his clear avoidance, her brow arches momentarily before she drops it and looks back to me.

Irritation begins to simmer beneath my skin, an angry inner voice shouting, *These are the fucking terms you set! At least respect me enough to stop pretending I'm not here.* But with a clearing of my throat, I shut the thought down. "I want to talk with you about something."

"With me?" Elora confirms, her voice growing higher pitched.

At that, Daje finally looks at me, his dark blue eyes meeting mine with hardly a glint of familiarity. Is it truly that easy? To simply decide decades of friendship is worth sacrificing at the expense of a love that does not—*cannot*—exist? *Is it really that easy to just let me go?*

Worthless. Kai's voice ricochets in my head unbidden, taking me off guard.

I scoff, knowing I should be more understanding and give Daje time to process... *this.* To mourn in whatever way he needs to because, despite his façade of indifference, I *know* he cares about me. I have always known that. But I'm angry. At him. At Kai. At myself. So instead, I bark, "You should go find Cass. There have been some developments, and he has a new task for you."

Daje nods, offering some quiet parting words to Elora that I don't hear over the way my heart thunders in my chest.

Elora slides her hands into the pockets of her tan trousers, her head tilting to the side. "What can I help you with?"

"I've been told that you are a bit of an expert when it comes to the books that line these shelves."

"O-oh, uh," she stammers, a shade of pink crawling up her face beneath her freckles. "I'm not sure about *expert*. I've just worked here for a while. Is there something in particular you're looking for?"

"Are you familiar with the Mirror that is used for the kingdoms to communicate with each other?"

Her eyes sparkle with intrigue at the question as she nods her head.

"I need every book that might mention the Mirror. How it works. Where it came from. How it was made. *Anything*."

She pinches her lips together, taking on a brief faraway look as if mentally running through a categorized list of books. But instead of offering up any titles we can start with, her curious gaze hardens. "I know I am not in the position to bargain for information, considering you are a princess and I am just a librarian, but no one else is telling me anything and I *know* something is wrong."

"You're going to have to be more specific."

Elora exhales roughly through her nose as she pushes away from the desk. She keeps her voice low as she leans in closer to me. "No one will tell me where Rhea is. It's like she's simply vanished, and that is *not* like her. And I can't even get an audience with Prince Nox." she huffs out another breath. "Those are my terms. I will help if you can tell me what is going on."

Part Two

I could do this. I *have* to do this. And if I lose myself a little along the way, then I could do that too.

Chapter Twenty-Three

RHEA

THE WATER HAS LONG grown cold in my bath, and my teeth chatter as I drag a finger over the murky surface. I need to get out, to dress and face whatever the king has in store for me today. Eve is waiting patiently on the other side of the door for me to do just that. Though maybe it is presumptuous to assume that she is simply being accommodating and not that she is terrified to interact with me. I wouldn't blame her if the latter were true, especially now. I see the way the staff and the guards that remain look at me, word traveling fast of what happened days ago on the beach.

I see my own remorse-laden reflection when I look in the mirror, the dark circles staining the skin beneath my eyes evidence of more than just too little sleep. My dreams, not that I can truly call them that, have ranged between finding myself strapped to a table, another branding iron hovering above me with the king's hand on my thigh, and reliving that day on the beach, hearing nothing but the screams of those men. Of my magic piercing through the Spell like glittering black serpents, obliterating an entire troop of guards in one terrifying swoop.

That had been the most surprising part of it all.

I had seen men killed at the hands of other men and not even that had prepared me for just how *easy* it had been to take a life. *Multiple lives.* Because it had been so damn *easy.* A simple command, and my magic had done the work of dozens. A quiet order, and something living had been reduced to only ash.

That was the brunt of my power, of the second half of the magic coiled within my veins. I can heal what has been lost, remake that which has been destroyed. Until the brink of death, I can nurse someone back with only my intention and that glowing white magic within me.

And yet...

I can also wither. I can decay and reduce and *destroy*. I can kill. I had, and it had been so *easy*.

I knew that dark power was dangerous. It's why I didn't want to even attempt working with it until I was properly trained. Who was I to be at the helm of such a perilous ship with no experience and no fail-safe? What made *me* worthy of carrying such massive power? Those questions are pointless now, but it doesn't stop them from rattling around in my head anyway.

I am a weapon now. Not just my magic, but *me*. I had seen it in the siren queen's eyes, the hunger for *more*. And in the king's, though his lust-filled gaze had come *after* he expressed his anger with me through his bruising fists. Confusing, considering *he* had been the one to agree with the queen's suggestion of killing the guards. But not even the sting of my newly given marks or the bite of his words after we returned could penetrate the dark space I had sunk into. Fifteen men had been wiped from this world in the blink of an eye. All because I had not done the one thing that Selene—that even Nox—had tried to convince me to do. I had not trained with both halves of my magic, choosing to suppress one in fear when I should have explored.

If I had done that, perhaps I would have been strong enough to fight off those who attacked Daje and I. Maybe I could have even sensed Nox's magic better, could have known that he wasn't on the beach, a newfound hunch based on the location of the attack. I couldn't remember much, but I knew the pathway we walked and the landmarks. We had made it most of the way to the beach, and that was much too close to attack me if he was there. But if he was at the palace? It would make sense why I felt him so strongly. It would make sense that they lured us so far from it. If I had trained with my full capabilities, perhaps I might even be strong enough to fight off the magical hold of this ring.

Fear had ruled my life in the tower before Nox ever entered it, and I wanted to believe that I had fully let that fear go once I was in the Mage Kingdom. But I was merely pretending, plucking at invisible threads and gathering up the ones I felt I could handle while leaving the others to rot with my avoidance. It didn't make them disappear, and it didn't make me better equipped. It simply made me blind. I had given myself a crutch, leaning on Nox in the moments I was too afraid to face reality, and in his love for me, he only gently pushed. Just as Selene had. In my ignorance, I had built up my walls and demanded that we wait.

I blow out a breath, halting my finger in the water as two things hit me at once. First, telling myself I had time to train had been nothing more than succumbing to the illusion that who I was—what I could *do*—affected me and me alone. Even before my Flame Ceremony, I knew my magic was different, and instead of acknowledging it, I tried to make myself smaller. I had successfully done what King Dolian—and the council and even Haylee—had attempted; I had erased a part of myself. The second is that this *wasn't* going to just be a matter of escaping back into the arms of Nox. What King Dolian had done... Who he has aligned himself with and the power that they both now wield is so much bigger than just my own plight. This is a new game, one that I certainly don't feel equipped to play, but one that I have no choice *but* to take part in. My magic is bound in my body, a body that isn't always in my control, but my mind is still my own. King Dolian isn't some all-knowing god walking amongst us. He is just a man. Despite how it might look now, he isn't infallible.

And I am not completely helpless.

Gentle knocks draw my gaze towards the door. "My Lady, I'm sorry to interrupt, but if you don't get out now, you will be late to breakfast." A pause and then, "I do not think it wise to prod at the king's already *terse* mood."

Great.

"Of course. I'll be right out." Standing from the tub, I shiver as my foot plants on the cold white tile, each step to where my towel hangs making more goosebumps bloom over my skin. The brand stings when the cool air hits it, and I glance at it briefly to make sure it is healing well. It's still red in some spots, the places where King Dolian had squeezed his hand over it only just barely scabbed over. The rest is a bright pink, but at least all the blisters have now gone away. Eve had helped clean the mark the night I had returned from the beach and despite everything that had happened—including how the king used her to get me to do what he wanted—she was still kind. Still gentle in the way she cared for me. It made my stomach ache, and I wondered if it secretly bothered her that she was stuck being a handmaiden to someone like *me*.

I ignore looking in the mirror as I pass, knowing that there are still plenty of bruises dotting my skin from my uncle's fury. He made sure to only strike me from the shoulders down, and as he stood over my heaving and crumpled form on the floor, a memory of Nox and I at the grave site for Immie unfurled in my mind. *One day, you will have your vengeance, Rhea*, he had said as he held me. I remember thinking the anger I felt then could be enough fuel for that—for vengeance. Yet what pulses beneath my veins now is so much more than anger, so much more than just wanting to make King Dolian suffer as I have. Because the idea of vengeance has never been about inflicting pain on *my* behalf. It is a way to repent for the lives my uncle has taken in my name. Alexi. Bella. Immie. Tienne. They all deserved so much more than to be unwilling pawns in a mad king's game. The same is true for Eve and anyone else the king uses.

When Nox comes for me, as I know he will, I am not naive enough to believe that he will not bring a reckoning with him. I *have* to make sure that it isn't all in vain. Perhaps I should fear, as past me once did, being cut from the same monstrous cloth as my uncle. That my newfound hunger for retribution against him might be a slippery slope to fall upon. But all I can think about are the lives King Dolian took—mercilessly. And as I wrap a towel around myself and head towards the door to my chambers, I decide that maybe being a little merciless towards monsters isn't such a bad thing.

⚜ ⚜

"How are you doing this morning, Lady Rhea?" Eve asks, her voice soft. A salt-tinted ocean breeze blows in through the open window in the room, stirring some of the light blonde hair that has fallen loose from her bun.

Dressed in a cream chemise, I step into the gown she holds out for me, its shade a lovely light blue. "Well enough," I answer, slipping my arms into the long gossamer sleeves, the fabric bundled with lace ties at my wrists. I run my hands over the white embroidery that decorates the thinly corseted bodice, noticing the pattern of stars.

She hums, lacing up the dress in the back before gesturing for me to sit at the vanity. "His Majesty has told me to inform you that after breakfast, you will have your first lesson."

"Right," I breathe out, twisting my hands together in my lap. The king had demanded that, before we could return to the castle at Vitour, I needed to be worthy of my *status* as his soon-to-be queen. Apparently, that involves taking actual lessons until he finds that to be true. I had snarled, reminding him that I would never be *his*, and to my surprise, he had only smirked as his eyes dragged down my body slowly. But I could do this—I could pretend to be enough of what he wants in the hopes that he lets his guard down. The sooner we return to Vitour, the sooner I will be reunited with Nox.

Gods, I *miss* him. I can't even imagine what he is doing now. How he is handling... *everything*. I suppose that isn't totally true. Nox had once told me he would drown the world in shadows if it meant I was safer. Despite what he's said, I know that he cares for his people. For those innocently caught between his wants and desires and the expectations thrust upon him by his title and the council. I do not doubt Nox would choose me over them, that he will come for me as soon as possible, but I *hope* that it will not come at the cost of anyone else. Or that the damage caused when he leaves won't be irreparable.

I shiver from the note of dread that settles in my stomach just as Eve finishes my hair.

"All done." She pats my shoulders gently, drawing my gaze up to hers in the reflection of the vanity mirror. She doesn't look much older than I am, and the urge to ask her about herself dangles on the tip of my tongue. But then I think of the crescent scar on her palm. Of the way the king so ruthlessly handled her. As if sensing my hesitation, she steps back and clears her throat. "I will be meeting with you later today for a tea lesson. Before that, you'll meet with Mia who will instruct you in dancing."

A sigh leaves me as I stand and thank her, though it morphs into a pained groan when my hip begins to throb. How long has it been since he branded me? A week? Nearly two? Time has bled from one day to the next, each one spent with me trying to tap into a part of myself that feels foreign. I suppose every part of me does now with the presence of another's magic suffocating my own. My heart pounds in my chest as we exit my room, each beat reverberating in my skull like an ominous drum.

I could do this. I *have* to do this. And if I lose myself a little along the way, then I could do that too.

"What news is there from my advisors?" King Dolian asks from my left, his question directed to Simon who occupies a seat across the table in front of me. Thankfully, there have been no follow up nightmares involving him.

"Nothing of note. There was a small skirmish in the city center, but it was dealt with quickly by our guards."

"What over?"

"A few of the shop owners refused to pay their taxes. Apparently, they are unhappy with the newest increase."

With my stomach already leaden being near the king, I lazily push the food on my plate around, my interest piqued by Simon's words.

"They think running a safe kingdom is something that can be done on will alone. Their coin goes directly back to them, ensuring no one enters our borders without our knowing," King Dolian sneers, his chair creaking as he adjusts his position in it.

A short huff leaves me, hidden by the sound of my fork scraping along my plate. I don't have to understand politics and the intricacies of *running a safe kingdom* to know that he spews nothing but falsities. Nox had infiltrated his kingdom—his godsdamn castle and the tower attached to it—without issue. I highly doubt he is the only one capable of doing such a thing.

"They also worry about the Cruel Death."

King Dolian's fingers drum on the table. "What is the total number of deaths this week?"

Simon takes a drink from his chalice before answering. "Twelve. All men under the age of twenty-four."

A few seconds of silence pass, and I glance the king's way to find him already looking at me, lines bracketing his mouth. "Send out a missive immediately to every province. Able men twenty-five and under are being enlisted. We don't have time to wait for those who volunteer. We need our numbers robust for what may lie ahead."

My grip tightens on my fork. It hadn't been twelve deaths in the kingdom but twelve in his precious *army*. The Cruel Death had always been something I felt far removed from, living as I did in the tower. Without frequent updates from Alexi and then Nox, I wouldn't have given it much thought. And recently, I'm ashamed to admit I hadn't thought about it at *all*. Still, the image of Tienne's emaciated body flashes in my mind, sending a chill down my back.

"Word has also come from the Mage Kingdom." Stupidly, I eagerly look to Simon. He smirks, as if acknowledging to us both that I was too obvious in my interest.

"And?" the king drawls.

"It's quite interesting. Princess Bahira has returned from her stint over in the Shifter Kingdom."

I glance over to King Dolian then. Though he feigns nonchalance, I've studied his face up close for *years*. I don't miss the way his eyebrow twitches or how his jaw hardens at the news. In contrast, I draw in what feels like a deeper breath than I've taken since I woke up here. Nox having Bahira will be good, as he and his sister are close. I hadn't gotten the chance to really know her yet, but Bahira didn't strike me as someone who would tolerate the council's interrogations and controlling tactics towards Nox. She would make sure he was careful and taken care of.

"Did she come home alone?"

"It appears that way," Simon answers, taking another drink before he looks back at me. "Care to share what you know about it?"

I arch a brow, sitting up straighter. "I don't know anything."

He grins—though it barely constitutes one. "There is also news of Prince Nox. Rumors state that he's sick, apparently in some sort of deep sleep that he can't be woken from."

What? I'm careful to let the thought stay inside, despite how my hand falls limply to the table, fork forgotten.

"The mage council is quite worried over him, as are the king and queen. It appears they are blaming the loss of your stolen bride as the reason for the downturn in the prince's health."

"We can only hope it continues to decline," the king mutters under his breath.

It happens so quickly—the way my anger moves from a spark to an inferno, consuming me as I glare at him. It burns through rationality, and like a caged animal, I snap my jaws at my jailor. "*Fiancée,*" I say, enunciating the word slowly to ensure he *feels* the power I put behind it. I hope it strikes him down to his very marrow, a poisoned arrow aimed directly at his heart. "Not a stolen bride, not someone he had to shackle in order to keep her at his side, but someone who *chose* him. Who still does. Who *always* wi—"

"Enough!" Simon shouts as King Dolian stands, his hand already reaching out to grip on to my arm. I'm yanked to my feet, my chair toppling over as I'm shoved into the edge of the table, the sharp corner hitting me in the exact *wrong* spot. I cry out in pain as electrifying heat flares over my hip, sending a tingling sensation of pure agony out in all directions from the brand. Dishes slide out of the way, my glass toppling over and spilling water onto the white tablecloth.

"Leave us," King Dolian commands.

Simon complies, and within a few seconds, I'm left alone with my uncle.

One of King Dolian's hands grips the side of my hip while the other drags down my back, the tug at my scalp indicating he's fingering through my hair.

"Let me *go*," I growl, attempting to push myself back.

He responds by pressing his hips closer to me, driving me farther into the table. His hand travels towards my backside, where he squeezes the flesh, an unintelligible sound vibrating from him. My body tenses as my eyes widen, blood rushing past my ears as my throat tightens.

"How many times do we need to have this conversation, my darling?" he sneers as his body drapes over mine, suffocating me. "How many fucking times do you need to be reminded, Rhea? You were *never* his. Even as you had your little dalliance, you always belonged to me. Every *fucking* part of you." His hips push harder, and white flares behind my eyes as I cry out at the feel of him. He's always invaded my personal space but not so intimately. Not like this.

Desperate, I reach out for the fork on my plate, squirming despite the way he's caged me in. But he simply commands me to stop moving, and with the swell of magic that pours over my mind, my body obeys. "Can't you see how lucky you are? You now have a king where before you only had a prince."

I can't draw in a deep enough breath, air trapped somewhere between my throat and my lungs as his fingers tighten on me. "St—" The word is cut off by a break in my voice as a *clap* rings in the air, followed by a stinging sensation over my backside. Stunned, I slam my eyes closed and reach for anything to pull me out of this moment. Any crevice in my mind that I can get lost in until I no longer feel the king above me or the table beneath me. I slip through those cracks in my shield and settle into the darkness waiting for me.

"Your Majesty, Lady Mia is ready for Lady Rhea's dance lessons." Xander's voice slices through my mind, throwing me right back into the present as King Dolian shifts his weight. I open my eyes and find the king's commander's gaze focused on King Dolian above me, his mouth set in a grim line.

"Of course," King Dolian says, peeling away from me. My hands grip the edge of the table, and I quickly push myself up, a wave of dizziness threatening to topple me. "Make yourself presentable, darling, and then the commander will escort you to your first lesson of the day. I will see you for dinner." He leans in, causing me to flinch, but all he does is place a kiss against my temple, lingering for a few seconds before drawing away. His footsteps echo out, and I stare down at the disturbed plates and my knocked-over glass, my mind slow to reconcile what just happened. He had just—

"Lady Rhea, are you alright?"

"I'm fine," I say, forcing the words out as I straighten myself and run my shaking hands down the front of my dress. No clothing had been removed. I hadn't been... violated like *that*. I repeat it again, avoiding the guard's stare as he leads us out of the dining room and down the hall. *I'm fine.* We continue down a new corridor, a door left open to a room with wood floors and walls lined with mirrors. Xander stops in front of it, his hands clasped behind his back as he introduces me to the dance instructor, an older woman named Mia who smiles warmly and beckons me into the room.

"I'll be right outside," Xander says, his gaze lingering as I walk past him.

I'm fine.

Mia immediately leaps into proper instruction for the types of royal dances, congratulating me on my engagement to the king. We start off with something that I think is meant to be easy for a beginner, but all of her instruction is lost to the same two words that repeat over and over again in my head:

I'm fine. I'm fine. I'm fine.

Chapter Twenty-Four

RHEA

As someone accustomed to reliving the terrors of my day through my subconscious while I sleep, I would think that the occurrence of nightmares wouldn't be something that throws me so off-kilter. Yet night after night, my mind finds new ways to taunt me. The vivid imagery conjured is enough to propel me awake at the latest hour, starlight streaming in through the window and highlighting the sweat coating my skin.

Last night, it had been another torture session with Simon, his menacing stare boring into me while an array of lethally sharp silver instruments did the same. I felt every slice, every split of my skin, as I silently begged for him to stop. It was always the same feeling—a weightiness to my body that left me unable to move. My voice couldn't be heard beyond a whisper, and yet I swore Simon relished in the squeaks of sound that could slip past my dry and cracked lips. When I woke this morning, my hands clung to the comforter as my mind tried to rationalize how everything had felt so viscerally real while looking at my *mostly* unblemished skin confirmed it was only a dream.

Sleep is beginning to feel like a luxury I can no longer afford, my eyes heavy with exhaustion every morning and yet impossible to close every evening as I fight to stay away from what I know is unavoidable. I still feel as if I'm floating in some middle space, not quite sure if I'm tethered in reality. But even as horrific as the nightmares are, my last encounter with the king had proven to be even more harrowing.

Setting my tea cup down on the small saucer in front of me, the clanging of porcelain rings out loudly enough to make Eve cringe from where she sits across from me. I offer her a sympathetic grin as I slide my hand back onto my lap beneath the table, my nails digging into my palm. In truth, I had been distracted for each of our lessons the past few days, her instructions getting lost in the way my mind refuses to release the feeling of how King Dolian's hands felt on my body. It was no worse than what he had done the day after the branding, no worse really than any of the other ways he liked to touch me. Yet, for reasons I cannot explain, I felt more vulnerable pinned between him and the table. With his hands gripping at my hair and at my—

"I think we've done enough for today," she says while laying her white napkin on the matching linen-covered table.

"I'm sorry. I know I make terrible company." I take in the display of tea and food in front of me, actually seeing them for the first time since taking a seat for the day. The cream-colored teapot and cups are painted with a lovely floral pattern, while the food is arranged upon trays made of silver, reflecting the sunlight that shines in through the windows behind me. It's the same set up it has been for each of our lessons so far, and my distracted silence is once more present between us like an unwelcome guest.

She shrugs, standing from the table and clasping her hands out in front of her. "We all have days when we are more ourselves than others." I follow suit, catching her gaze. "I imagine it must be hard to be away from what you've come to know."

Did she mean in regards to my life in the tower? Or after? It occurs to me then that I have no idea what those who work here have been told about me, if they know *who* I am beyond just being the king's betrothed. I swallow as I look away from her, gaze trailing once more over the delicacies placed in front of us.

"These are my favorite," she says abruptly, reaching over to grab a small yellow cake cut into a square. "They are called honey cakes, and they remind me of the ones that my grandmother used to make. Though hers are much better than Emelia's."

I smile as I think of Alexi and his story of sneaking me treats from the grumpy baker. Despite everything—the circumstances I find myself in and the way my body aches with things seen and unseen—I do feel a small bit of joy at the memory of the only father I ever knew.

Eve takes a bite of her cake, shutting her eyes as she slowly chews. "So good," she murmurs, her hand covering her mouth as she gestures with her chin to the platter. "Try one!"

My stomach picks that exact moment to grumble, reminding me that I didn't eat much at breakfast and hadn't chosen anything else to eat when I sat down for tea. With careful fingers, I pick the cake up and bring it to my mouth, biting off a corner as the flavors of honey and vanilla burst on my tongue. How novel it is to recognize those flavors now, after having similar enough treats in the Mage Kingdom. "It is delicious," I say as I chew, already raising the small square back towards my mouth.

"Before I came to work for the king, I used to help our neighbors with their bee farm. Did you know there are hundreds of different types of honey? Their flavors are nuanced, only slight differences based on the floral pollen collected by the bees." She opens her eyes again, her smile wider than before. "There is nothing like harvesting your own honey."

"Do you get to see your family often?" I ask before taking another bite. She briefly looks surprised, as if she hadn't expected me to engage in the conversation, and the thought makes the cake in my stomach sour. Keeping my distance is the smart choice, but loneliness combined with exhaustion makes for a powerful motivator. I know what it is to be forced to only listen to my own voice for days at a time. Even with the risks, it is nice to hear someone else's for a change.

"I used to," she says, pausing before adding, "but it has been a few months since I've been home to see my sister. I'm from Fairven, a smaller town just on the outskirts of Vitour."

"Are you not allowed leave to visit her?"

Her focus drops to her hands, where she draws her thumb across her palm. But before she can answer my question, footsteps in the hall widen her eyes. She quickly wipes her hands on her apron before clasping them in front of her. Her urgency sparks my own, and my heart pounds in my chest as I watch her attempt to school her face into neutrality. But her posture softens when the owner of the footsteps rounds the corner, his dark eyes immediately landing on me.

"Commander," Eve says, her relieved tone not one I'm sure I share yet, "what can we do for you?"

"Hello, Eve. I'm here to escort Lady Rhea back to her room."

"Eve can take me back," I say quickly, my eyes bouncing between them.

"I wasn't asking."

I study the lines of his face, wondering if the familiarity I see is from all the times he watched as the king beat me in the tower or something else. Just like the last time I saw him, he isn't wearing his full guard uniform, instead dressed in the same armor that covers his torso that Nox wore when undercover. Longing hits me, swift and fierce, drawing tears to the corners of my eyes before I blink them away.

"Manners, Xander. We talked about this," Eve says, crossing her arms over her chest. "You'll make no friends with an attitude like that."

"Good thing I have enough friends, then."

The look he sends her is somehow a cross between fondness and annoyance. *Interesting.* I don't know Eve, certainly not enough to judge her character in any way, but I do find it odd that she is so *friendly* with *him.* Though maybe this is part of life for those who work for the king. Those who spend day in and out in proximity with each other likely form friendships of all different natures. Perhaps Xander and Eve are no different. Or, maybe, the fondness I had seen in his eyes goes deeper than that—to something... *physical* in nature.

Eve turns towards me, her hip popping out to the side. "You don't have to go with him if you don't want to."

Xander grumbles under his breath, tipping his head up to the ceiling. "No, you do not. But I would appreciate it if you did. I'd like to talk with you, and with the king currently preoccupied by his meeting with the siren queen through the Mirror, we have time." He looks directly at me. "Please."

I sigh but pinch my lips and relent with a nod.

"Great! I will clean up here and see you tomorrow morning," Eve says to me. She pats Xander's arm and then turns to face the table. Xander pivots, making enough space for me to walk past him and out into the hall.

"We can walk and talk," he says. I keep a few feet between us, Xander doing his best to match my pace despite how long his legs are. His hand on his sword flexes occasionally as we walk, something I've noticed him do before. I had thought it might be a way to remind me that he has the ability to kill me, as if I need such a message, but now I think it is a nervous tick. He doesn't seem conscious of the fact he is doing it.

"What is it you wanted to talk about?"

He keeps his gaze forward when he answers. "I meant what I said last week about helping you. About *wanting* to help you."

I keep my steps steady, even as my heart thunders in my chest. "Again, how do I know this isn't a trick?"

There is a slight downturn of Xander's lips, the only indication of his displeasure. Then again, that could just be his normal face. "I'm not trying to trick you. I have no *need* to."

"That's not exactly reassuring. What need did Simon have? What need does the king have? Those men do it because they can. Because they have power and they want to wield it. Or they want more of it. Between the two of us, the power tilts in your favor—"

"Only because of that," he interrupts, pointing to my hand that holds the ring.

"A very important *that*," I counter, drawing my thumb over the pearl, its temperature cooler than the air around us.

"There is still your title."

"I have no title here."

Xander chuckles, the sound relaying his frustration. "Were your parents not the former king and queen? Are you not the heir to the Mortal Kingdom's throne?"

I meet his exasperation with my own. "Am I not under the control of an uncle who wants to marry me? One who has beaten and tortured me so often that I—" I blow out a breath through clenched teeth, settling my emotions. I cannot afford to be baited into a conversation that might be used against me. "Surely, debating the merits of my supposed title is not why you wanted to speak with me."

We round a corner, the gray stone walls adorned with black sconces, their flames not yet lit.

"No, it isn't." Yet he offers nothing else as we continue on in silence, my apprehension with the guard building as we eventually near the door to my room.

"Well, this has been a strange—"

"I'm sorry."

My mouth snaps shut while my gaze lands on his, assessing the tone of his words. They aren't said with anger or sarcasm but with genuine regret. Confusion spikes within me as I stop walking and turn to face him fully.

"My apology will never be enough to offer you. For all you've been through, for all I—I've allowed," he stammers, drawing a hand down his face before tucking a strand of his onyx hair behind his ear. "But it is owed to you all the same. As is my offer to help you now. It doesn't change what happened before, but I have no intention of watching you suffer the same fate again, and I've made too many promises to those I care about to break them." His eyes drift away from mine, but I only have one response to everything he's said.

"Why? Why would you expect me to believe that you just want to help me after *years* of doing nothing."

"I don't, and I'm glad to see that what I've been told about your intelligence is true." I scowl at that, watching as Xander reaches into his back pocket to pull out a small book, its cover bound with black leather. "But I'm going to give you two things that I hope might sway you into, at the very least, believing that my interests lie solely in what is best for the Mortal Kingdom and its people. Not the ones that prance about the castle, but the workers and servants. Those who live and breathe our shops and goods in Vitour and beyond." He checks once more over his shoulder, ensuring that we are alone before he lowers his voice. "There is a revolution brewing, both within the castle walls and beyond. One built on the backs of those workers and servants."

My heart leaps to my throat as I stare at him. "They wish to see King Dolian removed from the throne?" He nods. "How do you know this?"

At that, his façade breaks just enough for the smallest uptick of his lips to creep through. "Because I am leading it. And please know that me telling you this is no small feat," he says, likely reading my stunned unease. "If you go to the king with this information, if he suspects any movement at all against him, more than just my life will be on the line. Years of preparation, of building and planning and bowing to a king I do not consider mine, will be undone." There's nothing but truth in his gaze, and perhaps it makes me foolish, but I find that I believe every word he says. That I *want* to.

Still, I doubt Xander bringing up my claim to the mortal throne earlier is coincidental. "I will not be used as a pawn in your rebellion," I tell him, measuring my words carefully. "I may be the rightful heir, but I do not want to rule *here*. And as long as this ring is on me, I cannot wield my magic as my own."

His posture relaxes slightly, his thumb dragging across the soft black leather of the book still in his hand. "I tell you about the rebellion only so that you have something to use as collateral, to prove that we have equal footing. Beyond that, it would be my preference that you leave here as soon as possible. Your power, what you did at the beach..." He trails off, shaking his head incredulously. Guilt and sadness crackle in the air around me, threatening to pull me under again. "I don't mean it as an insult, but that sort of power should only be wielded by those who understand the weight of having it. Who understand the consequences of using it. King Dolian isn't that person."

"And you believe me to be?"

Xander tilts his head as he appraises me. "I do."

It shouldn't matter, the approval of this guard, but something in me warms at his answer. At how he gave it without hesitation. I eye the book again, gesturing to it with my hand. "I assume this is the second thing?"

"It is." He places the book in my hands, a gentleness in the exchange that makes me hold it a little more carefully.

"What is it?" I ask, inspecting the outside but finding it void of any title or words.

Xander takes a small step away, his hand returning to the hilt of his sword. "His death haunts me nearly every single night." Breath rushes from my lungs, a sharp tension snapping into place between us. "As does the image of you cradling his head in your lap, his blood pooled around your body."

I look away, squeezing my eyes shut.

"After we retrieved his body, I was tasked with going back to his room at the barracks to clean it out. I found that tucked beneath the mattress and the frame of his bed." My eyes whirl back to Xander. "That is his personal journal, and I thought you should be the one to have it."

Chapter Twenty-Five

KAI

Do you have any idea how often I come with your name slipping past my lips?

I groan at the memory of those words, of how she felt in my hands when she uttered them. My hips rock as I pump my cock faster, a poor attempt at recreating the night we claimed each other for the first time.

The hot water of the shower pricks at my back like a million little darts, but the sensation is lost to the images that play in my mind. That *have* played in my mind since the moment she left. Her light brown skin gleams beneath the glow of a flame gem, those wild curls begging for me to dig my fingers into them. To wrap them around my fist and tug until her neck—her body, her *everything*—is bared to me. *Only* to me.

You won't stay out of my fucking head.

I know the feeling of that all too fucking well. To think of Bahira is to subject myself to the greatest pleasure, evidenced by the need to work out my lust in the shower first thing in the morning. I have never met a female who inspired such crazed desire within me—one who made me ache for her nearly as often as she spiked my anger. One whose mind was the most beautiful part of her, despite the way her body might as well have been crafted from my very dreams.

My stomach muscles clench as I move my hand faster.

Kai. Her voice scrapes over my mind and down my spine, igniting me as my release barrels through me. I come hard, her name mixed with a grunt as I rock my hips until every part of me is wrung empty. "Fuck." Resting my forehead against the tile, I play through every intimate moment we'd had together while I catch my breath.

She is the sweetest torture; she always has been. Even when my attraction to her was something I fought as hard as I could, when it confused me as much as it made me curious. But thoughts of Bahira also lead down a darker path, one tainted in the whispers of her lies and the brashness of my response. One that reminds me that weeks have passed since I watched her ship sail away, and I have yet to hear from her. One that has me wondering if what I remember of our interactions is actually true or if the connection between us was imagined. A fabrication of a lonely mind and wanting a woman I couldn't fully have.

Once I'm as settled as I can be, I finish washing up and step out of the shower, wrapping a thick cotton towel around my hips.

Word had spread about Bahira and Kane's encounter with my uncle and his rebels, and in the wake of Tua's betrayal—and his subsequent death—each day has been spent weeding out those who want to continue his vision and see me removed from the throne. Far too many of my people have been apprehended and thrown in the dungeons, their fates to be decided by a committee of my choosing. Jahlee's eyes had glinted in feral delight at the mention of the new council, though I had to disappoint my sister when I told her I needed her brand of expertise elsewhere. That expertise being her excellence at making people so uncomfortable that they begin to spill their secrets. With Haloa's protection, Jahlee has spent time in Molsi identifying rebels and their sympathizers. A task that is not only necessary but allows my sister the freedom I know she desperately craves.

Truthfully, getting her out of the palace and into the city was only *partially* due to feeling guilty about cooping her up here before. But, she more than proved herself during the rebel attack on the palace, taking down male, female, and animal alike with an ease I hadn't given her credit for. Alternatively, when she didn't have anything else to focus on, all of her energy turned on me and how I was going to rectify things with Bahira.

I was able to fend her off the first week, citing Bahira's travel back to her kingdom and the time it would take her to get settled and make sure all was well. But as another week passed with no word from the mage princess, it got harder and harder to stave off Jahlee's urging, especially when it wasn't just her that wanted to hear from Bahira. I gave in, calling out to King Sadryn not once or twice but three fucking times, only to be met with silence.

After dressing, I comb through my hair with my fingers, pulling the strands back before taking a seat at the edge of my bed, wallowing in the thoughts of my mistakes. I had a lifetime of saying and doing the wrong things, yet the look on Bahira's face as I called her *worthless* is a memory that doesn't just haunt me more than anything else, it sits like venom in my veins. Burning through my body like penance.

I should have said more to her before she left. Should have insisted that she understood I was wrong—so *fucking* wrong—for ever insinuating what I did. She had changed me, simply because of who she was. Her brilliance and strength, that determination that sometimes drove me through a fucking wall and other times made me ache to wrap my hand around her throat and fuck her until we both forgot all else. Her sharp tongue and irreverent nature. All of it pushed me to do better. To *be* better. With her, there were no limits to the type of king I could be, only the ones I put on myself.

She had been mine for a brief moment in time, and then she was just *gone*.

Tilting my head back, I allow another few seconds of her face in my mind before I push it all down and stand, getting dressed before exiting my room. Two guards stand in the hall in front of me, another one of Jahlee's insistences. Though this one was easier to accept, considering there had already been multiple attempts on my life.

"Your Majesty," they say in unison as I walk past them. I manage to grunt out a greeting before heading to the east wing for an unofficial meeting with my newly appointed advisors. The palace is bustling, preparations for the belated autumnal celebration underway.

A cackling laugh echoes from ahead of me, and I can't help my smirk when I spot my sister engaging with a few males who look worse off for it. "If you thought this was me being unreasonable, then you have no idea what I am capable of!"

"Lady Jahlee, there isn't—"

"Princess," I rumble, cutting off the shorter of the two who stand across from Jahlee. "You are speaking with *Princess* Jahlee. Or have you forgotten how titles work?" His throat works with a nervous swallow, his fear thick in the air between us as he tips his head back to look up at me. Jahlee snorts, rolling her eyes in feigned annoyance, though I don't miss the small smile that tugs on the corners of her mouth.

"My apologies, Your Majesty—"

"It isn't I who was slighted. Direct your regret to the person you've wronged."

He sputters out an agreement before bowing to my sister, his companion doing the same. "I truly meant no harm; it's just the princess is asking for something to be added to tonight's festivities that will be impossible to make in the time allotted."

My brow arches as I turn towards Jahlee, who only offers a shrug of her shoulders as she rocks back on her heels.

"She wants an ice sculpture of you, Your Majesty, and I just don't think we will have the time!"

"An ice sculpture..." I let the sentence fade as I catch Jahlee's smile widening. "That, of course, *is* unreasonable and not something that is necessary to begin with. Pretend she never said a thing about it." Both males nod furiously before bowing again and bolting down the hall. Jahlee laughs at my side, drawing my gaze. "An ice sculpture? Really?"

"*It isn't I who was slighted,*" she mocks in return, her voice dropping low in an attempt to sound like mine. "I can see your new role as king is going to your head."

"I've been king for years, Jahlee."

She waves her hand in the air between us before tossing her wavy dark brown hair over her shoulder. "You know what I mean." Looping her arm around mine, I let her turn us in the direction of the dining hall. "Are you ready to see your new advisors?"

"They aren't in their roles yet *officially*," I remind her, walking past a few workers who offer more greetings with the use of my title. Though I push for that level of respect for Jahlee, having it given to me so frequently is something I am not yet used to.

Prior to the outing of the rebels, Tua had never encouraged those around us to address me with the level of respect—and fear—one might assume for a king. At the time, I thought he was trying to make me seem more approachable. Like I might not care so much that I was ruler, only that I wanted to help my people in whatever way I could. Now I recognize it for what Bahira saw so clearly in her limited time here: a way to undermine me. To present me as someone weak.

"They've been vetted enough, and with how little the pool of candidates was to choose from, I should hope that they are good enough for the job," she says, her movements carrying an excited energy as we near the open door to the dining hall. She's right about the lack of qualified males and females I could choose that had *enough* knowledge to fill the roles left by the previous group of rebel supporters. The corner of my mouth lifts as I think about Sir Duarte and Lady Aisha—the previous Masters of Coin—sitting in the dark and dirty cells beneath the palace. Their arrest had felt a hell of a lot more satisfying than any of the others.

Jahlee and I enter the larger dining room, drawing the gazes of those gathered around a large table. The scent of baked goods and fresh fruit linger in the air, and I scan those already seated as I take my own chair at the head of the table.

"Good morning, everyone!" she sings, plopping down into a chair to my left.

"Must you always be *so loud*," my cousin drawls from his seat at the opposite end. Dark circles stain the skin beneath his eyes as he narrows them in Jahlee's direction. She only smiles in response, flashing all her teeth as she wiggles her fingers dramatically at him. She had not wanted Kane to be part of anything new we are building. She believes that he had nothing to do with what his father planned, but her disdain for the male who had often treated her like shit is a slight she has no interest in forgiving. Not that I blame her. Unfortunately, Kane's presence is a necessity for both him and me. It shows those who support me that he can be trusted, and though it pains me to admit it, I need him. Kane may be an annoying prick on his absolute best day, but no one knows how to work a crowd of nobles better than he does. He's also knowledgeable on the laws and policies of our kingdom in a way that only someone who was actually raised to be king can be.

"Shall we begin?" the Master of Laws and only remaining advisor from before Tua's death, Lady Miranda, says. She leans forward and rests her elbows on the table, her snow-white hair pulled back from her face. Its color reminds me of *another* female whose presence has disrupted the kingdom. "Is everyone here familiar with everyone else?"

Jahlee kicks my foot under the table, her brown eyes comically wide as she silently conveys a message to me. She makes sure to also mouth the words *you should say something* in a way that is obvious to anyone looking in our direction. I fist my hands as I exhale roughly, turning back to face the shifters on either side of the table, varying levels of amusement dancing in their eyes.

"I'll introduce everyone, then." I shoot a glare at my sister when she snorts. The chair directly to my right is empty, but following that is Lady Miranda. Next to her is the newest Master of Coin, Sir Garreth. He had come at Lady Miranda's recommendation and is a noble male who has no history of ever working or siding with Tua or his rebels. And he passed Jahlee's thorough interrogation, though what that actually entails, I have no clue. At the end of this row is Kane, his role essentially the same as it was before, the voice between Crown and shifters. He will stick to speaking with those of a higher economic class, while Jahlee and Haloa will be the true eyes and ears of the working class of our kingdom. Across from him sits the new Master of Ships, a gruff female who refuses to go by anything other than Noe. Her time spent in the sun on the docks and on ships has aged her beyond her years, but her face is familiar—one I recognize from childhood—and her ability to shut Kane up with a single withering look makes her an invaluable asset. I introduce the last two members of my trusted advisors, Alon and Malik, both positions that oversee my guards and armies. While our kingdom has not seen adversity with any other since The War Of Five Kingdoms, my father made sure that there was a sizable army kept at the ready. It was one of the few things he didn't bother keeping secret.

I lean back in my chair when I'm finished, brushing my fingers along my jaw as Lady Miranda dives into her proposal to tweak some of the laws.

My thoughts can't help but to wander to my father, the late king a subject I *loathe* acknowledging but one that seems to constantly be present now. To know that he did something to my mother that not only affected her but me and Jahlee as well, leaves an ache in my chest that pulses right next to the empty spot left by Bahira.

"Those of a certain class are not going to like that change."

I look to Kane, my lips drawing down in a frown. "What change?"

The eyes of the entire table fall on me, making an itch take root beneath my skin.

"Daydreaming again, King Kai?" Kane taunts, his fucking grin making my magic thrum in my blood. "I bet I can figure out who is occupying your thoughts—"

"Hey, Kane, remember when your dad betrayed our king and his kingdom? Remember when he was more than willing to sacrifice you to whatever end and a certain female had to rescue your pathetic ass from the dungeons after she had just fought off two of his minions?" Jahlee cuts in smoothly. Kane growls as golden rings form around his irises, his fingers straining against the tabletop.

"Enough," I snap, making half the occupants at the table jump. My chest rises with a deep breath before I gesture to my right. "Lady Miranda, please continue." The Master of Laws doesn't skip a beat and repeats her idea for bringing more jobs and aid to those who have been affected by the blight and who don't come from wealth. Kane's comment about the nobles not liking the proposed plan comes from Miranda's idea to tax the richest at a higher percentage than they are now.

"We need allies more than ever, and alienating the ones who have the largest influence is not going to win you any favors," Kane says.

"If numbers are what you seek, it is important to remember that the vast majority of the people who make up this kingdom are those who have to scrape by doing whatever manual labor they can while trying to get help for their children from their neighbors who are in the exact same position. The blight does not just affect the rich."

"Of course it doesn't, but while the numbers may favor your idea, the truth is the economic stability of this kingdom rests solely on the nobles who own its business. Who spend their wealth at the shops and currently give their money to the Crown willingly."

I lean forward, forcing my annoyance at this conversation to not bleed through in my voice. "Are you saying they will resist and ignore if they are told to pay more?"

My cousin shrugs, drawing a disgruntled noise from Noe. "Maybe. There has been a lot of change, and while I agree that we needed to show we would treat traitors of all status equally, you *did* throw an exorbitant amount of our kingdom's wealthiest into the dirty cells below us. Their family members will not soon forget that."

Lady Miranda exhales loudly as her back meets her chair roughly, Jahlee mirroring the movement to my left.

"What do the kingdom's reserves look like at the moment?" I ask, ignoring the way my cheeks want to heat at the embarrassment that floods me. I hadn't cared to know before, hadn't *needed* to with Tua at the helm. Now I feel as if I'm an outsider to my own throne, daring to play catch up in a game where I fucking gave myself the disadvantage.

"There is enough to sustain the kingdom for a few years on just that alone, but..." Sir Garreth swallows, drawing a hand over his shaved head. "We would have to adjust our spending if there were to be a protest of some kind from those who, as Sir Kane pointed out, provide the majority of our funds."

I nod, my muscles tense as I think over my response. "We keep things as they are right now—allocating funds for those who ask for them—while encouraging the idea to the nobles that taxing them at a higher rate is beneficial."

"And how do you propose we do that?"

My eyes narrow at my cousin's question, my patience already strung too thin to pretend to be diplomatic. "Use your talents in your role to make it happen."

He clenches his jaw but speaks no further protests. The conversation moves on to other topics, including a new collection of rebels that were found and brought into the dungeons.

"They set fire to a few shops on the main street in Molsi. Some of the residents were able to apprehend three of the five males spotted at the time of the attack, but the prisoners have been *reluctant* to give any information up," Sir Alon, a male whose width rivals my own but who stands a full foot shorter, informs me.

"I will make a stop to their cells this evening and see if I can persuade them to speak." I ignore the way Jahlee's gaze burns into the side of my head, moving the rest of the meeting along. It ends unceremoniously, everyone filtering out with instructions on what moves to make next, except for Jahlee and Lady Miranda. I give the latter my attention first.

"I don't mean to overstep, and if I am, please tell me, but I wonder if you might have considered getting an assistant of sorts to help you," she says, interlacing her fingers in front of her. Her posture is regal in a way that speaks to her schooling and training, a female who is perhaps just as tired of standing on the sidelines as I have been.

"Do you think I could benefit from one?" I ask genuinely, crossing my arms over my chest.

She nods, leveling her brown eyes at me. "I have no doubt that as we continue to rebuild after the stain your uncle left on this kingdom, there will be more and more things that divide your attention. Having someone at your side who can help you filter through the information and tasks expected of you might ease the burden."

"How would this be different from what Tua did?"

"She wouldn't take the responsibilities on herself, only organize and list them out for you in whatever method you tell her to."

My brow arches as I tilt my head to the side. "She?"

"Ah, yes," she laughs, smoothing a hand down the front of her white dress. "My oldest daughter, Inessa, is in need of work now that she has graduated from schooling. She's hardworking, clever, organized, and not one to mince words." She adjusts her stance, looking more nervous than when I interrogated her about her possible involvement with Tua. "I know this screams of nepotism, and perhaps that is true, but I do think she would make a wonderful asset to our team."

I finally spare my sister a glance, the many gold bracelets dangling on her wrist jingle as she waves her hand in the air in what I *think* is approval.

"Have her report here tomorrow with you." Miranda smiles, dipping her chin before leaving the room to just Jahlee and myself. "Spit it out," I tell her, watching her lips purse and then flatten out at least three times.

"You can't torture the rebels."

Surprise crinkles my forehead. "I thought you would be open to getting whatever information we can by whatever means necessary." I am sure I had seen her eyes gleam with an eagerness to do so herself at times.

"*I am*. What I mean is that *you* shouldn't be the one to do it." She takes a step towards me, the movement fluid as if she is dancing instead of walking.

"We need whatever information from them that we can get. You know this."

"And as I said before, I have no qualms with that. I just do not want my brother losing the last of whatever moral compass he has because he's doing something he hates."

"Who said I hated it?" But the question is a stupid one, because my sister knows me better than anyone. She knows what my father had a reputation for. His ruthlessness as king did not begin or end with using my mother or altering her pregnancy or threatening Jahlee. Or the numerous ways he tortured me.

"Honestly, Kai, don't embarrass yourself. You already do enough pretending with how you're feeling about Bahira. Don't think you can trick me into believing that it wouldn't bother you."

Unwilling to get dragged into another conversation about Bahira, I shrug my shoulders and gesture with my chin to the door. "As king, it is my duty to ensure I do whatever it takes to keep our kingdom safe." I move to leave, only to be stopped when Jahlee grips my arm.

"Fine. Do what you think you must, but do not take on guilt because of it." The fierceness in her voice reminds me of our mother, and I have to swallow down the knot that forms in my throat. Keeping my gaze forward, I nod my head and wait for her to release me.

She does, only to join my side as we exit the dining hall and walk right into Siyala.

Chapter Twenty-Six

KAI

"Have you heard anything?" Her voice—deeper and smoother than it had been before she disappeared four years ago—commands my attention as Jahlee and I stop short in front of her.

"No."

Jahlee sighs, while Siyala's eyes narrow, their amber color brightening. "I thought you said we could count on your lover? It has been weeks since she left, and there has been no word on Rhea—"

"She is not my *lover*—" I interrupt, though it doesn't deter her rant.

"The Mage Kingdom is not even answering your calls through the Mirror. Either something is wrong, or she is purposefully ignoring us."

"Bahira wouldn't do that!" my sister cuts in.

"And you know her so well?" Siyala snaps, looking to Jahlee before shaking her head. "I knew I should have gone with her." My cousin's frustration isn't misplaced, and though her concerns are valid and mirror my own, I don't know how to respond.

Siyala's changed since she disappeared, and while that is to be expected, the jaded way she has shared her viewpoints isn't. Her survival in the Mortal Kingdom for four years is a mystery that not even she can answer, and she's been reluctant to give many details beyond the fact that she was well cared for in her animal form by Rhea. It's my understanding that she hasn't shifted once yet since being home.

Jahlee wraps an arm around Siyala's shoulders, flicking her white braid behind her back. "Bahira is a good one, Cousin. I'm sure whatever the reason is for her not reaching out to us, it is an important one. Kai will keep trying to contact the Mage Kingdom." She sends me an arched brow as if to say, *right?*

Meeting both of their gazes, I nod and ignore the pit that makes its presence known in my stomach again. "I could reach out to the Mortal Kingdom and see if—"

"No!" Siyala *growls*, raising invisible hackles along my neck at the power that infuses her voice. I note the clenching of her fists, the way her chest rises with a deep draw of breath that she holds, as if she is trying to halt the urge to shift. Jahlee's fingers tighten around her shoulder, but Siyala jerks out of my sister's hold. "It would risk too much." My gaze meets Jahlee's as Siyala shakes her head before running a hand down her face. "Just tell me if you hear from Bahira." She spins on her heel and heads towards the stairs, ignoring Jahlee when she calls out to her.

"She is still young," I murmur, facing my sister. "And we cannot imagine all she has gone through."

"Because she won't tell anyone! She keeps her thoughts to herself as they build and build within her. She's going to burst if she doesn't talk about what happened." Jahlee throws her hands up in frustration at the small chuckle that escapes me. "But it's not just her I'm upset with. Are you sure you're using the Mirror properly?"

My smirk falls as I lift a brow. "I am."

"Then why hasn't anyone answered? Why hasn't Bahira reached out to us?"

"The Mirror worked just fine when I reached out to the Mage Kingdom for help with the blight in the beginning. And when Bahira used it to contact her family before. This is... a choice they are making to not talk with us." It's the first time I've acknowledged the thought out loud, and Jahlee is all the more agitated for it.

The tip of her nail jabs into my chest as her eyes gleam with a fury that could rival any shifter's, even with her lack of magic. "What did you say to her when she left?"

"Goodbye." My hand wraps around her wrist to stop her attempt to hit me.

"*Asshole!*" she shouts, stumbling back when I release her. "Did you tell her how you feel about her? How you *really* feel?" The effort it takes to hold her glare makes that pit within me open wider, swallowing whole all the emotions this conversation brings up. "You didn't, did you? Gods, Kai! Would it have been *so* hard to be honest with her? With *yourself?*"

"What if I was? What if I *did* tell her how I felt and left it up to her whether she decided to include me in her life or not?" My voice rumbles down the hall, low and menacing as Jahlee's eyes widen. "As I said before, it is a *choice*. One I am not interested in ruminating on any further. I will reach out to the Mage Kingdom because I promised Siyala I would until we hear that Rhea is okay. Beyond that,

Bahira has made it abundantly clear she is not interested in anything I have to offer her."

I brush past, ignoring her soft call of my name. My admission circles round and round in my mind, Bahira's face accompanying it before I'm able to get control and squash it. It doesn't matter that I can admit to myself silently in the darkest depths of my mind that while I don't have any experience with romantic love, I think I felt it with her. I think I knew, briefly, what it was to lay my armor down at the same time as someone else, leaving me raw and exposed in a way no one had ever seen before. I can admit those things and still acknowledge that it was nothing more than a slip in time. A single star glimmering in the night sky, there and gone in the blink of an eye. Because Bahira has made it clear that her future does not include me, and maybe it's time I try to come to the same conclusion.

A haze surrounds me for the rest of the day, even when I visit the dungeons to interrogate the rebels. After an hour of interrogation on Sir Duarte, the promise of fresh water and a meal made of more than just meat scraps and bread *finally* got him talking on where there are still rebel strongholds throughout Molsi. I had anticipated that there would be larger pockets where shifters were still planning my demise. I *hadn't* expected the sheer volume that Sir Duarte alluded to.

But he had least given me the locations of meeting points that the rebels were known to utilize.

With the sun now set and a midnight storm shaking the palm trees outside the palace, I stare up at the ceiling lost in thoughts not of remorse or—thankfully—a certain mage princess but instead of what I had found two days prior.

Turning my head to the side, I look over at my nightstand and the five leather-bound journals stacked upon it. The words lining the pages taunt me, but despite the fact that I had found the journals that belonged to my father, I haven't had the strength to open them. Tua had done well enough hiding them, tucking them into a compartment hidden behind one of the bookcases in my father's room. And though I am so damn curious to know how the hell he altered any part of me, discovering exactly what he did to my mother is something I know I must be ready to read.

With a deep exhale, I turn my back on the journals and stare out one of the windows. Allowing sleep to slink in slowly, it cradles me as surely as my loneliness does, and despite the way I hear her calling out my name as I straddle the line between sleep and consciousness, I ignore the lure of the woman whose missing presence may as well be a blade to the heart.

Chapter Twenty-Seven

NOX

MY SISTER KNOWS. SHE has to. The wary glances she keeps sending me, ones that don't only contain concern but an unspoken threat, are too coincidental for her *not* to know. Then again, do I really expect anything different from Bahira? The woman was born to dissect things until answers emerged from whatever it was she fixated on, and as she, Elora, and I continue combing through books, searching for any clues on how to repair the Mirror that my magic had broken, it's clear that her fixation is primarily on me.

In the days that had passed since I woke up—officially—from my time in the Middle, I have never felt more lost. Like a spirit haunting my own home, I am trapped in the knowledge that nearly all of my worst fears have come true. When I was undercover in the Mortal Kingdom, nothing terrified me more than the thought that if I didn't complete my mission, my people would suffer. It didn't take long being near the king to realize that his loyalties lie not with the mortals he was sworn to protect but with his own self-interests. If someone like him had a tool powerful enough that mages could feel the brunt of its power an entire kingdom away, there was no telling what he would do with it. No telling what someone with a penchant for violence would be willing to sacrifice to get more.

It is no secret that he hates mages, and every night when the same nightmare plagued me over and over again, all I could think about was how many lives would be at risk if I didn't figure out what he had in time. It felt like I was constantly sprinting into darkness, something unknown and unseen following me and gaining speed with every step that I took. I was nearly paralyzed by the fear of it all, desperate for answers just as I was desperate to go home. And then I met her.

Sometimes, I wonder if Rhea truly understands just how much she changed me. If she realizes just how much she *saved* me. Loving her isn't just the easiest thing I have ever done, it is a godsdamn privilege. It is an honor that I don't deserve but a vow I will willingly ink in blood every single day for the rest of my life. As long as she is by my side, I have everything.

When I woke from the Middle to find that my nightmares were no longer hypotheticals conjured by my mind, no other responsibility I had sworn to uphold mattered. They are now firmly placed in line behind my dedication to Rhea, to the true Void queen. It doesn't lessen my horror to know that King Dolian doesn't just have the love of my life, he has the weapon I had been terrified of from the very beginning. Rhea isn't a helpless woman, but she isn't just a mage, either. She carries within her the magic of past goddesses, at least in comparison to the power that flows in everyone else's veins. She *is* a weapon, and I can only hope that she has found some way to utilize her magic to protect herself until I can get to her.

That is what I know my sister is dissecting as she stares at me over the book she is skimming. She had asked me not to do anything stupid, but retrieving my fiancée from the monster who once more caged her is anything but that. It is destiny—one that I am bound to fulfill.

"Maybe I pulled the wrong books," Elora says with a sigh, taking her glasses off to rub the bridge of her nose. She had berated me when I came with Bahira today to help them comb through books, and though I know it comes from the same place of worry that is festering in my own chest, it doesn't stop the bite of her words from piercing through me. *How could you let this happen?* Bahira had snarled something in my defense, but I *need* Elora's anger. I deserve it. I had questioned her loyalty to Rhea in the beginning, and she had shown my fiancée nothing but friendship and love. The tears that lined her eyes as her fists curled at her sides and her cheeks deepened to a furious shade of red had been real. She cared for Rhea, and though she didn't know every detail that often kept me awake about Rhea's history with her uncle, she knew enough to surmise that every fucking second spent with him would be tortuous ones.

"We've only just begun," Bahira counters, laying her book down on the table. It joins the others Elora had chosen a few days ago as a starting point for discovering how the Mirror was made. While Bahira's interest in fixing the Mirror seems to drive her, my own has waned. I doubt King Dolian will even use the Mirror until he is sure Rhea is securely in his grasp. *When she is back at my side and I have her in every way* you *cannot, it will be you who dies a slow and painful death.* I grit my teeth, hard enough to send pain shooting up my temple. His ego will give him a false sense of security, and I plan to exploit it thoroughly. Even if my magic is still not back to its full strength.

I adjust in my seat, aching muscles in my back making me grimace as I try to pull my magic forward for the hundredth time to no avail. Disquiet whispers in the back of my mind, questioning why it is still so depleted. It had never taken long to replace the magic I used. It was always an instantaneous thing, and now... I force my anxious thoughts back down and focus on the book in my hand.

"It's just frustrating. The Mirrors have been a defining pillar for each kingdom since the dawn of their existence, and yet so little is known about how they were formed in the first place. If we can't find what we need..." Elora sighs as she leans back in her chair, folding her arms over her chest.

"You're being dramatic. Don't presume we've failed before there is reason to," Bahira counters, her gray eyes moving from Elora to once more land on me. "And you should eat more." She gestures to the platter of fruits and vegetables laid out at the table's center, roasted meats and buttered rolls also mixed into the array.

"Keeping tabs on my eating habits?" I ask, brow arched.

She rolls her eyes. "Someone has to." Then, a little more quietly, she adds, "How are you feeling?"

A loaded question if there ever was one. I'm desperate and miserable. A void lives in my chest, the threads that once connected me to Rhea now left in a tattered mess, as if each one was pulled until it violently snapped. Above all of that, terror and agony bleed together until it's a constant fiery pressure that leaves me persistently aching, nauseous, and irritable. "I'm fine."

"If you're trying to be convincing, you aren't doing a very good job," Elora drawls, earning a snort from my sister.

"Let's focus on what actually matters and not on whether my stomach is satisfied."

Bahira's eyes narrow, but she thankfully doesn't press the issue any further. Silence once more settles between us, the library closed to the rest of the kingdom while we pursue the information we need. Selfishly, my mind wanders to Rhea instead of focusing on the words in front of me. I try to picture scenarios where she is safe. Where maybe one of the head maids like Erica has recognized that she is back in the kingdom and has taken measures to ensure Rhea has everything she needs. Would King Dolian put her back in the tower? I doubt it, but I suppose when it comes to him and his obsession with her, there is an unpredictability that I hate to factor in. Despite my best attempts to assuage my guilt, I keep coming to the same demand that rings throughout my head: *Go get her.*

"What does the Mirror look like?" Elora asks abruptly. "When it's in use, I mean."

"It changes from solid glass to something like liquid silver," Bahira answers. "And it ripples like water that's had a pebble skipped across its surface."

"Was it the same in the Shifter Kingdom?"

My sister nods, her eyes taking on a faraway look just like every time the subject of the shifters and her time there comes up. I wonder if she even realizes she does it. If she finds it as ironic as I do. I'm not the only one holding things back. Though it does make me curious, wondering what could have transpired there. Why the council is dead set on making her relive every detail, calling her into meetings just as frequently as they call me. I suppose this time I can't blame their devout interest in me.

"Is there any other conduit for magic besides dragon stone?" she asks, drawing twin looks of curiosity from Bahira and I.

"Not that I'm aware of." A line forms between Bahira's brows. "Which begs the question..."

"What was the Mirror made of? Because last time I checked, dragon stone only comes in black and white. Not silver," Elora finishes for her.

"And nothing else will hold mage magic long enough to be used in such a way," I murmur, dragging a hand through my hair and holding the strands at the top.

"Assuming the Mirror is made with just *any* mage magic. There's a chance that we may figure out the material but not have a way to imbue it again. The magic that must have been in that Mirror..." Elora pushes up to stand from the table. "It was ancient. Likely something that came directly from Olymazi itself."

"Or the gods." It isn't until I have two sets of gray eyes on me that I realize I spoke my thoughts aloud.

"This coming from the same man who once told me that the gods and fate were nothing more than things people blamed when they made the wrong decisions."

I shrug, joining Elora in standing and sliding my hands into my pockets. There isn't enough time, nor am I in the mood, to explain the Middle and everything that I had seen there. I will, when Rhea is safe and at my side again, tell Bahira and my friends all of it. But it feels like a tale I am not made to tell without her voice blending together with mine. "Am I not allowed to change my mind?"

"You are," Bahira answers immediately, standing and leaning her hands down on the table in front of her. "But I know you, and I know that you wouldn't merely change your mind unless you were presented with something that proved otherwise."

Damn her. I shoot her as big a grin as I can muster and back away, gesturing with my head towards the library's exit.

"We aren't done here, Nox—"

"I have somewhere else I need to be before the sun goes down." I turn and stride down the long rug centered between the windows of the library and its many bookcases, ignoring my sister's grumble and the way Elora chuckles.

Metal, warm from sitting in my pocket, brushes against my fingers, and I slowly slide the object up until it's resting between my thumb and palm. I hold it there as I pass through the foyer, the last rays of sunshine spilling in through the gaps of the trees dancing on the glittering black stone floors.

Excluding the higher presence of guards, the palace has been quieter than ever. Something I think I am directly to blame for. Where palace aides once smiled and offered friendly greetings as I passed, they now eye me warily, their lips drawn into tight lines. Not that I blame them. What I had done to the healers—what I was *going* to do in order to get Rhea back—doesn't paint me in a favorable light with my people. I'd be lying if I said I didn't care. Of course I do. But there was truth in what I told Rhea—that I'd sacrifice everything when it came to her. There is no line I'm not willing to cross, no depravity I won't sink into in order to bring her back home.

I climb the steps up to the third floor, the post on the landing occupied by two guards I don't recognize. Barron had disappeared, neither Cass nor my father had been able to locate the longtime member of our palace guard. My parents had met with his partner while I was in my deep sleep, the man rightfully beside himself. So far, no interviews with his fellow guards nor search parties conducted have yielded any clues to where he had gone. He had been someone I trusted, someone I considered safe for Rhea to be around, and reconciling that he might have aided in her capture for King Dolian slices deeper than I want to admit.

The sound of my boots is muffled on the carpet as I make my way down the long hallway that ends with the room I share with Rhea on the left and the entrance to the secret garden on the right. I can't say why I keep coming here, to the place that holds such a perfect memory. Pressing my hand against the wall, I immediately find the inset stone and push, stepping back as the hidden door opens with a creak and lets a rush of cool air out from the dark stairwell. My heartbeat picks up, pulse fluttering in my neck, as I slip past the threshold and shut the door behind me, submerging myself in total darkness.

I reach for my magic again, never once using it to help me navigate the stairs before and now feeling like I need it in order to make it to the bottom. But only flickers of my power rise, not even enough to be visible in my palm. My chest tightens, and my pulse grows faster, a sprinting of my heart that rushes blood to my ears and breath past my lips. My steps are slow down the stairs, and as I round the last turn, my eyes find an empty space at the bottom, knowing that she wouldn't be there yet hopelessly wishing that she was. I can't put into words what the absence of her feels like. How can one describe what it is to be without a home? A heart and soul? My hand closes around the ring in my pocket as I push open the door that leads outside, golden sunlight flooding my vision as a gentle breeze whips tendrils of my hair over my forehead.

The garden is as lovely as it always is, the unblemished stone pathway that leads out into the heart of it reflecting more of the sun's setting rays in front of me. I follow it, forcing my pace to stay leisurely and ignoring the demanding urge to run. *Not yet.* The path curves to the left, taking me to a small bridge that overlooks the aquamarine stream below and then to the tree that anchors the garden.

The air is heavy with the perfumed scent of flowers, their petals gleaming with white crystals that flare just outside my peripheral vision. The floral bundles attached to the curved branches sway in the cool air, sending lavender-colored petals to the ground. I stand right where I did when I asked Rhea to marry me, the tree as my background and the rest of the garden in the forefront. I had spent so much time in this place as a child, its refuge one that allowed me to stay hidden while also being a safe space to explore my magic without the council critiquing my every move. And now it holds the memory of the moment she said yes. Of the joy that shined on her face and the way her body molded to mine as if this was all she could ever need. As if *I* was.

My knees hit the emerald grass, the ground's warmth bleeding through my pants as I pull my hand from my pocket and open it in front of me. Rhea's engagement ring sparkles out here, just like it did on the day I gave it to her. Cradling it, I rest my hand against my thigh and let my head hang between my shoulders. I know the consequences of what I'm about to do. How it will likely leave my family in chaos. How the council will use my actions as an excuse to strip us of our right to the throne. I understand that I *do* have a choice, that waiting is a smarter, more strategic move. I know all of this, yet none of it will change my mind. None of it will stop me.

Squeezing the ring tightly enough to imprint it on my skin, I enjoy one more moment of silence before everything comes crumbling down.

Chapter Twenty-Eight

ARIA

WHEN IT COMES TO the actions of the siren queen, nothing is ever done without intention. My mother knows how to rile a crowd just as easily as she draws a male to his death, and she does both with the kind of flourish that sends my heart sinking to my stomach with dread.

She had gathered my sisters and I the night before last, asking for updates on the research Dyanna is helping her with—something to do with the type of magic the mages possess—and on the missing sirens. I had no information to give her, but neither did Sade, and our mother had simply glared at my older sister long enough that her displeasure with us all was clear. I know we can't come back to her empty-handed again, but I have no clue how I'm supposed to pretend to find them while actively knowing where at least *one* of the sirens could be found. I had gone to my cave of treasures that night to leave Nia a message, begging her to give me *something* that I could turn in to the queen to give the illusion that progress was being made. I intend to head back after the address to see if she responded.

I glance to Lyre at my left, taking in the swell of her belly. So much is dependent on me learning how to protect her. To protect her babe. I *need* something from Nia to appease my mother for now so that I can continue meeting with Myla without fear of being watched.

Queen Amari bangs her trident on the dais once, silencing the excited sirens in front of us. "My subjects, welcome. Welcome." Her voice booms over the throne room, and every siren flinches from its power. From the way it rolls through the water as strong as any current. My mother has always commanded attention and fealty, but our people's zealous love for her has grown. As if they too can sense a shift happening in Olymazi, one they intend to benefit from. "Thank you all for coming today," she begins, looking out over the crowd. "In my time as your queen, my goals have been simple: to keep our people from fading away beneath the surface and to make those who trapped us here pay. The War Of Five Kingdoms should have *never* happened, but because of the arrogance of men, we were forced to raid the land and fight to take what was rightfully ours. It resulted in our banishment by the traitorous mages, stuck behind a Spell constructed by their queen. Well, I have just learned that the mages have been keeping a secret all this time." The crowd murmurs to each other while their eyes stay locked on my mother. "They can pass through the Spell without losing their magic or life."

Voices raise as the females in front of the dais lift their arms in frustration, shouting out their displeasure at this discovery. I have no doubt that my mother has known this information long before we watched Rhea use her magic on the beach, and I'm terrified to wonder why she is choosing *now* to share it with everyone.

The queen taps her trident on the white stone again, and the sirens quiet once more. "I know, it is shocking to learn that we have been lied to. That others have given themselves an advantage while we are left with only scraps. Our numbers have steadily been declining, the rate of reproduction lower than ever. We have been suppressed beneath the surface for over two hundred years, and now our kind is bearing that weight in the form of a weakening species. Just as those above *wanted*."

Jewel-toned heads nod ferociously. Their frenzy coaxes anxiousness within me, and my heart rattles in my chest as I watch them.

"But there is hope on the horizon, my beloved sirens." Her voice softens, and everyone leans in a little closer, chomping at the bait she dangles before them. "Soon, we shall have what we are owed. Soon, our kind will again walk above water without fear of persecution or death. Without fear of the Spell! But, before that can happen, I need your support. I need my subjects now more than ever!" My pulse beats at my throat, the steady undulation of my tail growing a little choppier. I cast a sideways look down the line of my sisters, noting Allegra's smugness and the stern set of Sade's brows. Dyanna has her hands clasped behind her back, her gaze lost on something above the crowd. Only Lyre returns my look, the same concern I feel reflecting back in her amethyst eyes. "Turn to your sister next to you and ask yourself, are you willing to do whatever it takes to keep her safe?"

They respond with a resounding "Yes!"

"Look at your queen and ask yourself, are you willing to do whatever it takes to keep *me* safe?"

Screams of agreement answer.

"You are loyal to your people. You are loyal to me, and so I know it will honor you deeply when I say that, beginning today, one siren from every family will be asked to join their legion sisters, if they have not already."

Years of practice not reacting to my mother's words or actions fails me in that moment, as my eyes grow wide and my head snaps to look at her, catching Allegra's waiting glare as I do. Joining the Queen's Legion has always been optional; never once in our history—not even during the war—has it ever been forced upon a siren. But what had the sirens in Eersten said while I was traveling to the Northern Island? That our mother had ordered that some of them be taken into the legion as payment for not having the number of offspring required? Why would she do that? And why would there be more needed beyond that?

Lyre's shoulder gently brushes mine, a reminder to reel myself in. My eyes scan over the throne room, and while most of those gathered here seem to be exuberant at the idea of joining, I spot a few whose forced grins I recognize. If only because of how many of my own smiles I've had to fake as well. But they are few and far between, and as the majority of the sirens cheer and speak excitedly of what is to come, I can't help but wonder if anyone—Allegra and Sade included—knows what the queen is truly planning.

The cave is blissfully empty when I enter, the soft light of the crystals I have tucked onto the natural stone shelves highlighting the trinkets within. The waters are cooler here, making a shiver bloom over my skin as I swim towards the shelf where the hidden note for Nia was left. It's been replaced, and when I unfold the letter, a gold chain clasped with a purple gem unravels from it.

Nia's letter is brief, offering the necklace as proof of a trail to follow. She tells me to say it was found on the northeastern edge of Lumen, and I can only assume it means that she has led the seamount sirens elsewhere. When I reach the final sentences, my heart skips a beat as I skim over the words.

As you can imagine, staying on the run is a costly endeavor. I've taken some of these treasures as penance for your inaction to help us pay for shelter and food. The longer you take to retrieve our weapons, the longer we will be forced to hide. And the longer I will keep removing and selling your little trinkets.

"No," I whisper to myself, looking up from Nia's letter to inspect the shelves. With so many items lining the walls, one might have assumed that I wouldn't have a clue which ones have gone missing. But as I look around, I spot the newly empty spaces. A jeweled bracelet that had been stored next to the lion's head pin is now gone. Some daggers I had laid side by side are absent, the empty space between a bundle of rings and a small mirror showcasing their absence. More gaps between items become obvious to me, and I slump onto the cave floor, crushing Nia's note in my hand.

I shouldn't care. These items were never mine, just odds and ends I pulled from the ocean floor. Old things that belonged to someone who once lived and was now nothing more than bone and decay in our waters. I shouldn't have cared, but I did. *I do.* Because collecting these things has always been about more than just displaying them. It was my way to pay tribute. To try and absolve myself, in a way, for the cruelty of my kind. Of my mother and sisters. Nia had taken something precious and reduced it to its weight in coins, and while I understand that they are desperate, I'm angry that she decided on *this.* That she stole my cave and then stole the memories in it.

If I can no longer ease my conscience this way, what other redemption is there for me? But then I remember Lyre and her hands on her belly, a babe she already loves enough to risk everything for. Perhaps my time trying to appease my guilt is no longer meant for the dead but for the living.

Picking up the necklace Nia left, I destroy her letter and leave the cave, eager for my next meeting with Myla—if only to be one step closer to keeping someone I love safe.

❧ ❧

Myla's attitude today rivals all of my previous interactions with her, a feat that feels like it should be etched on the stone walls of the cavern we are training in for future generations to read. The fae, who I thought had already shown me what her ire looked like, had apparently unlocked a deeper level of hatred in our time apart. Every question I ask and every time I stumble with my footwork, I'm met with a scowl that could rival a dragon's. If the winged beasts even do such a thing. She's hardly spoken a word more than necessary, nothing beyond "here" as she handed me a black button-up tunic when I first arrived.

The fabric is stiff against my skin, the length of the clothing suggesting that its owner is larger than Myla. Perhaps it belongs to a former lover. Maybe it's that of the male who rides the blue dragon.

"Focus." Myla's voice snaps me out of my thoughts and to where she is standing in front of me, her arms folded over her chest.

She wears her all-black uniform, the tattered cloak hanging from her shoulders pinned in place by bronze chains. A dragon insignia decorates one shoulder, and it makes me wonder if Myla has her own dragon to ride. My gaze travels down the long lines of her body, the curvature of her muscle noticeable even beneath the leathers that she wears. From the clothing to her obvious mastery of weapons, even the lithe way she moves, all points to a female who's been turned into a predator. I might find it admirable, if her attitude didn't thoroughly sour any feelings of admiration.

"You're wasting my time." Her boot gently taps the inside of my ankle, the one that works my scarred foot. "This is your weakest spot, which isn't saying much considering the whole of you is nearly just as bad."

My cheeks burn at her jab, even though worse has been said about me. Done *to* me. What was the weight of a few more words added on top of an already crumbling structure? "Can you show me how to do it again?"

With effort, she bites back whatever piercing retort she has and resumes the stance she wants me to mirror. I follow suit, the muscles in my legs and feet straining to hold the position as her eyes move over my body impassively, down and up, before she lifts her arms in front of her. "Make fists and show me your guard."

I don't know what exactly she means by *guard*, but I mimic the way her elbows bend and how her arms block from her chin down to her chest. Even with Myla's legs bent slightly, her height still forces my chin up to make eye contact with her. But she avoids holding my gaze, instead focusing on all the parts of my body she clearly finds unsatisfactory. I can understand her hatred of my kind, even if I don't know why *she* specifically carries it so strongly, but her disgust when she looks at *me* leaves me feeling two feet tall. It's why I can't keep myself from asking, "Why do you hate me so much?"

Not even the length of a breath passes before she answers. "Sirens started a war that led to the death of members of my family." Her dark eyes lift to meet mine for a moment, and they pierce through me like the cold waters of winter. "Don't let your guard fall," she says, dropping her gaze.

I lift my arms up again and put that small bend in my knees that Myla has. "You had family that fought in The War Of Five Kingdoms too?" I ask carefully. I can't tell her I am a siren princess, my self-preservation warning me that if she knew, she would likely defy the rules of the life debt between us and kill me anyway, no matter the cost. I had lost Mashaka. I live in constant fear of losing Lyre. Perhaps this can be a unifying thread between us. At least enough to soften her anger towards me.

"We aren't talking about this."

Or maybe not.

"How are you so stiff? I assumed that one of the sirens' only admirable qualities was that they were elegant in the way they moved. Yet you're proving me wrong with every minute that passes in your presence."

"I am not used to doing this"—I drop my guard to gesture at my body—"on land." Not that I was used to doing anything like this in the water either, but voicing that doesn't seem wise.

"This is such a fucking mistake," she growls, prowling to the other side of the cavern. "I would have more luck trying to teach a dragon to wield a sword." She looks over her shoulder at me. "At least then there would be some honor in that."

Pressure builds behind my eyes, my frustration mounting behind an already weakened façade. "Well, maybe if you were a better teacher—"

Her eyes flare, and in a movement so quick I can't even track it, she unstraps one of the daggers sheathed at her thighs and hurls it. The dagger's zips right past me, and my responding gasp is already seconds past the sound of the dagger hitting the stone at my back. I look down when I feel something tickling my foot to see a small collection of my ruby strands dusting the floor around me.

Mouth agape, my gaze snaps back to hers. "What are you—"

But Myla is already moving again, the look on her face so intense as she closes the distance between us that I retreat from it—from *her*. "My patience is thin, Little Siren. A fragile thread that has frayed nearly to destruction, so I need you to understand that I mean it when I say that I am *already* tired of watching you flounder beneath my instruction." Our chests heave in tandem, the small stream of sunlight coming in from a gap in the rocks above us highlighting that bronze dragon on Myla's shoulder. I can't help but look at it, the sight of the beast forged in metal serving as a reminder of just who this female is. Her lip peels back with a snarl as she adds, "You claim to have a reason for wanting to train, to fight, but you have given me nothing to work with beyond a doe-eyed gaze and a less than functional body."

Beneath the shame her words conjure, the embarrassment and voice inside my head that agrees with her, a small spark of something hot and fierce ignites. I *do* have something to fight for. *Someone* to fight for. And as my eyes narrow in on hers, I wade into unknown waters for the first time *ever* as I stand up for myself.

Chapter Twenty-Nine

ARIA

"**Y**OU ARE NOT THE only one who has to *suffer* through these meetings, Myla," I growl. I actually *growl*, the smooth resonance of my voice echoing around me as my magic pulses at my throat. Her expression doesn't change, the practiced way she leaves her emotions tucked beneath indifference only making that spark within glow brighter. "I am not like *you*. I was not just born with the ability to carry myself as if no one else matters, and even if I was, you have *no* idea what I have gone through. What I have been forced to do, no matter how much I didn't want to."

She laughs, but the sound skates over me like a serrated blade. "You think I did not have to work for the abilities I have? That they just came naturally, without effort?"

I give her a pointed look. She may have needed to learn specific skill sets, but her very being was built for lethality. Whether she wants to recognize it or not, she has an advantage that I don't. Especially here above the surface of the water.

Myla shakes her head, her hands bracing her hips as she turns to the side, once more avoiding my gaze. "I have had to fight for every single thing in my life. Every bit of freedom that is given so easily to so many who are undeserving of it. And that's what this is—what training and learning how to fight gives. *Freedom.*" Her lips form a perfect line as she leans in a little closer. My nostrils flare at the scent of her, noticing for the first time that she smells like vanilla but harsher. As if the sweet plant had been thrown in the fire, tainting the ashes with its floral familiarity. "Hear me when I say this, *Aria*. The most dangerous person you face will always be the one willing to do whatever it takes."

The way my name slices from her mouth prompts a shiver to work its way up my spine, and I find I can't look away from her. Even as shadows gather in her eyes.

"What are you willing to do to get whatever it is you want? Who are you willing to *become*?" She pulls back from me, cool air rushing in as I inhale deeply. "Only when you can *show* me the answers to those questions will I stop considering our lessons a waste of my fucking time. Life debt aside, I can't make you care enough about what is motivating you. Only you can do that. Start in the first position," she says, gesturing with her chin to my legs.

It takes me a moment to follow her instructions, my mind still trying to latch on to everything she's said. And everything she didn't. But I attempt to push it all away as I try to focus, except for the two questions that hit exactly where that spark inside of me glows. *What are you willing to do to get whatever it is you want? What are you willing to become?* I might not have known before Lyre, might not have had a concrete enough answer that was worth fighting for. Because without my sister, there is only me, and I'm certainly not worth the effort it is going to take to survive escaping from beneath my mother's trident. But for Lyre? For her and her unborn babe? I could do it because they *are* worth fighting for.

⁕⁕⁕⁕⁕⁕⁕⁕

Myla climbs onto the back of the dragon, ignoring me even as the fae male with her offers a friendly smile and wave of his hand. While I had grown up fearing males—avoiding them as much as possible because of what being near one meant—I can't help but return his friendly gesture with one of my own. I watch as the blue dragon carries him and Myla back through the shimmering Spell, its own scales reflecting light in a glittering display of iridescence. Once they are small specks against the mountainous backdrop of the Fae Kingdom, I return to the water and begin my journey back to Lumen.

It's evening by the time I arrive, clutching my satchel with the necklace tucked firmly inside it as I make my way through the palace to find Sade. When I can't find her in the main areas on the first floor, I swim up to the second, stopping in front of the door to her room. My knocks go unanswered, and I am in the middle of trying to scrape enough confidence together to brave visiting the garrison to see if she is there when the hair on the back of my neck lifts and dread unexpectedly pools low in my stomach. I spin around, bubbles rising from my swishing tail, and can't contain that shriek that tumbles out of me when I come face-to-face with Lore.

"Aria," she purrs, swimming close enough to plant her hands to either side of me on Sade's door, her chest brushing against my own, "I've been looking for you."

I swallow roughly, Lore tracking the movement of my throat. "Lore," I rasp, pressing back against the cool glass of the door.

She tilts her head to the side, letting her eyes drift down to my mouth where they linger as she draws her tongue out to swipe her bottom lip. "Where were you? I couldn't find you in any of your usual places. Not even the ones you try to hide in." Her face nuzzles into the crook of my neck as she drags her tongue along my skin, cold water immediately rushing in to wash the warm touch away.

But I still feel it, even as I push her back with a hand against her chest, her lips forming a pout. "What's the matter?"

"I— Nothing. I just— I'm looking for my sister." My hand gestures to the door behind me. "I have something for her."

Lore's eyes—their golden color stark against her dark skin—shine with an all-too-familiar look, making my thoughts race back to our last interaction together. I drop my hands from her, letting my talons push out from the tips of my fingers. "Surely, you can spare a few moments for us?" she drawls, lifting a hand from the door as she takes note of my talons, letting hers show as well. She drags the dark claw down my arm slowly, watching the goosebumps that bloom behind it. "You're always so reactive to my touch."

"I can't," I manage to squeeze out from the cavity that forms in my chest, my head growing dizzy. I don't want her to touch me. I haven't wanted her touch in a long time, not since the day she stood in the crowd of people gathered the very first time I was forced to perform my duty as a siren daughter. Every time I look into her bright eyes, I see the moment she watched with a small smile on her face. She didn't cheer as the other sirens in the crowd had. She didn't glare at my mother for forcing the person she said she loved to do something she clearly did not want to do. No, that luminous gaze stayed pinned on me while the rest of her body remained impassive. Inactive. Unwilling to risk her flesh to save my own. No one had ever done it—no one except Mashaka.

She leans in again, forcing my arm to bend beneath her strength as she grasps my chin in her hand. "We both know that fighting against this is pointless. Especially when I can see the way I affect you, Aria. Words are one thing, but our bodies..." Her lips find my neck again, just above my gills, and I squeeze my eyes shut.

The most dangerous person you will ever face is the one willing to do whatever it takes. Myla's words taunt me, bouncing from ear to ear. It is something ruthless like my mother would say, but gods, if it doesn't invoke a different feeling coming from that fae. I had let not just Lore, but my mother and Allegra and nearly every other siren I had come in contact with have their way with me. I had *let* them and now... Holding Lore's gaze, I wrap my fingers around her shoulders, the tips of my talons making her release a hiss as I drive them into her skin. Strangely, my magic gathers at the base of my throat, throbbing with the quick pace of my heart as those words repeat. That spark, small but undeniable, flares again, and I open my mouth, prepared to refuse her. To *truly* refuse her, but I'm denied the opportunity when a different voice booms down the hall.

"Please don't fuck in front of my door." Lore and I both turn to see my sister swimming in place, her shell armor adorning her shoulders and chest, while her helmet is tucked beneath one arm.

"We were just about to leave—"

"I found something while out on my search today," I interrupt Lore, dropping my hands to my satchel and biting back a sigh of relief when she swims back a few paces to make room for Sade to come between us. "Belonging to the seamount sirens, I think. I can show you now if you're ready."

Lore's eyes narrow, but I turn my gaze to Sade, whose own look of suspicion is much more tolerable. The three of us float in the hallway, an awkward tension pulling so tightly that for a moment, I'm afraid Sade is just going to dismiss me and leave me to Lore's demands. But she resigns with a clenched jaw and jerk of her head towards her door, unlocking and opening it. "Show me."

Adrenaline rushes through me as I bolt into the room, looking over my shoulder at Lore. She forces a smile to her face, giving me a look that promises I'll be seeing her again soon, before Sade closes the door and my shoulders inadvertently sag with relief. Perhaps this is what I deserve as punishment for what I had done as a siren. Though the intention differs between what I was forced to do and what Lore has repeatedly chosen to do, does it matter? If, in the end, there is an unwilling victim, do the details of what drove the perpetrator make a difference? I don't know. I stare at the door while Sade begins removing her armor, and it isn't until I hear her helmet bang onto her vanity that I realize I haven't moved since we entered.

"Aria." Her voice—rough and tired—draws me out of myself. Reaching into my satchel, I glide through the water to her, watching her shake out her braids from the tie they were held in. Though Sade is five decades older than me, it would be impossible to tell from looks alone. Her nose is a touch more slender than mine, and I have freckles dotting my cheeks where she doesn't. But, like all sirens, she has an inherent beauty that makes it impossible to look away.

"I found this today, northeast of Lumen," I tell her as I hand her the gold necklace, hoping that Nia is right in her assumption of Sade's interest.

She turns it over in her hands, taking in the way the gold loops together, and the purple gem attached to it. "I know this necklace," she finally says, a look I can't decipher contorting her features. "It belonged to our grandmother originally but was given to Nia's mother before the war."

I don't acknowledge her response, afraid of giving too much away. Instead, I focus on closing my satchel, catching sight of my dagger's bone-white hilt before I do.

"Northeast you said?"

"Yes. Tangled in a spindle of coral."

She nods, laying the necklace down on her vanity before moving to the bed. "It was likely from when they first left the seamounts. Whenever they were tipped off." She speaks quietly, as if she is working out the details aloud to herself. "I doubt it is from any recent activity."

"Why?"

Sade groans as she collapses onto the silk-covered eelgrass, her eyes immediately falling shut. "Because I have reason to believe they've gone northwest." At my answering silence, she draws a single eye open, lifting the accompanying eyebrow as she does. "It's simple, really. The seamount sirens are a large group, but they can't stay together, or it would be too easy to spot them. You and I aren't the only ones going out to search for them." A yawn interrupts her. "As such, they will need to move in smaller groups so as not to draw attention. And they would want to get away as fast as possible and find somewhere to hide on the path with least resistance. If they go northeast, they'll have to go around the fae side of the Continent, and this time of year, the water is only going to be colder and more rough that way. It'll be dangerous for any of the offspring and elderly who cannot keep up."

Sade's gaze catches on my hands fidgeting with the strap of my satchel, and I force them to still.

"But if they go northwest? There's plenty of small outposts for them to hide in. No one will think they are anything but sirens traveling back and forth, selling wares or whatever excuse they come up with." *Shit.* Nia had all but exclaimed this was exactly what they were doing. "And then there is Eersten." My blood runs cold, the tips of my nails digging into the scales at my hips.

"What about Eersten?"

My sister pushes herself onto her elbows as she studies me, her brows creasing together for a moment before she releases them slowly. "Ah, yes, you would have likely stayed there on your way to the Northern Island. A feat, I have to say, I did not think you would accomplish."

"Thanks," I mutter, to which she actually chokes out a noise that sounds like a laugh.

"Don't sound so offended, Little Sister. The look on Allegra's face when she learned you had returned was worth its weight in gold. But Eersten has always been a place that has caught our mother's attention because of the sirens that live there. If the seamount sirens think they can hide there, they are wrong."

Sade then dismisses me from her room, citing that the reason she is so tired is because of the *fucking disaster* the Queen's Legion has turned into after our mother's announcement.

Reaching my room, I groan as I lay on my bed, placing my hands over my eyes and replaying the day's events in my head. If Sade already suspects Nia's next move with the seamount sirens, there is no telling how quickly she will find them. Can I truly stand by and watch as the siren queen slaughters them? *The most dangerous person you will face is the one willing to do whatever it takes*. Myla's voice echoes in my mind, and as sleep eludes me, a single question taunts me well into the next morning: Who am I willing to become?

Chapter Thirty

MYLA

THE OPAL BROTHEL IS the best one in Khargis, and that isn't exactly saying much. A bar makes up the front of the establishment, the only drinks served the kind that hurt going down. Leading to the worn wooden bar top is a collection of mismatched tables and chairs, occupants gathered around them as they scout which female to claim for the evening. While cleaner than its competitors, this place in the center of the poorest district of Khargis is still filled with the normal assortment of trash. Rich males doing a terrible job hiding their extramarital affairs from their wives. Drunks spending coin they don't have on bodily pleasures instead of feeding their children. Lurking in the corners are those of an even seedier variety—males for hire that work efficiently and don't ask questions. They are mirrored by females whose gift for blending in allows them to hear all. And then there is me. A princess shunned by her own kingdom. Believed to be a curse set upon the fae for their discretions during the war. A punishment from the gods.

I toss back my shot of liquor, enjoying the way it burns as it coats my throat.

To believe in the existence of *gods* is to admit that you are alright with someone fucking with your life, controlling you as if you are nothing more than a puppet attached to taut strings. I have enough of that existence here in the corporeal plane of my kingdom. I don't need it from some made up illusion of power that has never been seen or heard from. *The will of the gods* is what Father Yamin calls it during his pretentious hours' long sermons, and that will is something only he and the other high-ranking holy males of the church can decipher, apparently. Our people are to continue begging for forgiveness, continue showing their piety in order to find redemption from the equivalent of ghosts in the skies. I may have tarnished every decent bone in my body over the last half a decade, but even *I* believe that threatening torture to get good behavior isn't a way to lead the people. I could laugh at the hypocrisy.

The bartender—a fae who looks no older than myself with greasy black hair and beady little eyes—props himself up on the counter across from me. "Another drink, princess?" I snort and shake my head. He uses the nickname as an insult, noting that because I don't look as if I haven't showered in weeks, I must be as *high maintenance as the royal family living in their fancy stone palace*. It is ironic, and yet I hope the silly nickname won't come back to bite me in the ass. "Your favorite is here; she's just off with another customer."

I clench my jaw, my fingers curling into my black leather pants as I look away. Of all the brothels that dot the landscape in the bowels of this city, I always return to this one. It seems my repeated presence is beginning to breed a sense of familiarity, and for the sake of my larger mission, I can't allow it to continue. I delay leaving, ordering one final shot to avoid having to squat for hours on a nearby roof as I wait for my target to exit the bar he likes to frequent, when I'm hit with the scent of blackberries. My body immediately relaxes, the aroma working to help me draw in a calmer breath. *Fuck.* Familiarity indeed.

There are no excuses now—this will have to be my last time here.

Turning from the bar, I spot the owner of the delicate scent. She gives me a small smirk and quick nod of her head before disappearing down the hallway that leads to her room. The bartender behind me chuckles as I drop a few coins for my drinks with a glare. While known for his lewd comments and lascivious gaze, Ayan has never actually touched anyone without their consent. Word in brothels spreads easily amongst the females who keep it afloat, and no one has ever complained of having a negative experience with him. It's the reason he's still alive.

My boots stick to the floor as I walk down the dark hallway, leaving the noisier half of the brothel behind for where the actual business takes place. Each door I pass contains a cacophony of noises—moans and grunts and the occasional muffled plea. My delicate sensibilities had been scandalized by all the different ways pleasure could be found when I first came here. But I had been different then, a little more full of hope and a little less intrigued by the darkness that wrapped itself around me.

The door to Karina's room is left ajar, and I quietly push it open and slip in, the scent of blackberries intensifying—along with the smell of the others who have been here. "I'm just going to wash up!" she shouts from the small bathroom attached, her voice echoing off the tile.

"Take your time." In truth, I had plenty to kill before I needed to leave. The target I am hunting tonight will spend an ungodly amount of coin at the bar, likely harass a few females while he is there, and then have his carriage take him to the *other* side of Khargis. Where the homes are as elegantly crafted as the palace itself, built into the mountainside so they can look down upon those who live and work at the mountain's base.

Karina's soft voice hums from the shower as I sit on the edge of her bed and begin untying the laces of my boots. Her room is always clean, the sheets on her bed swapped between customers. Candles of every shape and size are placed throughout, making shadows dance on the walls. Karina hadn't been my introduction to sexual gratification, but she had been the first to see me as more than a paying customer. It's been years of indulging in her company—something that brings me pleasure that I don't often allow myself. But it has to end tonight.

The shower finally turns off, and the rustling noises of Karina drying herself encourage me to move a little faster. Steam billows out of the bathroom, the mist parting when she steps through, her naked skin flushed from the shower. "It's been a while," she says, running her hand through her white hair, the stark color an anomaly amongst the fae. Her dark skin is interrupted by patches of pure white, creating a unique and beautiful pattern that I've traced my tongue over time and time again. She crawls onto the bed, night-colored eyes meeting my own as she braces her hands on either side of my shoulders. A necklace dangles in the air between us, and I lift my hand to caress it between my fingers.

"It has, and you will not see me again after this."

She watches as my brows draw low when I realize that the necklace is made of *seashells*. Their flat surface is dotted with ridges and specks of iridescent color. Just like Aria's scales. Karina chuckles. "What thought is causing such a serious face?"

Flashes of Aria's luminous skin, her scales inset along her body like some magical piece of art, come to me unbidden. I let go of the necklace and instead weave my hand into Karina's hair, guiding her down to me. There is nothing sweet about the way our mouths collide, the taste of her flooding my tongue as her body drapes over mine and I use her to chase away the images of the ruby-haired siren who has become the bane of my existence. Her fingers trail down my body, sliding into the indent of my waist before coasting over my hip and then finding the warmth between my legs. There is a comfort in the way she touches me, as much as I hate to admit such a vulnerability.

Karina had given attention to what I liked from the very beginning, only because it was her job to. I paid her well and got out of her hair the moment we were done, and she gave me a momentary break from the constant fear I lived in before I knew what it was to *be* a weapon. To find some sort of solace in the fae I killed who actually deserved it. But before I was Khargis's Shadow, I was just a pathetic, lost female, teetering on the edge of a blade that promised to slice me no matter which way I moved. The events that led to my full ostracization began with a sweet-talking pair of lips and a head full of silky raven hair. And in the destruction, I realized that love could never be anything more than a weakness. I had fallen in love once—let myself be bared to another because I had believed that, no matter what, she held my heart as carefully as I held hers. Never again would I be so weak.

"Is this truly the last time?" Karina says softly, dragging her lips over my neck and down to my collarbone.

"Yes."

"Then we will make sure you are properly taken care of before you leave." Nothing more is spoken as she kisses her way down my body, her head settling between my widely spread legs. I squeeze my eyes shut and let myself melt at her touch, let myself pretend for the briefest of moments that I'm somebody with a soul. That I have freedoms that aren't hidden in the shadows cast by my father's rule. I give myself this single illusion of happiness.

Later, I slip back into the darkness of the city, my hood pulled up and my mask covering the lower half of my face as I return to my purpose. With my blades strapped to my body, I *am* the weapon the vulnerable need. And until I can bond a dragon, that will have to be enough.

❧ ❧

My gaze flicks to where Sir Dae hangs attached to the metal hook and chain—unconscious with his feet dangling a few inches above the ground. The flame gems I have placed around the room highlight his sharp cheekbones and full mouth while strands of black hair frame his face, the rest of it pulled back into a neat braid. As far as males who have hung in front of me go, he might be the prettiest one I've ever caught. The bastard had put up a decent struggle, though, and our scuffle in the alleyway had not only left me surprised that he knew how to fight at all but also with a bruised rib and a swollen eye where he had landed well-timed punches. I try to avoid hits to my face at all costs because, even though I am mostly hidden beneath the veil I am required to wear in the palace, I never know when Leesi will show up to dress me. And I am under no preconceived notion that she would keep the discovery of a mysterious wound on me to herself.

Sir Dae's body jerks as he gasps for a breath, *finally* regaining consciousness. I pace around him as he slowly wakes and observes his surroundings in a calmer manner than I would have anticipated. Most immediately panic, their bodies recognizing the danger they are in before their minds do. But this male just looks around the darkened chamber as if he's mapping out every corner in his mind to see which will yield his best chance at escape. Maybe he is. The thought brings a smile to my face.

"Hello." I drop my voice deep enough to hide its femininity, beginning one of my favorite games. "Welcome to my workshop."

"Where am I?"

"In Khargis," I answer, walking around him until I'm at his back. I wait for him to thrash, as they all do, to keep me in his line of sight. But the male stays still, his breathing *relaxed*.

"Not just Khargis, but in the lower district," he counters, halting my steps. At the silence that builds between us, he adds, "This area has a certain *odor* to it. It clings to the buildings and the people, making it very distinguishable to a sensitive nose."

I resume my pacing, letting a hand slide to one of the daggers strapped to my thigh. "Fair enough, though the smell can't be too offensive to a male who spends so much time in this district." I keep my eyes trained on him, smirking beneath my mask when he tenses for the briefest second before relaxing again.

"So you've been keeping tabs on me."

"Oh, much more than that, Sir Dae." I stop once I'm in front of him again, drumming my fingers along the outside of my leg. "I know that you run a collection of businesses in Khargis, ranging from clothing shops to apothecaries to the occasional bakery and tavern."

"Diversifying one's income is never a bad thing."

"I *also* know that you have a wife and children at home, and yet when you aren't working, you spend your evenings here. In the lower district you seem to despise so much."

He lets loose a chuckle, and my vision flashes red before I tame my ire. "My family is taken care of. They want for nothing."

"Except a loyal husband and father."

He laughs again, shaking his head before laying it against his arm, flexing his hands where they are restrained above his head. "Spoken like someone who has longed for something they could never have. My wife's class was lower than my own. Marrying her was seen as a *kindness*, and she acts as such. Our children attend the finest schools and have full bellies every day. They will grow up and lead as the next generation to carry my name. My loyalty to them is in all that I provide, not what I do to chase my own pleasures once they sleep."

"Do you allow your wife to *chase* her own pleasures while you are gone?" The flattening of his lips answers my question before any words can leave his mouth. "Precisely. Your claims of generosity, I'm afraid, fall upon deaf ears. Because I know what your so-called *pleasures* are." The sound of my dagger sliding from its sheath draws his gaze to my thigh.

"There is nothing wrong with partaking in a hobby to relieve stress."

I tilt the blade in my hand, letting the light from a nearby flame gem reflect off of the sleek metal. "I think the females you brutalize would disagree."

"And I think that the opinions of birds matter not to a cat."

My jaw clenches, but I force my movements to stay steady—controlled. This game is mine, and while Sir Dae may be a skilled opponent, his moves are limited to only what he aims to rile out of me. There's a sadistic thrill at having someone who counters my moves enough to keep me entertained. Even if I know that, in the end, the justice of my blade will still prevail.

"You know, so many of those from the higher districts don't believe you to be real, despite the way your reputation precedes you." I watch him track the movement of my blade as I toss it up in front of me, catching it by the hilt and then doing it again. "I know, down here, they treat you as a hero. Their vigilante come to rescue them from the evil that walks among them. But up there, up the mountain where the sidewalks glitter with gold and the air isn't tainted with a rotten stench, the fae that *matter* can't believe anyone would waste their time killing scum over some childish idea of *righteousness*."

"What makes you think there is any sort of morality to the way I kill? Perhaps I just enjoy the sound they make as I flay their skin from their muscles."

"I don't doubt that plays a part. It is quite a *unique* feeling to force someone to confront death early, isn't it? All the confidence in the world can shatter easily once someone realizes that their next breath might be their last. There is something *intoxicating* about it."

I get close enough for Sir Dae to see into my eyes. To see, even in only the amber light of the flame gems, the way they glisten at the prospect of doing just that. "Glad to see we are in agreement." I flick my wrist to angle my dagger, and like a hot knife through butter, I dig into him as I drag a line across his chest.

Chapter Thirty-One

MYLA

HE HISSES A SHARP sound through his teeth, crimson blood pooling beneath his finely tailored tunic. "Fucking bastard!"

I click my tongue and resume my walking, wiping my blade on his clothing as I do. "I thought we were on the same page? To think I found someone who might understand me," I tease, my words met with a forced laugh.

"We are surely more alike than you think."

"Shall we compare? I'll go first. I enjoy killing those who believe themselves to be exempt from any kind of consequence. Your turn."

The sound of blood dripping into the dirt sends a jolt of satisfaction through me, but it's interrupted when Sir Dae speaks through a labored breath. "I enjoy giving value to females who, otherwise, would be nothing more than a waste of space and air."

I snap forward and cut into his chest again, creating an 'x'. *Control.* I am in control.

"Rape and torture hardly seem like things one should be grateful for, let alone find value in," I respond.

He attempts a shrug, grunting as he moves. "It gives them a story, and I pay them handsomely for their time."

This time, it's me who laughs as I round his hanging body, coming to his side. "A story? What is a story to someone who is no longer themselves because of what you've done to them?"

"It's more than they had before."

"Pathetic," I growl, digging my dagger into the space between his ribs. "The way males think themselves above the world."

A deep noise rumbles from his throat, but he doesn't whimper in pain. "Why should we believe differently when the gods themselves designed it this way?"

I am *sick* of hearing about the gods and their so-called *divine* rule. Sick of the males who believe these gods speak directly to them and for their own benefit.

And I am fucking *tired* of not hearing this male scream.

I slam the blade into his ribs until the hilt meets his skin, finally rewarded with a guttural shout that echoes off the walls. As if realizing that he can make such a noise, he begins shouting again, his previously calm demeanor evaporating.

"Look at that," I muse, yanking the blade out and then wiping his blood on his cheek, laughing when I see the tear that stains the skin there. "You bleed as equally as any whore. As any female or peasant or anyone else you believe yourself to be above." Reaching up, I tug the black cloth covering half my face down and let my natural voice come to the surface. "And you'll die the same as them too."

Sir Dae's eyes—glossy and red—focus on my features, bouncing back and forth between my delicately pointed chin and the fullness of my lips. I'm denied the shock and surprise I'm yearning for when he scoffs instead, lifting his head away from mine. "When you're caught and the kingdom realizes it is a female who has been pretending as you have, they will show you no mercy."

I nod as I stand before him, my fingers clutching the frayed hilt of my dagger. "I'm beyond mercy, and as you mentioned yourself, no one cares about what I'm doing."

"If you kill me, they will care."

I smile wide enough to show my elongated canines. "Because you're so important?"

"Killing me has consequences beyond just saving those no one else cares about. You're an *amateur*, and it shows."

"Maybe," I acknowledge. Sir Dae *is* one of the most high profile targets I have ever gone after. It had taken months of meticulously tracking the victims with my informant for us to figure out who was responsible for leaving them in such horrific states. Because of his noble name and the money associated with it, Sir Dae has been able to pay to keep mouths shut. I can only threaten so many people before *I* become at risk of being exposed. Maybe killing him will amplify that risk. But maybe I don't fucking care.

His torture is slow and meticulous as I cut into is soft flesh over and over again. Yet, for all the pain I inflict, not once does he beg me to stop, and when he finally stops breathing and new blood stops layering atop the old, I find that the usual sense of relief I feel after a night like this is absent. Instead, something I can't quite name takes residence in the hole in my chest. Something darker and more like dread than I've ever felt before. I push it down, leaving it to fester within me like everything else while I work on disposing of Sir Dae's body.

I wrap my cloak more firmly around my shoulders, the fabric doing a half decent job at warding off the late-night chill. Stars flicker above me, the silver light of the moon shining down between the pines as I make my way from my warehouse to Bali and Sunis's cave. There are still a few hours until the sun crests, and while my body aches and my head pounds in time to my steps, I still can't shake that ominous feeling. It chased me the entire journey to the dragon fields, disappearing when I looked over my shoulder only to descend upon me again the moment I turned back around.

Despite the way I turn over Sir Dae's words in my head, searching between them for the reason I feel so *off*, I keep coming back to the same question: What if he was right? Being Khargis's Shadow isn't a completely altruistic venture. It is becoming someone in the dark that I can't be in the light. I am feared. I am respected. I am *someone*. What if tonight, I had thrown that all away *because* there is no line I am unwilling to cross?

The scent of sulfur is strong when I finally break from the trees and step onto the gravel outside of the cave. To my left are more mountains and dragon caves, though they are far enough away that if any beasts are residing within them, I can't tell. To my right, the dragon fields extend for acres. Like the last time I came, piles of remains smolder beneath the remnants of dragon fire, dotting the land in a haunting yellow glow.

I blow out a breath, wincing at the pain at my ribs, and plant my feet on the ground. "Bali!"

Leather wings rustle, a deep rumble answering my call, but I realize too late that it isn't coming from the darkness in front of me. It's coming from *behind*. Heat in the form of a menacing exhale blasts my back, doing nothing to the shot of fear that slides down my spine like ice. Swallowing, I turn slowly, hoping that giving my back to the cave is the smarter choice, and come face to face with a dragon from the Hiravar line. I stare down the bumps and ridges of his snout, his nostrils angled as he snarls at me, showing off his jagged teeth—some of which are stained with blood. These dragons are the smallest of the three types, but that knowledge is inconsequential when he can still swallow me whole. Round dark green scales frame a pair of glossy, luminous yellow eyes, and I only hold the dragon's glare for a moment before I drop my own to the ground.

Everything Navin has told me about dragons and everything I have read about the different breeds myself rushes through me at once, the information categorizing itself as I recall what the fuck I am supposed to do in this situation. With an active bond, there is a given level of protection from another's dragon. Without that connection, however, I am no better than any of the unlucky piles of singed bones out on the dragon field.

The ground shakes beneath my boots, sending shockwaves up my legs as a deep growl draws my attention over my shoulder and to the cave. Expecting Bali, I smirk as a black-scaled dragon emerges, the silver light from above pouring over her. Except it isn't the domineering dragon I know rules these fields but her smaller daughter.

"Shit," I whisper, watching as she winds her head from side to side, a warning growl showing off her still very menacing and very sharp teeth. Her claws dig into the ground, sending pebbles and dirt flying with each step she takes. Though she is a younger dragon, her Khar lineage makes her just as big as the green dragon, and when she gives him another thundering roar of warning, she snaps her wings out to the sides, making her appear even larger. Hunching low on her front two legs, she pauses like a cat waiting to pounce. Sandwiched between the two of them, sweat pools on my palms.

The Hiravar dragon doesn't back down, flaring his own wings out as he raises his head, taking a defensive stance against Sunis. My feet are moving before I mentally tell them to, running to the side to get out of the Hiravar's way. The air stirs above me as a green tail slices through it, and I dive onto my stomach, my body connecting with the ground harshly enough for stars to flare behind my eyes. My ribs scream in protest, air punched out of my lungs until I'm left gasping.

Sunis swipes at the Hiravar's chest, her claws scraping against the rough, leathery skin devoid of scales. The green dragon whines, the sound piercing as he backs up a step. A ridiculous amount of pride surges through me as Sunis advances, communicating her displeasure through a series of gruff growls. Pushing myself up to stand, I catch the attention of the Hiravar, his head snapping towards me while those yellow eyes narrow into slits. The sight is terrifying, and I lay my hands on my vest where throwing daggers are sheathed on instinct, despite knowing they will not help me at all. My heart pounds in my throat as I cast a quick look to the cave Sunis came from and to the forest that leads back to the palace. Both options are less than desirable, but staying here will get me killed, and I'd rather not have Sunis fighting for me without our bond in place.

With my decision made, I bolt to my left.

My arms pump at my sides, the roar at my back pushing me faster while my boots pound against the uneven ground as I sprint towards the forest. I don't need to see to know that the green dragon's attention is locked on me. I can feel it on my skin, a primal unease coating me. *Faster.* My thighs burn and my throat goes raw from the air that rushes past it, death lurking a half step behind me and gaining speed.

Pain flares at my ribs from running, just as I realize the ground isn't vibrating with the steps of the dragon chasing me. The moment the thought forms in my mind, I drop to the ground, my arms covering my head as an immense heat more powerful than any sun blasts above me. I scream into the dirt, sure that this is the end.

A rush of cold night air blankets my skin as the dragon fire disappears, but any relief I feel is temporary when I hear what can only be described as a night-shattering howl. Lifting my head, I ensure I truly am alive and not melted into my leathers before pushing up onto all fours, craning my neck to look back at the two dragons. My eyes widen as I watch the Hiravar advance on Sunis, pushing her back towards the cave. *Where he can trap her.* I'm up and running towards the chaos again before I can think it through. Sliding my blades from their sheaths at my ribs, I push myself faster, my ankles nearly twisting as I run over sticks and rocks. The Hiravar swings his tail and strikes Sunis, the dark liquid staining her front making a scream rip from my throat.

He lunges again, sharp teeth closing around her neck and making her roar in pain. She tries to shake him off, but the dragon holds firm, lifting a front leg and dragging his claws over her chest. Fuck, he's going to kill her.

I reach his back foot, jamming my dagger between his round scales. Even though the blade is much too small to cause significant damage, it draws the dragon's attention to me, his head snapping back towards me as he releases Sunis. Those vertical pupils flare wide when he opens his mouth to reveal a flame of swirling orange and yellow and red. I pull the dagger out, sweat sliding into my eyes as I jam it again into a different spot, hoping Sunis takes advantage of the distraction to fly away. The green dragon fills the entirety of my vision, so when I hear wings beating, I assume it's Sunis taking to the sky.

But I'm wrong. I hear her before I see her, a bone-rattling roar filling the air before the ground shakes from the impact of her landing. Bali wastes no time charging forward, and I'm forced to abandon my dagger when the Hiravar moves to defend himself from her. Rolling to my side, I pop up to the left of Bali, bolting to Sunis as I watch her mother sink her teeth into the attacking dragon's neck, inducing a blood-curdling whine. He swings his tail again, aiming directly for Bali's flared wing. But she adjusts effortlessly, keeping her hold on his neck as she snaps her wing in and tips her body to the side. The three spikes scrape against her scales, missing her softer underbelly. She growls around the blood of the now destroyed scales on her opponent's neck as he tries desperately to free himself.

Standing in front of Sunis, I dare a closer look at the wound on her chest. The Hiravar's claws shredded her skin, but the gash doesn't appear too deep, the blood leaking from it already beginning to slow. My stomach settles as I release a breath. *My dragon won't be dying today.*

The green dragon still struggles against Bali's hold on his neck, and it occurs to me then that if she wanted him dead, this would have been over the moment she landed to defend her offspring. No, she is toying with him. He may have been testing his fate against Sunis confidently, but against Bali? All he's done is anger a stronger power.

Bali lifts onto her hind legs with a growl that sounds almost frustrated, the weight of the dragon in her jaw inconsequential before she slams him onto the ground, the weight of her body crashing into his side. The sound he releases is like nothing I've heard one of the beasts make before, and the silence that follows is even more deafening.

Taking a step forward, I see Bali's eyes snap to mine as she finally releases the green dragon, leaving him injured but alive. Fury burns in her gaze as she prowls towards me, but I keep my weary body still. Moving to stand over me, Sunis makes a series of deep chittering sounds while her mother approaches.

Several tense seconds pass, and Sunis bumps her snout against her mother's in some unspoken conversation. Whatever she is trying to communicate makes Bali relent with a flash of her teeth aimed at me before she stalks into the cave. The tension in my jaw releases, only to travel up to my temples, throbbing to the beat of my quick pulse. Sunis lowers her head when I step out from underneath her, tilting it to the side like she did when nudging at her mother. One serpent-like eye stares at me, and though I can't explain why, I lift my hand and lay it against the side of her face. Both of our eyes close at the contact.

Navin described the bond as a slow build of power, like watching the sun rise, until it suddenly snapped into place. He said each pairing has a different look, feel, and color to their bond, its uniqueness dependent on the fae and dragon themselves. Even with my eyes closed, I sense Sunis settling down in front of me. My heart begins to pound for a different reason, excitement amplifying each beat as I search my mind for that bond. A pathway to Sunis that will forever be mine and mine alone.

Each inhale draws her scent towards me—fire and brimstone and ash. I take another step closer, the heat of her mouth so powerful that new sweat layers over the old behind my neck. A line forms between my brows as I search the darkness of my mind, empty hands grasping at nothing over and over and over again. Sunis makes that chittering noise again, and I say her name under my breath to calm her as I peer deeper into my mind. *There!* A flicker in the dark, like a wayward star come to life. I stretch my mind towards it, watching as its size grows and morphs, flashing from white to gray and back again before taking on a slightly pink hue. As if recognizing I am there, the movement halts, the pink light suspended and frozen in time. My stomach lurches, and my hand on Sunis trembles, pressure building behind my eyes as desperation washes over me. *Finally. Fucking finally, it's—*

Sunis pulls away from my touch, and the connection between us severs in an instant.

Chapter Thirty-Two

MYLA

THE GREEN DRAGON WASN'T down long before he stood and hobbled into the dragon fields, ignoring my presence completely. I don't know how much time passes as I stare at the mouth of the cave Sunis retreated into, both daughter and mother now nestled safely within its walls. It's long enough that my disappointment morphed into anger which has now settled into some pathetic version of acceptance. As if I have any say in the matter. "It is progress," I mutter to myself before tugging my hood up and turning towards the forest. I'm halfway there, moving slowly as exhaustion and pain settle into my bones when two dragons crest the treeline ahead of me. I drop into a low crouch, hoping that my black attire will help me blend into the rocky ground as I watch the dragons slow down, making their descent to the middle of the dragon fields.

Shit. Measuring the distance left until I can hide within the pines, I prepare to launch myself forward when the sound of *voices* stops my movements. What are King's Riders doing out on the fields? My brows furrow as I try to recall the last time I saw dragons enter the fields with their bonded. But in the years I've come here, not once have I ever seen anyone other than those sentenced to death.

One of the dragons turns towards me, its head lifting high in the air as it begins to sniff. "What are you doing?" its rider asks, stretching an arm clad in black riding leather out as he pats the blue-scaled dragon on the side of its back. "You smell something? *Someone*?" The rider peers in my direction, his eyes scanning from side to side. But I'm in a pocket of shadows between the moonlight, invisible to them unless their dragons decide to investigate. A growl, low and full of warning, rumbles from the cave on my right. The males on their dragons stiffen while their beasts each take a step back.

"Let's hurry this up. I've got a female waiting for me back at the palace," the other rider says, his voice gravelly as he guides his dragon past a still burning pile of remains.

"Why are we even doing this anyway? It's the third time, and Shah's old dragon hasn't fallen for the bait once."

"I don't ask questions, and neither should you. The king wants us to leave the bait here, so that's what we are going to do."

Bait? I watch as they walk farther out into the field, pausing in the darkness, their voices drowned out by the distance between us. The chill of the night air permeates my leathers, my joints stiffening as I stay crouched and wait for their departure. Eventually, wingbeats punctuate the air and signify their departure.

I stare out at the space the riders vacated, my curiosity drawing my steps towards it even as I mutter, "This is fucking stupid." I have never before stepped onto the fields, but my curiosity drives me forward at their mention of Bali.

A beast rumbles not too far off in the distance, so I pick up my pace, finally reaching the spot where they stood. The scent of rotting meat is pungent in the air, and I lift my hand to my nose to try and stifle some of the stench. It takes me a moment to locate the offender—a decaying pile of dead deer. Swallowing down the bile in my throat, I survey the ground around the pile, but nothing looks different or out of place. Nothing except the waiting meat.

Saliva gathers in my mouth at the foul rotting meat. How curiously annoying that I can gut a fae without blinking an eye but decaying animal turns my stomach. Moving past the initial scent of maggot-infested deer, I draw in a deeper inhale as I take a step closer, this one rich with the metallic smell of old blood. Old blood and— I freeze, inhaling again as a second scent layered beneath the blood catches my attention. It's faint, only just barely noticeable, but the pungent and acrid floral notes are undeniable. "Belladragis?" I whisper.

It is one of the few plants that are poisonous to fae, even in small amounts. Its nectar looks innocuous enough, a honey-colored liquid that isn't quite as thick. But a teaspoon of it will lead to full-body paralysis for days. More than that? Immediate death. Dragons are bigger, their bodies tougher than our own, but I imagine that in a high enough dose, the effects would be the same. Which begs the question, was my father trying to paralyze Bali or kill her? *And why?*

It's something I ponder as I make quick work of setting the tainted meat on fire to ensure neither dragon consumes it before finally leaving the fields.

When I finally emerge from the dark tunnels near the palace, I pocket the small flame gem I use for light and climb from the dragon's landing platform onto Navin's balcony. The moon is lower in the sky, the sun close to peaking above the mountaintops. In my exhaustion, I don't realize that there is someone standing on the balcony already, not until Navin steps forward, his finger pressed against his lips.

"What—"

"Do you not see the universal sign for *be quiet* that I'm giving you?"

Navin rolls his eyes as mine narrow, and he leads me to the corner of the balcony. He's still dressed in his flight leathers, twin swords strapped down his back and his hair thrown into a messy ponytail. He looks over his shoulder as he whispers, "Leesi came looking for you earlier."

I match his low tone. "Why?"

"I don't know, something about—" Navin halts when he turns back around, sniffing the air twice before his face twists into a grimace. "Why do you smell so bad?"

I look down at myself. "It's dragon blood." Sir Dae might be splashed on me too.

"It's dragon... *Why* are you covered in dragon blood?"

"Navin, we don't have time for this. What did you tell Leesi?"

He wipes the hand that was holding on to my arm on his thigh, making no attempt to hide his disgust. "First, I told her you were visiting Mother." *Fuck.* That might have been a mistake. "Then, when she returned an hour later, I told her you were already in bed asleep. She said something about Father Yamin and began pounding on your door, eventually fishing out a key." His hands brace his hips as he shakes his head. "I tried to stop her, but she knows you weren't in your room, Myla, and I don't doubt that she's already informed both Father Yamin and the king."

My frustration battles for dominance against my exhaustion as I growl and tip my head back, staring up at the predawn sky. "Has she returned from telling them?"

"Not yet—"

"Let's get back inside before she does." Brushing past Navin, I open the slider and slip inside.

"Wait! What are you going to tell her when she comes back?"

I shrug, heading to Navin's bathroom so I can change. "I don't know. Maybe that I was in the library. That's far more believable than saying I was speaking to Mother." I squat to untie my boots before kicking them off.

"I had to think of something quick," he retorts as a drawer opens and closes in his bedroom followed by footsteps. Taking off my cloak, I tug on the laces of my vest, loosening them enough to pull it off entirely before letting it fall to the floor. My trousers join it. Grabbing a black cotton towel from where it's hooked on the stone wall, I wrap it tightly around myself, grabbing a second one to lay my weapons on.

"If that is you thinking quickly on your feet, I'd hate to see you in battle."

"That's rude. I'm great in battle."

I layer dagger after dagger onto the towel from my vest, moving to the sheath on my thigh and sliding the curved blade there free. "You've never been in battle."

"What happened to your ribs?" His voice takes on a solemn tone, one that relays his concern for me and makes tension build between my shoulder blades. I drop my gaze to where his meets my skin, a large and ugly welt peeking out from where the towel gapes at my side.

"Likely a wound from Sir Dae."

Navin makes a choking noise, stepping farther into the bathroom. "I'm sorry, did you just say Sir Dae. As in, *Sir Dae*? The fucking owner of the biggest collection of businesses in the entire kingdom?" His incredulousness makes my annoyance flare. Well, that and the fact that I am injured, covered in foul-smelling blood, exhausted, and have missed out on an opportunity to bond with Sunis.

At least I got fucked tonight. Though even my time with Karina feels like a godsdamn week ago. "I did."

"Fuck. *Fuck*, Myla. This is a big deal. You can't just—"

"I *can*," I snap, abandoning my daggers in the towel as I stand and take a step towards my brother. "And I already *did*. So you can save whatever self-serving, idiotic nonsense you were about to spew at me because it won't change anything. Sir Dae was a conniving asshole who brutally raped and tortured females for fun. *To release stress,* he said. The kingdom is better off without him."

Navin blinks once, then twice, his stunned silence piercing my already pock-marked heart. I look away and bend down to secure my weapons in the towel before standing again, ignoring the chemise he holds out for me.

"I'm too filthy to wear that." Confirming that the space connecting our bedrooms is still empty of a meddling maid, I pad across the carpet, a hot shower and my bed sounding more and more like a cure to this fucking nightmare of a night the closer I get to my door.

"I can't just turn off caring about you," Navin says at my back, halting my steps as I reach my hand out to the door handle. "After everything you've been through"—I squeeze my eyes shut, wishing he would stop and not say anything else—"I can't just turn it off like you can." Too many words pile up on my tongue but none that I am willing to let out. When the silence lingers, Navin sighs from across the sitting room. "Good night, Myla."

"Good night." I push the door to my room open and close it quickly behind me, not giving myself a chance to linger on his declaration. Hiding my weapons in the armoire, I toss the towels in my hamper before turning the shower to the hottest it will go. I try to wash the night off of me as best as I can, but a hint of something still lingers when I step out. Like the ominous feeling I had after killing Sir Dae, I can't quite name what remains, only that it leaves me uneasy.

Looking into the bathroom mirror, I'm pleased to see that no bruise marks my face from my scuffle earlier in the evening, only a small red mark that is tender to the touch but at least easily hidden beneath makeup. Dressing in a long-sleeved nightgown, I brush my teeth and hair and then crawl into bed, exhausted down to my very marrow and yet unable to find the relief of sleep.

My brother's voice tortures me as I toss and turn. I know Navin cares about me far more than warranted. He is good, deserving of more than the life our father has laid out for him. Though I know he would never say it, I wonder if in moments like earlier tonight, he regrets teaching me how to fight. If he wishes he would have stood by as I destroyed myself instead of intervening.

But he hadn't. He saved me from myself, saved me when no one else *wanted* to, and for that, I will never be able to repay him. Whether I deserve it or not, I have a life debt owed to him too. Bonding a dragon and freeing him from the duties of being the crown prince is the least I can fucking do, and no matter what comes tomorrow with Father Yamin or the king, no matter how I wish I could kill Aria instead of train her, I will not yield and I will not fail. Because Navin is wrong, I can't simply ignore how much I care about him. I am just better at making him think that I don't.

Chapter Thirty-Three

RHEA

C OOL AIR BLOWN IN from the ocean stirs the thin fabric of my chemise, the golden light of sunrise dashing across a vibrant pink and purple sky. Sitting on the window ledge, I clutch the black leather journal tightly in my hands, its spine resting against the tops of my thighs. The journal's contents—Alexi's words and thoughts, his hopes and dreams and sadness and anger—are precious, each paragraph worth more than all the gold a treasury could hold. I knew Alexi, all the important parts of him anyway. I could decipher a look on his face or filter out the words he wasn't saying between the ones he was. He was my guard, and he was my father. He only visited me for an hour at a time, yet I felt like I had gained a lifetime of knowledge from him.

But between the pages of this journal, written in short, precise capital letters, were things I had never heard Alexi express before. His impression of our first meeting, and his thoughts that led up to it. His frustration with the king and how he kept me locked up. His prose was the most beautiful when he mentioned his wife, both before and after her death. Alexi had been so brief when he talked about Alanna, as if he could only handle the memory of her in small pieces before her loss became too overwhelming. I suppose, to a degree, I understood that. I could relate to the feeling of an empty spot at my side that someone had once filled so thoroughly.

I had tried to pace myself when Xander gave me the journal, knowing that this tether to a man long since gone would be short lived. But as I began reading, the words morphed from simple writing on a page to his voice inside my head. I could nearly *feel* him sitting next to me, a look on his face that somehow balanced stern amusement.

His writing was inconsistent. Sometimes there were daily updates, though the entries were much shorter and written like a list of events. Then months would go by, the only clue that time had passed in the content of the entry itself, as Alexi never wrote out the dates. A few entries had years between them, the most notable taking place after his wife's death. His writing after those time gaps was always the most elegant—the most thoughtful. Like he had kept everything he wanted to say locked within until no more would fit, and it all came tumbling it out. Those were my favorite ones to read because *that* was a side to Alexi he so rarely let me see. I know it was because he was shielding me, only wanting to present the version of himself that he thought I needed. He was selfless in that way.

But reading through his heartbreak—his turmoil at coming to the decision to no longer be my guard and then the ravaging guilt afterwards—made me realize just how much I wished I could have gotten to know Alexi outside of our confines as guard and princess. I loved him, but I so often felt alone in the way I thought and felt. What I longed for. To learn that he experienced those same emotions... It shouldn't have surprised me, but it did. It makes me all the more grateful to have had a man in my life who never shied away from sharing himself with me. Who always reassured me that everything I was—with all my broken pieces—was everything he wanted. *Every version of you is one that I want,* Nox had told me. He had also shown me, in so many unspoken ways, just how deeply he meant what he said.

Another breeze slips in through the crack of the open window, making the pages of the journal flutter. I only have a handful left, having read in my spare time between the king's demands of me and my lessons with Eve and Lady Mia.

Xander and I hadn't talked about what he revealed the day he gave me the journal, and I hadn't given him an answer about letting him help me get free of the king. It isn't that I don't want help, and it isn't even that I necessarily distrust him. It's the image that is burned into my mind—him holding Alexi by the hair as the king spears his sword through my guard's chest. It is him—cold and calculating—the morning after as he tells me to move so he can take Alexi's body. It is him—his eyes, specifically—as they meet mine during a beating from the king, no emotion at all etched into their dark depths. Xander has been a fixed presence in my subconscious as someone who aided the king in hurting me. I don't know if I can reconcile who he appears to be *now* with the version of him in my head.

Over the course of the week, when I wasn't taking dancing lessons or being forced to learn table etiquette, I had tense meals with my uncle. He toyed with his control over me, commands ranging from drinking wine until my eyes blurred and my mind went numb, to forcing me to endure his touch by sitting in his lap as his hands caressed my sides. I preferred the effects of the alcohol, even if I woke the next day paying for it. At least then, I couldn't remember what he said or did.

Sometimes, Simon was there, his sneer ever-present. My skin crawled with disquiet whenever his gaze lingered on me, as if he wasn't looking at me but *through* me.

The nightmare of his tools slicing through my skin haunts me nearly every night, and sometimes I wake coated with sweat and confused. My nerves acting as if those nightmares are real, even as my body bears zero evidence of them.

Proof of the brand, however, is very much existent. My hip still aches with the raw tenderness of it, the swollen and puckered skin one I avoid looking at as much as possible.

Every day after my mandatory lessons, I retreat to the library. I no longer read for the pleasure of escapism, instead scouring the shelves for any possible clue on how to free my magic. The problem is not only do I not know where to even *begin*, but the books at my disposal are mostly fiction. It makes Xander's offer all the more tempting.

Simon has given the king no new updates from the Mage Kingdom in my presence. Nothing new on Nox and his family. As the end of another week comes into view—marking this as my third week since waking up here—dread begins to creep inside my chest. Whispers of the same question repeat in my mind: *Why hasn't he come for me*? Even though I know, rationally, that he has no idea where I am. That he could still be stuck in that deep sleep Simon had claimed he was in. That there could be a myriad of things keeping Nox exactly where he is. But those rational thoughts do nothing to coax away my apprehension.

It is a different kind of torture to know *exactly* what I'm missing out on. To not just hope and wish for something better, as I did for so long in that tower, but to have actually tasted that freedom only to then be stripped of it, leaving something bitter in its wake.

Between the external *and* internal conflicts that savagely demand my attention, Alexi's journal has become a sweet spot of reprieve. I don't want it to end, and so, as I sit on the window ledge as the sun finishes rising in the sky, I go back and revisit some of my favorite entries, saving those last few pages for the day I might be able to read beside another.

❧❧❧❧❧ ❦❦❦❦❦

Eve is hurt. She tried to hide it when she entered my room this morning with breakfast and word that the king had a meeting with the siren queen through the Mirror, meaning that I was to eat alone. She favored her right leg as she walked, her back hunched just a small bit forward as if she couldn't draw herself up fully. For the first time since I met her, she wore her hair down. It hung low to just below her mid back, but when she had absentmindedly tossed the strands over her shoulder as she prepped my outfit for the day, it revealed a collection of bruises along the side of her neck. She must have felt me looking because she stiffened for a moment before immediately bringing her hair forward to cover them.

I decided then to keep my question on how she might have acquired them to myself.

Eve's personality is bright and often reminds me of Elora. It is easy to find myself sucked into her orbit during our otherwise banal tea lessons. Even as I worry about the oath that scars her hand. Perhaps it will be my own loneliness that creates my downfall, but I find that with every one-on-one that we have, another part of me softens towards her. Especially at the excitement in her voice when she speaks about how proud she is of her younger sister. At the sadness that sometimes tinges it when she talks of the premature death of her parents. And then there is the yearning I sense when I ask about her next visit after taking a sip of tea. She gave a half answer: She isn't sure when, but she hopes it will be soon. But it was the way she said it, speaking like one would talk about an impossibly large stack of books one hopes to read. There was an air of longing to it—like it wasn't quite a tangible reality—that made my stomach sour. Is she stuck here because of me? Am *I* the reason that she can't see her family?

"Are you not hungry?" Eve asks, crossing my room from where she's organized my dresses in the closet to where I stare out the window at the roiling sea. My appetite since arriving here has fluctuated between casual hunger to outright revolt at the thought of food. A pity, considering the meals I had been served at the very least *looked* like they would taste incredible.

"Not really."

Eve nods and crosses her arms over her chest. "Which kingdom do you think it belongs to?" she asks, nodding out to a ship that is bobbing over the choppy waters.

My mouth quirks as I stare at it, the vessel much too far away to make out any sort of kingdom insignia. "Mortal Kingdom would be boring," I tease, my grin growing when she laughs.

"Shifter, then?"

"Could be. Back home, there was a lot of talk about the Shifter Kingdom." I don't know why, exactly, I say that, and the silence that descends is proof of Eve's own shock that I've spoken about any part of my life before. In my pursuit of making sure I don't say anything that might be used against me, I often only speak about surface level things. My dance lessons or the latest book I read. This is a deviation—a shift in conversation driven by the fact that I *miss* my friends. I miss having people to talk with that I can trust. I miss my *life*.

"*Is* the Mage Kingdom your home?" she asks, so quietly at first that I wonder if she meant to voice it all. But I hear the unspoken question, the same one Xander gave me with his eyes when we spoke of his secret movement. *You are heir to this kingdom's throne; is this place not your home as well?*

"Are you aware of who I am?"

She takes her time answering, reading between the lines of what I've asked. "That you lived in the tower until you escaped a few months ago? Or that you are the king's niece?" At the mention of my relationship to my uncle, shame forces my cheeks to heat and my gaze to drop to the window sill. Eve shifts her stance subtly and unfolds her arms as she clasps her hands together in front of her, rubbing her thumb over the opposite hand's palm. "I only know because of Xander. The other servants and guards here know as well, but they all have been sworn to secrecy with blood oaths—some a second or third time."

I release a rueful laugh, tucking windblown strands of hair behind my ear. "This is not something I ever wanted." For them. For *me*.

"I imagine it isn't."

"For a long time, I don't think I truly understood what a home was." Emotions knot thickly in my throat, my fingers drumming along the sill nervously. "I knew the logistics of it, of course, from what I had read in books. I could paint an imaginary picture in my mind of how it might look, what it might feel like. But it wasn't until I left that tower that I actually experienced what it meant to have a home. To have a constant and safe place to land every night. My imagination didn't do it justice because having a *true* home is one of the most beautiful things about being alive." And, gods, I miss my home so very terribly.

"And you found somewhere to land in the Mage Kingdom?"

"Not somewhere. I found it with someone." I glance at Eve from the corner of my eye.

She studies me carefully, her lips pressed into a relaxed line, but something edgier takes root in her gaze. "You sound very homesick," she finally says.

I turn back to look at the ship, the sun having moved past the horizon. "You have no idea."

Eventually, Eve reminds me of our schedule for the day, and we leave the room to see Lady Mia. Though the brand is covered in gauze, each step tugs at it, and I'm nervous to see what it will feel like after dance lessons. Eager to get my mind off of both the brand and the fact that I let Eve see a vulnerable part of me, I ask, "How do you know Xander?"

"We met when I first started working at the castle," she says, lacing her hands together in front of her white apron. "He helped me acclimate to my new surroundings."

"Really?" I don't hide the surprise in my tone, and it draws a light chuckle from Eve.

"I know he is a little rough around the edges, but outside of his role to the king, Xander cares for others. At least more than anyone else in his station does."

I hear her surety, that she believes what she says, but does she know all that his role entails? Would she still have that appreciative look in her eyes if I told her everything he bore witness to? How his hands were also stained with Alexi's blood? She may have identified me as this kingdom's true heir, but she had no idea what my life beneath the king's rule had entailed. No idea just how sadistic said king could be. Though a part of me wants to disprove everything she claimed about Xander as true, a different voice stops me.

The best piece of advice I can give you, Little One, is to remember that, often-times, when we think we have seen everything at face value, there are still pieces lingering in the dark.

I can't treat Xander as if the past never happened, but I also can't discount the fact that, like me, he is trapped. His cage may be bigger and less intimate, but does any of that matter to the person locked inside it?

I sigh as we round the final corner that leads to Lady Mia's and then suck it back in, my steps faltering when I see Xander himself waiting by the door.

Chapter Thirty-Four

RHEA

"Lady Rhea. Eve," he says in greeting as we approach.

"Xander! We were just talking about you," Eve says, her cheeks lifting high with a smile. He regards us both with what seems like only mild interest, his gaze then casting out into the hallway.

I notice that he isn't wearing any armor today. Without the bulk of the gold that all the guards wear, this is the first time I'm seeing him as *him*. I'm not sure what I expected him to look like beneath, not that I had given the idea any thought, but I'm somewhat surprised by how... *sturdy* he is. His chest is broad, and the muscles of his arms are well defined. He takes up space as if he needs more than what is necessary for one person, the notion making me snort as I finish looking him over.

"What?" he asks, a brow arching.

"Nothing."

Eve watches us with a smirk that borders on full delight before clearing her throat and gesturing with her hand. "Are you here to help Rhea learn some waltzes?" she jokes with a laugh, the noise dying along with a little part of myself when he doesn't refute her assumption.

"You're here to *dance*?" I ask, far too loudly.

He lowers his brow, facing contorting into resignation. "Unfortunately."

"But the king..." I trail off, resisting the urge to look over my shoulder in case I find him lingering there like a malicious spirit. Eve looks down at her feet as Xander's gaze hardens.

"He is busy planning with Simon for the rest of the day. He also requested that should you need a dance partner beyond Lady Mia, I be the one to fill the role."

I frown as I meet Xander's gaze. King Dolian is jealous beyond reason. Why would he suggest that Xander—a guard as Nox had been—be my dance partner? Before I can ask just that, the door to the room opens, and Lady Mia throws her hands exuberantly up into the air.

"Are we hosting lessons out in the hall today?" she asks, pointing a slender finger at me. "You! Come. And you too." She points to Xander before spinning on her heel, sending her red dress fluttering out around her ankles.

"I'll see you for tea," Eve says, giving me a reassuring smile before narrowing her eyes at Xander. "And you be nice." She doesn't wait for Xander's response—a brief twitch of one corner of his mouth—before she takes off down the hall and disappears around a corner.

I slide my palms down the front of my dress, Xander tracking the movement before his gaze flicks to Lady Mia and then back to the hall. I see his mind working, likely trying to find a way out of this. But I have questions for him, and this might be the only chance I can ask them without fear of interruption from the king.

"Come on," I say, lifting my chin. "We might as well get this over with."

"How thrilling it is to have a real dance partner for you," Lady Mia says, turning to face us as I walk to the center of the room, Xander letting the door shut behind him when he joins us. "Let us start with a slow waltz to warm up."

She claps her hands before turning to face the wall of mirrors in front of us, her eyes bouncing between Xander and I. We approach each other at the same time, Xander holding his hand out for mine. I lay one palm over his and gently press the fingers of my other onto his opposite shoulder. His touch is faint at my waist when we begin the set of steps for the waltz. Lady Mia claps her hands in time to the beat, watching our feet in the mirrors as Xander leads. It takes approximately six steps before I step on him for the first time.

"Lady Rhea, a new record for you! Focus on what I taught you. Dancing should be fluid. It shouldn't feel like you're checking off a list."

"Sorry," I say, staring at one of the buttons on Xander's chest.

"Look at how the commander moves with such graceful ease. Copy that."

I refrain from snorting. Looking up to Xander, I find his attention fixated on a point above my head. "How did you learn to dance like this?" I ask.

"My mother." He doesn't say anything more, but I watch the way his jaw clenches, his gaze flicking to mine for a brief moment before returning. "Have you thought about what I told you?"

I accidentally step on his foot again, making his fingers tighten just a fraction around me—the move pulling at the tight skin on my hip—while Lady Mia lets out a disapproving hiss. "I have." I take a few moments to gather my thoughts, Xander thankfully giving me the time as we continue dancing. He guides us a little farther away from where Lady Mia is still clapping, but I keep my voice low enough for only him to hear. "You say you want to help me, but how can you do anything more than I can do on my own? Won't the king be suspicious of you? Especially around me? And with your blood oath?"

Xander's eyes meet mine again. "He trusts me more than he trusts any of the other guards." I purposefully run my thumb along the raised crescent-shaped scar on his palm. Xander amends his last statement. "Within reason."

"You still haven't explained *why* you would risk anything to help me at all," I breathe through the discomfort of the brand being tugged on.

"Shouldn't the offer of help be enough?" I step on his foot intentionally. He grimaces while Lady Mia chastises me. "Helping you *leave* the Mortal Kingdom is better for everyone."

Having satisfied Lady Mia with our warmup, she instructs us to move on to a faster-paced waltz as I give Xander a nod. If he is telling the truth about his underground movement against the king, I can't even begin to imagine how my being here has disrupted that. "Can you communicate with the Mage Kingdom behind the king's back?"

"Not from here, but possibly once we are back in Vitour."

My heart pounds harshly in my chest at the thought. "Do you know when that will be?"

Lady Mia claps her hands three times in quick succession, indicating the end of the dance. She praises Xander with a bright smile before it falls as she looks to me, her displeasure woven into each critique she gives me. I stuff my frustration down, reminding myself that she is acting on the command of the king and that my poor performance will be seen as a direct reflection of *her*. She stays too close for Xander and I to continue our conversation, instructing us through another series of faster-paced waltzes that he executes perfectly.

When we are finally given a break, I pull away from him and take the small linen towel Lady Mia offers to wipe off the sweat on my brow. The brand stings from the sweat, and I bite down on my tongue to keep from crying at the fact that I can't ever get a reprieve from the reminder that it is there.

"Well done, you two. Fewer mistakes this time, Lady Rhea. I will let the king know that this arrangement is preferred for everyone involved." I pinch my lips together as Xander's brows drop low, clearly this *arrangement* is not one *he* prefers. She tosses us both a smile before opening the door to the room and leaving the two of us.

Xander wastes no time diving back into our earlier conversation. "To answer your question, we leave for Vitour soon. In just over a week."

Anticipation grabs hold of me, claws digging in deeply. *Only a week*. I don't want to draw attention to the excitement that suddenly rushes into my veins. Being in Vitour doesn't mean the king will be less vigilant over me. In fact, I don't doubt he will find a way to ensure that his eyes are on me as much as possible when we return. It's the fact that Nox is familiar with Vitour and the castle. He can find me there.

"I want to help you, Lady Rhea, not only because it is better for my interests or because it is the right thing to do, but because I *owe* it to you." He goes to rest his hand on his sword only to remember he doesn't have it. He lets it fall back to his side as his eyes meet mine again. "So rarely have I come across people that are *good*, but you are."

My throat tightens as I stare at him, my breaths shallow. When I finally relent with a quiet *okay*, his shoulders relax. But then his expression hardens, shifting into the commander and the king's Trusted once more.

"There is something else that you should know that is happening this week."

I swallow, my fingers curling into my palms. "What?"

"The siren queen is coming to meet with King Dolian again and has... *requested* that you be there."

⁂

Xander meets me at my door to escort me to dinner later that evening, his expression grim.

The king is already waiting for me in the dining room when I enter, Simon sitting in his usual spot across from the chair assigned to me. Ignoring the king's gaze as I take my seat is arduous. Every part of me feels inexplicably exposed to him, despite how I've changed into a dark blue dress with sleeves that drape down my arms and a neckline that covers up to my collarbones. I'm only in my chair for a few seconds before two servants are there. One gathers my food, while the other pours wine into my glass.

"Drink it," King Dolian demands, a cold lilt to his voice that makes every one of my nerve endings go on high alert.

My heart races as my hand automatically reaches for the drink, the cup cool in my clammy palm. I meet his eyes over the lip of the glass as I tip it up, noting how they are glassy and how red lines the whites of them. Opening my mouth, I tense in anticipation of the bitter taste, my stomach already churning. But the wine tastes sweeter—*fruitier*—than before. Almost as if it's...

I look to the corner of the dining room, where a dark-haired servant is waiting next to a small table that hosts a tray of different glass pitchers. One is clearly full of water, but the other two look identical, as if they are both filled with the same cherry wine. My eyes then flick to where Xander stands at the opposite corner, his hands clasped behind his back. But where the servant kept his gaze down towards the floor, Xander's eyes meet mine. He gives me a small nod—the move hardly perceptible—and I realize at once, this is him helping me. Because it's not wine but juice that fills my cup.

195

"Something wrong with the wine, Lady Rhea?" Simon asks. I take another small gulp of the juice, grateful the magic lets me set the glass down on the table.

The last time the king forced me to drink wine, I had gotten drunk from it. I can't remember how I acted or what I said, and I hope his intention isn't to do the same thing tonight, because I'll have to fake it now that juice fills my cup.

"Nothing at all," I answer, picking up my fork and stabbing it into a piece of roasted potato.

The rest of the meal proceeds in stilted silence. King Dolian doesn't speak, hardly moves except to lift his hand for more wine. I watch as the servant chooses the pitcher filled with red liquid on the right and walks over to the king, refilling his cup for the third time since I've sat down to eat. As he retreats back to his corner, Simon's voice halts his steps.

The king's advisor looks at me, his crooked mouth resembling a smirk. "Lady Rhea, your cup could use a refresh." The servant's eyes grow wide for a quick second as he looks at me before he rounds the table behind the king and stops at my side. He keeps his pour steady, despite the nervous energy I can feel wafting off from him.

"Thank you," I say out of habit, earning a quick glance from the man. As the man attempts to return to his station, King Dolian snaps his hand out and grasps his wrist.

"What did I tell you about *looking* at her?" he drawls out slowly, the alcohol slurring his speech. The servant keeps his gaze downcast, and when King Dolian stands, clumsily bumping into the table while knocking his chair to the ground, I follow.

"Lady, let the king handle his animals," Simon says from his chair, his hands clasped beneath his chin.

I ignore him, pleading with my uncle. "It is my fault—"

"He looked at what is *mine*."

"*I* thanked him for the wine. If you want someone to be mad at, let it be me."

"You already make me *plenty* angry, darling," he snaps back, shoving the servant away as he takes another large drink from his chalice. Then, under his breath, he murmurs, "She always did that too."

My heart thunders in my chest as I ask, "Who?"

"Luna. She cared about those who shouldn't have been seen. Who deserved *none* of her attention."

I struggle to find something to say, watching as his gaze fogs over. I know he's thinking of my mother, running through the memories they had together. But I wonder if his memories of the two of them are tainted by his own greed and lust and anger. When the haze of the past clears and only that of the alcohol remains, his eyes find me again. There is no mistaking the look that's there now. His cheeks flush red beneath his beard, matching the bloodshot pattern of his eyes. I curl my lip as I look away.

"Simon, has Lady Rhea heard the latest update from the Mage Kingdom?" he snarls.

"No," Simon answers with a withering smile. "I don't believe she has."

"Then let me be the one to tell you, *fiancée*, of how the precious life you miss so much has devolved since the last time we spoke." He kicks the chair out of his way and stumbles towards me, wine spilling out of the cup still in his hand. "It appears the mage prince has awoken from his slumber, not ill with health but with *magic*." My breath catches in my throat, and I squeeze the soft, velvety fabric of my dress in my hands. What did he mean *ill with magic*? "But that's not all. Your most perfect prince also hurt three of the healers that were sent to help him."

I'm careful to not let my composure slip, biting my lower lip to keep from responding. Nox wouldn't. *He wouldn't.*

"Let us not forget that his sister has been outed as a treasonous wench who sold her body and the kingdom's secrets to the shifter king," Simon adds from his seat. I don't dare look at Xander, not as both of the other men examine me for my reaction. "There is word that they are going to strip the Daxel family of their power."

"Unless, of course, he agrees to marry someone better *suited* to be queen at his side."

I hold my breath in my chest as my knees threaten to buckle. *No.* This can't be true. It is a ploy to break me. These are lies, nothing less.

"You look as if you don't believe us," Simon, correctly, points out. "Perhaps you need proof."

"How can you prove what you say? Unless you plan to bring me to the Mage Kingdom yourself, I will find hearsay about other kingdoms hardly much more than that."

The king hums as he takes another drink, setting the chalice down on the table. I stay still while he drunkenly steps towards me, stopping when he's close enough for me to smell the alcohol on his breath. "And what if I could show you exactly where the information comes from?"

I lift my eyes to his. "You said they weren't answering the Mirror."

His smile is watery, tainted by the alcohol and his own evil intent. "Xander!" he shouts, making me jump. "Bring Stephan here."

A hesitation and then, "Stephan, Your Majesty?"

"He arrived earlier this evening. Bring him here so he can share with Lady Rhea everything he knows." Xander hesitates before he relents and leaves. I try to comb through my memories, grasping for when I might have heard that name before. But no one comes to mind. The room feels stifling in the presence of the king, trapped between his lascivious stare and the equally horrible one that comes from Simon. "You *do* look just like her," the king says, lifting his hand to cup the side of my face as I tense. "Do you have any idea of the restraint I possess?"

I pinch my lips together, nails digging into my palms as my chest heaves unsteadily. He stares at my mouth, possession and desire mingling as he leans in even closer. Gods, if he tries to kiss me... He can force me to reciprocate, and the fact that he *hasn't* yet leaves me terrified. It doesn't feel like a question of *if* he will do it but *when*. King Dolian slides his hand from my face to my hair. He opens his mouth as if he is going to say something more, but then the creaking of Xander's armor sounds in the hallway. It's followed by a male voice that doesn't sound particularly thrilled.

"Just remember, you asked for this when you showed me that you did not trust my word. That you did not trust your king. *Your future husband*." He removes his hand and backs away, going only far enough that his wine is once more within reach. "Stephan, step forward."

A man approaches wearing a white short-sleeved tunic and thin dark trousers. His black hair is rumpled as it hangs at his shoulders, as if Xander pulled him directly from bed. At first glance, I have no idea who he is, but there is something about him that holds my attention. Candlelight from the chandeliers above dances along his high cheekbones, but it's what it highlights that sends my heart careening into my ribs. *Gray. His eyes are gray.* There is only one kingdom that eye color originates from.

He folds his arms over his chest, and like slipping a final puzzle piece into place, the act ushers in a memory. My throat grows dry and tight, an invisible hand squeezing it as I stare. The recognition must show on my face because the man dips his chin and offers me a cunning smile. "I'm afraid that the prince was not *actually* at the beach."

Everything within me deflates, my knees actually buckling this time and sending me collapsing into my chair. This is the man who directed Daje and I away from the palace. He isn't just a guard for the mages—if he is truly one at all—he is a *spy*. An informant for King Dolian.

He is the reason I am *here*.

Chapter Thirty-Five

RHEA

"You," I gasp, forgetting everything in favor of the anger that simmers precariously beneath my skin. At this moment, I don't care about the trouble it might cause me, all I feel is the rush of that burning fury at the man who had tricked me. Who had put me on a path to more pain and sadness. And for what? What did he gain from doing so?

"Now, darling, be nice to our guest. We do owe our reunion to him, after all."

I grip the armrests, my upper lip peeling away from my teeth. "I thought you hated mages. I thought they were to be executed if they were ever found in your kingdom." My uncle blames the mages for my parents' deaths. I know he hates the fact that Nox is one, that he had been bested by one snooping about his kingdom right under his nose. That I had fallen in *love* with one. That I *am* one.

"You are correct," he answers, holding out his hand for the servant to give him more wine. The man grabs one of the pitchers containing crimson and rushes over to fill his cup. "But when you fled your tower—when you left me—you made me *very* desperate." Despite his drunken stupor, King Dolian's posture is perfect, the hand not holding his wine slipping into his pocket. "I would do *anything* to get you back, even listen to Simon when he suggests that working with a mage to infiltrate their kingdom might be our best bet."

My attention goes to Simon and the smug arrogance surrounding him as he stands on the other side of Stephan. "The king is wise, and he knows when to keep his enemies close. As luck would have it, we had already captured Stephan entering our kingdom."

"Lucky, indeed," I hiss.

Simon's eyes narrow, but it is King Dolian who continues. "Stephan is smart, in spite of where he was born. He accepted the deal we offered him. In exchange for his life—for his freedom—he would help us get you back home."

Home. How I hate that word coming from him. As if he could ever know what it is. Turning to Stephan, I ask, "Why?"

He shrugs, the picture of nonchalance. "The Daxel family line has wrongfully been on the throne for far too long. They lack leadership. They lack the gumption to put the people first." His eyes take on a darker note, pulling from a memory locked somewhere deep within him. "They act as if the Mage Kingdom is exempt from any consequences."

"And which of their actions are so horrible you deem them worthy of stealing the prince's betrothed?" *Careless.* I know better than to thoughtlessly throw those words around, so I'm not surprised when the back of the king's hand cracks across my face. I lay my hand over my stinging cheek, my eyes bouncing to Xander's for a moment. Bright anger glows there, but I know he can't act. Neither of us can.

"You were *never* his, Rhea."

"You might not have realized it, trapped as you were within their very clutches," Stephan says, not quite interrupting the king, but close enough to it that Simon sends him a disapproving look. "But for those living outside of Galdr, life is quite different. Sure, King Sadryn doesn't rule with cruelty. But neither does he rule with a spine. I had already agreed to help King Dolian when I learned that the prince was going to defy the council and marry you—*an outsider*—anyway. That his parents supported it." He shakes his head. "Returning you back to your own kingdom was the right thing to do."

"I am mage!" I shout, slamming my hand onto the table. "That kingdom—"

"Your Majesty, we have an early morning tomorrow," Xander interrupts, perhaps saving me from myself. From earning yet another slap. The king sighs as he brings his glass to his lips. His face contorts, gaze snapping from the chalice to the pitchers in the corner.

"This wine is..." He looks to the servant in the corner.

"Well, this has been a *delight*, but I'm exhausted from traveling, and I'd like to get some sleep before I do it all again." No one says anything as Stephan leaves, but his exit draws the king's unfocused attention from the servant as he looks instead to Xander.

"Send a note to Commander Valence tomorrow," he says as he stumbles towards the archway that leads back to the hall, "I want the castle ready for our arrival and the guards on alert should anything happen before then. Simon, walk with me."

"Yes, Your Majesty," Xander answers, adding, "I'll return Lady Rhea back to her room."

I stand, and catch Simon's gaze, letting the anger simmering within slip out. "Shouldn't you be following your king?"

Simon merely smirks, darkness hidden within it. "Enjoy your evening, Lady Rhea. May your night be free of that which haunts you." He doesn't even look at Xander as he leaves.

"What the fuck was that supposed to mean?" Xander asks under his breath.

I shake my head, my thoughts tumbling relentlessly as we walk. No part of me believes the things Stephan claimed because none of it makes any *sense*. The Daxel family is beloved by the people, nothing in all the interactions I had seen proved anything different. Nothing except for the council. But Stephan had also spoken of those who did not live in Galdr, and I had not traveled outside of the spaces that Nox took me to. Gods, and I am supposed to be their *queen*? I had not made *any* effort to get to know the people that I would be ruling over, either by blood or by marriage. It is another crack in my armor exposed—one that the king, Simon, and Stephan had taken advantage of so *easily*.

"Rhea." Xander's fingers gently tug on my elbow, and I take in the hallway we are stopped in. *When had we stopped walking?* "Are you okay?"

"I—" My response gets swept away by the weight of everything that has been revealed. By my own insecurities and the way I hate not knowing where Nox is or if he is okay. By the crushing and relentless *loneliness* that somehow feels worse than when I existed in a tower with only Bella at my side. To my absolute horror, a sob chokes it way up my throat. I cover my mouth, squeezing my eyes shut as I turn away from Xander.

"Hey, uh, are you—" He stumbles over his words from behind me, his voice muffled from the ringing in my ears.

Stop crying. I repeat the command over and over, but I'm helpless to stop it. I try to claw at any tether to reality that I can find, but I'm a stranger in this place. To myself right now. There is *nothing* that I can anchor to because my anchor isn't *here. He isn't here.* That leaves me bereft, smothered in the waters of my own grief and anxiety and *anger*.

And apparently, it is time for it all to come rushing out in front of a man I hardly know and barely trust.

My feet begin moving again, my body led by a firm but gentle hand on my shoulder. I expect to be taken to my bedroom, but as I blink away the tears that line my eyes, I'm met with the double doors that lead to the library. "What are we doing here?"

He opens one of the doors and ushers me in, pitch black greeting us until Xander pulls a small flame gem from his pocket. "I thought you might want to be somewhere that is calm but not your room. A change of scenery, I guess." There is a hesitancy to his answer, like he isn't quite sure if he's helping or hurting the situation. "I can bring you to your room if you prefer—"

"No, a change in scenery is perfect." He guides us to the back of the library, where we settle down between two bookcases. Xander sits opposite me, lit by the flame gem laid by his feet. Tilting my head back against one of the shelves, I close my eyes and force each of my breaths to be slower than the one that came before it. The air is filled with the scent of worn leather and old paper, of ink and something earthier. As if the dirt between the stones is somehow seeping through the cracks. It is comforting and foreign all the same. Xander sits with his legs extended in front of him, his ankles crossed and arms folded over his chest.

For a while—minutes or an hour, I'm unsure—we sit in the silence together.

When my heart no longer feels as if it's trying to escape my body, I draw my knees into my chest and lay my cheek on top of them, ignoring how the movement pulls at the brand. "Thank you."

Xander tucks his onyx hair behind his ear, shaking his head. "No need to thank me. I have experience with those kinds of... *attacks*."

"Attacks?"

He blows out a breath, adjusting his position and making the armor he wears creak with the movement. "When it's like your mind is trying to convince you to fight. That if you don't, you'll die. Go up in flames despite the fact that you're sprinting from them."

"Mine feels more like I'm drowning," I tell him, staring off into the darkness that the flame gem doesn't touch. "It's like I'm adrift in choppy waters, the current constantly trying to pull me under. And I kick and kick, promising myself that relief is coming. That I just need to hold on for a little while." The weight of Xander's stare falls on me, but I avoid meeting it. "But if I'm honest, I've been kicking for a very long time."

Though there is still a wild mix of emotions within me when it comes to this guard, I am grateful for the silence he offers in response to what I've said. We sit for so long in the library that eventually my eyelids begin to droop and he suggests that we go. "I will walk you to the foyer, but I should leave you there and let you make your way back alone. Just in case."

"Right." It would be one thing to explain that I simply couldn't sleep and went for a walk around the residence. It is another entirely to be caught with Xander in the middle of the night, no matter how innocuous our meeting is. Quietly, we make our way from the library to the foyer and say goodbye.

My room is dark when I enter it, a chill in the air seeping in from the open window. After closing it, I grab my nightgown from the armoire and head into the bathroom to wash and change, forced to look at the brand as I take off the blood-stained gauze covering it. I pinch my lips together to ward off anymore tears as I stare at the ugly mark. Ignoring the acknowledgment that I am forever changed by it. Once changed, I crawl into bed and cover myself with the comforter.

Though sleep tries to draw in around the corners of my vision, I force my eyes to stay open for as long as I can. Staring at nothing but letting my mind wander into a place that is neither here nor there but somewhere in between. Like when I visit the Middle, except it's my poor attempt at pretending that Nox is actually here with me. Reality without him is almost too much to bear, but sometimes, my dreams are even worse. At least when I am awake, I understand clearly that he isn't here. But in my dreams? There are moments when he is standing in front of me, those gray and silver-flecked eyes seeing me as wholly as they always have. Where I can swear I smell autumn woods and his voice is a pleasurable thrum along my skin. Then he's ripped away again when my eyes open, and the surroundings of my room remind me where I am.

And yet when my eyes finally fall closed and I sink deeper into the bed, my mind goes right to him. A beacon of my heart, his face is all I can see. All I want to see. I tumble further, escaping to a world where it's only him and I. Together in a field, his lips on mine. Wrapped up in a bed, limbs tangled and breaths shared. And, gods, I miss him so much that I don't care that as soon as the sun hits my face through the window in the morning, the illusion will be shattered. That the sharp pain of his loss will roll in anew, a wound healed and then cut over and over and over again.

Chapter Thirty-Six

BAHIRA

SWEAT SLIDES DOWN MY back as I arc my spear from left to right, forcing Haylee to retreat a few steps. She grips her sword tightly in both hands, her keen gray eyes studying me as she bounces on her toes on the soft grass of the training field. I had been surprised when she offered to meet me here, but maybe the fury that contorted my expression when I ran into her near the palace entrance had been enough for her to realize I needed to blow off some steam.

What I really need is to wrap my hands around my brother's neck.

Haylee lunges forward, the tip of her blade aiming towards my middle before I block it. "Stop holding back."

Her chest heaves, the sunlight shining over her dark blonde hair, the strands braided into a coronet around her head. "Not all of us want to spar to the point of maiming, Bahira."

I slice an upward motion, metal hitting metal when she lifts her sword to block. A frown tugs on her lips when she's forced to retreat as I come at her again. And again. My anger feeds my movements, making our surroundings disappear until I'm no longer on the training grounds but somewhere new altogether. I'm no longer fighting Haylee but a faceless entity in the form of everything that threatens to unravel me. Wood and metal bite into my palms, the reverberation of each of Haylee's countermoves traveling down my arms and settling between my shoulder blades. Yes, *this*. The physical pain of a well-fought match. In sparring, there is nothing left up to hypotheticals. Nothing left to the hypotheses of experiments that have yet to yield meaningful results. There is only steel and flesh and will.

I spin my spear and lunge towards her, a growl vibrating deep in my throat.

"Gods above!" she shouts, dodging to the left as she rolls onto the ground, landing on her knees. I'm already there, the tip of my spear beneath her chin, the sun highlighting me from behind. "I surrender." Her sword falls to the grass, and her hands lift in front of her. "Don't kill me, please."

I snort, lowering my spear as I suck in a deep breath and reach a hand down to help her up. "I wouldn't kill you without a reason," I tease, pulling her up and then bending over to pick up her sword. It's the same weapon all the guards of our kingdom have, a beautifully crafted silver blade set into a black hilt with a sun and moon carved into the front.

"You had a murderous look in your eyes. One I've only ever seen you give to Gosston or, occasionally, Daje," she says, grabbing the sword. "Speaking of which—"

"No," I interrupt, twirling my spear until the tip is pointed down and stabbing it into the ground. "I don't want to talk about him."

Haylee smirks, grabbing a canteen of water and taking a drink. "I take it you finally gave him an answer."

My time away had given me clarity I didn't know I needed in many areas of my life. I don't want to question Haylee's intentions as my friend—considering she has been in my life for nearly as long as Daje—but I can't deny that there were times I could have used her support, unwavering and in a way that spoke to the ease of the friendship I thought we had, and instead, I had been met with a snarky comment. A push towards what I so clearly didn't want. A lack of the support I so desperately *did*. Even now, I turn the intention of her comment over and over in my mind, wondering if there is something hidden there beyond just genuine curiosity. "I did," I answer simply.

"He isn't taking it well." A statement, not a question.

I eye her as I wipe the sweat off my brow with my sleeve, grateful for the gust of autumn-chilled air. "You don't have to act as if you haven't spoken with him."

"I haven't since the night you told him," she says, her hands bracing on her dark brown leggings, her white form-fitting shirt soaked with sweat. "But one doesn't need to engage in conversation with the man to realize he is hurting."

I clench my jaw and look out to the obstacle course built on the west side of the training field, pops of colorful magic bursting in the air from the mages that navigate it. "This is the consequence of the terms he set. He demanded something I cannot give him." My gaze moves back to hers. "And I'm done talking about it."

She raises her hands in front of her, surrendering to the seriousness in my voice. "Fine. Then tell me how your brother is doing at least."

I sigh. I don't want to talk about him either. Not the way he slipped a note under my fucking door last night nor how his actions will set off a chain of completely avoidable events. I don't want to recall the way my parents' faces fell as I handed them the letter. Their pity for him was my bitter anger. I know Nox is hurting, that being away from Rhea while she is likely in dire circumstances is eating away at him like a sickness. I know, but I can't understand his recklessness. I can't forgive it. Not at a time like this.

Our family's legacy is balanced in the hands of men who seem all too eager to crush it, and Nox has given them all the ammunition they need to squeeze and squeeze. Because last night, he left on a mission to save Rhea. Alone. Without magic and still healing from whatever ailment has drained his strength. He left his family to go on a suicide mission, and he had done it *knowing* what it would usher in.

When I give Haylee a look that relays I'd rather talk about anything else, she groans and plops down on the ground, leaning back on her hands. "You have to give me *something,* Bahira! We have hardly spoken since your return from the Shifter Kingdom! I don't even know what you did there or how you liked it. No one else will tell me anything about you *or* Nox, despite the fact that we're practically family." She shakes her head, a small grin lifting the right corner of her mouth. "Friends are supposed to *share* things with each other."

"Then share something with me," I counter, taking a seat across from her.

She tilts her head in thought, as if rifling through an imaginary filing cabinet to find the right thing to tell me. "Well, Arin and I had another fight." I roll my eyes. That is nothing new. The two had been linked together for years but were never more than a couple of convenience according to Haylee. "Beyond that, my uncle forced me to attend more council meetings than ever before. He's convinced it will help me learn to love the *political* side of things. You know how he is with his plans for me."

I hum as I nod my head. Haylee's parents passed away from illness when she was only five years old, and her uncle, Councilman Borris, had taken over her care. He is an irascible man, one that often causes contention when there is no need for it, but he had done well raising his niece. Haylee, by any measurement, is strong. Smart. Cunning in a way that only a woman surrounded by powerful men can be, and while she had never expressed that she wanted a life in politics, neither had she shied away from any of the training her uncle signed her up for.

"I even attended the meeting they held to question Rhea."

"Really?" While, technically, anyone has the right to sit in on the questioning of a potential partner to a royal, it is *unusual* to have Haylee attend, considering the council wants her to marry Nox instead. Something I had been surprised and a little hurt to learn from my family and not from Haylee herself.

My expression must relay my emotions because Haylee leans forward and rests her elbows on her knees. "It wasn't that I was keeping their plans a secret from you; it's just that I hadn't really expected my uncle, let alone the council, to *enforce* it like they have." Her gaze falls to the soft pillow grass, her fingers tugging on the blades as she continues. "Nox and I have only ever been friends—"

"I've seen you act more like siblings," I interject, lifting a brow.

Her responding laugh is choked out. "I don't know about that. He's *your* brother, and just because I didn't want to discuss the intimate details of how I viewed Nox with you, doesn't mean that I harbored only benign feelings about him."

Stunned, I sit up a little straighter. "You like Nox?"

"It sounds so silly to put it that way, but what is there not to like? He's strong. Powerful. Loyal to a fault." Her eyes finally lift up to mine, light pink staining her cheeks. "I'd have to be without my faculties to *not* be attracted to that."

"Does he know? How you feel?"

"No," she answers quickly, going back to toying with the grass. "He came back already in love with *her*, so it seemed a lost cause to tell him. What would a childhood crush matter in the face of the love of a woman who held his heart as if she had pulled it from his chest herself?"

I study her and the sincerity of her words. But what can I say as someone entangled in my own mess of relationships and *feelings*?

"Anyways, enough about *me*. It's your turn. Tell me *anything* about your experience in the Shifter Kingdom," she says, gesturing with an elegant roll of her wrist.

"My time there was flawed," I begin, watching as a group of people led by Dilan walk onto the grounds, emerging from the thick forest. "On the way there, the ship was attacked by sirens, and somehow, I was lured into nearly jumping off the deck."

A line forms between her brows. "From the siren song? They only affect males, though."

I shrug, unable to explain it myself. "I'm not sure, but I felt the call of it in my mind. It was this undeniable urge to go to the sea. The magic washed over me as if I were caught in a giant wave, and I was only able to surface again when Kai pulled me away from their song."

"Kai?"

"The shifter king," I amend. Her eyes widen, her mouth forming a perfect "o" as she smacks my leg with the back of her hand.

"So you and the king..."

"It wasn't like that. We had a business deal, and me dying while under his care would have nullified that. He was merely protecting his assets."

"I bet he was doing something with your *assets*," she murmurs under her breath, winking as she draws out the beginning half of the word.

I glare at her, but it's eased by the snort I make. As much as I want to pretend that the way I feel about Kai is something that can be pushed away, a more prominent part of me simply wants someone else's advice on the situation. Selfishly, I also want an ally. Someone to hear everything I have to say about how Kai and I had caught fire with an intensity I had never before experienced, only for us to crash and burn just as brilliantly. A friend all my own to say, *Yes. He was wrong, and you were right to be so wary of letting your guard down. Even if you lied to him. You aren't worthless.* The urge is so strong that I open my mouth, prepared to let the entirety of our story come flowing out.

"Oh, look, it's Arin. And Daje." Haylee points to where they are standing and like being punched in the stomach, my breath is stolen from me. Along with anything I might have said. I follow Haylee's gaze to the edge of the training grounds. Daje walks with his head down, listening to whatever Arin is saying at his side.

"That's my cue to leave," I tell Haylee, standing and brushing the grass from me as I yank my spear out of the ground.

"You owe me more conversation," she says, wagging her finger in front of my face. "Even if it takes an overly intense sparring session from you to get it all out."

I give her a smile that doesn't quite reach my eyes, its guardedness going unnoticed before she pats my shoulder and takes off in Daje and Arin's direction. I turn away, but not before I see the surprised look on Daje's face when he spots me.

Heading back towards the edge of the forest, intent on dipping into my workshop in hopes I can distract myself with *anything* before the council inevitably finds out about Nox leaving, a familiar face catches my attention. Dark skin and short black hair. A body that isn't quite as big as Kai's but is large enough to exude the type of dominance that I crave. Max stands tall as he spars with another mage, his blue magic glowing intensely in one hand while his other is wrapped firmly around a long sword. His eyes meet mine as he blocks an incoming attack, his parry quick before he holds his hand up and turns in my direction. "Bahira!"

I fight off a smirk at the obvious look on his face, cocking my hip to the side as he jogs over to me.

"It's been a while," he says, his chest heaving while sweat rolls down the side of his neck and under his tunic.

"It has," I drawl, twirling my spear idly at my side. "Looks like you're just as eager of a fighter as before."

"Well," he chuckles, his hand going to the back of his neck, "perhaps I just need the right motivation to win." The innuendo hangs between us, Max dangling my challenge from the last time we were together.

I click my tongue, faking my sadness. "I told you, I don't ever repeat."

"Oh, come on," he says, stepping nearer until his body blocks out the sun. He drops his voice low, and the hair rises on the back of my neck because of it. "One more time could be fun."

Undoubtedly, it could. It might just be the thing I need to get myself free of the way a certain male torments my thoughts. "Maybe…"

The rest of the statement fades away as the image of Kai's hands on me comes rushing in. The feel of his teeth scraping along my neck, the breathless way he called me *princess*. Neither term of endearment nor insult but something in between. How his body moved on me and *in* me with the kind of precision that had never made sense. Because how could a stranger know me so intimately in such a short period of time? How could he disarm so *easily*? I shake my head and take a step back from Max, watching as his smile falls and his eyes dim.

"I don't do repeats," I say again, walking past him to head back into Galdr.

Chapter Thirty-Seven

BAHIRA

I AM STARTING TO hate the fucking scent of blood.

Staring at the glass jars lined up in front of me, I fight the urge to throw them against the wall. To watch the glass shatter as assuredly as my sanity has. Leaning back against the counter in my workshop, I cross one ankle over the other and place my hands over my eyes. A noise entirely born of frustration rumbles in my throat before I slide my hands down my face and let them fall to my sides.

Starla and I conducted another set of experiments. One that was supposed to serve as a control for future tests, but now... My eyes flick to the jar of completely decayed leaves that is flanked by two more containers. The left is blooming with life, the blood droplets rust-colored on the large bright green leaves that have grown from a brand-new stem. The right also contains the same coloring though it isn't as fully flourished. Looking at these jars is confirmation of all the data I've managed to gather in the past few months when it comes to the relationship of blood and magic. Everything excluding what Tua had alluded to with Kai's father and his mother. But I can't correlate the evidence presented to me with anything other than a recognition of the truth: My blood does not contain magic. With the jar at the left containing my father's blood and the one on the right containing Starla's, the decay of the one at the center holding *my* blood is all the more evidence of that truth.

Despite my morose mood, I almost let a smirk slip at the thought of my newest young aide. She had gathered the leaves for my experiments and watched as I cut my palm just enough to let some blood drop into one of the jars. When she then held her own hand out, palm up and waiting for me, I scoffed and shook my head. "Absolutely not." I should have realized that Starla, a girl cut from the same cloth as myself, would have seen it as a challenge before proceeding to grab the knife from the table after I cleaned it and cutting her palm herself.

I had wanted to growl at her, but before something angry ever made it past my lips, I took notice of the look on her face. The way she wore her pride on the surface. She had just wanted to help. Though I *did* make sure she knew that, going forward, disobeying my orders would result in her spending the day dress shopping with the girls from her orphanage. As far as threats go, that one seems to be the most effective.

Focusing back on the glass in front of me, I release a breath and reach for the middle jar, dumping its contents and setting it in the sink. I do the same with the others, knowing that based on the results of the Shifter Kingdom experiment, I no longer need to watch for further reaction. Eventually, the plants will get what they can from the blood—or the magic *within* the blood—and then they too will decay.

Once I've cleaned, I take a seat in front of my desk, recalling what I know of magic in general and how I reconcile that with my suspicions about the Spell. I had gone to Councilman Arav requesting his help choosing two scouts to collect data about the declining magic from some of the border towns along the Spell. It had been a risk, of course, entrusting him with *any* information, but I know that Arav loves his people. That he always has their best interests at heart and really, I had been working on the issue of our magic well before anything happened between Kai and I.

Despite the way frustration nips at my heels, so does a small amount of excitement. Finding answers to unknowns has always been my favorite way to work my mind. It's only been in recent years—as the stakes grew impossibly higher—that I've allowed uncertainty to chip away at my confidence. If I truly don't have magic, if it's nowhere to be found within me, then my mind is the only power I hold. And, *fucking gods,* do I want to be the one to solve this.

Reaching into a desk drawer, I open the journal that I keep my notes in, flipping through to the pages with the graph of declining magic throughout the kingdom. From the earliest records I read to the more recent ones, I study how the dots are imposed on the graph. Looking at the trending line and the way the cities closest to the Spell had their oldest mages losing their magic completely, it can't *just* be a random coincidence.

I lean back in the wooden chair. The Spell was put into place by the queen of Void Magic, and she sacrificed her life in order to do it. Since her death, no queen of Void Magic has been found. Could the Spell be why? All magic has a cost—a price to pay for its sustained use. I can only imagine what that price would be to sustain the Spell for over two hundred years.

Except, I don't *have* to imagine.

"Shit," I whisper, looking back down at the journal. What could sustain the magic of the Spell for so long? The magic of *everyone* else on this continent.

The cost of keeping the kingdoms separated, of the magic being wielded for so long—even if its wielder is no longer *alive*—would be astronomical. And it *is*.

If Void Magic is powerful enough to change an entire continent, what would it need to sustain itself? The magic of all peoples seems like a damn good theory.

⁂

I can't believe I haven't punched Councilman Arav yet.

After leaving my workshop, I spend my walk home lost in thought. When I reach the palace, I pass a collection of guards stationed at its entrance. More fill the foyer, and it isn't until I register the heavy silence in the air that I focus my attention on them.

And the way they are *staring* at me.

"Princess Bahira," one of them says, his hand resting on the hilt of his sword strapped at his waist. He steps forward, the others fanning out on either side.

"Yes?" I drawl out, taking a small step back.

"You've been summoned to the council room. Your parents are already there." The guards on either side part, creating a gap for me to go through. A breath catches in my throat, my eyes dipping to the guard's light hold on his weapon. Deep within me, anger stirs like kindling to a flame. I force my feet to move, my steps loud as I walk past him. I expect that to be it, but the guard turns and follows me, the others falling in behind him. *Fucking gods*. Clenching my jaw, I keep my chin parallel to the ground and my shoulders rolled back, intent on letting that fire loose on the ones waiting just past the council doors.

Cass stands guard there, his light blue eyes meeting mine as I near. He offers me one quick glance, enough to relay his concern, before his face returns to a stoic mask. I slip behind my own shields, not allowing room for fear as I enter. I see my mother's face first, tight lines bracketing the corners of her mouth when she looks at me. Concern shines in her gray eyes, tired circles marking the skin beneath them. My gaze naturally goes to the head of the table, expecting to see my father ready to command the room. But my heart skips a beat when, instead, I meet the indignant gaze of Daje's father.

Despite the glare he gives me, his posture is relaxed. His hands are in front of him, fingers interlaced as if this spot at the table is more comfortable than even *he* anticipated. I narrow my eyes, jaw locked as I run my gaze over the rest of the council members. A few have the humility to at least look shocked, while others obtain that nearly smug intolerance that twists Kallin's face. Hadrik, my father's oldest friend, is the only one who looks outright horrified, his head resting in his hand and ruffling his salt and pepper hair.

"Bahira, thank you for joining us," Councilman Kallin says, gesturing to the empty seat between my parents. My father sits one seat removed from Kallin's right, Councilman Borris filling in the gap.

"Seems I did not have much of a choice, as you ensured our own guards escorted me here," I say, no shortage of anger coloring my words.

"Well, seeing as one Daxel sibling has proven to be a flight risk, I figured it was smart to ensure the other isn't given the opportunity to be one under the circumstances as well."

My nails dig into the edge of the table, but I don't give him the satisfaction of snapping.

"Cassius, close the door, please," Kallin commands. "And make sure that no one enters until I declare this session ended." My friend doesn't respond, but I hear the creaking of the hinges as he follows Kallin's command. Yet, just before the door shuts, a voice in the hall shouts Cass's name. I turn in my chair as the door swings back open. It isn't Nox that walks through, but who does still sends the air rushing from my mouth. "Son, what are you doing here?"

Daje's chest heaves as he uses his sleeve to wipe sweat from his brow, his clothing stained from grass as if he sprinted from the training grounds. "You tried to have this meeting without me," he says around an exaggerated inhale.

His father doesn't deny it, instead leaning his elbows on the table as he looks at him. "Your presence is not necessary."

"Says *you*," Daje snarls as he rounds the table, taking the empty seat of the still sick Councilwoman Mora. The tension in the room takes a razor-sharp edge as Daje slams down into his chair, his gaze stuck firmly on his father's.

"This is a council issue," Councilman Osiris says, his face already taking on a red hue. "You have no right—"

"He does, actually," Hadrik interrupts, his shrewd gaze on his fellow councilman. "The inquisition you intend to conduct upon our royal family permits anyone to attend as a character reference, as long as they have a close relationship with the accused."

The words "inquisition" and "accused" scrape against my skin like a rusty blade, the rawness making a breath hiss through my teeth. But Daje seems to calm at Hadrik's explanation, giving the table a curt nod of his head. "That is why I am here. Much, it seems, to my father's dismay."

Kallin laughs, the sound rougher than if it were an outright growl. "Hardly. I have nothing but the utmost respect for our royal family. I just question if having *you* volunteer as a character reference is a wise choice. Considering your *history* with the princess."

A few snickers bounce around the table, igniting my fury as I snap my head towards Kallin. "Excuse me—"

"There is no history between us," Daje interrupts. I don't turn to look at him, especially not at the way his tone carries that statement. Something a little sharper than resignation. "We were friends and nothing beyond that. But I have been in the Daxel family's life for the entirety of mine. I believe my opinion has weight and should be considered in whatever it is you're about to accuse them of."

"Fine," Kallin finally concedes. He reaches for a stack of papers, orange magic glowing from his hands as he sends them to every seat. I pick it up, beginning to read as he continues. "The purpose of today's meeting is to discuss the risks to the kingdom's safety that the current ruling family has imposed. The most recent infractions include sharing secrets with another kingdom, an act of treason committed by Princess Bahira Daxel, and the willful defiance by Prince Nox, who has now left despite being ordered to remain within our borders while recovering."

My hand tightens around the paper, crinkling it as my gaze flicks up to meet the councilman's.

"Let us begin."

Chapter Thirty-Eight

BAHIRA

"COUNCILMAN, ACCUSING A ROYAL of treason based on the grounds of a letter sent by someone *not* in power from another kingdom is quite the reach," my father says, dropping the letter from Jahlee that Kallin passed out to everyone. My pulse beats at an accelerated rate as I watch the councilman mull his response over. At times, I almost forget that he is related to Daje. That he fathered a son who, for all his faults when it came to *us*, is still a genuinely good man. Daje cares, and I have to assume he got that trait from his mother, just like his sapphire eyes.

"It is. Which is why we don't take the accusation lightly. Perhaps if there had been less evidence of this family's willingness to not only hide things from our council but to outright *lie* to us, then we might not have even considered the princess capable of such an act. But as it stands now, we have reason to believe that more than just the exchange in services as laid out by the deal inked in blood took place between the mage princess and the king of the shifters."

"I did not share anything that would ever pose a risk to the safety of our people," I say, my voice steady. "I have only *ever* acted in the best interest of our kingdom."

"No one else has attempted to address the magical blight as Bahira has," my father adds, his profile strong as he looks down the table. "She is a pillar in our kingdom for her academic studies and her prowess as a warrior."

"Those are not the only things she is known for," Councilman Borris says in a low drawl. Confusion filters through me as a few of the other council members, including Arav, adjust in their seats uncomfortably.

My father's voice is cold—*deadly*—when he encourages Borris to continue. "What do you mean?"

"Oh, gods above, Sadryn. You know. It is not the first time it's been brought to this table."

"What are you talking about?" I ask, leaning forward to catch my father's attention. His eyes soften when he looks at me, but it's my mother's voice that sends a chill up my spine.

"How *dare* you," she seethes, her voice an octave I've never heard before. "To even suggest that the topic merits mention here is disgraceful. It's *unprecedented* and—"

"These are unprecedented times as you are well aware, Alexandria," Kallin interrupts, and maybe it's for the best that I don't have magic because I would fucking *strike* the councilman down where he sits if I did. My fist curls on the table, but my mother covers it with her hand. Her eyes are hard when I turn to face her, and a look that says, *don't give them a reaction* is written across her face. But I'm still unsure of what the fuck they are even insinuating.

"What the princess does outside of her official duties, and who she chooses to do them with, is of no concern to this council nor is it *anyone's* business." My father's light purple magic faintly outlines his silhouette. Horror begins to creep in, my fears confirmed when I shoot my gaze to Daje who doesn't look away for once. It's the unintentional pity I see in his eyes that makes my cheeks heat.

How fucking dare they. To act as if who I fuck has any merit on who I am as a person. As if it should undercut all of the other things I've done in service to my kingdom like some negative footnote in the story of my life. Furious doesn't begin to cover how I'm feeling, but it's what twists within the rage that keeps me biting my tongue.

All my life, there has always been an asterisk to everything that I've done. I am Bahira Daxel, Princess of the Mage Kingdom. *First born without magic.* I am a scientist. Researcher. Academic. *Haven't figured out how to fix the magical blight.* I am a skilled warrior who has bested all of my opponents. *Cannot fight against magic.* Back and forth, for the entirety of my twenty-two years of life, I have been split upon a scale of impossibilities and inadequacies. And I am done—so *fucking* done—with pretending like I'm more shield than woman.

"If you can't even speak this supposed *offense* to my face, then at least have the decency to look as ashamed as you are trying to make me feel. You may look down on me for what you perceive me to lack or for not being whatever this fairytale vision of a princess is, but make *no* mistake, I am not afraid to slice off your acidic tongues and feed them to you in return." The silence that covers the room is subtle enough to make goosebumps bloom over my skin but strong enough to send shards of fractured egos spilling out onto the glittering stone floor.

I *hate* that Councilman Kallin is the one that breaks it.

"Tell us what occurred in the Shifter Kingdom, Bahira," he says, as if the past few minutes have not transpired. As if it is nothing more than an item on a checklist, and now it is on to the next thing.

I have always *known* where I stand with the council, but it isn't until this moment that I *understand* it. How foolish I was to believe that I might gain any of their respect with nothing more than what I thought were the best parts of me. My mind. My tenacity. My strength. Now my family's ability to remain on the throne rests in my grasp, and the only thing I can offer them is the truth.

Kallin's fingers tighten around each other. "And we want the *unabridged* version, please."

Memories of the past few months slam into me, and I try to force myself to detach any sentimental meaning to them. Because unlike Nox, I will choose my family first. Even if it means giving over parts of myself that feel as if they aren't mine anymore. I draw in a deep breath and look directly at Daje's father, prepared to recount my stay in the Shifter Kingdom in full when the words clog in my throat. The wrongness of giving these people—a council *intent* on retaining power that never should have been theirs to claim in the first place—parts of me turns my stomach. I once again question what they might do with the information that Kai's kingdom is in turmoil. That rebels have weakened his stance as king. And while that naïve part of me still wants to cling to the idea that we as mages are good and kind and opposed to violence, the hardened woman I've become is screaming within that trust is something to be given until it is betrayed. I may have trusted the council at one point, but now, as I glare at Kallin with a malice that has me itching for my spear, I admit to myself that there is no *fucking* way I would trust them with Jahlee's life. With Kai's.

But giving them *nothing* is not an option.

"Princess—"

"I was kidnapped by the king's uncle and kept prisoner in a dungeon," I interrupt, Kallin's stunned gaze worth admitting this piece of information. I take the silence that follows to launch into a version of my time in the Shifter Kingdom, highlighting once more my attempt to help with their blight—which I only reveal has to do with the length of time they are able to shift—while sprinkling in more of my personal experience with the king's uncle, Tua, and his few rogue separatists who didn't want Kai to be king. I leave out the salacious details between Kai and I, but I insinuate enough to hope that they believe I'm telling the truth.

I recount how Tua knew I didn't have magic and had tried to kill me *multiple* times in an attempt to start a skirmish between our two kingdoms, and how Kai then killed him because of me. My stomach churns, my heart pounding against my ribs wild as a caged animal, while I let everything come pouring out that might paint me in an unfavorable light but will keep Kai and his kingdom safe. When

I'm finished, I force myself to stay upright, despite how every inch of me is begging to collapse.

Worthless.

Well, I wonder if I should add *betrayer* to that too.

"As compelling as all of that is, how can we be sure she isn't omitting anything?" Councilman Osiris asks, spittle flying from his mouth.

"She isn't." Daje's voice is clear—firm—and his eyes don't shy away again when I look at him.

"Son, I know as her friend, it is your inclination to believe her, but we need to ensure that nothing that may harm this kingdom was given to the shifter king. Particularly after learning of the nature of his *relationship* with Bahira."

Gods, do I really want to punch him.

"I've known Bahira for nearly my entire life. She is telling the truth." He speaks so confidently that, for a moment, I forget. I forget about the ultimatum that led to our friendship separating. I forget that despite his vote of confidence, he ignored what must have been so clearly obvious because he thought he knew me better than I knew myself. Maybe, to a small degree, he does. Or *did*. Jahlee had pointed out how I had blind spots in my life, things I thought were one way that, upon reflection and time away, proved to be another. I had seen it firsthand in the way Kai spoke to me, how he treated me before he knew the lies that I hid behind. He, like Daje, saw parts of me that no one else ever had. One man just represented my past while the other... He was just a footnote.

"Even if you thought Bahira was not being truthful, how would you rectify that?" my father asks, tapping a finger on the table. "What would you propose we do to question her?"

"There are ways to get information we need from those who refuse to talk," Borris says, the corners of his mouth curling up. "You know this."

The tapping on the table ceases, and the hair rises at the back of my neck as *both* my parents begin to glow with their magic. "You lay one hand on her, you *foul* creature, and I will ensure it is the last thing you *ever* do." It's my mother who delivers the threat, but I keep my gaze pinned on Haylee's uncle. If he makes a single move towards me—physical or with his magic—a death at my mother's hand would be a *mercy*.

Kallin sighs as he runs a hand down his face. "That is enough for today. We will resume questioning tomorrow morning when hopefully *everyone* is ready to cooperate." He sends a pointed look my way. I fight the urge to roll my eyes, standing when Kallin turns his attention to my father. "Three groups of guards have been sent to retrieve Nox."

That stops me in my tracks.

"On whose authority?" the king asks, standing from his chair and bracing his hands on the table.

The council is quiet, all save for Daje's father who stands as well. "The councils. We voted on it earlier today." Hadrik's eyes narrow, a vein throbbing in his forehead as he stares at his fellow councilman. I know Hadrik well enough to know that if he didn't tell my father before the meeting, there is a reason. Likely one that originated from Kallin. "They were told to return him here by any means necessary, short of killing him of course."

"His magic is still weakened. He *himself* is weakened! To send *our* guards after him like he is some type of criminal—"

"He is!" Borris booms, slamming his hand on the table. "He defied our orders to leave that lying *whore* of a woman. He defied our orders when he left his kingdom to chase after her, clearly willing to draw a line between choosing her and choosing the duty he was born for. He—"

"Why did you call her a liar?" I ask, interrupting his rant. His face turns a hideous shade of red as he begins to sputter something, only stopping when Kallin holds his hand out.

But it's Councilman Arav who answers my question. "She claimed to be from Santor, which as you know borders Galina. Someone tipped us off that no record of her there existed." His light blue eyes, a shade darker than Cass's, glitter beneath the light of the chandeliers while his lips pull definitively to the right. "I had my own people confirm it. She was lying about who she was."

My father shakes his head. "You did not think to come to me with that discovery?"

"I did not think you could be trusted to tell your son that the woman he so clearly loves is a fraud. I think when it comes to him—to both of your children—you do not approach them with the thoughts of a king. You approach them with the actions of a father, and while it is admirable, that behavior can be dangerous. It can make you blind and complacent."

I turn towards the door, my boots heavy against the stone as I push it open, nearly running into Cass on the other side. I had said practically those same damn words to Kai, even though the circumstances are so very different. Yet here stand men ready to rip a family to shreds over the perception of a king who could not choose between his children's happiness and the duty his council swears he owes to the kingdom. It is madness. *Lunacy.*

"Bahira."

I know instantly who calls my name, and I freeze halfway down the hall while I wait for him to catch up. "You were right," I tell him when he comes into view, stepping to my side and crossing his arms over his chest.

"What do you mean?"

"When we rode together to Starla's Flame Ceremony. What you said to me." He doesn't answer, though something shudders in his expression. I bank my anger, storing it deep within as I face him fully. "You said that I should be wary of the rumors that surrounded my *sleeping habits,* for they could ruin my reputation. That it would *tarnish* it. It must please you to know that you were right."

He frowns, letting his hands fall to his sides. "Nothing about *any* of this pleases me, Bahira. Absolutely *none* of it."

I let my gaze rake over his face and find that I believe him.

Needing to be anywhere else, I head towards the front exit of the palace, passing the guards at the doors and those at the bottom of the stairs. Both groups eye me warily, but there must not have been direct orders from Kallin to keep me here, so with their stares heavy at my back, I follow the stone pathway that leads out into the forest until the palace is no longer in sight.

I navigate the closely growing trees, taking a hidden path that I've traveled a hundred times over as a child until I pop out at the edge of Galdr's center plaza. Folding my arms over my chest, I brush past those mingling between shops and aim for the tavern tucked into one of the large albero trees.

The door swings open as I step through and release a breath, pathetically grateful that, unlike everything else in my life, this establishment hasn't changed since the last time I was here. It's crowded, loud and boisterous voices coming from the tables dotting the space. A few curious eyes glance my way as I head to the bar, but no one attempts to speak with me as I take a seat and order a drink. One shot turns into two and then three and four, a pleasant numbness settling over me. I ignore that inner voice that tells me this is a pathetic way to deal with my problems and order a fifth shot.

"Hello, Bahira."

Fuck me. I give the man now at my side a look that relays my annoyance, only to find that he misses the cue. Gosston's eyes are bloodshot, evidence of just how much time he's already spent here. I ignore him as I down my next drink, wincing from the taste before lifting the empty glass to signal the bartender for another.

"Well, isn't this a familiar sight—the princess come to drown her troubles!" he drunkenly shouts. The men around him laugh, except for one. *Max.* He stares at me with wide eyes, like a child caught stealing in a candy store. Gosston leans in close, his breath hot on my cheek. "Just like the last time I saw you."

"Funny," I drawl, tapping my nails against my shot glass as I look at him. I take in his messy curly black hair and his glassy gaze, my nose wrinkling in disgust. "Because I remember you on your knees before me the last time I saw you."

The men let out low noises of amusement, and Gosston's lips lift into a sneer. "Thanks to *Daje.* I had you at my mercy like the magicless whore you are before he swooped in to rescue you. Ever the fucking savior."

"Call me a whore again," I say, gripping the shot glass in my hand. "Go ahead."

"Maybe don't do that," Max pipes up from the back of the group. But the rest of the men around him egg Gosston on, obliging to the alcohol in their veins that is encouraging them to act like the fools they are. Gosston rolls his shoulders back, stumbling into one of his friends before they help straighten him back up. Adrenaline sparks like lightning within me, my muscles tensing as his lips form the words I hoped they would.

"Magicless *whor*—" Glass shatters on the side of his head, sending him sprawling onto the floor where his blood leaks onto the stained and worn-down wooden planks. The tavern falls silent as I flex my hand, hissing at the sting from the shards of glass embedded in my palm. Gosston's friends all stare with mouths hung open, only Max brave enough to step forward. He looks down at Gosston, nudging him with the edge of his boot before his gaze finds mine, a brow raised.

I offer him a wide smile as I turn back around and signal the bartender. "He should have kept his mouth shut."

Chapter Thirty-Nine

NOX

I HAD MADE THIS journey what felt like a hundred times. Had traversed these woods when I was undercover, leaving behind my life as Nox and returning to my secret mission as Flynn. Traveling alone with only my thoughts had been the exact thing I needed to transition between the two, regardless of which kingdom I was returning to.

This time is different.

Despite how I have pushed my body to walk from before the sun rises to long after it sets, I know based on landmarks that I'm not progressing as quickly as I need to. Pain radiates from my upper back, encompassing both shoulders and settling deeply in my chest. It's as if I've gone through battle, exhausted myself to the point that my body can't remember what *normal* feels like anymore. I'm sure sleeping on the forest floor for the past three nights isn't helping.

But I'll take every ache and pain, every discomfort this continent has to offer, if it brings me to her.

Letting out a long exhale, I tuck an arm under my head and stare up at the night sky. Stars dot it in a beautiful array and the sight reminds me of what I saw in the Middle.

When Rhea and I left the Mortal Kingdom, I assumed it would be the last time I'd traverse these woods. To do it again without her by my side is only a cruel reminder that there are others out there that want to harm her. And through her, *me*.

I replay what I remember from the night of the ball, over and over until I've run my mind ragged, but I'm no closer to knowing who took her. And that thought makes sleep—even with exhaustion—elusive. Sighing, I sit up and pull my pack closer, undoing its leather strap. Inside a small black velvet pouch rests on top, and I untie it to reveal a flame gem. I use it to search for the one item that I hadn't deemed necessary for this trip, but instead simply wanted to keep close.

I had been stumped on what to get Rhea for her birthday, finding that everything I saw in the local shops of Vitour were not worthy of being held by her. She had lived through hell and had done such a damn good job at hanging on to her humanity that everything else seemed so mundane in comparison. It was as I was perusing a bookstore that the idea struck me. I knew she would be free of that tower, even if she ended up staying in Celatum and refusing to come with me. A journal would allow Rhea the privacy of writing her thoughts out but also give her a way to document her new life.

And now, I stare at it like it holds the secrets of a long-forgotten goddess. I trace a finger over her name, back and forth until I'm afraid I'll rub the gold right off. Flipping the cover open, I reread the only page I dare to look at. The one that I wrote on before I gave it to her. I skip over my own handwriting, the words on the page ones I know by heart, and move down to the space beneath my signature. When I was still too afraid to give her my real name because losing her meant accepting that she knew all of me and rejected it. That, perhaps, in the moments I had never let anyone else see, there was truth to the thoughts that ate at me. Being prince and carrying the weight of my kingdom on my shoulders had always felt like a privilege, a self-sacrificing one but one that I was all too happy to hold. But at that moment, as I was writing out what I felt and how she had changed me, I didn't feel selfless. I didn't feel motivated by keeping my kingdom safe or returning to my life back home. I just felt *her*, and I only wanted more. This letter wasn't just a confession of deeply rooted feelings; it was a line drawn in the sand. It was the moment I tossed everything that I was out and vowed to be whatever she needed.

It was when I became selfish.

And there, written in her beautiful and distinct script, were just three words repeated: *I love him. I love him. I love him.*

I'm not sure when she wrote it, if it was right after she learned of my true name or if it was later after we had become even more. But the timeline didn't matter so much as the words themselves, and if I can't hear them in person from her, then I will read them. Because to be loved by Rhea is to bask in the sunlight, and I am terrified that if I don't get to her soon, I'll find myself once again in the dark.

Morning comes quickly and brings with it a heavy rainstorm. My magic is useless, nothing more than a small trickle of power balling in my palm when I call upon it. But I use what I can to cover the top of my pack, protecting the contents. My eyebrows draw low as I clench my jaw, the strain of holding the magic causing a headache to bloom.

My boots crunch over the dead leaves that coat the forest floor, the sound muffled by the rain. If I can push myself, I should be able to reach Vitour in another handful of days. Still too slow, but given that my body cannot seem to handle anything more, it will have to do.

The rain falls harder as the day continues, and I pull my traveling cloak around me more tightly, tugging down on the hood to help shield my eyes. Mud makes it harder to hike, my steps sliding over the wet foliage and then suctioning to the ground. I finally reach a thickly woven canopy of trees, providing a small dry patch for me to rest in. Leaning against the rough bark, I close my eyes and try to slow my racing heart, furious that I'm too taxed to continue without a break.

Leaves rustle nearby, and I assume it is from the falling rain until a snapping branch draws my eyes open. I scan the trees ahead of me, reaching to palm the dagger sheathed on my belt. My breath rattles as I slowly draw it in, sheets of rain falling so heavily I can only see a few yards ahead of me.

Turning to face the way I came, I squint into the distance. The magic I'm holding falters, and for the briefest second, I feel it—the presence of another.

Then pain erupts at the back of my head before everything goes black.

❦

She tastes like honey—like sunshine and melodies and other things that I'm not poetic enough to describe but that fill me so wholly, I know I'll be starved once she's no longer on my tongue. Leaning back, I stare at her swollen lips. Desire and yearning and love fiercely flood my veins as my gaze rakes over every perfect inch of her. She's the most beautiful thing I've ever seen, and I'm desperate for her to know just how much she means to me. Just how much her forgiveness is a treasure I'll never part with.

"I love you," I rasp, leaning in to taste her again. Mouth searching and heart screaming, I move down over the curve of her jaw to her neck, the warmth of her skin awakening every part of me. "There is only you, Rhea. Only you."

"I love you," she says, her hands moving from my hair to my shoulders, fingertips digging into the muscle. "Nox, I love you."

Gods, when she says my name, my true fucking name, it takes everything not to lay her down and ensure she'll scream it over and over again. There is nothing like hearing her moan, nothing like feeling her body against me as she does. "My name from your perfect lips is a godsend."

I want to worship her. In whatever way she'll have me. In control or on my damn knees begging for a single piece of her, it's never mattered to me. There may be a list of gods one could pray at the feet of, but the only altar I'll willingly choose is hers. I flick my tongue against her collarbone, waiting for the small gasp I know she'll give me as a reward. But instead, cold rushes in. Water splashes my cheek and then my forehead, an icy chill invading my bones.

Rhea slips through my fingers, turning into mist before fading away completely. Someone begins to whistle—the tune coming from above me. My surroundings grow hazy, swirling like the galaxies in the Middle as everything blurs and I'm once more alone.

⁂

Whistling. Someone is whistling. The thought stirs me awake from my dream fully and into a reality where a terrible ache at the back of my head throbs in time to my heartbeat. I force my eyes to open, only to immediately be pelted with bitterly cold drops of rain. Reaching for my magic, I direct what small remnants of it I can to that ache, the pain only mildly relieved. Moving my hand to my face takes far longer than it should, and it isn't until I've wiped away the rain that I realize the whistling has stopped.

"Welcome back to the land of the living, Your Highness," a voice from above says. I arch my neck, looking at three figures that morph into one and then back to three again squatting in front of me. "Sorry for the hit, but I was afraid you'd give me a decent fight."

When my vision finally focuses, I meet the gaze of a man. One who I don't immediately recognize. "Who are you?" The words come out groggy and slurred.

"I'm afraid I can't tell you that. See, it would ruin my plans, and there is nothing I despise more than ruined plans." He brushes a long strand of rain-slicked raven hair from his face. "Though finding you was a happy accident."

I take in our surroundings, relieved to find that we are still in the forest but it's impossible to tell exactly *where*. My eyes go back to his, and that's when I notice their color. *Gray.* "What kingdom are we in?"

He smirks, smug satisfaction wafting from him as if it were his fucking magical signature. "Mortal, though I'm afraid we're no longer heading to Vitour. That's where you were going, right?" He squats down, elbows resting on his bent knees. "Going to save *her.*"

My lips pull back from my teeth. "You made a mistake stopping me."

He laughs, reaching to secure two ropes before standing. I follow the length of them to where they connect to a makeshift stretcher made of branches beneath me.

"You know, I didn't think it would be so easy." He brings his hands out wide, adopting a boisterously deep voice as he taunts, "The great and powerful Prince Nox Daxel! With the magic of the *gods* in his veins!" Licking his lips, he drops his arms to his sides and stares at me, something shifting in his expression. "You're a legend in the kingdom. Fuck, you're a legend outside of it too. It's funny, isn't it? How quickly the mighty can fall."

I don't respond but press back against the branches, hoping to feel the outline of my weapon. Disappointment surges when I realize he's taken it, along with every one of my possessions except for my clothing. My pack is tied at my feet, at least. I can only hope he hasn't gone through the items there. I take stock of my faculties, noting that in addition to the ever-present pain, my limbs also feel entirely too heavy. Any other time, he'd be dead. My shadows racing in from every corner to strangle the life from him. Or I'd simply do it with my hands. Unfortunately, he is right. I didn't sense him *at all*, and now I can't even *defend* myself should he attack me again.

"Oh, I recognize the look in your eyes," he acknowledges, putting the ropes in one hand before digging the other into his pocket. "But I recommend you tuck those murderous little thoughts back into your mind for now. Based on how weak your signature feels—hardly existent at all—and the fact that you're all but limp on my comfy stretcher, you'd likely just hurt yourself."

"Why don't you come a little closer, and we'll test that theory out."

He chuckles, removing his hand from his pocket to reveal a cloth and a small vial of liquid. "That's the spirit, Your Highness! I can see why she likes you." Everything in me stills, honing in on the man as he steps between muddy puddles and clumped leaves to stand near my head, squatting once more.

"What the fuck did you say?"

His cockiness morphs into something darker, his eyes matching the tone. "She is beautiful, I'll give you that. Though I like them a little less mouthy."

Fury grips me, tossing me in its flames as I reach out to grab him. But my body is so weak, my reaction time even more so, and he's able to deflect me easily.

Uncorking the vial, I watch as he pours a light purple liquid onto the cloth before corking and pocketing it again. "Your effort is valiant, *My Prince*, but there are larger games at play. Ones that require your *fiancée* to be elsewhere." He holds the cloth up, looking from me to it and back again. "I'm sorry for the side effects of this tincture. Gelsemium is quite the nasty flower." Quick as lightning, his hand covers my mouth and nose, and I take a full breath in, an herbal bitterness filling my mouth and lungs.

I struggle against his hold, every warning bell in my body screaming to fight. To do something—*fucking anything*. It starts with my tongue, a tingling sensation that deprives it of feeling when I try to push it to the roof of my mouth. Then it moves down my throat to my chest. My arms are next, followed by the rest of my torso and legs. The last bit of movement I feel is my toes wiggling in my boots before they too become numb.

The man watches, his smile growing after a few moments when he realizes I'm completely immobilized. Patting my shoulder, he pockets the cloth and grabs the ropes again in both hands. "Time to go back home." My eyes fall of their own volition as he begins to drag me through the forest.

Chapter Forty

ARIA

THE SUN IS BARELY up when I leave Lumen and set out to meet Myla. My heart races in anticipation of our lesson, despite knowing I'll be met with something *less* than enthusiasm from her. Her deep-seated hatred of the sirens is warranted; after all, hadn't I also begrudged all that my kind had done? Could I really blame her, knowing it is possible that my own mother had a hand in murdering her family? The cutting looks and blade-like words from her hurt, but my kind had done irreparable damage to her family.

Her fury had sparked my own and inspired me to stand up for myself for the first time. And it had felt... *freeing*. That spark of bravery had left its mark. It is small progress and not nearly enough to protect Lyre and her babe when it comes time to leave, but after a lifetime of feeling like my failures were measured in magnitudes, I am hungry for even small victories. And I'll take them wherever I can get them.

I spend the rest of my journey replaying the defensive techniques. Between our last visit and this one, I had practiced them in the safety of my room at night, sometimes only allowing myself a few hours of sleep so that I could practice for longer.

I transform when I reach the shallow waters of our meeting spot, and my skin prickles with awareness when glowing yellow dragon's eyes land on mine through the Spell. A familiar fae male sits atop the blue dragon's back, between a set of rather imposing looking spikes. He pats the side of its neck, and I wonder if the massive animal can even feel it through those hard scales.

I plant my feet on wet sand just at the water's edge, waiting for Myla to slide off of the dragon and make her way to the rocky cavern. Already anticipating a scowl to mar her otherwise elegant features. But as the dragon lowers, its eyes still pinned on me, there is only the one rider on its back. Glancing around the beach, I don't see Myla at all, and when I bring my attention back to the dragon, the fae male is strutting towards me, his hands raised in front of him.

"I come bearing a message for you," he says, passing through the Spell.

I take a step back towards the safety of the ocean. "From Myla?"

He nods, lowering his arms to his sides. "Please don't use your magic to send me into the water. Lan here is a baby, and he'd probably die without me." As if the dragon understands the fae, he lets out a low growl, opening his mouth to show off his incredibly large teeth. I swallow, my wide eyes drawing a chuckle from the fae. *Maybe Lan* can *understand him through their magical bond.*

I give him a nod. It's not like he knows my magic is useless against him anyway. "As long as you stay over there, then you will be safe."

He smiles, his face a beautiful mosaic of high cheekbones and angular eyes. Dark full lashes frame them, and his long black hair only adds to his distinct look. "Excellent. My name is Navin. I am Myla's brother."

"She has a brother?" I blurt, earning a playful scoff.

"Of course, she hasn't spoken of me. Myla's never been one for open conversation, if you hadn't noticed." I can't help but snort at that. Navin's smile widens. "Anyway, she is unable to come today."

I grip my satchel, the soft eel grass smooth against my palm as I stare at him. "Why?"

"I'm afraid I can't say. But she should be here next week."

I shake my head and look down at my feet as cool air brushes against my skin. "I can't wait a whole week," I lament. Not with how my mother is clearly planning something big with the Mortal Kingdom. To delay an entire lesson—to not have the next bit of knowledge and skill needed to ensure I keep Lyre safe—one week could be the very difference between our escape and our capture.

"I might have a solution," Navin offers, drawing my gaze. He studies me, clasping his hands behind his back. "What if *I* teach you for today?"

I grip the strap of my bag more tightly. "You? But the life debt—"

"It wouldn't count towards that. Only Myla's lessons will. But if you're wanting the extra instruction..." He shrugs, smirking into the wind that blows his long hair behind him. "I would be happy to help."

"Do you know how to fight?" I don't know why I ask, one look reveals that he very clearly has experience at least *training* for a fight. He's packed with lean muscle beneath the black leather he wears, the style similar to Myla's.

I expect a sharp remark, but Navin just laughs, the sound soft and inviting. "Who do you think taught Myla?"

I grin at the image of Navin teaching someone like the aggressive fae as I think over his offer. There is a chance he could use my proximity to do something insidious. Yet every time I have seen Navin, he has always offered me a kind gesture. He seems to get under Myla's skin more often than not, and he believes me to have *normal* siren magic. I doubt it would get me very far, but I also have my dagger in my satchel. All I need is to get out of the cavern and into the water if he tries to attack.

Navin's dragon, Lan, stretches his wings out, their near translucence brilliant even beneath a cloudy sky. Veins of black spread like cracked porcelain all throughout his wingspan, breaking up the hues of blue. Where the wing bends on either side, there is a single sharp talon—similar to the ones that grow from my fingers, only much larger. *Gods*, he is massive.

Seeing my focus, Navin says, "Lan here won't be a problem. In fact, I'll probably tell him to go hunt for an hour."

That helps make my decision. "Alright, Navin. I will train with you."

He pumps a fist in the air before turning to look at Lan, the two seeming to communicate for a brief moment before the dragon crouches low and then leaps into the sky. He lets out a deep roar that rattles my bones before banking right with an elegant sweep of his wings, flying towards the dark and misty mountains in the distance.

Navin leads us into the cover of the cavern, reaching a hand into the bag strapped to his chest and pulling out a black tunic, which he then tosses to me.

"Did Myla tell you to bring this?" I ask.

He shrugs, gesturing for us to walk towards the cavern. "No. She actually doesn't know I'm doing this."

"Bringing me a tunic? Or training me?"

Navin climbs up the large boulders to get the platform, turning to reach a hand down to help me up the last few feet. "Both, I guess."

I remove my satchel and lay it against the wall before slipping the shirt on. It hits my knees but is softer than the last one Myla brought. "How did you know I would agree?"

"I didn't," Navin answers, tying his hair away from his face. "But I hoped."

"Why?"

"Because if you were desperate enough to withstand a life debt with my sister, I figured you must have a reason for wanting to learn." He folds his arms over his chest as his gaze works over the cavern. "And I want to help."

"Thank you," I say sincerely.

His own sincerity shines back as he dips his chin and then lifts his hands up in front of him, taking on the defensive posture Myla taught me last week. "Show me what you know so far."

I go through the series of ducks and blocks that I know, grateful the swim here warmed my muscles up. Navin spots the same weaknesses that Myla did, but he's much nicer about how he corrects them. He doesn't outwardly ask about the scar on my foot, though I see his gaze bounce to it a handful of times. "I was attacked by rogue sirens," I decide to tell him, lifting my arm to block a slow punch. Navin's teaching style is calm, his body movements elegant as he runs through another round of punching combos for me to practice avoiding.

"Rogue sirens?" he questions, drawing my attention to his leg as he sweeps it out in an attempt to take me down. I step back to avoid it, bouncing on the balls of my feet as we begin to circle each other again.

"In my queendom, sirens who break the law are banished from Lumen and all of the surrounding cities and towns. They are forced to wander, without the home or community that my kind craves."

"That's a fitting punishment, I suppose," he says, extending his right arm out and smiling encouragingly when I quickly block it. My own cheeks lift, and I duck beneath the next arm that he swings out. "In my kingdom, anyone found doing *anything* remotely against the king gets sent to the dragon fields."

I blanch, lifting my guard too late to block his punch. Luckily, he's moving slowly enough that it merely brushes against my cheek, marking the spot that would have gotten hit were he actually trying to take me down. "Sorry."

"Don't apologize, this is all part of training. Talking while we warm up and while you're still learning is a great distraction, but just remember the basics. A hit like that from an opponent who knows what they are doing will take you out. Be vigilant. Stay focused, even when you're trying to hold a conversation. Let your strength start in your core and then draw the other muscles in towards it. That's where your power originates."

I nod, lifting my arms again as I work to engage my stomach muscles. "I imagine the dragon fields are not a place one walks out of alive."

"No," Navin says, his expression falling as he sweeps his leg again, a little faster this time. I'm able to bounce back, blocking the immediate right punch he sends in my direction. Pride blooms within me, and my next steps are lighter because of it. "Unfortunately, our father isn't known for his mercy."

I cringe at the thought of being killed by a dragon, my focus so wrapped up in what I'm doing that I don't realize what Navin said until a few rounds later. "Wait—your *father*?"

He nods, bouncing on his feet while mine fall flat to the stone. He extends his arm out again but stops it halfway when he realizes I'm not holding my guard up anymore. His eyes regard mine, a confused expression wrinkling his forehead. "What?"

It takes me a few tries to get the words past my lips, and when I do, they come out hushed. "Y-your father, *Myla's* father, is the king of the fae? Myla is a *princess*?"

"Oh, fuck," Navin grumbles, tilting his face up to the sky. "I probably shouldn't have said anything."

Oh gods. My hand covers my mouth as my magic pools at the back of my throat, responding to my panic. I hadn't just bound myself to any fae but the *princess* of the fae. And she hadn't just bound herself to *any* siren but a siren *princess.* I can't decide if it's terrible luck or unfortunate irony, but either way, it leaves me momentarily speechless as I stare at Navin. If anything happens to Myla while she is with me, what will they do? Do they know the details of our deal?

"Hey, it's okay," Navin murmurs, walking to me and placing a gentle hand on my shoulder. "Just... pretend I didn't say anything." My gaze shoots up to his, and he winces. "Right, terrible advice. But Myla doesn't wear her status like other royals do. She would prefer that you not know about it, but since you now do, I can guarantee she would want you to act as if she is the same cranky fae she always has been."

"And what of your father? Does he know of the deal? What if he decides to punish me by doing something to my kind for trapping his daughter into this life debt?" My voice shakes, a mixture of worry and anger gnawing at my throat.

"He doesn't know about your deal with her, and even if he did, he wouldn't care enough to interfere. In fact, he'd probably hope that you failed," he grits out, his fair cheeks flushing pink.

"What?"

Navin steps back, heaving a sigh as he turns to look out at the ocean. Sunlight streams in from the holes in the stone surrounding us, highlighting the different medallions on his leather uniform. They glint, bronze metal flaring. "Myla is a princess, yes, but in our kingdom, that means practically *nothing.* Just— Promise me that you won't say anything to her. That you will treat her as you have been." He turns to look at me, onyx eyes pleading. "Please."

The ocean breeze brushes against my cheek, stirring my curls. I take in Navin's stricken expression, the words he gave me, and what I know of Myla from my own experience before I nod. "Okay. I promise."

Chapter Forty-One

ARIA

LYRE RUBS HER BELLY absentmindedly as she stares at the ceiling from where she lays on my bed. "So another trip to meet with the mortal king?" she asks, and my shoulders hike towards my ears. I had made it back from my impromptu meeting with Navin just as my mother had summoned us. Dyanna and I are to accompany her to the Mortal Kingdom once more.

"It appears so," I say, returning my focus to the sea glass in front of me. Dropping the last blue piece into its designated pile, I grab the large white stone that will serve as the canvas, its flat top smooth. An image takes form in my mind, and without examining *why* my brain conjured *that* up, I lay the first glass piece down. "And it's just Dyanna and I joining her this time."

"It makes sense, doesn't it? Sade commands the Queen's Legion, and with all the new recruits being added, it would be pure chaos for her to be gone even a few days."

It is true enough. It took nearly two days to reach the Mortal Kingdom where the king waits, and that is with very little stopping.

"Mother has spent quite a bit of time in Dyanna's library."

I lay another piece of sea glass down, this one black. "Has she found whatever it is she is looking for?"

"It's hard to say," Lyre answers, turning to lay on her side. Her lavender braids have grown during her pregnancy, their ends now past her collarbones. "Though based on how Dyanna looks when I catch her at the end of the day, one would think the queen was torturing her the whole time."

I snort, laying another black piece down. "You know how Dyanna is with her books." She works in the library that houses all of Lumen's important literature,

233

only accessible with permission from the queen, yet no one dares to enter even with said permission without first gaining Dyanna's. She can be as vicious with the protection of her books as our mother is with, well, everything else.

"I suppose that is true." She chuckles before lapsing into silence. Scooting closer to the edge of the bed, Lyre watches as the bottom edge of my art piece begins to take shape. "How is the search for the seamount sirens going?"

"I found something that belonged to Nia when I was out covering the area Sade assigned to me," I lie, tucking my braids behind my ear. "Though Sade believes that the location I found it in is either old or it was left there as a distraction."

She drums her fingers along the bed. "You were gone for a long time yesterday."

I drop a piece of sea glass as I clear my throat. "I was out looking for the sirens. Why, did someone ask for me?"

Lyre sits up, draping her fin over the bed. "Lore was looking for you."

My fingers curl in towards my palms, and though slight relief rushes through me at having missed her, it carries a kernel of annoyance. Lore believes I am *hers* and hers alone, regardless of the fact that she hasn't been mine in a very long time.

"I was able to distract her with a mission to Sade. Our sister owed me a favor, and I called it in then."

My eyes flutter closed as I drop my chin to my chest. "I'm sorry. You didn't have to do that. Lore is…" I don't know how to finish that sentence. Lyre knows of our history, and in the beginning, Lore and I were not exactly secretive about our attraction to each other.

"Aria, you know that you can talk to me about anything, right?"

I nod, rolling black sea glass between my fingers. "I do."

"Good. Because if we are truly going to do *this* together, we need to have complete faith that the other has our back." Her hands frame the swell of her belly. "I will protect you, and I know you will do your best to protect us."

"I will," I vow, reaching to lay my hand gently on top of hers. "I'm working hard to ensure I'm the strongest I can be when the time comes. I won't let you down." Though I mean them, the words feel hollow. I have no experience to back them up, not in the same way Lyre does. She made the effort to protect me anytime she feasibly could. All I had done was cower.

But Lyre just smiles softly, dropping her gaze to where her babe rests safely. "I know you won't. You've never seen yourself the way I have, Aria. It isn't a burden to protect you. It's an honor. One I don't intend to stop."

The throne room is filled with legionaries when I enter, Dyanna and Sade on the dais with our mother.

"Aria." The sharp tone of her voice ushers silence in its wake, every gaze turning to land on me as I make my way up the center aisle. I bend at the waist when I reach her dais, and she pounds her golden trident on the stone floor three times in response. "Rise, Daughter," she commands. I let my eyes slowly travel up to her waiting gaze. "Have you found anything new in our hunt for those traitors?"

"Nothing new since the necklace, Your Majesty. But I will."

She arches a dark brow, leaning forward on her throne as her onyx talons catch a ray of sunlight coming in from the surface. "So sure, are you?" The females around me chuckle, and blood rushes to my cheeks as I hold my mother's glare. "You have made me question your loyalty to this queendom—to me and the crown that graces my head—far too many times in the past."

Jaw and shoulders relaxed, lips flat, spine straight, and attitude vicious.

"Don't abuse the leniency and grace I grant you now to the point that I begin to question that loyalty *again*." With a nod, I swim to join my sisters as our mother addresses the room. "I have gathered you all here for something very important. As you know, I have been working diligently for *you*, my lovely subjects, to reclaim what should have always been ours from the Mortal Kingdom." The legionaries cheer, beating their spears against the helmets of their shell armor. "And now the time has come for me to enact the next part of my plan. Today, you will travel with me and my two daughters to visit the king of the Mortal Realm."

The excitement in the air shifts as the eyes of the sirens ahead of me look from the queen to each other and back again. I harbor the same confusion they do. To go to the surface was one thing, but in such a large group? And in front of King Dolian and his guards? What could my mother *possibly* need her legion for up there?

"I know there are questions, but the answers you seek are better *seen*. Gather whatever you will need for a multi-day trip and meet me here in half an hour." She rises from her throne, looking down at her people as she projects her voice even louder. "Soon, we make history!" The Queen's Legion rushes out of the throne room, and my mother turns to face my sister. "Sade, I will be borrowing a section of my legion today."

Sade's sunset eyes narrow just slightly before she dips her chin. "I can see that. May I ask *why*?"

"You may, but like I told them, the explanation is better seen than told. Once I can confirm that my theory is accurate, then I will bring along another group. You may come with me once most of my legion is... *tested*."

My sister tilts her head, orange scales shimmering. "Tested with *what*?"

To that, our mother just smiles as she descends the dais before turning to look at me. "Our scouts have relayed that a mortal ship carrying supplies to the Shifter

Kingdom will be crossing over our waters during our journey. You will join them on their hunt." She tips her trident forward, the jagged diamond spires scratching my skin as she presses it into my chest. "Do *not* disappoint me." She gives Dyanna a look that beckons her to follow as she elegantly moves through the water to the exit, leaving Sade and I alone.

I don't look at my sister, afraid that my feelings will be obvious on my face. Gods, I haven't been on a hunt since I had come back from the Northern Island, and I have *never* gone on one without Lyre. Panic churns my stomach as it whirls through me. *My magic won't work. I'll be found out and, if I'm lucky, killed right away. If I'm not...* Queen Amari knows where to hurt me the most.

"You look like you are going to puke," Sade drawls from my side, the striped helmet cradled in her arm indenting her dark skin.

Jaw and shoulders relaxed, lips flat—

"You don't want to hunt," she guesses.

I bite the inside of my cheek, folding my arms over my chest. Sade is not one I can trust enough to voice my fears to. She's never been outwardly cruel like Allegra, but she's also *never* treated me as if I'm anyone of importance in her life. Like the rest of the queendom outside of Lyre, I'm nothing but a nuisance to her. A failure of the Malika line. *Who are you willing to become?* I jerk at Myla's voice in my head. At how easily it eviscerates the self-loathing and doubt. Sade looks at me expectantly, a single brow lifted. "It is no secret that hunts are not my favorite," I finally answer.

She snorts, lifting her helmet and positioning it over her head. "Yes, well, being a siren often means enduring a lot of things we'd rather not."

I blink, sure I heard her wrong.

Sade grips her trident, undulating her hips as she moves down the center aisle, pausing to look over her shoulder when she's almost at the door. "Hunts with the legionaries are messy because the females are more *ravenous* than others. It's easy for things to get obscured in the madness. Wouldn't want you to end up skewered on one of their spears." Sade leaves, and I stare at the door for a long while after she is gone.

Did she just... help *me?* No. No, that is impossible. *Improbable.* When chatter from the gathering legionaries knocks me from my stupor, I move to join them outside the palace.

My mother waits at the front of the crowd, the cunning smile on her face making my skin crawl. "Sirens, let us go forth and make our ancestors proud. Let us right the wrongs brought on by men. Let us claim victory with our *teeth*."

The legionaries take off, and I find my place next to Dyanna as we follow behind them on our way to the Mortal Kingdom, where only the gods and my mother know what is waiting for us.

Chapter Forty-Two

RHEA

STEPHAN HAD LEFT THE morning after my introduction to him. Though King Dolian and Simon were careful with what information they shared in my presence, I surmised from what they *did* say that it would be a few weeks before Stephan would return.

As the days passed and the next visit with the sirens loomed nearer, I found myself both terrified with anticipation and utterly *bored* with the monotonous execution of my schedule. Every day, I had dance lessons with Xander—a male who might have been willing to help me but who certainly wasn't keen on lively conversation—and tea lessons with Eve, who luckily *was* keen on such things. The bruises I had noticed on her were yellow now, and sometimes during our one-on-one time, I thought about asking her what *really* happened. If someone here was hurting her. If that someone might travel with us back to Vitour after this meeting with the sirens. But every time the words bubbled up my throat, I swallowed them back down. Eve was good about respecting my privacy, taking note when I dodged a question and never bringing the topic back up again. I at least owed her the same courtesy. While I still couldn't let my guard down fully around her, I found myself looking forward to her bright smile and cheery attitude.

After tea lessons, we would part and the rest of my day would be spent scouring books in the library, hoping that I could figure out how to release siren magic from the ring—based on what the siren queen had said during her last visit. On one occasion, Xander found me reading between stacks of books, and he quietly relayed word from his men back in Vitour. There was rumor that the Shifter Kingdom underwent some sort of mutiny and the king, Kai, had been nearly overthrown. My concern had immediately shifted to Bahira before I remembered that she was back home. But then Simon's words danced in my mind, worry for her being accused of treason making my stomach churn.

Neither Xander nor the king and his advisor had any updates on Nox. I was torn over what to believe because either Nox *had* attacked healers and was sick and possibly magicless, *or* he was fine and simply hadn't figured out where I was yet. Both options provoked spiraling thoughts that left me feeling impossibly more anxious.

But I tell myself that I can't let my unease over so many unknowns occupy all of my thoughts. All I can do is focus on my next steps here. On staying out of the king's hands and away from his advisor's leering glares.

It is all easier said than done.

The wind whips my hair across my face while I stare out at the gray ocean, its color reflecting the morose storm clouds above it. Another chilly gust scrapes along my nose, and I'm grateful Eve insisted I wear a velvet long-sleeved dress today, the dark blue material warding off the cold everywhere it covers me.

I wipe my palms on my dress, the soft material soothing, as King Dolian adjusts the crown on his head. He stands to my left, a whole step ahead of me and everyone else here, as if the crown alone isn't enough to differentiate himself. As if the sirens are unaware of who he is. Though I hate to acknowledge his presence at all, I *have* studied the way my uncle presents himself both in the residence and outside of it when speaking to others. His posture is always perfect, his look the same elegant, refined royal taste I have come to know. But in fleeting moments, ones I was sure he didn't realize he showed, I saw beneath the façade to a small and lonely man with a twisted viewpoint on the world and enough power to change it for the worse. I know he thinks this kingdom owes him something because of what happened between him, my mother, and my father. And I harbor zero doubts that he will do whatever it takes to claim everything he wants, including me.

But even now, as he stares out at the choppy ocean waiting for Queen Amari, I see the nerves that he tries to hide. He spins the ring matching mine on his finger, rolling his shoulders back for the tenth time since we arrived on this freezing beach. I should delight in the fact that there is somebody out there who has this effect on him, but all I can think about is her last visit. The way Queen Amari had relished watching me kill those guards. I wonder if King Dolian's unease is a sign that the siren queen holds much more sway over him than anyone realizes.

Xander stands to my right, dressed in his golden armor with enough weapons strapped to him that it's a marvel he can walk properly. In sand no less. Behind us stands the Spell and, behind that, a line of guards only ten across. I can feel their gazes at my back, their silent judgment making me fidget to the point that Xander turns his head to look at me. I had killed so many guards the last time, ones I imagined were friends of those behind me. I can't blame any of them for the glares.

"They're fucking *late*," the king growls, tugging on his vest, its color abhorrently matching my dress.

Simon is noticeably absent, left at the front door to see us off with orders to ensure our boat is ready to leave by tomorrow afternoon. The carriage ride had been a bumpy one, my knee constantly hitting into the king's no matter which way I positioned my body. Each touch—no matter the layers of clothing between us—did nothing but send revulsion through me and make the brand on my hip itch with awareness. I hate the mark, hate the man who gave it to me. Hate that I'm trapped here, a mouse scurrying in a maze only to find dead end after dead end.

I don't realize how hard I'm gritting my teeth together until pain shoots up my temple.

There is an audible gasp behind me, and when I cast my gaze out to the sea, I see three heads rise from the water. I watch in awe as the sirens emerge, their transformation a waterfall effect that starts at the crowns of their heads and moves over their bodies with ease. Their scales seem to *retreat* into their bodies, leaving only the faintest glimmer of color over their dark brown skin. While the queen and the one standing to her left have curls in long strands that cover their chests, the bright pink hair of the siren on the right only just touches her collarbones. Her expression is one of boredom, as if making an entrance onto the beach completely nude is part of a normal day for her.

Maybe it is.

"Your Majesty," King Dolian says, his posture stiff as he stares at the queen. She gives him a brilliant smile in return, one that neither reaches her eyes nor reads as anything remotely sincere.

"King Dolian, thank you for meeting us here." Her eyes land on me, a callousness in them that makes me go rigid. I once read that there are parts of the ocean untouched by the sun, places so dark and deep that not even the sirens had ever dared to explore them. That's what her gaze reminds of—a place devoid of *light*. "And for bringing Lady Rhea."

"It is a pleasure to see you, of course," the king says coolly, cocking his head to the side. "But I am curious what is so important that you need to speak in person instead of through the Mirrors." The queen's eyes snap back to his as she flattens her lips. The ruby-haired siren to her left works a rough swallow down her throat.

"Watch your tongue, Mortal King. I have killed men for far less."

"Kill me, and all of our deals become void," he retorts, sliding his hands into his pockets. Xander adjusts his stance at my side, the creaking of his armor drawing the gazes of both sirens that flank the queen. I study them, bouncing my attention back and forth. The pink-haired siren's features are harsher, her bright pink eyes boring into Xander's while her sharp jaw clenches. It's a look that mimics the queen's, and it makes me wonder if they are related. The other siren's eyes don't match her hair, their orange hue similar to the king's. Her features are softer, and dark freckles pepper her cheeks. When her gaze meets mine, there is no malice or even curiosity there. All I see is the same trepidation reflected on her face that I feel inside.

"Luckily for us both, killing you is *not* in my best interest. Not yet anyway." The queen grips her trident—a dark golden weapon tipped with jagged-looking diamonds larger than my arm—flipping it so that the sharp ends point directly at the king. The sound of blades sliding from their sheaths slices the air behind me, but Xander holds out a hand, halting the guards' reactions to the threat. "Look at how they react so strongly to protect you. What a *loyal* army you have."

King Dolian says nothing, his posture still like a statue though his hands flex where he's stuffed them in his pockets. "They do as they are told."

"As all soldiers should." Despite the sea and wind dancing around us, the queen projects her voice loudly enough to be heard. "Did you know that we keep a legion under the sea?"

Xander's hand drops to one of his sheathed swords, his fingers squeezing the hilt. The pink-haired siren traces the movement, baring her teeth at him in warning.

"I'm not foolish enough to assume a realm—even one beneath the surface—would leave themselves vulnerable should this damned Spell ever come down," Dolian replies.

"The Spell," Queen Amari repeats slowly, looking at where it gleams behind me. "Such a troublesome nuisance, isn't it? One would think that, in the two hundred years since it was cast, a mage would have been able to bring it down." Those terrifying eyes move to me again. "Though why would they test something that is of no consequence to them?"

My heart pounds in my chest, panic filtering in the longer her question lingers between us. Of course, she knows the mages' secret. She would have known the moment she saw me use my magic on the beach. It's the way she looks at me, as if I'm something to be *devoured*. Something that she can sink her sharp black talons into and claw away at until I'm nothing but pieces for her to use. King Dolian clears his throat, taking a small sidestep so that he partially obscures me from her.

"What are you getting at?" he asks.

The queen just smirks, the strands of her midnight hair stirring as a powerful gust of wind rolls off the ocean. Then she lifts her trident high in the air, sunlight catching the diamond tips and casting small flares of rainbow light onto the sand. Again, the guards stir behind me. Again, Xander holds off their response. With the king's new position in front of me, I can't see the pink-haired siren, but I can see the other one. She watches the queen with intense concentration, her talons gently scraping her hips in quick motions.

"Gods above," one of the guards behind me says, the sentiment echoed throughout the group and even by Xander, his softly murmured curse only barely hitting my ears.

When I lean a little to the side to have a clear view of the ocean, I gasp too, though I'm unsure of what I'm actually looking at. It starts out with tan-colored points rising above the thrashing water line before they grow into giant... *shells*. The kind I had only ever seen drawn in books. They are larger than I could have possibly imagined, and it isn't until they rise about a foot from the water that I realize there is a *person* beneath. Like some sort of macabre helmet, the shells—variations of brown and tan and white—mask the sirens' heads and some of their faces as they rise from the ocean, transforming into their mortal forms beneath what appears to be shell *armor*.

The king takes a step back, his hand wrapping around my wrist. "What is the meaning of this?"

"Do not panic, dear king," Queen Amari cajoles, walking until she is only a hand's width away from him. He keeps his gaze keenly on her face, though he squeezes my wrist so tightly my fingers flex from the pain. "They are not here to harm you."

Row after row of armored sirens emerge from the sea, an entire *army* of them. The females, each with the same soft curves as the queen and her companions, wear expressions that suck the air right from my chest. By the time they finish lining the beach, I count upwards of fifty sirens. Almost all of them hold metal spears while a select few carry miniature tridents, and *all* of them send us steely jewel-colored glares.

"Bring your fiancée forward," the queen says, dropping her voice lower. King Dolian, to my astonishment, obeys immediately. He tugs me a single step forward until I'm right at his side, his grip growing tighter. I hiss a breath out through my teeth and attempt to pull away from him to no avail. The queen's mouth curves deviantly. "You will let the girl go."

Without hesitation, his fingers leave my skin. I draw my arm up to cradle it against my chest, but the queen snatches it first. Her touch is cold, and though she's retracted her talons and only mortal nails remain, I swear I can feel the prick of them indenting my skin.

"We have work to do, Lady Rhea, and I don't want to waste another moment."

"What work?" I rasp while she positions me at her side, forcing the ruby-haired siren to move farther down.

"I know that mages have the ability to pass through the Spell." Her gaze slides to mine, but I keep my lips pinched closed. "And I have a theory that the reason that is possible is because their magic *heals* them from the Spell's side effects."

Again, I don't respond, my heart pounding near my throat.

"Today, we are going to test that theory."

"I—I can't *do* that," I sputter, shaking my head. "It won't work. My magic doesn't—"

"Have you tried healing another in this way?" she asks.

"No, but—"

"Then you cannot speak to whether it will work or not. I have willing subjects, ready to fulfill their duty to their queendom," she says quietly, leaning in until her nose nearly touches mine. "And I have a king under my control just as you are."

My blood runs cold as her eyes dip down to where my hands press against my stomach. To a ring of golden coral topped with a pearl. One that matches the king's, though his is striped with ocean blue. Gods, in some poetic and dreadful twist of fate, she is using the *same* magic to control him that he is using on me. That's why he didn't resist earlier. She was *commanding* him. Does the king realize that's what she's doing? Does the same rush of magic flood him that does me? Noting my discovery on my face, Queen Amari smiles brightly and turns back to face her subjects, forcing me to do the same with a tug at my arm.

"My sirens, now is the time you have been waiting for. *Now* is the first day of retribution! For today, we will finally take our first step on mortal lands in over two hundred years!"

Chapter Forty-Three

RHEA

"**T**HIS WILL NOT WORK," I say a little louder, drawing Queen Amari's attention again. Shaking my head, I bare my palms to her. "My magic cannot *do* that."

"I have been alive a long time, *girl*, and I have seen the impossible made possible." Her voice carries over the wind and sea, echoing out over the beach until her sirens settle. "I have seen shifters battle in their animal forms. I have seen dragons take flight and crowd the skies. I have seen mortal men go back on their word." Her eyes flick to King Dolian briefly before they settle back on me. "And I have seen mages use their magic to tear kingdoms apart."

Goosebumps unravel over my body, making the hair at the back of my neck rise. "I am not one of *those* mages." Yet, even as I refute her claim, something deep in my gut stirs. It was a queen of Void Magic who cast the Spell, but that doesn't mean the magic *I* have could make it safe to cross over.

She reaches out and tucks a strand of hair behind my ear, the tender move impossibly at odds with the merciless look on her face. "We will find out which one of us is correct."

My heart revolts like a caged animal. "Your people will die. *Please.*"

Her hand falls away as she straightens her posture and grips her trident tightly. "That is a risk I'm willing to take." She beckons a volunteer forward, their teal eyes meeting mine after she takes her helmet off. She appears no older than I am, and my stomach drops as I look to Queen Amari again.

"Please, I can't—" But my pleas are overshadowed by her next command.

"Use your magic to heal her so that she may go through the Spell unharmed."

A roaring fills my ears, and I squeeze my eyes shut, grasping for a foothold. Reaching invisible hands out to my magic as if I can force it back into submission. But the powerful wave of the queen's order keeps building, standing over me like a vengeful god waiting for the chance to pounce.

And then it does.

The cover to the well of my magic is removed, and my power comes rushing out from where it's been trapped. A scream rings out on the beach—*mine*—as my back arches and the familiar hum of my power settles into every muscle. Seeps into every pore and nerve ending and space between my bones. I open my eyes wide, my vision haloed in bright white light as one of my arms lifts. With a grunt from the force of it, my magic bursts from my fingertips and hits the armored siren in her chest, her body filling with my power. Glittering light bleeds into her veins, lighting them beneath her dark brown skin. It makes her look like fracturing marble, and fear punches through my chest at the thought that my magic might shatter her.

Yet, in the same breath that I worry for the siren's life, another emotion takes root.

It has been *so long* since I've used my power. So long since I've felt it alive within me. And it feels... *good*. Wisps seep away from the path of the siren and begin slithering over the sand, my magic feeding me information, sensing the world around me as it tries to decipher my intentions. It leaves me overwhelmed and desperate as I claw for more of it, never wanting to lose this connection again. I just want *more*, and that want smothers the small voice of reason in my mind that is trying to remind me that what I'm doing is wrong. That this is *wrong*.

The queen takes a step towards me, her pitch-black eyes narrowing with deep suspicion. She doesn't order me to stop, and *that* makes a smile not my own curl my lips upward. Only when the siren is completely glowing with veins of white light does my magic slowly begin to recede on its own, pulling the remnants that have crept out around me with it. Disappointment and longing pull at my chest, and I cling heartily to this intrinsic part of myself. I don't want it to disappear again. I don't want to lose the connection to it. But the power of the queen's command ebbs away and, with it, so does the connection to my magic.

"How do you feel?" Queen Amari asks her siren, the latter staring at her open hands as if the magic I've sent through her will come manifesting out of her palms too.

"I feel... the same," she says between the quick rise and fall of her chest. "Or *mostly* the same."

"See? My magic will not make her live through crossing the Spell. She—"

"Go through the Spell," she orders. When the siren hesitates, she bites out a "*Now!*"

No. "Don't!" I shout, my hands trembling in front of me. "Please, don't go through. It will *kill* you." The siren's knuckles turn white from how tightly she grips her spear, but when the queen gives her a look that can only be described as *murderous*, she begins walking again. Air squeezes from my lungs, and I spin to face King Dolian. Nausea burns my throat as I grip his forearms, shaking him slightly to get his attention. "You cannot allow this. She will *die,* and I can't—" My voice breaks, and tears crest and then fall, dotting my cheeks with their warmth. "Please. *Stop this.*"

The taste of salt coats my tongue, drying my mouth out as I wait for him to answer. His hazel eyes are honed in on me, and he adjusts his stance so that he faces me fully, reaching up to cup my face in his hands. *Something* flashes across his expression, an emotion strong enough to furrow his brows as he pulls me in closer. Then it's gone, leaving only the familiar villainous curl of his lips. "There are a great many things I will do for you, Rhea. Many things I *have* done for you." His grip on me tightens when I try to back away. "But this *has* to happen."

"Why?" I cry, trying to look past him as the siren gets within a few steps of the Spell.

Dolian drops his voice to a whisper, his lips a breath away from my own. "Because all of those things I did for you had a cost." My heart sinks as ripples dance across the Spell when the siren passes through. "*You're* the reason this is happening." Tugging my head forward, he presses his mouth onto mine harshly. My hands plant on his chest as I attempt to push him away, but he only digs his fingers harder into the sides of my head, his tongue attempting to pry my lips apart to grant him full access.

"Your Majesty, look!" Xander's voice booms behind me, and the sharpness of it makes King Dolian draw back. His eyes widen as he drops his hold on me, and I immediately spin to face the Spell, seeing the siren on the other side of it.

"How do you feel?" Queen Amari shouts, pushing past the king and I.

"I feel..." The siren licks her lips as she shakes her head. "I feel fine."

My mouth falls open, and if it weren't for the fact that my knees are locked by the adrenaline from what has just happened, I would collapse onto them.

"Try singing," the queen urges. "See if her magic altered your power at all." King Dolian tenses, a protest already spewing from his mouth, but Queen Amari silences him. "She will not lure your men beyond just testing her magic," she growls over her shoulder, turning back to look at the siren. "Go."

A seductive melody fills the air, the siren's notes dulcet and rich. The mortal guard closest to her lowers his sword until the tip digs into the sand. His expression falls lax as his lids grow heavy.

"Gods above," Xander whispers from his new place at my side. I glance at him just as he takes a step towards the Spell.

This can't be happening. It *can't* be. Perhaps there is a delayed reaction or... But no. I've read enough books to know that when one crosses the Spell and steps into a kingdom they are not from, the magic begins taking from them immediately. Elora had confirmed the same during one of our reading sessions together. If the siren were truly suffering from the consequences of crossing the border, it would be obvious.

But if she is alive and well, then... *Oh gods.*

"That's enough," Queen Amari says, and the siren ends her song, releasing the men from her magic. Xander shakes his head, as if clearing a terrible thought, while King Dolian draws a hand down his face, the color leached from it. And something about seeing him—the man who holds so much power over me—frightened by what just happened, lodges dread in my throat all over again. "Well," the queen starts, turning to face us, "it looks as if the mages have been keeping quite a few secrets."

"Indeed," King Dolian grumbles.

"Let us not waste any more time, then." The siren queen prowls through the sand to stand between her two companions, both of whom have a sickly sheen to their skin.

"I think we've spent enough—"

"Quiet," she drawls, interrupting King Dolian before slamming the end of her trident down. The king stiffens, the result of her magical order flooding his body. There's no pleasure to be found in the fact that he's turned from captor to captive, however. Not when the monster holding the leash is *worse* than even him. "Come, Lady Rhea," she beckons, crooking her finger at me. "We have much to do."

❧❧❧❧❧ ❧❧❧❧❧

The cost for using my magic comes once we leave the beach and are in route back to the residence. My eyelids are heavy, and my body slumps against the soft velvet bench as I grip its edges.

"Did you know that your magic could... *do* that?" King Dolian asks, his voice deceptively soft.

I roll my head to the side as it pounds in time to the horse hooves outside. "No."

His fingers curl and then straighten on top of his thigh, as if he's restraining himself from touching me. "I don't know if it is foolish to believe you, but I do," he finally says, looking out the opposite window of the carriage.

I don't respond, my body losing its battle against the fatigue that presses in from all sides,

"Rhea, if I had tried to stop the queen's attempt to have you heal the siren—however impossible it would have been—would it have changed how you feel about me?"

His question is so sincere that it *almost* stops the bitter laugh that travels up my throat. Instead, I let the sound tumble out as I turn my head to look out my own window. *None* of this would be happening were my uncle not so corrupted. And now that corruption is pulling at me, shredding me apart piece by piece until I'm certain that all that will be left at the end is as vile and fickle as he is. "There is *nothing* you could do to change that."

Nox had said he wanted *every* version of me, but what will he think when he learns what I've done? When he *sees* for himself the marks from my time here that I cannot hide. I'd barely scratched the surface of my own redemption with everything I had gone through at the hands of the king before I was taken, and doubt bleeds through my shield, reminding me that Nox has not yet come. Even though it's not logical for him to know where I am. Even though Simon and Dolian had relayed that he himself might be injured or sick. *He hasn't come.*

I think the king might respond, or perhaps the voice I hear is someone else, but it all blends as I fall into nothingness.

Part Three

Time moves differently when pain is the only thing you can feel.

Chapter Forty-Four

RHEA

"**S**UNSHINE." NOX'S VOICE RINGS out in the dark as I spin where I stand, turning round and round while searching for him.

"Where are you?" I shout, blindly reaching out in front of me. "Nox!"

"I'm here," he whispers, sounding even farther away than before.

I take an unsteady step forward, my bare feet hitting cool, wet stone when a flicker of golden light catches my gaze. It's in the distance, just out of reach, but if I move a little more—

"Rhea!" He screams this time, propelling me into a sprint. Tears crest my eyes as my chest heaves, but I can't stop. I'll lose him if I stop. The golden light grows brighter as it moves like a tattered flag in the wind. My hair whips behind me, and I pump my arms harder, stretching a hand out—to reach for what, I'm not sure. The light sharpens the nearer I get, morphing from a simple golden glow into something linear. Something that looks like... like a rope.

"Nox!" I scream, limbs tingling with magic as I reach towards that tether. Its warmth brushes along my fingertips, a pleasant hum emanating from the light, but right as I'm about to grasp it, sure that it must lead to him, I'm yanked back.

Cold, slithering magic wraps around my torso, pinning my arms into place at my sides. I struggle to get free, screaming for Nox. For anyone to help. But my pleas fall on deaf ears, and as I'm dragged farther away, the light once more shrinking into something undefinable, darkness creeps in until it suffocates me completely.

I suck in a breath as the shadows fade until I'm in my room. How did I get here? Staring at the ceiling, my brows furrow when I try to swallow, my mouth parched and tasting of something herbal. Its bitterness makes me gag, but when I attempt to sit up to go to the bathroom, my vision swirls as white sparks across it and my body stays firmly in place.

"Ah, she's finally awake." A silhouette appears at the foot of my bed, backlit by hazy silver moonlight and shadows that dance along its edges. But I don't need to see his features to know whose voice this is. This scenario has played out enough times in my dreams for me to understand. Simon picks an instrument up from the metal tray that is always at the bed's corner, and I force my eyes closed as my heartrate spikes. "I had wondered if perhaps using so much magic today would leave you in a catatonic state. I'm glad to see you only needed a few hours of rest. How are you feeling?" he asks.

"This isn't real," I whisper, startled that my voice carries sound. It hasn't the past few times he's haunted my dreams. Clearing my throat of that bitter taste, I repeat, "This isn't real."

"Surprised you can talk?" He sounds closer, and the question prompts my eyes back open, the swirling darkness of my bedroom making my head pound. Simon stares down at me from where he now stands at my feet. "Did you know that the fae have their own version of gelsemium? They call it belladragis. The flowers are beautiful and quite deceiving in their strength." The right side of his mouth lifts. "Somewhat like you."

The tool in his hand glints, its flat shape like a blade except it's thinner than any I've ever seen before. "This isn't—"

"When you slice their little petals open, they secrete a liquid that, while awful in taste and smell, works as a true paralytic." My blink is slow, and Simon moves from my feet to my hip in the time it takes my eyes to open again. "What will we see when we slice you open?"

His silhouette lifts an arm over his head, and even though I expect the pain to come, as it has in every dream, nothing prepares me for the way it erupts over my thigh when he plunges his instrument in. My scream echoes out and reverberates in my head, as if I'm trapped in a cave with my own nightmare.

"Are you paying attention, Princess Rhea?" I groan when he yanks the blade out, prompting more white stars to flare across my vision. "Today, you did something that could be considered miraculous. Spectacular. Godly, even." My eyelids flutter as I stare at the ceiling, a dark green glow washing over it for a moment before the sound of Simon playing with his metal tray again draws my gaze back down.

I look over my body, attempting to wiggle my limbs beneath my velvet dress. But I don't move. I never do. "Wake up," I rasp, Simon once more hovering near my hip.

"Tell me what secrets you're holding within." He shows me the new tool he's plucked, but I can't focus on it, not as I watch him raise his arm over his head again. "What else can your magic do?" He doesn't even give me time to answer before he plunges the newest weapon down, hard enough that I'm sure he hits bone.

I scream, the horrid noise wrenched from me as quickly as my lungs empty of every speck of air. "Wake up!" I heave, tears streaming down the sides of my face as shadows swirl above me. "Wake up!"

Simon pulls his tool free, examining my blood that coats it as a sadistic smile lifts his cheeks. "Is that what you think is happening right now? That you're in some sort of dream?"

This isn't real. This isn't real.

"Oh, I'm afraid that this is *very* real and, until you give me the answers I want, so too is the pain I will inflict on you. So before we continue, do you want to confess what else your magic can do?"

My lips quiver as I track his movements, tears blurring his figure from one to two then back again.

"What else can your magic do?" Simon asks again, his sharp voice piercing my heart.

"I don't— Nothing beyond normal mage magic." His movements are a blur when he drags the blade over my knee, warmth spilling from the split skin as metal scrapes against bone. I scream until my throat is raw, until my own voice vibrates in my skull. *Wake up. Wake up. Wake.* Up!

"Don't *lie* to me," he says curtly. "I will always know if you do." Again, he cuts into my skin, agony filling every empty spot within me as my vision glows white around the edges. A soft, unintelligible whisper plays in my ear, there for only a few seconds before it's gone again, replaced with Simon's voice. "Tell me *everything* your magic can do."

My consciousness begins to dwindle, and I silently beg for it to take me out. To ease me into a space where I can be numb. Through a hazy white veil, a green light forms over my leg. Right where Simon's hands are hovering. It doesn't make sense, but then again my dreams lately never do.

"I want to tell you a story." My eyes threaten to fall closed as warmth flares at my thigh, a pleasant sensation trickling there. But I'm stuck here, unable to move. Unable to *leave.* "Roughly five decades ago, a boy was born into the Mage Kingdom. He was a curious one, always tinkering with the world around him. But nothing fascinated him more than the intricate nature of the mage body. He could read all day about how it functioned, and he did. While his friends played with their magic and studied things like politics or history, he learned about the brain and the nervous system. He found himself eager to learn if the magic mages wielded was the reason they were so superior."

"He wanted to know if what made them different could be seen *within* the body. If it could be dissected. His obsession drew him into a relatively reclusive life, but one that fulfilled him enough because he let himself explore those curiosities. For years, he did what he knew he was born to. He memorized the inner layout of the body, and it was even more marvelous than he imagined."

My awareness sharpens when Simon's voice grows strained, that green light flickering beneath his palms. The sensation of something familiar—something I've felt before—wanes from my muscles and the once aching bone until there is... *nothing*. No lingering pain. It's almost as if...

"But something else happened as he pursued this knowledge. He discovered a certain kind of joy in pushing someone to their limits. Each individual had a breaking point, and once they were past that, well, they'd tell you anything if it meant finding relief."

He draws in a deep breath as he turns his head towards me. Even with the silver light from outside cutting a line over his face, his dark eyes don't look *mage*. But I knew there were those in the Mage Kingdom who didn't have gray eyes. Cass, Daje, and Councilman Arav to name a few. But Simon... I swallow the bile that rises in my throat. Gods above, the reason I awoke without evidence after our encounters wasn't because they were dreams. It's because Simon *healed* me of all that he was doing. He *healed* me. "You're mage," I grit out.

He smiles as he moves to that metal tray again, fingers trailing over the instruments there. He ignores my question. "As you might imagine, finding subjects to experiment on was a task all its own. It's why I became so knowledgeable of the plant life around me. It's harder to convince someone by getting them drunk or cornering them in an alley, but when I can slip something in their drink so that they can't fight back? Well"—he plucks a thin steel *pick*—"that's an entirely different sense of euphoria."

"This is madness," I whisper, trying to mask my fear but failing when my voice breaks. "If the king finds out what you are doing to me, that you are *mage*—"

"*I* am the king's greatest asset!" he screams, rushing to me between one blink and the next, his profile outlined green from his *magic*. His lips peel back in a snarl, white teeth flashing as he hovers over me. "I fled here when my own kingdom tried to execute me. When they turned my own family against *me*. King Sadryn did not even *consider* seeing how my research could help our people!"

A sob claws its way up my throat, a leaden feeling blanketing me and my useless limbs.

"I settled in Vitour first, making a name for myself because of my knowledge with plants. My reputation earned me jobs from wealthier clients, greedy noblemen and women looking for tinctures that played to their vanity until one day, one of the males joked about wishing to kill his wife without being caught. Of course, I knew exactly how to do it. How to make it look like she had simply passed away from something unknown. Thus, a different reputation was born, one that eventually earned me council with the king." Simon stands tall, his jaw set tightly as he looks down at me. "King Dolian offered me a place at his side if I could prove to him my worth. So I did. First by quietly poisoning those who opposed him. Then, by capturing and torturing any who dared to threaten his rule as king. I have never let him down with the intelligence I gather or by my methods, and *you* will not be the thing that breaks that streak."

"I will tell the king," I rasp, a final plea of desperation. King Dolian harbors a twisted affection for me. I can use it, exploit it, to get him to *believe* me.

"I will give you one more chance, Lady Rhea, and then I will move on to more *persuasive* measures." He presses the tip of the pick into my arm, not enough to cut through skin but enough to serve as a warning that he will. "Tell me everything your magic can do and what the Mage Kingdom was using it for."

A whimper escapes me—one that I can't hold in as I use precious seconds to sink into that dark, imaginary place before he continues his torture. I scramble as I push everything I have to fight for to the forefront of my mind like a shield that I can hide behind. The air stirs, and I think of Cass and his playful smirk. How his eyes—so beautiful and clear—always held mirth. Green magic swirls around Simon, and he sends it to my door, sealing the edges. I scream as the pick slams into my arm, easily shredding through skin and muscle and bone until I just *know* it is protruding from the other side. A sickening squelch sounds when he yanks it back out.

"What are the mages doing with someone like you? Someone as powerful as Prince Nox?" His hand comes down again, and I don't hear the noise I make beyond the ringing of my ears.

Elora. I picture her sly smile and her boisterous laugh. The way she reads a book with her entire body hunched over it as if she can dive into the pages themselves. Blood pools beneath my arm, spreading slowly towards my back. I think of her kindness, of how she immediately believed me when I told her how I came to the Mage Kingdom. Of how she held the secret without question.

Simon grips my chin, forcing my gaze to his. Anger dances within them, visible even in the dark, but that's not all. Determination flickers in their depths, and that is far more frightening. "What else can your magic do?" He jerks the metal still lodged in my arm, and my breath is robbed from me as a primal noise ravages my throat. "Tell me!"

I retreat deeper into my mind, passing memories of Sadryn and Alexandria and their utter joy when we announced our engagement. Of Daje's proud expression when we sparred and I took him down. I pass by all the small moments in my brief time away from the king, every new experience that was beginning to shape the kind of woman I might become. And then I stop at the sight of sparkling gray and silver eyes. At the smirk of his perfect mouth and the wave of his onyx hair. Everything narrows down to the image of Nox—not as my lover or my friend. Not as my guard or my fiancé or my prince. But as my home. My safety.

Simon's breaths grow heavy, and he releases my chin and pulls the pick out, tossing it onto the tray with a wet *clang*. "Perhaps I was unclear," he says, flashing his magic as he moves his palms over my arm. Healing me again. "But I take pleasure in dragging this out. And I have nowhere else to be."

My gaze returns to the ceiling as his magic eventually fades. All the while, I savor that image of Nox. Me curled into his embrace. The way my heart would steady to match the beat of his. Simon continues his ministrations, asking the same questions and healing me right when I'm on the verge of passing out. Then the torture begins again, a new instrument plucked from the tray every time.

Something fractures deep within me the later into the night we go, and when Simon heals me for the final time as the sun is beginning to rise, I know that the damage he's done is the kind that cannot be mended. Still, I find myself using the last dredges of my defiance, unwilling to give that new crack in the foundation of my soul a name. To feel it is one thing, but to acknowledge the thoughts that it ushers in? The ones that scream that *true* freedom is only one well-placed slice of a blade away? That terrifies me more than anything Simon or the king or the sirens can do. Because I can block them from my mind, hard as it is, but my own voice? I don't know if I am strong enough to ignore that, and its quiet offer of sweet release has never been so tempting.

Chapter Forty-Five

RHEA

WE ARE LEAVING FOR Vitour today. *Those weren't just nightmares.* I'm finally returning to a place where Nox can find me. *Were they all real?* Perhaps I can find a way to break free of the king there. *How many times did Simon heal me only to torture me again?*

My thoughts volley back and forth as I stand beneath the warm water of the shower, my heart racing in my chest. I look down over my body, fingers tracing lightly over the scabbed brand, its tenderness beneath the water mild. My gaze drops lower, to my thighs and then my knees, staring at the smooth skin as my chest tightens. For weeks, nightmares had haunted me. Ones that were anchored around Simon and my torture, but also ones where it was the king. Had those been real too?

I bring my fingers to my temples, squinting my eyes shut against the ache that throbs between them. I hadn't slept at all, enduring hours of Simon's questions and subsequent inflictions of pain. And I had no evidence to show for it. Nothing that I could take to the king to prove that his advisor was lying to him. That he was torturing me.

I turn my head to look out the small window in the bathroom, its angle showing only the clear blue sky. Maybe King Dolian might have helped me without proof, but I had likely sunken that ship after what I told him on the carriage ride from the beach. Now I can't imagine he will believe *anything* I say. I should have been smarter in my approach, playing someone more pliant to get the king to let his guard down instead of openly defying him when I could. But how could I suddenly be expected to heel when every part of me wanted to lash out like a rabid animal? When I could feel so acutely the weight of the invisible chains that bound me? Then again, so much of myself had already been sacrificed to the king on behalf of others. In *spite* of my wants and desires. What was another piece added to the pile?

With a reluctant sigh, I turn the water off and exit the shower, wrapping a towel around myself before heading to the door. Eve is laying out a dress for me on the freshly made bed, her mouth is pinched into a forced smile as she turns to face me. I didn't know exactly how long Simon had been gone before she arrived in my room, only that I had been laying unmoving for so long that I didn't realize the paralytic he had given me had worn off.

"How are you feeling?"

I shrug, walking to the armoire to grab a chemise and some undergarments before rounding the bed to stand in front of the dress. I stare down at the comforter, at how it fits perfectly over the bed, hiding what occurred the night before. Not that there would be evidence of how I bled. Before Simon left, he had used his magic to *move* me, revealing a plastic lining that prevented any blood from seeping through to the sheets. It had hidden what he was doing just as easily as his magic did. Then he removed the dress I was wearing and the garments beneath, hardly sparing me a glance before putting a new chemise on me and laying me back on the bed. Truly as if I had merely dreamed the events. "I'm fine."

"Lady Rhea, are you injured?" I look over my shoulder to where Eve has moved to a bundle of fabric on the floor. My bedsheets, I realize. She sifts through them, grabbing one and lifting it up as she looks at me. It takes me a moment to answer her, a quick shake of my head all I'm able to give. But I can tell she doesn't believe me, and when she holds the sheet up, her brows pinched in concentration, I see why. Crimson dots the cream fabric. Eve asks again if I'm alright, but all I can do is stare at those red stains, that hollow feeling inside of me yawning wider.

❧ ☙

Leaning against the railing that edges the deck, I look out over the ocean, its calmer waters gleaming beneath a layer of the Spell that Xander told me goes down several feet past the surface. The sun is warm above me, countering the cold air that grazes my skin. Eve had accompanied me on the ship, showing me to my room which was unfortunately near King Dolian's. The latter had not so much as *looked* at me while we boarded, instead going right into a private meeting with Xander and Simon. It was all fine by me, the less attention he gave me, the better.

But eventually, he had summoned Eve, the handmaiden's fingers curling in on her apron as she offered me a small smile before leaving. I wondered what the king might need from her for a few moments before I collapsed onto the soft bed that smelled of lavender and clean linens and *finally* drifted off into sleep. To my relief, it had been completely dreamless, and when I woke, I wandered back up to the deck, intent to spend as much time as possible outside of my own head.

Bootsteps sound behind me, and I tense, looking over my shoulder only to see Xander walking in my direction. He's armorless, though a golden sword shines at his hip and a small dagger is strapped to his thigh. He stops a few feet away from me, turning so that his back is to the ocean as he leans against the railing and folds his arms over his chest. "How are you holding up?" He doesn't look at me when he asks the question, instead studying the deck around us. I move to get closer to him so we can engage in a *normal* conversation, but Xander shakes his head subtly. "Better it appears we aren't talking to each other in case someone reports it."

"Would it be odd for the king's commander to engage in conversation with his supposed fiancée?"

Xander arches a dark brow. "Have you met said king?"

I force a grin at that, though it dwindles in the wind as I look back out over the water.

"So," Xander says, breaking the silence, "how are you doing? Really?"

"Fine," I answer, swallowing down the other words that attempt to follow in opposition. "Everything is fine."

"Has anyone ever told you you're a shit liar?"

I scoff, tightening my fingers over the cold metal railing. "That's rude."

Xander offers a barely perceptible shrug of one shoulder. "Doesn't make it any less true," he teases, his lips just briefly quirking before his voice grows serious again. "Eve is... *concerned* about you. Because of what's happened."

My chin drops to my chest, an invisible noose tightening around my throat. "The beach?"

"Amongst other things. I am limited in *how* I can help you, but that doesn't mean that I can't or won't. I know you don't trust me fully—and I'd honestly be disappointed if you did—but I can promise you that I mean it when I say I want you away from the king and back with the mage prince."

"You can say his name," I assert, though my voice comes out haggard. I turn my head to see Xander's gaze already on me, a question lingering there. "No one ever says it, and I just—" My words choke off under a stilted breath. It's a silly thing, really, to care that they always refer to him like some mysterious entity. One shrouded by the lies and secrets he wore to keep himself safe as he tried to find the source of the magic. As he tried to find *me*. But when was the last time I heard his name spoken outside of the confines of my own mind? "He is real," I say, more to myself.

"He is," Xander affirms, leaning in a little closer. "I'm hoping that once I can check in with my men in Vitour, I'll have some more information to give you regarding him."

"Is Stephan the one giving you that information?"

"Some of it," he answers honestly. "The rest is from a collection of small towns that border the Mage Kingdom. I've found that having multiple sources produces the most accurate information."

I nod right as a wave crashes into the ship, momentarily knocking me off balance. I hit my hip against the railing as the ship evens out and grunt at the bite of pain that licks around the brand. "*Gods*," I hiss, squeezing my eyes shut while I breathe through the lingering soreness.

"What's wrong?"

"Nothing," I bite out as I lay my hand gently over my hip as if that alone will soothe the ache there. "It's nothing."

Xander looks unconvinced but thankfully doesn't press the issue. He does, unfortunately, bring up a different one. "We need to talk about what happened yesterday."

"Which part?"

His brows furrow again as he looks out over the deck. "You *healed* sirens," he says with a hint of incredulity. "What else could have happened that was more noteworthy than that?"

Right. Because Xander doesn't know about Simon and the torture and the way I told King Dolian I would always hate him. All of those things had inexplicably happened in a single day, yet it feels as if a part of me has been stuck in each of those moments simultaneously for weeks.

"I didn't know my magic could do that. I truly thought they were going to die."

"I gathered as much," he says gently, and that knot in my throat grows bigger. "But I do think you need to be aware that now that the king knows what you can do, he's going to figure out a way to use it to his own advantage, especially if it means regaining the upper hand from Queen Amari."

I flex my fingers over my hip. I hadn't even considered how I might be used in this way. "If I can heal the sirens..."

"Then it stands to reason that your magic will work on *any* being," Xander finishes for me as he pushes up from the railing. "You've just become Olymazi's greatest weapon."

Or its downfall.

"I have a system back in Vitour. More men I trust, more ways to gather information securely. Our options will be greater. We just need to survive whatever His Majesty has planned next until we can get you free of his hold." His use of the word "we" makes my heart thump strangely. Does he truly think of us as a team? At my nod, he takes a step, making to walk away before pausing. "Eve is a good one," he blurts, almost as if he hadn't quite planned on those words spilling out.

"What?"

"Person. She's a good person. If you need someone to... *talk* to about things, you can trust her."

"Says the male with the same scar on his palm that she has."

His eyes meet mine then, both of us looking over our shoulders at the other. There's no judgement in his, and I watch as he deliberately unmasks his expression layer by layer, letting me see his sincerity. "Our imprisonment may not have been as literal as yours was and *is*, Lady Rhea, but it doesn't make it any less real. It doesn't mean we are not still unwilling participants in all of this."

Xander doesn't linger, walking to the other side of the ship where a staircase leads below deck. I stay for a moment longer, letting his words seep into me as guilt roars within, before I decide to explore the ship to pass the time. As I make my way across the deck, following the same path Xander took, my gaze snags on a few of the posted guards. One looks at me with outright curiosity, his eyes roaming over me like doing so will show him the inner workings of my body. *Of my magic.* Another's stare is more condemning, his light blue eyes narrowing harshly as I pass.

The farther that I go, the more looks I receive, some so sharp they prick right between my ribs. I abandon the idea of exploring and head back to my room, collapsing on the bed once more and forcing my eyes to close. But sleep eludes me, and instead, the faces of the guards play on repeat behind my lids. They have a myriad of reasons to be wary of me, none greater than that I had *killed* so many of them not long ago. And now? Now I had made it so an enemy that they cannot defend against is able to walk unharmed through the Spell. Of all the things I have done, forced or not, I can't help but feel like those moments on the beach will be the ones that haunt me most of all.

Chapter Forty-Six

RHEA

WHEN THE SHIP DOCKED, I wasn't expecting to be greeted with unnerving silence. Instead of a bustling port filled with other ships, we landed somewhere private. I suppose it made sense, given who was on the ship with me, but I had dared to hope that a busier location would be easier for someone to get lost in. To *hide* in. That it would be easier for Nox to wait in the shadows. It's those thoughts that hover over me as I walk at King Dolian's side in the sand, a swarm of guards protecting us from all sides.

There are trees that surround us as we cut a path through the beach, though I wouldn't call it a forest like in the Mage Kingdom. They are more sparsely planted, certainly not leaving many places for someone to hide. Especially not with how many of the King's Guardsmen are spread throughout the landscape in all directions. My shoulders slump unbidden as realization settles.

"I see you are beginning to understand that there will be no rescue today." The king's breath is warm against my ear, and I close my eyes against him and the confirmation that Nox isn't here. *But of course he isn't here.* At the sound of marching steps, my eyes open again, and I watch as guards trickle out from the treeline ahead.

One of them walks to where Xander leads our procession, the two men dipping their heads to speak quietly before Xander nods and the other man returns to the other waiting guards. "The area and path to the palace are secure, Your Majesty."

The king looks to me, his eyes slowly dragging down my body and back up again, making sure I feel their caress as thoroughly as I have felt his fists. "Then let us return *home*." His emphasis is a reminder that is not needed. Despite being the place where I lived the majority of my life, it will *never* be home.

King Dolian wraps his fingers around my arm and tugs me towards him, my chest bumping into his as he leans down and whispers in my ear. "I want to make something abundantly clear. You will follow all the same rules as at the residence. You will not be able to leave any part of the castle grounds without me at your side." Magic infuses his words, a roaring filling my head at his commands. "I have been too soft on you, Rhea. I see now. That changes here." Placing a kiss on my cheek, he steps back and walks to join Xander at the front, leaving me alone as his guards surround me again.

We climb worn wooden stairs to a road, carriages pulled by horses waiting for us. I expect to be put in the same one as King Dolian, my body already tensing at the idea of being stuck in such close quarters with him, but instead, I'm led to the one behind his. The carriage is a pristine white, gold details in the shape of flowers and vines are painted along its edges. Taking my seat on one of the small velvet-lined benches, I pull the matching curtains back and stare out of the window into the surrounding trees as a guard closes the door. But moments later, it opens again, and Eve climbs in.

"Hi," she says, taking the bench across from me, an easy smile gracing her face. "I figured you might want some company as we ride through Vitour."

"We'll be riding through the city?"

"Sort of. The king prefers to travel on the outskirts of the city center. Mostly because it is safer to do so."

"Safer?" I look back out the window to the guards that mount horses and the ones that line up on either side of the carriages. You'd have to be a fool to attack when this many guards are present. *Or extremely powerful.* My chest heaves as I push that thought away.

The snap of the reins ring out before the carriage lurches forward. The journey is long in the sense that my anxiousness makes it difficult for me to sit still and short in the way my anticipation builds at what might be waiting for me when we arrive.

The first portion of the trip is filled with meadows, tall trees dotting the landscape every so often. But, after a while, it morphs into a collection of rugged looking homes, smoke curling from chimneys and people milling about as they tend gardens. Children run right up to where the guards walk alongside us, but the men ignore their smiling faces until the children are called back. My fingertips press against the cold glass as I watch the families study the king's procession, looks of uncertainty marring their faces.

"This is Amnois, a small town that provides much of the produce that the palace consumes," Eve says into the silence that's filled the carriage.

"The fields are so large," I respond, looking at the rows and rows of land dedicated to growing fruits and vegetables. "I know I have no reference for this sort of thing, but it seems like enough land to supply the kingdom."

"Maybe not the kingdom, but certainly a large portion of it." At the bitterness I hear in her voice, I turn away from the window to regard her. "The king does not allow them to sell to anyone outside of nobility. There are smaller farms dotted throughout the landscape, but Vitour and its outskirts have the biggest population. They have limited options when it comes to food."

"Can they not grow it themselves?"

Eve's eyes soften, but the pity in them makes me shuffle in my seat. "They can if they have enough land. They also need someone to tend it, but that task falls to the children since, in most instances, both parents work. Even then, there are limitations put in place by the Crown. You can only grow enough to feed your family, and if you are caught with more than is deemed *appropriate,* then you're punished."

"I had no idea." Even with my brief freedom in the Mage Kingdom, I never took it upon myself to learn how life operated for those not in the vicinity of the palace. Part of that was circumstances outside of my control, but part of it was because I had been, selfishly, content in my own little bubble.

Eventually, we reach the outskirts of Vitour. We aren't close enough to see more than the tops of the establishments, trees obscuring some of that, but it fills me with a longing that is reminiscent of my time in the tower. I hate that my first glimpse at the city is while I'm trapped within a carriage.

The paved road turns to cobblestone, and the castle looms in front of us like a menacing beast made of depressing gray stone. Its peaks reach high into the sky, rounded windows of stained glass breaking up the stone and depicting images that are too far away to make out. A stone wall encircles the perimeter of the castle, connecting to a portcullis, the spiked gate already drawn up and guarded heavily.

We enter beneath a stone archway into a scene that looks like a fairytale pulled straight from the pages of a book. A garden filled with more flowers than I know how to name stretches far, red cobblestone walking paths visible in each row. Branches from wide trees dotting the gardens hang low enough to brush your fingers against their deep green leaves. Stone benches are scattered throughout—as are fountains that showcase statues of men and women, each one more intricately carved than the last.

As I take everything in for the first time, it's easy to forget exactly what this place is. What it represents. It's a confounding sort of beauty—one that easily draws me in like a well-timed distraction. For so long in my tower, I fantasized about what the castle might look like. Without even stepping foot inside, I can admit that not even my imagination paid homage to the grandiosity of this place. That realization frightens me because it only solidifies the knowledge that the power King Dolian has isn't just limited to the ring on my finger. His threat from earlier plays in my ear, making the hair rise on the back of my neck as the carriage rolls to a stop.

Eve exits first, standing off to the side while a guard extends his hand out to me. His brown eyes are kind when they meet mine, not holding any of the hostility I felt from his companions. "Lady Rhea, my name is Brisk, and I'm to show you to your rooms." Taking my fingers in his, he guides me out into the cool afternoon air, my next inhale laced with the scent of flowers and something even sweet, like a dessert. King Dolian and his Trusted guards must have already exited, but his absence doesn't bring relief, instead making my stomach ache as I follow Brisk with Eve at my side.

My steps are less sure-footed the farther inside the castle we go, my attention bouncing from one corner of the entrance to the other. If I thought the outside of the castle seemed monstrously big, the inside somehow feels bigger. Draped in red and accented in an unfathomable amount of gold, the Mortal Kingdom's castle is a monument to opulence. The stone walls are painted white and covered with tapestries and art. Windows framed within pointed arches let sunlight stream in abundantly and rugs of woven gold and crimson line the tiled floors, the stone beneath them glittering white and tan.

Brisk guides us to the left towards a large spiral staircase, the banister a gleaming wood that is soft beneath my hand as we begin to climb. By the time we reach the third floor, my heart is pounding in my chest as I pathetically struggle to keep my breathing even. Muscles burning as we continue forward, I take in this wing of the castle. It's far quieter than the levels below us.

"This entire wing is for the king's betrothed," Brisk says as we pass a wide tapestry depicting a woman with long blonde hair lying on the beach, the water splashing around her hips. Her face is serene, a gentle smile tugging on her lips as her arms are thrown above her head. "Eve will remain at your service whenever you have need of her, though there is a team that will be fully dedicated to you for bigger events. The king's quarters are on the opposite side, if you turn back towards the staircase and then follow the hall to the west."

Knowing where the king's chambers are lets me know which way *not* to go, but I nod anyway as we come to a stop in front of a white door, a gold flower embedded at its center.

"This door will take you to your sitting rooms; from there, you will see two more doors—one that leads to your sleeping chambers where there is a bathroom," Brisk says as he steps back to make room for me to enter.

"I'll convene with the other staff and make sure all of your belongings are brought here from the Windseren," Eve adds with a smile. "And I'll bring up some refreshments."

I reach out to open the door, but my fingers pause on the handle. "Brisk," I call out, halting the guard's steps. "You said there were two doors. What is the other one for?"

I quirk an eyebrow when a blush stains his cheeks, his hand rubbing at the back of his neck. "Uh, it's for meetings with the king." At the confusion still present in my expression, he adds with subtle innuendo, "*Premarital* meetings."

My blood runs cold, and I quickly turn back to face the door, waiting until I hear Brisk's steps begin down the hall before I push the door open and step inside. Heart pounding in my chest for a different reason, I stop in the center of the sitting room, my eyes roaming over the space. Floral patterns cover the rugs and the upholstery, gold a dominant color from the sconces on the walls to the chandeliers above. A coffee table made of light wood is intricately carved with flowers at its edges, and the glass slider that leads to a balcony is covered with sheer white curtains, embroidered roses trickling down over the material. The room is grand—so much more than any sitting room in Nox's home. But where Nox's rooms had felt intimate and safe—had felt like *him*—this space is cold. Desolate. A room meant to be shown off, not to settle down in.

The two doors Brisk mentioned were set on either side of the sitting room, and it had been pure luck that I chose the one to my left, which led to a bedroom just as lavishly decorated as everything else but more importantly, was attached to a bathroom. We had only been on the ship for just over a day, but I can feel the salt in a thin layer over my exposed skin, and nothing currently sounded better than a hot shower.

A stained-glass window across from the shower paints the bright white space in splashes of yellow, orange, and red. The image is a roaring lion, its mane wild while a crown floats a few inches above its head, rubies inset on its front. My hand falls to my hip unbidden as a tightness crawls up my chest before I grip the fabric of my dress and pull it over my head, taking the chemise beneath it. My fingers tremble as the culmination of the past month—a godsdamn *month*—crests all at once now that I've found myself alone in a new place. I focus on the task at hand, turning the shower on and waiting for the water to warm, when I catch my reflection in a nearby mirror.

My first thought as I examine myself, turning to face it and then stepping close, is that I don't look as different as I feel. My fingers drift over my collarbones and lower, feeling the way my skin seems thinner as it stretches over my bones. My gaze inevitably falls to the brand and how it is scabbed in some places while a pink hue has taken over others. I prod the flesh around it, the wound still tender enough to make me wince as I study the way my body now looks off balance. No other scars mark me, something that has me as equally disturbed as it does relieved, but this one speaks enough on its own.

It certainly will to Nox.

The thought ushers me away from the mirror and into the hot shower, steam quickly filling the room. As water drips from my hair and over my body, my thumb pushes at the ring on my finger, spinning it as I reach for my magic. I'm not sure why I do, why I hope that anything other than that hollowness that resides within me will answer. Sometimes, I think I might feel something rising to meet my call, just a spark before it's suffocated again. I could laugh at how I ignored my magic for so long when I lived in the tower. How I forced it into an illusion of submission when I lived in the Mage Kingdom.

When Eve announces her return in the bedroom, I finish cleaning myself and turn the shower off, forcing my regrets down until I can't feel them anymore. It takes a moment to find the towels in a cupboard beneath the sink, but once I wrap the soft yellow cotton around me, I exit the bathroom, finding Eve in the adjacent closet.

She smiles warmly when she sees me as she hangs a pink gown on the metal rod that runs from one wall to another. "How are you feeling?"

I try my best to match her grin, eyeing the dresses as I step further into the closet. "Fine. And you?"

She huffs out a half-hearted laugh, grabbing another garment from a trunk on the floor next to her, it's shade green. "Kind of you to ask, but I'm more concerned about you." I can feel her gaze on the side of my face, my stomach fluttering with nerves that I just *can't* acknowledge right now. "Rhea—"

"Are all of these dresses from the Windseren?" I ask, clearing my throat awkwardly as I finally meet her soft blue gaze.

She pinches her lips together, chin tipping down as she shakes the dress out and then grabs a metal hanger from the rod. "No. A lot of these the king had made for you months ago." I grip the edge of the towel at my front as I stare at them. *Of course he had.* "There are a few personal items in the second trunk by the bed that I wasn't sure what to do with. I figured I'd leave them to you to make sure they are put away in places you approve of."

It takes me a moment to catch her subtle hint, but then I remember Alexi's journal that I had wrapped into one of the gowns as we packed. *Gods*, if anyone else had found it... But Eve had made sure she was the one to help me unpack. I blink back the rising pressure behind my eyes at her kindness. That's all she has ever been with me. The softness of the gesture smooths a rough edge within me, one that had been desperately clawing at my chest ever since I stepped foot off of the boat.

"I also brought some food freshly made from the kitchens. I noticed you didn't eat anything on the ship, so you should try to replenish now." Her voice drops a little lower, as if the next words hold more weight. "It's important to keep up your strength." Her gaze moves back to the dresses as she reaches down into the trunk for another.

"Would you like to share a meal with me?" I ask, feeling foolish for doing so while dressed in nothing but a towel with my wet hair draped over it.

But Eve simply gives me another genuine grin. "Let me finish up here, and then I'd love to."

When she meets me back in the sitting room, I'm dressed in one of the longer-sleeved gowns I swiped from the closet on my way out. It's a lovely pale pink color, sequin beading working around the bodice in a pattern that reminds me of vines of jasmine. I gesture for Eve to sit across from me at the small four-person table set off to the left, and together, we enjoy the first few minutes of our meal in silence.

It's a simple enough spread, warm bread and roasted chicken, vegetables glistening in butter still warm enough to have steam wafting up from them. I let my mind wander as I eat, wondering how I might convene with Xander in a way that won't rouse suspicions now that we are in the palace. I know he vowed to help me escape, but I would settle with an update on Nox first.

It startles me when Eve clears her throat, putting her fork down gently on her plate. "If I were to show you something that under *no* circumstances could be found out by the king, would you swear to keep it a secret?"

Intrigued, I lay my fork on the table, my stomach feeling full for the first time in a while. "I want to say yes," I begin, leaning my elbows on the white tablecloth. "But this ring prevents me from disobeying the king in *any* way. If he asks me about it, I will have to tell him. The magic will *make* me."

Eve nods as she thinks, leaning back in her chair. "It's worth the risk. You should know, just in case you ever need a place to hide." My brows draw together as her face grows serious. "Tonight, I'll show you."

When we've both eaten our fill, Eve excuses herself to attend to some other duties, and I'm left alone to pace this foreign space until night falls. I'm told I have permission to explore the castle as long as a guard is accompanying me. Apparently, one will be stationed outside of my rooms at all times. My annoyance at that is the last thing I remember before drifting to sleep on the stiff couch in the sitting room, waiting for Eve to come.

Sometime late into the night, a gentle hand shaking my shoulder wakes me. "Come on," Eve whispers, helping me to stand. "We shouldn't be gone for too long."

I assume we are heading back out into the hallway, but Eve stops me, instead pointing to my bedroom.

"This way."

My steps are uncertain as I follow her into the darkness, watching as she slides a hand along the wall across from the bed. One I note isn't made of stone but wood. She pauses at a clicking noise, and then a portion of the wall swings backwards.

"We'll have to navigate the dark for a bit—"

"What is this?" I interrupt, my eyes squinting as I try to peer closer into the opening.

Eve looks over her shoulder at me, and I realize that she isn't dressed in her maid's uniform, instead donning a black tunic and pants. "These are the secret tunnels," she says nonchalantly. "It's how Xander and his rebellion have been gathering right under King Dolian's nose."

Chapter Forty-Seven

RHEA

There's an entire system of tunnels within the castle, and Eve only shows me part of it as we walk hunched over to accommodate the low ceilings. "Every few feet, you will see a series of paint smudges that indicate what part of the castle you are nearest. Green means the back of the castle, near the largest hedges and garden. Blue means you're at the castle center and have the chance of popping out in a variety of different rooms, some of which could leave you in more precarious situations than others." Her voice is low as it echoes against the stone around us, the golden glow of the torch in her hand casting just enough light to show one of those colored smudges.

"What does red mean?" I ask, letting my fingers trail lightly over the mark.

"Those are for Xander and his men to mark passageways that lead to abandoned rooms that they can convene where the likelihood of being caught is low to none."

"How did he even discover these?"

"He's never told me, and the others don't bring it up, so I'm not sure." I shiver at the much cooler air as Eve comes to a split in the passageway. One is marked red and the other blue. She turns left, following the blue paint smudge. I glance to the right but see nothing except for shadows, so I turn and follow Eve. "I like to imagine these were servant passageways or maybe a secret hideout for kings and queens long past," she muses, dragging her free hand along the wall.

"It is strange to have them here at all." But even I know that this castle is particularly old. From what I had read, it housed the very first king of the Mortal Realm, at least as far back as records dated. I'm sure hundreds of years ago, when there was no Spell protecting the kingdoms from each other, there was likely a need to move with such secrecy.

The ground begins to slope up, and my thighs burn again with the effort. Finally, with more sweat beading my brow than I'd like, Eve guides us to what appears to be a dead end. "If you look here," she says, holding the torch closer to the wall and pointing with her finger, "you can see the faint outline of the door." Her voice is a soft whisper, and when I lean forward, I can just barely make out the door. "I think you might enjoy having unfettered access to this place."

I don't have time to question her before she pushes at a metal bar attached horizontally to the door, the sound of stone scraping lightly rending the air. She tips her ear forward as she listens before opening it the rest of the way. I shouldn't be surprised that she's taken me to a library, but a kernel of wonder warms inside of me when I see the spines of books lit by nearby flame gems. I follow her out of the tunnel, brushing my hands on my dress as I stand up tall and take the room in.

"Oh my gods," I whisper, stepping in farther as Eve shuts the makeshift door. Rows of shelves extend nearly floor to ceiling, stretching towards the opposite end of the room for as far as the eye can see.

"I'm glad to see my hunch was correct."

I let a small laugh tumble out of me as I struggle to take it all in. It's more books in one space than I've ever seen before.

"This library is *technically* only open to those King Dolian allows in, and since everyone is out celebrating the king's return to Vitour, no one will be here."

"*Celebrating*," I murmur in disgust, as if his absence is one to be missed.

Eve chuckles before blowing out her torch and setting it by the wall. "Come on, I'll show you my favorite spot."

Our steps whisper against the thick rugs lining the floors, my gaze tracking the towering bookcases on either side of us. They stretch up so high that even having flame gems attached to every shelf doesn't make it easier to read the titles at the top. I can't help but let my shoulders relax the deeper between the stacks that we go.

"I came here a lot when Xander first showed me the tunnels and how to navigate them," Eve says, keeping her voice soft. "There were nights that I couldn't sleep, and though my quarters here are nicer than most in my position, they still felt so small and suffocating." I suppose we aren't too different in that regard. I watch as a small smile tugs at the corners of her mouth, her unbound hair pulled over one shoulder. "Though it isn't home," she starts, that smile growing larger when a small spiraling metal staircase comes into view ahead of us, "it's nice to have a space like this to escape to. It's why I wanted to show you." We climb the steps up to the second floor, where more bookcases are built in neat rows, hundreds of books lining them. Black metal chandeliers hang from above, holding little glass bowls with a small flame gem in each.

"I'm surprised it isn't gold," I say, gesturing with my hand to the fixture.

"Between you and me, I'll be happy if I *never* see the color inside any residence ever again. It makes me all the more happy to know that the humble home I share with my sister is a patchwork of mismatched lights and furniture. A little chaos is something I never thought I would be desperate to return to."

"Will you get to go home soon?" I ask. "Now that we are closer to your home town?"

She takes her time answering, and in her silence, I observe the rest of this floor. We had ended up at an indoor balcony, after exiting the staircase and following a long aisle. A metal railing—spindles twisting as they reach from floor to banister—closes in a half circle of space, and beyond that, the first floor of the library sprawls out in front of us. It's even more grand from this viewpoint. At the edge of the library are three stained-glass windows that vertically span nearly the entire wall, each one depicting beings that look too ethereal to be mortal. Their bodies are lithe, wrapped in strategically placed fabric. One is male, his dark skin outlined by a faint glow. The other two are female, one with the same skin tone as the male and the other a color closer to mine. The latter's hair is bright blonde, nearly appearing white as it wraps around her down to her hips. I'm lost in the beauty of their details when Eve finally answers my question.

"As much as I long to go home, I don't think it will happen any time soon."

I turn back to her as she takes a seat on one of the chaises, and I follow suit choosing a deep maroon one. "Why is that?"

"The king is very *particular* about this sort of thing." I wait for her to elaborate, but she only adds, "It just isn't the right time."

The offer to speak to King Dolian on her behalf scratches at my throat, but I push it back down and sink into the chair. "Besides your sister—I'm realizing I have never asked her name—is there anyone else waiting for you?"

"Her name is Elsa, and there is someone else," she drawls before pinching her lips closed as if she hadn't meant to answer the question.

I lift a brow, shifting to lay on my unmarked hip as I look at her with anticipation.

Huffing out a laugh, she hugs her knees to her chest. "We've known each other since we were children—his parents own the bee farm I told you about. He's... *lovely*. Kind. Smart. Strong. A flirt in all the ways a girl could want without it becoming a burden." My finger toys with one of the buttons on the tufted chair as she speaks, the longing in her voice matching what I feel inside.

"Are you two together?"

"He wants us to be, but"—she shrugs a single shoulder—"the nature of my job has always made it difficult to do so."

"Does he get frustrated by what you do?" I ask. I imagine being forced to stay away for however long the king wants would be taxing on a relationship. Especially when Eve presumably couldn't welcome her own guests into the castle.

"The opposite," she says, surprising me. "Edwin has always cheered me on, even when I didn't think I was worthy of it."

At that, I sit up a little, making sure to hold Eve's gaze. "Why would you think you aren't worthy?" Eve is earning a living for herself, choosing to be away from her sister in order to better support her. Those sacrifices are not easy to make and certainly not ones to make someone unworthy.

She clears her throat, uncertainty tugging her brows together. "Prior to coming to work at the palace, I had a different job. It's how I met the king originally."

"What—" A loud bang sounds, and our conversation is quickly abandoned in favor of scrambling off of the chaises and ducking onto the floor. Voices float to us from below, and I cast a wary eye to Eve who holds her finger to her lips before crawling towards the railing. I watch as she scans the library, her shoulders hiking before she slowly retreats backwards when the voices grow nearer.

"It seems like some of the nobles have snuck away from the party for a *private* rendezvous," she whispers, gesturing to head back towards the staircase. "We better go before we accidentally get spotted." Once we are safely hidden by the massive bookcases, we quicken our steps until we reach the stairs and then slow down as we pause every few steps to listen for voices. I let Eve get ahead of me and follow as she guides us back to the last row of books, the hidden tunnel straight ahead.

"We have to be quick," she says, the voices doubling until I'm unsure just *exactly* how many people are in here with us. "I'll light the torch again once we are safely inside."

I nod and then watch as she reaches to grab a nearby book from its perch on the shelf. "What is that for?"

"A distraction, should we need it. Ready?"

I stick closer to her as we dart out from the safety of the bookshelves, exposed to whoever might be here as we run to where the torch is laying in front of the opening.

"Did you hear that?" A female asks, murmuring far too close for comfort following the question.

"*Shit*," Eve whispers, pressing her fingers along the outline of the hidden door until it clicks. She adjusts her grip on the book she took from the shelf. "Hurry, go!"

I quickly move into the tunnel, leaving enough room for Eve to follow behind.

"Hello! Is someone here?" a male shouts. To my utter disbelief, Eve *heaves* the book across the open space we just ran through and into one of the bookcases, a loud smacking noise reverberating out. Then she ducks into the tunnel, pulling the wall back towards her with the metal bar.

She doesn't move, and with our surroundings now pitch black, I have to use the sound of her breathing to figure out how close she is. Muffled footsteps sound on the other side of the wall, and I move to scoot deeper into the tunnel when Eve's hand gently lands on my leg, prompting me to stay where I am.

"One of the books fell," the male says, a hint of annoyance in his tone. "Come on, let's go back to my place. It's creepy in here."

When we hear retreating footsteps, Eve strikes a match and fire immediately casts its glow over her as she lights the torch and then shakes the match to extinguish it.

"You threw a book," I say to break the tension, the comment making Eve smirk.

"I *did*, but we needed a distraction!" she argues, her voice only a whisper.

"At the sake of a poor book?"

For a moment, I can tell that she is unsure if I'm joking, but then her features relax, and she shakes her head in amusement. "Listen, I'm all for not harming books *unless* it comes down to me versus them."

I can't help but snort and shake my head, a lightness in my chest that feels foreign now.

We don't speak much on the way back, and when Eve stops at the door that leads to my bedroom, she says her farewell. "I can't be seen in clothing not handmaiden appropriate in the halls," she says by way of explanation. "I'll use the tunnels to make it back to my own floor."

I dip my chin as I press along the door like Eve did, finding the section that clicks open. "I'll see you tomorrow, then."

"Tomorrow. Goodnight, Lady Rhea."

"Rhea," I correct, opening the door and carefully stepping through. Turning, I bend over until I can fully see her face again. "Just Rhea is fine."

Chapter Forty-Eight

RHEA

WHATEVER REPRIEVE I MIGHT have had from the king disappears days later when Eve arrives at my room with a new gown and orders to ready me for dinner. My stomach stays in knots as I slip the icy blue dress on, its sleeves sheer. White lace details in a floral pattern twirl up my arms and across my chest, meeting right in the center where a white silk ribbon is tied into a bow. The sheer lace continues over the rest of the dress, flaring out slightly at my hips while the blue silk beneath it stays formed to the slight curves of my body. Dread tickles the back of my throat as I look at myself in the mirror.

Eve stands behind me, combing my hair before sliding in two silver barrettes, one on each side of my head. "Do you know who is supposed to be in attendance?" I ask, toying with the ribbon. I watch her reflection in the vanity mirror as she purses her lips.

"I'm not sure. Usually, the king invites his closest council members as well as a few influential nobles that reside in the castle. But this situation is... *different.*" A line forms between her brows. "He's never brought someone he's courting to a meal like this before."

My next question is out before I can think better of it. "Has he ever *courted* anyone before?"

"Not that I'm aware of."

My next swallow is bitter at the thought that he hadn't ever introduced a potential partner to court because he was waiting for me. He had always claimed me to be his, had always alleged that my destiny was at his side, and now he is getting *everything* he's ever wanted.

Those thoughts are still loud when Xander arrives, the commander relieving Brisk of his post outside my door. Xander keeps his steps slow so that I can walk beside him easily, and like all of our communication in a public setting, he talks low while keeping his gaze forward. "I have news from the Mage Kingdom," he says.

My heart leaps into my throat as I force my steps to stay steady. "And?" I prod, sneaking a glance up at him. A muscle flutters at his jaw, doing nothing to calm my nerves.

"I received a missive from Stephan. He's back in the Mage Kingdom."

My brows draw low as I look back out at the hallway in front of us, the stairs coming into view. The urge to ask Xander if he knew how involved Stephan was with my abduction burns at my tongue, but even if he did, Xander wouldn't have been able to do anything about it. So I keep the question inside.

"Stephan sent a letter that arrived early this morning," he says, his fingers flexing on the hilt of his sword. "In it, he talks of the council and their pursuit of whether or not Princess Bahira committed treason in the Shifter Kingdom."

"And?" I whisper.

"Stephan said the council still seems divided, but beyond that, the kingdom is beginning to speculate about what is going on inside the palace regarding the prince—*Nox*." I push back at the unease that creeps up my chest, staying silent to let Xander continue. "Apparently, he hasn't been seen outside of the palace, and those who *have* describe him as looking ill. And then there's the fact that he was found in the city of Celatum."

Celatum? "We stayed the night in Celatum after we escaped the tower," I respond, before I turn over what Xander said. *He was found*. "They caught him?" Gods, was it the king? Is Nox trapped *here* somewhere? Could the king have already—

"Nox was caught by Stephan and brought back to the Mage Kingdom," he cuts in, halting my spiral but nearly starting another. My flats click softly against the steps as we continue down to the main level, the distant noise of chattering finding my ear. Xander remains quiet so that I can process what he's told me.

"One man brought him back?" I ask eventually, my gaze tracking over the long red banners that are looped overhead as we walk through the grand foyer. And *Stephan*? He's mage, of course, but Nox is... *powerful*. Strong. A warrior. Even sick, he is still formidable enough to fight off *one* man. I had seen him forgo magic altogether to fight off a band of guards after our escape.

Old portrait-style paintings line the wall to my left, the stern faces of men staring back at me from each one that I pass. Xander slows his steps, eyes peering farther down the corridor as servants and other guards pass us. "I didn't want to come to you with this, Lady Rhea." The trepidation living in my chest grows arms and legs, stretching out to clutch at my ribs as Xander nervously taps the hilt of his sword. "Stephan brought him back to the mage palace under the influence of gelsemium. It's a—"

"I know what it is," I interject, my hand resting against my stomach as my chest rises and falls quickly. He had been *drugged*. Kept paralyzed while Stephan dragged him back to the council and away from *me*. Nox had been coming for me. *He—he had almost made it to me, and I—* "I can't breathe," I gasp, tears springing to my eyes as I lean back against the wall, my vision blurring.

Xander murmurs something lost to the way there is a roaring in my ears, and takes a step closer. It would still look suspicious for us to be this close, and it endangers Xander more than anything if someone like Simon or, gods forbid, the king himself sees us like this. *Get it together*, I chastise myself, but the words clang uselessly inside my head. *Nox had been coming for me.*

"La— *Rhea*." Xander's voice is calm, but the urgency in it isn't missed by me even in this state. "It's going to be okay. We'll figure out how to get this ring off, and then you can go—"

"What if we can't?" I lift my shaking hand out in front of me and stare at the unassuming pearl dotting the top of my finger. "What if there's always something to stop me from leaving? To prevent him from coming for me?" I bite down on my lower lip, and squeeze my eyes closed. Hope is an easy thing to hold on to when the adversity threatening it is still new. When you can clearly remember what life is *supposed* to be like and carry only the eager determination to return to it again. But, like I had told Xander that day in the library, I've been treading tumultuous waters for such a long time. And I'm tired. I'm so, *so* very tired.

Xander scans the hall in silence as I try to compose myself. Eventually, he gives me a look that I know means we have to go, and I force my feet to move as he resumes guiding us to wherever it is we are going.

"I don't make promises lightly, and I certainly don't give my word on *any-thing* unless I'm sure I can make it happen. So *hear me* when I say that I will get you out of here, but I need you to not give up. To *want* to keep fighting to leave." An ache begins to pulse at my temple, the sob I've kept trapped inside desperately trying to claw its way out. I want to fight, to believe that he can get me away from here, but if not even *Nox* could help me, what hope does Xander have? What hope do *I* have? "I hate to change the subject, but I think it's important that you know you're about to enter an entirely different situation than anything you encountered with the king prior, and though I know it's going to go against *every* instinct you have, you need to be submissive to him in there."

He jerks his chin towards the looming gold double doors, the kingdom's sigil centered on each one. *Submissive.* Did I have any other choice at this point? When I don't say anything, Xander continues talking.

"There's something else—"

"You are quickly becoming my least favorite person right now," I say, clinging to a small bit of levity as our steps begin to slow. Xander doesn't react to it.

"King Dolian is a selfish, single-minded man, but he—*unfortunately*—is not stupid. He knows that there are some present in the castle that will recognize you simply by how you look."

I arch a brow, my hands clasping nervously in front of me. "Because I look like my mother?"

"Exactly like her," he says, earning a glance from me that questions how he *knows* that. "The king got rid of all the portraits that showed her, but I remember stumbling across one as a boy—" Xander abruptly pinches his lips together before shaking his head. "Anyway, there are those who are old enough to remember the former king and queen, and though you will not find an ally in them, the king will put to rest any rumor that you're his niece by halting it before it starts."

"And how is he supposed to do that?" One of the double doors opens, and a man even larger than Xander steps out, his eyes shrewd beneath his helmet. They land on Xander with open malice before they drift to me, narrowing as we come nearer.

"You're late."

"Lady Rhea needed extra time to get ready." The guard scoffs as he looks me over, making me bristle beneath his glare. "Do you need something else, Jerrick?"

The man towering before us snickers, his hand falling to grip the hilt of his sword. "No, Commander," he grits out, reaching to hold one of the doors open for us.

I want to ask Xander to wait, to explain what he meant earlier, but there isn't time as he ushers me through the door and into a great hall. The tile color changes to glittering black, my eyes bouncing from it to the hanging red banners above us. A dark wooden banquet table, large enough to fit multiple dozens of guests, is centered in the room, and everyone seated around it pauses the moment the door shuts behind us, making my heart leap into my throat as their eyes jump to us.

"Ah. There she is." My body tenses at the king's voice, two servants rushing over to the head of the table to pull out his gaudy chair. Gold glimmers from its edges as he rises, his gaze on me felt even with the distance between us. "Rise." At the king's command, everyone rises from their red velvet-tufted chairs, all bowing their heads in deference. Xander leaves my side to stand at his post across the room, but the spot next to me is quickly filled by a different man. He's dressed in finer clothes than the servants but nothing nearly as extravagant as the guests that surround the table.

"Introducing, His Majesty King Dolian's betrothed, your future queen of the Mortal Kingdom, Lady Nele."

Chapter Forty-Nine

RHEA

A shocked sound croaks past my lips as I turn to look at the man, my brows raised towards my hairline. *This* is what Xander had meant? That the king is going to convince everyone that I'm not his niece by simply calling me a different name? As if that alone could erase the features of both my mother and my father from my face? "My Lady," the man says, looking at me expectantly as he offers me his arm. I stare at him, dumbfounded and yet oddly *numb* to the fact that I was going to have to *pretend* to be someone else at the king's behest.

When the man clears his throat, his eyes bouncing from me to where I know the king is waiting for me, I put him out of his misery and wrap my fingers on his outstretched arm. I feel the stares of those around the table as acutely as one might feel a blade on their skin, even with their chins resting on their chests.

"You look beautiful, my darling," King Dolian says, leaning in to kiss my cheek as he forces my hand off of the man's, and into his own. When I don't respond, my gaze roaming anywhere but to him, his fingers wrap around my chin and jerk my head forward, forcing our eyes to meet. "You will answer to Lady Nele, and you will regard me—as both your betrothed and your king—with the respect I am owed in front of my people." I swallow roughly, wincing when he squeezes his fingers more tightly around me. But I don't agree to his terms. I don't have to, because the magic of his command has already made the decision for me. He lets his grip tighten a fraction more, a cruel smile tilting his lips before he finally releases me and guides me to an empty chair at his right.

Before I'm even fully seated, a servant appears and reaches for my glass. I stare blankly at the crimson liquid he pours before turning to actually look at him. I had hoped to see the same man who served me juice instead of wine at the previous residence, the one who clearly was working with Xander. But it's a different man, one still too young to be at the whim of the king but whose eyes don't hold any of the other man's kindness. When he retreats, I find King Dolian watching me, his finger tracing the edge of his chalice.

"Sit." At the command, everyone around the table returns to their seats, easily falling back into the conversations they were having before as if my arrival, and the announcement of my betrothal to the king, is something easy to move on from. But for them, it is. "*Drink*, Rhea," he commands, and my hand automatically reaches for the glass. Tipping it towards my lips, I take a gulp of the bitter wine, waiting for the magic to demand I take more but finding that it retreats after the first drink. I keep the cup pressed to my lips a little longer to pretend I'm drinking more before setting it down, my anger slipping out.

"I *hate* wine."

King Dolian's cheeks lift in amusement, his eyes moving to his finger lingering on the rim of his chalice. "Yes, I suppose *juice* is a much sweeter beverage. Though it might be harder to find here than it was before." My spine goes rigid when he leans over, his hand covering mine and holding it tightly when I try to pull away. "Did you think I wouldn't find out? That you could outsmart me?" He tilts his head, a breath lodging in my throat as I work to keep from reacting. "Such a shame you were willing to sacrifice yet another life in order to disobey me. Simon was able to persuade him to answer almost all of our questions except how you were able to convince him to help you."

No. No. No. I know exactly what Simon's *persuasion* looks like. And that servant— He had been so young. But King Dolian is watching me for a reaction, and I'm afraid if I give him one, he'll start asking questions that will lead to Xander and his mission being exposed. I don't know much, but what I do know... It would endanger the lives of good people. Of Xander and Eve and countless others.

"Perhaps this is a conversation better had in the privacy of one's quarters," he says, releasing my hand to trail his knuckles down my cheek. I search for my magic as if it's still within reach of my fingertips, a panicked response that I do without thinking. But, of course, nothing answers. King Dolian studies me, keen eyes seemingly seeing right through me, even as another voice I recognize calls his name from his other side. "I *will* uncover every secret you're keeping from me. Even the ones that were given life in your tower. Keep drinking, my darling. The night is young, and there is still so much I want to do with you."

I take another drink of the wine, catching the gaze of Simon who sits across from me. Our connection is brief before he turns and speaks to the king, but it still stokes my anxiety higher, the hand not clutching my cup gripping the fabric of my dress at my thigh. Despite making a show of introducing me to his court, no one attempts to speak with me. I'm spoken about, whispers trickling in from the seats next to me by those either too drunk or too obnoxious to care that I can hear them. I know the king watches me from where he is sitting, but even he doesn't bring me into any of his own conversations. I'm invisible here, nothing more than a prop. A shiny toy for the king to gloat that he's gotten and then shoved back in a corner to rot behind his shadow.

The evening passes measured by my sips of wine, the alcohol's effects dulling some of my senses in a not unpleasant way. The magic never lets me get more than a few minutes between gulps before I'm tipping the rim of the glass to my lips again, picking at my food in between drinks to try and keep myself from getting too drunk.

My thumb presses at the pearl ring, and I wonder not for the first time exactly what magic is in it that gives the king such control over me. When Nox was training me, he had talked about not only the importance of balance when it came to having magic but also that of being intentional when wielding it. Is that how the magic of the ring works too? Intentionality? King Dolian had given a lot of commands, and most of them *had* been very specific, but like with the wine, there were... loopholes. How did the magic differentiate between what I was forced to follow and where there seemed to be a little bit of room for interpretation?

I scan the table as I think, letting my gaze roam between sips of wine, and watch the noblewoman across from me lift her cup in signal. A servant is there within seconds, refilling it without being given so much as a *courtesy* nod. When he moves the pitcher from one hand to the other so he can serve her a second helping of food, I catch a glimpse of the scar on his palm. What did the wording for the blood oaths the servants gave sound like? Eve had admitted that when she was commanded to help ready me, she had to obey, but there were varying degrees to which she usually helped me. Had I inadvertently tested the magic of the blood oath's boundaries with her then? And then there is Xander, his oath preventing him from outright killing the king, yet he is able to stage an entire rebellion right beneath his nose. The magic that binds them is different than that of the ring, different even than my own. But what if the rules that govern one, govern them all? What if *I* can figure out loopholes in the king's commands? Not always—not every time—but in instances like this with the wine. Can I try to find a way to mitigate the effect of the command without alerting King Dolian?

"So, Lady Nele," the woman across from me calls, her voice a high trill against the backdrop of all the others. It startles me, after having endured the majority of this meal alone with my thoughts. I look her over, finding that she is pretty in the way all those with wealth and the means to have whatever they want can be. Her hair is a deep auburn and curled into tight ringlets that hug her head. Her lips are painted bright red, while black lines her eyes and colors her lashes. A teal dress accented with glittering silver shimmers as she adjusts her body to face me fully, her freshly filled glass of wine held aloft in her hand. "We are all *dying* to know how you and the king met. You seem so..." Her pause is weighted enough to draw the gaze of said king, as well as Simon and a few others around us. "Unexpected," she settles on.

Well if there was ever an opportunity to test the magic, now might be it. "Actually—"

"We met when I went to visit Celatum after the princess's abduction," King Dolian interrupts, making my grip tighten on my fork as I bite down on my tongue. *Gods above, how* dare *he.*

"Oh yes, such a tragedy," she says, shaking her head dramatically. "And to know it was one of our *own* who abducted her? Absolutely repulsive. At least you made sure he was taken care of when you caught him."

"Taken care of?" I ask.

"Well, yes. The king's Trusted apprehended the rogue guard and disposed of him quickly."

I can't help the laugh that rises, a soft bubbling of noise that might not have slipped out had I not had wine filling my belly. Those watching my interaction with the noblewoman stare in confusion, their eyes—like hers—darting to King Dolian's.

"Darling, I'm not sure our guests understand what is so funny," he warns, smiling even through the warning laced in his tone.

"Is... something the matter, Lady Nele?"

"Of course not," I say, a slur to my words as I put my cup down harshly. A little of the wine spills onto the table. "I just can't believe that through all the king's safeguarding of the princess, it was just a *guard* who had taken her. That it was a guard who bested him."

The noblewoman stutters, her brows rising high on her forehead. A few of the men surrounding me huff a noise as they scowl at me, but I turn to look at my uncle. And though I hear Xander's warning in the back of my head to stay submissive, to not agitate the king, I find that I just... I don't *care* what he does to me anymore. The list of violations he had already conducted was long, what was another beating? Another incestuous look? Warning bells flare, but in muddled thoughts, they are easily pushed to the side.

"This guard *easily* captured the princess of the tower. Set her free of her stone prison and led her to places she surely only dreamed about," I say to him, an unnatural hush falling over the table. "He did *all* of that right under your nose—"

"I think the wine has made Lady Nele's tongue a little more adventurous tonight," Simon interrupts. "No one tells a fable quite like a woman." His words earn an awkward and tense chuckle from those closest, the noblewoman across from me staring down at her plate as they do. I open my mouth to retort when the magic commands me to drink. My fingers wrap around my cup but I'm halted with a hand on my forearm before I can bring it to my mouth.

"That's enough," King Dolian says before standing, moving his hand up to my arm as he tugs me up from my seat. "Let's go to your room." It's not a suggestion but a command, and one I'm forced to obey as my feet begin moving. The room spins as my head pounds, and I bring a hand up to frame my temple against the sudden onslaught of dizziness as the king practically *drags* me to the double doors.

"Your Majesty, I can escort the lady back if you would like to stay with your guests." Xander's voice comes from behind me, but the king only tightens his grip and pulls me forward. A breath hisses through my teeth.

"That won't be necessary, Commander. Remain at your post."

There's a pause, Xander's steps still following behind us as we enter the hall. Then, "I'm sure your guests—"

King Dolian abruptly halts and jerks me around until we are both facing Xander, his chest heaving at my side. Anger *pours* off of him so thickly that it makes the hairs on the back of my neck rise in warning. "What is this?" he snarls, taking a step towards Xander. "I have given you an order. That doesn't leave room for rebuttal!" I yelp as I'm once more pulled forward, my feet tripping over themselves. "Is it her? Are you wanting to spend time *alone* with my betrothed? With your future fucking *queen*?"

The seconds are tense as they pass, a ringing in my ears growing louder as Xander keeps his gaze pinned on the king. I see his nervousness, though, in the way his fingers flex around the hilt of his sword. And I beg the gods that he doesn't look at me. That he makes the right choice to leave me to handle the king on my own because his rebellion is already at risk by what I know. If the king thinks *anything* at all is happening between us, he could force me to tell him every interaction I've had with Xander.

Xander, both to my relief and slight horror, does just that. "No, Your Majesty. As I have proven to you over and over again, my allegiance is to you and you *alone*." He lifts the hand that had been on his hilt and forms a fist, laying it across his chest.

King Dolian doesn't move at first, his grip still tight and his gaze still flaring with irritation. But then he lifts his chin, looking down his nose at Xander. "Yes, I suppose if there is *anyone* I can trust to not try and fuck her, it is *you*." Xander says nothing, but his look of disgust speaks for him. "Go back to your post."

We're already on the move again before I can watch Xander retreat. I don't try to wrench my arm from the king's hold as he marches us back through the foyer and presumably up to my room. I have to think—have to try and work this to my advantage. But coherent thought is lost in the haze of the alcohol. We reach the staircase and begin climbing, the king's steps loud at my side the entire way up.

Only when we've reached the corridor of my wing does he stop, shoving me up against the wall as one hand wraps around my neck and the other slams the stone next to my head. "Have you *fucked* the commander?" he asks, magic behind the question.

"No," I answer quickly. The pull of the magic recedes, and in my drunken stupor, I add, "Not that it's *any* of your business—"

The hand gripping my neck squeezes more tightly as he shakes me, the back of my head bouncing off the stone wall. "*Everything* regarding you is *my* business," he snarls in my face, moving his other hand to my shoulder, his fingers draping over the curve of it as his thumb sweeps low on the fabric of my dress, right over the top of my breast.

I struggle beneath his hold, my hands closing around his wrists as I try to pull his own away, only to be met with a command to stop moving. My arms fall down to my sides, lifelessly hanging there as he leans in to brush his lips against mine. "You think you're so clever, Rhea, don't you? That somehow you and you alone are enough to change what I've been working towards for twenty-two years." His hips press into mine, and I suck in a startled breath at the feel of him against me, the hand at my shoulder sliding lower, until it's cupping the flesh beneath the dress. "I should have demanded answers from you before, but I wanted to believe that you would come around." He groans low in his throat, and I press myself further back into the stone wall, as if I can sink into it to get away from him. But he only closes any miniscule distance made with a deeper press of his hips forward. There's no command to work around here because I'm completely at his mercy, unable to get away. I swallow as fear chokes me, my mind racing beneath the lull of the alcohol. "As I mentioned, my leniency is gone, and now I demand answers. Did you know that your magic could heal?"

Water pressure builds in my ears, the answer spoken before I can think. "*No.*"

"Do not *lie!*"

"I'm—I'm not!" I shout, my eyes growing wet as tears spill from them. The magic pushes at me again to answer him. "I didn't know. How would I?"

"Then how else did the shifter live in your tower?"

I blink, my breath sawing in and out of me.

"How else did the shifter *live*? Answer the question!"

"I don't—" The power of his command pulses inside my head, but I have no answer for him. I have no idea what he is even talking about.

His eyes bore into mine, the nearness of his body suffocating me. But when I fail to give him an answer he scoffs and pulls back abruptly. "You truly don't know, do you?" I press my hands into the stone behind me as he laughs, the levity in it absent. With my head hanging low, I focus on trying to breathe through how his phantom touch still lingers on my body. The tips of his pristine boots enter my vision before his fingers are grasping at my chin and tilting my head back, forcing me to look up at him. "She was a *shifter,*" he says, the words a slow drip from his tongue.

"I don't know *who* you are talking about."

His head tilts to the side, a few strands of hair falling over his forehead. "Your fox. The white one who *lived* with you. All this time, you thought you had a pet, but what you *really* had was a shifter woman." His tone is one of condescension, false pity contorting his features.

"No," I scrape out, the word rough in my dry mouth. "No, that can't be."

"She was. I saw the creature myself in the dungeons on *many* occasions when the commander and I needed to question her."

"Wha—" My mind spins as I try to make sense of his words, but Bella being not only a shifter but *alive* is impossible. I had lived with her for years, and I had seen her get shot right in front of me. Had seen the guards close in on her as Nox pulled me away. Through the throbbing in my head, a memory of our escape into the Mage Kingdom crystallizes. Yes, I had seen her get shot, but there had been a flash of blue light before the guards surrounded her. I hadn't actually confirmed she was dead— *No.* No, Xander surely would have told me if Bella was alive.

King Dolian smiles at the torment on my face, one of his hands gently brushing the loose strands of his hair back while the other releases its hold on me. "She was *interesting* in her mortal form, with hair as white as snow. She lived for a while after her capture, frothing at the mouth behind bars like any wild animal. But when she couldn't be broken, when she wouldn't give the commander or I what we needed, she ceased to be a problem at all."

"You're lying," I rasp, shaking my head. This is his brand of torment—nothing more than a game of manipulation.

The king ignores my accusation, his savage satisfaction at the way this information has broken me undeniable on his face. "Tomorrow, I will take you to my army, and you will do for them what you did for the sirens. What you must have done for that shifter. If this is to be your cursed mage magic, then I will use it to *my* kingdom's advantage. Rest easy, my darling, knowing that what you've done—what you *will* do—will change Olymazi as we know it. The good and bad—it all rests on your shoulders."

He then orders me to go to my room, my swaying body stumbling down the hall as I make my way to the door marked with a golden flower. Magic rages through me until I'm past the threshold, the door firmly shut behind me before I lean against it. I don't believe him, *can't* believe him, yet that conviction runs hollow as I reminisce on my time with Bella in the tower. As I realize, with a shocked gasp, that there *had* been a time when I healed Bella. *One time* I had flooded her body with my magic, my intention to save her from the arrow, but it had done *so* much more than that. I remember when Alexi brought her to me, and I had mistaken her lethargy as sadness about being locked in the tower. Really, she had been suffering the effects of passing through the Spell. She was dying because she wasn't in her own kingdom.

I had saved her that day, only to doom her to something more horrific.

I close my eyes against the tightness in my chest as I slide down to the ground, sitting back on my heels. *But when she couldn't be broken, when she wouldn't give the commander or I what we needed, then she ceased to be a problem at all.* Bella had survived her time in the tower with me. Survived trekking through the woods and running from the guards, only to get shot and shift back into her mortal form before being dragged back here. Thrown into a dungeon and *tortured* for information that I could only assume was about *me*. And then she died alone. All because she knew *me*. Because I had saved her and damned her in the same moment.

And Xander? Xander had *known*.

Chapter Fifty

ARIA

O F ALL THE THINGS I thought I might have to fear on this journey, I naively assumed working around the hunts would be the worst of it. But Sade's unlikely advice prior to us leaving for the Mortal Kingdom had worked. The hunt of the mortal ship had been successful—though it had taken the smaller group longer for their magic to ensnare those on the ship. When they finally leapt to their deaths from the deck of the supply vessel, the legionaries descended upon them with a fury. It wasn't a large crew, which meant there weren't enough to go around. The females fought with each other, vicious snarls and even a few clashings of claws had erupted. And I had been able to slink away, hiding nearby until the chaos calmed and I could return and act as if I had done what was expected of me.

No one batted an eye. No one berated me for proof. I was all but invisible as consumed as they were with their own urges.

I had felt lighter as I transformed into my mortal form and walked onto the beach. But I had been wrong. So very wrong.

Rhea's magic was unlike anything I've seen before. Unlike anything I've ever *heard* of. I had watched her kill with it, and I had watched her heal. And she had clearly suffered for it both times. As I sink beneath the surface of the water, passing through the thick layer of the Spell, a sense of wrongness coats my skin.

I watch the legionaries look over themselves as my mother instructs everyone to return to Lumen, Dyanna swimming at her side. They wear their legion-issued shell armor and clutch their identical spears, but I see the unsure way their hands roam over their scales and tails, looking for anomalies as a result of Rhea's magic.

My chest tightens as my tail undulates in the water. There are now sirens—ones trained to fight and obey only the siren queen—that are able to pass through the Spell. There is no telling just how she might use them or who might be destroyed for standing in her way.

❧ ☙

It's late in the evening the next day by the time we enter Lumen, and though my body is begging me to collapse into my bed, I need to go to the treasure cave and see if Nia has left any new communication for me. Slowing my pace, I drop far enough back that I can no longer see the queen and Dyanna through the legionaries ahead of me. Once we reach the palace grounds, I break from the group—my heart beating in my throat—as I pivot in the direction of the cave. But I only make it a few lengths before a powerful voice calls my name.

"Aria? Where do you think you are going?" *Jaw and shoulders relaxed, lips flat, spine straight, and attitude vicious.* I repeat my mantra as I turn to face her. Legionaries float on either side of her, both with similar shades of ruby-red scales as my own. But where my scales slowly shift in an ombre pattern to yellow and then green, theirs stay red down to the delicate fins that tip their tails. Trident in hand, my mother comes towards me, her dark eyes relaying no emotion. "I asked you a question, Daughter."

"I thought I might see Lore," I blurt out. It's the only thing I can think to say that might not immediately be picked up as a lie. Lore lives near the legion garrisons that are stationed away from the palace. Queen Amari tilts her head, black braids snaking around her shoulders and the crown she still wears on her head, and for a moment, I worry that I've been caught.

But my mother's expression turns unnervingly soft, the small smile forming there unnatural. "A small bit of advice, Aria, before you go off to meet your *lover.*"

Nausea curls in my stomach at that word. Lore would *never* be such again.

"Remember that rarely is a choice of the heart ever the right one. Loyalty. Honor. Duty. Those are the things that should guide you in life. *Those* are the traits that will ensure your safety."

"Yes, Mother."

My chest is tight as I watch her and her legionaries swim back towards the palace, and once she is out of sight, I let my shoulders round and drag a hand over my face. Shaking my arms out to dispel the rest of my nervous energy, I swim the rest of the way to the cave without interruption. Passing through the long strands of floating kelp that hide the cave's entrance, I let my eyes adjust to the lack of light in the space as I root around for a crystal I keep in my satchel. Its light is a faint yellow, but it's enough for me to see. My heart dips beneath my ribs when I notice nearly an entire shelf of memorabilia is now gone. Lifting a small rock nestled between a ring with a blue gemstone and a gold necklace, I find the note she's left. My hand shakes as I unroll it, settling on the cave floor so I can use one hand to lay it out flat and the other to hold the crystal.

Aria,

Sade has begun sending out legionaries to systematically comb through the outposts, including the ones that lead to Eersten. Three of our own were caught, and I can assume they've either been killed or brought back to the prison. It's only a matter of time before the rest of us—offspring included—find ourselves in the same position. Without those weapons, we will not stand a chance.

I have given you time to prove your claim that you want to help, that you care, and you have managed to fall even shorter than I dared to give you credit for. No more waiting. No more excuses.

I suppose you'll find out soon enough whether or not your queen truly cares so little for blood.

-Nia

"Shit," I whisper, eyes closing as I tilt my head back.

I have no idea how old this letter is. Nia could have planted it the day I left for the Mortal Kingdom, or she could have left it today. Then again, even if she planned on *somehow* telling my mother about this cave—about how I've helped the seamount sirens—the queen was also gone. That left notifying Allegra or Sade, the latter of which could use that information to figure out that I'm not actually looking for the seamount sirens like she believes me to be.

Tipping my head forward again, I open my eyes and crumple the letter in my hand. "Think, Aria."

Part of me just wants to run. To cut ties with everything and everyone and disappear until I'm nothing more than a forgotten word washed away in the current. But then I think about Lyre and my promise to her. Her hope for the future with her babe. I think of what my mother is capable of—of what she is already doing to ensure she gets what she wants. Her legion is lethal, but at least right now, they are preoccupied. With her attention on healing her legionaries, there is still time for me to take advantage of the temporary distraction.

The most dangerous person is the one willing to do whatever it takes.

I'm not willing to run from this—not now.

Still, to get their weapons, I will need to not only find them in the legion's arsenal, but I'll also need to sneak them out. Considering they are guarded day and night, this is a mission that I need to admit I can't do on my own. Especially not with Nia attempting to make good on her threats. I let out a resigned sigh and tuck the crystal back into my bag. It is time to ask for help.

Ten minutes later, my heart thrashes against my ribs as I swim back to the palace. I can't tell if the feeling of being watched is there because it's *real* or I'm just nervous for what I'm about to do. The front of the palace comes into view and again, I repeat Myla's words.

The most dangerous person...

I have never been considered dangerous to anyone, but that certainly doesn't mean that I never *could* be. That perhaps even I—in all my perceived weaknesses—have the potential to be someone formidable. The thought bolsters me, and I decide now that if Nia has already gone to Sade or Allegra in my mother's absence, I will fight them to maintain my freedom. I don't want to be someone that *needs* to rely on others. I want to be someone that *I* can rely on.

With that thought in mind, I abandon the old mantra, the one that hid me behind a shield as fragile as glass. *Jaw and shoulders relaxed, lips flat, spine straight, and attitude vicious.* I thought that mantra was one that could hide what I believed myself to be, the antithesis of what I truly was. I am not the most vicious. I am not the strongest or smartest or most capable at fighting. But to protect Lyre? To repay the debts of my mother's unfounded bitterness to those who deserve the chance to live a life free from her wicked revenge? I can forge a new shield for that. One constructed of the confidence that has just started to blossom. One that is layered with those words Myla had spoken to me. Strengthened with the fact that I love my sister more than I hate myself.

Just because I have failed *so far* doesn't mean that I *am* a failure.

I swim above the manicured sea floor near the palace, glowing anemones and plants lit with bioluminescence dotting it. When I reach the pathway that leads to the palace entrance, I spy Karina and Hova guarding it. They cross their spears in front of the door, and I adopt the bored look I always give them. But this time, I'm not pretending to be tougher than I am. They may have more training than I do, but I'm no longer afraid to draw blood if needed.

"Well, if it isn't Princess Aria," Sarina drawls, narrowing her topaz eyes at me. "What are you doing here?"

I cock my head to the side, brushing my braids back over my shoulders. "I live here."

Hova snorts, but doesn't remove her weapon from my path.

"General Sade declared that with two pregnant princesses residing within the palace, we must show extreme caution with who we let past these doors." The corner of Karina's mouth lifts in a mocking smile. "We all know that Princess Aria has never exactly *fit in*."

My fingers curl into my palms as I resist the urge to let my talons show as my magic begins to gather low in my throat. I stare at them, my muscles tense with the anticipation of an attack when Hova lifts her spear and swims back to her side of the door.

"Let her through before you earn Sade's wrath. She's been crankier than usual." Karina relents though doesn't mask her snicker of disapproval. I roll my shoulders back and swim past them, their attitudes forgotten at the chaos that immediately greets me.

Inside, the palace is bustling with more sirens than I have ever seen here at once, despite the late hour. And all of them are legionaries. *Shit.* My eyes dart from female to female, my pulse fluttering in my chest as I wait for the moment they realize I'm among them. If Nia has already informed Sade or Allegra of my betrayal, then surely, they will apprehend me the moment they see me. Yet, though a few of them look my way, they spare me nothing more than a cursory glance. I cautiously glide forward, water and bubbles sliding along my skin as I make my way through the throng of gathered legionaries. If they aren't here for me...

"They say they can pass through the Spell now!" one says as she swims by me.

"Can we trust it? How do we know it is actually *true*?"

More murmurs of the Spell—of the first group of legionaries that came back *changed*—ring in my ear as I pass, the reason for those gathered abundantly clear now. An involuntary shiver draws my shoulders up to my ears. My mother hadn't wasted time informing everyone of what Rhea did.

I pass by the yellow sea glass door of the throne room, stopping in front of it for just a moment before the sound of Allegra's voice on the other side sends me scrambling to the ramp up to the second floor. Lyre's bedroom is on the opposite end of the hall from my own, and relief hits me when I find her door open, my sister sitting on her bed.

"Aria," she says, giving me a soft smile. I shut the door behind me as I enter, taking in her room as I make my way to the bed. Its layout is similar to my own, only larger and decorated with pale shades of purple, yellow, and pink. On the wall behind the bed is a mosaic of crystals made to look like a flaring sun. Their light is subtle, setting the room in a soft glow of gold. Unlike the barebones room of Sade's and the mismatched quality of mine, Lyre's space is one that represents her.

"How are you feeling?" I ask, settling in next to her.

"Tired," she answers with a chuckle, leaning back on her hands, "but well." Her eyes shift to mine. "How are you?"

"Fine." She sends me a look that says, *liar*, but I shake my head and gesture to her belly. "And the little one?"

"She's moving a ton now. Particularly while I'm trying to sleep." I laugh, my own tension seeping away while I watch emotions play across her face. *Happiness. Excitement. Joy.* But then her smile shrinks and her brows draw low over her eyes.

"What is it?"

"Whatever Mother is planning has me nervous," she starts, shifting to sit up. I join her, my gaze meeting hers in concern. "It was one thing when what she preached was all talk—the ramblings of a female lost in her own rage. But to hear that she is one step closer to getting what she wants... Aria, I don't know if it's safe for us to do this anymore."

My throat constricts tightly. "What?"

"She is becoming more powerful, and if she gets what she wants on land? There is no telling the lengths she'll go to in order to ensure her reach into every part of Olymazi. That will include us," she says, her hands cradling her belly more tightly.

"We can do this," I counter, my hand laying on top of hers. "Lyre, I promise. We *will* do it."

"How? How can we hope to hide when she's been growing her legion? Every day, more are forced to join, and now that they will have the ability to walk through the Spell and *live*? This is more than we ever could have planned for. More than *I* can ask of you—"

"I've been meeting with a fae." The confession comes tumbling out of me, but I don't panic at what I've said. Instead, I feel *lighter*, a weight lifted from my chest.

Lyre's mouth opens, then shuts, her brows scrunching together. "*What?*"

I leap into the tale of how Myla and I met, what I've been doing in the weeks since that fateful day, and how it is strengthening my hope in our escape. "She hates me, but she's fulfilling her end of the deal," I tell her, clutching the silky strands of sea kelp that stuff her bed.

Lyre's expression doesn't shift from her initial shock, and when I finish telling her everything related to Myla, I wait through glacial seconds for her to pass judgement on me. But then a smile breaks over her face, her amethyst eyes sparkling as she draws me in for a tight hug.

"You actually fucking obtained a *life debt* from a fae?"

"Does everyone but me know what that is?" I ask, laughing when she draws back and wraps her hands around my shoulders, giving me a gentle shake.

"What is she like? *Myla.*" She says her name as if its syllables are foreign on her tongue.

I tip my head to the side as I picture her. Her cutting looks and even sharper tongue. The way she makes me feel like I'm impossibly naive. "She's brutal," I start, making Lyre frown. "And mean. I'm the spike in her side that she's forced to live with until the deal is met and she can dig me out. But she's also ruthless in a way that is inspiring." Myla's anger towards me is as earned as it is frustrating, but I don't think even she realizes that her curtness draws out a defiance of my own.

"Aria." Lyre's voice pulls me from my own head, my heart rapidly beating for an entirely different reason. One I can't even begin to reconcile with.

"Sorry," I rush out quickly, clearing my throat. "But we can do this together, Lyre."

"I have to say, Sister, I underestimated you."

"It's alright—"

"No, it isn't. I've tried my best to protect you in all the ways I thought wouldn't be obvious to our mother. And I know that it still hasn't been enough. *I know that.* But despite what you think about yourself, you are so much stronger than you've ever given yourself credit for. Than *I* have given you credit for."

Emotions clog my throat and threaten tears to form in my eyes, but I fend them off as I duck my head. "There is one more thing," I whisper, earning a surprised chuckle.

"What, are you going to tell me that you've struck some sort of deal with the shifters now?"

"Not exactly. This has to do with Nia and the seamount sirens." The mention of them sobers the moment. Lyre's spine straightens as her face shifts into a serious expression so quickly, I could almost laugh.

"What about them?"

"Nia found my cave a while ago and has been using its existence to blackmail me. She tasked me with retrieving their confiscated weapons." I go on to tell her about the note I found earlier, how the threat was clear. *It might already be too late.*

Lyre's eyes are sharp, her attention wholly focused on me. "Why didn't you say anything sooner?"

"I didn't think there was anything you could do to help me. I also felt like, perhaps, this was my penance for not trying to do more, as Nia said. Our mother drove her own people out to live in squalor, all because of a grudge she's held for over two hundred years. Nia's chosen path may not be the most savory, but she isn't necessarily wrong in what she's trying to do."

"And what is that?"

"She wants to remove our mother from the throne."

Lyre scoffs, running a hand through her lavender braids. "Even if she could somehow manage that with her ragtag team of sirens, who would then be queen? Her? Because you know as well as I do that she isn't going to ask you or I. She'll kill Allegra and Sade and likely keep Dyanna only to use as an information pet."

"Does it matter? As long as our mother is gone?"

"*Yes*," she answers curtly, making me startle back. She closes her eyes, moving a hand to cradle her belly. "You have to think long term about something like this. Our mother is horrible by *every* standard, but she is a monster we *know*. To help put someone new on the throne, someone who already hates our family, would be just as dangerous. We don't want to escape one tyrant only to be at the whims of a worse one."

"So what should I do, then?"

"We get the seamount sirens their weapons. *Together.* But we use them as a bargaining tool with Nia. She's holding too much over your head without any real *proof*. Even if she told Sade or our mother about the cave, there is no way to tie you to it unless you have personal items there." I shake my head. Everything the cave once contained were items I found. Nothing of it is actually *mine*. "We get the weapons, and then we ask for our guaranteed safety through whatever she and her sirens are planning. Safety whether we stay here or continue forward with our plan to leave."

My apprehension with not only this plan but entangling Lyre in it must show on my face because my sister sighs and reaches over to grab my hand.

"Didn't I say this will only work if we trust each other? I'm pregnant, Aria, but not incapable. I'm still as vicious as I've ever been. Perhaps even more so now." She pats her belly. "We are not weak." Her eyes sparkle with undeniable determination. "Let us plan the beginnings of a coup."

Chapter Fifty-One

MYLA

COLD STONE BITES INTO my knees, sending a shiver up my spine. My feet have long since gone numb, and the lack of proper blood flow makes them tingle as if they're being pricked by small needles. I have lost track of how long I've been here, of how many days have passed. Did the sun rise twice? Three times? The days wouldn't matter so much if I wasn't due to meet the siren soon, and anger gnaws at my chest just as hunger does my belly. I don't want to miss a meeting and delay fulfilling the terms of my life debt.

After Leesi reported to Father Yamin and the queen that I was missing from my room, I had prepared for this eventuality. I don't regret spending time killing Sir Dae, nor do I regret visiting the dragon fields afterwards, but past experience makes my body tense.

A shadow passes through the sunlight streaming in from a small square window as a bird lands on the windowsill. I watch as it hops and tilts its head, and maybe it's because I know what's about to come, or maybe it's because I'm so fucking tired, but the sight of a small creature living its life oblivious to the archaic rules of the fae and made-up gods makes pressure build behind my eyes. But tears won't fall—they never do. Not since the first time this happened.

I jolt when the door to my cell in the church's wing opens, its hinges letting out creaks of protest. His robes hiss along the stone floor, and I fight the urge to yank away from the finger under my chin. My eyes lift to meet Father Yamin's, and though a frown paints his face in a shade of disappointment, I see beyond this forced emotion. As he studies my gaze, I hope he sees what my face won't show as well. I think he does, and maybe I am cursed by the fucking gods he loves so much, because were we in any *other scenario, I would have* him *hanging from a hook in my warehouse. Drowning in the glee that his blood spilling from his body would fill me with.*

"Princess Myla, you know that I do not take pleasure in watching you suffer." Liar. *He releases my chin, and I force my spine to straighten, despite the way my back and stomach muscles scream to just give in. "But you bring the wrath of the gods upon yourself when you do not follow the rules for a noble female."*

"Royal," I croak, my throat stinging from the lack of water over the course of however many days I've been here. "I'm royalty, not nobility." There's a single moment of silence, one that prefaces what I know is coming, but I relish it all the same with the tiniest quirk of my mouth. Then agony flares at the back of my head, stars bursting over my eyes as my body is forced forward from the impact of the hit. The taste of iron blooms over my tongue.

"You will watch *your tongue when speaking to me." His hand lands harshly on my shoulder, yanking me back into an upright position as his fingers dig in. "This is the last time I will ask before I take you out into the temple where a crowd is already waiting." Despite how I try to fight it off, disquiet twirls in my stomach, shortening every inhale. "Where did you go that night, hmm? We know that you were not in your bedroom, and despite the way Prince Navin insists you were on the grounds, we both know he will do whatever it takes to protect you." Father Yamin lowers into a squat before me, showing off the wooden baton he hit me with. I stare at the black char marks, swirling lines, and scripture passages burned along its length. Crimson stains the side of it, the fresh glisten making my teeth gnash together. "Tell the truth for once, Princess Myla, and this can end here and now," he whispers, forcing his lips into a reassuring smile.*

My head dances as my vision blurs, the bastard growing from two people to three and then back to one. But I know how he plays his games now, and punishment comes no matter what I say. "And I will tell you what I've been telling you. I woke from a nightmare and needed fresh air, so I went to the queen's garden and sat for a while. When I came back, I was informed by Prince Navin that you assumed me to be missing. But I was not aware that walking around one's own home was a crime." I've repeated the story so many times, I'm almost starting to believe it myself.

His eyes brighten, that excuse of a smile blooming into a real one. Despite what the bastard claims, punishing me is a favorite pastime of his. "Very well." He stands and pulls a black veil from one of his robe pockets, ensuring that, even in punishment, I will remain faceless to the people. Once the veil is in place, he walks to the door and beckons two of the brethren in, their cream robes indicating that they're still initiates. Unlike the black robe of Father Yamin, which indicates he's reached the highest level. Closer to the gods or whatever the fuck. "Pick her up." The males obey, and I'm hoisted up by my arms, my feet left to drag behind me as we begin our procession out of the cell.

The journey to the temple attached to the north wing of the palace is short, and when I see the rich onyx doors through my veil, my pathetic heart slams against my ribs. *It's just the lack of water and food and movement and stress release. There is nothing to fear here because I am fear itself.*

The males at my side grip with brutal strength, adding to the collection of bruises already marring my body. Though bruises will be the least of my concerns after this.

Father Yamin pushes those dark doors open, the click when they lock into place silencing the hushed whispers from inside the temple. I glance down at my body, the robe they've covered me in cinched tightly at my waist. When the Divine Father's helpers begin to drag me again, I force my feet to try to match their steps. But days of waiting on my knees for judgement has left me too weak to hold myself up. It's all part of their plan to shame me.

I stare at Father Yamin's back as he strides into the temple with the confidence only a male who holds both king and kingdom in his hands could have. Because despite how my own father may be the face of rule and order, it's Father Yamin who whispers into his ear. I'm brought to the very center of the temple where a wooden pole connects from the ground up to the ceiling, every inch of it covered in the same swirls and holy words as the father's favorite baton.

"Your Majesty, King Kamon, it is an honor as always to be in your presence, under the watchful eye of Khaos and His temple which we stand in."

The king smiles at the father, silver-ringed fingers drumming along his jaw for a long while before he looks my way. Of course, he isn't looking at me so much as he is assessing the way I'm about to be punished. "Tell me what you have decided."

Next to him sits my mother, her face as emotionless as glass. Her black hair is tied on top of her head in a beautiful pattern, silver picks ending in bright red tassels crossing over each other in the bun at its center. She doesn't bother to look at me. On the other side of the king is Navin. Deep despair alters his expression as he leans forward in his throne, gripping the very edge of the armrests so tightly that all color is drained from his knuckles.

"As you know, Your Majesty, the customary punishment for one who purposely disobeys the codes of our kingdom and will of the gods is death." Navin's eyes grow wide, and his chest stops lifting with breath. Neither king nor queen react at all. "But death, while freeing the princess from her sins, will not help us earn the gods' favor. Your daughter was sent not only as a message but as a test. A measurement with which to gauge our repentance as a kingdom."

I look away from my brother, instead focusing on the detailed, carved dragon wings that bracket my father's throne.

"So it is as a humble servant of our gods that I suggest another round of twenty-five lashes, as was the punishment for her first offense." A few murmurs ring out from the crowd, but I'm not at all surprised. The last time I was in this position, the father had been all too eager to split my skin open. At least my back is already a mess—these new wounds cannot make it worse. "In addition, I believe we should de-veil the princess."

My gaze snaps to him as gasps *sound around the room. Father Yamin holds his chin high, his hands clasped calmly as if he hasn't just asked openly to break away from the very tradition he holds dear.*

"And what is your reasoning for such a suggestion?" the king asks, his eyes lowered in boredom as he brings the hand at his jaw down to the throne's armrest. Calm and collected, completely unaffected at the thought of his daughter being whipped.

"Your Majesty, Princess Myla has shown that her dedication to repentance and not repeating her sins is unreliable. Perhaps a drastic measure such as this will be enough incentive for her to remember that when she disobeys the gods, they will always retaliate."

I almost laugh at the father's hyperbole. But taking off my veil and revealing my face is dangerous. Anonymity has been my biggest aid in remaining Khargis's Shadow. No one knows what the princess looks like, but they might *have seen the Shadow. Some of those people could even be in this room, not that anyone here would admit to spending time in the bowels of the city. Still, my heart gallops in my chest, and I finally look back at my brother, his eyes expressing what mine can't.* Fear.

Movement lures my gaze to my mother, and I watch as she slides her hand over my father's, giving it a light squeeze before returning it to her lap. He dips his chin in a nearly imperceptible movement before drawing in a deep breath. "If you think it would impart a better lesson for my daughter—"

"You can't be serious!" Navin interrupts, causing another roll of gasps that echo against the stone walls. "This goes directly *against everything we claim to hold value in." His hand shoots out in my direction. "Regardless of what the princess has done, the punishment should be befitting of the crime, and de-veiling her strips her of more than just a cloth over her face. It takes away any future prospects for her to marry."*

I don't react, letting my fury stoke me from within—a flame that grows infinite in its heat. I know he's just using my most valuable card to play, but my worth as a person being dwindled down to nothing more than some male's future wife only makes that flame grow hotter.

"There is still time to make advantageous deals for Myla's hand, even as she is tainted." His voice wavers on the final word.

Fuck, I'd rather just out myself fully than be referred to as if I'm not here, but my logic outweighs my emotions, so I keep my mouth shut.

"While I can appreciate your steadfast adherence to tradition, in this case—"

"No, Prince Navin is right," the king interrupts Father Yamin, his voice sharp. "Administer the lashings, and then we can all get on with our day."

It's as simple as that. It brings me a small amount of joy when Father Yamin's expression stumbles, unable to hide his anger and embarrassment for a few heartbeats before composing himself.

Assuring my veil remains, the two brethren who dragged me here make quick work of removing my robe. The air is cold as it hits my skin, my hands rebound around the wooden pole. From the corner of my eye, I watch as my brother leans over to our father, whispering something harshly in his ear. The king just sends him an icy glare in response. Navin flexes his jaw, his eyes dropping to the floor where they stay as the sound of the father's whip uncoiling brings my own focus forward. Metal scrapes along the stone as he slowly drags the iron-tipped ends of the whip back, and my body reacts and draws taut at the sound.

"Princess Myla Ryuu, you are being punished today for lying to the brethren of Khaos, god of Time and Void, about your whereabouts three evenings ago. As decided by Khaos, and the gods that rule with him, you will receive twenty-five lashings."

My breath trickles in through my nose as I stare at the unfortunate passage burned into the wood in front of me. May Solana's light guide you to the Afterlife.

The rustling of Father Yamin's robe seems to stop time itself, a distended few seconds where there is nothing but the beat of my heart and the hiss of breath between my clenched teeth. The words on the pole blur as my mind begins to flash through random memories as a distraction. Sunis and the dragon fields. The men who left bait for Bali. Aria and the way her hair glints like a jewel beneath the dappled sunlight of the cavern. All at once, everything fractures, the impact of the whip slicing through my skin luring me back into the present with world-shattering agony.

My eyes snap closed as my chest pushes against the pole, my nails digging into it. The next lash chokes air from my lungs. The next makes my eyes sting. I stop counting around ten, my body sagging against the pole enough that the father pauses for me to be repositioned.

"Get up," someone calls, feminine but not my voice. At least, I don't think it is. A snap rends the air as warmth trickles down my back and pools at my knees. "Get up!" they say more urgently. I groan, the scent of iron heavy with every gasp, churning my stomach as blood drips down my torso and hips.

"Get. Up. Myla."

My eyes fly open, strands of black hair covering them as my fingers grip not the wooden pole but something softer—a pillow.

"Come on, you've been in bed for three days. You need to get up." *Navin.* He brushes the hair away from my face, concern forming a wrinkle on his forehead. "You're covered in sweat. It's even soaked through the bandages." He has the audacity to look slightly ill at that. "Let's get you cleaned up and moving."

"I'm not healed enough to move," I argue, my voice raspy. *It had only been three days since the whipping?* But I shouldn't be surprised by that, time moves differently when pain is the only thing you can feel.

"No," he sighs, tying his long hair back. He's wearing his sparring leathers and a plain white undershirt. "But you must."

"You cannot expect me to train in this condition," I murmur, closing my eyes and sinking my face deeper into the pillow. *Snap.* Another drag of the barbs against my ravaged back. *Snap.* There's no air, and I can't *breathe. Snap.*

"I expect so much of you, Myla, and this is no exception. You aren't weak or helpless or unworthy. You never have been. Now get up. We have work to do." The bedsheets rustle as he stands and leaves my room, the door remaining open behind him. I groan, but when the sound of the whip cracks again in my mind, I move.

And just like he did the last time the whip met my skin, Navin gets me out of bed and forces me to meet a new day.

Chapter Fifty-Two

MYLA

Five days later, Lan's wings beat hard against the wind as we soar to my meeting with the siren. The sun reflects off of his blue scales, flaring directly into my fucking eyes. My back screams at the jostling as we fly, but I clamp down on the pain that rolls through me and instead focus on the next task at hand. This will be my third lesson with the female who had saved my life, having missed last week after the lashings. At least now she would know what it was like to wait alone on a beach while the other didn't show.

Navin's shoulders tense where he's sitting in front of me, and I watch him place a hand on Lan's scales as he and his dragon communicate. I scan the black mountains surrounding us, misty clouds hovering close to their peaks. I haven't been able to visit Sunis in a week, and the thought that my father could be trying to capture her mother is an incessant alarm in my mind.

"Lan has a lot of concerned energy today," Navin shouts over his shoulder. "He keeps pushing it through the bond."

I lean in closer so he can hear me over the wind. "Any idea why?"

"No."

I look past Navin to Lan's head, watching as he tilts it to the side as if he's trying to get a better look at something.

A different set of wingbeats cleaves the air to our left, just as a low rumble vibrates down Lan's body. My stomach hollows and sharp pain shoots through my back when we bank right, Lan tucking his wings in with a leathery *snap*. Then we're in a freefall, diving through the mist as air stings my eyes. Fighting against the force of the fall, I crouch low over Navin's back, gripping tightly to the leather strap holding me in place. As abruptly as the dive began, it ends when Lan flares his wings out, catching his weight as he moves into a glide.

"There was another dragon," Navin says after a long bout of silence, both of us needing a moment to catch our breath.

"Any idea who would be this far out?" It isn't unusual to have smaller units of King's Riders patrolling near Khargis. But I hadn't known them to travel this far. At least, I hadn't *assumed* it from my father's meetings that I had snuck into.

"No idea, but whoever it was, Lan didn't seem familiar with them. His energy bordered on nervousness, and that's only the case if he's around a bigger dragon or one that he doesn't know."

Interesting. While it would be foolish to assume all bonded dragons know each other, Lan had grown up on the dragon fields, much like Sunis, before choosing my brother as his rider. Most of the bonded chose to stay on or near the fields because its landscape makes finding livestock easy. Yes, wild game is plentiful too, but out in the mountains is where the unbonded dragons roam. While fights between dragons are rare, hunger can make even the most docile among them irate. Was it an unbonded that Lan had sensed? Or simply a larger black dragon that had flown too close?

"We're almost there," Navin shouts, jerking his head forward where I can already see the ocean through the Spell. It only takes a few minutes for us to reach the magical border, the tingling sensation of passing through drawing goosebumps over my skin. Lan circles the beach as he prepares to land, and I turn my gaze out to the shore, where I catch a glimpse of dark skin and ruby-red hair. "Aria's here."

"I, too, have eyes."

"I bet you do," he says with a laugh.

"What is that supposed to mean?"

"Nothing at all, Dear Sister." Lan hits the sand a little harder than usual, and the impact forms stars behind my lids as I growl out in pain. "Shit, are you okay?"

"Fine," I grit out, grabbing a tunic for the siren from a pack attached to Lan's back. Undoing the straps that secure me, I carefully hoist myself up. But there is no such thing as *careful* when your back is a ravaged, fiery pit of still-healing jagged lashes. Traversing along his bumpy ridges, I climb down Lan's front leg, leaning against it when I slip and land in the sand in a crouch. Squeezing my eyes shut, I breathe through the lancing pain. While my enhanced healing has stitched the skin back together, it's what is damaged beneath that still radiates with excruciating tenderness. By the time I stand again, Navin has dismounted and is making his way to the edge of the water.

"It's nice to see you, Navin," she says to him as she waves, her eyes bright with excitement.

Wait...

"How do you know his name?"

She jumps at the bark in my voice, her eyes flitting to my brother with a familiarity that I don't like.

"I may have spent some time with her last week when I came to tell her you wouldn't be coming."

"You saw her last week?"

"I did. *And* we spent some time training together."

I'm going to kill him.

He takes one look at my face and rolls his eyes. "Oh, come on, Myla. It would have been rude to leave Aria waiting." He gestures to the siren, who at least has the intelligence to take a step back towards the ocean.

"Unbelievable," I snap, tossing Aria the tunic. Something insidious rises as I turn to face Navin fully. "And *when* did you take the time to visit her?"

His expression softens, a hand reaching out to my shoulder before I jerk away. "Myla—"

"Just go." I brush past him towards the cavern, tension rippling from my temples to my jaw. Once beneath the dome shape of the stone jutting out from the mountain, I run a hand down my face, wiping the sweat dotting my brow. Distant wingbeats let me know that Navin has left, and I'm annoyed to realize that behind my anger—and something that feels a lot like *jealousy*—guilt settles like a stone.

The siren makes her way inside beneath an arched break in the stone, the white tunic hitting her mid-thigh. Her hazel eyes assess me, running over my body in quick sweeps before she adjusts her stance and folds her arms over her chest. "Where were you last week?"

I let my fingers drum against the dagger strapped to my thigh, Aria's attention dropping to watch the movement. "Navin didn't tell you when you had your little practice session?"

Her brow furrows as she looks up at me. "No. All he said was that you were preoccupied."

"Preoccupied," I repeat. "What else did he say about me?" I watch her throat work as she clasps her hands behind her.

"Nothing of importance."

I tilt my head to the side as I step into her space, her scent—salt and something warm and *sweet*—trickles in the closer I get. "You're a terrible liar.". I study the way she watches me, her pulse fluttering at her neck while her full lips pinch together.

"I'm not lying. You can ask Navin yourself." My brother's name coming out of her mouth sends a jolt of awareness through me. I had never wanted this siren involved in my life more than what was needed to fulfill the life debt. But Navin couldn't help himself, sticking his nose into places it didn't belong. And this siren... I growl as I step back and make my way to the platform where we train, climbing the large rocks quickly and ignoring the gripping pain at my back as I do.

I had left Opal Brothel, left Karina, because they had started to feel too *familiar* with me, and yet somehow, a fucking *siren* now knew more about me than she had any *right* to. Aria climbs up behind me, taking the bag crossed over her body off and laying it down on the ground. Our gazes meet over the length of the platform, and she inhales deeply before opening her mouth to speak.

"Start with your warm-ups," I tell her, watching as her expression falters into something mirroring disappointment before she steps into the center of the cavern and begins.

Two sets of exercises later, she pauses to wipe a light sheen of sweat from her brow, and I feel her eyes on me where I lean against the cavern wall. "Why aren't you doing the moves with me?"

Disregarding her question, I instruct her to go on the attack. She waits for me to join her, a sparring partner required to truly practice, but my aggravation with Navin—with myself and the siren—keeps my feet rooted in place. When it's clear I'm not going to move, she sighs, her hands coming to her hips.

"It's awkward doing this by myself." Those alluring eyes narrow on me. "Are you sick?"

"Keep punching. Balance your weight better on the balls of your feet."

She scoffs, tucking her curls behind her ears before obeying. Or at least, she tries too. While she moves through the combos I—and apparently Navin—have taught her, she favors the foot with the jagged scar across it more than the other.

"You keep a lot of secrets," she says between breaths.

"Only from those who don't deserve to know."

Aria frowns but returns to her jabs silently.

"Lift your right arm and step back a little farther with your left foot," I instruct.

She steps back, but her foot angles too far in, causing her to wobble and throw her arms out for balance.

"Flatten that back foot—"

"Can you just come and *help* me?" she snaps, her talons pushing from the tips over her fingers. I draw a brow up at the outburst, a taunting rebuttal pressing at my lips before the abrupt urge to *move* and help her overwhelms me. *The oath.* Fuck, the magic is demanding that submit to her plea.

Her eyes flare wide as I uncross my arms and walk towards her, biting back a wince. "Draw your heel out wider," I say, gently tapping the side of her foot with the tip of my boot. "Until your strength increases, you need to be more aware of how each part of your body is moving. If I would have attempted to hit you while you took up that positioning, you would have fallen flat on your ass."

"My foot— I can't press it flat. The muscles won't work.".

"What animal would leave a scar like that?" I ask. The question hadn't exactly slipped out, but I have been curious to know what could leave such a jagged mark. It was like a smaller version of the scars on my back. Had she been subjected to a whip too? My hands involuntarily clench at the thought before I force myself to relax them.

"How about you tell me one thing about *you*, and I will answer your question?" she counters.

I smirk as I round her front, lifting her arms to put her guard back up in front of her. Her skin is warm beneath my fingers, in contrast to the chill in the air from our proximity to the ocean. "How about I challenge you for real and then *force* you to tell me when I win?"

She rolls her eyes as she distributes her weight between both feet. "These will be long hours together if we don't have anything other than fighting to talk about," she urges, tilting her head. "Would it be *so* bad to get to know each other? Tell me about your life in the palace, and I'll share how your lessons actually helped m—"

Her words are silenced when my head snaps in her direction, my brows drawn low over my eyes. "Why would you assume I live in the palace?"

"I—" She drops her guard as she stumbles backwards, but I follow her retreat until she hits the cavern wall, one of my hands bracing near her head. "I was just guessing."

"Don't *lie*, Aria." My eyes search hers, but there is only one way she could know. "Navin," I growl.

"He didn't mean to let it slip," she whispers, showing me her palms in the space between our heaving chests. "He was helping me train and—"

"So what? You know *one* detail about me and now think you're entitled to it all? That we are somehow *friends* or equals? Because let's get *one* thing straight, Little Siren. I'm neither a friend nor someone you can trust. I'd sooner watch this oath between us fail and *kill* me then share anything personal with the likes of *you*."

Her fingers curl in towards her palms, but where her bravery when speaking with me before was nonexistent, something now sparks in her gaze. A brightly lit ember that backlights the hazel.

"I wish I had let you *drown*." Her bottom lip trembles with the admission, my gaze drawn to it. This close to her, I can see the dark freckles that dust her cheeks and the bridge of her nose. I take note of the way her long lashes frame her eyes, their shape doe-like.

Air doesn't quite meet my lungs on my next breath as I show her my canines in a snarl. "That makes two of us."

Her mouth drops with a gasp, but I step away before she offers whatever apology is dangling on the tip of her tongue. Walking to the other side of the cavern, I give her my back as I close my eyes. *Control.* I need to gain *control.*

"Do you hear that?" she asks softly, her steps gentle as they pad in my direction.

"Hear wh—" A shadow passes over us, the distinct sound of beating wings drawing my gaze upward. "He's early," I murmur as I walk to the edge of the platform, intent on letting Navin know *exactly* how I feel about him sharing details of me with Aria when my boots halt at the sight of the dragon I can see through one of the holes in the wall. *Fuck.*

Ducking back, I squat low and palm my dagger, inspecting our surroundings for a spot to hide should we need it.

"What is it?" Aria asks, joining me on the ground.

"I'm not sure, but the dragon out there is not Navin's." I push my own discomfort out of the way as I focus on identifying who is out there. Aria doesn't move at my side, keeping still as she peers down to one of the openings carved into the rock.

The black dragon's scales glisten as it lowers itself to the sand, its yellow eye visible in the cutout. I tilt my head slowly and catch a glimpse of silver that makes me grow rigid, my teeth grinding together before I carefully take a step back. "It's a King's Rider," I murmur, returning to scan the platform. But there is no crevice big enough to slip between, nothing but the beach in front of us and the pool of water behind us.

"I don't know what that is," she whispers back, panicked eyes meeting mine.

"No one good. We need to hide—" I blink as I remember who I'm talking to. *What* I'm talking to. "You can use your song."

Her head draws back as her brows rise towards her hairline. "What?"

I look back out to the dragon and his rider, only seeing the former as I answer her. "You're a fucking siren. Use your song to lure him in."

When she doesn't respond, I glance in her direction. Aria's eyes are still blown wide, but it's more than just fear of the guard and his dragon. She carries the same look as the males who meet the end of my blade.

"My song," she starts, licking her lips and then swallowing. "I can't— It doesn't work."

"What do you mean it doesn't work?"

"It *doesn't work* on males."

I stare harshly at her, too many questions rising that we don't have time to answer. Especially as the dragon lets out a low growl, it's eye clashing with both of mine when I turn to look for the guard. "*Shit*," I hiss, jolting backwards as the King's Rider appears at one of the openings of the cavern.

We are sitting prey, and while taking on a single rider would not be an issue normally, in my current state, I'm not positive our fight would end without me in a worse position. And that is before his bonded dragon is taken into account. But the rules of the life debt demand I do *something*, and as the dragon lets out another rumbling growl, closer than before, I realize that we've officially run out of time.

Chapter Fifty-Three

MYLA

"Can you swim?" The question pulls me from my focus on our impending discovery, and I give Aria a look that conveys as much. But she repeats herself, leaning in more closely. "Can you *swim*?"

"Yes—"

"Good, come on." She grabs her bag, and I move to follow, unsure of how the fuck she is going to sneak past the rider and his dragon to get to the ocean when she gestures towards the pool of water behind the platform. I stop, heart pounding as we stay crouched low.

"What are you doing?"

"We need to get in the water." Her voice is overshadowed by the dragon's chuff behind us, the King's Rider speaking low to his bonded but still close enough for me to hear. *Fucking stars above.*

"How is that—"

"Myla"—her opposite hand grips my wrist, fingers squeezing tightly—"I need you to trust me."

The scoff that leaves me is automatic. There is no world in which that can happen. In which I want it to.

Her eyes plead, more orange than hazel now as the gleam. "We don't have time. I can help us both, but you can't fight what I'm about to do. At all."

"I—"

"Is anyone up there?" The male's voice reverberates off the stone, and Aria's eyes grow wide at the sound.

"Please." The single word is whispered, her lips trembling as she drapes her legs over the platform, the dark water before us rippling from the contact.

Stupid. This is so fucking stupid. I'll be the first fae willingly led to their death beneath the water. But the sound of rustling leather permeates my logic and rationale. Aria sees my silent, reluctant agreement because she wastes no more time tugging me into the water.

It's colder than I thought it would be as I suck in a lungful of air before our heads dip below the surface. I keep one hand on the dagger strapped to me, Aria's fingers still wrapped around my other wrist to keep us tethered.

The sunlight seeping in from cracks in the ceiling is meager, but there is still enough to see the vines of jasmine crawling up the walls and, beyond that, the larger holes in rock. Beneath the surface, the Spell shimmers behind us as it cuts through the water, and lower in the dark water, tunnels that I assume lead back out to the ocean are just barely visible.

"Keep treading water, no matter what else happens." My gaze collides with Aria's, my mind struggling to reconcile the fact that she is *speaking* to me beneath the water. Her curls are now replaced with tightly woven braids, glimmering gold beads decorating some of them. The braids suit her just as well as her curls. Still wearing the white tunic I brought for her, it floats around her, giving view to the scales that have grown brighter at her hips and thighs. My gaze traces down her body to where a tail has replaced her legs, the color of her scales shifting from that brilliant red to golden yellow and then to a light green. It's mesmerizing watching the way she moves, her body as fluid as the water that surrounds us. Every bit of grace she lacks above the surface is made up for in her siren form.

When her gaze flicks upwards, I follow suit, the sight above making me pull my dagger from its sheath.

"He can't see us," Aria says, her voice softer and more melodic than before. But even with her assurance, she pulls me a little farther down. The male searches the water from above, and I suppress my urge to kick back towards the surface, my lungs beginning to burn from holding my breath. Even in the water, the deep and throaty growls of the dragon that hails from the Khar line can be heard, and I know that we will not leave this beach alive if we are spotted.

My heartbeat is loud in my head, and the urge to take a breath grows stronger. The rider above pulls back from the platform's edge, and once he is out of sight, I begin kicking to the surface, white stars bursting to life across my vision.

"No!" Aria shouts, swimming until she's right in front of me as one hand plants on my shoulder, the other gripping tightly to a dagger that I've never seen before. "I can still sense them up there. You can't—"

Shaking my head, I push her back and mime a choking gesture. The weight of my soaked cloak and boots makes it difficult to tread the water, and when Aria says to wait, panic begins to set in despite the way I try to push it away. *We're trapped here.*

"I think they might be testing us to see if we'll break the surface," she says, her gaze holding mine.

I'm trapped here. The thought makes my lungs contract, every sensation abruptly feeling like it's too much as I again struggle to kick upwards.

"Remember when I told you not to fight me? Now is that time." She moves closer to me, keeping her hold on my wrist as she gets close enough for her chest to brush against mine. I jerk back, tugging on my hand as my heart flails in my chest, those spots in my vision growing while darkness creeps in along the edges. "I'm not going to hurt you." It's Aria speaking, I know it is. I watched her lips move. But her voice... it comes out like a song. A melody of notes that is as pleasing to my ears as any I've heard sung in the palace by performers. "I promise," she adds, her eyes glowing brightly.

Then her mouth presses onto mine.

Her thumb gently slides along the sensitive skin of my inner wrist, eyes still boring into me when the tip of her tongue pushes against the seam of my lips. *What the fucking stars above is happening?* I keep them clamped shut, Aria's face in front of me almost fully blocked out by the darkness invading my vision. My kicks become lazier, the weight of my body heavier as the thumping of my heart reverberates in my skull.

"Please, Myla," she says against my lips, her own panic reflected in that ethereal voice. I don't know if it's her fear or my own that motivates me, but I submit and open my mouth to her. The moment her tongue sweeps in, caressing against my own, my lungs expand. There is no breath of air—there is *no* air at *all*—but the sensation of breathing fills my chest anyway, the stars in my eyes slowly vanishing. *This* is the magic of the sirens. More than just luring males to them, they have the ability to keep them *alive* beneath the water.

As the oxygen rushes into my system, it heightens everything around me. The coolness of the water at my back and the warmth of the siren at my front. The softness of Aria's lips—the slickness of her tongue—each sensation bottoms my stomach out while simultaneously filling me with the primal urge for *more*. Aria makes a soft sound as her fingers twitch around my wrist, her lids lowering halfway while her body arches just slightly towards me.

This is survival, and I am only acting on my instincts when I plant my hands on her hips and tug her closer to me. It's only *her* magic that drives my tongue deeper into her mouth, desperate to know if that slight sweetness that lingers is how she tastes everywhere. It's a lapse of judgement, one that blurs reality until there is only the feel of Aria in my hands. On my lips.

Suspended in the cold waters of this cave, time itself halts, bowing down to this moment between us that should be impossible. And then, like a punch to my gut, it all rushes back in. The palace guard and the dragon. My distrust of the female in front of me. My eyes fly open—I'm unsure of when they even *closed*—and I rip myself away from Aria, ignoring the way her eyes flutter open too as I kick my way up, gasping for a breath the moment my head breaks the water. She doesn't stop me, surfacing a few seconds after I do, her gaze heavy on the side of my face as I scan our surroundings.

"Myla, I—"

"They're gone," I interrupt with a relieved exhale, kicking until I reach the platform.

"Do you need help—"

"I think you've done enough," I snap, my back muscles contracting in pain as I hoist myself up, my clothing waterlogged and boots squishing as I come up to stand.

Aria is silent as she exits the pool, her transformation back to her mortal form happening behind my back as I ensure the cavern is empty on the other side of the platform. But when she speaks again, it's the anguish in her voice that sends tension rippling over my shoulders.

"Myla, I'm *sorry*. My magic— I didn't mean to make you—" She exhales in frustration from behind me. "I thought I was only using enough to ensure you could breathe beneath the surface. Just enough to keep you alive."

I press my palm into the curved blade at my thigh as I turn to face her, recoiling at the *shame* I see on her face. But on land, *I* am the weapon. *I* have the advantage. *I* am the one *she* should fear. Not pity.

"I'm sorry," she says again, and my restraint falters.

"That is enough!" I brush past her as I barrel towards the rocks to climb down to the sand.

"No," she rasps, rushing to keep up with me. "I stripped you of choice, and that was never my intent. I promised you could trust me and then—"

"I was never going to trust you, Little Siren," I interrupt, jumping the last few feet despite the way my body protests. The salt from the pool has settled into the tender wounds at my back, and I breathe through the sting of it with gritted teeth. "We are done discussing this." When I turn to face her again, her mouth is open as if she is poised to discuss it further, but a nearby roar silences her protest, her hand diving into the bag still strapped around her and producing the dagger I saw before.

I slide my own blade out of its sheath as we both peer to the sky above through one of the holes in the rock above. When the skies remain clear, I step back from the opening and put my blade away. Aria still holds hers in her hand, her shoulders hiked towards her ears. I study it in her grasp, noting the longer, more slender blade that is similar to the one I lost in the Hiravar's leg. "Never would have pegged you as a female who carries a weapon."

She exhales an incredulous laugh, holding the blade out in front of her to show me. "I'm not usually."

A line forms between my brows as I stare at the hilt, the off-white color tugging at a memory in my mind. I have seen a weapon like this before, down in the vaults of the palace where relics and treasures are stored. "That is a dragon bone hilt," I whisper. It's an item that was made before the war. Swallowing at the sudden tightness in my throat, I lunge for the dagger, easily taking it from Aria's grasp. My gaze flashes up to hers as I spin it in my hand, pointing the blade at her while my next words come out as a low growl. "Care to tell me why the *fuck* you have a dagger that belonged to my father?"

Chapter Fifty-Four

BAHIRA

GROWING UP AS PRINCESS of the Mage Kingdom, I never believed there would come a time I had to sneak around my own home. When I looked at guards and the council that surrounded my father with suspicion. When I *lied* to keep another kingdom safe because the traitorous thing beating behind my ribs was more loyal to a male hundreds of miles away than it was to the people I had vowed to keep safe here.

Perhaps that is a hyperbolic way to describe the situation I find myself in—sneaking through darkened hallways that I *shouldn't* know the location of behind the council and my father's back—but unfortunately, the woman I once pictured myself becoming truly was nothing more than an illusion. A storybook character created by a younger me that thought if I worked hard enough, I would get everything that I wanted. Reality had a way of crushing dreams faster than anything else, and mine had officially died the moment I came to terms with the results of my experiments.

I, Bahira Daxel, am well and truly magicless. At least, according to my blood. I trap my breath in my chest at the silent declaration just as a figure emerges from the shadows cast by spelled flames flickering in sconces on the wall. That thought, as well as ones of Kai, gets pushed as far from my mind as possible, to be dealt with at another time.

"I know I shouldn't be surprised that you were aware of the archives' location," the familiar voice says, mirth woven into his tone.

"Then don't be," I retort, adjusting my pack's straps on my shoulders.

Hadrik chuckles as he steps into the light, the white of his hair shining beneath it. "I suppose I know your father well enough to assume he would have told you how to at least *get* here."

I hum in thought, stepping into the hug that awaits. "Seems cruel to torture me with the knowledge of it, knowing damn well I can't access it on my own." Especially now that I know exactly what it takes to open the door.

"Or," Hadrik says with a pause, pulling back enough to see my face and resting his hands affectionately on my shoulders, "perhaps he knew you could figure out how to get around its... *safeguards*."

"I'm afraid I've disappointed him then." Smiling, I gently pull away from his grasp to turn and gesture to the end of the hall where I *know* the entrance to the archives is, even if I can't see it. "It makes sense that it would be layered with magic. Long ago, mortals, fae, shifters, and sirens might have snuck into the palace to walk these halls."

Hadrik reaches into the pocket of his trousers, tilting his head in thought as does. "And I wonder if it will return to a time like that again."

I take in his appearance—one that's as haggard as I feel and as exhausted as everyone in my family looks. My heart aches as I think of all that he has endured as the very council he is a part of questions the integrity of the man he grew up alongside. The children that he would do anything for as if they were his own.

"I wish there was more we could do," I whisper. To him. To myself.

Hadrik's gray eyes soften in the amber light, a sad smile tugging on his lips. "If anyone can figure it out..." He lets the sentence trail off as he opens the hand that had been in his pocket, revealing a silver key.

"This is it?" The metal is cold beneath my fingertips when I lift it from his palm, turning the ornate key over under the light. At the top are three circles laid over each other, and on the bottom are three tines of different lengths. Carved into the metal is a crescent moon overlapped with a flaring sun, the celestial symbol of Void queens past making a shiver run over my body.

"I'll have you know that it took great effort to retrieve this key."

I make sure to meet his eyes when I respond, "I know. And if you are found out, I will—"

He shakes his head. "You will do *nothing*, Bahira. I knew the risks involved with taking the key from Kallin's office, and I willingly accept whatever punishment should he find out. Now, come," he says, holding his hand back out. "We shouldn't linger where we might be so easily spotted."

Laying the key back into his waiting hand, I let him lead the way down the hall, my own fingers curling inwards as the hair rises on the back of my neck when a phantom draft caresses me. "It's fucking creepy in here."

"Perhaps part of the archives' self-defense," Hadrik muses, his profile falling into darkness between spelled flames. "Or maybe its curious charm."

"You speak of it as if it's living."

Hadrik's magic, a blend of blue and green, rises to his palm and floods the key, making it glow too. "It is imbued with the magic of Olymazi, a magic even more wild and raw than our own," he says, lifting his hand to light the hallway. "It has to be sentient in its own way to honor the vows of those who bind their blood to it. To stay in places like this, places suspended in magic even when they shouldn't be."

We reach what looks like a dead end, nothing but dark stone in front of us. I brace for something to happen, my heart pounding in my chest. The darkness surrounding us is thick, only broken by Hadrik's magic reacting to the key.

"The archives are as ancient as the palace. As the Mirror is—*was*." I cringe at his correction, Kai's voice threatening the edges of my mind before I push him out of it.

Above us, a bright white light glitters against the stone. It's small, about the size of an orange at first, but then the light splits. Two flares arch in opposite directions, curving out about two feet before dropping straight to the floor. In the brilliant light, the outline of a door appears. It's wide enough for us both to walk through, but Hadrik holds a hand back in warning as he takes a step forward, angling the key over a lock.

"The last time I opened the archives was for your father," he says quietly. "The night after his coronation." The lock lets out a *click* as he pushes the key in fully before taking his hand off and stepping back.

"He hasn't come back since?" I ask, my eyes narrowing on the key as it begins to *vibrate*. "Do you see—"

"Yes."

Leaning forward, I watch as the vibrations grow stronger, the magic glowing brightly enough that I have to squint my eyes. The key abruptly turns, the sound echoing out and startling both Hadrik and I back a step. Slowly, as if it's being pulled by someone on the other side, it cracks open and then stops. The white magic sputters out at the same time Hadrik's fades around the key, plunging us once more into darkness.

"Was that *normal*?" I ask, feeling Hadrik walk forward when his arm brushes mine.

"It wasn't as *lively* the last time I was here," he drawls, and I hear the sound of metal sliding against metal as he pulls the key from the lock. "Perhaps, the magic was excited by your presence."

I snort and put my hands out in front of me, looking back over my shoulder once to make sure the entire hallway hasn't been left in darkness. The spelled flames lining the walls farther down still blaze as they did earlier. Turning back around, I take another slow step forward, my fingers connecting with the cool metal of the door.

"Ready?" he asks.

"As I will ever be." Together, we push the door open on silent hinges and step past the threshold into the ancient archives. The air pressure shifts, as does the temperature. It's colder, enough so that my eyes water as they adjust to the difference.

"One more step," Hadrik advises. We take it together, and the air *snaps*, two flames coming to life in the darkness in front of us.

"What the fuck is this place," I rasp, brushing rogue strands from my ponytail away from my face. I inhale and immediately get thrown into a coughing fit, my eyes tearing up again from how long it takes me to catch my breath. "And what is that gods awful smell?" It is hard to even categorize it as bitter or rotten or musty. It's some horrific combination of the three, and I'm now *completely* understanding of why my father only deigned to visit this place once.

"Something ancient," he says, answering my first question. Hadrik walks towards one of the flames, which I realize is actually a small torch affixed to a pillar. He grabs one, gesturing for me to take the other. "These are spelled not to burn you," he explains, wiggling his fingers right over his flame to demonstrate. "To your left, there will be a wooden trough attached to the wall. Put the flame down in it."

I turn at the same time he does, each of us moving in opposite directions as I walk the expanse of the room to the other side. Using the light cast by the flame, I find the trough and set the torch down. Within seconds, the flame *spreads*. It moves forward, lighting up the wall as it continues for a few feet before dropping down out of view.

Hadrik's steps towards me echo out against the rough stone as he makes his way back to me, the same trail of fire lit on his side. Together we walk forward, the golden glow of the flames descending down the length of a long staircase, giving light to the steps and expansive space that lies beyond them.

"Welcome to the archives," he says reverently at my side. "Here, take this." I look at his proffered hand and the key that rests upon it, my gaze then lifting to his. "When you are finished, return the torches to the pillars, and the flames will extinguish. You will need the key to leave, but there is no magical exchange that takes place in order to exit."

"You're not staying?"

"I shouldn't. Kallin has had his eyes on your family *far* too closely for my liking. I want to make sure he doesn't realize you are somewhere you shouldn't be. Even with much of his focus on your brother."

I nod, even as my stomach twists. Nox had been dumped on the palace steps nearly a week after his departure to the Mortal Kingdom. It had been a shock for the guard who found him on his morning patrol of the grounds, and even more so for our family when the healers told us of his condition.

My brother had always been the strongest amongst us, but they said his magic is still depleted and his body weakened to the point that even sitting up causes his chest to heave. Perhaps my anxiety and questions surrounding him would be remedied by speaking to him, but the council decided to station guards outside of Nox's room. All of them with the directive to not let *anyone* in. Given Kallin's propensity to find my family at fault for everything lately, Hadrik is right to not give them something else to suspect us of.

"Thank you, Hadrik. For your help."

He smiles at me before turning for the exit. "Always, Your Highness. Be mindful of your time in here. It's easy for it to pass more quickly than you realize." He freezes halfway out the door, leaning away from it as he meets my eyes again. "If you walk far enough back, you'll find the owner of that peculiar smell." His departure is marked by the locking of the door, an unnatural silence settling over me as I slip the key into my pocket.

"That wasn't at all an ominous fucking thing to say," I murmur, pausing to wait and see if anyone—*anything*—will answer. When nothing does, I release an exaggerated exhale and curse my unbridled curiosity as I begin to descend the steps.

❧❧❧ ❧❧❧

For a massive room filled with thousands of items that's rarely ever visited, it's surprisingly tidy. Bookcases carved into the walls house more than just tomes—though the sheer number of volumes had me cursing out loud and then immediately hoping some ancient being didn't smite me for it. Something about this place, whether its ancient origins or something more, has me looking over my shoulder quite often, the feeling of being watched making my skin crawl.

Trinkets and carvings of every type act as bookends; some are clustered together as if their owner couldn't be bothered to do anything but dump them there, while others are neatly filed away row by row. The juxtaposition of the two tugs at my lips as I think about a past king or queen coming here to preserve a part of their history. I wonder if my father might place something here, if Nox will. Though I'm unsure if the latter harbors an interest in the throne anymore.

Eyeing one long wall of books, I sigh as I start at the first bookcase, reaching up on my toes to grab the very first book in the highest corner. I spend what feels like no short amount of time thumbing through the pages of multiple books, looking for mentions of blood magic or even of the Spell. Yet, for as ancient as these books are, they don't have mention of *either*. I look back up at the bookcase, and bite back a groan when I realize I've only made my way through *two* fucking shelves.

"There has to be a better way."

Stepping back from the wall of books, I scan it thoroughly, attempting to guess how it might be organized. I've found that most are less like factual texts and more like personal accounts. The coronation of a new queen, a new trade deal with another kingdom. While interesting enough on their own, they aren't the type of information I *need* right now. Spinning in place, I eye the equally long wall of books on the other side of the room. *Damn it.* I might die from old age before I *ever* find anything relating to the experimentation with blood. And though the two scouts Arav selected to gather information for me in the small towns lining our border have already left, I would still like to gather as much information about the formation of the Spell as I can while I wait the weeks it will take for their return.

It seems *both* feats are impossible.

"If you were a book about blood and magic," I murmur to myself, walking towards the center of the room where tables hold every manner of artifact, "where would you be?" My fingers drag over a dagger, its jeweled hilt indicating its decorative use. In fact, most of the items here look more ornate than useful, blending together metals and gems in ways that make them gleam but render them wholly impractical.

Beyond the tables, larger than life statues loom, the details so intricate that I shiver at the feeling that some watch me as I move. Most of the statues are female, some even carved with diadems on their heads. While most shine in white marble or gilded metals, a few of the statues are made of an entirely different stone, the glossy black surface of it making me itch to run my fingers along it. Dragon stone was one of the most beautiful materials to carve, showcasing the curves of the subject as easily as it shows the finer details like eyes and lips. My skin prickles as I near those, the flames playing over them in a way that almost makes them glow *white* at their centers.

I continue down the length of the room, rummaging lightly through the items on top of the tables when a *thump* rends the air. My hand automatically reaches for my spear, but it would have been suspicious if I was walking anywhere except to the training grounds with the weapon, so I left it back in my room. A choice I hope I don't come to regret.

Seeing a thin blade on the table in front of me—dragon stone hilt with slightly curved steel blade—I reach out and grab it, turning my back to the tables as I face the noise. Patting the key in my pocket, I breathe a sigh of relief, only for another breath to immediately tighten my chest. As far as I know, there is only *one* key available to the archives. If the noise didn't come from someone *outside* coming *in*, then there is someone already *here*.

Panic floods through my veins for a few seconds before I lock into my training, my body following suit as I bend my knees to keep my steps light and hold my dagger out in front of me, the blade almost parallel to my forearm.

The center walkway is long, and though my steps are quiet, the persistent beating of my heart is loud in my ears, my eyes glancing from side to side. When I finally reach the end, the flames on either side of me flicker, growing dimmer as if to shroud this part of the archives in shadows. *Great*, Hadrik was right. The magic here *is* sentient, and it's fucking with me.

My next inhale is a struggle, my stomach urging me to gag as nausea burns the back of my throat. The smell is *worse* here, and gods above, I can practically *taste* the rotten stench. Something definitely died back here, and I swear that if Hadrik knew that and wanted me to see a dead rat or something equally as disgusting, I *will* punch the old man square in the face.

Continuing forward, I lift my arm higher in a defensive position, keeping my steps quiet. After a few more feet, the pathway hooks to the right, the flames following suit and guiding me into a different room, this one darker than the rest as the light dwindles down to barely that of a candle. Another *thump* sounds, this time from behind me, and though my shoulders hike, I'm too focused on what I see ahead of me to turn around. Because I sincerely doubt that whatever ghost or being trying to scare me from behind is more impressive than the creature laid out in front of me. A *dragon*. A half-decayed one, but a dragon nonetheless.

"What the fuck?" I whisper, leaning forward as I stare at the dead beast.

It looks as if it's been dropped from the sky right in this very spot, legs sprawled out from its body while its wings drape out to the sides. Half of its body glows a light gray color, the magic *glittering* like it had around the entrance to the archives. Almost as if the magic is fading, as if there might have been enough at one point, but now time has begun to take parts of it, leaving only felled black scales and white bone to shine beneath the meager flames. Still, even as half a corpse, the dragon cannot be described as anything other than *magnificent*. And it makes absolutely *no* sense that it is here. In a room deep beneath the palace, in a kingdom not its own.

I allow myself another few moments to ogle it, sure I'll never again get to see such a creature up close, before I retreat towards the main room. Rounding the curve back, my eyes catch on something lying on the floor that wasn't there before. Positioning my borrowed dagger once more in front of me, I approach it carefully before squatting down and retrieving a leather-bound book that bears no title. There's no identifier, nothing beyond a small sun and moon stamped into the leather at the bottom right corner.

Glancing side to side, I take note of the distance between the bookcases and where this book lies, unease once more pressing at my back. Standing, I return my weapon to the table I swiped it from and lay the book down, turning to the first page. Though there are no visible signs of aging—likely spelled by the magic of this place—I can tell this book is old simply by the language used. Not just old, but *ancient*. It speaks of a Void queen who I know from the history books had ruled *at least* two thousand years prior.

I turn the pages, my eyes scanning them quickly as I temper my excitement, only to a phrase that makes me gasp.

Blood mingling has been a curious topic as of late, it reads. *Though curious about the interaction of mixing bloods in this way, we must be careful that we do not accidentally create harm between the two subjects. Raw magic is wild and unpredictable, but it can be wielded correctly under the right circumstances.*

My finger trembles as I lift my head, looking back to the spot on the floor where I found the book. *Or where the book was placed.* The thumps I had heard, was that the archive's magic? *Giving* me the book that I might need. *If you were a book about blood and magic, where would you be?* Hadn't I asked that *out loud?*

"Fucking archives," I mumble, closing the book and slipping it into my pack. My steps are quick up the stairs, the sensation of being watched once more nipping at my heels, but I do as Hadrik instructed and return the torches back to the pillar before pulling the key from my pocket and inserting it into the lock.

Anxious anticipation presses at my ribs as I wait for it to unlock, terror that Hadrik had been wrong when he said I didn't need magic to exit. But the key turns without any of the flair from before, and the moment the door opens, I pull it back out and slip over the threshold, shutting the door behind me. I all but sprint back to the first floor of the palace, never quite shaking that ominous presence at my back.

Chapter Fifty-Five

BAHIRA

I'M HESITANT TO BELIEVE that the council has forgotten about calling me in for another round of interrogation, but I suppose if anything could pull their attention, Nox's return would do it. I should be elated, celebrating the fact that, at least for now, they seem entirely content to believe my account of what happened in the Shifter Kingdom. Yet something about their newfound lack of interest in *me* doesn't feel like relief.

In the days since I visited the archives, there's been no hint that any of the council members are aware that Hadrik let me in. I returned the key to him the next day, relaying the events of what I had found and what the archives had... *given* me. To my annoyance, Hadrik didn't seem all that shocked. "I told you there was old magic there," he had said with a shrug of his shoulders.

"Yeah, well, you could have informed me about the fucking *dragon*," I had bitten back.

"And spoil the surprise? What kind of self-proclaimed favorite uncle would I be if I did that?" The mischief in his eyes kept me from retorting, but he promised to return the key at the first opportunity *and* to keep my visit a secret from my parents. The less unscrupulous acts that they knew about, the less the council could berate them for. I'd officially turn down my royal status if it came to that before I'd allow my father to have his crown stripped over something *I* had chosen to do.

Nox on the other hand...

I clench my jaw as I enter the healers' wing. Word had come from Sarai this morning that Nox was ready for visitors. Knowing my parents would be there first, I opted to read from the ancient book, finding more mentions of the term *blood mingling* but as of yet no explanation of what that actually was.

Sarai had also revealed what those working within the palace thought about the rumors surrounding Nox. "They are afraid," she had said quietly, her hand holding mine as a concerned line formed between her brows. "They don't know all the details, but what has been allowed to spread doesn't shed a favorable light on His Highness." Sarai had been gentle with her news, but it didn't soften the blow I felt knowing that there were those in the palace that feared him now. Perhaps even feared our family.

The line of guards that comes into view ahead is only six deep, but their presence at Nox's door feels *wrong*. As I near, one of the guards breaks formation, stepping in front of them and turning towards me. "Princess Bahira, you—"

"I've been told my brother is awake, and I'm—" My statement is cut short when I brush past the guard and abruptly stop in front of the door, surprised to find it already open and Nox up and walking. And also not alone.

"I don't think it is asking too much to just *consider*—"

"It's out of the question," Nox says, something *off* about his tone. It's his voice, but it isn't. "I'll tell you the same thing that I told the council. I will not marry anyone but Rhea."

"Even if they *strip* your family of the throne?" Haylee barks back, her cheeks turning pink. "Because I'm telling you, they will. You are smarter than this, Nox."

"*Don't.*" The single word is fired like a weapon, one that makes Haylee straighten where she stands at the foot of his bed. Unlike the first room Nox occupied during the events after the ball, this one is larger and contains a small kitchen in one corner as well as space for a loveseat and a four-person table. Nox braces his hands on the white stone counters, his head drooped between his shoulders.

Haylee lets out a soft sigh, oblivious to me standing here as she makes her way over to him. She reaches out her hand to rest on his back, letting it hover over his right shoulder before dropping it to the middle of his back instead. Nox tenses, his head snapping towards her, and the look in his eyes... My breath catches in my throat. I'm not sure I've ever seen my brother look so fucking *feral*.

"I'm sorry," she whispers, leaning in closer to him. "I just want to keep you and your family safe. I don't want anyone else hurt by this—this *disconnect* that is happening between the council and the king." She tilts her head, holding his gaze. "We've known each other for a long time, Nox, and I would never ask you to give me something that isn't yours to give. All I'm asking for is the *illusion* of it."

"And all *I'm* telling you is that it will *never* happen."

I clear my throat to announce my presence, Haylee taking a large step back when she spots me before smiling. "Bahira! Look who is finally well enough to move around."

"I can see that," I reply, entering the room as Nox stands, turning to lean back against the counter. "How are you?"

He shrugs, a loose wave falling over his forehead with the movement. "Can't say I've been worse."

A half-hearted smirk is all I can muster as I fold my arms over my chest, my eyes bouncing awkwardly between Nox and Haylee. She lingers for a moment, her body still leaning towards him as if caught in his gravitational pull, before the silence registers.

"I'll let you two talk," she says, smiling at Nox before walking towards me. "Perhaps we can meet later?"

I nod, and she brushes her hand against my arm before she exits, closing the door behind her. I let my smirk fall as I say, "I half expected to find Councilman Kallin hiding in here."

"The bastard hasn't left me alone for more than a few hours at a time since I—" His hand shoots to his temple.

"Are you alright?"

"I'm fine," he murmurs, reaching into a nearby cabinet for a glass and filling it with water. "Just a headache." I watch him down the glass and set it on the counter, his gaze then jumping to mine. His eyes look bloodshot and *odd*—the silver in them dulled to a darker hue. I swallow back my worry as I look him over, taking in how he's slightly hunched and sweat clings to his temples. The paleness of his skin and the circles under his eyes.

"You look like shit."

His responding laugh is quiet, a hand moving up to brush the strands of hair away from above his eyes. "It's great to see you too, Bahira."

It's the gentleness of his voice that relaxes my shoulders, but even that small relief isn't enough to stop the next words from tumbling out. "You left." The accusation is thick despite how my voice cracks. "You knew what would come of it, and you left anyway."

"I did, and if you're looking for some sort of apology, you'll be waiting forever for it. My only regret is that I did not return with Rhea."

Anger sparks as I take a step towards him, Nox watching my movements with tired eyes. "Not even knowing that it would cause chaos? That our father might lose his crown, or that you might never get it? That we are being treated as *criminals*?"

He shrugs, infuriating me further. "It wasn't our family's crown to begin with. It belongs to someone else."

"How can you be so short-sighted?" I ask, taking a step towards him. "Do you think that your actions will truly bring you closer to Rhea? That, even if you were *somehow* able to rescue her from King Dolian, the council would forget it all and just *allow* you to keep your crown without consequence?"

His jaw clenches as he looks away. "I'm *saying*, I don't want the crown at all, Bahira. The title, the throne, whatever you want to call it. It was never meant to be mine."

I inhale sharply, my head jerking back. "What the fuck are you even talking about? It has only *ever* been yours."

"That was before," he says, his hands bracing the counter on either side of him.

"Before *what?*"

"Before her."

"Well, I guess fuck what that means for everyone else, right?" I snark, earning a glare from him. But, brother or not, I'm not going to sit by while he makes an ass of himself. And certainly not when our family's power is on the line. Whatever is left of it. "It's not that I don't sympathize with you, Nox, about wanting to get her back. I *do*. It's that you went behind our back to do it."

Several moments of silence pass before Nox walks to the table and pulls out a chair, sinking into it as if standing has been too exhausting. "I know," he whispers, cradling his head, his elbows resting on the tabletop. "I didn't keep it secret because I didn't trust you with the information. I did it because—"

"You thought—accurately, I might add—that we would try to stop you."

He nods, leaning back against the chair and tilting his head to look up at the ceiling. "I am desperate, and I'm afraid of what that desperation will turn me into."

Nox is so good about hiding his true emotions. He'd have to be to survive undercover for as long as he did. But, looking at my brother now, I see everything he's struggling with laid bare on his face. His own anger and sadness and guilt. His *terror*. It propels me to the table too, taking a seat and placing a hand over his.

"You don't know, Bahira, the horrors she's gone through. You don't know all that might happen now that she's back in his grasp." His throat works with a rough swallow. "She is strong—she always has been. So much stronger than she'd ever give herself credit for. But I failed her. I *let* her get stolen from right out of my home. I trusted—*blindly trusted*—that she would be safe here, and that is a mistake that I won't ever make again." His eyes find mine as he lifts his head. "Even if it means hurting you—hurting our family—to ensure it."

"Is that what Rhea would want?" I ask. At the look he gives me, I lift a shoulder and add, "I genuinely don't know, Nox. Is it?"

His sigh is weighted. "No, it isn't. She would undoubtedly ask me to work to ensure our father remains king. She wouldn't want anyone to get hurt, certainly not in her name." His lips quirk upwards. "Her reaction would be very queenly, even if she doesn't believe herself to be one."

I snort. "I suppose she'll be happy you don't want the throne, then."

"She'll be queen either way."

"Hard for her to be queen if the heir to the throne doesn't want to be king," I counter, a brow arched.

He has the audacity to aim the expression back at me. "Not if the throne is actually *hers*."

"What are you talking about?" I ask, sitting upright. "The only way she could have any claim to it is if she marries you." I shake my head, a laugh tumbling up my throat. "Not unless you're insinuating she is the next Void queen or some—" I snap my mouth closed at the expression on his face, my eyes growing wide. "No. *No*. She wasn't even born here, Nox. It's impossible for her to carry Void Magic."

"It isn't," he says, leaning forward so he can keep his voice low. "We did her Flame Ceremony before the ball."

"What? Do our parents know?"

"No."

"Fucking gods, Nox!" I whisper-shout, standing from the chair to begin pacing the room. "Why haven't you said anything sooner?"

"It isn't my information to share," he answers, his gaze shooting to the door. "Rhea wanted time for us to talk about what that blue flame *meant*. But I can't trust that I won't get myself killed trying to bring her back, and she'll need as many allies as we can give her to claim the throne."

My pacing halts. "You aren't going to get yourself killed," I tell him. *Command* it of him.

But he shakes his head as he stands, rounding the table and placing a hand on my shoulder. "I need you to promise me something."

"As soon as you agree, you won't get yourself killed."

He smiles, but it's clearly an attempt to pacify me. It has the opposite effect. "Promise me that, no matter what happens to me, you will stand by Rhea as your queen."

My eyes bounce back and forth between his as too many rebuttals fire off in my head. "Nox—"

"Please, Bahira. I have never asked you for anything, but I'm calling in all the favorite brother points I've accumulated."

"You're my only brother," I whisper, something desperate clawing at my chest. When his eyes stay pleading, I groan and give in. "I promise."

Relief visibly relaxes him, his hand squeezing my shoulder before he releases it. "Thank you. I know this is likely the worst and most *ironic* time to ask this question, but how are *you*?"

A short laugh bursts from me, and even though uncertainty and anger still hum beneath my skin, I shake them off in favor of simply having a conversation with my brother. "Fine enough. I didn't expect coming home from the Shifter Kingdom would mean entering *chaos*, but I suppose I've never been one to thrive in monotony."

"And your time on the shifter island," he says, tilting his head. "Did you find what you were looking for?"

"I—" I knit my brows as the memories of a deep voice and golden-brown eyes play in my head, the reminder that I had found so much more than I went looking for leaving me feeling hollow. "I did, and I didn't," I answer, making Nox grin. The urge to tell him overwhelms me. Perhaps it's because I know I can trust him, or simply that, in the havoc since I've been home, this is the first time I've felt safe enough to let my guard down. Either way, when I begin to recount my time there, Nox listens intently, and although I keep the same intimate details to myself like I did with the council, I tell him everything else. The rebels and Kai and our goodbye. At some point, I find tears tracing down my cheeks and wipe them away with quick hands, embarrassed that I'm feeling so deeply. Embarrassed that there is so much *to* feel regarding Kai and the island he rules.

"Gods, Bahira," he finally says after taking it all in, cradling his head in his hand. "I feel like a shit brother now."

I chuckle, but it's short-lived when a guard knocks on the door. "Your Highnesses, Councilman Kallin has requested Prince Nox's presence in his office," he says through the wood. Nox drags a hand down his face and moves to step towards the door, only to falter as he sways.

"Are you alright?" I ask, rushing to help steady him.

"Don't worry, I'm fine. Just a little off after... *everything*." *Right*. We hadn't even talked yet about what happened while he was gone and how he was caught—or his magic, though it sounds like that still isn't back to normal. And, gods, I still haven't told him about Siyala, and her connection to Rhea. I don't know when the right time might be to share those details, but now certainly doesn't feel like it.

We walk together to the door, my hand gripping his wrist as I stop him before he reaches for the handle. "Be careful, Nox. I really do not want to be an only child."

He manages to laugh before sending me a wink. "At least you'll always have Cass."

Chapter Fifty-Six

NOX

I STARE AT THE back of the guard's head as he leads me to Kallin's office, the handful of his companions following behind me drawing the gazes of the palace workers as we pass. I don't blame them for the fear their expressions carry. I *had* harmed three of their own, and no matter my intent, no matter whether I was acting in my right mind or not, I was forever changed in their eyes now. I doubted that would change even if they learned the truth of everything.

For days, I had been dragged back towards the Mage Kingdom against my will, drugged beyond clear or conscious thought for more than an hour or so at night. Only then, when the man who attacked me would stop to rest, would he let enough of the herb he gave me fade so that I could hear him speak. Just enough that I could comprehend what he was saying before he would pour more onto a cloth and force it to my nose and mouth, its bitter taste blanketing my tongue and throat until there was only a hazy darkness. I became lost in the shadows I normally commanded, and I was powerless to stop any of it from happening.

I slept through most of the days, which was a blessing of sorts. If I couldn't fight back, then I was grateful for the opportunity to dream of all the ways I might shred this man—one who admitted to seeing Rhea with King Dolian—apart piece by piece. My rage was an inferno confined to the limitations of my magic and body, both of which had failed me. In getting Rhea back. In fulfilling the promise I had made to her to never let anyone take her from me. Even though it pained me to accept the truth, during those long days when I was nothing more than a sack of flesh being pulled through the forest, I came to realize that Cass and Bahira and my parents had been right. I should have waited to leave until I was stronger.

But between those barely lucid moments, I began to plot. I knew that coming back here would bring a new set of rules from the council. That it would likely usher in the removal of my father from the throne. My actions had affected everyone *but* the person I needed to get to most, and I wanted to care. Deep down, I know a small part of me does, yet it doesn't change the fact that, the moment I am strong enough, I will leave again. I will further toss my kingdom into chaos.

In the meantime, there is work to be done.

If I cannot leave to get Rhea, then I will make *damn* sure that I spend every waking second searching for those who hurt her. Finding out who plotted against us and ensuring that the next breath they take is their last. And I have to start with the guard who found me in the woods. The one who kept me bound and weakened, drugged except for the late hours when he would rummage through my pack and pull out Rhea's diary. When he would then read her intimate thoughts and feelings. He had taunted me with them, reading entries from when Rhea was upset with me after I had threatened Daje. When she had admitted she felt her magic morph into something ugly at the thought of me being with someone else. When she had written about her fears of becoming queen and feeling unworthy of the role.

As he read, the guard had laughed, and I realized that there was a depth to rage I had previously not met. I didn't recognize him, and even now, his physical details are fuzzy. But his voice... *That* is burned into my mind with a permanence I want to hate but am secretly thankful for. I will find him—force Kallin to tell me who he is—and then I will make him tell me every single thing he knows about King Dolian. About those in my own fucking kingdom that are working for the monster. Once I have wrung every detail I need from him, I will kill him slowly. Methodically. In a manner befitting the way he had hurt Rhea.

My temples throb with every step, matching their cadence as I roll my shoulders back, only to clench my jaw from the pain that radiates deep in those muscles. My magic sputters within me, nothing but a tendril of shadow hardly enough to feel, let alone manipulate. But, gods, how I have tried to muster more. To pull at that fragment until I thought I might tear myself apart. The only thing that answered was pain, one so bad that I begged Galen for something to ease it within me. Even now, I can feel it taunting me like a call on the wind, a warning that it's coming to consume me once more.

I have become a stranger to my own body.

"Councilman Kallin, Prince Nox is here to see you." The announcement by the guard in front pulls me from my spiral, and I remind myself what information I need from Daje's father. Kallin lets me in, allowing me to step past him and into the office I have always loathed.

"Your Highness," he says in greeting from where he sits behind a dark brown wooden desk. His hands are stacked and resting beneath his chin, his dark eyes calculating as he stares intently at me.

He isn't alone. Galen stands off to the side, nearly in the corner of the room. "It is good to see you up and moving about."

I take the seat across from Kallin, biting back a wince when I press back into the chair. "It is good to be up," I respond, crossing my ankle over my knee. "Though I am surprised that you have summoned me, Councilman. It was only this morning that we last spoke."

"I knew your family would be eager to see you, and I wanted you to have time to visit them before things inevitably become a bit more hectic for you. Besides, as I told you over the course of the last few days, there is much work to be done."

I fight back the instinct to curl my fingers in towards my palms at his words, instead forcing a bored look to my face. "What, exactly, do you have in mind?"

He takes his time answering as he studies me, Galen shifting back and forth while he waits. "Public perception is an important element to keep tabs on for a ruling family," he starts, letting his hands rest on the desk as he leans forward. "If our people do not believe in the king—in those they've entrusted with the highest powers in the realm—then it will cause cracks in our foundation." His lips form a straight line. "If we do not have their trust, then we will earn their chaos. I have vowed too much of myself in the name of keeping this land safe to ever let that happen." Galen nods at his side, joining his hidden hands in the large sleeves of his healer's robe. "I'm afraid the court of public opinion is at an all-time low for the Daxel family."

"My father has always put them first," I answer calmly, despite the irritation that heats my skin. "Have they so easily forgotten the many decades of peace that not only he but his father and grandfather and so on have ushered in?"

Kallin's brow arches. "It is easy to keep the peace when peace is all that you have. For centuries, we have been willing to let others fight out their differences while we—*mages*—kept to ourselves."

"There are no threats now that there weren't before."

The councilman chuckles as he studies me, the sound condescending. "I think we both know that is no longer the case."

I lay my hands on the armrests of my chair, my grip tight on the wood. I glance at Galen, his own expression twisted into pity aimed directly at me. "They can't possibly believe something that isn't true. Everything that happened after the ball should have been contained to only those who witnessed it and have since been sworn to secrecy *or* those deemed important enough to have been told. Which, if memory serves correctly, would only be the council members and royalty."

"And most of it has. But I'm afraid that it's quite hard to fully contain the happenings in the palace. Our informants are reporting back that while the details of your attack on the healers haven't leaked, those of Lady Rhea and her *mission* here have. There is a very real fear amongst our people that their king and queen do not have their best interests at heart when they have *proof* that they hid information about Rhea from us. They are scared that you will throw our kingdom into war over a woman."

I squeeze the armrests hard enough to turn my knuckles white, anger filling every vein as my jaw ticks. Did the councilman know where Rhea was? Did he help King Dolian plot her seizure? Though my eyes narrow, I keep the accusations locked inside. Kallin is calculating and manipulative. While I may be unclear on if his dislike of Rhea led to him helping with her abduction or not, I can't let him rile me to the point that I lose access to whatever information I need from him. So I swallow every bitter thing I want to say and relax my grip on the chair.

"We have the opportunity to get ahead of this, Your Highness. To show the people that while poor leadership will not be tolerated, we can provide them the same level of contentment they've come to know." Galen nods in agreement.

"And how do you propose we do that?"

"Your father will be asked to formally step down, and you will take his place," he answers matter-of-factly.

I exhale slowly, having anticipated that Kallin would suggest something like this and still not quite prepared. "The people love him—"

"They have," he interrupts, leaning back as he watches me. "For many years, your father has been a dutiful servant to the Crown. Yet even the best amongst us can falter over time. Sadryn was a wonderful king for the past but not the one we need for the future. That title belongs to you."

"And if I don't want to be king?"

He sighs in disappointment. "Then we will see to it that the Daxel line is removed from the throne and you are all stripped of your titles. A formal investigation will be launched into the secrets kept from the council regarding Lady Rhea and your fake betrothal to her, with the intent to prosecute anyone who was involved in the hiding of crucial details about her. We will show no leniency in our interrogation of your sister and her treasonous acts." At the mention of Bahira, a crack in my façade shows, and Kallin capitalizes on it. "The council will temporarily take over control of the kingdom under the laws that provide us the ability to do so and we will use those powers to ensure that anyone *not* found to be working in the best interest of the kingdom will find themselves rotting in the cells beneath the palace."

"This can just be a small bump in the road, Prince Nox," Galen adds.

A small bump in the road. It's an effort to not send my fist into the desk. I don't care about the title or the throne, but I'm not naïve enough to believe that having those things won't make my own mission easier. If this is *all* I can do until my magic or strength return, then I can force myself to play along. Even if, in the end, I'm worse off for it. How I suffer is inconsequential to getting Rhea back. "Fine," I grind out, the annoyance in my voice only half-faked. "What do you need me to do?"

Kallin clasps his hands together in front of him. "I knew you could be reasoned with, Prince. I believe, with your total cooperation, we can remind the people just how loyal to them you are. After all, are you not the same man who went undercover to ensure their safety? The same one who promised to use his blessing of immense power to keep his kingdom safe?"

"Except they don't know that I infiltrated the Mortal Kingdom for four years," I retort, stretching my neck from side to side. "And my magic is still depleted."

Kallin looks over at the palace healer. "Galen believes you shall be back to your full strength and magical capacity soon." I look to the healer, noting his tight smile as he nods. "Until then, we will announce your intention to take your father's place. I anticipate he will show some... *resistance*. All well-intentioned of course, but you will need to convince him that this is the best step."

"*Of course.*" The pain in my head throbs more harshly, and I bring my fingers to press in at my temple.

"And then, shortly after, we will announce your betrothal to Councilman Borris's niece."

My lungs seize, my eyes narrowing on his as my lips pull against my teeth in a snarl. Even in my game of pretend, this is a line I *will not* cross. "Absolutely *not*."

"Prince Nox, it is imperative to show our people that you have their best interests at heart, particularly with the rumors surrounding Lady Rhea." Anger rises, coloring my vision red as I stand abruptly from the chair, my chest heaving. The room spins, and I plant my hands on his desk to keep myself upright. "You don't need to marry her right away, but the betrothal—"

"I said *no!*" I shout, wincing as my voice reverberates through my skull.

"Galen," Kallin says calmly, calling the healer to my side.

"Your tonic, Your Highness." He holds out a small glass vial containing the pink liquid he's been giving me since my return. I hesitate, its foul taste enough to preemptively sour my stomach. "No need to suffer when you don't need to," Galen insists, his hand drawing nearer. "This will help bring you closer to feeling yourself again."

Swallowing the saliva gathered at the back of my tongue, I relent and take the vial from him, uncorking it before bringing it to my mouth. The liquid goes down in one gulp, my eyes squeezing shut at the wave of nausea that immediately follows. Galen takes the empty bottle and pockets it.

It only takes a few seconds for it to coat me in a pleasant haze, quieting enough of the aches and pains that they become a murmur in the back of my mind. The righteous anger that had heated my veins moments before gone with them.

"We will revisit the betrothal talk another day," Kallin says, his voice sounding farther away. "For now, let's plan your ascension to king."

Chapter Fifty-Seven

RHEA

MY FINGERS DRAG ALONG the rough walls of the tunnel yet again, my eyes wide as I traverse them in the scant light of my small torch. While I wouldn't say I'm getting familiar with the system within—and in some instances *beneath*—the castle, my exploration of the dark space is easy to navigate thanks to the paint markings every so often on the wall.

The first few times, I had gone straight to the library, sneaking in how Eve had shown me and hiding on the second floor with some books that looked somewhat promising in my quest for finding a way out from the ring's hold on me. There had thankfully been no more near misses with others sneaking into the library for a late-night rendezvous. As the nights passed with sleep proving more and more evasive, I took my restlessness to the tunnels, deciding to follow the dashes of blue paint—markers that signified the castle's center—until I eventually came to a small door. After listening for a few minutes, I decided to risk opening it and found myself in a silent, empty room that seemed to be the equivalent of a storage space. Curiosity and lack of anything better to do got the best of me, and with my torch propped in a large glass vase, I rummaged through the boxes and trunks. It held gowns that were moth eaten, tunics that smelled more of mold than they did of linens, and a few books whose pages were too yellowed and ink-faded to read.

All in all, I found nothing of real value to me, and so I left down the tunnels to find another.

I looked forward to this nightly routine, especially when it provided an escape from the inevitable. *Eventually*, I would always return to my room and fall asleep. And there, nightmares and horrors alike would ravage my dreams. Daytime was no better, as the reasons for my terrible dreams accompanied me for meals—blood and flesh and inescapable.

The hidden door is cold against my ear as I press it there, listening for voices and footsteps. When I hear none, I carefully push it open and step into the dark space. Though my feet are slippered, the gentle scrape of the soles on stone seems to ring out in a way that sends a chill of warning down my back. I keep my steps slow and steady, surprised to find a wall of curtains in front of me, reaching high enough to touch the ceiling. The satiny fabric also extends the entire length of the space but I'm able to find a gap between to pry them open, holding my torch far enough away to ensure that it doesn't set anything on fire.

My steps halt just past the curtains at the sight of a golden throne, the flame reflecting off its ornate edges. *The throne room.* Swallowing, I proceed forward, holding the torch high enough for light to stretch out a few feet all around me. Even with only being able to see a portion of it, I can *feel* the room's massiveness like how it might be to walk into a cave. This is a room I've yet to be dragged into by the king, and as I force myself to start walking again, I take in his massive throne. The top is pointed with a crown of its own, spires stretching far past my own height. It's upholstered in velvet a rich, royal shade of red, matching the rubies inlaid on the chairs back. I admire the way the gold twists and curves along it as a tempting idea forms, but I quickly push the thought from my mind.

"There is no way this thing is comfortable," I murmur beneath my breath.

I have never had the inclination to sit on a throne—much less one currently occupied by my uncle. Ruling may have been my right by blood and apparently magic, but it was never an option I would have chosen if given the opportunity. It certainly isn't something I can see myself doing now, even if I manage to escape. For all his faults as a man and king, my uncle commands every room he steps into. I have seen it here in the castle with the nobles and men he keeps close to him, and I had seen it on the one excursion King Dolian insisted I join, claiming there was something he wanted to show me in Vitour. I endured the ride in the confining carriage with him, tolerated his fingers dragging back and forth on my thigh as he spoke of the next event we were to attend together. I forced myself to believe that, perhaps, getting a closer glimpse of the city I could see from my tower might strengthen my resolve or even just confirm the idea that there was still so much outside my own cage that I had yet to explore and experience and *learn.*

But as we passed through Vitour, what I saw was not people living their lives freely. It was *worse.* I saw haggard men and women and *children*, working their merchant carts as their skin clung to their bones. I had read about poverty, of course, and heard from Xander and Eve how the king's taxes had left people worse off, but to see it with my own eyes only reinforced the fact that I was a fool for *ever* entertaining the idea that I could rule. I was ashamed that there was an entire class of people I hadn't so much as said *hello* to, and when we finally got to our destination and King Dolian revealed that he wanted to *test* if my magic worked on those suffering from the Cruel Death, that shame only manifested into something darker. More jagged and rough. It consumed me again, a current constantly tossing me in choppy waters. It was made worse when my magic worked to heal those suffering, filling their cheeks out with life again and drawing them from the edge of death they were teetering on.

Turning away from the monstrous chair, I wildly—*unexpectedly*—come face to face with my own reflection across the dais. A scream lodges itself in my throat as I stumble backwards, bumping into the throne and nearly falling over its armrest. I lay a hand over my chest, my pulse pounding at my neck as I stare at the large standing mirror, my wide-eyed likeness looking back. What an *odd* place to have a mirror—

"Gods above," I whisper, gripping the torch more tightly as I take a cautious step forward. This isn't just a mirror but *the* Mirror. The Mortal Kingdom's Mirror.

I recall what information I can as I take another step. Rulers give their blood to the Mirror when they become king or queen, activating it to their command. Some rulers choose to do the same with their descendants, as Sadryn had done for Nox and Bahira, allowing them to command it as well. Before King Dolian, my father held the crown. And before both of them was their father. While I'm not King Dolian's direct descendant, I *am* of his blood. But I have also never given my blood to any Mirror, here or back in the Mage Kingdom.

That fact alone should rein in my budding excitement but that is the thing about hope—it only needs the smallest spark to grow. It rears wildly when the Mirror flickers at my presence as I close the remaining distance. The hard surface then ripples just like it had when Sadryn used the Mage Kingdom's Mirror.

My bottom lip trembles along with my fingers, my torch sputtering from my shaking hand as I try to work the muscles that control my voice. I intend for the command to come out well, *commanding*, but instead, the words only trickle past my lips, hardly louder than the brash beating of my heart. "King Sadryn of the Mage Kingdom."

The Mirror ripples again, waves of silvery glass moving as if I've dropped a pebble onto the surface of a lake. I press my lips together to keep in the eager noise that threatens to pry them apart, my entire body leaning closer to the Mirror as if proximity is all that is needed to power it. Seconds pass by in a slow drip of time, each growing more weighted the longer no response is given.

"The Mirror is always guarded. *Someone* is there—someone *has* to hear this." Saying it out loud does little to calm my nerves, only driving home what King Dolian had taunted me with in Windseren. *Perhaps they are purposefully ignoring me.* I shake my head, physically dispelling the emotion that idea draws up, and I try a different approach.

Inhaling deeply through my nose, I make my voice louder and more steady. "King Sadryn of the Mage Kingdom." The breath stays trapped in my chest as I watch the Mirror react to the command, my eyes bouncing over its cloudy gray surface as I wait for the fog to clear.

And I wait.

And I wait.

And I wait.

I don't realize how tightly I'm clutching the torch until the heat makes my hand grow sensitive. I don't realize just how much hope rested on this moment until defeat knocks the rest of the air from my lungs. And as I step back and watch the Mirror harden again, its surface becoming nothing more than reflective glass, all of the small nicks I've accumulated in my time here gather into one gaping wound, uncontrollable sadness bleeding from it and washing away that small flicker of hope.

Logical reasons for why no one answered—for why no one *has* answered—bounce violently around in my mind, never quite sticking long enough for me to grasp. They can't seem to penetrate past that one shield of doubt that the king shoved into my head. And what if he was right? What if, in order to keep his kingdom peaceful and his council happy, King Sadryn decided I'm *not* worth the risk that my presence would disrupt?

And Nox...

It isn't until my back hits the cool silk drapes behind the throne that I realize I've walked backwards into them. My hand rushes up to my cheek, brushing away the tears that have fallen.

I return to the tunnels and follow them back to my room, extinguishing the torch and propping it up against the wall. My eyes scour the room, searching for something—*anything*—for me to anchor on to. But I find nothing.

As the days pass, I don't venture again into the tunnels. I don't go back to the library. I don't do anything but stare out at the night sky and the twinkling stars I once thought were waving hello to me. And I say nothing to them in return.

Chapter Fifty-Eight

KAI

SWEAT BEADS DOWN MY temples as the brisk morning air stings my chest and the new tattoos there. My magic pulses beneath my skin, but I tamp it down as I duck the incoming punch from Haloa, spinning and barely avoiding the harsh swing of Jahlee's sword from the other side.

"Damn it. I almost got you!" she shouts between heavy inhales, angling her long sword again as she begins to circle me.

"You do know that *maiming* our king would be a punishable offense, yes?" Haloa asks as he advances on me, swinging his fists in a quick combo of punches. I throw up my arms and block them, cursing myself for taking up Jahlee's invitation to train so quickly after adding to the tapestry inked on my body.

"Those rules don't apply to me because I'm his sister," she says from somewhere behind me, making my brow arch. I catch a flash of my cousin's white hair as she attempts to attack my blindside before I spin and duck, sweeping her legs out from under her. Siyala stumbles to the ground, letting out a growl of frustration.

My answering smirk falls quickly as I look up to see Jahlee's sword arcing through the air towards me. *Fucking hell.* I duck and roll, snatching my sword from where it was discarded in the grass and turning back with only enough time to stop Jahlee's blade a few inches above my face.

"Ha!" she laughs, light brown eyes glinting with mirth. "Got y—" I kick the side of her knee, making her drop. Jerking my sword upward, the momentum forces her grip on her own weapon to slip, and the hilt of the sword falls directly into my waiting hand. "Fuck!"

Jumping to my feet, I see Siyala surge towards me, gold ringing her irises. "When was the last time you shifted?" I ask.

Haloa closes in again, landing a kick to the side of my thigh that makes me grunt. I shoot him a disgruntled look as I toss Jahlee's weapon to the ground, but the bastard simply shrugs his shoulders.

"None of your business," Siyala snaps, swinging a fist for my side. My breath rushes from me as I lunge out of the way, grabbing her wrist and twisting it with one hand while lifting my blade to block another far too zealous attack by Jahlee.

"It *is* my business when your refusal to shift is making you a hazard to be around."

"I'm fine," she says, attempting to kick out only to wobble on her standing leg. Spending years in her animal form has done her no favors when it comes to her strength or balance. It isn't just that our physical bodies change during a shift. We are present in our minds, but everything else becomes lost to the animal within. Four years is a long time to be in such a state.

The four of us continue to weave around each other, exchanging blows and dancing away like we've practiced this choreography a hundred times before. Jahlee and Haloa are here by choice, while Siyala is here because I commanded it of her as her king.

"Stop *kicking* me!" Jahlee shouts after I do just that, having the nerve to look affronted as if she isn't actively trying to slice me open. Throwing her sword on the ground in a tantrum she then collapses onto her back, her chest heaving as she stares up at the graying sky, a storm rolling in towards us. "I'm done."

Haloa laughs as he abandons his fighting stance to stretch an arm across his body. He's become an invaluable asset to me and a good friend to Jahlee. Siyala moves to grab a waterskin from the grass, and I eye her as she does, taking in the way her brows are pinched towards each other. "Have you spoken to your mother?"

She tenses as she drinks, pulling the waterskin away and wiping her mouth with the back of her hand. "She wants me to come home and *work*. Like I'm not needed elsewhere."

"You're not. There's nothing you can do for Rhea from here. And your attitude is just making everyone else around you miserable," Jahlee says, and I let out a sigh.

Fucking gods. I run a hand through my hair, catching Haloa slowly backing away towards the palace.

"This sounds like a family thing, so I'm just going to—" He doesn't even finish his sentence as he spins on his heel and breaks into a jog. My brows lower in annoyance—and faint amusement—before I return my attention to my cousin.

"I don't care what anyone thinks or feels about me. Until I know Rhea is safe, until your *precious* Bahira proves herself to not be a fucking liar, I'm staying here at the palace."

Anger pulses beneath my skin, the immediate response to her tone about Bahira hot and striking, but with a deep breath, I force it back down. "You won't let us write letters to the Mage Kingdom—"

"For fear it may hurt Rhea!" she insists.

"You don't want me to reach out to the mortal king," I continue, watching her fists curl at her sides.

Jahlee stands and sheaths her sword, her gaze locked on our cousin.

"You know there is nothing else we can do *but* wait, and *that* can be done at home with *your family* just as easily as it can be done here."

"You guys are my family," she retorts, though the sentiment is tainted with anything but sweetness.

"Then you should heed our advice. You need to shift—"

"I spent four *fucking* years trapped in my animal form!" she shouts, her eyes flashing gold as her neck strains. "You have no idea what it is like to be *stuck* like that. To be this fearsome animal and to still be *helpless*. To have to watch as someone you care about is hurt over and over again. And you can't do a *fucking* thing about it!"

I watch tears crest her eyes, her harsh expression faltering beneath them.

"What happened over there, Siyala?" Jahlee asks softly, sitting up.

Siyala's mouth opens and closes twice before she pinches her lips together and rolls her shoulders back. The transformation is so fast, it's almost admirable. "Nothing that bears repeating." She doesn't spare us a second glance as she turns to follow Haloa. "I'll be around if you hear anything."

Jahlee waits until Siyala is out of earshot before she lets out a heavy sigh. "She's going to explode if she doesn't talk to us about what happened."

"We can't force these things," I respond, though I know she's right. "We have to give her time."

Jahlee scoffs, fixing her hair into a ponytail high on the top of her head. With her slight curls draping down over her shoulders, she is the spitting image of our mother, and my chest warms and then ices over at their similarities. "And what is that look for?"

"Nothing." I reach down and grab the sheath for my sword before gesturing for Jahlee to follow. "Come on. We have a meeting to attend, and I want to shower first."

She rolls her eyes but follows, blowing a stray hair away from her face with a flutter of her lips. "You just want me there to protect you from Noe when she finds out that you're going to lower some of her budget."

"Everyone is getting budget cuts until we roll out the new tax," I counter, walking on the stone pathway and passing the various busts of past shifter kings, including the one of my father. "But, yes, you make an excellent buffer."

She snorts as we climb the steps into the palace, the bottom level bustling with activity. It has been since I opened the palace up to all visitors, allowing access to anywhere on the first floor.

"Your Majesty!" a soft voice calls from our right, followed by the sound of running steps. I watch as Inessa, Lady Miranda's daughter and my new assistant, jogs to us. She smiles—one that mirrors her mother's—as a slight flush pinkens her cheeks. Tucking a strand of dark brown hair behind her ear, she clears her throat and holds up a small collection of papers. "I'm so sorry to bother you, but I have some last-minute proposals that need your signature."

"No bother at all, Inessa."

Handing the missives to me, I begin to read through them as she turns to talk with Jahlee.

"How did your training go?"

Jahlee sighs as she waves her hand in my direction. "Your king likes to *cheat*. Hitting defenseless females and all."

My hand freezes mid signature as I lift my gaze to her and arch a brow. Inessa stifles a laugh. "I never would have assumed King Kai was anything other than honorable."

Jahlee cackles at that and launches into a series of stories about me, each more embarrassing than the last. I quickly sign the rest of the papers while merely glancing at them before handing them back and ushering Jahlee forward as Inessa laughs and waves goodbye.

"I like her. Don't fire her," she says, poking my arm.

I chuckle as we come to the stairs that lead up to the second floor, a brief memory flashing of Bahira standing in this exact spot. It was the night that Magda's body was found in the palace, and Bahira had spent hours offering her silent presence while I contemplated if being king was worth it. If it was just better to hand the seat of power to Kane. Or even Tua. Pushing the recollection away, I clear my throat. "As long as she keeps doing her job well, I have no intentions of replacing her."

"Yeah, but we know how you get. Your particular brand of grumpiness is more of an acquired taste." I lift the corner of my mouth while we climb the steps. "It's why it was so shocking that someone as amazing as Bahira fell for you." My lips flatten as I give Jahlee a warning look. One she immediately ignores. "Then again, she's nearly as stubborn as you are."

"Jahlee—"

"You'd think that two grown ass adults would be able to speak *openly* about how they are feeling—"

"Stop—"

"I just hope my letter knocks some sense into her—"

I halt, a slight buzz sounding in my ears as I turn to look at her. "What letter?"

"Shit." She continues up the stairs to the landing, her steps quickening as I trail behind her.

"*What* letter?" I repeat, and I know if I were to look in the mirror, my eyes would be glowing.

Turning to walk backwards so she can face me, she holds her hands out in front of her. "I may have possibly—*definitely*—sent a letter to the Mage Kingdom."

A growl rumbles from me as Jahlee quickens her pace. "Why would you do that?"

"I wanted her to know that we care about her. That if she's worried about reaching out through the Mirror, she shouldn't be." She swallows, her expression cautious as she finally stops walking. "And I asked her mundane questions." She shrugs.

"Did you write about the blight? About the rebels or how I'm working to properly claim my throne?"

"I honestly can't remember."

"*Jahlee*," I snap, my jaw flexing. My sister always means well, so even if her methods suggest otherwise, I know that she leads with her heart. But politics is not her forte, and without knowing what the *fuck* is going on with the mages and mortals, what she wrote could be an issue of security for the island.

"Hey, she wasn't just the love of *your* life! She was *my* friend too. The only other person in this godsforsaken world that understands what it is to be *different*."

I knew Jahlee and Bahira had found a sort of camaraderie in being magicless. The first of their kind in their respective kingdoms. But it doesn't excuse going behind my back. My mind then catches up with the rest of what she said. "She isn't the love—"

"Spare. Me. The. Fucking. Bullshit, Kai Vaea," she seethes, taking a step towards me and jabbing her finger into my chest. "I sent her a letter because I had things *I* wanted to say and things I knew *you* couldn't say." At the fury in my eyes, she lowers her hand and releases a breath. "Though, I admit, I did not think about how it would look if someone *other* than Bahira read the letter."

The look I fire at her is nothing short of incredulous. Bahira seemed to trust her family, but she had spoken often of those who viewed her as less than. I hadn't fully grasped the scope of it all until days after she left, when it became clear to me that she deserved so much better than her kingdom had offered her. Then even *I* could offer her.

"With the mages not answering my call through the Mirror, and our next exchange of supplies not for another few weeks, I am blind to what is happening beyond our kingdom, Jahlee." Drawing a hand down my face, I cross my arms over my chest. "I know you meant well, but going behind my back is the sort of thing that breaks trust. I'm not just your brother. I am your king." Though she keeps her defiant stance, I bear witness to the way my words dim the light in her eyes. Tension pulls my shoulders back. "Meet me here in thirty minutes."

Forty minutes later, I sit at the head of the table in our newly renovated council chambers, my officially sworn in advisors split almost equally on both sides. Inessa sits in a chair behind me, ready to take notes for the meeting, while an empty chair at the very end reveals Kane's absence. Jahlee is at my left, eyeing Kane's spot angrily. He hadn't bothered to show for the autumnal celebration either, and I know if it weren't for the fact that I asked her to stay and act as a buffer, she would already be out looking for him. Eager to give him more than a piece of her mind.

"Welcome to the first official meeting under my rule," I start, clasping my hands together as I rest my elbows on the table. "I understand you all have reports for me, so let's not waste any more time."

Noe edges forward in her seat, her mouth drawn tight as she glares at me. "The budget cut to our forces needs to be reversed."

"Everyone is going to have to make sacrifices until we have voted the tax through," I answer.

"Our ships are the lifeline of the island, *King*, and hiring shifters to operate them is what keeps most of the working class afloat. To cut that budget is to punish them," she says, shaking her head. "I would advise you to think long and hard over whether that is the type of precedent you want to set."

Fuck.

"Dramatics are unwelcome here," Lady Miranda replies smoothly. "As His Majesty said, there will be no part of our kingdom that will be unaffected until we can right the ship, so to speak."

"Don't try to win me over with nautical puns, Miranda. What changes will be happening to your precious *laws* that could affect the livelihoods of the most vulnerable?"

Jahlee snorts, earning the entire table's attention. "I like when you all bicker. Much more fun than the last group."

I send her a warning look and earn a roll of her eyes in response. So much for being my fucking buffer.

"As a matter of fact, the tweaking of the laws I have presented to King Kai is meant to enhance those most affected by the late Tua and his rebel forces." She lifts the paper she brought up in front of her and begins to read off of it, the changes to the laws ones that Inessa had gone over with me earlier in the week. "Anyone whose business has been tampered with by the rebels will receive aid from the Crown to rebuild, including a monthly stipend to hold them afloat until they can become profitable again. Those who have had the working family member affected by the blight will also receive aid so that no shifter will have to choose between earning money for their family and raising their young. In addition, we've drafted harsher consequences for those found to be in collaboration with rebel activity." She lays the paper down and clasps her hands above it. "While I don't think anyone in this room would argue that these changes are unnecessary, there is a cost to doing so. And until Kane can work whatever influence he has with the nobles to quell any sort of upheaval at the new tax, then as mentioned, sacrifices must be made."

I scan the faces of my advisors, noting that while none of them look particularly thrilled, neither do they protest what Lady Miranda has stated. "Change is going to be difficult on us all," I tell them, leaning back as I fold my arms over my chest. "But our goal is to work towards unification. Your input and your value to this council cannot be understated." I swallow, pushing past the uncomfortable knot in my throat. "It is crucial to my rule. None of this is possible without you all."

Jahlee thrusts a thumbs-up in my direction, a wide smile brightening her face. It eases a bit of the weight from our earlier conversation off of my chest.

The meeting continues with each shifter laying out their agendas to cut their budgets while doing the least amount of harm to the people we are trying to help. At the end, everyone is excused with plans to meet in a few weeks and officially vote on the tax bill. I make my way to my new office, the space a familiar one that still contains Bahira's scent. Jahlee follows, her hands clasped behind her back.

"That went quite well," she says as I unlock the door and we enter Bahira's experiment room. "It seems everyone understands their role."

"Indeed." Walking over to the desk, I open the top drawer and reach for the large dagger I have hidden there, affixing it to my belt. "All except for one."

Jahlee gasps, clapping her hands together in front of her. "Do we finally get to kill Kane?"

"I'm not going to kill him." *Yet* goes unsaid. It all depends on where the fuck he is. "And there is no *we*. You and Haloa need to return to Molsi and scout more of the rebel spots Sir Duarte told us about."

"You never let me have any fun." She pouts but spins on her heel and dances towards the hall. "But if killing Kane *does* become an option, you better not do it without me."

I watch her leave before taking a deep breath and exiting the room behind her. I'd prefer not to kill my cousin, but trust is in short supply, and I'd be foolish to let mine be stolen so easily.

Chapter Fifty-Nine

KAI

IT DOESN'T TAKE LONG to follow his poorly hidden trail, Kane having been spotted in a town known for trouble just outside of Molsi. Since it's nearly impossible to hide my identity, I trudge down the worn streets as my wolf, my teeth clamped on to a pack filled with clothing. When I reach the most questionable tavern I've ever seen, I quickly shift and dress before entering. With my magic still pulsing beneath my skin and lighting my eyes, I interrogate the bartender, his lip trembling while I tower over him, and he relays the secret location of the last place on this damn island my cousin *should* be.

"Thank you for your cooperation," I say, dropping a pile of coins onto his countertop before returning to the main street, the gaze of every shifter that passes hot on my skin. Thankfully, the walk to the edge of town is quick, the distance eaten up by determined strides as I come to the dilapidated building called *The Dog House*. Rotted wood and black-stained stone make up the exterior, and something about its simple façade—two windows and a door—makes my hackles rise the closer I get.

Reaching for the handle, I jerk the door once, only to find that it's locked. A ragged voice shouts through the crumbling wood. "What is the password?"

I growl and contemplate just kicking it in. "Open the fucking door."

"Ha! Nice try, but that was last week's password. There is a new one for this week."

Tilting my head back, I steady myself with a breath as my wolf threatens to burst out. "How about, open-because-your-king-stands-on-the-other-side." Using my influence as king has never been something I enjoy, but if Kane truly is in this place, then it's better I don't waste time getting him out.

"Oh sure. Like you expect me to believe"—the door handle jiggles as the click of a lock sounds—"that *His Majesty*, King Kai, would deign to show his ugly mug here—" The door swings open, and a pair of brown eyes meet mine, their owner's mouth sputtering to a stop. "Holy fuck, you're big. I don't envy the male that has to go against *you*." He shuffles back, swinging his arm dramatically out in front of him. "I'll let you pass without the code if you promise that you'll win your fight. I haven't been lucky with my bets."

Ducking my head, I step past and enter a dingy room, a single flame gem casting just enough light to see a small staircase straight ahead. "What were you saying about the king?" I ask, the floorboards shuddering beneath my weight as I walk towards it.

"Well, some of us are more blessed than others in the looks department."

I look over my shoulder. Scraggly hair hangs at his shoulders, looking as if it hasn't seen a comb in a while. He smiles as I study him, eyes sparkling with happiness or alcohol. It could go either way. "See what I mean? You and I could pass as brothers, we're so handsome. But, alas, our ruler is cursed with looks no better than a mangled rock. I'm sure he's an acquired taste for some, being king and all."

"I'm sure." I turn and head down the stairs encased in darkness. The sound of shouts and cheers grows the farther I descend, and it isn't until the last few steps that I can see what the hell I'm walking into.

The air is thick with sweat and ale, and the ground is made of mostly dirt, except where large pits are dug out. Chain links connected to wooden posts surround the pits, and shifters of every gender and size push against them as they revel over whatever is happening below. Animals meander throughout the space, and as I move to inspect one of the pits, I brush against the side of a large jaguar. It snarls at me, but I push my power forward until my eyes glow, and the shifter scurries away. Standing behind a shorter male, I look down just as the crack of bone rings out. Burning hell, these are fighting pits. I've heard the rumors of places like this, where those down on their luck—or worse, those with nothing to lose—come to find some solace. I just didn't believe them to be like *this*.

I am going to kill my cousin. To work out some stress is one thing, but to come here and risk his life as though he isn't essential to our kingdom running efficiently... If he hasn't been beaten to shit, then I am going to do it myself.

I make my way through the throng of people, using my height to check over the raucous crowds and look down into the pits they surround. It isn't until I've crossed all the way over to the other side that I find him. Leaning against an aged wooden beam, I fold my arms over my chest and watch as Kane stands in conversation with a shorter male—one who has every inch of his skin tattooed in the traditional shifter lines. All except for his face. My newest tattoos start to itch under the sweltering heat of this place, but I avoid scratching at my chest and instead watch as Kane nods his head and begins to stretch out his arms.

The shifters to my left cheer loudly, drawing my gaze over to the pit. Money is exchanged, and ale spills from their mugs as they clang them together in victory. A male with a shaved head is pulled from the pit, his unconscious body tossed to the side as if he's nothing more than a piece of trash. The victor of the match pulls himself up, revealing a male nearly as large as me in height but who has me beat in width. He doesn't even look *phased*, sweat curling the short strands of his black hair the only indication that he participated in the fight.

I bring my attention back to the pit Kane was standing next to, only to find he isn't there. Pushing off from the post, I reach the edge of the growing crowd, their whispers hushed as they look down at its occupants.

"A new challenge is about to begin!" a male shouts from somewhere across the pit. "You know the rules—no interference until one of them is either knocked out or"—he drags his thumb across his throat—"*dead*. Challengers, enter the pit!"

Shouts and cheers rise as fists pump into the air. I shoulder my way through the tightly knit horde, earning grumbles of protest until they turn and catch sight of my face. In a rare moment of vanity, I'm hoping the silence is because they recognize me and not because my features are *undesirable*. I groan at the thought, the urge to punch myself only abating when I see Kane drop down into the pit. His ankle rolls, and he nearly goes down, his body wobbling when he attempts to straighten himself out. I stare down at him as my jaw clenches, noting his already swollen lip and the giant bruise that stains the skin at his ribs. *The asshole has already fought tonight.* Kane draws a hand down his face before shaking his head and bouncing on his toes.

The volume increases when Kane's contender makes his way through the crowd, their bodies moving to give him an unobstructed path. Pain shoots up my temples when I grind my teeth. It's the unphased male from the last fight—the one whose previous opponent *still* hasn't woken up.

He drops down into the pit and eyes Kane, rolling his head side-to-side as he stretches his neck. His muscles speak to combat training of some kind, and while Kane is naturally physically gifted, and I know he *does* train, it's like staring down at two different species. My heart pounds as I clench my hands at my sides. He's going to get himself fucking *killed*, and while my fondness for my cousin only stretches so far, his work with the nobles is needed. There may also be a miniscule part of me that isn't eager to lose what little blood-related family I have left to stupidity.

I move to shout his name and force him to leave when a bell rings out three times and both men leap into action.

Fuck.

"Yeah! Kill him, Manu!" someone to my right shouts, his drink spilling over onto my shoe. His glazed eyes lift to meet mine in a watery smile before he chugs his drink and then drops the pewter mug right into the pit before returning to cheering for the opponent.

Despite the evidence of Kane's fight and his earlier off-balance actions, he rushes at Manu quickly, sending a right hook into the behemoth's side that makes the male grunt. Kane paces back a few steps, lifting his arms to block as he dodges Manu's fists before lunging forward and swinging one of his own up. It connects beneath Manu's jaw, snapping his teeth together loudly.

But despite the hit, Manu counters with unparalleled speed, sending a combo of punches into Kane's chest that makes my cousin stumble backwards until he falls on his ass. Spectators around the pit scream ravenously as they lean against the chain barriers. Manu doesn't go in to finish Kane, instead creating distance between them so that Kane has time to jump back to his feet.

"Come on, pretty boy. Don't be afraid," he taunts, crooking his finger. The dare has the desired effect, and like a damn fool, Kane charges at Manu without any finesse. He lowers his shoulder and jams it into Manu's torso, but Manu stays upright.

Kane's sides are left open as he draws his right arm back, fist poised to punch his opponent's jaw. But Manu grabs his wrist and *twists*, a crack sounding that makes my cousin immediately drop to his knees as he screams out in pain. Breath is pulled from me as I watch, my magic rising along my neck as gold frames my vision.

Manu pumps his arms up over him, egging the crowd on as they chant his name.

"Stay down," I growl under my breath, remembering that the match doesn't end until Kane is either knocked out or dead. But the idiot stands, cradling his dominant arm to his chest as he snarls at Manu.

"We aren't done yet, asshole!" He wobbles where he stands, sweat dripping from his temple. "Come on! Or are you too much of a *bitch* to fight me properly?"

Manu chuckles, flexing his right hand out in front of him as he begins to prowl towards Kane. "It's going to be pleasurable ending your pathetic life!" he shouts, a sadistic grin peeling his lips back. "After all, it's what your *father* would have wanted." My blood runs cold as I narrow my stare on him, Kane momentarily stunned before he lets out a growl of his own and lunges again.

The other male latches on to Kane's arm as he sprints towards him, using the momentum to send a knee directly into his gut. Kane's breath sputters, but Manu doesn't taunt him with space this time. He laces his fingers behind Kane's neck and pulls his face down into a brutal knee jab, the crunch of Kane's nose echoing out over the screaming crowd.

Dirt billows out where Kane's body falls, Manu delivering a kick to his side that rolls him from his stomach to his back. "Stay *down*," I say louder, elbowing a few males off who push into me. Kane moans, turning onto his side before lifting to his hands and knees. Manu positions himself at Kane's head, leaning down to say something that I can't hear against the thunderous noise surrounding me. Tugging on Kane's hair, Manu sends another powerful punch into his jaw, rocking my cousin's entire body before he collapses to the ground.

Sure he'll stay down this time, I push my way around the perimeter of the pit to a gap in the fence, ready to drag him out of here myself when the crowd breaks into wild cheering again. I snap my gaze down to where Manu stands over Kane, my anger flaring when I watch my cousin stumble to his feet. Manu punches him, dropping Kane to his knees again.

"Pathetic," Manu says, wiping Kane's blood off on his tunic. "I'll do what even Tua was too weak to."

Magic pulses down my torso and to my arms, but I bite down the urge to shift as my hands grasp the chain fence.

"Fuck. *You*," Kane quips, blood spilling from his mouth. Manu smiles, its deviant curve tugging on me to act. I don't let myself second guess my actions as I jump over the fence and fall the ten feet down into the pit, landing in a crouch.

The crowd *roars*, their excited footsteps rumbling through the earth and reverberating over my body with every step that I take as I close the distance to my cousin. Manu's too lost in his eager rage to notice me, and I use the advantage to quickly step up at his side and grab his wrist mid-air. Chants of protest ring in my ears, but it's Manu's eyes I stare into, gold rimming his irises. "Enough."

His gaze widens for a heartbeat, recognition stealing his breath, before he snaps his teeth at me.

"Kai?" Kane murmurs from behind me. I drop my hold on Manu and spin to face him, an angry snarling of words pressing at my lips. "What the fuck are you doing?"

"Get up. We're going." I reach under his arms and pull him up to stand, taking most of his weight as he leans into me. I march us towards the other end of the pit, content on throwing his nearly limp body up into the crowd if that's what it takes.

"You can't *leave*." Manu's voice is an arrow hitting true, silencing the crowd as it echoes out. "It's against the rules."

"Do you think I fucking *care* about the rules of this shithole?" I snap, earning a rolling tide of low murmurs.

"No, I doubt you do, *Your Majesty*. But they are the rules. Anyone who enters the pit can only exit by winning or being knocked out or killed." I grind my teeth together.

"It's true!" the male who announced the fight shouts, leaning over the fence. "Technically, Kane is still locked into this match. And so are *you*."

"Let go of me," Kane drawls at my side, attempting to push away from me but failing *miserably*. "I don't need you." I ignore him as I think over what the fuck to do. I don't want to fight either of them, but to blatantly use my title to act as if *I* am above the rules—even in a place like this—can't be the option either. "Let go, Kai."

"Shut up, I'm trying to think."

He snorts. "Don't act like you wouldn't enjoy punching the shit out of my face."

"I definitely would, but as king—"

"I'll kill you both! What do we think? Does the victor get to be king?" Manu shouts, lifting both arms into the air and spurring the crowd into a manic state.

A low noise of annoyance rumbles up my chest. "Of all the fucking places, Kane, why here?" He forces himself away from my side, stumbling out in front of me and wiping the sweat and blood from his brow.

"Knock me out."

I glare at him and shake my head. "No." Now that Manu has outed who I am to the entire room, I can't make another mistake. Not here. I have to show these people—*my* people—that I can be the king they need. One steady and rational. One intelligent and... *worthy*. And fist fighting here would not—

"I can still taste her sometimes." He smirks, dried blood staining the corners of his mouth. "I can still feel the way her body pressed against mine. So hot. *So* insistent and needy."

My heart stills, and even though I know he is just trying to rile me up, the words immediately bring my anger to the forefront. "*Don't*," I warn.

"Gods, she knows how to work her mouth doesn't she?"

"*Kane*."

"I'm tired of waiting!" Manu shouts.

"Her skin was so soft, and had you not interrupted us? I would have fucked her senseless. I still wanted to, up until the moment she left."

My animal bares its teeth within me, snapping at the way he talks of her. She is mine. *Mine*. Every part of her belongs to me, and *every* pathetic part of me will always be hers. No matter how I try to fight it, that will always remain true.

"You're a *worthless* king, Kai Vaea!" Behind Kane, Manu charges towards us.

"Bahira," Kane says slowly, tasting her name as if it is his to do so. "So *fucking* sweet—"

It is not a conscious decision but a primal one when I send my fist into his jaw, knocking his body to the ground where he lays unmoving. My chest heaves as my vision hazes over, and then pain explodes on the side of my face.

Chapter Sixty

KAI

I STUMBLE BACKWARDS, AND another hit pummels my face, making my ears ring. The crowd becomes a buzzing sound, but I blink away the sting of sweat—or is it blood?—dripping into my eyes just in time to see the next swing of Manu's fist.

I duck, finding my bearings and sending a punch directly into his side. Just below his ribs. He bellows out in pain, eyes fully golden now as he growls. I don't hesitate, still fired up from Kane's words. Picturing his hands on *my* Bahira. Bringing her pleasure that was only mine to give, even if she wants nothing to do with me now. I kick at his chest, but it doesn't send him flying back nearly far enough. *Worthless,* he had said. Just like *I* called her.

She had given me all of herself. I had seen her unguarded and bare. Her armor laid down only for me to raise my own and send a spear of bitterness through her.

I charge after Manu, only a breath away from shifting. My magic tugs within me, sending a shiver of energy down my spine. Manu smirks, raising his guard and blocking the barrage of punches I send. He attempts to speak—or maybe he actually does—but I can't hear it above the voice that screams at me to fix everything that I've fucked up. My kingdom and my relationships. Myself and *her*. I want to be worthy of everything I have, even knowing that none of it should have been mine to begin with.

Manu's leg sweeps mine, striking right at the knee and dropping me onto it. But before he can capitalize on it, I spin and balance on one arm as I send a kick to his jaw. *That* brings him down, blood already blooming where the skin is thinnest against bone. Pushing him onto his back, I bracket his hips with my knees and punch at his head. Over and over again, until the pain in my knuckles turns numb and the features of his face morph into a mash of blood and bone.

It takes me longer than it should to realize he isn't fighting back. Too long to notice that the crowd has simmered down its raucous cheering to simple murmurs. By the time my magic fades and there is only *me* at the forefront, Manu is dead. I push myself up, using my forearm to wipe the blood off my face before turning to where Kane is still out. Squatting, I hoist him up and over my shoulder in the near silence of the fighting pit, wishing with every part of myself that I could disappear. A rope ladder is thrown down, and I take its aid, climbing to the top. The shifters ahead of me part, their wide eyes scanning over my body as I pass, but it's the condemnation I see in their eyes that makes mine lower.

The beat of my heart sets a punishing rhythm as I begin the journey back to the palace, the taunting disappointment of my people chasing my shadow the entire way. Kane stirs as I walk up the long driveway to the front entrance, and only when he complains about being carried do I set him down.

"Did you win?" he asks through swollen lips.

I don't bother giving him a response, but based on the rules of the pits, he makes his own conclusion.

"Good."

Anger still simmers beneath my skin at what he said, but the walk here has calmed me enough to not act on it. Together, we enter the palace, though I slow my pace to keep at Kane's side. Assuming he'll head towards the healer's office, I question him when he goes in the opposite direction. "Where are you going?"

"None of your business."

"Kane!" He stops his retreat, taking his time to turn around. I take in the state of his face, how he favors one side and cradles his arm in the other. "Why were you there tonight?"

His gaze drops to my feet, shame briefly tugging his shoulders down as he frowns. Silence stretches taut between us. "Are you asking as my cousin or as my king?"

I blink, pressing my lips together before releasing them. "Whichever one will give me the truth."

He cackles and draws a hand through his gnarled hair. "Do you ever hear their disappointed voices?" he asks, moving his stare towards a far window overlooking the jungle.

"Whose?"

"Our fathers. I hear them sometimes, even when I know I'm alone and it's merely a trick of my mind. But it doesn't soften the blow of their words or the cadence of their discontent. It doesn't matter that the voices filtering in are sometimes theirs and sometimes my own played through their mouths." He goes quiet for a few moments before clearing his throat and looking to me. "My father was leading an entire movement to kill you and take your throne, and I had no *fucking* idea. I hope you believe me when I say that."

"I do. You'd be dead already if I didn't." Bahira had told me what Tua said to Kane, and the story of how he had tried to get Kane to kill me when I was a child. He may be a pain more often than not, but I believe her story. I believe *him*.

"All this time, I thought my arrogance would bring me to people who accepted me. Regardless of the fact that the throne you sit on was promised to me. Regardless of the fact that my father couldn't look me in the eye without relaying the magnitude of his hatred towards me. In the end, all I did was blind myself—blind *you* through my own anger and jealousy—to what was really going on. People died. You almost *died*. *She* almost died." Kane drags a breath in and holds it before slowly letting it out. "If you're asking as my king why your advisor was there, then I don't have a good enough reason for you not to remove me from my position immediately. And I do not blame you for doing so if that's what you choose."

"And if I'm asking as your cousin?"

His glassy eyes hold mine. "I'd tell you, it's the only way to make their voices stop."

"Your Majesty!" Footsteps pound on the stone behind me, and I glance away from my cousin to look over my shoulder, finding Inessa running towards me with wide eyes.

"Yes?"

"It's the Mirror. You've been summoned through the Mirror." *Bahira*. Hope bursts in my chest, and when I turn to tell Kane we'll continue this later, I find that he's already retreating down the hall.

"Your face," Inessa whispers at my side. Her fingers lay over my arm gently. "Are you alright?"

"Fine," I murmur, releasing a breath.

She nods before retreating a few steps. "We should hurry, Your Majesty. They've been trying to call you for a little while now."

"You can just call me Kai," I tell her as I follow her around a corner and into the main foyer on our way to the throne room.

She slows her pace to drop back to my side, her chin drawing down to her chest. "Thank you, Kai."

I offer her a tight smile as we approach the double doors, a wolf and oryx carved into them. The symbols of two kingdoms—one run by my father and one attempted to be run by Tua. I ignore how my stomach sours and push one open on silent hinges, the throne room quiet except for the shuffling of steps from Lady Miranda and some guards.

"Your Majesty—"

"I'd like to do this alone," I bite out, striding down the center of the room, shadows dancing from the lit torches all around us.

Lady Miranda crosses her arms over her chest as she studies me, Inessa moving to stand at her side. It's not that I don't trust her or anyone else to be here. It's that I don't know what I will do when I see Bahira's face for the first time, and I'd rather not have an audience as the mage princess brings a king to his knees. She nods once and heads towards the door, her daughter joining her as the guards follow behind.

"I'll grab some ice for your face!" Inessa shouts, and then the doors shut behind her.

The Mirror's solid surface ripples when I step closer. Each magical wisp in the glass pulls towards the edges, and as the image they are hiding grows clearer, my heart plummets into my stomach. In front of me is not Bahira, nor is it anyone from the Mage Kingdom. Standing with his hands in his pockets and a troubling smirk on his face is King Dolian, ruler of the Mortal Kingdom.

"King Kai, it is wonderful to finally have a face to put to the name," he says, tilting his head. "Though it looks like you've had a rough day." The light of whatever room he is in glints off the gold embroidery on his vest and the matching embroidery of the dress the woman standing next to him wears. Her head is bowed while her hands are clasped in front of her, but it's the stiffness in her posture that makes my eyes narrow, unbidden fists forming. When I don't respond, he adds, "I was talking with my council today, and we realized that we cannot pin down your exact coronation date. When was it you became king?"

I lift a brow. "Likely after you did." The answer makes his smirk falter for a brief moment, while the woman to his left leans her body slightly away from his. He takes one hand out of his pocket and wraps it around her hip, tugging her into him and pinning her there.

"Where are my manners? King of the shifters, may I introduce you to my fiancée, Lady Nele."

The woman's shoulders rise towards her ears, but she keeps her gaze down until the king leans over and whispers something in her ear, and a line forms between my brows at this overall *odd* fucking exchange. Her chest rises and falls slowly before she finally lifts her head and meets my eyes. Hers are a shade of green I've never seen before, one that reminds me of the rarest flowers that grow on the island, their roots planted at the edge of a volcano.

I dip my chin at her, taking my time to study her and the way familiarity strikes me even though I'm *sure* I've never seen her before. Much like those rare flowers, her beauty is a delicate one. Those green eyes glow against fair skin, honey golden hair framing her face where it falls over her shoulders. But there's a certain *hollowness* about her beyond the way darkness stains the skin beneath her eyes and her cheeks hug the bone beneath them. "It is a pleasure to meet you, Lady Nele."

She forces a smile before the king's fingers flex against her hip and it twists into a wince.

"What can I do for you, King Dolian?"

"What can you tell me about Princess Bahira of the Mage Kingdom?"

I mask any emotion his question evokes, even as Lady Nele sharpens her gaze on me as if she's intrigued by my answer. "I likely only know what every other kingdom does." Knowing that mages can pass through the Spell may be a secret that my father somehow came by, but it certainly isn't one I am willing to share with anyone else. Not when it could harm the people of the Mage Kingdom. *Not when it could harm* her.

King Dolian chuckles. "Come now, Your Majesty. Let us not start off with any lies between us."

I offer him nothing but a blank stare.

He sighs, shaking his head as if he's disciplining a difficult child. "I know, as you do, that mages can cross through the Spell without loss of life. I know that Princess Bahira spent months in your kingdom and is currently being investigated for treason after a letter from you was intercepted by the king's council."

The hair on the back of my neck rises as my magic floods my veins. *Treason?* Is that why they haven't been answering my call? Because they believe that she'd somehow *endangered* her kingdom by being here?

"I see I've rendered you speechless, but it doesn't matter. Your silence is answer enough. The reason I'm truly calling is that I need to know, one ruler to another, if you are planning on allying with the mages to attack us."

"No."

"Not very reassuring, is he?" he retorts, leaning over to kiss Lady Nele's temple. She doesn't react, instead keeping her gaze fixed on mine. "Perhaps information shared, then. Why did you enlist in the help of the princess?"

"Why do you need to know what I seek in my spare time? Or *who* I seek to spend that time with?" I inflect enough innuendo in the last statement to bring a slight blush to Lady Nele's cheeks and a scoff from the king's mouth. *Good.* I'd rather him be disgusted than continue to dig too deeply.

"You expect me to believe that there aren't enough of your own kind to fuck, so you've taken to pillaging women from other kingdoms?"

I snort as anger curls over my spine. As if Bahira would let *anyone* touch her without her consent. "Better to sink into someone willing than to force someone who isn't, don't you agree?"

Lady Nele's stare widens, her lips pressing into a thin line.

"I see this was a waste of time, then, Your Majesty." His sigh is dramatic, but the anger that colors his cheeks gives him away. "I suppose, I hope that our paths never cross."

"I don't know, King Dolian," I start, leaning in closer as I grip on to a little more power until my eyes are glowing gold. "I have a feeling things between us have only just begun."

His smile is anything but friendly as he tugs the woman out of view and the Mirror grows misty again.

My hands brace my hips as I sort through the information I've learned. Jahlee's letter had been intercepted, and whatever she wrote in it is now causing problems for Bahira. It's clear King Dolian has someone inside the Mage Kingdom, someone close enough to the Crown. And I have no doubts that Lady Nele is actually Rhea. Siyala had given me a description of the woman King Dolian imprisoned in a tower.

In one short conversation, two worst-case scenarios are now confirmed: Rhea is back with the mortal king and Bahira is worse off because of her time here. The urge to leave the island hits me hard, as it has every day that has passed, but leaving my kingdom now feels impossible. And telling Jahlee and Siyala what I've learned? They would be devastated.

I spend a lot of time replaying the events of the day in my mind as I lug myself up to my room to bathe. I never wanted to be king, but I thought that perhaps, with enough determination, I might be able to make it work. To dull everything that made me sharp and dangerous into something more refined. Something deserving of the power that flows in my blood. But if today's events are any indication, I can't reform myself any more than I can control the tides.

I am Kai Vaea, king of the shifters and a damn *fool*.

Chapter Sixty-One

BAHIRA

THE CLOUDS OVERHEAD TURNED gray quickly, my view of them unob-structed from my spot on the training fields, an archery target in front of me. My mind needed the quiet that only physical movement could provide, and though I used to find myself tumbling into the bed of another at a moment like this, the thought of hands on me that do not belong to a giant male with a wicked mouth and warm brown eyes is as unappealing now as it was weeks ago.

Blowing out a breath, I nock my arrow, pulling it back until I feel the bow-string's resistance, the strain on my muscles a welcome distraction. Seconds pass as I wait for the right moment to release, my heart beating softly against my ribs as I allow my eyes to fall closed. *Breathe.* I tune into my surroundings—the cool air scented with rain from the incoming storm, the soft fabric of my cloak as it brushes against my bare arms. One by one, each part of me settles in the present where there is no over-reaching council. No threat to my father's throne. No faraway shifter king occupying all of my thoughts. No experiments or worries about the Spell or a broken Mirror. There is only me and the weapon I'm holding.

I release the arrow, the sound of it traveling through the air and hitting the target bringing a smile to my face.

"A perfect shot." My eyes open at the sound of Haylee's voice behind me, and I turn to watch her crest a small hill as she makes her way to me. "I forget sometimes just how talented you are with other weapons because you prefer the use of your spear."

I smirk, dropping the bow to my side while I reach for the quiver at my back, pulling another arrow from it. "You've likely got me beat in the sword department," I counter.

"You flatter me."

It isn't exactly flattery. Haylee is a talented warrior with training as extensive as my own. As her friend, it makes me proud to know that she could hold her own if it ever came to it. She stands in front of me in black trousers and a dark blue long-sleeved shirt, crossing her arms against the cool wind that pulls strands of her dark blonde hair free from her usual braided coronet.

"How are you, Bahira?" she asks, tilting her head to the side. "And I want the *real* answer. Not the one you give everyone else."

"You know things are... *precarious* right now. The most they've ever been." I turn back to face the wooden targets, my previous arrow sticking out of the center of the farthest. I prepare to nock the next one, rolling my shoulders back and adjusting my stance. "I'm just trying to put current fires out before new ones start."

"That's putting it mildly." She watches me line up, my fingers pulling the bow string back as I inhale deeply. "Is one of those fires your brother?"

I arch a brow on instinct, keeping my gaze on the target. "He certainly isn't making things easier."

Not that I could sincerely blame *only* him. My brother has been kept busy by the council, and while I'm grateful that their focus on him has drawn them away from me, there's something odd about how much time they are spending with him. Even my father has been kept on the sideline, the council claiming that they are simply assuring that Nox is doing well enough to deal with the public pressure that's been building ever since the ball. Including the fact that a body had been discovered and a guard had also gone missing. Toss in the rumor-fueled gossip that both of those things happened the same night Rhea supposedly *abandoned* Nox, and I suppose I *can* understand why they are preparing him. Still, understanding it doesn't mean that it also doesn't feel *wrong*.

Releasing the arrow, I watch it hit its mark just slightly off center. *Damn it.*

"May I?" Haylee asks, holding her hand out for the bow. I grab another arrow, giving that to her as well.

"Why were you so insistent that Nox get engaged to you?" I ask as she nocks her arrow, her stance opposite of my own.

"I'm sure that interaction with your brother seemed odd. Given our last conversation."

"It's more that I'm confused by the whole thing." I expect a quick retort or a witty response, but instead, Haylee keeps her gaze forward, spending way too much time readjusting her stance. I take a step closer to her, worry gnawing at my gut. "What's really going on, Haylee?"

Her brows furrow as another cold gust blows through the training field, pulling a few more tendrils of hair from her makeshift crown. "Have you ever felt trapped?" she asks, the corners of her mouth drawing down as if she doesn't like her own question. "I suppose it's insensitive of me to ask *you* that."

I let out a rough laugh, following her gaze to the targets in front of us. "We already know my feelings on being magicless. It's nothing you haven't heard a hundred times already. But what has *you* feeling trapped?"

She sighs, planting her feet more firmly as she lifts the bow. "Did I ever tell you that when I was growing up, my uncle would take me on tours of your palace?"

"You didn't."

"It was the only time we ever had one on one. So often he was busy with the council or pushing me into another class, another lesson. But, occasionally, we would walk the foyer, and he would point to the different paintings and tapestries, explaining the history of your family. Of the Void queens that came before them." She begins to pull the bowstring back, her bicep flexing. "And we *always* stopped to linger in two rooms, one of which was the council chambers. At first, I had looked around that room in awe. *There is power to be had in this room, Haylee,* he would tell me, a hand gripping my shoulder. Not like a father would—he's never cared about me enough to even *pretend* about showing that level of emotion—but for him, for the relationship between us, well, I cherished it. I lived for the attention he gave me because it came so rarely. In those moments, he taught me just how valuable status and reputation was to gaining power and, in return, what opportunities arose from it."

I swallow roughly. I knew that Councilman Borris had been hard on Haylee. Growing up, she often complained about the pressure placed on her to be the best at everything she attempted. I had thought it was nothing more than Borris preparing her for life as a future council member.

"Don't pity me," she says, and I shake my head, my mouth opening to explain that having empathy isn't the same as pitying her, but she cuts her eyes towards me. "I would not change the way he raised me." The arrow sings through the air as she releases it, and it embeds in the center target right next to my own. "The bastard may have been brutish, cruel at times even, but he wasn't entirely wrong in his approach. I have spent a lifetime trying to appease him, trying to prove that I'm worthy of him taking me in instead of letting me go to the orphanage when my parents died. I have obeyed every single rule in order to be valuable in his eyes. And though you may hear that and immediately think me a fool, I see it for what my uncle taught me: If I want something badly enough, I have to work for it."

A storm of emotion swirls in her gray eyes as she turns to me, pressing the bow into my hands. "What is it that *you* want, Haylee?" I ask.

The wind whistles between us, the pillow grass of the training field swaying as we stare at each other. "I want freedom," she whispers, lifting her chin. "And I will do whatever I need to in order to get it."

Haylee offers me a small smile before she brushes past, only making it a few steps before I ask, "What was the other room?"

"What?"

"You said your uncle would always take you to two rooms in the palace. One was the council chambers. What was the other?" This entire conversation had started because I wanted to know why she was pursuing Nox despite knowing his heart was elsewhere. Despite *claiming* hers was as well. But the woman who looks at me now isn't some lovestruck fawn trying to win over a man who isn't interested in her. That fact makes my stomach sink with realization. In all the time I've known Haylee, I've never once thought her a liar. But secrets don't always come in the form of lies spoken—I know that all too well. Sometimes, betrayals happen in what is kept hidden. In what is never said.

"It was the throne room," she says, turning to head back towards Galdr.

My eyes shut, my hand going lax around the bow. My mind begins to run through all of our previous interactions, going as far back as when we first met as children. Had Haylee befriended me because she saw a girl being picked on and felt bad? Or had she, even then, seen me as nothing more than an opportunity? She wanted freedom, and the only way for her to gain that was through power. What was more powerful than befriending the princess of the kingdom?

My eyes open, my lips pursing as I stare in the direction she disappeared. "Marrying the prince."

The palace library is practically empty—only the sound of pages turning disrupts the otherwise oppressive silence. Sitting at Elora's desk, I wait for the red-headed librarian to show while I peruse a book that talks about the first instances of imbuing dragon stone with magic. It's not a firsthand account, more of a researcher's thoughts on why it makes such a great conduit for our magic. One interesting theory is the makeup of the onyx mountains themselves. While the Fae Kingdom's temperatures are generally cooler than ours, since they are farther north than the rest of the Continent, their mountains are rumored to have warm *cores* made of more than just rock. The author theorizes that this is why the dragons settled there as opposed to anywhere else on the Continent. It's an interesting hypothesis but not exactly what I'm looking for.

Still, there have been a few noteworthy pieces of information on imbuing stone and the history of the practice. Laying the book face down on the table, I stretch my arms as I yawn and stand, rounding the desk to where Elora keeps paper and pens for note taking. I grab a black pen and find a notepad, laying it on top of the desk as I flip through the pages to find a blank one.

Most of them contain Elora's thoughts on whatever book she is currently reading, one of which included *doodles* of the characters kissing. I continue to pass pages of drawings and quickly jotted notes when a name catches my eye. Pausing, I hold the notepad open and reread to confirm what I saw. *Rhea Maxwell.*

"What the fuck?" I whisper, scanning the length of the paper and its back side. By the time I've finished reading everything, my heart is racing in my throat.

"Hello, hello!" My head shoots up as her voice rings out from somewhere down the center aisle.

Moving quickly, I rip the two pages out and fold them before stuffing them into my pocket and putting the notebook back in the drawer. Elora rounds the corner a second later, carrying a large bag of books. She looks as she normally does—like she's in a rush but the place she is hurrying to is just the next chapter of her current read. With her unassuming personality, it would be easy for her to fly under the radar as the rat within our kingdom. She already had the trust of Nox, of Daje and Cass too. What information has she been privy to?

"Okay, so I was incredibly bored last night at work and started thinking about other materials that could mirror the... *Mirror*." She snorts as she heaves her bag onto the desk with a *thud*, beginning to pull books from it. "Glossy, reflective materials, regardless of whether we know if they hold magic or not. And that brought me to glass." She pushes her glasses up her nose where they have slipped, medium gray eyes meeting mine with excitement.

"Mages can't imbue glass," I remind her, keeping my voice level despite the way my fists clench at my sides.

"Right, we can't do it to *our* glass. But what if there was a special type of glass from the Fae Kingdom? Just like how there is dragon stone?"

"It's never been recorded." Not once.

"Well, not in the texts we have *here*," she counters, leaning a hip against the table. "But that doesn't mean it doesn't exist. Or that it might be kept secret by the fae or hidden in texts that I don't have access to." Her eyebrow lifts, and she tosses her plait over her shoulder. "What if there is dragon *glass* and that's what we need to fix the Mirror?"

"A fair guess," I tell her, rounding the desk. "I'll see if Elisha has anything that might cover it in the Galdr library." Or if the *archives* do.

"Wait, right now?" she asks as I pass her. "I thought we were going to look through these books together!"

"I had something come up. I'll meet you here tomorrow." I leave her grumbling behind me as I make my way out of the library and into one of the main halls, my muscles tense. I need to show someone who knows Elora what I found, who can at the *very* least tell me if I'm overreacting or if we should have her questioned immediately. Nox is too close to the situation to ask him to judge fairly, and that leaves only one person I trust that I can ask.

Daje.

Chapter Sixty-Two

BAHIRA

I TILT MY HEAD to look up at the small house built into the wide banya tree, the leaves above it hued with tips of ruby and gold, the transformation from summer to autumn in full effect. I was surprised to learn that Daje had moved out of the home he shared with his father, that he had apparently done it while I was in the Shifter Kingdom, if what Cass told me is true. Tugging my cloak more tightly around my shoulders, I climb up the two flights of stairs, the landing extending into a wide balcony that leads to the front door. I don't give myself any more time to second guess before I cross the distance and knock.

His answer is almost immediate.

"Bahira," he says, startled blue eyes flaring. "What are you doing here?" Just enough of the setting sun peeks through the treetops to gild the front of the home with golden light, painting his skin the same color and giving him a lovely bronzed look that he'd love a compliment on from anyone other than me.

"I need to talk to you."

His chin drops to his chest as holds my gaze, hand running over his shaved head. "I don't think that's a good idea—"

"It isn't about us," I add quickly, then wince when I realize that doesn't sound any better. "I mean, it has to do with Elora. Just give me a few minutes, and then I'll leave. We can even talk out here if it makes you more comfortable."

Letting loose a sigh, he steps back and waves his hand. "Come on in."

I take a step, immediately hit with the soft scent of leather and burning wood from the fireplace near the entrance. "When did you move here?"

"About two months ago." His feet pad softly on the rug in the main living area, a tasteful dark green and tan pattern matching his light furniture. "Would

359

you mind…" He gestures towards my boots, stopping me from moving past the entryway.

"Of course." I remove them as he makes his way down a hall to a small kitchen, where I hear him rifle through a cabinet. I pull the notes out of my pocket, laying them on the dark wooden coffee table before I peer around at the decorated walls. Art hangs in golden frames, and a tapestry that depicts a night sky with moonlight dancing over the water is tacked to the wall across from me.

Daje returns with two glasses of water, setting mine on the table and then taking a seat in the dark brown leather chair to my right.

"Whose idea was it for you to leave?"

He lifts a shoulder as he crosses an ankle over his knee. "Mostly mine, but he certainly had no qualms about it. It was something that was a long time coming. Living with him began to feel suffocating, and I could no longer pretend that I was separating the father from the councilman." He scratches at his jaw. "Not that there had ever really been a difference."

I nod, unsure of how to respond. Harping about the havoc his father is causing within my own family certainly doesn't seem like the right thing to do.

When a bout of uncomfortable silence lingers, he asks, "What do you want to talk about? You mentioned Elora?"

I reach to grab the notes I stole, handing them over. "I was in the library waiting for Elora to show up when I stumbled upon this in one of her desk drawers."

He looks up at me, arching a brow. "You stumbled upon them while they were tucked away in a drawer?"

I wave my hand as I roll my eyes. "Semantics. Look at what they say."

His gaze lingers on me a beat longer than necessary before he blinks and focuses on the notes, taking the time to read them carefully. The farther he gets, the more tension forms between his brows. By the time he's read it all, his fingers are trembling. "This… This makes it seem like she figured out Rhea wasn't from here."

My fingers curl into my palms. "And that she told Councilman Arav."

"I never—" He tosses the notes back to the table before bracing his elbows on his knees, holding his head in his hands. "*Gods*, am I really this terrible at reading people? Elora and Rhea were friends. I saw them interact. I saw how Rhea lit up when they were together. No, we have to be missing something. Have you spoken to her yet? Or to Nox?"

"No. I didn't want to confront her in case she tried to run and hide after being found out. And Nox is too wrapped up in Rhea being gone to think rationally at the moment. I was afraid that if I told him—"

"He'd go into accusation mode. Yeah, that's an accurate assessment." It's my turn to lift a brow at the way he sounds almost *familiar* with that sort of behavior from my brother. Daje gives an airy chuckle. "I may have accidentally walked in on them using the Mirror because I thought they were speaking with you. Turns out, it was King Dolian on the other side. Nox was *not* happy about the potential risk of Rhea being outed to the council—not that I blamed him then or now—and he threatened to kill me. Even brought out his shadows and everything."

"You're kidding." I've *never* seen Nox use his shadows on anyone, certainly nothing beyond practicing with them, and even that was... *rare.*

"Yeah, it was honestly incredible, even if it scared the shit out of me." I hum at the lightness in his voice, this comfortable familiarity between us like nothing ever changed. As if having the same thought, Daje clears his throat and gestures to the notes. "Though I would have to assume that if Nox was worried about Elora at all, he would have brought it up to both Rhea *and* Elora. I'd speak with him before confronting her. Just to be sure."

I nod, folding the notes and pocketing them. I don't know why I say what I do next, why I let the anxious words tumble from me. "I'm worried about him. He left without telling anyone, Daje. Then he gets dumped on the palace steps, like someone returning an escaped animal. His magic is still *broken*, and—" I cut myself off, emotion clogging my throat as I stare up at the wooden ceiling.

"I saw him earlier, talking with my father. His signature is still *off.* I can't imagine how that feels for him to suddenly be cut off from his power, to know that something isn't right with it."

I look back at him, folding my arms over my chest. "I just can't help but feel like change is coming," I say softly, shaking my head, "And I don't know what my life—my family's life—is going to look like by the time the dust settles."

Daje watches me intently from where he's hunched over his knees, his gaze softening just slightly. When silence once more invites itself between us, I take that as my cue to leave, standing and slipping my boots back on.

"I'll always support your family any way that I can," he says once I've opened the front door, the cool night air nipping at my cheeks.

I look back over my shoulder at him, and offer him a weary grin. "I know."

✥✥✥✥✥ ✥✥✥✥✥

The next day, I find myself once more fuming inside the council room. Councilman Kallin has again taken my father's spot at the head of the table. I eye the rest of the council from my seat, my parents positioned to my left. Leaning lazily against a wall like a shadow himself is Nox, his gaze lost on something down at his feet. I had heard him leave his room late into the evening last night and had fallen asleep while waiting to see if he returned at all. When I knocked on his door the following morning, it was clear he already left again. Or hadn't returned back to his room at all.

I lean in towards my mother, my fingers resting on her arm to get her attention as I look around the table and whisper, "Is Councilwoman Mora still sick?" Gods, she's been absent for a few months now.

She keeps her gaze on Daje's father, speaking only loud enough for me to hear. "I have questioned everyone who has come in contact with her—from her personal aides to her friends and neighbors. The only consistent story I'm being told is that she hasn't been seen in *months*." I jerk my head back. *How can that be?* "And that her home is empty."

"Could she be the mole?"

"I don't know, but I'm afraid something isn't adding up between both her and Barron missing. We must remember to tread lightly, especially with what they are getting ready to announce."

"What are th—"

"Cassius, shut the doors." Cass obeys Kallin's command, posting up at the right of the door and resting his hand over the hilt of his sheathed sword.

My mother pats my hand. "It'll be alright." Her voice is deceptively calm, and it instantly sets me on edge.

"Let us get right to the point. Ever since His Highness, Prince Nox, has returned from his mission in the Mortal Kingdom, things have transpired in our kingdom that have left a lot of this council scratching their heads. Our goal as advisors to the Crown is to make sure that the people's safety is at the forefront of their ruler's mind." He shifts his beady eyes to look at my father. "Sadryn, you have been a dutiful servant for many years in your role as king. Were it not for recent events, you might very well have continued to have our support for many more."

"No," I whisper, my body going rigid. They are going to officially remove my father from the throne. And with Nox's disinterest in it, they'll erase the Daxel line altogether. We'll be relegated to nobles, still able to live within the palace if we choose, but the access to *more* information will be left completely up to the council's discretion. Our words will hold no weight. We'll be at the whim of whoever the council puts in my father's place.

Kallin's eyes move to me for a second, long enough for the corners of his mouth to twist down, before he looks back out over the table. "As of a vote yesterday, the result of which was six to three—Hadrik, Arav, and Balen as the dissenters—we are removing King Sadryn Daxel from the throne immediately."

My eyes shoot to my father, his face set in a stern sort of apathy that I would believe if I didn't know him so well. His finger taps idly on the tabletop for a few beats before he stands and brings his hands behind his back. "It has been the greatest honor of my life being king. I have approached this role and my duty as I approach all things that I love—with honor and respect and the utmost dedication." I hate the way his voice cracks as he stares down at our mother, as if she is his tether to steady ground. "Thank you for guiding me as king when I needed it, and though I cannot say that I am happy with the council's decision, I will abide by whatever course of action they choose to take next if it is in the best interest of the kingdom." He takes his seat again, lacing his fingers through hers as she rubs the side of his arm with her other hand.

Nox steps out of his broody corner and into the light cast by the chandeliers above, and it takes everything in me not to audibly gasp at his appearance. He somehow looks even more exhausted than when I saw him a few days ago, with dark circles beneath his eyes bruising his pale skin. My gaze narrows on him, but he pointedly ignores me as he holds Kallin's glare. "Let's get this over with."

The head councilman clears his throat, gesturing to Nox. "The council also voted on whether Prince Nox, the current crown prince, should be allowed to step fully into his role as king, considering his *many* missteps the past few months."

Pointless, considering Nox just told me he doesn't want it.

"It has been decided by a unanimous vote that Prince Nox will be allowed the title of King of the Mage Kingdom effective immediately."

My lips part as I stare at my brother, wishing he would fucking *look* at me so I might be able to decipher where his head is at with all of this. But he simply folds his arms over his chest and leans against the edge of the table—right where Councilwoman Mora would be seated.

"This is a *trial* run, Your Highness," Councilman Borris says with evident disdain. "Perform your duties as *we* see fit, and you'll officially be declared king once a reasonable amount of time has passed." He lifts his chin, a barbed smile pulling his lips apart. "And once you've regained your magic, of course."

"And if I don't feel like following all of your precious rules?" Nox retorts, and I think I see sweat gleaming at his temples. His forced nonchalance is worrisome, as is the way his body seems to be curling in on itself.

Councilman Borris's face turns predictably red as he takes the verbal bait Nox has dropped for him. "Either you do things *our* way, or we will lock you up and—"

"Councilman!" Kallin barks, silencing the sputtering idiot across from me.

"I'm sorry, did you say *lock* him up?" A chair scrapes the ground behind me where Daje and Haylee are sitting. They had been two last minute additions to the meeting, one forcing his way in while the other had been invited to attend. Daje stands, his hands fists at his sides. "You were going to *imprison* the prince—"

"And why wouldn't we?" Borris interrupts him, lacing his sausage fingers together. "He repeatedly disobeyed the council's orders regarding that *woman*, his actions leading to security breaches that put the entire kingdom at risk."

"And let's not forget the three innocent people he viciously *injured*," Councilman Osiris jumps in, his lips in a taut line. "Prince or not, *royalty* or not, no one is above the law. *No one* will be allowed to put the kingdom at risk."

"Rhea is *not* a security threat, I can assure you," Nox says, and despite the fact that his power is drained and he is noticeably weaker, everyone at the table still stiffens at the threat in his voice. "And I did not wish to harm *anyone*, though I regret immensely that it happened."

"I will make sure to relay your *regret* to the family members," Borris says under his breath.

I push away from the table, my chair screeching over the stone floor. "How *dare* you—"

My mother gently grasps my wrist, drawing my attention as she shakes her head. "He's not worth it," she whispers.

"Bahira, a word, please." Nox jerks his head to the door, already walking towards it. I shoot every council member a glare, only sparing Hadrik who sits at my right, before I follow Nox, Cass giving me a wide berth as we pass. My brother strides to the opposite wall, leaning back against it as his gaze lands on mine. "You need to calm down."

"You did *not* just tell me to calm down, asshole," I snap, taking a step before halting at the smile that curls his lips.

"No. I mean, I *did*," he laughs, holding his hands out in surrender. "But I don't mean it. You have every right to be upset."

"I know I do!" Taking up a spot at his side, I tip my head back against the cool stone. The hall is empty, save for a few guards who are lingering at the very end near the main foyer. "Were you lying about not wanting to be king?"

"No," he answers immediately, turning his head to look at me. I meet his gaze with my own, noting the way his eyes have shifted to a darker shade of gray, those silver flecks even less noticeable than before. "Everything I told you is true."

"Then why? Why pretend to appease them?"

Nox sighs, running a hand through his hair. "Borris wasn't joking when he said my options were to do as they say or get imprisoned. This way, they have the illusion of getting what they want and the kingdom won't go to someone who will contest Rhea. It's what you suggested from the very beginning."

"And what do you get?" He smirks, and I aim a pointed look in his direction. "I know you're not doing this simply because it will make things easier for the time being. That hasn't exactly been your style lately."

"I get the freedom to do what I need to. The last thing that will help Rhea is me being locked in some dungeon while I wait for my body and my magic to figure their shit out. I have a plan."

"You're being vague, and I just want you to know that it didn't get past me."

He laughs, but the sound is sullen. "Nothing ever does." Pushing away from the wall, he lays his hand on my shoulder, squeezing it gently. Though he seems in better spirits, I can see how he wears his exhaustion heavily, his eyes bloodshot and cheeks sunken. "I'm sorry we didn't give you a heads up beforehand. It took everything just to warn our parents before the meeting. I'm only doing what I think is best in order to help bring Rhea home."

I lay my hand over his, squeezing his fingers. "Are you alright, Nox?"

Even though his words bring a modicum of comfort, they also stir my unease. Nox is practiced at keeping secrets—he had to be for his mission in the Mortal Kingdom. This just *feels* different, even if I can't exactly pinpoint why. But if he says he's got a plan, then I believe him. I just have to hope it doesn't include anything reckless enough to endanger himself... *again*.

"I should go back in there," he says, dropping his hand from my shoulder.

"Shit, wait!" I dig my hand in my pocket, fishing out Elora's notes and handing them to him.

"What is this?"

"I think it may be proof of our mole."

Chapter Sixty-Three

BAHIRA

A STORM BASHES THE windows outside Daje's home, where I wait awk-wardly with him and Elora for Nox and Cass to arrive. The latter keeps trying to catch my gaze, while the former is doing everything possible to avoid it. Not that I blame either of them. But I refuse to let Elora talk until Nox is here, which makes for tense silence considering she doesn't know *why* she is here.

"You know, when you asked if I wanted to come over tonight, this is not exactly what I had in mind."

I look over at her, taking in her outfit and how her unruly red waves are pinned up in a pretty updo, tight curls framing her face. She's wearing a deep green corset, ribbons of the same color cinching her waist. It's paired with a long khaki skirt, the fabric dusting the tops of her satin-slippered feet.

"What exactly *were* you hoping for?" I ask with an arched brow, right as Daje says, "I'm sorry. I had to be vague." He rubs the back of his neck, glancing for the hundredth time to the door.

"Well, clearly, there was a miscommunication because unless you are about to suggest the most uncomfortable threesome I've ever been a part of, I'm thinking it's time for me to go."

"You can't leave," I tell her.

"What other threesomes have you been a part of?" Daje asks.

I roll my eyes and sink farther into his couch, kicking my feet up on the coffee table. I hear a single noise of protest come from Daje and grumble under my breath as I place my feet back on the wood floors. "Where the fuck is Nox?"

"Yes, where is *His Illustriousness*? He hasn't shown up in days to help us search for information on the Mirror, and I'm starting to feel like I'm the only one who actually gives a shit about bringing Rhea home."

"If you care at all," I counter.

Her jaw slackens as her eyes go wide, but before she can squeak out whatever protest is on her tongue, the door opens and Cass and Nox come barreling in, dripping all over Daje's floor.

"Shit," he sighs, running to gather a bundle of towels, two going to the floor and the others to my brother and friend.

"What took you so long?" I ask, moving to sit on the edge of the couch.

"Fucking Kallin," Nox swears, dragging the towel over his face. "The bastard knows exactly when I'm not in the mood to speak with him, then ensures that he's present at that moment. Between his and Galen's hovering, I haven't had a moment to just *breathe*." Huffing, he carefully places the wet towel on top of the one on the floor to catch the water dripping off of him. "I've been chosen to give the closing remarks for Father's transfer of power ceremony."

Everyone in the room cringes, except for Elora, who lets out an entirely animalistic sound. "What? Your father is stepping down?"

"He is," Nox answers. "It will be announced in a few days."

Elora's hands fall to her lap, her nails digging into her palms. "And what, you'll take his place?" she snarls, her intensity startling me as she stands. Her steps are measured carefully, though she doesn't release the fists she formed. Daje attempts to block her path, but she pushes him out of the way until she's right in front of Nox, her face twisted in anger. "You would dare make a move like that without Rhea?"

"You don't know what you're—" My words are halted when Nox holds his hand out.

Elora's eyes widen, the whites of them fully visible. "Does this have to do with Haylee? And what she offered her?"

Daje leans forward. "Wait, what did she offer her?"

"It doesn't matter!" Nox barks, a muscle pulsing at his jaw. "And it doesn't have a damn thing to do with that."

"Oh, well that's just great, then," she says, jabbing a finger in his chest. "So instead of rescuing her, you're going to *play king* here?"

"You should really stop talking before you say something stupid," I retort, slipping into a space between my rage and my need to know what Elora did with the information she gathered on Rhea. "*More* stupid, I mean."

"No, *you* need to stop acting like we don't have someone we love in the hands of a monster!" Elora's chest heaves, her eyes turning glassy as she looks back at Nox. "Tell me what is *happening*!"

Nox shuts his eyes as he breathes deeply, composing himself before reaching into his pocket. "That's why we are here," he says in a voice much too gentle, but one that I can tell is sincere. "I promise I will tell you what I can, but first, can you please explain this?"

"What— These are from my notes on Rhea," she says, unfolding the papers. Her gaze flicks back up to Nox. "What do you think you're looking at?"

"That's what we wanted to ask. We need to be sure," he answers.

"Sure of *what*? I told Rhea that I had attempted to look her up in the city she was from because I wanted to know if she had living family members she was unaware of."

"Did you also tell her that you shared your findings with Councilman Arav?" I ask, the weight of everyone's attention following.

"I never told him." A line forms between her brows as her eyes dart to every other face in the room. "Is that what you all think? That I ratted Rhea out to the council?"

"None of us believed it—" Daje starts, but Elora shoots her hand out in my direction. "Okay, *some* of us believed that you might have done it, but only because Bahira doesn't know you like the rest of us do."

"Elora, Rhea told me that you knew about her not being from Santor and that you didn't say a word until *she* brought things up with you. I believed her then, and I believe you now. But we had to make sure. When it comes to finding out who betrayed us, no one is presumed innocent."

Cass steps forward, folding his arms over his chest. "I've seen the two of you interact enough to know that you wouldn't intentionally hurt her."

She catches his meaning, and her shoulders droop. "The council found out because of me?" Nox nods, and Elora backs up until her legs bump one of the chairs and sinks down into it. "If they found out, who else did? Is that why they were so insistent that you not marry her? Because they knew you were lying about where she was from?"

"I think so," Nox answers, his anger evident in the way his tone drops.

"Do you think they are the ones who also gave her to King Dolian?" She asks the question out loud, but she aims it Daje's direction.

He swallows and runs a hand over his head. "I don't know. My father never mentioned anything about her being from the Mortal Kingdom or about King Dolian. If he or any of the council members knew, I have to hope that they wouldn't stage a fake attack just to return her to him. Especially knowing that she *must* be mage if she can cross over the Spell."

"Well, if their plan was for Haylee to marry Nox, then Rhea was just in the way. Why question anything when you can just return her to where she came from?" Elora counters, dropping her crumpled notes on the table.

"I will find whoever orchestrated working with King Dolian and ensure that they pay," Nox says, pinning his gaze on Daje. "No matter who they are."

Daje nods grimly.

"So, now that everything's out in the open, what's next?" Cass asks, taking a seat next to me and throwing his arm over the back of the couch. His clothing is still soaking wet from the rain, and a quick glance in Daje's direction reveals he is *less* than enthused about it. "Might as well take advantage of our covert meeting."

I shoot Nox a look because not *everything* is out in the open, but he subtly shakes his head. Apparently, he's set on Rhea being the one to break the news that she is our newest Void queen.

"What is the status of questioning the guards?" Nox asks, folding his arms over his chest.

"Daje and I have been carefully combing through the ones present the night of the ball, but it's no easy task. Kallin has been relatively helpful in confirming which ones were there, but so far, our questioning about Daje's attack hasn't gone anywhere. Based on those we have questioned, I don't think they were involved with anything nefarious concerning Rhea."

"Again, I wonder if involving any council members at *all* is a good idea," Elora says, the corners of her mouth downturned.

"We don't exactly have a choice, especially now. My father has made sure that the council has eyes and ears everywhere. *I* can't even move through the palace without him knowing about it."

"There are ways," Nox says, a dark glint shining in his eyes before he blinks, and the look dissipates. "In any case, we continue looking for the mole *and* ways to repair the Mirror. That's still our biggest priority while I wait for my magic to return to its full strength."

"I might be able to help with that last part. At least, I have an idea of something we might be able to try, based on my experiments in the Shifter Kingdom. I just need someone willing to have their blood mixed with yours."

"Please tell me you aren't considering messing with blood and magic," Daje jests, planting his hands on the back of Elora's chair.

"Fine. Then I won't."

"It's forbidden," he adds, unhelpfully, when he realizes I'm not joking.

"Because of something that supposedly happened thousands of years ago, which I'm still trying to piece together the details of. I was hoping a visit to the archives would be more helpful, but the book I found isn't *complete*—"

"You went to the archives?" Nox interrupts.

"Yes, but that's not important. Back in the Shifter Kingdom, Kai and I explored the use of blood to treat shifters who were stuck in their animal forms. It had mixed results, but with Kai only being shifter, it makes sense it might not work correctly. It could be different if we try with mage blood."

"First name basis with the king?" Daje asks, his eyes holding mine as I watch his mind work to come to a conclusion that I'm not sure I can avoid anymore. At least he merely looks curious and not like he might be sick.

Cass whistles, and I'm unsure if it's to break the tension or simply because he finds this whole thing amusing. I look back to Nox. "I think it's worth exploring."

"I trust you," he replies, and gods, if that doesn't ease something in my chest.

"I'll give up my precious blood. Wouldn't be the first time a woman asked for it." A different kind of awkward silence follows, and before Cass can clarify *that* bizarre statement, Elora thankfully changes the subject.

"I think I might have some news on the Mirror front. Assuming Bahira hasn't updated you already on my newest hypothesis?"

"I was a little preoccupied with thinking you had betrayed Nox and Rhea." Elora narrows her eyes as Cass attempts to cover his laugh with a poorly timed cough. "Which I was clearly wrong about. I apologize."

"What have you found?" Nox prods.

Elora repeats everything she told me in the library—adding that, since I've seen her, she's delved into information about dragon fire, and while there isn't any reference to something called dragon *glass*, the fae believe the fire from dragons to be a magical property. "Fire melts rock and sand and turns it into glass. We already know that the Fae Kingdom's geographical makeup lends itself to being hospitable for dragons. What if rock or sand combined with dragon fire creates glass able to hold our magic?"

"It's sound reasoning," I concede, leaning my elbows on my knees. "But unless you have a live dragon you're keeping secret from us or connections in the Fae Kingdom, I'm not sure how we're going to procure this glass."

"Maybe we don't need to ask a fae," Nox says, beginning to pace. "Maybe they have the dragon equivalent of lightning fossils littering their beaches near the mountains."

My eyebrows draw up as Cass laughs, while Daje looks at Nox like he's insane. "Yes!" Elora shouts, clapping her hands twice. "Exactly that! But, you know, the dragon version."

Daje rounds the chair and asks, "What are lightning fossils?"

Elora lays her hand on Daje's arm, her excitement spilling into her voice. I watch as his body tenses slightly but then relaxes, as if he isn't quite used to being touched like this but it certainly isn't unwelcome. Elora explains what lightning fossils are— lightning hitting damp sand. The heat of the lightning melts the sand, and cool ocean water hardens it into glass. "If dragon fire met sand on the beach at any point, then we might be able to find enough to repair the Mirror."

"Let me see if I understand this correctly," Daje starts, his gaze moving to my brother's. "You are suggesting that we sneak into the Fae Kingdom and risk encountering beings that are known for their brashness and their access to fucking dragons, all in the hope that we *might* find some random dragon glass on their beaches."

"Essentially," Nox answers, earning another chuckle from Cass.

Daje groans and drags a hand down his face. "Let's say that scenario plays out perfectly and we make it back home alive. Then what?"

Silence answers as everyone's gazes drop to the floor. *Then what?* How did we take this hypothetical glass and turn it into a new working Mirror?

"We'll deal with that part of the plan once we have the glass," Nox finally answers, his fingers massaging his temples.

Daje scoffs but offers no further argument. "Fine. Who is leading this suicide mission?"

"I will—"

"No." I cut my brother off, shaking my head. "You can't. And before you try to argue with me, consider the fact that you've agreed to be king. They will likely not let you go and just as likely kill you if you attempt to leave anyway."

"She's right," Cass adds, a dagger now twirling over his knuckles playfully while he looks at Nox. "It's too dangerous for you to go right now. Stay and play by the rules while continuing to look for the mole." He catches the dagger by the hilt and stands, sliding it into the sheath at his thigh. "I'll go."

"As will I," I stand, bumping Cass's shoulder.

"Nope, you have to stay too."

I whip my head to look at him, my hands falling to my hips. "What? *Why?*"

Cass's eyes soften, lowering his head so that our conversation is somewhat private. "Because Nox needs someone here that he can trust, and *I* need someone here who will make sure he doesn't do something stupid."

"You know that I can hear you," Nox growls.

A protest battles behind my teeth, but I shove it down, coming to the same conclusion as Cass. Nox is fragile right now, in more ways than one. The last thing he needs is almost everyone he cares about leaving him to the whims of the council and the weight of his own guilt. "Fine, I'll stay."

"Excellent." He clasps my shoulder. "Who else?"

"Obviously, I'm going, as the entire idea was *mine*," Elora says, standing up and brushing her skirt off. "It'll be good to get my mind off of everything I can't control here."

Cass nods and then looks at Daje. "What about you?"

Daje's eyes travel over his living room as he draws in a deep breath, letting his cheeks puff out before releasing it. "I'll go on your suicide mission—"

"Dragon Quest! Glass Adventure!" Cass interrupts, pumping his fist in the air.

Daje rolls his eyes but adds quietly, "A change of scenery might be nice."

So we begin to plan.

Chapter Sixty-Four

BAHIRA

I ALWAYS PICTURED THE day my brother became king as one where the skies were blue and the sun was bright. There would be colorful flags decorating Galdr's city center, birds chirping loudly as if even the animals could not contain their excitement, and everyone from around the kingdom would gather in celebration as they watched a man that I knew loved his kingdom receive his crown.

Reality, as luck would have it, is much more bleak.

There are no brightly colored banners of celebration, no birds rejoicing or sunlight warming us. The skies are gray, swollen rain clouds threatening to unleash upon us and the crowd of thousands that have gathered. While my wool coat keeps most of me warm from the bitter chill heavy in the air, my cheeks have gone numb. But I keep the soft smile plastered to my face as my father finishes up his last remarks on what it has meant to him being king. Over four decades of dedication have come to an abrupt end, all because of a council who believes that our father put his love for his family over his dedication to the realm. Maybe, to a degree, that is true. There are non-negotiables to Sadryn Daxel when it comes to my mother, Nox, and me. But if paranoia were manifested into something tangible, it would be the members of the council who act as if there is a threat that my father has refused to prepare for. While they're getting what they want—a somewhat compliant Nox, at least from the outside, stepping into his role as king—it doesn't come without a cost. One that only our family seems poised to pay.

Nox and my mother flank my father where he stands behind a podium that is centered on the stone stage of the outdoor amphitheater, the field where the Summer Solstice celebration was held not that many months ago. I stand to Nox's left, keeping my gaze anywhere but on the first row where the members of the council sit, leering. I had managed to avoid them in the days since Daje, Cass, and Elora left for the Fae Kingdom, tasked with finding something that might not even exist. If Councilman Kallin is at all worried about his son's life, he has yet to express it in any capacity.

Nox, however, has been more tightly strung in their absence than I have ever known him to be. His worry for Rhea is etched into every line on his face, his eyes taking on a dark glint and hands inadvertently forming fists at his sides—as if some sinister idea has formed, and it's taking everything in his power not to act on it. Every morning since our interaction in the hall, I wake up half expecting to find he's once more snuck away to try and get to her and then feel an odd pang of concern when I find him attending the council meetings or having breakfast with our parents in the queen's dining hall. He is in no condition to do anything until his magic is back, but the fear that's gnarled its way around my stomach feels like a warning. Nox is biding his time, but only he knows the real reason why. And as much as I love and trust my brother, he has already admitted that Rhea is his top priority, no matter where the chaos of choosing her might leave the dust to settle.

Clapping and cheering draws my attention back to the center of the stage as my father steps to the side and Nox takes his place. He clears his throat, looking at the crowd of people that return his stare with a certain kind of awe that leaves a chill on my skin unrelated to the weather. Those close to Nox say they can *feel* the difference in Nox's signature, how his magic has changed in the wake of Rhea's disappearance. Can the people ahead of us feel that as well? Scanning their faces, I wouldn't think so. Then again, there are traitors among us. My gaze lifts to the guards that line the crowd as Nox begins speaking.

"Thank you all for the lovely welcome," he says, lifting a hand to silence them. I don't miss the crease forming between his brows at the movement. He grips the sides of the podium he stands behind, knuckles drowned white beneath his skin as he looks out over the crowd, his expression unreadable. "Times of transition can be monumental. None more so than a shift of power from one leader to another. I have spent my life in preparation for this moment, and yet it doesn't quite feel like I'm ready for it. The truth is, I'm not sure there are *enough* preparations one can make when stepping into such a significant role. What I can tell you is that I love my home, and I will always do what is necessary to keep her safe." The crowd shouts their approval, their love for my brother obvious. But Nox looks out to them with an emptiness that sinks my stomach.

He finishes his remarks, the words clearly practiced and without flare, and then Councilmen Kallin and Borris join him, Hadrik following behind and holding the ceremonial crown that will be placed upon Nox's head to signify his ascension to the throne. It sits on a red satin pillow, the gold gleaming despite the clouds overhead. At the center is the sigil of the Void queen, a crescent moon of glittering black gems and a flaring sun of brilliant white diamonds. Smaller diamonds and onyx gems alternate around the crown, and the sight of it being placed on my brother's head fills me simultaneously with pride and dread.

The crowd cheers as Nox turns to face them, Borris clipping a deep navy velvet cape lined with white fur and embroidered with gold thread on the matching tunic Nox wears. Kallin bows to Nox, Hadrik and Borris following suit as do my parents and I. The mages in front of us pound their chest three times before raising a fist in the air, shouting in unison "Long live the king!"

"It is such a momentous day," Kallin says from the podium. "For a new king has been named, one of the most powerful our realm has seen since The War Of Five Kingdoms!" Applause rings out, and I watch as a few of the guards that wait at the edges of the stage subtly shift their positions a few steps closer. I turn my gaze to the opposite side, noting those guards are closer as well. "There is more good news to be shared!"

Confusion furrows my brows as I look at my parents, both of whom bear the same expression of uncertainty. Nox stands completely still, his face hidden behind a cold mask of apathy.

"As you know, who the king picks as his queen is a matter that cannot be taken lightly. The role deserves to go to someone who has shown that she will support *your* king, *her* king, in ensuring that he upholds the vows he takes when that crown is placed upon his head."

Movement draws my attention to the side of the stage, to a woman with dark blonde hair and flowing pink gown. The rise of my anger is immediate, my fingers curling in towards my palms.

"Though her name might come as a shock, given the *previous* betrothal announcement, her face is one you will recognize. She is a devoted daughter to the realm, a woman whose entire life has been in service not only to the crown but also to you, her people. Sometimes, it takes making a mistake in order to see that the right choice has been in front of us all along. Therefore, it is my absolute honor to announce the newly betrothed couple, King Nox Daxel and Lady Haylee Valen!"

I clench my jaw to keep my mouth from falling open, a dull ringing taking residence in my ears as I watch Haylee cross the stage in a floor-length gown, the fabric clinging to her curves and flowing elegantly in the wind as she passes me. Her eyes connect with mine, and I wish could say it is fear or uncertainty or, fuck, even *sorrow* that I find in them. Instead, her expression mirrors those of the council. Contentment. Peace. *Entitlement.* Gods a-fucking-bove, she *knew* this was going to happen. Those flooding the amphitheater go *wild*, their applause deafening as Haylee stands next to my brother. She attempts to wrap her hand around his forearm, but even in his apathetic stupor, he manages to adjust the cape so that it covers his arm and she has nothing to grasp.

I expect rage. My body tenses for it, preparing to leap in front of my brother should anyone dare to attempt restraining him. But for all the gusto with which he defended his love for Rhea mere days ago, it's gone now. My eyes leap from him to our parents, both of whom watch the situation unfolding with barely reserved shock, before they finally land on Kallin, and it takes every *ounce* of control I possess not to leap across the stage and send my fist directly into his jaw. He smirks, as if he can see the murderous thoughts I'm holding back.

We walk off the stage in a procession, the crowd's cheering discordant in my ear as I watch guards surround Nox and Haylee. I wait off to the side for my parents before I continue walking to the line of carriages that are waiting.

"What was that?" I whisper, keeping my gaze forward and my shoulders back. The council walks behind us, Hadrik somewhere in the mix. I need to speak with him about accessing the archives again, sure that the rest of the journals explaining the connection between blood and magic are there. Hopefully some regarding the creation of the Mirror as well. But with the chaos of Nox's ascension to king and his own descent into someone I don't recognize, focus on my research is scant.

"A show of strength," my father answers just as quietly, my mother dipping her chin in agreement. "By announcing it as he did in front of the kingdom, it's setting a different kind of precedent."

"But you said Nox and Rhea announced their engagement at the Autumnal Ball," I counter, watching as Haylee leans over to say something to Nox ahead of us. "The only precedent this sets is that Nox can apparently propose to two women."

"It's the way Kallin framed the betrothal," my mother says, turning to face me. "He called Rhea a mistake. This paired with the rumors that have made their way outside the palace walls about her leaving him and Barron's absence, he's effectively ensured that when Rhea returns, she isn't met with excitement."

"He wasn't wrong when he said that the people *know* Haylee, either," my father adds on, bringing my mother's hand up to his lips. He kisses the back of it as their steps slow, their carriage coming into view. "She has been around the palace since Borris took over as her guardian. She's made herself known outside of it too."

That was true enough. Haylee had woven herself not only into the community but our own family as well. From the very beginning, Haylee's life had been leading to this moment, and whether she always wanted this or was simply set on this path by her uncle, it doesn't matter. Because at some point, she decided that the power she would gain from becoming queen was worth the cost of whoever it hurt to claim it.

If she is willing to accept those casualties, what else is she capable of? *Could she be the mole we've been looking for?* The thought alone makes me cringe, and I pick up my pace until I'm at Nox's other side just as they are about to reach the royal carriage.

"We need to talk," I blurt, garnering both of their attention.

"Bahira! Was it not a lovely ceremony for your brother—"

"Shut the fuck up." My brashness draws a few curious glances in our direction, but I'm beyond the point of caring. I wait for Nox to meet my expectant gaze, nearly gasping from shock when he finally does. Pink colors the whites of his eyes, the bruising beneath them the darkest I've ever seen. The normal glow of his skin inherited from our father is dimmed, leaving him looking pale and as if he hasn't seen the sun in months.

He lets me guide him towards his carriage, ignoring Haylee's protests from behind. Once he's inside, I turn to find her standing close, her arms folded over her chest.

"Don't do this," she says, keeping her voice low. "This doesn't have to be something that you fight, Bahira. Use your talents and time on things that actually matter, just as I will do with my own."

I chuckle, nodding my head as I hold her gaze. "Is that what you told yourself? When you pretended to befriend me? When you listened to my plights and my personal thoughts? When you looked Rhea in the eyes and promised that you just wanted to help? That you didn't love her fiancé?"

Her eyes widen in surprise.

A bigger laugh erupts from me. "Gods, you are either incredibly naive or supremely stupid." I lean in close, enjoying the way she tries to hold her position against me even as fear flashes in her eyes. "There will come a day when your betrayals catch up to you, and you won't get everything you want, but you *will* get everything you fucking deserve. And when that happens, I just hope I'm there to watch you fall."

She scoffs, attempting to push past me into the carriage. My hand closes around her arm, fingers digging into the skin as nearby guards take a step towards us, their hands already on the hilts of their swords.

"Don't even fucking *think* about coming into this carriage."

Jerking out of my grasp, Haylee takes a step back, finally showing me her true self as the fake kindness falls away from her expression. "You will regret this, Bahira."

I don't spare her another look as I climb into the carriage and sit opposite of my brother. He offers me a weak grin, the weight of the crown on his head looking too heavy for him to bear. "What is going on, Nox?"

"Nothing. Everything's f—"

"If you say that everything is *fine*, if you lie to me, not even being my favorite brother will save you from my fist. I've already punched one king; I'm happy to do it to another." Though anger colors my voice, it only makes his shaky smile grow, a small bit of fondness in the broken sight of it.

"Please, Nox. Talk to me." I scoot to the edge of the bench, unsure of exactly what to do in this moment but knowing that I can't just *leave* Nox to whatever fate is currently being laid out for him. Not when I can see the torture of how it is affecting him, how it's tearing him apart slowly.

For a long while, he doesn't speak. The carriage lurches into motion, the outside blurring through the window as we journey back to the palace. My anger is soon swallowed by rising fear, panic a tip-toeing monster that creeps along the edges of my mind. We're nearly home when he lets out a sigh. It's a weary sound, like a breath one might exhale before closing their eyes for the final time.

"I thought I could outsmart him."

"Who?"

"Kallin. All of the council, really. The guards and whoever else they've employed to keep an eye on us. *On me.*" I don't speak, holding myself still for fear that if I so much as reach for him, he'll stop talking. Nox's gaze is locked on his hands on his thighs, his palms facing him as he shakes his head. "I understand that in my current state, I'm no help to Rhea, but I thought—" A rough swallow moves his throat. "I suppose it doesn't matter what I thought I could do because Kallin figured it out. Or someone broke my trust. *Again.*" He shakes his head, the carriage slowing as it rolls to a stop.

My voice is hardly a rasp when I ask, "What did you try to do?"

When his eyes lift to mine, appearing dark and hollow, a shiver rolls down my spine. "If I could not be the one to get to her, then I thought maybe a small team of guards could." My heart leaps to my throat when the carriage door opens. "They were caught only a few miles outside of Galdr by men Kallin had sent. Rhea remains in hell, and I—" His chest rises slowly with an inhale, as if the act is almost too arduous. "I will never forgive myself for it."

I watch my brother exit the carriage and wonder about the polarity that exists with being in love. The warmth and softness of being held in its embrace and the cold, jagged danger that is born when it's threatened.

Chapter Sixty-Five

DAJE

I T HAD ONLY TAKEN us forty-eight hours to put together a semblance of a plan to present to the council for how to repair the Mirror. Elora pulled excerpts from texts that mildly supported her theory that there could be something known as dragon glass on or near the northern fae beaches. Together, she and Nox explained that it might be the right conduit to replace whatever material the Mirror was originally made with. Councilman Arav asked about the magic—the Mirror operated on ancient power, nothing close to anything a *normal* mage might have. But there was one of us here whose magic wasn't normal, and Nox's parents were already looking at him when he explained his theory that *his* power might work. There was a healthy dose of skepticism in his voice as he spoke, and I wasn't sure if it was due to the fact that his magic was still mysteriously depleted *or* if it was because he didn't believe it would actually do anything.

"And who do you plan to take on this mission to secretly infiltrate another kingdom?" my father had asked, a judgmental lilt to his voice that almost made me laugh. As if he had not orchestrated for Nox to do the very same damn thing in the Mortal Kingdom. A part of me wondered if he even wanted the Mirror to be fixed.

"I will go. I've been studying dragon habits and our maps on the geographical layout of the land," Elora said, her fingers nervously gripping the spine of one of the references. I found my gaze trailing over her side profile briefly, her fiery red hair draping down one shoulder in a barely held together braid. Like she couldn't be bothered to put more effort into it when there was research to do. In a way, it reminded me a lot of another's dedication to her cause. I internally cursed where

I'd allowed my thoughts to drift, returning my attention back to the long table in front of me and the eight men and one woman sitting there.

"I'll be going as well," Cass added from my right where he stood next to Nox. That drew raised brows from a few of the council members, their gazes snapping to my father.

"That's a surprise, considering your job is to protect our newest king," he said, his hands lacing together where he rested them on the table. "Would it not make more sense to stay here? We can choose another guard to go."

"Because of the *sensitive* nature of the mission and the fact that the possibility of death is extremely high, I would prefer only those that I trust go, those who truly understand what's at stake," Nox countered, crossing his arms over his chest. It was hard to reconcile the man who had drawn his power in tight ropes around me for merely the *idea* of a perceived threat with the one who stands before me now, sweat dotting his temples as if he's struggling to support his own weight.

"It makes sense." That agreement had come from Councilman Hadrik. *He* definitely appeared worse in the days since King Sadryn was forced away from the throne. I didn't blame him. He had been blindsided by his fellow council members—by *my* father—and given that he was Sadryn's oldest friend, I didn't doubt that there might be some animosity there that wasn't before.

My father nodded, as did everyone else at the table. "Then the two of you have—"

"Three," I had cut in as I drew my hands behind my back. "I'll be going as well."

Borris and Osiris had cut a glance to each other as Councilwoman Naji raised a brow in question. My father looked me over as he always did—like I was something to dissect. An experiment he could shred apart and mold into something new over and over again, expecting a different result but only finding disappointment in what always remained—*me*. "And what purpose do *you* serve on this mission?"

"Daje is going to help ensure everyone's safety but also act as liaison should anyone give them trouble in the border towns," Nox answered. "Being raised as he was, he'll know exactly what to say to any who might question their presence." Given the secretive nature of the mission, it was not like we could send a missive of our impending arrival.

"Daje's expertise will be needed as we are quite dumb," Cass added, drawing a scathing look from Elora.

"Speak for yourself," she murmured, tucking her book in at her hip. My lips quirked as her gaze met mine, pink flushing her cheeks before she looked away. My father had caught the interaction, his eyes bouncing from me to Elora before an unsettling expression contorted his face.

I prepared for his denial and mentally dug my heels in to fight back, but to my utter surprise, he simply said, "Fine. Then the council gives the three of you our blessing to go north and hopefully retrieve enough of this dragon glass to repair the Mirror."

And that was that.

Now, a day later, we traverse on horseback through the thickly wooded forest, Elora riding in front of me after paling with one look at the beautiful mare offered to her. Apparently, riding had not been one of the many things she'd taught herself.

"How are you doing?" I ask, trying to keep a reasonable distance between our bodies, a tough feat considering there isn't much room.

"Fine, and you don't have to keep asking. It's not like *I'm* the one being ridden."

"Not with that attitude," Cass drawls, earning a snort from Elora and a look from me. He winks, and I shake my head and look forward. "Don't worry, Daje, you're not exactly my type."

"I didn't realize you had a type. I just assumed you fucked anything that moved," I retort. Elora laughs as she looks back at me, her cheeks rounded from her smile.

"It must pain you to know that my standards are at least high enough to exclude you."

Elora tosses her hair over her shoulder, the scent of spicy cinnamon and vanilla hitting my nose a breath later. "If you guys are going to keep flirting like this, I'll have to insist that I continue this mission alone."

"I'm not flirting with him," I say, gripping the leather reins tightly.

Cass brings his horse—a light brown mare with a white mane and tail—closer, a mischievous glint in his eye making me tense in anticipation. "It's true. I've seen him flirt. It's way worse than this."

I might kill Cass before this mission is done. Though Elora tries to hide her laugh, the way her shoulders silently shake gives her away. I lean forward, just enough to speak low in her ear. "Don't encourage his antics. He feeds off the attention."

"You sound more like his dad than his friend," she counters, keeping her gaze forward.

"Ouch." I lean back again as she laughs and draws her hand down our horse's mane. Feeling the weight of his stare, I turn my head towards Cass. He lifts a brow in question, his eyes darting towards Elora. I ignore him and look to the road ahead.

Everyone's parents had met us outside the stables to see us off, all except for my father. His noticeable absence must have drawn pity from Sadryn because his hand had found a home on my shoulder as he handed me a map of places that were safe to stop at.

"Because of the increase in missing mages near the Fae Kingdom's border, they are more aggressive to faces they do not know," he had said, squeezing my shoulder gently. "Don't assume that they will trust you simply because you are mage."

I had heard about the missing mages from my father. But once he had realized that I could not be coerced into believing that Rhea had attacked me to stage her own escape, he had iced me out of everything.

"How much farther until we reach Kilmere?" Elora asks.

"A few more hours. Though we might want to pick up the pace," Cass answers, his hand gesturing to the gray clouds showing through the gaps in the canopy. "I'd rather not have to guide the horses through a storm."

It's silent as we urge the horses to move faster, the day quickly melting into night before we reach the outskirts of Kilmere. Much like the training grounds, the small city is built in a clearing, the night sky opening up wide as we break through the treeline. Wind gusts in our direction, the air significantly chilled and carrying the scent of rain. Cass guides us to a two-story inn, its wooden sign lit brightly by two spelled flames flanking it. Green vines creep up its sides, a large pirang tree behind it with twisting branches that reach high overhead and are decorated with small spelled flames in glass orbs. The roads are fairly quiet, most patrons either already inside the various establishments that dot the roadway or home given the late hour.

"There's a stable at the side of the inn," Cass says, but he throws his hand up to stop us. "No sense in all of us going to do the work of one. Why don't you two secure our rooms, and I'll get the horses settled and meet you in the lobby."

Nodding, I climb down from my horse and hand the reins to Cass before turning to help Elora down. Her hands plant on my shoulders as mine land on her hips, her body swaying when her feet hit the ground. "Are you alright?"

"Fine. It's just the longest I've sat uninterrupted before. My legs are used to moving."

"Don't you read a lot?" I counter, waiting until she steadies herself before pulling my hands back.

She laughs, turning to pat our horse on its side. "I do, and I've adapted. Reading while staying still is for the weak. I prefer to read and walk. Or shop. Or dance."

Grabbing my pack from the saddle, I throw it on my back before reaching for Elora's, its weight significantly heavier from all the books she brought with her. I lug it over one shoulder, shooing her outstretched hand as we move towards the inn. "Sounds like a dangerous way to read."

She pushes her glasses up from where they've slipped down her nose before pulling the ends of her cloak in, wrapping herself up in the thick wool fabric. "You see it as dangerous, while I see it as practical. I can't sit all day, and I can't *not* read either. So I combine both." She turns to look at me, offering a sly grin. "Multi-tasking is a bit of a specialty."

I stumble a step at that look, making her laugh. An unfamiliar feeling pulls at my chest, but I swallow it down as I quickly open the door and usher Elora through. The warmth of a fire burning brightly in a hearth hits us, and my muscles immediately relax, the ache of riding all day beginning to catch up with me.

The lobby is tastefully decorated in shades of dark blue and green, its tan walls brightened by the amber light of spelled flames that lie in glass sconces every few feet. A desk is centered against the wall across from the entrance, and behind it, a woman around my age drums her fingers along the dark wood as she watches us with bored eyes. Dark ringlets frame her face and spill over her shoulder.

"Hello," I say, crossing the space and dropping Elora's pack at my feet. She comes to stand next to me. "We'd like to get three rooms, please."

The woman tilts her head, peering past my shoulder at the door before straightening. "Unless my counting is significantly worse than I thought, there are only two of you here." As if to prove that, she points first to Elora and then to me, pulling her red-painted lips to the side. "Two."

"Our third friend is putting the horses in the stable," Elora says, leaning her elbows on the countertop. "I like your dress."

"Ah." The woman turns, giving us her back as she scans a row of cubbies behind her, humming a tune that I don't recognize. "It's late for travelers to be here, and before a big storm no less." She ignores Elora's compliment as she squats down and looks at a row near the floor.

"We are coming from Galdr, on our way home to Palatos."

"Palatos," she repeats, reaching into one cubby and then standing, her hand darting into another. "So you aren't from around here?"

My gaze darts to Elora's before I slide a hand down to the dagger strapped at my hip, hidden by my tunic. "Not here in particular—"

Turning back around, she slams two keys on the table before reaching for a large notepad to her right and flipping to the last page. Her gray eyes lift to look at us, skepticism making them narrow. "Why don't I wait until your *friend*—"

The door to the inn flies open, and before I have time to react, Cass is striding in, throwing a flirty smirk to the woman behind the desk. "Abi, my darling, it is good to see you."

I cast Elora bewildered look, only to find that she's smiling at whatever the hell is going on here.

"Cass? Oh my gods, how wonderful! Are they with you?"

Cass throws his arms over our shoulders, his leather vambraces chilled from being outside and seeping the warmth right from my body. "Yeah, they are. We need some rooms before we continue on to Palatos," he says, at least ensuring our fake story sounds consistent. "We'll take your *finest*, of course."

Abi pouts her full lips, her brown skin gleaming beneath the light of the flame hanging above her. "I'm afraid we only have two rooms available, love."

"That's fine," he answers, releasing Elora and I to pick up her pack from the ground. "We'll figure out the logistics. Perhaps you could have some dinner sent up, though?"

She smiles as she hands him the keys before resting her chin in her hand. "Will do. Your rooms will be down the hall to your right and up the stairs. Rooms ten and eleven." Cass offers her a mock bow and a wink before spinning on his heel. "And my room is on the first floor, room one, if you find that you're in need of a distraction before bed."

I nearly choke on my next breath, but Cass sends her a wink that makes her blush, and then we head towards the stairs, climbing them in a single file line until we reach our designated rooms.

"Elora, ten will be your room," Cass says, dropping one of the keys into her waiting palm. "And Daje and I will take eleven."

"Are you sure?" she asks, grabbing her pack from him.

"Of course," I answer, yanking the key from Cass's hand and shoving it into the lock. "We'll see you in the morning." Pushing the door open, I take in the single bed that makes up most of the room and groan.

"It's about to get cozy, buddy." He pats my back as he brushes past, dropping his pack onto the floor and digging out some clothes. "And I call dibs on the shower first."

"How do you know that woman downstairs?" I ask, closing the door and setting my bag down on a threadbare armchair.

"Nox and I stopped here on our last trip to Palatos," he answers, a bundle of clothes in his arm. "And Nox was being broody about missing Rhea, so I gave him some space and found myself invited into Abi's." He wiggles his eyebrows at me before turning towards the door on the other side of the room.

"She's great. Makes for a good listening ear if you want to go speak to someone about Bahira."

I halt opening my pack to scowl at him. "Why would I talk to her about Bahira?"

"Since Bahira's been home, it's obvious that you guys aren't on good terms. And, it's none of my business—"

"You're right. It isn't."

"But you need to figure your shit out so it isn't a distraction."

I arch a brow. "A distraction to *who*?"

"You. Her. Nox and the council. Anyone within a five foot radius of you two." He pauses under the doorframe to look back at me. "Elora."

I turn my gaze down to my organized pack, carefully lifting my clothing until I find my sleeping pants. "I don't know why you think she would care."

"You're not entirely a fucking idiot, Daje, so stop acting like one." In the silence that follows, I swallow and lift my gaze again. "She's a good person, and she deserves better than to be caught up in whatever fucked up feelings you're dealing with. I've seen the way she looks at you, and I've seen the looks you give her."

Fucking observant bastard.

Cass smirks as if he heard my thoughts. "Just... don't be an idiot."

"Sound advice," I mutter as he goes into the bathroom. Taking a seat on the edge of the bed, I draw a hand down my face. I *had* noticed the lingering glances from Elora, but I'm ashamed to admit I hadn't given them a second thought, not with my mind so preoccupied with the shit storm that had become my life. Cass is wrong; I *am* a fucking idiot.

A set of knocks draws me from my thoughts. When I pull the door open, fully expecting to see Abi with our dinner, it's Elora instead. "Hey," I blurt out, heat rushing up my neck.

"Hi," she says, her lips pulled into a wide smile. With Cass's voice playing in my ear, I suddenly become very aware of how close I'm standing to her. How close *she's* standing to *me*.

I shift, folding my arms as I lean a shoulder against the doorframe. "Everything alright?"

"Yeah. Yes, of course," she stumbles, lifting up a small book in her hand. "You mentioned on the ride here that you would be open to reading some of the books I packed, and I thought I might bring one over in case you can't sleep. Or don't want to sleep." She holds the book out to me, its gold-foiled lettering shining beneath the light of the spelled flames. Its cover reads: *Our Neighbors to the West: What we know about the Fae.* "I've already read it, but it's always good to have a second pair of eyes in case I missed something."

I sincerely doubt that she would have. What I know of Elora is that she is as steadfast as Bahira when it comes to finding answers. Plucking the book from her hand, I tuck it into my side. "Thanks. I'll get started right away."

"Perfect." She pinches her lips together, drawing my gaze to her mouth. I watch them slowly release, too much time passing before I look back up. Only to find her watching me. *Godsdammit, I hate Cass.* Something flickers over her expression, but she backs away and tosses a hand in the air before I have time to sort it out. "Okay, goodnight!"

I watch her walk back to her room and shut the door before banging my head against the doorframe. "I'm going to kill Cass."

Part Four

Just because what is inside of us is dark doesn't mean that it holds less value than something light.

Chapter Sixty-Six

ARIA

Somehow, I've acquired a dagger Myla claims was once owned by her father. It's the weapon I found at the bottom of the sea months ago as I was beginning my journey to the Northern Island, and yet, *impossibly*, it belongs to the father of the very female I'm now bound to. One who looks like she'd rather drive that dagger into my chest than entertain the idea that it was random luck or divine intervention that made it end up in the hands of her *enemy*.

"Did you bring it?" I ask. Myla had not returned the dagger to me during our last visit, and though a small part of me recognizes that maybe she does have *some* claim to the weapon, a bigger part wanted what I had begun to think of as *my* blade back. When I had broken through the chaotic waves of the ocean, their wildness due to an impending storm, Myla had already been waiting inside the cavern. She didn't offer me a greeting in response to my own, just tossed me a dark red tunic and stood with a bored gaze. It's the same look she's giving me now. "I want it back."

"What are you willing to give me for it?"

My mouth drops as a frustrated noise rumbles from me. "It is *my* dagger! You stole it from me."

"You don't get to claim I stole something that was my family's to begin with," she counters, folding her arms over her chest. I drop her gaze as I chew on my bottom lip. My entire life, others have easily dismissed me as nothing but an annoyance. And I had let them. Myla's defiance of our life debt, her clear disdain for me, bothers me, because I haven't done anything to warrant it. Nothing beyond being a siren. If she finds it acceptable to treat me this way, then what's to stop me from reciprocating?

"I didn't take you for a thief," I say as I look back to her, mirroring her stance. "And certainly not one who preys on those *weaker*."

Her lips quirk a fraction. "And you know me so well?"

"I don't know you at *all*, despite wanting to," I bark, throwing my hands out to the side. "You have your secrets, and that's fine, but you actively choose to spend our time together being *miserable*. And cruel. Those are choices *you* make, while *I* have been nothing but kind to you." Something shifts in her expression, a muscle at her jaw pulsing with the steady beat of her heart. I can't help but study the way her midnight-black hair is tucked behind her delicately pointed ear, the shape of it perhaps the only soft thing about her. Everything else is as sharp and finely honed as the blades she wields, including the vicious curl of her barely there smirk. The memory of our mouths fusing together surfaces uninvited. It had felt so different from any other time I've used my magic, and I had spent the evening afterwards trying to figure out if that was good or bad.

"You know what your problem is?" she asks, her boots scuffing softly against stone as she approaches. "You're too *soft*. It's a weakness. A gaping hole within that you're *begging* for people to cut deeper into."

My heart catches at the defensiveness of her tone, but I wanted a reaction, so I don't back down. "Give me my dagger."

"Take it from me. That's what you *want* to do, isn't it?"

"You don't think I will?"

"I *know* you won't—just as *I* know you." She stops a few feet away, her cloak fluttering in the gusty wind traveling through the cavern. "The weak are always easy to read."

My talons grow from my fingertips, my vision spotting as my breaths quicken. *Who are you willing to become?* Anyone that Lyre needed me to be. I *was* weak, but now... now I have *purpose* in my veins where before there was only hopelessness. My upper lip lifts in a snarl, sharpened canines smaller than the fae's across from me flashing with the movement. "Fine. If I take the dagger, all of our remaining lessons —including this one—will double in length. No questions asked. No delaying our deal to try and get out of it."

"And if I keep the dagger in my possession, then we shave two lessons off our timeline."

I growl at her in frustration. Maybe I had walked right into that one, but if Myla wants to see just how far I am willing to go to protect those I love, then I am happy to show her. "Deal."

"Oh, Little Siren," she says, her voice dropping low as she prowls towards me. "While confidence certainly looks better on you than the usual meekness you hide behind, in this case, you lack the skills to back it up. It will be your downfall."

I wait until she's crossed half the distance between us, my talons curling into my palms. "And overconfidence will be yours." My voice rings out as I start to sing, the notes low and melodic from where they vibrate from deep in my throat. I had thought long about our *kiss* between my meetings with Sade and conversations with Lyre this past week. Because my magic wasn't useful during hunts, I had allowed myself to become *afraid* of using it. Sure that once someone else realized that my song only lured females, my life would be cut short.

Maybe now is the time to reclaim the magic I have shunned as the weapon it was meant to be.

I retreat as Myla pushes forward, the fact that she is fae making it easier for her to fight against my song at first. But then her next steps falter as her eyes glaze over. With only a foot between us to spare, she comes to a stop and doesn't move again.

I let my song fade and drag in a breath, though it does nothing to calm my wildly beating heart. "I don't know if you can understand me while you are under my song; I suppose I've never been given the opportunity to ask." I drop my focus to the bone hilt of my dagger strapped to her thigh and pull it free. Holding it up, my eyes meet hers. "The thing about shutting out even the *enemy*, Myla, is that it makes you blind to their strengths. I don't like using my song, and I do apologize for using it on you for a second time, but I won't apologize for becoming who I need to be in order to keep my sister safe. And I have *you* to thank for that."

This close, it's impossible for me not to lose myself in the stunning brutality of her beauty. It's the kind that demands you take notice, each feature drawing you in closer and closer until you realize too late that you're caught in her web.

She blinks away the glassiness in her eyes, but though her anger immediately surfaces, it's accompanied by an emotion I *never* thought I would see from her—*fear*. She doesn't even acknowledge the fact that I've taken my dagger back when she grits out, "Second time?"

I guess that gives me an answer to just how aware she is while under my song. I clasp the weapon tightly and move my hands behind my back. "Yes."

"When, Aria? Because by my count, you've lured me under your influence by your lips once and now by your song *once*."

I shiver at the use of my name, but shame sits heavily in place of my magic. I had done what I needed to prove to Myla that she couldn't walk all over me, but it doesn't change the fact that, at my core, I acted no differently than any other siren.

My eyes bounce between hers as I try to formulate the right words. "I used it on you when I found you floating in the sea during the rogue siren attack. You woke and were disoriented, and you kept trying to kick me. I attempted to calm you, but eventually, I couldn't swim and dodge your attacks, and I didn't want you to fall off the raft and through the Spell. So I sang to get you to calm down."

She gives herself the length of one breath to glare at me before she steps away, retreating to the other side of the cavern, her expression tight. Rain begins to fall outside, lightning flashing before a wave of rolling thunder follows. I quickly bend down to grab my bag and place the dagger in it, my fingers trembling. Myla doesn't move, doesn't say anything as the rain falls in heavier sheets, water leaking in through the gaps in the ceiling.

The storm intensifies, the thunder rumbling the pebbles around us as lightning continues to flare. I stare at Myla's blank face from where she is now seated on the ground, her legs bent in front of her and her arms propped on her knees. My mouth opens and closes as I struggle with what to fill our own silence with. I don't want to leave and miss valuable training time but it's clear that our interaction perturbed her, and that shame within me whispers that it's my fault that it has.

"Myla?" I shout over the rain, crossing the platform to get to her. The hair rises on my arm as light flashes right outside the entrance, the answering crack of thunder forcing my hands to my ears. When the ringing stops, I look up and watch as Myla climbs down the platform, her boots planting on the sand-covered rock below. "Where are you going?" When she doesn't answer, I scramble behind her, my bare feet hitting the ground just as she reaches the edge of the cavern's entrance. "Myla?"

"I have to walk to where Navin will be able to retrieve me with Lan. This close to the storm, it will be unsafe for the dragon to land."

"You cannot go yet." The words come out as half plea, something souring in my gut at how lost she looks.

Myla's eyes cut to mine. "Why don't you *sing* and make me stay?"

The wind shifts, sending a wall of rain directly into our faces and forcing us to take cover deeper into the cavern. "I don't want to do that. Despite what you may think about me and my magic, I don't enjoy using it."

She releases a broken laugh, the sound slipping through tense lips. "No, you'll just resort to it when you need to trick someone."

My lips part on a gasp, and I take a step towards her. "Don't act like you would not do the same if you had the ability," I say quietly, fire lit in my belly as I point to my chest. "Not just *my* life depends on these lessons, and time is a luxury I do not have. You made it clear that you wouldn't bargain fairly with me, so I took the opportunity you laid at my feet. I simply pretended I was *you*, and this was the result. So if you want to be upset with anyone, start with yourself. Because you showed me what ruthlessness looks like, and how could a *Little Siren* such as myself resist such a tempting opportunity?"

The storm batters the beach around us as we stare at each other, the weather only partly to blame for the tension in the air. But that hollowed look in her eyes dissipates, and though the terrifying darkness in them returns, so does the slightest amount of surprised mirth. "I don't think someone has ever simultaneously complimented and condemned me in the same breath."

I roll my lips together to keep myself from smiling. Pathetic as it is, that small bit of pride I hear in her voice is enough to ward away the cold from the storm.

With an exhale, she palms the other dagger strapped to her thigh and slides it free of its sheath. It's curved, unlike any blade I've ever seen, but held in her hand it's just a natural extension of *her*. "If time is of the essence, then we certainly shouldn't waste it. Get your blade."

I turn and climb back up to the platform, releasing my trapped smile at the slight emphasis she uses on the word *your*.

Chapter Sixty-Seven

ARIA

MYLA IS RELENTLESS IN her pursuit to show me just how easily she cannot only best me in a fight but outright *kill* me. Not that I had any doubts, but the soreness in my back and hips just adds proof where none was needed. If this is her getting payback for using my song on her, then I suppose it is deserved.

Rain still blankets the beach in harrowing sheets, its noise louder than the angry crashing of the waves at the shoreline, the tide moving in closer to the rocks inside the cavern.

"Move, Aria. We need to keep our muscles warm," she chides from above me, my breaths heaving while I stare up at the now darkened rocky ceiling above us after a particularly nasty takedown.

"Just. One. Minute." I gasp for breath between each word, dagger still clutched in one hand while my other rests limply on my chest.

"In a fight, you will not get a minute to rest. You'll have to push yourself to give everything that you have, and sometimes, you'll be asked to give even more."

I sit up, cold stone biting into my thighs as the tunic rises to my hips. "You speak as if you've experienced it."

She doesn't answer, instead curling her fingers as she beckons me forward. "Up."

I groan as I stand, pulling my thick curls away from my face and letting them tumble down my back. Myla readies her stance, bending her knees slightly as she holds both arms up, one hand clutching the hilt of that strange blade.

"Are the initials on the hilt of my dagger your father's?" I avoid saying *king*, as the question already seems like one she won't answer.

She steps to the side, and I mirror the movement, stepping into a puddle made from a leak in the ceiling. At least Myla's glare has lessened from murderous to disdainful. "How about if you can draw blood from me before our lesson is up, I'll tell you?"

Frustration surges at how every interaction has to be some sort of deal, as if the act of giving basic information costs Myla something beyond just engaging in conversation. I'm too exhausted to pry anything out of her, so I agree, and we continue sparring. Half an hour later, I'm no closer to her answering the question. Sweat beads at my temples despite the cold, and when Myla lunges forward, I throw up my arm at the last minute, our blades clashing. I hiss out a short breath as pain flares. I must have caught the tip of her dagger.

"Why did you hesitate?" she asks, standing to her full height and dropping her guard.

I follow suit, cradling my arm to my chest while I inspect the wound. "I was running through the blocks you taught me earlier and panicked. I didn't want to accidentally stab you."

She blinks and cocks her head. "I thought the entire point of this was to try and draw blood from me."

"Well not the *entire* point," I counter, grateful to find that the small nick on my arm has already stopped bleeding. "That would be defending myself. But if I draw your blood, Myla, I want to do it because I'm actually good enough to catch you off-guard." Using the edge of my tunic, I dab the small drip of blood away, only noticing that Myla hasn't answered when the howling of the storm lingers for too long. Lifting my gaze, I find hers already on me, scrutinizing me in a way that strips me bare. On the surface, her face is set in the same cold rigidity, but beneath it, just barely noticeable, is a warmth that forces a knot in my throat. "What?"

"You can't stop to think," she says, her voice rough as she lifts her weapon again and bends her knees. She jerks her chin towards me in a command to get into position. "If you do, you'll be dead before your next breath. You need to practice so that these movements become instinctual, especially with how differently they'll feel beneath the surface."

I nod, inhaling deeply as I watch her. Myla's movements are quick, no pre-emptive thought given. Just fluidity that speaks to the years of practice she's had. Why would a princess in a kingdom with dragons behind the protection of the Spell *need* to be so well-versed in battle? Do the fae know that mages can pass through the Spell unharmed? Does she know about Rhea, and her ability to *heal* others from the effects of the Spell?

Myla strikes, her movements quick as she attacks. My muscles are fatigued, but I manage to block every one of her attempts. "Good," she says, swiping again. I jump back and smack into the wall. Myla closes in, and our arms cross, blades singing as they meet. She leans her weight towards me, a small quirk to her lips. "Seems I've got you cornered."

I reach with my other hand and curl my fingers around her wrist. "You once said that a desperate person is the most dangerous, because they are willing to do whatever it takes to win."

Myla nods. "I did, because it's true."

I swallow, and her eyes dip down for a moment before they draw back up. "My reason for wanting you to teach me how to fight was born from watching a friend die so that I could live, and it grew into something powerful when I learned someone I love needs my help to stay safe."

"Your sister?" she guesses. I'm confused how she would know about Lyre until I remember letting it slip while she was under my song.

"Yes. I have always lived in fear, from the moment I understood what the emotion meant. I've been desperate for a long, *long* time, but I didn't have the tools to act. I didn't realize how I could weaponize that desperation. Until now." I hold Myla's gaze, one of her brows arching before it abruptly halts and she grunts out in pain. "Sorry," I say with a wince as my talon pierces her wrist.

"*Fucking* stars," Myla grumbles, watching as my talon slowly retreats. She steps back and pulls the sleeve of her black shirt up, revealing only one small mark that has split the skin. "Surprising creature," she murmurs under her breath, sheathing her dagger at her thigh and pulling her sleeve down.

I smile as I roll the dagger in my hand until the initials are facing her. "Who is L.V.?" I ask.

Myla reaches into a pocket on the side of her vest, pulling out something wrapped in a black cloth. When she peels the fabric back, a warm glow is cast out from her palm. *A flame gem.* I had only ever read about them, the rock holding light from the sun. She walks to where there is a dry area of sand further away from the cavern entrance, setting the flame gem down before she takes a seat herself, her back against the wall. "L.V. stands not for my father's name but for the last queen of Void Magic, Queen Lucia Vasiris."

My brows rise as I follow her, taking a seat next to her, the gem now centered between us. "And how did your father come into possession of it?" I ask, pulling the tunic over my crossed legs to cover them as much as possible.

Myla's face turns contemplative, a rare show of something other than anger. "My father was on friendly terms with the last mage queen prior to the war. It is said that as the war began to get closer to their kingdoms, Queen Lucia called for an emergency meeting with the fae under the guise of joining forces against the mortals, shifters, and sirens. She gave him this dagger when he arrived as a token of their friendship, but then sirens flooded the meeting grounds and began to sing. My father was able to get his dragon off the ground before he became enthralled by their magic, but many of the males he traveled with did not." Her gaze lifts to mine, expression grim. "Including my older brother, Shah. He had taken possession of the dagger from the queen. When my father realized Shah had not followed him into the sky, he turned back and searched by air. But my brother was never seen again. That dagger proves that he was likely pulled into the sea by one of your own, left to rot there like he was nothing more than carrion."

My lips part, an apology paired with a lame explanation about how siren history differed bubbles up my throat, but she holds her hand out, her eyes dropping to the dagger in my own.

"May I see it?" When I hesitate handing it to her, she sends me a deadpan look. "If I wanted to steal it, Aria, I would. Besides, as you demonstrated *twice* today, you're not defenseless without a blade."

No, I think to myself. *I suppose I'm not.*

She inspects it when I hand it over, a pensive line carved between her brows. "According to my father's account, this dagger had originally been a gift *to* Lucia."

I tilt my head in thought. "It's hard to imagine any of the rulers being friendly enough to give gifts," I say, watching her trace the engraved letters with the tip of her finger.

"It's hard to imagine my father being anything other than the callous male he is today," she counters almost to herself as she grips the bottom of the hilt, the tip of the dagger pointing towards the sky. Giving it a twist, a rusty sounding *click* rings out. Myla carefully tugs, and the hilt separates from the blade, revealing a hollow center that she holds up to inspect. "Dragon-made things can be imbued with magic as long as the item stays intact."

"Is that a dragon-made blade?" I ask.

"The hilt is dragon bone. And look here." She pauses to show me the inside of the hilt. Unable to see what she is pointing at, I scoot closer until my knee touches her shin. She tenses and then adjusts her leg, moving just out of reach. I swallow the swell of confusing disappointment that rises. Tilting the hilt so that light pours into it, she shows me a name etched into the silver: *Kamon*.

"That is your father?"

She dips her chin. "I half expected something to happen when I opened this." A well-timed burst of white light from the storm illuminates the sky, drawing her gaze to mine. I smile when the thunder rolls in next, briefly drowning out the noise of the wind and rain. Myla quickly looks away, twisting the base back into the hilt before handing it to me. She easily slips back into her icy disposition. "I imagine Navin will not be able to come until the storm has fully passed through the mountains, which will take some time. I'd say our lesson is done for the day?" Though it's phrased as a question, it sounds more like a command. One that doesn't leave room for argument.

I exhale through my nose, turning my head to look out at the choppy waters of the sea. In truth, I am too exhausted to train any more today. But I do not *want* to go. Myla is just as dangerous—as ruthless and mean and self-serving—as any of the sirens below. But here, in this space that isn't a home for either of us, there is safety in not having to pretend to be anything other than I am. She has seen me weakened and on my back, and she has seen my secret magic. And she can do nothing with that information but keep it to herself because—based on how she reacted to the guard that came last week and what I've come to learn from Navin—I'm betting she isn't supposed to be here. Certainly not with the likes of me.

"What do you know of mages?" I ask, leaning an elbow on one of my crossed legs and propping my chin on my hand. When she doesn't answer, I sigh. "Will every conversation cost me something in order for you to engage?"

Myla's focus stays on the storm, but she subtly arches her brow. "It should." Despite what she says, there is no bite to her answer. Leaning her head back against the wall, her chest lifts with a breath. "Do you mean in general? Or are you asking for something more specific?"

I picture Rhea, but I hold off on telling Myla about her. At least until I can decipher what she knows first. "What do you know of their magic?" I ask, figuring the broad topic is safe.

"They can manipulate what Olymazi keeps tucked in her soils and mountains. Raw and wild magic that is only accessible to them and those who make deals in blood." She tilts her head to look at me. "And life debts, I suppose."

Heat inexplicably rushes up to my cheeks under her gaze, so I drop mine to where my fingers play with the fabric of my tunic. "Don't you think it's strange that of all the ways the kingdoms are split with magic, the mages received something less specific than the others?"

"It does seem unfairly balanced if you ask me."

I shrug, letting my lips curl into a smile. "At least we aren't mortals." The joke earns me a snort, warmth flickering in my chest at the sound.

"My turn," she says, looking at me straight on. The tips of my fingers press into my calves, the weight of her full attention on me making me want to squirm. "Are there others of your kind whose magic is as unexpected as yours?"

"Not the same way. There are some sirens whose songs have begun to fade. Some who can no longer transform. But none whose magic can draw females in. At least, none that I'm aware of."

She ponders that before asking, "When did you discover you were different?"

"The first time I went on a hunt," I answer, pushing past the uncomfortable tightness in my throat. "Hunts are when sirens go out looking for ships to sink. It is... an *integral* part of our lives. Non-negotiable. The siren queen is ruthless in her expectations that everyone partakes in this, or there are consequences."

Myla makes a noise caught between a scoff and a growl, so I keep my gaze forward to avoid what might be her condemning gaze.

"And what consequences might those be?" There's enough judgment in her tone that I hear what she really wants to ask: *How do you punish someone who is already a monster?*

"Banishment. Being forced to live outside of Lumen in caves carved into seamounts. For some, it is death." My voice grows quieter. "And for others, her punishments are more tailored. More humiliating. She has a keen ability to take one look at you and see *right* through you. Down to your bones, exposing every weakness you have to her. If there is any part of you that harbors goodness—that harbors *light*—she snuffs it out. It's like being in a nightmare, except you can't wake up, and there is no escaping those looming consequences. There's no relief, except the occasional blip in reality where you might feel like your body is your own again, untouched and unsullied. Or when something small reminds you that, despite the cold, dark pit that has opened up within you, you're still *you*. To some degree anyway." I chew on my cheek, dropping my gaze to the scar on my foot. "But it's only a blip. Just a small fragment of time before the real world comes rushing in, and you're once again thrown into the depths of what it means to *be* in a place that does not like or want you."

Her silence is damning, and I blink back the annoying tears that have beaded in the corner of my eyes. In the quiet, we listen to the storm settle, and when the sun finally breaks through the mottled gray, I sigh and push myself up. I gather my bag, placing the dagger within it before slipping the tunic over my head. When I turn to hand it to Myla, I find her already standing, her hands clenched into fists at her sides as those dark eyes land on mine. Forcing air into lungs, I walk towards her and hold the tunic out to her.

"I will see you in a week."

She clutches the garment without looking at it, a muscle flexing along her slender neck. I turn and sidestep a puddle, making my way to the exit and silently berating myself for letting so much show.

"Aria." Her voice is raspy, as if she can't quite get herself to use it wholly.

"Yes?" I answer, looking over my shoulder.

"Just because what is inside of us is dark doesn't mean that it holds less value than something light." She takes a single step towards me, then stops. "We may be composed of the consequences of other's actions and words against us, but they do *not* get to define who we are. Only *we* decide that."

Chapter Sixty-Eight

RHEA

S WEAT COATS MY FOREHEAD and back, the trembling of my hands now joined by the chattering of my teeth. But what ails me isn't due to the weather.

Xander adjusts his stance on my right, shifting his gaze to me every few minutes it seems, but I avoid it as I have since I learned about Bella being a shifter and his involvement with her death. "We're almost done," he murmurs, his arms crossed over his chest as wind blows his dark hair across his face. "It's a smaller group."

I'm sure that statement is meant to be helpful in some way. I'm so *tired* that I don't know if I even have enough in me to heal another two guards, let alone another few *groups* of them.

When I don't respond, Xander runs a hand through his hair. "Tell me what's going on."

I keep my gaze on the incoming men, all without their armor. They stay clustered together, their expressions ranging from confused curiosity to utter disdain. That has been a recurring theme since I started healing them at the king's request. I don't pretend that I don't know the reasons why.

Xander and I are stationed near the guard barracks to the west of the palace, hidden from view of the castle's occupants. The barracks themselves are a stand-alone gray stone structure that houses only the guards at the palace while the rest of the king's army lives closer to Vitour, so I had been told. I had known from history books that because mortals lacked direct access to magic unlike the sirens, mages, shifters, and fae, that they had been given strength in numbers and the ability to reproduce more easily. I had known, and yet seeing the sheer *size* of just one part of King Dolian's army had been shocking.

"Look at them all," the king had said from a private balcony that peered out over just *one* of the army's training spaces in the distance. "Aren't they magnificent?"

In truth, they were. The men that sparred with each other—doing target practice with arrows or perfecting their skills with all manner of weapons—*were* incredible. Bodies in motion were stretched far and wide, hidden from the view of my tower because of the angle of the castle, but now spread out in front of me in a way that reminded me of an overflowing anthill.

"This is only a *fraction* of the power I hold," he continued, drawing his lips up as I stared at the rows and rows of men. All prepping as if war was not some impossibility but an *inevitability*. "You will heal them all."

With the command from the king, I was brought here for the first time some days ago. While healing the sirens had been a slower process, the king demanded that I heal more than one man at a time, and thus, groups were brought to me, their size growing daily. Some were outright *terrified*, begging me to stop once they saw the magic glowing in my hands. Many tried to run, while others attempted to attack me. Xander had brought men that he trusted for protection, including Brisk, who still guarded my door every day and accompanied me when Xander couldn't, and together, they were able to keep the men contained. I had to pretend their terrified screams were innocuous.

I tell myself now that I'm not actually hurting them. If anything, I'm giving them a better chance at living a more *normal* life—one without fear of dying once they pass through the Spell. But that is nothing but a lie, a placating statement whispered by the part of my mind that doesn't want me to completely fall apart. These men are bound to the king, servants to his will alone, and if I know anything about my uncle, it is that his vengeance is a slow burning flame. With his army healed, he can march into any kingdom he wants.

I've lost count of the days that have passed. What's the point in keeping track when each one is spent either forcing me to reach a depletion of my magic that I have never felt before or in the company of people who have the king's favor and look at him as if he's some sort of god and I'm the roach he's affectionately taken in? Sometimes I feel as if I am standing outside of myself, watching things happen *to* me. I can't admit it—out loud or in my own head—but the numbness that accompanies those moments is welcome. It is relief, a temporary pause in the battering of the churning sea I'm stuck in.

"Rhea." Xander's voice cuts through my wandering mind, and my eyes snap to his. "Are you okay?"

I nod and refocus my gaze on the men in front of me, magic pooling in my hands.

"So the rumors *are* true," one guard says, a scar bisecting his eyebrow and crossing his eye, the iris a milky-blue color. "The king's whore is actually a mage."

"Watch it," Xander snarls threateningly. "This is your future queen, and His Majesty has *demanded* that you respect her."

I try to smile in the only form of gratitude I can muster, but the movement feels foreign. The muscles atrophied from lack of use.

"You know what she did, Commander," another man says, elbowing his way to the front and eyeing my magic with an accusatorial glare. I swallow and push down the ever-present screams of the men I killed to the back of my mind. "A *mage* as queen? After King Dolian insisted that mages were the root of all our kingdom's plights? Seems a little suspicious, doesn't it?"

"I don't question the king's choices, and neither should you."

Gods, his loyalty to the king seems so believable. But had he thought that when he was tasked with killing Bella? Had Xander really just viewed her as another casualty to further his own cause? Did he make it quick? Was the last thing she saw the same cold and unforgiving gaze he had given me after Alexi died?

That's what makes interacting with him hard now. I know he has so much to protect, beyond just himself. That people are relying on him and his secret machinations to create a better life for *all*. But I am tired of those most important to me being sacrificed. I'm petrified that anyone who gets close to me is inviting death to their doorstep. And, despite myself and the memories that haunt me, I have grown to like Xander. In another lifetime, perhaps, we could have had a friendship built on organic trust. But now his hand has caused the deaths of those closest to me, and I just don't know if I have the strength to separate his two personas.

I'm just *so* tired.

"She is going to use her *gift* on you so that you can pass through the Spell without harm. There are no ill side effects. It will feel strange at first, but it will be over quickly, and then you can return to your duties," Xander shouts, and the guards all tense. It's funny to hear him repeat the line about how my magic will feel, considering he hasn't been healed. Nor has he requested to.

My magic vibrates at my fingertips, the sensation traveling across my arms and chest where it connects to that deep well within me that I now have limited access to. Falling into the only sort of reprieve that I can conjure under the circumstances, I allow my eyes to close and, with a slow breath, release my magic towards the guards. There's an instant sense of *relief* as I pull more power up, warmth tingling all over my body. Unbidden, the corners of my mouth rise as white light pours from me, and I don't need to see to know that the guards' bodies are lit from within, bright streaks running through them as if their veins are made of lightning.

Despite the chilly air that cascades over my body, I tilt my head back and bask in the sun's rays. I get lost in the heady rush of using my magic. Why had I ever fought this? Why had I *denied* myself this connection when I should have been celebrating it? My chest flares hot as my fingers twitch, almost like my magic is answering. *Yes. It could always feel like this.*

Help me, the rasp of my voice echoes in my mind. *Help me*. Cold rises from my stomach, and for the briefest of moments, I feel them both—life and death. It all settles heavily on me, an answer to my pleas. Then, having met the requirement for healing the guards, my magic abruptly dissipates until I'm completely severed from it again. My eyes flare, hands still outstretched towards the glowing guards. I can't help the quiet whimper of longing that slips out before my knees crash into the grass, knocking the air from my lungs.

"That is the last for today." Xander's voice booms before he squats next to me and waits for the men to leave, the garden falling silent except for the sound of my heaving breaths. "Rhea—"

"I'm fine." I grasp the final drops of my energy to push myself up, only to nearly topple back over. Xander steadies me, and I allow his touch for a few seconds before stepping out of it.

"Did the king hurt you that night?" he asks, the words rushed and so unlike him that I whip my head in his direction. "You know I have people in this castle that I trust. One of them saw you and him in the hallway outside your room and..." He takes a breath. "Did he hurt you?"

My gaze falls to the ground, the shouts of those men on the beach echoing more loudly in my head. It's at least preferred to the memory Xander brings up. "You're asking a question you already know the answer to."

"I am trying *everything* that I can, Rhea, to get that ring off of you," he says, a desperate edge to his voice. "To work around the king's magic so that you can—"

"I know," I interrupt, my thumb pushing at the cool pearl ring on my finger. I had tried to find *something* too, only to come up empty handed.

"Come with me to meet the resistance. See the men and women anxious to help not just me or you but all of Vitour. All of the Mortal Kingdom."

"I don't think that is a good idea," I answer, stepping past Xander towards the castle. Every part of me aches, my eyelids growing heavier with each step. Behind the pain and exhaustion, a hollowness lives within me. Reminding me that I'm nothing but a blank canvas for the king to paint his worst plans on. A shell of a woman, more than ever before.

"Why not?"

"It isn't safe." Not a lie, yet not my whole reasoning.

"Look, it's none of my business—I know this—but I want to help you. I know it was hard hearing about Nox—"

"That's not— He isn't— This isn't about him." Hearing his name spoken out loud flusters me.

"Then tell me *what* happened."

I stop, my chest already heaving as I squeeze my eyes shut. I don't want to do this right now, but I force myself to turn and face him. "I know about Bella."

Xander's eyes grow wide with shock. "What do you know about her?"

"King Dolian told me *everything*. How she was held in the dungeon. The torture you both inflicted on her. *Her death*." My voice shakes, but the anger loses out to my fatigue.

Xander doesn't move, doesn't seem to breathe as his eyes bounce between mine. I turn and resume stalking to the palace, Xander's steps falling behind my own a few moments later. He follows me silently to my room, where Brisk takes up his post. Shutting the door, I cross the sitting room to my bedroom, undressing just enough to crawl back into bed, where I shut my eyes and beg for sleep.

I manage to avoid dinner with my uncle, and later Eve's knock at my bedroom door stirs me from a light sleep. Her blue eyes flare with something that looks like concern when I open the door, but she masks it beneath a pretty smile as she waves a small white paper bag in front of me. It's nondescript, but even if it weren't for the sweet scent emanating from it, I'd recognize it. It's from the confectionary shop Alexi used to visit.

"The king asked that I pick up some things at the city center, so I just *had* to have you try the chocolate creams there!" Turning, she returns to the sitting room and lays the chocolates out of a napkin on one of the tea tables, talking about the flavors of each one. When she realizes I haven't joined her yet, she lifts her gaze back to mine. "What's wrong?"

"What isn't?" I scrape out, and immediately regret it. Her expression dims as she takes a step towards me, her hands nervously fidgeting with the white apron of her dress. Despite the late hour, she's still working, and guilt barrels into me for that. Because I can't bear to wipe the smile from her face completely, I force my lips into a grin and walk to the tea table, taking a seat on the ground before grabbing a chocolate at random and popping it into my mouth. "Tell me again about how you keep avoiding Edwin's propositions," I say as I chew.

She laughs, her shoulders relaxing before she undoes her blonde hair from the tight bun she keeps it in, and launches into another take of her and the man who loves her. But even the light conversation doesn't change how the chocolate tastes like ash in my mouth, nor does it chase away the numb feeling that pricks at me when we finish and she bids me goodnight.

Lying in bed, I stare at the ceiling for a long while, until my eyes grow watery and eventually close. I sink into welcome darkness, and quietly hope that it will hold me in its clutches forever.

Chapter Sixty-Nine

RHEA

*T*HIS IS A DREAM.

I know it by the small details—the way the air is just a little too warm and my body is just a little too relaxed. Sun gleams above me as I drag my fingers along delicate rose and carnation petals, the softness something I once only fantasized I would get to feel. But this flower garden isn't one I'm familiar with.

"I wanted to talk with you, but with your magic blocked, I cannot call you to the Middle."

"Selene?" I mean to speak her name, but instead, I hear my voice echo in my head.

"Yes."

I reach the end of the row of flowers, staring out at a white structure that is covered with long green vines, tiny white flowers dotting them every few inches. There's something striking about the building, something I might recognize, but when I try to examine it, my body moves on its own command and turns down the next row in the garden. This one is filled with more roses, lilacs and lavender also planted in neat lines. The scent of them is in each breath I take.

"This is not real."

"No, it isn't." Her voice rings out, and gods, I could cry at the sound of it. At how it soothes a part of me that has felt so desperately alone these past weeks. "I'm sorry I could not reach you sooner. Manipulating his magic is not easy, and were he to figure out I've even done this, *it would likely upset him."*

"Who?"

"The one who occupies the Middle with me."

I reach the end of the row and, this time, continue forward, my toes curling into the thick blades of grass. A treeline of thickly woven branches waits before me, and as I reach it, I brush my hands over the rough bark. It scratches at my palms, but the sensation isn't unwelcome because with it comes the nostalgia of being home.

"Why does this place feel like I've been here before?"

"I cannot say," Selene answers, her voice thick with sadness. I look around at the fallen leaves littering the forest floor, different shades that remind me of my favorite time of year. And of my favorite person. "You miss him?" she asks, then chuckles as if realizing how absurd the question is.

I stop in front of a particularly thick tree. The center is carved out but only enough so it's the right size for me to fit into. "Yes. His missing presence haunts me every waking moment and every time I close my eyes." My fingers dig into the bark as I hoist myself up, nails scraping while I tuck into the hollow, the action driven by something instinctual. A small blanket and a book are already laid out and waiting for me. "Is this what it is to love?" I ask. "To hurt and rejoice all in the same breath?"

"You will see each other again," she says after a moment, and I wish I didn't hear her twinge of uncertainty.

I sit cross-legged on the blanket, noting my strange clothes. They are tattered, cinched high on my ankles as if I've grown too big for them. My gaze lifts and snags on all of the etchings on the inside of the tree, my clothing now forgotten. The drawings are done by someone with a much steadier hand than my own. My nail traces the outline of one, its shape like the tree I sit in, branches stretching high overhead where they touch the edges of a cloud. Beyond the cloud are small dots that I think are stars, a thin line connecting them all.

"Constellations?"

"Yes. Ones that are visible from Olymazi."

I smile as my finger follows the lines, that same contentment I felt entering the woods blooming in my gut again.

"Rhea, we don't have much time, but I want to make sure you know something."

"And what is that?"

Selene sighs, and the scenery around me flickers—as if lightning has struck close by. "I know that you have struggled with being forced to use—and not use—your magic."

I laugh, the strained sound the only response I can muster.

"I know my word choice is poor, but even as you endure horrible things, you must remain strong. Resilient. Your fortitude will continue to be tested, but I have faith, Rhea, that you will find freedom. You've already withstood so much, and I am so very proud of you."

I lean my back against the tree, a different carving catching my eye. "I can't help but feel like there is bad news following all of that."

Her long bout of silence is damning. "As you know, I cannot say anything that would violate the deal I made, and though I can see glimpses of the future, it has always come in fragments. More often than not, I can't make it into a complete picture until right before the event happens."

"That must be frustrating." My head tilts to the side as I trace the outline of... a tower. *Stone bricks make up the exterior, its base set near a body of water. There is no bridge depicted, but vines trail from a balcony where two figures—one taller than the other—are standing. Goosebumps break out over my skin.*

"It is, because my magic is changing. Warping as his *does. And making it very difficult to see what I've always been shown before."*

My hand brushes against the book near my feet, its cover turned away from me. "And what is it you've been shown before?"

"You."

A voice calls out in the forest but I don't pay it any attention as I pick up the book, my brow scrunching at how low large it looks in my grip. I stifle a gasp when I turn the book over, revealing its title.

"There you are!" A woman's voice startles me, and the book falls onto my lap. "I should have expected to find you here!" Light brown freckles dust over fair skin, her hair an unmistakable shade of honey blonde.

"Of course, Mama. It's my favorite spot." A child's voice rings out and it takes me a moment to realize that it's come from me. Or, rather, the body I seem to be occupying.

"Selene, whose dream is this?"

The woman outside smiles before extending her hand out for me. "Come on, my Little Sun. Papa has made your favorite for dinner." I climb from the tree and take her hand, a new emotion roiling through me. It takes a moment to realize it is joy.

My surroundings flicker again, and abruptly I'm no longer the little girl but a stranger watching as she and her mother walk away, their identical honey-blonde hair swaying against their backs.

"Selene—"

"I am bound by what I can say, and my magic will no longer show me glimpses of your future. But, Rhea, I need you to know that no matter what happens, you aren't *alone. I am always here with you, and when you return to your full power, I will be with you then as well." Her voice softens, and my vision through the girl's eyes flickers again, only this time it doesn't return to normal. "Remember your bravery and strength. Remember who you are at your core." Gray bleeds into my surroundings, taking over until everything becomes washed out.*

"I don't understand. Why did you show me this?" But even as I ask the question, I feel Selene fading away as the ground beneath me disappears and I begin to fall and fall and fall.

My eyes open with a start, sweat sticking my hair to my temples in clumps. I pull the strands away from my face as I sit up in bed. Pushing the covers off of me, I stumble to the wooden side table where a pitcher of room temperature water sits with a crystal cup. My hand shakes as I pour, but I wait until I've gulped it down and made my way to the small balcony off the sitting room before I replay the events of my dream... or *whatever* that was. It had been visceral, as if I was both living it and watching it happen from afar. The woman—the mother—could have passed as my own with how similar we looked. But even more startling was the nickname she called her daughter—*my Little Sun*. And then there was the book. *The Little Sun* had been in this dream, and it wasn't just a copy of it—it was *my* copy. It had the same colored foiling, the same dented right corner.

What was Selene showing me—something from the past or something from the future?

I close my eyes against the breeze, my fingers clenching the stone railing. This is the first dream I've had in... I don't know how long that wasn't egregiously awful, but sadness lingers at the fact that it wasn't a dream of Nox. Or even one of Alexi or Bella or—

Bella. Gods, what was her real name? Did the king or Xander even ask?

What would the shifter king do if he learned one of his own was *murdered* by King Dolian? I shiver as I recall seeing King Kai. He is every bit as menacing as one might expect from a land of half beasts, but he only ever gave that dark and threatening gaze to King Dolian. When his eyes shifted to me, something softened in their amber glow. Or perhaps I was imagining it; after all, this is a male who used his knowledge about mages as a bargaining chip to force Bahira to his kingdom. I know her to be smart, but what could she do to defend herself against someone like *him*?

King Kai looked formidable on his own, but what kind of power lies in the nation of shifters? If I could heal *them* to pass through the Spell, would it be enough? I bite down on my lower lip as a darker thought takes root: What if *I* am enough to stop them? I have never wanted to use my magic as a weapon—not even when it would benefit me. But if that line has already been crossed against my will, what does it matter? If I make it out of this kingdom with any part of my soul intact, maybe it will be worth sacrificing to ensure neither King Dolian nor Queen Amari can force anyone to do something against their will again.

By the time my mind quiets enough to fall back asleep, the sun is peeking over the horizon. With my skin sufficiently chilled from the bitter air, I step back into the sitting room, turning to close the slider, when an unfamiliar voice halts me.

"Lady Rhea."

I spin, my heart leaping as I meet the dark eyes of a man. His messy blond hair hangs over his forehead, as if he's run his hand through it over and over again. Dark circles color the skin beneath his eyes, and his rumpled clothes look as if he hasn't changed in days. I swallow, my body tense as our gazes hold. He stands in the sitting room just past the entrance, the door behind him open. My eyes leave his to check for Brisk, but either he's not at his post or he *is*, and didn't stop this man from coming in.

"You killed my brothers." Even with only the early morning light, I can make out his murderous expression. The way he grimaces and his body moves as if it takes all of his effort. He steps towards me as his fist tightens around an altered bow, the pressure making it creak beneath his grasp. "They were the only family I had left, and *you* killed them."

"I didn't kill anyone—"

"Don't lie," he interrupts, pointing the bow towards me, an arrow already nocked and drawn within it. "The men came home with rumors about your magic turning our comrades to *ash*. That *you* drained their life!" he shouts, his entire body trembling as he closes the distance between us by another few steps. I counter by moving backwards, my back hitting the glass slider.

"I didn't mean to," I whisper, my heart beating furiously as I chance a single step to the left. "I was forced to do it."

The man's laugh is jarring as he jerks the strange bow in my direction. But his smile falls quickly, and his cheeks become stained with tears. "They were all I had. It was the three of us just trying to save up enough to live somewhere quiet. We were only supposed to be in the guard for another year at most."

I suck in a breath, blinking back the pressure that builds behind my eyes. "I'm sorry. Truly, I'm so sorry."

"Your apology isn't going to bring them back! Nothing will!" he snarls, sweat gleaming over his brow. "The king expects us to just accept your magic without question when we know *nothing* about how you might poison us with it!" A shadow forms right outside the door, drawing my gaze as Xander peeks his head around the doorframe. "I asked for an audience with the king so I could share what so many in the guard think—that trusting a *mage* is a mistake. And he *denied* me, sending that bastard Simon to say he was *too busy* to meet with me."

My breaths shorten as I take another step to the left, but the man mirrors it. "Your brothers and your friends did not deserve their fates," I rasp with a shaky breath. But I can tell my words fall short as resignation settles over his tear-streaked face.

"They deserved more than *you*, and now the king will know what it's like to lose someone he loves."

The room descends into a cacophony of noise—the sound of a click and *whoosh* of air, a sword being drawn from its scabbard and the pounding of footsteps. I watch in slow motion as Xander enters, sword in hand and angled towards the man. Pain flares hot and bright in my chest as I'm knocked backwards, stumbling into the slider before collapsing to the ground. My pulse beats loud in my ears, each second ticking by rhythmically as I lift my head to find Xander now right in front of me. *How did he move so quickly?* He drops his sword, falling to his knees beside me. The man behind him staggers out into the hall, blood draining from his face.

Why aren't you going after him? I try to ask, but I can't get the words out. Xander's hands land on my shoulders, and he guides me onto my side before shouting something behind him. Cold pierces the tips of my fingers, and I flex them out in front of me, half expecting my shadow magic to be spilling from them.

"Rhea? Rhea, can you hear me?" His voice is muffled, as if he's speaking underwater as he leans over me, a hand pressing at my back. My chest *burns*, and I try to move my hands closer to brush away whatever is causing it, but Xander pins them to my stomach with one of his. "It's okay. We're going to get you help." His voice shakes, and then he lets go to bring his hand to my chest, pressing down on it so hard that I scream. Or, I try to. A strange noise comes out instead. "Fuck! Rhea, look at me."

I try to ask him what's wrong but gag when the taste of metal floods my mouth. It makes me cough, sending liquid splattering onto the floor in front of me and dotting Xander's trousers.

"Don't talk. Just focus on staying awake."

My next inhale is gurgled, and my gaze drifts down, my vision going double as I stare at the fletching of an arrow, blood seeping out where it's impaled me. All at once, sound comes rushing in, scent and sensation following close behind. Another broken sound meant to be a scream wrenches out of me, taking all the fight I have in me with it.

Blood dribbles from my mouth as the ground vibrates with more footsteps, and my lids grow heavy. *Tired. I'm so tired.*

"Hang on, Rhea," Xander says, giving me a gentle shake when my eyes start to close. "No, come on. Stay awake!"

My lashes lower again as I groan, exhaustion smothering me as the numbness at my fingers travels up my arms. If I can just fall asleep, I won't have to feel this pain. Won't have to hear that man's words bouncing around in my head, a tomb filled with the screams of those I had killed. If I can just *sleep*—

A different voice sounds, this one panicked as its owner settles in front of me. They say something—command it of me. But there is no fighting the way death blankets me, its alluring darkness calm and quiet and final.

Chapter Seventy

XANDER

"Get the fucking healers here *now*!" I shout at the men who stumble into the room after the king. All but two go right back out, running to collect the women from the infirmary.

"Use your magic and heal yourself," King Dolian commands, leaning close enough that his lips brush Rhea's cheek. I fight back the urge to push him away from her while applying pressure to the injury. "I command you to use your magic and heal yourself."

Rhea lays lifeless, her lips beginning to pale.

"Move your hands," King Dolian commands, his eyes feral as he stares at the arrow. "Now!" I slowly lift them, blood staining my fingers as I brace for more of it to come spilling out. The king tugs on the ripped fabric of her nightgown, exposing the wound at the bottom of her ribcage. "Look. She's starting to heal herself!" He points at her skin that is indeed *knitting* itself back together.

My relief is temporary as I feel the tip protruding from her back. "We need to get the arrow out before her body seals it in. Otherwise, it could still kill her." I tell him, reaching for the dagger strapped to my belt.

When the king doesn't protest, I begin sawing at the body of the arrow.

"You better hope this doesn't kill her, or your life is forfeit as well."

"Of course," I murmur, working faster as I watch the skin around the arrow heal more quickly than before. *Shit*. I manage to keep my hands steady as the blade finally saws through the wood, and I waste no time pushing it until I can fully grip the shaft at her back and pull it out. White glows at the center at the puncture mark as the jagged skin closes, leaving no evidence behind. My gaze flicks back up to Rhea's face, and already, her lips and cheeks are regaining color.

"Do you know who did this?" King Dolian asks as he stands up, staring at his hands before pulling out a handkerchief from his pocket to wipe her blood off his hands.

"It was a guard, but one whose name I don't know. Our men were drawn to a commotion on the main floor, and it left Rhea's room temporarily unguarded." Anger flushes the king's cheeks red, but I don't give him a moment to question who was supposed to be stationed here before I continue. "I was coming up to secure her door when I saw it was open, and heard him speaking to her about his brothers. They were in the guard and died on the beach." I don't need to explain which day; it's burned into the minds of everyone present. Including the asshole in front of me.

"And you didn't kill him when you realized he was threatening her?" he asks, clenching his fists at his sides.

"I entered the room and stabbed him, but he had already fired. The choice was kill him or save her." And I had been a step too late. If the king hadn't arrived when he did—if she hadn't been conscious enough to hear his command—the outcome would have been cataclysmic. Particularly when Nox found out. Though, I have no updates on the prince and the Mage Kingdom. I push *that* problem away to deal with later and look back to King Dolian. "We'll find him, and I'll ensure that his heart stops when it meets the tip of my blade."

"No," he counters, staring down at Rhea. "Keep him alive. I want his death to be painful. I want it to be drawn out and merciless. I want her to enact her revenge."

The healers finally arrive, the two best women we have gently pushing me out of the way so they can take a look. But other than the blood left drying on her skin and the floor in front of her, there's no evidence of the arrow's puncture.

Stepping back, I nod at the king before heading towards the exit, meeting my personally appointed second in command where he waits in the hall. "Brisk, please tell me you guys fucking caught him."

"Not yet, Sir, but our men are scouring the castle and the grounds." Brisk's strides keep up with my own as we move, guards spilling into every open space as they search. It takes a few minutes in the chaos to cross the castle and reach the King's Guard's wing, where we have a command center stationed. Brisk keeps his voice low when he says, "I'm sorry, Xander. I heard screaming and ran. Rhea never leaves her room, and I just—"

"She's alive," I interject, my jaw tight. "Let's hope that means the king won't request your head."

He bristles but manages to nod. "I'll get some towels for you to wash up with."

"Thank you." Brisk darts to the right as I continue forward. Tall wooden double doors engraved with the Mortal Kingdom sigil loom in front of me, parting when I near. The command space is like a second home to me and where

I spend most of my time when I'm not the king's glorified errand boy. Five guards are waiting within, two of whom are part of the king's personal Trusted, still ranking below me. The other three are men I've hand-picked as part of my resistance, who I trust implicitly. "Status report."

"Our men have checkpoints at every castle exit and on the roads leading to Vitour. We've identified the guard as Sterling Brown, brother to Rainer Brown and Captain Oliver Brown. All three men were set to leave at the end of their contracts later this year," Grayson, a guard a decade older than me, explains. White streaks through his beard and the mop of brown hair on his head, but his gaze is just as sharp as ever, and he's shown his loyalty to me on more than one occasion.

"So I've heard," I respond, leaning against the table that houses a map of Olymazi and wooden figurines representing the beings and different threats each kingdom possesses. Dragons for the fae, random animals for the shifters, a carved sun for the mages to represent their magic, and a fin over the ocean for the sirens. "Tell the men to keep their eyes sharp and their wits about them. Sterling is one of us. He'll know the tactics we are using to hunt him, and he will try to evade us until he's sure we've given up. Force him out of hiding before that happens."

"Yes, Commander." Grayson exits the room, another of my men in tow, and my mind jumps to possible locations Sterling could be hiding. It hasn't been long enough for him to have exited the castle grounds *yet*.

"Did he kill her?" asks Jerrick, one of the king's Trusted and a man I've hated since I first met him, crossing his arms over his broad chest. Dark brows draw low over his eyes, his sharp features conveying a permanently disgruntled look. "Based on the blood that stains your hands, I'm betting he did."

I ignore the urge to look at the crimson staining my skin. "He hit her in the chest, but she was able to use her magic and heal herself before the arrow took her life." Brisk returns with a pile of hand towels and a bucket of steaming water. "I suspect she'll make a full recovery."

There's a significant weighted pause from Jerrick, a muscle ticking in his jaw before he glances at the map. "Thank the gods for that."

I begin to clean off my hands. "Indeed."

But Jerrick's pseudo relief is easy to see through, as is the pitying look of the man standing next to him. Silas is another Trusted who's in his third decade and known for the brutal way he battles. He has no problem slicing through another body, innocent or otherwise, civilian or not. While our forces haven't seen much action since the introduction of the Spell, it doesn't mean that there haven't been civil disturbances. Occasionally, a small group of mortals upset with the king will rise up, unaware that a larger group is silently biding their time. Sometimes, my men *try* to make them aware, only to be met with incredulous disbelief because of our proximity to the Crown. Our movement is underground, secret to everyone who hasn't gone through rigorous questioning to prove that they have the same goals. It's the only way we can protect ourselves. It doesn't mean we don't try to recruit everyone that we can, but for the safety of the current members and the overall mission, we can't beg people who aren't willing to risk something to join.

"Do we have anyone guarding the lower levels that lead to the wine cellars?" I ask, reaching for another towel and tossing the stained one to the ground.

"No, but do we really think Sterling is suddenly fancying some wine for his adventures?" Jerrick asks.

"We check every avenue." When neither moves, I toss the second towel to the ground and grab a third. "We have a man who tried to murder our king's fiancée, a woman who is now protected under the same vows that we gave King Dolian. Should I relay to His Majesty that perhaps it is time to test his guards again and see which of you might break?" Jerrick glares at me as fury radiates off of him, but the threat is enough. He and Silas are silent as they stride out of the room. I wait until the door shuts before I let my shoulders relax, Brisk and a guard named Anderson flanking me.

"Almost had me believing you truly care about the king," Brisk says, running a hand through his short blond hair.

Anderson chuckles, both hands grasping the edge of the table. "So it's true? Her magic saved her?"

I nod, making sure my hands are as clean as they can be before looking over the map. "The king was able to reach her in time before she... *succumbed* to her injuries."

"You sound relieved by that," Anderson says from my left, drawing my gaze.

"Why wouldn't I be?"

He sighs, the sound as exasperated as I feel. "She's a threat."

"Rhea— The *princess* isn't a threat to anyone," I counter, stumbling over my words like an idiot. It only causes Anderson to dig deeper into his stance.

"First name basis now?"

"For gods' sakes." I reach a hand for the siren figure, moving it from Lumen to our beaches. "It's my fault you're weary of her because *I* planted that idea in your head. Now I'm telling you I was wrong." Rhea had been a threat, at least a perceived one, months ago. But not now. Not after her interactions with Eve or how she carries her regret and guilt over the lives taken on the beach and those healed against her will. Not when I've seen what forgiveness from her *might* look like, if she's able to fully give it all. I would understand if she couldn't—just as I would have understood the same of Siyala. My chest clenches at the thought of her, her golden eyes bright in my mind.

"She's mage, and she has the only *legitimate* claim to this kingdom's throne."

"A throne that she has told me she does not want."

Anderson releases a laugh, while Brisk shakes his head, giving our companion a warning look. "And you believe her? Knowing what you saw, what the king has done to her, you believe that she wouldn't take that throne at the first opportunity? That she wouldn't enact retribution the moment it becomes available?" He leans across the table until I'm forced to give him my attention. "We have worked too damn hard for too fucking long to have an outsider sit on that throne once King Dolian is removed."

"Do *not* talk to me about the struggles we've faced as if I have not lived through them," I snap, a fist forming on the table. "No one cares about what we are doing *more* than me. No one has as much invested in making sure that our plans do not stray more than *me*."

Anderson's chest heaves, and Brisk comes around to lay a hand on his shoulder, giving it a light squeeze. "Hey, man, he's right. Xander has spent far too much time preparing to let it slip from his grasp. If he says the princess isn't a threat, we have no reason not to believe him."

Heated seconds pass, and for a moment, I think Anderson might continue to fight me on this. But with a sigh, he nods, his chin falling to his chest. "I'm sorry. It's just that we are so close, and I didn't think we would have a wrench thrown in our plans quite like this."

"She's no wrench, trust me." I move the sun figurine closer to the border of the Mage Kingdom, right where it touches our own. "All she wants is to get home to her *real* fiancé."

"If there is still a *fiancé* to return to," Brisk mutters under his breath, drawing our gazes. "What? You read the latest missive from Stephan. Sounds like the council is one strike away from just imprisoning the guy."

"Let's hope, for everyone's sake, that doesn't happen." I need to help Rhea get that fucking ring off so I can get her back home to Nox before whatever is going on in the Mage Kingdom becomes *my* problem too.

The doors open, a young guard popping his head inside. "Commander, we caught him."

My spine straightens. "Where did you find him?"

"Hiding in the throne room." My brows lift towards my hairline. I would have expected him to have been found in the gardens or on his way to Vitour. "He was waiting for the king."

"Well, *shit*," Brisk says, his mouth tipping down into a frown.

"Shall we get him ready for public execution?"

"No. The king wants to make a spectacle of his death. Tell the men to bring him to the dungeons. I'll go down and interrogate him once he's there." The guard nods and slips back into the hall.

"Would have made our jobs easier if he had been successful in any of his attempts to take a life today," Anderson says, and I bite back the urge to remind him to exclude Rhea from that statement. Of all the people I want to see rot in this castle, she is not one of them.

"The blood oath would have just killed him. It was a fool's choice from the start." I run my thumb over my own crescent-shaped mark, tension gathering once more in my shoulders. "We aren't ready yet anyway," I say, checking that all of my weapons are in place before heading to the doors. "To move before we are would spell disaster. We wait until the right moment, and then we'll take down the king and every one of those bastards like him."

Chapter Seventy-One

RHEA

I NEVER GAVE MUCH thought about what death would look like, but I hoped for something that resembled life. A part of me wondered if there would be an existence that mirrored the living one. Not quite the same—as it is death, after all—but one that I could find my own happiness in. Maybe I wouldn't remember what had come before, but I would innately recognize someone who was important to me. Like my mother and father. Alexi and Bella. Tienne and Immie and anyone else killed in my name. I thought it might be a peaceful place.

I'm disappointed to find it isn't any of those things.

And how ridiculous is that? To know that I'm dead and not be saddened by the fact that I've left everyone I love behind. Knowing that there is nothing and no one waiting for me on the other side. There is just darkness cradling me, a mother with her babe. And what I wouldn't give to see my own. To converse with her and learn who she was. To ask her what it might have looked like if things were different—if she and my father would have lived.

An ache takes root in my chest, but when I try to touch it, all I see is blinding white light. It fills my body as if I am *made* of it. The power of the sun, the moon, and the stars flows through my veins like my very blood, though the life it gives me is not that of any world.

This is the cost. It comes as a whisper, gentle in my ears and silky across my skin. *And the price you must pay.* The light within me pulses, warm and bright. *This is the cost.*

My awareness shifts to something in the distance, a different flickering light. It's not quite a flame but something thinner. Something... *golden.* On instinct alone, I reach for it. Even as that voice trickles over me, commanding that I am the price to pay, I still reach. *A golden thread.* My fingers brush along it, plucking it like a stringed instrument. Instead of music, it glows brighter, matching the intensity of my own light. A thread... A *tether.*

It is the price you must pay, the voice whispers, deep and resonant.

But I don't want to. My chest begins to burn, forcing a hiss through my teeth. I glow brighter, light seeping from my body and into the darkness that surrounds me. I clutch that golden tether, and a jolt of longing and love—such *desperate* love—sears me from within, pushing more light out until it almost overtakes my vision. But there, in the center of it all and reaching out from my chest, is a second golden thread. It connects with the first, sending a cascade of warmth from the crown of my head to the tips of my toes.

The scent of autumn woods fills my lungs. Silver-speckled eyes flare open in my mind. In my ears, a heartbeat not my own echoes. The threads pull taut, and my back arches. *Rhea...* I know that voice—*his voice.* I would know it anywhere. The thread pulses, a connection just on the edge of forming, and then everything goes dark.

⋆⟡⋆

"Lady Rhea, are you awake?" A feminine voice rouses me this time, and though my eyes are closed, I know where I'll be once more when I open them. *Alive.* I'm *alive,* and that should be a good thing. Except all I feel is a great sense of loss, a mourning for something I don't understand. It takes great effort to pry my eyelids apart, soft glowing light from a small chandelier coming into focus when I finally do. "There she is."

Her sigh of relief draws my gaze to her, and though it takes a few moments for my groggy mind to catch up with who I'm seeing, eventually, it does.

"You might remember me. My name—"

"Erica," I interrupt, earning a bright grin from her.

"That's right. It is lovely to see you again, though I wish the circumstances were different."

Her comment sobers me quickly, and I cast my gaze out to the room. Though the walls are painted a shade of white, the gray of the stone beneath peeks grimly through. A reminder of where I am.

"They've caught the man who hurt you," Erica says, her fingers gently wrapping around mine and giving them a squeeze.

I nod, though I don't feel any solace. *You killed my brothers.* My throat constricts, and screams echo in the back of my mind. "Will you help me sit up?"

Letting go of my hand, Erica eases me into a sitting position, and my head screams in protest at the movement. Fragmented memories surge as I look down at myself, the nightgown I had seen stained with my blood now replaced with one a light pink color. Only a slight tenderness remains beneath my ribs, signifying that my magic healed the worst of it. A thought crosses my mind, and I dive my hand beneath the blanket and the soft satin I'm wearing to the brand on my hip. My hopes fall flat when my eyes trace the rough lines still on the skin there for a few seconds before I push the nightgown down.

"The healers and I washed and changed you prior to the king visiting. Though he was unable to stay long, as rumor has it he is preparing to make a spectacle of the man who hurt you."

Of course he is.

Only when Erica snorts do I realize I said the words out loud. She eyes me carefully, blue eyes piercing through me in a way that makes my skin burn, before she walks to a nearby pitcher of water and fills a glass for me. "I'm sorry," I murmur between sips.

"Whatever for?" she asks, tucking a lock of her blonde hair behind her ear. She's dressed in the same uniform that I last saw her in, the day after Alexi's death. The memory is a visceral noose that I fight to loosen.

"Tienne was a lovely woman, and were it not for the king's interest in me, she would still be here." I had hardly allowed myself to think of Tienne—her death setting off the chain of events that ended in my capture.

Erica looks down at the bed, smoothing her hand over the wrinkled dark green comforter. "She was my best friend. The epitome of kind, but fiercely protective of those she cared about. I loved her very much." I glance down and away from the grief that's as evident on her as it was on me the last time she saw me. "But you do not bear the weight of her death, Lady Rhea. That stain belongs on *him*, not you. You will release yourself of the pain of that burden. If not for yourself, then for Tienne. She would be outraged if she learned that you feel that way."

I'm overwhelmed by the gentle sternness of her voice, and how it commands me to do something that I'm not sure that I can. So, like a coward, I bring the glass up to my lips and hide behind a drink of water.

"Now rest," she says when I hand the glass back to her, and though the last thing I want is to lay in bed while my mind roams, I nod and sink lower, pulling the covers up to my chin. She ensures there is water close by before pausing at the side of the bed. "I always thought there was something different about him, you know," she starts, tilting her head to the side. "And then he suddenly was asking for excuses to bring you things. 'Do you think she would want a treat from the kitchens?' he'd ask. 'When was the last time she got anything other than supplies?'" She mimics a deep male voice, moving about the room as if it needs any sort of tidying. It doesn't; in fact, I'm sure this space is the cleanest room I've ever been in. "Tienne suspected there might have been something going on, and she made sure to relay to him that if he hurt you, it would be the last thing he ever did."

"Who are you talking about?"

She chuckles, pausing to look over her shoulder, her smile brighter than before. "Flynn. Or, should I say, His Highness, Prince Nox."

The quirk of my lips is small. "He always told me the gifts were from you both. In fact, he even insinuated you were using him as an errand boy."

"I imagine he wanted us as scapegoats if you decided you wanted nothing to do with him," she says, facing me fully as she joins her hands in front of her. "Is he good to you?"

If you're in pieces, I want every fucking one of them.

There is only you.

Our love is not a beginning or an end but an infinite constant.

Nox's voice wraps around my mind, and for a moment, I feel the delicate fluttering of butterfly wings taking flight in my stomach. "He's very good to me. The best."

"Well, then, consider me part of the team that will do whatever it takes to make sure you get back to him."

The corners of my mouth draw down as I think of all the risks involved. "Nothing that would get you in trouble with the king."

Erica doesn't respond beyond a playful wink before there's knocking at the door. With a sigh, she moves to open it, revealing a fidgeting Eve.

"You're awake!" she shouts when she meets my gaze, a deeper voice murmuring something behind her.

"Yes, but she needs her rest—"

"She can come in," I interrupt, sitting back up and tucking the comforter around my waist. Eve is at my side quickly as her eyes roam over me. Behind her, Xander stands in the doorway but doesn't enter. Instead calling Erica over to speak with her in a hushed voice.

"Rhea, you're truly alright," Eve says, taking a seat on the edge of my bed. "I was tasked with cleaning your room after, and"—color drains from her face—"there was just so much blood."

Regret rises like a tide within me at her worry. "It appears I was able to heal myself," I tell her, my gaze jumping to Xander's. Despite the way everything feels grayed out—*hazy*—I'm still curious to know one thing. "How *was* I able to do that?"

"King Dolian commanded you when he arrived," he answers, walking to the foot of the bed.

I gaze down at my hands. At the ring that sits atop one of my fingers. Foolish as it was, a small part of me thought that maybe under duress I could access my magic. It wouldn't be the *best* way to use it, but if it meant getting free... I blink away the pointless thought. Imagine my hand swiping away at that seedling of hope.

"I've been ordered to let the king know when you've awakened," Xander says, bracing his hands on his hips. Erica scowls at him. "But I wanted to warn you first."

There's a skip in the beat of my heart when I ask, "Warn me about what?"

"King Dolian intends to make the death of the man who attacked you a public event. And he wants you there when he does it."

The next morning comes far too quickly, and though I skipped breakfast, nausea still threatens to expel the meager contents of my stomach.

"I can't believe he is making you watch," Eve says from behind me as she runs a brush through my hair. King Dolian had ordered her to spend extra time on my appearance this morning, so that I might be *presentable* enough to watch a man's execution. "It is cruel."

"It's his idea of showing me he cares," I respond, my voice hollow even to my own ears. I had expected to wear black, sure that was the only appropriate option. But the king had a crimson dress made for me, the cut of it dripping from my body as if made of liquid. It follows the contour of my delicate curves, gold lace edging the long sleeves where they flutter around my wrists. The neckline dips just enough to show the top of my cleavage, but Eve layers multiple jewel-laden necklaces to conceal as much of the skin as possible. I swallow the bile that rises to the back of my throat. "If he knew anything about me, he would know that I do not want this. I would *never* want this."

"I know," she says quietly, laying the brush down. I stand, my heart racing as I grip the back of the chair and look over my reflection. But I don't see me so much as I see the color of blood. Red and red and red. Splashed over my body and leaking to the floor. Staining skin a shade too pale. "Hopefully it is quick," she says, wincing. "In any case, I can be here once it is over if you like. Perhaps we can sneak into the library to get your mind off of it all?"

I force a grin as I nod, appreciative of her offer even if that place is no longer the refuge it once was. Eve's reassuring smile is the last I see as I step into the hall, Xander and Brisk waiting to flank me. As we begin to walk, another two guards join us from behind.

"Is all of this a result of the king's command?" I ask Xander under my breath.

"No. This is a result of *my* command. I trust each of these men with my secrets. You can trust them with your life." He spares me a glance, ensuring that I understand his intention. And even with my complicated feelings about him, I do. "I'm not going to pretend that anything I say will help make the next few moments more bearable. I don't know exactly what the king has planned, but

I've bore witness to enough of what he deems entertainment to know that it will involve making a spectacle."

My entire body bows under the weight of those words. I hold no fond feelings for the man who tried to kill me, but neither do I want to watch my uncle torture him on my behalf. We walk for a while, the occupants of the castle thinning out until we arrive at a set of gilded double doors, and Xander holds his hand up to halt the guards stationed there from opening them before he turns to me.

"We will not be able to interfere," he says, remorse heavy in his gaze. "But you will not be alone."

My eyes bounce from one man to the next, each of them offering a small nod. "Thank you," I say quietly. But even with Xander's assurance, and those of the men around me, dread still holds me within its clutches.

"Get ready," Xander says quietly before dipping his chin for the guards to open the doors. My heart pounds as I dig my nails into my palms, unsure of what I'm bracing for. But as I walk forward with Xander at my side—his own hand resting on the hilt of his sword—and we pass the doors, my brows knit together.

"What the fuck?" Xander whispers, confirming what I see. That this is not some strange dream.

Like the rest of the castle, this room is painted in red and gold, fabric draping from beam to beam making it look like a bleeding sky. Gold flecks the cream tile floors, and as I take another step forward, it's hard not to feel two feet tall under the sheer magnitude of this place. Especially because there is no one else *here*.

Heavy steps sound behind us, and Xander rips his sword free as he spins, the light from flame gems reflecting off of his golden armor. Guards spill through the doors, a sea of glinting gold as they file off to the sides and stand at attention, their hands clasped behind their backs.

"Guard!" Xander shouts at a man a few inches shorter than him with short blond hair. "What is your order?"

"I invited them here." My breath catches in my throat at his voice, that feeling of dread squeezing more tightly as the king walks in next, followed by Simon and men I recognize from my forced dinners with the king but whose names I cannot remember.

"Your Majesty," Xander says, bowing deeply. I don't join him. "What is the meaning of all of this?"

"This"—he waves his hand to the guards behind us and the men seated near the throne—"is about showing what happens when you hurt something that is *mine*." Each of his steps are measured, just as they had been before he killed Alexi. Like they had been when he would taunt me before hitting me in the tower. He walks to the center of the room and stops, while Simon and the rest of the men continue to the far wall, where rows of benches staggered in height like this is some sort of stadium and they are here to enjoy a spectacle.

The doors to the room close, the sound making my stomach sink. King Dolian's gaze bores into mine as he reaches a hand out to me.

"Come, darling. Let's show my men who you *really* are."

Chapter Seventy-Two

RHEA

"Come now, Rhea, this is a time of celebration!" he shouts, eyes growing wide as I continue to ignore his outstretched hand.

"Lady Nele," I counter, curling my fingers in to hide the way they tremble. "Isn't that who I am supposed to be now?"

My uncle's façade slips, his smile cracking as his true nature peeks through. "Everyone here already knows who you are. These guards? Given blood oaths to not speak a word to anyone." His hand sweeps grandly over the line of men that stand along the wall. "And these ones? My council?" he says, turning to face the men sitting on the benches. "Well, they hold no objections to my want of you."

I scowl as I look at them, heat flaring at my chest and rising up my neck. *Is this true?* I want to ask. *Are you truly alright with your king marrying his niece?* And maybe I look poised to ask just that because, abruptly, King Dolian's grip is on my arm, tight and unforgiving as he pulls me hard enough to spin me around, my hands planting on his chest.

"If you are looking for someone to save you, I'm afraid you'll find our company lacking. There is no one coming for you, Rhea. No one who cares whether you live or die or who you fuck or what crown you wear." His eyes flare as the skin beneath his short beard flushes red. "There is only *me.*"

"And yet you will *never* be enough."

Still clutching my arm, he slams his opposite palm across my cheek, snapping my head to the side. My legs wobble beneath me as ringing fills my ears, my vision hazy and eyes watering. King Dolian pulls me closer, my shoulder hitting his chest as his lips brush against my temple. "You think *they* will help you?" I look to the men, that void inside of me growing when I see Simon, his hand propped against his jaw and that sadistic gleam in his eyes that I knew all too intimately. He and the others sit and watch, varying degrees of enjoyment playing across their faces. "He's not coming," King Dolian whispers, breath hot on my skin. "Just as easily as he gained his interest in you, he lost it the moment you left him. Like the vermin he is, he's already moved on to the next most appetizing thing."

I grit my teeth together, drawing up invisible shields as if they can save me from invisible arrows. But the king has already laid his traps in my mind, and I blindly step into them. One right after the other. *Nox not answering the Mirror. Nox not being in Vitour when I returned. Nox not wanting me. Nox moving on.*

King Dolian's fingers grip my chin and tilt my head up roughly, forcing me to look in his hazel eyes. "It's time to earn your title, darling. Bring in the prisoner!" he shouts, making me jump.

I spin out of his hold to look as the doors to the room open again, and two guards haul the slumped man through. His head hangs heavily between his shoulders, blood—old and new—stains his bare chest. The scent of sweat is thick in the air when they force him to his knees in front of us. This was Sterling, the guard who would have killed me were it not for my magic. I attempt to step backwards, but only manage to bump into the king.

"Commander, hand Lady Rhea a dagger," King Dolian commands.

My eyes widen as I look from Sterling to Xander, a breath trapped in my chest. His face is completely placid, devoid of any emotion. And, yet, he still asks, "Your Majesty?"

"Give the lady one of your daggers. *Now.*"

"Your Majesty, I don't know that giving her a weapon—"

King Dolian releases me to stalk towards Xander, reaching for one of the blades stored on his belt. "Let me remind you, *Commander*, that I do not have you here because I value your opinion. You are muscle to do my bidding. *Nothing* more." He pulls a large dagger free, and though Xander tracks the movement, he doesn't intercept.

The king turns towards me, spinning the blade gracefully until the hilt faces me. "Take the weapon, Rhea."

There is no magic behind his words, so I shake my head, blood rushing in my ears as I struggle to speak over my racing heart. "You're insane," I whisper, swallowing the urge to scream. "Whatever this is, I will have *no* part in it."

"Do you truly think you have a choice?" he bellows, his intensity knocking loose a new thread of fear within me. There is only so much one person—one *mind*—can endure before it crumbles completely. My nightmares already bleed into my reality. My dreams are no longer a place of refuge but just another way for me to hurt. Over and over again, I have been pummeled by my uncle's rage and jealousy and lust, reduced to nothing but a collection of mismatched rubble, never to be fit together again. Never to be *whole.*

Yet I recognize that, through *all* of that, I have remained. I have persevered, sometimes against my will. Has it all been just for this? Just to add another scar on top of an already unrecognizable body?

King Dolian faces the guards who stand as impassively now as they did when they entered the room. "This is the man who attempted to *kill* your future queen. He viciously attacked her in her bedroom, and were it not for the quick actions of the healers, she would be dead! She is owed vengeance, and today, she will take it. Let this serve as a reminder to *all* of you that you do *not* touch what is mine!"

His attention returns to me, gaze feral and eyes bloodshot.

"I will not do it," I growl past the tight feeling encircling my throat.

"Then what is his life worth to you?"

"What?"

"This man who tried to kill you." He grips Sterling's hair, yanking his head back. A gasp slips from me at his bloody and swollen face, one eye completely shut while blood actively leaks from his bottom lip. "What is worth giving up so that he may live?"

"I— I don't—" I shake my head again, my lips attempting to close around words that won't form. What he's asking is an impossible question with a terrible answer. And King Dolian knows that.

"Here is what I propose: his life for a night in my bed." He releases his grip on Sterling, dragging his hand down his trousers before returning to stand next to me.

"Excuse me?" I whisper, my palms growing clammy.

"Well, I will have you on our wedding night regardless, but I have waited a long time, Rhea. I have been thinking of why you fight me so, and I realized that while holding to tradition may have worked if our relationship were at all traditional, what we have between us is new. *Uncharted.* As such, it must be approached differently. Waiting is only tearing us apart." His eyes take on a sickening gleam. "I'm simply a man wanting to drink at the fountain of his beloved."

I rear my head back as I wade through my grief and cling on to the last remnants of my defiance. "If you think I will *ever*—"

"I don't *need* you to agree to it, and you know this," he cuts in. "So? Is a night without you fighting me before we are officially wed worth sparing the life of the man who tried to kill you?"

"I—"

Sterling tries to pull away from the guards holding him, his body thrashing until one of them sends a boot right into his ribs. A crack rends the air, and Sterling is reduced to whimpers.

The room narrows as I struggle to breathe, my fingers diving into my hair. I don't value my life above anyone else's, but what King Dolian is demanding... How could I agree to that? A shriveled part of me wishes he would just *command* me because at least then my culpability would be reduced to not being able to stop him. But *this*? This is not a choice. This is a consequence. This is the king demonstrating that no matter how vile and foul and *evil* I find him to be, he has the depravity to dig deeper. To show just how black his soul is.

"Perhaps it's for the best that you'll never see *Prince Nox* again. After all, what would he say to learning that you not only have my mark *on* you but *inside* of you?"

"Fuck you." The words erupt without restraint, and regret immediately fills me when he steps forward and drags the dagger down Sterling's cheek in one fluid movement. Sterling screams in pain, the hoarse sound adding to my anguish as I watch blood bloom. I look to the guards. To the advisors watching and, finally, to Xander. His jaw clenches, the only tell he lets slip, but even he doesn't move to interfere. No one does.

"Come on, darling. Time is wasting."

I can't kill him, but to *willingly* give myself to the king? *Gods*, I can't. It's selfish and cruel—*I'm* selfish and cruel—but I can't do it. "Please, don't do this," I beg. Foolishly, I beg.

King Dolian snarls, and I know I've lost before his next words are even spoken. "If you will not give me what I want, then you will coat your hands in his blood. *Extinguish him.*" This time, magic backs his command. It rushes over me, thick and suffocating, as it stuffs my own wants and desires back and forces me to reach for the dagger in King Dolian's hand. I hold it the way Cass taught me, devastated that the memory is now tainted. My morality frays at the seams as the inches between the tip of the dagger and the man's chest disappear, all because I did something I never should have—I chose *myself*.

My hand shakes around the hilt as I take aim. *Extinguish him* whispers in my head, the command reverberating as if trapped. *Extinguish him.* My eyes widen as I suck in a breath at the thought, and with hardly any distance or time to spare, I plunge the dagger not in the center of his chest or near his heart but higher, beneath his clavicle with the blade pointed straight back. It will hurt, as evidenced by his blood-curdling scream—but the siren magic flooding my veins doesn't protest the attempt. By incapacitating him, I've *extinguished* his importance to the king. By hurting him, I've *extinguished* the need for vengeance. It's a loophole, but I realize too late when I pull the dagger out and my gaze meets the king's, that it isn't one that is going to save Sterling.

"Clever," he murmurs, stepping behind me as one hand rests on my hip, right above the brand, while the other clutches where I hold the dagger, forcing our fingers to interlace. His lips brush my ear, my body stricken with fear as he whispers, "But you only succeeded in prolonging his death." He positions us closer to Sterling, commanding one of the guards to hold the prisoner's head up so that my eyes are forced to meet his. When I try to jerk away, the action driven by my desperation, King Dolian forces me into submission with magic. "Don't fight against me, Rhea. Look into his eyes as we do what must be done." So I do. Together, our hands drag the dagger across Sterling's throat, flesh splitting as his blood spurts out and coats my dress.

Though my chest heaves as if a scream is building, there is no sound. None that tumbles from me and none that I hear in my head as something dark and twisted shifts within. Sterling collapses to the ground, his eyes frozen open and forever burned into my memory. I had killed before, but it was never this intimate, and it isn't until this moment that I realize I've been clinging to an innocence that was only mine to claim by semantics alone. But now even *that* is gone.

As Sterling's blood begins to pool around his body, King Dolian tugs me to the left, keeping his body behind me as if I am a shield before he shouts, "Bring the next one in!"

There is the sound of footsteps and creaking armor, distantly I'm aware of the doors opening and someone else entering. But it's all as if I'm trapped in honey, every movement just a fraction too slow. My own thoughts struggling to keep up as I stare and stare at Sterling's lifeless body.

Suddenly, a woman is in front of me, kneeling in a tattered skirt as her head hangs low. Her blouse might have been a lighter color but is now the shade of dried blood. I drag my gaze up to her face, her lips cracked and swollen, her eyes faring no better. She looks from me to the king, her own attention slow to notice Sterling on the ground next to her. But then she does, and her lips part as a harrowing scream shatters the fog over me. All at once, the world rushes back in, sharpening the edges of my vision until my skin breaks out in goosebumps and I feel the heat of the king's body at my back.

"Let's try a new bargain," the king says from behind me, grip tightening on my hip. "This woman is guilty of consorting with the criminal who attacked you. You will drag your knife across her throat"—the woman whimpers through her tears, her gaze still locked on Sterling as she struggles to break out of the guards' hold on her—"*or* you can say that you love me. That you are *mine* in every way that matters." He buries his face into the side of my neck, lips sliding along the sensitive skin there. "Vow in blood that you belong to *me*, and she lives."

The woman in front of me blurs, and it isn't until I blink that I realize it's because of the tears pouring from my eyes. Despite how I hear my heart pounding in my chest, I don't feel it. As if the organ has detached itself and is now outside my body, a stranger pounding on a former home's door. And that's how I feel, how I've felt, for weeks now. Like an interloper in my own life. But, whatever this version of me is now, even she does not want to do this. But how many people would King Dolian sacrifice to gain something that is not his—that never was? How many lives would I *let* him claim so that I can hold on to the one thing I desperately want to keep for myself? For Nox?

His rumble of disappointment at my reluctance is the only moment I get before he commands me to kill her. The magic of his demand overpowers me, and while the guards hold her in place and her dark brown eyes plead with mine, I slide the sharpened end of my blade across her neck, the king's hand aiding in the kill. *Skin splits. Blood splatters.*

Her body hasn't even hit the ground when King Dolian yells, "Bring in the next one!"

"Stop!" I cry, turning to face him, my arm twisted at an uncomfortable angle as he keeps me in his grasp. My entire body vibrates as my chest heaves, air cold against my cheeks from the tears that track down them. "Please, *stop!*"

Behind me, Xander's voice cuts through the incoming footsteps and the high-pitched crying of the next person the guards have brought in. "Your Majesty, *surely,* a ch—"

"Do not speak another word if you hope to make it out of here with your head still attached to your body," King Dolian interrupts, his gaze bright with feral intensity before he turns it down on me, making me flinch. "Give me what I want, and all of this will end."

The crying behind grows louder, its cadence panicked.

My eyes bounce between his as my vision fills with tears before clearing, over and over again. His fingers flex over mine, the blood of Sterling and the woman having seeped between our hands and making the skin there sticky. Yet I hesitate. My hands are *stained* with the blood of two lives, the fate of a third dependent on *me*, and still, I hesitate.

And the king notices. Though he is shorter than Nox, at this moment, he towers over me, a monster trapping his prey and waiting for the right moment to strike. It comes not by his hand or with the dagger we hold jointly. It doesn't even come by his tongue. No, the king turns me slowly, his hand returning to the permanent reminder of his ownership over me, and forces me to see the third victim in his deranged game.

This time, *screams* of protest scrape up my throat. This time, I try to fight him, but the magic keeps me from doing anything more than shaking my head. My knees threaten to buckle, and I think I might hear Xander or perhaps one of the other guards speaking or shouting, but it's all discordant in my ears as I stare down at not a man or a woman but a *child*. A child who is kicking and screaming. Whose bruised eye is nearly swollen shut. One who looks up at me with pleading brown eyes, his blond hair messily strewn over his forehead in stringy clumps.

"A new compromise," King Dolian breathes near my ear, his voice soft but laced with warning. "You must give me *something*, Rhea, that shows your loyalty to me and this kingdom. After all, is it not *yours* too?"

It's the first time he's ever acknowledged my claim to the throne, but it doesn't matter. Despite his words, it isn't mine. No kingdom is, and after today, no kingdom should ever be.

"This boy's life is in your hands, and what I want from you is fairly simple. Vow to me that you will *obliterate* anyone that says they will take you away from me. Away from the Mortal Kingdom."

My mind whirls around his words as they surround me, the consequences of them firing off like a distant siren in the back of my head. But in front of me, there is a boy no more than ten, his body finally giving out and sagging in the guards' hold as his chest rises and falls too quickly. And there is no choice in this, there never was, but that's always been part of King Dolian's game. Giving me the illusion of choosing when the only options were always curated by him.

"Okay," I whisper, swallowing back the nausea that rises. The king doesn't respond, and when I turn to look at him over my shoulder, suspicion narrows his eyes and brackets his mouth. "I will vow to never leave you. Vow to being yours, and you can command me to kill anyone who tries to take me away from you. Who tries to take me away from this kingdom." There are no loopholes in my wording, no skirting around the magic that will lock me into this deal. But I can give this version of myself to him. I can stop pretending that the person here worthy of being saved is me. Still, the king does not move beyond a twitch of his fingers at my hip. "Command me," I say, wrapping the words up as a plea while staring into his eyes. "And let the boy return to his family."

"The boy is free to go," he says, gesturing with his chin to Xander. "Come. You'll be our witness. The rest of you, clean them up." Plucking the dagger from my hand, King Dolian hands it to Xander, whose eyes try to catch mine as he takes it and returns it to the sheath at his belt. But I won't risk the king suspecting anything between us, so I keep my gaze down as I'm tugged away from the carnage I've created.

But the boy's cries draw my attention back over my shoulder, and I watch as the boy falls to his knees and turns to look at the dead woman lying next to Sterling. "Promise me that you will return him to his parents," I say through the broken beating of my heart.

"I'm afraid that is impossible."

I turn to look at the back of King Dolian's head as we pass the guarded doors, a cold sweat breaking out over my body. "Why?" Behind me, the boy begins to wail again, the sound pained. Torturous.

"Because you just killed them."

Chapter Seventy-Three

RHEA

I T STARTS WITH THE king's command, magic drowning me as he speaks. Then, with Xander standing guard, my blood drips onto the courtyard outside, King Dolian's joining it as he clasps my hand and I make my vow. White magic—magic not unlike my own—flares from the ground and swirls up to our hands, wrapping around our wrists before sinking into our skin. Its warmth tingles for a few seconds before it dissipates. I feel no different, yet everything has changed.

You just killed them.

His words ricochet inside of me.

You just killed them.

A part of me is dead now too.

Chapter Seventy-Four

ARIA

I T HAD TAKEN A few weeks for Lyre and I to develop a plan that we both felt comfortable with to get the seamount sirens their weapons back. With her order to stay in the palace because of her pregnancy, Lyre was limited on what information she could gain.

Or she should have been. As it turns out, my sister's resourcefulness has no limits.

Since informing her of Nia's many threats, which hadn't yet resulted in me being apprehended and dragged through the palace to face my mother, Lyre has not only learned how many weapons are being stored in the Queen's Legion's arsenal but where we can find them. In the same amount of time it's taken me to reconcile knowing what the shape of Myla's lips pressed against my own feels like, Lyre has accrued more information about the arsenal than I even know what to do with.

"How in the Five Realms did you do this?" I ask her as we sprawl her notes out on my bed—detailing the number of sirens guarding the arsenal, a drawn map to them, and ideas to draw both Allegra and Sade away to give us time to haul the weapons out.

Lyre shrugs, leaning back on her hands, the swell of her belly prominent. "It's easy when plenty of females owe you favors. Or when they hate Allegra." Her lips quirk to the side. "There are a lot of sirens who fall into the latter category."

I pinch my lips together to keep my smile from growing. "So this is it, then?" I ask, looking from my sister to the mess of notes spread out before us. "We're really going to do this?"

"It's well thought out and the best we can do given the dire circumstances. Just because Nia hasn't made good on her threat *yet* doesn't mean that she won't. And while I still think it would be difficult to tie it all to you, I don't want to risk it. We empty out as many of their weapons as we can while the guards are distracted." She taps the map she's drawn, arrows indicating the hallways to follow when we enter the building. "Hopefully enough for the seamount sirens to do something with, while avoiding getting caught ourselves."

"Hopefully," I repeat, pursing my lips. "Are you sure it will be safe for you to sneak out without our mother noticing?"

Lyre nods. "The queen's attention has been solely focused on building the legion's numbers and bringing them to the Mortal Kingdom to be healed. Between that and her research with Dyanna, there hasn't been much focus given to Allegra or I. Something that annoys our older sister to no end."

"And the plan for Allegra?"

"I only need to have dinner with her as we've been doing since Mother sequestered us," Lyre answers, gliding from the bed to turn and begin cleaning up the papers detailing her plan. "After that, I will pretend to go to bed and sneak out and meet you at the back of the arsenal. Where a legion raft and extra armor will be waiting."

I try to crack a smile, even as anxiousness makes my fingers nervously tap against my scales. "I still don't know how you managed to arrange that."

"There may be more sirens joining the legion, but it doesn't mean that things are running smoothly. Sade alone is doing the work of ten females as she tries to ensure that the newest legionaries are trained properly. This is pulling tenured females from their normal posts. They're being replaced with those less knowledgeable, and mistakes are bound to happen." With a shrug, she gathers up the remaining plans and tucks them into her satchel. "Sade will be busy enough with the newest recruits in the evening that we don't need to worry about her. This will work, Aria."

I follow her to the door of my bedroom, my heart already in my throat in anticipation. But though I'm nervous, hope still winds within me. We will get Nia and the others their weapons, and then I will have one less thing hanging over my head. "I'll see you tomorrow," I tell her.

⁂

Conch shell armor is so much heavier than it looks.

The helmet is tight, my braids stuffed into it to help conceal my identity. While my markings could be considered unique, with the armor covering my hair and the top half of my body, I'm hopeful I won't stand out. Lyre swims next to me, the armor covering everywhere except the swell of her belly down. Sirens not of nobility are expected to continue their normal duties until they give birth, so she won't draw any attention simply because she is pregnant. Covered as we are, we should look like any other legionaries requesting access to the arsenal. Well, all except for the hollow out Queen's Clam raft that floats behind us, attached to our waists with straps.

Though we are silent, my heart dances wildly in my chest as we approach the front of the round building that stores all the weapons of the Siren Queendom, one of the legionary spears in my hand while the other I force to remain down at my side. Tall spires top the structure, the outside made of crushed seashells, sea glass, and rock. Like the other buildings in Lumen, it sparkles a brilliant white, glowing despite the late hour. Identical structures flank it on both sides, one a garrison housing all of the Queen's Legion who choose to stay there and the other a command station for the queen and her generals—though my mother prefers her throne room in the palace for those meetings.

I had met Lyre here exactly as planned, after her dinner with Allegra and my own quick journey to the cave. There had been no new letter from Nia, but the one I had left her the week prior was gone, so I know she visited.

Slowing our pace until we stop in front of the two legionaries on guard, I will myself to calm down. All I have to do is stay quiet while Lyre does the talking. I had faced down an angry fae female and come out on top *twice*. Biting my tongue should be easy enough.

"State your business, legionary," one of the guards commands, her yellow eyes glowing beneath the coverage of her helmet.

"We were sent by General Sade to collect weapons for the new recruits." Lyre's voice is perfectly steady, her answer given without a second thought.

"I was not aware of such a request." The yellow-eyed siren moves forward, eyeing the raft we are tugging behind us. Her fellow legionary—a female with braids a brighter orange than Sade's—grips her spear more tightly, her eyes bouncing between us and her companion.

"The order was just given," Lyre says, shrugging her shoulders as she throws a thumb over one of them, pointing in the direction of the garrison. "It's chaos over there."

The yellow-eyed siren smirks, nodding her head in agreement. "That it is." She looks us over again, her attention making awareness prickle on the back of my neck. When she returns to her post, my stomach drops only for it to lurch in relief when she and her companion begin pulling on the chains that heave the arsenal gate up, the entrance only a little wider than the raft Lyre and I pull behind us. "Make it quick."

Lyre and I both nod and swim inside the moment the gate is fully up, neither saying a word until we hear the gate close again. I take in our surroundings, the multi-colored light of crystals mounted on the walls showing the many hallways connected to the main one we are in. The walls gleam in the same white as the outside, nothing distinguishing one hall from another. That is purposeful, a way to trick those who come here that don't belong. If not for Lyre's ability to get information, it would likely take us the entire night to find what we are looking for.

"That was too easy," I whisper, pulling up the memory of the map as I try to orient myself. I had memorized the path to where the weapons are stored, and soon, we'll have to take a right, going down a long corridor that will eventually split in two.

"It was," Lyre adds, making my anxiety spike. Could the guards have deceived us? Only let us pass because they know we'll be caught here, where there is no denying our involvement? "Relax, Aria." Lyre's fingers grip my arm, giving me a gentle shake. "Let's stay focused and move quickly."

I pull my shoulders down away from my ears, fingers flexing around the spear I'm holding. *Who are you willing to become?* Whoever I need to be, and right now, I need to be someone confident in this plan.

"It's quiet," Lyre observes, eyes darting from side to side. We had expected at least a handful of roaming legionaries, but then again, this space was meant for storing things. It's not like the items could get up and walk away on their own.

Studying the map proves useful, and it only takes us a few minutes to find the collection of weapons we're looking for, their rudimentary look distinguishing them from those issued by the legion. "What if the guards ask to check the raft as we're leaving?" I ask.

"We'll figure that out when the time comes." Unbuckling herself and pulling a tarp from the raft, Lyre swims over to the stacks of spears, the light of a single white crystal shining down from where it's centered in the room. "Let's hurry before our luck is tested." We rush to gather as many of the weapons as the raft will carry before we cover it with the tarp, securing the fabric to the shell. Once we're both buckled back in, we return the way we came—bracing for an interruption, for a legionary to question us, but finding nothing but still empty hallways.

When we reach the gate, we both pause, glancing at each other, likely with the same thought: *Please, don't let there be an ambush waiting on the other side.* Lyre rolls her shoulders back as she lifts her chin, knocking on the gate to signal that we are done. A few seconds pass, and then I hear the legionaries on the other side pulling the chains, revealing the outside inch by agonizing inch. I wait until the gate is fully lifted and a clear view of the outside is visible before I allow myself to begin to hope that we've been successful.

"We've got everything Sade requested," Lyre says, urging us forward. "We'll be on our way."

It takes concentrated effort to keep my movements graceful, each part of me strung tight as I'm sure my heartbeat is loud enough for the legionaries to hear.

"Legionaries," the yellow-eyed siren shouts. Lyre and I pause, our eyes connecting in fear before looking over our shoulders. "Keep those guarded closely."

"Of course." Lyre and I waste no time moving forward again, the stares of the legionaries at our backs like flames licking at our skin. We swim just above the ocean floor, the bioluminescent plants a glowing array of pink, green, and yellow along the path to the garrison. "A little farther," Lyre whispers, nodding to where the path has fallen into shadow. Though my gills draw in oxygen from the water, suffocating fear is thick in my throat.

"I never should have let you do this," I whisper as the cover of darkness blankets us, and Lyre guides us to the left, away from the building and towards the direction of the cave. "It was stupid to risk—"

"You do not control me, Aria; just as I don't control you. Now *hush*." Her tone doesn't leave room for argument, so I keep myself vigilant as we make our way to the outskirts of Lumen. The journey feels twice as long, and my stomach has knotted itself ten times over by the time the cave comes into view.

"I have to take this off," I tell Lyre, tugging on the helmet until my braids float freely.

Lyre chuckles and gestures towards the silky sea kelp that floats in front of the hidden entrance as we near. "We can set the raft here and quickly unload it. Then we'll be back to the palace in no time."

We both unbuckle and remove the tarp, grabbing a handful of spears before pushing past the sea kelp.

My eyes take a moment to adjust to the darkness, only to come face to face with Sade.

"Well," she drawls, tilting her head to the side, her loose orange braids tied in a knot that hangs over her shoulder. A trident nearly as large as our mother's is gripped in one hand, and my stomach completely bottoms out when she points it at me, her face serious. "You have some explaining to do, Sister."

Chapter Seventy-Five

ARIA

"**F**UCK." LYRE'S TALONS GROW from the ends of her fingers, prompting me to do the same as my stupid magic blooms at the back of my throat. Sade appears to be alone, Lyre and I could attack her at the same time. But even as the thought enters my head, logic crushes it. Sade is the *general* of the Queen's Legion. Where Allegra's strength comes from her willingness to be as ruthless as possible, Sade's has been crafted and honed for *decades*. War may have never been fought in our lifetimes, but looking at Sade, you'd never know. From top to bottom, she is built for battle.

"It appears we have a Malika family special," Sade muses, an eyebrow lifting at the loot in her arms. "Though I'm afraid I will have to add a few guests to the mix." I look over my shoulder as the sea kelp parts to reveal two legionaries dressed in full armor, both with their spears. Deep yellow eyes meet mine, and pressure builds behind my eyes.

"Hello," the yellow-eyed siren taunts.

"Again," the other adds. It's the two legionaries that were guarding the arsenal.

My gaze meets Lyre's, and I almost scream at the defeat I see waiting in her eyes. We were set up from the very beginning. Somehow, Sade *knew*, and if she does, then so does the queen. My panic is a tangible thing, wrapping its rough hands around my lungs as my desperation tightens its fingers. Lyre's plan to raise her offspring, to live a life free of our mother, is gone now. Both of our lives now forfeit in the wake of this betrayal to our mother.

My eyes burn as the two sirens flank us, Sade's voice battling against the hum of magic that buzzes in my ears. "We have a lot to talk about—"

A legionary reaches to grab Lyre, the other wrapping her hand around me, and something within me snaps as an angry growl unleashes itself from my throat. "Stop!" I shout, my power infusing the command as my chest heaves and I jerk myself away from the legionary closest to me. I drop all but one of the spears, gripping it tightly even though I have no idea how to wield it properly, certainly not enough against these three trained females. But, surely I can buy enough time for Lyre to escape. "Lyre, go!" I yell, my voice a fraction calmer as I spin to take aim at the legionary holding her.

Except, when my attention falls to the yellow-eyed siren, she isn't taking aim at Lyre or me. She isn't even gripping my sister anymore. Instead, the siren is motionless. Unmoving.

"Aria..." Lyre whispers, her eyes blown wide as her mouth hangs open. I turn my own gaze back to the siren that flanked my side, only to find her frozen too, her body beginning to sink to the bottom of the cave. My brows crease in confusion, but my focus on the legionaries is abandoned when Sade moves closer.

"Don't hurt Lyre," I plead, holding the spear out in front of me as I block Lyre from Sade's view. "She didn't choose this; I forced her into helping me. Mother doesn't have to know—"

"Aria, stop," she says roughly, halting my panicked rambling. My expression falls, this nightmare truly coming to life right in front of me. Sade lowers her trident, her defensive stance completely melting away. It's not like she needs it facing me. Who am I but a weak—

Who are you willing to become? I stare at Sade, my heartbeat loud in my ears and magic pulsing at my throat as I abandon the spear. *Anyone Lyre needs me to be.*

My fingers curl, talons gleaming from their ends as my brows lower and I face my sister head on.

"No," Sade warns, pointing at me. "Don't you dar—"

I don't give her the chance to finish before I rush towards her. Most of my lessons with Myla have been building the basics and focusing on defending myself. We hadn't gone over how to properly attack an opponent, how to spot their weaknesses and exploit them as Myla so easily did with me. Without any of those skills—gods, likely even *with* them—I am not going to beat my older sister. But I'm not looking for victory; I'm looking to give Lyre a chance to escape. And while I have no real plan other than to *attack*, there is enough desperation flaring to life within me to, at the very least, make me a fucking nuisance.

The first swipe of my claws is met by Sade's trident, and I spin out of the way to avoid her incoming attack. Only it never comes. I don't allow myself to question why before I move back in, my biceps bulging and fingers flexed as I claw at her face. Her chest is protected by the armor, so when she blocks me again, I move lower, talons connecting with the scales of her tail. Pride surges through me when I manage to snag a few, pulling them from the softer flesh.

"*Ow*," Sade growls, her knuckles growing white from gripping her trident.

The cry that leaves me is filled with raw turmoil, my magic thrumming along with it. Sade's brows rise towards her hairline, and this time when my arm descends in an arc towards her face, she catches my wrist and spins me around, pinning it behind me. Her other arm is quick to band around my chest, and before I can open my mouth, her hand clamps over it, silencing me.

"Aria, stop!" The plea doesn't come from Sade but from Lyre. My focus shifts as she swims towards me, her hands framing my face. My muffled cries beg for her to get away as I struggle against Sade, but Lyre leans her forehead onto mine. "It's alright. It's going to be okay."

My body crumples in on itself as I sob, my failure crushing my chest.

"Everyone needs to calm the *fuck* down." Sade's voice rumbles down my back, making me stiffen. "We don't have a lot of time, and I need to make sure we are all on the same page before we leave this cave."

What?

"Aria, I'm going to let you go under the assumption that you *aren't* going to use your magic on me."

Why would I... Lyre's hands fall away from my face as she watches me, concern bright in her amethyst eyes. *Oh gods*. My magic... I look at both legionaries, their unmoving bodies now laying on the ocean floor. But that is impossible. Siren magic doesn't work on other sirens, and I hadn't— *Stop*. I had shouted the command at both, had felt the magic rushing up my throat—

"Aria, will you use your magic?" Sade asks, halting my spiraling thoughts. I shake my head, blinking away the remaining pressure behind my eyes as she releases me from her hold, feeling slowly returning to the hand that was pinned behind me.

The three of us watch as the magic—*my* magic—begins to wear off the legionaries, their fingers wiggling followed by their tails, until they are slowly swimming back up to us from the cave floor, their expressions disoriented as they look from Sade and then to me.

I knew my magic would only work on females. That has been proven over and over again. But in no realm of possibility did I *ever* believe it would work on another siren. That had never happened before. Not once in the millennia that the sirens have been a part of this world. Then again, neither had there been a record of our magic luring females.

"We are going to bring the rest of those weapons inside," Sade says slowly, reaching down to grab her trident from the floor. "And then Althea and Cali, you will return to the garrison, and then you two," she says, pointing to Lyre and I, "are going to explain what your plan regarding the seamount sirens is."

"I don't understand," I say, shaking my head as I settle close to Lyre, my talons still drawn.

Lyre echoes my confusion, asking, "Why are you helping us?"

Sade sighs as if annoyed, but I don't miss the way her eyes gleam in excitement. "Turns out you two aren't the only Malika sisters working against Queen Amari."

Lyre's room feels smaller than the last time I was in it, though it might have something to do with our older sister's presence. Having gotten rid of her armor and weapon, Sade leans back against the wall next to the door, her tail flicking gently side to side while her arms are folded over her chest. I sit next to Lyre on her bed, my fingers curling over the edge as I take in the information she's given us.

Nia *had* made good on her threat, passing information to Allegra about my cave of mementos and my involvement in helping them. Allegra had come to Sade, unsurprisingly calling for her to immediately apprehend and present me to the queen.

"She wants your blood," Sade says matter-of-factly. "And she's already gone to the queen with the supposed tale of your betrayal."

My eyes shut as I hang my head. There might still be time to run, but where would I go? Would I just *leave* Lyre? Leave Myla in the middle of our lessons? Did the latter even matter anymore now that I only had two options in front me: certain death or being bound to my mother's side at all times?

"You have a plan." Lyre's voice is calmer than my own thoughts, and I'm about to respond that I have *zero* plans when I look up and see that she is talking to Sade.

"Obviously. Allegra's been a thorn in the queen's side ever since being made obsolete," Sade says, the corner of her mouth twitching in amusement. "It's been quite hilarious watching her descend into madness."

"I don't understand. She's been pregnant before. She *knew* Mother was going to force her to stay here in the palace."

"Yes," Sade says, her sunset eyes meeting mine, "but our mother has never been so close to having everything she's ever wanted before. And if there is anything our eldest sister hates, it is being excluded from Mother's plans."

"And if there is anything Queen Amari hates, it's having to repeat herself," Lyre chimes in.

Sade nods in agreement. "Allegra is desperate to be a part of *any* conversation with the queen, and Nia dropped the perfect information into her lap. Or that is what Allegra believes anyway."

"Can we back up?" I ask, pushing off the bed to begin swimming in front of it. "How did you know we would be at the cave tonight? That we were going to come for the weapons? *Any* of it?"

"I knew something was going on the day you brought me Nia's necklace. Nia never would have left it behind for us to find of her own volition."

My brows scrunch as I look at my older sister. "You knew it was bait meant to get you off their trail."

"Yes. My legionaries had already combed the area I gave you thoroughly after the sirens left the seamounts. The odds of *you* finding that necklace after them were low." At Lyre's scoff, she amends her words. "I didn't say they were impossible; I said they were *low*. No offense, Aria, but you aren't a trained soldier. I gave you a section of the outskirts of Lumen to search because I knew that you needed an excuse to get away from the palace." I jerk my head back, my eyes widening as a noise between a yelp and a cough leaves my mouth. *Does this mean she knows about Myla?* "Well, that and the fact that I already know where the seamount sirens are."

"And the cave?" Lyre asks, seemingly alright with the barrage of information that Sade's just shared—unlike myself.

Sade shrugs, not bothering to smother her smile. "When I realized that Aria had to be in contact with Nia, I began following her. Our baby sister is not very good at making sure she's alone before she goes to her super secret cave of forbidden items."

"That she is not," Lyre says with a chuckle of her own, sending heat flaring to my cheeks.

"Sorry, I'm not some super spy like *you*, apparently," I retort weakly. Sade snorts, while Lyre attempts to cajole me by holding my hand. But despite my embarrassment, I meant what I said. Sade has managed to fool everyone about her loyalties. Another realization has my head snapping to her. "It was you, wasn't it? The one who warned them that the legion was coming."

The mood in the room sombers in an instant as Sade unfolds her arms and lets them hang loosely at her sides, her fingers curling inward. "Yes." Her eyes take on a distant look. "The call to attack had been given so abruptly, I didn't have time to do anything but send Cali ahead of the rest and hope that they listened to her warning. Thank the gods they did, but I knew they would have to abandon everything in order to get out in time."

The weapons. Their belongings. Everything needed for the offspring. All of it was left as the sirens fled the only place they had been allowed to call home.

"You say you know where they are now?" Lyre asks.

"They're in Eersten. Which is where the weapons and the items in your cave will go."

"You once told me that would be one of the first places Mother would look," I say, heart pounding in my chest as I recall not only what Sade said, but what the female I had met in Eersten, Izel, told me of how my mother was taking sirens to add to the legion. "Isn't it foolish for them to stay there?"

Sade's demeanor shifts again, something ruthless taking over. "Had you asked me a few months ago, I would have said yes. Our mother's devotion to finding and murdering the seamount sirens, as well as *anyone* who might oppose her reign, was undeterred. But now she is distracted with her plans on land. Her involvement with King Dolian has led to Allegra and I ensuring that everyone stays in line. With Allegra bound to the palace, I'm the one with eyes everywhere."

"So you can make sure that those in Eersten are overlooked when searching for the supposed traitors," Lyre surmises.

"Yes. Though Allegra and the queen are highly suspicious of the inhabitants because it's still the only place capable of hiding them. Izel will make sure that it stays that way, and she will have some time to focus on what is coming next while the queen is distracted." Izel, the teal-haired siren that lives in Eersten. "She will also make sure Nia stays put there."

"Does anyone else know?" I ask, sitting back down on the bed. "That you're pretending?"

"No. Only a handful of the legionaries that I trust and now you two. Every other correspondence I've had, whether it be with the sirens of Eersten or otherwise, has been anonymous."

"Why? Why risk it at all? The queen trusts you, and that is not something that has come easily," Lyre says, her voice hard. My eyes bounce from one sister to the other, something unspoken passing between them. With Sade in her seventh decade and Lyre in her fourth, there is a large amount of history they had together before I was born. But whatever situation Lyre is insinuating, Sade seems apathetic.

"At first, I *did* buy into everything our mother said. About our history and what was taken from us. About what we were owed and how it was our duty to take it by any means necessary. As our song began fading and our numbers reduced, it only strengthened that belief. For many decades, I was a faithful daughter in every sense." Sade looks away from us, her lips pursed in a harsh line. She doesn't have to add anything else. Somewhere along the line, things changed. Perhaps it was a single moment or many smaller ones strung together. Whatever it was, Sade is risking everything *now* to be here and to undermine our mother. Bravery doesn't have to be loud and flashy to be worthy.

"So now what?" I ask.

"Once we are sure the cave has been cleared, I will have to present you to our mother for the traitor accusations. It's the only way to appease Allegra and keep her from getting suspicious. I'll tell them what I found or, rather, what I *didn't* find." My throat works with a rough swallow, panic once more creeping along the edges of my mind. "And then your fate will be determined with a vote."

Great.

"But there is something we've yet to discuss," Sade says, looking right at me.

I nervously tap my fingers against the scales at my hips as I shift between her stare. Lyre offers me a small smile of encouragement. "I was sort of hoping you had forgotten about that."

Sade's brow arches. "Forget that your magic works on *sirens*? Don't think *that* will be happening any time soon."

"Did you know?" Lyre asks me, her gaze soft. "That your magic worked on our kind?"

"No," I rasp, just as shocked by the revelation as they are. "I swear it. I only knew that it worked on females, but I assumed that excluded sirens."

"Interesting." That's all Sade offers as she heads towards Lyre's door, apparently done for the evening.

"Sade, no one can know about Aria's magic. If the queen finds out—"

"You needn't worry about that, Lyre," Sade interrupts, her fingers closing around the door handle. "Another of Aria's secrets will be kept safe with me."

Chapter Seventy-Six

MYLA

I FUCKING *HATE* THE throne room. Beneath its silver adornments and drapes of deep red velvet hides a darkness. The punishments administered in this room begin and end in the shadow of my father's throne—his seat of power made of ancient dragon bones, masterfully crafted dragon wings flaring as if the chair itself is preparing to take flight. Beneath the glow of the chandeliers and above the glittering onyx floor, this room holds so much more than the aristocratic fae that currently mingle within it. It's where the condemned come to be judged, their fates locked in before they ever step foot in front of my father. It's the birthplace of my first set of scars, my once clean skin now a menagerie of markings that can be traced back to the moment I was dragged up the center aisle and thrown before the king.

It had been ten years, and the wounds still ache as if they are fresh any time I step foot in here. Ten years, and the scent of the burning wood and oil on the lamps still trigger me to the point my fingers tremble. Ten years and dozens of bodies that I have claimed in my own form of retribution, and I *still* fucking hate this room and everything it stands for.

But I need information that only the people here can give me.

Leaning back against the wooden wall of the small mezzanine overlooking the throne room, I stay back so as not to be seen by anyone below. This space is meant for musicians during celebrations, but today, it's serving as the perfect spot to eavesdrop. Plucking a green grape I swiped before climbing up here, I pop it into my mouth and listen to the chatter below. For now, it's nothing more than idle gossip, and with how rich they are, one would think they could at least *pay* to have something more interesting to talk about. Yet, as the night wears on and my bundle of grapes dwindles, I begin to wonder if forcing myself to endure this room is a mistake. Particularly as the remaining tenderness of my lashes makes me shift uncomfortably.

A pair of voices grows louder than the others, and when I strain my ears to catch what they're saying, I realize they are coming from the small stairwell leading to the mezzanine. Sucking in a breath, I pull my headdress into place and squat on the balls of my feet, dagger in hand. Leesi had forced me into a light green dress, the matching fabric wrapping around my head and half of my face a light enough material to breathe through easily. No one paid me mind as I meandered the halls before the party, my latest punishment only furthering my status as a social pariah. Not that I am complaining.

Crouching low, I listen to the scrape of boots on stone as they climb higher up the concealed staircase. My heart beats heavily in anticipation while my fingers roll along the hilt of my dagger, soothing movements that pacify the anxiousness of being discovered.

The footsteps come to a stop on the other side of the door.

"Tell me you have some positive news," a male asks, somewhat breathlessly.

A sigh responds, followed by the scraping of fabric against stone. "They are avoiding our border where we've been attacking them. We have to go somewhere new if we have any hope of fulfilling the king's quota of mages." My ears perk as I lean towards the door, picking up the steadier inhales of the second male. They're close enough that if they listened carefully, they would hear the sound of my breathing and heartbeat too.

"The king will not take kindly to that answer. We *have* to get close to the numbers he's asked for, or *you're* going to tell him we've failed."

The two bicker about who will be tasked with telling the king, and I consider outing myself just to tell them to move the fuck on when they finally change the subject.

"He killed one of the mages last night. I think it had to do with the failed attempt to get that black dragon."

I arch a brow at that.

"Damn. That means there are only two remaining. And we're supposed to get another five so he can test the big one?" There's a slow exhale of breath. "I know King Kamon is desperate, but this is madness."

"Quiet," the other barks. There's more shuffling, and I hold my breath, my blood heating at the thought of releasing pent-up energy that's grown restless within me. But when footsteps sound again, they are moving away from me, growing quieter until all I hear is the same revelry as before. *Damn.*

Sheathing my dagger, I sit back on my heels and let my elbows rest on my knees. *The king is taking mages?* To what end if they'll just die once they pass through the Spell? Does Navin know? And if he does, why the *fuck* hasn't he said anything? Perhaps his love for me is finally as compartmentalized as he thinks mine is for him. Swallowing a bitter taste at the thought, I release a breath, stirring the veil in front of my mouth. It's what I deserve, isn't it? To be iced out. No one as good as Navin wants someone like me lingering over them like a stain they can't quite get rid of. What was it I had told Aria? *Just because what is inside of us is dark doesn't mean that it holds less value than something light.* I don't know what possessed me to attempt to comfort her in that moment. To offer words that were soft for once instead of covered in thorns. It could have been the way she talked of her own experiences. It could have even been the fact that I found myself *resonating* with what she was saying. It is ludicrous to believe that I might have found common ground with a *siren* of all beings, and yet it is impossible to ignore that Aria had spoken to a sadness and loneliness and pain that I understood intimately. One that made my mouth twist in confusion because I didn't want to give a damn about her. I didn't want there to be familiarity between us.

The chatter below grows louder, knocking me out of my head. I crawl forward just far enough to peer over the edge, keeping low to avoid being seen. Watching as the crowd parts, I recognize the top of Navin's head immediately, half of his long hair pulled back into a knot. He cradles a silver guard helmet, armor adorning his body. It isn't unusual for him to wear the full gear of our King's Riders—the highest rank in the fae army—but he tends to only wear it when he's being sent on a mission or to patrol our borders. While my brother looks forward to the former, the latter he absolutely *loathes*.

"My son," our father says, his voice colder than the peaks of the mountain this palace is built into. "What information do you have?"

"I spoke with Sir Dae's wife and confirmed our suspicions. He's officially missing." Words of surprise and shock reverberate over the throne room. I grit my teeth, fighting off a grin. Parts of him were missing to be sure.

"Have you interrogated her?" the king retorts—leaving little to the imagination of what sort of *interrogating* he means. The King's Riders are not known for their manners or grace. Their ruthlessness matches my own. Navin, of course, is the exception, using the fear he inflicts as the crown prince before he'd ever raise a hand to a female.

"I did," Navin answers with hesitance I doubt my father notices. "She seems genuinely unsure of his whereabouts and can think of no reason why he would leave when their businesses and family are so heavily tied to Khargis."

"It's the Shadow," someone shouts, turning heads in their direction. "The bastard is hunting us and has been for a long time." Murmurs rise as the nobles show their assent.

"We have no proof—"

"We have a list of males of varying notoriety who have gone missing," another noble says, cutting Navin off. "Sir Dae is the most influential, but who's to say the Shadow will stop there? He's unpredictable. Picking victims at will. What if he turns his sights on our king?" At that, the fae below erupt in a flurry of panic, their panicked voices growing until my father holds his hand up, and the room immediately falls silent.

"Your worry over me is as unnecessary as it is insulting. As if I would allow a male who slithers under the cover of night to get the best of me."

My nails scrape against the wooden floor. The amount of gold I would pay to watch his face as he learns that Khargis's Shadow is none other than his abomination of a daughter is limitless.

"Your Majesty, the supposed *Shadow* is nothing more than a myth. If he is killing all of these people, where are their bodies? Where are the witnesses to the crimes?" Navin asks, cocking his head to the side. A flicker of warmth settles in my heart as he tries to dissuade the king from the notion that the Shadow—that *I*—might be a problem. He had asked me those very questions in the past, but I never answered them, leaving his imagination to fill in the gaps. "Even the most stealthy among us gets caught eventually."

Well that feels like a very pointed line. But there is no way Navin knows I'm here. Our communication has been limited the past few weeks, as he has been sent on more missions to patrol our borders.

It's obvious there are a few who disagree, their shaking heads and awkward silence giving them away. My father waits for the noise to quiet, the silver crown adorning his head catching the light when he stands and steps down the dais to place a hand on Navin's shoulder. "I have already allocated a group of guards to begin patrolling the lower districts. We must show our people that this *Shadow* cannot be allowed to terrorize at will. I assume this is a task you can oversee?"

"Yes, Father," Navin answers, and my gut sours.

"Excellent." He drops his hand and continues to the exit, the wide onyx double doors opening for him. I catch a glimpse of brown robes on the other side, Father Yamin's head dipped in a bow as my father joins him.

Turning, I begin my descent down the stairwell to the first floor, the exit hidden in a servants' corridor. Moving quickly, I stick to the shadows of the hallway as I make my way to my room. The night is still young enough for me to visit Khargis and warn my informant. The last thing I want is for the guards to take away my eyes in the city.

Opening the door to the sitting room, my steps halt as my gaze clashes with Navin's.

"That line was for you," he says from where he's sitting on the arm of the couch, drumming his fingers along its back. "In case you were wondering."

I don't question how he knew I was present in the throne room. If anything, I'm more surprised he beat me here. "Duly noted."

"You can't go to Khargis."

"And why is that?" I ask, closing the door behind me.

He shoots an arm out towards it. "You were in there, Myla. You heard what the king said. It's too dangerous."

"I'm not afraid of the King's Riders, and I'd think you'd have a little more respect for my skills than to believe they actually pose a threat."

"One-on-one? They don't. But our father was underplaying how many he sent. I checked with Commander Hinata, and there are dozens of guards already crawling around the lower district, more being sent as we speak. No streets are clear. There are *no* shadows for the Shadow to hide in." He stands and strides towards me, light playing off of his silver armor. "All it takes is for *one* of them to see you, and they'll sound the alarm until you're overwhelmed."

"I'll deserve whatever happens to me if I'm dumb enough to get caught."

"Myla"—his hand reaches out to wrap around my arm gently, snapping my gaze to his—"what is it that you want from this?" When I fail to answer, he shakes his head, hands covering his face before he lets them fall to his sides. "What happened to you was fucking horrible, Myla. What's continued to happen under the guise of a punishment by the gods is utter bullshit, and *you don't deserve it.* You never have. And I'm sorry. What Daiya did—"

I take a step back, every nerve ending on high alert for a danger that isn't even fucking here. It's a triggered response to that name—*her* name. I haven't allowed myself to think of it, let alone heard it spoken, in a very long time.

Navin's eyes soften as he watches whatever emotion I've let slip onto my face. "Myla—"

"You asked what I want from this? Why I keep risking myself for those people in Khargis? It's because if I do not have *this,* then I have *nothing.*" And there it is—a bit of the truth. Of the fear that I keep tucked deep within. The shambles of my life—the whippings and degradation and utter disdain with which I am looked upon—is worth enduring if what I do in response matters at the end of the day. If my defiance of the labels and rules my father and his father and all of the males who came before them have placed on the females of this kingdom actually *makes* a difference, then so what if my life is the cost? If the oppressed can see someone fighting *for* them, I have to believe it will inspire more of them to rise up. Even in the face of defeat. And, selfishly—psychotically—I *enjoy* being the Shadow. I enjoy watching those who have done awful and horrific things to others beg for mercy from the likes of *me.* It is a monstrous thing to heed the beckoning call of, but I accepted a long time ago that being monstrous doesn't mean I can't be a force for *good.*

How can I begin to verbalize all of that to Navin? Not even he, a male who has known me my entire life, could understand without judgement. Even if, deep down, I know that he wants to.

"I'm going." There are no other words spoken as I slip into my bedroom to change. When I step back out, Navin is gone. I shut down the replay of our conversation—the way he looked at me and the mention of *her* name. And because I need the distraction, because I need *anything* else to focus on, I picture a siren with ruby-red hair and soft doe eyes.

I don't allow myself to question why my mind goes to her as I open the glass slider and leave.

Chapter Seventy-Seven

MYLA

"IT'S A FUCKING SHIT show," Shen says as she paces her small living room, the bar beneath her apartment loud in spite of the late hour. I wrinkle my nose at the scent of stale beer that permeates the floor, Shen jumping when the sound of something crashing below shakes the walls. "Fucking assholes!"

"Their presence will remain because of what I did to Sir Dae," I say through my mask, my fingers dancing along the empty sheath at my thigh.

"He deserved everything that you did to him. I only wish I could have been there to give him a few slices and dices of my own."

I arch a brow, folding my arms over my chest. "Slices and dices?"

She rolls her eyes. "I don't know what you do, but you have enough daggers strapped on you that I assume you enjoy cutting into these mongrels." She exhales and plops down on the armchair across from me, tossing her glossy black hair over her shoulder. "In any case, if you're feeling regret about bringing the guards here, you shouldn't."

"They're going to make everything more difficult," I warn. They already had, and they'd only been here for a handful of minutes longer than me. "You'll have to be more careful when scouting."

Shen scoffs. "I'm *plenty* careful! The perk about being a low-born *nobody* is that I'm never noticed when I go out. And before you get all sentimental, I wasn't trying to garner pity."

It's my turn to make a noise of derision. "I do not pity you, Shen. And I'm not sentimental."

She smiles as she points her finger at me, one that has been cut off at the top knuckle. "Good. The last thing we need is the Shadow getting soft."

"That will never happen," I tell her, adjusting my weight where I lean against the wall. "Do you have any new information for me?"

Shen sighs, crossing one leg over the other beneath her black cotton dress. I observe her as she begins to update me on a few targets. She was still a teenager when I met her for the first time. It was an accidental moment on my second trip to Khargis, but it solidified what I wanted to do with Navin's training. Shen had been abducted on her way home from the market by two wealthy males who had been *scouting* for females in the lower neighborhoods. Witnesses had tried to stop them, but the males' security had fought them off. For days, they brutally tortured her, invading her body in ways that still make anger burn deep in the pit of my soul.

It had been dumb luck that I was sneaking through the forest into Khargis when I was, passing by a small shack the men were hiding a small group of females in. They were kept in a basement, but Shen had managed to hoist herself up to a small window, hitting it to garner my attention. When I discovered them, they were pale and sickly, bleeding and covered in fluids that made my stomach churn. They had been treated worse than garbage, yet they thanked me as I helped them break free of the literal chains anchoring them to a wall.

We moved quickly as I snuck them into Khargis, Shen leading us to the group home she had been raised in as she begged the females running it to give the others a safe place to clean up and sleep.

"What about you?" I had asked when she emerged with a bag slung over her shoulder, freshly showered but with a haunted look in her eyes.

"There isn't enough coin to take care of us all. I'll find somewhere else to go." It was a lie. There *was* nowhere else to go. As I watched her walk away, disappearing around a corner, I realized that justice wasn't something that had ever been doled out fairly in this kingdom. These males would never be caught, never have to face the way they had terrorized these females simply because they were born into money and their victims weren't. They knew that, and it made them feel invincible. It made them act as if they were gods.

That night, I returned home and gathered as much coin as I could, asking Navin to go to the royal treasurers for more under the guise of wanting to buy a small piece of land. I knew they wouldn't question him, and they didn't. The next day, I returned to Khargis, dropped funds off at the group home, and then found Shen.

"I have a job for you," I told her, as I showed her around the tavern that would become her new business. And her new home. "I want you to spy for me." She had been apprehensive at first, but when I explained the type of *clientele* I wanted her to get information on, it morphed into determination. For years, Shen has used the bar as a way to get information. She hasn't failed me once, and I've watched her grow into a female who knows her worth.

"You weren't in Khargis for a few weeks," she says quietly, halting my trip down memory lane. My gaze meets hers, dark eyes serious beneath the dim light of candles flickering around us.

"I was busy," I lie.

Shen hums but says nothing more, standing as she brushes the nonexistent lint off of her dress. "I should go back down and make sure those bastards aren't messing with Jarrin."

Jarrin is an older fae male Shen had hired to help run the bar. He treats her like a granddaughter, the two having met when Jarrin punched a male half his age for saying something nasty to Shen. I have trusted my informant's gut when it comes to who she allows in her bar, and so far, Jarrin has proven worthy.

"Thank you for the updates. You will likely see me less because of all the guards," I say, walking to her front door. My hand pauses on the handle as I twist to look at her. "Leave your correspondence in our usual place, and if at any point you think you're being watched, stop recon."

Shen smiles wider, her teeth flashing. "Don't worry about me, Shadow. I can take care of myself." She waits for me to open the door before breezing through it, the ruckus from the tavern below still bleeding through the floors.

Blowing out a breath, I make sure my hood and mask are in place before I follow, shutting and locking the door before disappearing into the night to watch over the city.

⚜ ⚜

Navin is quiet as we fly to meet Aria days later. I had only spoken with him once since our disagreement before the king decided to send him to patrol the borders. I want to believe that he was truthful when I asked if he knew about the mages or dragons. That he was simply acting on the information the king gave him and was flying with the King's Riders to make sure that our borders were secure behind the Spell.

When my boots hit the sand, Navin says nothing before he and Lan launch back into the air.

Heading into the cavern, my gaze catches on Aria as she emerges from the water, transforming into her mortal form while clutching her usual blue bag to her chest. Her hair hangs in ringlets around her shoulders, the ends brushing the curves of her hips as she trudges in my direction. The sun plays off the faint markings of her scales, rivulets of water making them glint even brighter. When her gaze meets mine, it's paired with a pinched look of concentration. There is no quick hello or far too friendly smile offered to me. There is only quiet as we reach the rocks to climb up to the stone platform at the same time.

Handing her the cream tunic I brought, I give her my back as I climb up first.

"What is your lesson plan for today?" she asks once she's joined me, dropping her bag down. I turn to face her fully, the faint shimmer of the golden scales just below the hem of her tunic catching my attention as she walks towards me. They glow against her dark skin, a warm contrast to the ruby color of her hair and the scales now hidden beneath the cream fabric. "Myla."

I blink at my name, my eyes lifting to find her gaze already on me. "Warm-ups and then more practice on defensive measures," I bite out, Aria's eyes widening at my tone.

It had been another late night in Khargis, followed by a short trip to the dragon fields. Sunis had been asleep, Bali nowhere to be found, and the frustration at yet another week passing without a dragon bond had kept my mind running long after my body collapsed onto my bed. Leesi had not come to my room this morning, not exactly surprising considering preparations for the winter solstice celebrations are underway. Every maid and servant will be working from dawn to dusk for weeks to decorate the palace. I had used the alone time to clean my blades before getting dressed and meeting Navin in the sitting room. Then I had endured the silent flight over.

That is why I can't focus, why my gaze keeps straying places it shouldn't.

"Can we do *more*?" she asks, her voice softly echoing out.

"More?" Clasping my hands behind me, I tilt my head, noting how the orange in her eyes is brighter.

"I need to learn how to attack. Both with a weapon and without. Defense is only half of fighting, and we've spent enough time on that for now," she says, and I find my lips fighting to smirk at the defiance I hear in her voice. At the determination that gleams in her eyes.

"I might argue that being proficient in defense is more important than having only the basics of attack down," I counter, beginning to pace the length of the platform. "You want to make sure you have each step down thoroughly before moving on to the next one."

"No," she whispers, and this time there is a flare of panic to it as she shakes her head, fingers interlacing nervously in front of her. "No. I don't have time to *only* know defense. I need to learn how to understand my opponent. Anticipate their weaknesses so that I can beat them." Her chest heaves and my steps halt, the distance between us smaller. "I need to capitalize on the fact that I'm underestimated. I want to *hurt* someone before they see me coming." She gasps for air, her body turned to the side so that I can only see her profile. Closing her eyes, her chin falls to her chest, red curls covering her cheek.

My eyes narrow as I replay her words, scanning her body, and this time, I'm looking for something specific. "Little Siren." My voice relays a calm that I don't quite feel as I take a single step towards her. "Did someone hurt you?"

"No. No, no one hurt me. I just— I need to know how to prevent the queen from... *Gods!*" Her hands dive into her hair, pushing the strands away from her face as she heaves a deep breath before letting a shaky laugh fill the silence. "I need a lifetime of training in only a matter of weeks! And it will likely *still* not matter because if the queen decides that my fate is to be bound to her side for the remainder of my days or worse—"

Aria pinches her lips shut, sealing in the rest of her words despite how I find myself hanging on for the next one. *The queen is deciding her fate?*

"I'm sorry," she says, turning to face me fully and forcing a fake smile to her pretty lips. "I know you don't care about my pathetic life story. Can we just focus on the basics of attacking an opponent today? Please."

She resumes wringing her fingers in front of her as she waits for me to answer. I push back the urge to tell her to *demand* I train her, not to *plead* for it. Does she not understand the power she holds in our bargain?

"Do you have your dagger?" I ask, reaching to my vest for one of my smaller blades. Aria swallows as she watches me, an array of emotions moving over her face before she nods and grabs the weapon from her bag. The one that belonged to my father and was last held by Shah. And one that, if the stories I've overheard are true, holds magic that can give its wielder temporary passage through the Spell by way of a blood sacrifice.

Returning to her position across from me, Aria's chest lifts with a breath, and then she bends at her knees and begins bouncing on the balls of her feet. Her grip on the dagger is strong as she holds the blade almost parallel to her forearm. "My muscles are warm from my swim here," she says, brushing her curls over her shoulders with her free hand. "I want to use all of our time learning new attacks."

"So eager to draw blood?" I ask as we circle each other, my blood thrumming with anticipation.

"You sound surprised. I thought you believed me to be nothing but a mindless, vicious monster. I thought you wanted nothing more than to slide your blade across my throat," she counters. Something warm blooms low in my gut at the focused look on her face as our eyes lock, at her taunting words. "What was it you said? You can't wait to send my remains to my *bitch queen*? Well, what are you waiting for?"

I tighten the space between us, moving in closer as I breathe through the thrill her words ignite. "Goading me will not end well for you, Aria."

Her lips pinch at my use of her name, and I berate myself internally for saying it. Names are too familiar, and I—

The thought disintegrates when she lunges for me. She actually *fucking* lunges. The dagger swipes at my face, and I lean back to dodge it, the air stirring where the blade slices through it. Aria pivots, bringing her weaker foot forward before plunging the dagger straight towards the center of my chest. I lift my blade to block hers, using my other hand to push at her wrist, sending her arm off course.

"Don't put all of your weight behind one move," I tell her, as we separate. "Not until you're sure that next hit is the one that is going to kill your opponent."

"How do you know that it *will* kill them?" she asks.

"It's a feeling. A knowing," I answer, watching as her expression shifts in thought. "When you see the right opening, you won't have a doubt that it will be *the one*."

"What if I get that opportunity with you?" she asks, her lips turning up.

"If I allow you to get close enough to harm me, by all means, take the opportunity." I hold my free hand out in front of me, fingers curling in towards my palm. "Now, come at me again, but this time, move more quickly. Your goal with these initial attacks is to try and catch me off-guard."

Aria prepares her stance, this time leading with her good foot as she exhales through her mouth. "Catch you off-guard? Can I use any means necessary?"

I arch a brow. "You can try." The rush of adrenaline is instant when her mouth widens with a true smile and she attacks again.

Chapter Seventy-Eight

MYLA

"**M**Y ARMS ARE ON fire," Aria whines from where she stands in front of me, sweat beading at her temples. She had continued to try to attack me, swinging her blade in nearly feral movements in her attempts to nick me. It was sloppy, but even with the lack of practiced finesse, I had to admit I was impressed. The female who had shown up to our first meeting is not the same one who stands in front of me now, dagger in hand, attacking as if *I* am her sworn enemy.

Maybe I am. Does her queen know about her visits here, and that is why she is deciding Aria's fate? And why the *fuck* do I keep coming back to that one sentence she said? If Aria were to die from something unrelated to our life debt, I would be free of our bargain. At least, I *think* I would. I'm not necessarily eager to find out, considering that if I am wrong, I would be dead too.

It is that line of thinking, and only that line of thinking, that leads me to ask, "Why is the queen deciding your fate?"

Aria punches at my extended hand, pausing when she makes contact to look at me with wide eyes. "Why do you want to know?"

"It seems pertinent for me to know," I answer, gesturing with my chin for her to keep going. "Stay light on your feet. Use your back leg and core to power the punch." I give her time to think her answer over as we move around the cavern, my muscles welcoming the heat building from the exercise.

"It's... a complicated answer," she says, her elbows dropping slightly. I reach out and use the tips of my fingers to lift her arms back up, putting her guard in place. Once she's steady there, I send a few punches of my own, pulling their weight back. She blocks them, wincing slightly as she does.

"Life is complicated," I say with a shrug, opening my palms to signal it's her turn to come at me now. "If it helps, there is not much you could say that would surprise me."

"I don't know if that is a good or bad thing." When I let the silence linger as an answer, she rolls her eyes. "I am being investigated for treason." I suck in a breath and choke on it, all while Aria swings her fists towards my palms, driving me backwards a few steps. "Oh my gods, did I catch you off-guard?"

I growl and then cough again. Fuck I *had* been caught off-guard. *Treason?* Clearing my throat to settle the coughing, I ask, "What did you do to warrant that?"

"What makes you think I did anything at all?"

I tuck an errant strand of onyx hair behind my ear before gesturing for her to continue punching. "Seems like a fairly major accusation," I answer. "Is your queen in the business of wrongly accusing the innocent?"

She exhales roughly, a dark expression flitting across her features briefly. "Queen Amari isn't known for being fair. She's merciless, and she extends that to anyone who she believes to be a threat to the Siren Queendom. To *her*."

"And she believes you to be that threat?"

She punches at me twice, each reverberation making her brows lower. "Someone told her I was a threat because they believed I wasn't doing what they wanted," she says quickly, as if needing to force the words out as fast as possible. "So now I must face judgement from the queen and her daughters."

Interesting. I don't know a thing about how the sirens run their queendom and certainly not about how they mete out judgement. *One-two. One-two.* We dance in circles, her hits coming as quick as her breaths and with more strength behind them.

"It's ridiculous, really. I didn't fight back when Nia demanded I stay away from the seamount sirens. I didn't fight back when she cornered me and ordered me to help her get their weapons."

One-two. One-two. We keep moving as Aria punches at my hands, her eyes focused where her knuckles meet my skin.

"I didn't fight back when she *stole* the items I had gathered, each one a remembrance of the lives our kind had taken. And she just *sold* them off, as if they were nothing at all. I didn't fight back when she threatened to tell the queen of my involvement with those that were banished. So *many* times, I didn't fight back. And for what? I have been beaten. Forced to do things that no being should, and still, that is not enough. For Nia. For my mother. For those the queen surrounds herself with." Aria's eyes grow glassy as her punches get sloppy, my hands trying to anticipate their direction so she doesn't hurt herself. "I was the *only* one trying to help her, and she betrayed me so *fucking* easily! I feel *trapped* between falling back into the siren I was and becoming one I am trying to be, and it's—" Her breath hitches when she sends an errant punch in my direction, the force of it making her stumble forward. I catch her wrist in one hand, letting her fall into my chest while my other hand lands on her hip to steady her.

"I'm sorry," she rasps, eyes wide as they meet mine.

I swallow against the strange tightness in my throat. I know all too well what it is like to not be enough for those around me. To feel trapped within my circumstances. Even now, even with how I spend my nights, I still feel the invisible bars of my cage surrounding me.

I suppose I never considered that someone like Aria might also understand what that feels like.

My fingers flex on her hip, her sweet, warm scent laced within my next inhale. The rise and fall of her chest against my own makes me *acutely* aware of just how close we are, even if the distance between our lips feels like miles. *Would she taste as sweet as she smells*? The thought appears unbidden, yet my body responds to it, heat pooling low as I draw in another breath. My mind betrays me further when it conjures up the memory of our kiss beneath the water, the positioning of our bodies not so different than it is now. And, fuck, if there isn't something about her that makes me want to test her reaction if I closed that small space between us. If I drew my lips against her own not because it was needed but because I want to.

Because I want her.

It's that realization—more than the warmth of her body against mine and the way she feels beneath my fingertips—that is more sobering than a punch to the gut, and as if I've been hit, I release her quickly and back away.

"Myla?"

My name comes out as a question, and I grit my teeth, pain flaring to my temples as if that will dispel whatever fucking chaos just arose inside me. Something within me yearns to erase the disappointed look on her face. To tell her that I understand, to some bizarre degree, everything she's said. That I might have been *wrong* in my assumptions about her.

But then my inner voice grows loud. It not only reminds me that, because of the sirens, I am forced to endure the brunt of my kingdom's wrath and disdain but also that I have been down this road before. My back bears the scars of that consequence. It's a stark admonition that warns of the dangers of believing I've found common ground with someone. Of believing I'm worthy of any kind of deep connection.

Aria continues to stare at me, her body frozen in the position I left her in when I stumbled away. My voice is rough when I finally find it. "You'll have to learn how to control your emotions when you fight. While the intensity will benefit you, the sloppiness will not." For a long moment she doesn't move, nothing beyond the working of her throat as she swallows. Then her expression shutters, and the tension between us dissipates as she nods.

"Teach me another combination of hits."

The rest of our time together is spent mostly in silence, the only words spoken when I make a suggestion to her form or show her a new combo. By the time Navin and Lan show up, I'm on edge, frustration coiling through my veins. Aria wastes no time returning to the ocean, giving my brother a parting wave before returning to the sea.

I climb on Lan's back, sitting behind Navin as I grip the leather strap and prepare for flight. Only, Navin lingers. "What?"

"I found something out, and I don't want to tell you."

I scowl as I stare at the back of his head, my fingers tightening around the leather. "What is it?"

"You have to promise me that you won't go all *Myla*—"

"*Navin*."

"—and try to intervene. In this instance, I have to *insist*."

I tilt my head back and close my eyes, letting the warm sun paint my face as I try to calm my annoyance. "*Fine*," I promise, rolling my shoulders back. "What do you know?"

"The king has increased patrols even more in Khargis and has extended the King's Riders vigilance to the air above the city as well."

"I know this, Navin," I say, unable to keep the ire out of my voice. "I'm quite aware of just how many of the bastards are in Khargis."

He sighs, heavy and full-bodied as Lan adjusts beneath us, a low rumble vibrating down his body. I fight off the urge to dig my heel a little harder into the impatient beast's side. "You asked me about the mages and the dragons and I wasn't exactly truthful with you when I told you I didn't know what was going on with them." A bitter taste blooms in my mouth at the admittance of his lie, even if it's hypocritical for me to feel that way. Maybe my silence relays that because Navin tries to fill it with a series of apologies before I get him back on track. "I didn't know at first *why* Father was kidnapping them, only that he was. He's kept everything close to the chest, only allowing Father Yamin the details about the dragons and mages—"

"Get to the point, Brother," I snap.

"It's the bonds," he says, leaning to the side so that his gaze can meet mine. "He's terrified that, eventually, the failing of the dragon bonds will happen to *him*."

I draw my brows together, shaking my head in confusion. "He believes *me* to be the cause of that particular bad fortune. What does that have to do with the mages?"

Navin's gaze is hard as it holds mine, his serious tone growing uneasy. "He's using the dragons to kidnap mages and bring them through the Spell. Then he's forcing them to test their magic on the dragons in an attempt to repair the bonds."

What? "That doesn't make any sense. Even if their magic *was* compatible, they'd die before he'd properly get to test it." That must be why he was giving his men a quota, why those males in the stairwell were so stressed about grabbing more mages. "He's a fool."

"Except there's something else you don't know," Navin says slowly, rubbing at the back of his neck. I lean forward, my eyes narrowed at my brother.

"Which is?"

"The mages have the ability to pass through the Spell. Without loss of life or magic."

I'm silent as I overturn Navin's words. I have no clue if mage magic *can* repair a dragon bond. Could it *force* a bond? Is that what they want Bali for? For Sunis?

"There is nothing you can do about this, Myla. Nothing you *should* do."

"I won't," I say, earning a sarcastic look. I don't try to convince him any further, so he sighs again and faces forward. Within a few seconds, Lan launches into the air, snapping his wings out and beating them hard to lift us higher. The wind whips at my hair, my eyes closing as I run through everything I've just learned. My father can try whatever he wants with the dragons that have lost their bonds. But Sunis? She is *mine*, and I'll be damned if I let that bastard take anything else from me.

Gravel crunches beneath my boots as I walk the outskirts of the dragon fields, my gaze turned up to the night sky. Mist floats high above me, the flicker of silver stars only just visible through it. The wind carries with it the scent of rain and the residual smell of something burning.

When I finally reach Bali and Sunis's cave, rare nerves rattle my stomach. What will I do if my father is successful in luring Bali away with the drugged food? If Sunis is taken as well? I don't want to be a sentimental fae, but the possessiveness over the dragon that isn't even mine is nearly overwhelming. Is it possible to have a bond with the creature without one actually forming?

My pathetic anxiousness is snuffed out when I hear wings rustling inside the cave. The ground begins to rumble, a pair of yellow eyes blazing to life against the dark backdrop. My gut says it's Sunis, and that's confirmed a few moments later when she emerges, her head low as she observes me. Holding my hand out, I release a trapped breath when she nudges her head against it, the roughness of her scales welcome against my palm. A low purring sound comes from her as she closes her eyes. I bring my other hand to her snout, rubbing before laying my forehead against her. "We're running out of time," I whisper to her. To myself. Stating the obvious out in the open.

A second dragon trill comes from inside the cave, and Sunis lifts her head away from mine as her wings ruffle at her sides. She backs into the cave until there is only darkness once more looking back at me. *They are safe here*, I tell myself until I scan the dragon fields and spot another large pile of dead goats and sheep just waiting to be eaten. Fingers curling into my palms, I gather some sticks from the nearby treeline, working quickly to light them one by one from a nearby flaming pile of *something*, and then toss them onto the tainted meat.

Rage flickers inside of me as I watch it burn, a sizzling in my blood that can only be alleviated by one thing. Putting my mask back in place, I tug my hood over my head and retreat back to the forest. Khargis was being infected with a different kind of poison, and I am more than ready to bleed it out.

Chapter Seventy-Nine

NOX

"**Y**ES, I WILL MARRY you."

I hardly have time to slip the ring on her finger before she's pulling my face to hers, our lips meeting beneath the tree that I had spent so much of my childhood daydreaming under. As a child, life outside of this garden had been chaotic and demanding. What else could have been expected for a boy given the most magic anyone had seen since before the war? This place had become a refuge, and now it would be even more than that.

Rhea leans away to examine the ring, her brows drawing together. "It's so very beautiful."

Smiling, I help her stand, marveling at the way the ring sparkles on her finger. It feels right, seeing it there. Knowing that I'm hers in every way that will ever matter. "The diamond was taken from a ring that has been passed down from queen to queen for millennia," I tell her, no shortage of pride in my voice. It had been obvious to choose the Mage Kingdom heirloom as her ring's stone, something that the council would collectively burst into flames over if they knew. But I wanted this piece of jewelry to not just represent my love for her. I wanted something that was worthy of being on her finger. Something that reminded her that her right to rule was the same as all those who had come before her.

There was only one place I knew of that might house the jewelry of past mage queens. Stealing the key to access the archives was easy enough, as was making sure the palace jeweler kept quiet about the ring. The turnaround had been quick, and for weeks, the ring sat hidden in a secret compartment in my room while I waited for the right time. In truth, I had known long before I asked that I wanted to tie my life to hers, but Rhea needed to experience a world outside of the tower. So I waited.

"You just took from another ring?" The cadence of her voice draws my gaze down to her, where her top lip is curling.

I tilt my head, an inhale catching in my throat. "Of course. You are to be the next queen, Rhea. You have every right—"

"Queen," she interrupts, avoiding my eyes as she looks out to the garden, her lips pressed into a thin line. "That's right."

I frown at the look on her face. The edges of my vision flicker, shadows rolling in like storm clouds as the forest darkens. Had she really been so disappointed?

"Rhea—"

"Are you ready to go?" She smiles, but it's the one she used to give me when we were first getting to know each other. It was meant to be reassuring, like I wouldn't be able to tell that it was a mask. Even back then, I spent way too much time memorizing every facet of her face. I could see through her attempts to pacify me, and this was no exception.

Her steps are soft against the white stone as she walks ahead of me, her gaze drawn to the ring on her hand as she holds it out in front of her. As if she can sense me watching her, she stiffens and drops it down to her side.

My heart beats wildly in my chest as panic creeps in. No, she was happy—ecstatic about the proposal. About becoming my wife. The shadows creep farther in, and so do my doubts. Is the memory I hold of that day actually what happened or a mere projection of what I wished to see? Sweat beads at my temples and on the back of my neck, my next breath hissing out through clenched teeth as pain radiates from the space behind my heart and down my torso.

My steps falter, and my knees crash to the stone, but Rhea keeps walking.

"Rhea— Ah!" The sound of her name makes that unbearable ache singe me from within, making air impossible to take in. I call for her again, watching as she continues towards the door with the stained-glass window, leaving me alone as darkness takes over.

It's my gasp of air that wakes me from the dream, my body launching upright as my hands slam down on my face, covering my eyes. It takes minutes for my heart to calm, the pressure behind my eyes threatening to explode with every breath I take. By the time I feel more in control, my body is coated in sweat and my stomach is revolting against the meal I consumed earlier. I barely make it to the bathroom before heaving it up, and when I'm finished, I hobble over to the shower, turning it to the coldest setting.

It was only a dream. A nightmare. A figment of my imagination. I had seen the same scenario play out in my head for weeks, and yet, like a splinter beneath my skin, I can't ignore it. Not the way I saw Rhea's happiness wither away at the mention of being queen.

Stepping into the shower, I plant my hands on the tiles in front of me, my head hanging between my shoulders as the icy water batters my back. *It was only a dream*. But Rhea did have doubts. When the guard who dragged me back here had read her private thoughts aloud, that had been made clear.

I curl my fingers in towards my palms while my heartbeat pulses in a rhythm far too fast. *No.* I pound a fist against the tile. "It was only a dream," I murmur, shaking my head. *Fuck. Was* she happy that I proposed to her? That she left a life of horrors only to be thrown into a chamber full of judgmental men and women who didn't think she was good enough to be my godsdamn wife? Who would want to stay in a situation like that?

Nox Flynn Daxel, you will be my husband.

My chest heaves while everything blurs in my mind until it's all muddled into something unrecognizable. *It was only a dream.* My magic—the small amount I can feel—rises, attempting to answer the call of my agony as I send my fist into the tile again, trying to ground myself. But my body is made of pain and my mind is shrouded in an illusion of time that I can't decipher as real or not. Blood streaks the tile, the crimson against stark white shocking me back into the present.

Blinking water out of my lashes, I push away from the wall, unsteady on my feet. Turning my hand over, I direct my magic to heal my knuckles, disappointed but unsurprised to find that I barely have enough to close the cuts. White bursts over my vision as I sway, my pulse just as erratic as my thoughts. I am too weak—too fucking *vulnerable* right now. It's why I attempted to collect guards I thought I could trust to go and retrieve her. I knew I'd be captured and killed at best or captured and tortured in front of her at worst in my current condition. But, somehow, Kallin had found out about my plan, and stopped the guards only miles outside of Galdr.

It was only a dream. I'm not sure anymore, but I know that I love Rhea. I know that I will do anything to ensure she is safe, even if I'm no longer with her.

I finish my shower and get dressed, grabbing a black cloak and clasping it over me. Heading out to the sitting room, I pull open the slider door and peer into the darkness. Cold air brushes against my face, my skin breaking out in goosebumps.

I've watched the guards over the past few days, mapping shift changes. Most are posted at the entrances, while small groups rotate to patrol the woods surrounding us. With the heavy increase in guard activity, there's no chance I can sneak out using any of the main doors, and while my secret garden feeds out into the rest of the forest, the thought of walking through that place right now is too much for me to bear.

Gripping tightly to the thick railing of the balcony, I heave myself up, crouching low as I scout out a path to the grounds below. There had been times in my youth when I had thoughtlessly jumped from a height like this, relying on the magic that flowed through my veins. After all, I had been praised for the power I had done nothing to gain; why wouldn't I act as if its presence would be an infinite thing? Why *wouldn't* I be a bit reckless with it?

The council saw that recklessness and mistook it as me wanting freedom, so they acted quickly. Growing up, my magic went from something that was solely mine to the shield and sword of the kingdom. Now that it can no longer be those things, I find myself free falling, staring down at the ground from a dizzying height and wondering if that is all my value had ever been. Or at least, all it was before Rhea.

A gust of wind shakes me, and I focus on my route down.

Though my progress is slow, my steps are sure as I scale the wall of the palace, vines draping from above helping to keep my balance while my feet find divots in the rock. By the time I make it to the ground, my breaths are labored and my head is dizzy as I lean against the stone façade. No, I certainly can't rescue Rhea in this state, but I don't need to go against a king and his army to bring her justice. The irony of that thought almost brings a smile to my lips. Rhea would *hate* anyone being harmed in her name, even those who deserve it. But I had promised her that I would destroy each and every realm, including my own, to ensure she stayed safe, and I had *failed*. All that is left now is to sacrifice the only thing I have remaining—myself.

Taking a deep drag of air, I pull my hood up over my head and push away from the wall, palming the daggers strapped to my belt and confirming they are secure. Leaves rustle beneath my boots as I dart into the forest, relying solely on my hearing to alert me if anyone is near since I can't sense their magical signatures. There is no moonlight to guide me, but I know these woods like the back of my hand. I move as quickly as I can, keeping to the shadows that I used to wield. When I finally reach a break in the canopy, I'm relieved to see that it's still deep into the night. I won't have long to linger here, especially if anyone recognizes me.

Colter is a very small village that is technically within the city limits of Galdr but has managed to keep its identity separate from the capital for centuries. Unlike the lights and bustle of the Galdr Square, Colter is known for only two things: seedy inns and bars. It's the kind of place you go when you want a distraction—when you want to escape. But it's *also* a place for hiding those who would rather not be found.

Cass and Daje had tried their best to comb through the guards that were working in the palace the night of the ball, but they hadn't been successful before their departure with Elora to the Fae Kingdom. Everything—from identifying those who betrayed us to rescuing Rhea—feels as if it is dependent on hypotheticals that become more out of reach with each second that passes. I am tired of waiting, tired of *knowing* that she is with *him,* reliving her nightmares all over again.

Though the possibility of finding the guard who laughed as he read Rhea's most private thoughts is low, something keeps bringing me back to this place. Hoping that maybe, over the men playing cards and the women lounging on their laps, I might hear the voice that haunts my waking thoughts.

The air shifts when The Shallow Inn and Tavern comes into view, and I ensure my hood is firmly in place before I open the rickety wooden door, ale and sweat immediately stinging my nostrils. When I first chose to scout the guards, my surveillance had been cut short when an intoxicated woman became upset that I declined her advances and tugged my hood down, exposing my face to the entire tavern. Luckily, in their various drunken states, no one batted an eye to my reveal.

Still, I stick to the edge of the tavern, choosing a seat at a back table that gives me a view of the entire space. As much as I can see beneath the sparsely lit chandeliers above anyway.

"Hello, darling," the barmaid says as she saunters towards me, her dark brown hair braided over one shoulder. "What are you drinking tonight?"

"A mug of ale." She smiles, moving closer as her fingers drag along my arm. I snap a hand out to catch her wrist, gently plucking her fingers off me. "*Just* the ale." She gives a fake pout but spins to head towards the bartender. Leaning my elbows on the table, I look out over the room, scanning the faces and hoping one of them strikes me as familiar.

Off duty guards are spread out—some only identifiable by the weapon strapped down their backs, while others are still dressed in their full leather armor. It immediately makes me think of Cass. My best friend has only been gone for a week, but I feel his absence acutely. What he and Daje and Elora are doing is crucial, and I can only hope that my magic begins strengthening soon, or their effort might be for nothing.

The barmaid returns, placing a frothing mug of ale down. I drop more than enough money to cover my drink onto the table for her, nodding in thanks. After she leaves, I return to scanning the patrons, hoping that, with any luck, the night might end in my favor.

Chapter Eighty

NOX

"COME ON, *MYSTERIOUS ONE*, put your next card down already." The command comes from the disheveled man across from me, his glassy gaze fixated on the cards I hold. The nickname had come when I refused to remove my hood, the "s's" slurring on his drunken tongue as spectators chuckle.

After spending most of the night scouting the main part of the tavern with no luck, I migrated to a smaller room where buy-in card games were taking place. I had moved from table to table, listening for that voice only to be disappointed. Eyeing my cards, I pluck out two that will give me the highest value match to those on the table and lay them down. The man across from me curses at my victory as he tosses his cards down, but the victory is worthless, as my time here hasn't yielded the one thing I hoped for. Scooping up my winnings, I grit my teeth at the pain shooting down my back as I stand from my chair. Waiting for it to subside, I float my gaze around the room. What would Rhea think of a tavern like this? I am sure she has never seen anything like it, and I can practically picture the way she would blush, how her eyes would devour every interaction with piqued interest.

Gods, I fucking *miss* her.

Though pain still throbs with each breath I take, the failure of the evening propels me forward as I weave past tables and the men gathered around them. I'm halfway to the door when someone steps abruptly in front of me, his shoulder smacking into my chest and causing me to stumble. He turns, hand bracing my arm while his own feet falter. "Sorry, friend. Got a little excited about my winning hand."

The sounds of the tavern come to a halt, a chill rolling up my spine. My knees lock, every muscle trembling as recognition barrels through me. Knowing my hood will cloak the top half of my face in shadows, I lift my gaze from to his face, where bloodshot gray eyes are framed by strands of black hair. His lips tip in a smirk, even as one brow lifts.

"Oh, come on, man. It was an accident. Surely not worth holding a grudge over." He gives me a playful shake before releasing me, prepared to step back to his game. *Does he really not recognize me?* I had replayed this moment over and over again, sure that when I finally came face to face with the man who had taunted me with Rhea's diary, who had kept me from getting to her, he would at least *remember* me. That he would look into my eyes and know that his reckoning had come.

Shooting my hand out, I squeeze onto his arm, halting him from moving any farther. Scraps of magic stir as fragments of a memory taunt me.

The forest is drenched in rain, wet leaves sticking to my boots. Pain flares at the back of my head, and everything goes black.

His eyes flare wide as he attempts to tug out of my hold.

A hard surface digging into my back, the sound of whistling piercing the air. Dark gray eyes.

"You should probably let go before we have a problem."

I can't move. Foreign hands grip the ropes of my stretcher. "Time to go back home."

Each breath I take is measured, my anger rising and baiting me to act on it. My freehand reaches back for one of the blades strapped to my belt but before my fingers can squeeze around the hilt, the man pulls out of my hold. It breaks the spell of my fury, allowing me to see through my anger. I *will* get the information I need from him. But not here. Not yet.

"What the fuck is your problem?" he shouts, drawing curious gazes in our direction.

"There's no problem," I murmur, my fingers curling in towards my palms. "Have a good night."

He huffs a breath but returns to his table, our interaction all but forgotten in favor of more ale and a new round of cards. Keeping my head down, I hail the same barmaid as earlier.

Her hip juts out as she looks me over. "Yes?"

I hold the pouch containing my winnings out for her to see, gesturing with my head back to the table where the guard is sitting. "That man with the dark hair, do you know what his name is?"

She narrows her eyes in either curiosity or amusement—it's hard to tell with the way her whole face scrunches with the movement—before she looks over my shoulder. My hand holding the pouch shakes, making the coins within jingle. She swipes it quickly, weighing its contents before a small grin lifts her lips. "That's Stephan. He's here almost every week. Sometimes, he disappears for a bit but always shows back up."

"I appreciate your discretion," I tell her, ignoring her wink as I brush past her towards the exit. Cool night air shocks some awareness into me, every instinct roaring to turn back around, to snatch the guard from where he is sitting and enact the vengeance that has been slowly burning me from within.

Stephan. The name doesn't ring any bells, and without Daje or Cass here, I'll have to be creative with narrowing down which section of the guard he is in without giving myself away. Darting quickly into a thick gathering of trees, I drop my hood, running a hand through my hair and wiping the sweat gathered on my brow off on my forearm. Squatting between two trees, I reach into my pocket and grab the small vile of pink liquid Galen had given me for my pain. Uncorking it, I down it in one gulp before leaning against a trunk as I settle in and wait for Stephan to exit the tavern, a plan slowly forming in my head.

Dawn has nearly broken by the time Stephan hobbles from the tavern. I keep my steps light as I follow after him, hiding behind trees while he walks a path through the forest. The tincture has all but worn off, and without sleeping at all, I worry I'm not being as quiet as I need to be. But if Stephan suspects someone is following him, he doesn't show it. And with the way he wobbles, I doubt he's aware of anything beyond getting home. He follows a small trail into a cluster of houses tucked into banya trees, smoke already billowing from some as warm lights glow from within.

Stephan's steps slow to a stop in front of a white and green home, his movements clumsy as he retrieves a key to unlock the door and goes inside. I make note of which house is his before I turn and begin my journey back. Vengeance has never been a powerful motivator for me before, but now it sings at the possibility of finally getting some retribution. I'll make him tell me everything he knows, and when I'm done, when I've wrung him of all his secrets, I'll show him just how little magic or strength have to do with being powerful. With being *terrifying*.

King Dolian couldn't have known that, when he took the one person I love most in this world, he effectively pushed me past the imaginary line of morality I had used to keep myself in check. Whatever I do, whatever I *become*, will be the direct consequence of that, and when the day that I can kill him as slowly and methodically as he deserves finally arrives, there will be no sweeter vengeance.

"Where the *fuck* have you been?" Bahira's tone is jarring, and it temporarily knocks me from the hazy, pain-induced stupor I'm in when I enter my sitting room. "And *what* are you wearing?"

"Good morning to you too," I counter, lowering the hood of my cloak. My hair tickles the tops of my eyebrows, the longest I've had it in a while. I brush a hand through it, tugging the strands back while exhaustion stings my eyes.

"Nox—"

"I'm surprised to see you here and not at your workshop."

"And I'm surprised to see you waltzing in as the sun is rising." She sniffs the air as I pass, her nose crinkling. "Smelling like alcohol. Where were you?"

Misplaced frustration boils to the surface, and I avoid my sister's gaze as I answer, "Nowhere." She plants a hand on my bedroom door, blocking me from entering. My gaze is harsh when I turn it towards her, drawing a frown to her lips. "Bahira, move."

"Tell me where you were, where you've been going, Nox. I know you aren't sleeping all night in your room."

"Your observational skills are truly unmatched. Well done. Now *move*."

Her jaw clenches as she tilts her head to the side. "That was rude."

"You don't need to concern yourself with me—"

"Oh, spare me this conversation, Nox," she snaps, leaning into my space. "Ever since I've been home, you've made it impossible for me to do anything *but* concern myself with you."

The tension in the air draws tight, and I *despise* it. Bahira and I have always been close, her sound advice and steady presence one that I'm grateful for. But for what I'm planning—for what I need to do—I can't have her sucked into it. Just because I am willing to become a monster doesn't mean she's deserving of the same fate by association.

"You are about to be the *king*, so the self-sacrificing attitude *has* to stop."

"I'm not a puzzle for you to solve, Bahira." Her eyes narrow but not before I see a flash of hurt. My throat constricts, the throbbing between my temples intensifying despite the latest dose of medicine. "I'm not here to make *your* life easier. I'm going to do whatever I need to get Rhea back. Like I told you from the moment I woke up, there is nothing and no one who can stop that from happening." I reach for the door handle and then swing it open, watching as her chest heaves with a frustrated breath. "Call me selfish. Self-sacrificing. Anything and everything in between. I don't give a shit. But do *not* stand in my way."

She steps back and lets her arm fall to her side, her chin lifting in a way that shrivels me. "You can attempt to push me away, but I know who you are, Nox."

Turning away from her, I pause beneath the doorframe, my hands on the edges to hold me up. "No. You know who I *was*." Then I step into the room and shut the door behind me, leaning against it as my heart races. I wait until I hear her walk away before I take a seat on the bed, picking up one of the dragon stones from the bedside table that Rhea imbued with her magic when she was practicing.

The stone is warm, the faint gray glow at the center making me wish I could sense the magic that is emanating from it—if only just to feel *her* again. I clutch it to my chest and lay down, my gaze on the ceiling above me. *Hang on*, I whisper in my mind. *I promise, I'm coming.*

Part Five

Love is a funny thing, isn't it? It has the potential to make people tip over into either a better version of themselves or something worse.

Chapter Eighty-One

RHEA

A *WEDDING.*

There was a point, not all that long ago, that I might have preened at the idea of planning a wedding. That the mention of such a thing would have made my heart flutter instead of having it fall to my stomach. I suppose there are a lot of things about my life that I thought I would be excited about that now just seem obsolete.

The days following what I had done in the throne room proceeded in a blur of healing the king's army in small groups and being forced to participate in preparations for my upcoming wedding. The servants are wary of interacting with me, but a few take pity and explain what is to be expected as they ask for my approval on things I cannot even drum up enough energy to form an opinion on. They assume my quiet demeanor is due to being overwhelmed with marrying the king. They can't possibly know that this entire ordeal is nothing more than a funeral procession and that each task they check off their list as they unknowingly prepare me to marry my own blood is nothing more than another step towards an already dug grave.

I move through the motions, certainly not blaming them for doing the job the king demands. I numbly try on a dress that is wrapped in shimmering white fabric. I let them pick a veil to match and simply nod to whatever flowers are put down in front of me. There is a cake tasting with the king at my side, every single piece as flavorless as the air that surrounds us. I can hardly find it within me to *pretend* to be present, only doing enough to not incite his wrath. I might have found it worth it to fight him every step of the way before, but I *had* underestimated him.

I had so foolishly assumed my uncle's cruelest measures were reserved for only me, and he had somehow proven that to be both false and true.

My defiance had destroyed the lives of so many others—a child completely innocent in all of this. A servant only trying to help me. Tienne and Immie. Sterling and his wife. In the end, that defiance destroyed *me* too. Who I am—all of my desires and wishes—has been washed away in the wake of what I couldn't stop from happening. He had taken those seeds of hope I had so carefully planted and torn them up one by one until there was nothing left. I want to blame him fully—to scream that his attempts to break me have finally worked. And yet, even in that recognition, there is another truth. One that reminds me all of this could have been avoided had I just trained with both halves of my magic. Had I not been lured out so *fucking* easily by my love for Nox and my own ravaging guilt over Tienne's death.

If I had spent the time I was free *actually* doing the hard things instead of just leaning into everything that felt easy and secure and safe, then maybe, the lives of those who I had irrefutably changed could have been different.

My *own* life would be different.

Reflecting on the past is a foolish endeavor, and I've already proven my inanity a hundred times over. Blood still stains my hands just as permanently as the brand has altered my hip.

Sitting on the settee with silver moonlight pouring over me, I stare out the glass slider to the dark sky above. Rain rhythmically pelts the castle, a bone-piercing chill accompanying it. Wrapping my silk robe around my body, I clutch the fabric tightly, wishing my hands were holding something else. *Someone* else. I had whispered to him in my mind so many times lately, only one question ever asked—where are you?

There has been no news from the Mage Kingdom, nothing Xander has shared as he walks with me to meet the next round of guards waiting to be healed. His attempts to talk to me about anything *other* than Nox are met with quiet but steadfast disregard on my end. It is rude—*bitter*—of me to still find it difficult to talk to him, but even if the heat of my anger *has* begun to cool, the truth is that I just don't have the energy to engage in *any* conversation. What did it matter when it was just us coming to the same conclusion over and over again? Xander claims he wants to help me but hasn't been able to figure out how he can yet. I want to escape, but there is no answer to getting the ring off. To somehow finding the loophole in the king's commands that are keeping me here. Until we have a solution to *any* one of those questions, everything else seems inconsequential. Just another cog in the wheel of my torture here.

Then there is Eve who, true to her word, was waiting for me to return after the horrors I committed in the throne room. After I was commanded to swear myself to the king in blood. She did not try to fill the silence that blanketed the room when I entered, understanding that sometimes, there were no words that could be said. Instead, she took one look at the blood streaking my hands and chest, the rest blending into the crimson gown I had worn, and started a hot shower. She waited in the sitting room while I scrubbed my skin raw. As I washed my hair twice over, too lost in what had happened to notice that the water had grown cold until my body was trembling beneath it.

When I emerged from the bathroom, a cup of hot tea was thrust into my hands, a blanket wrapped around my shoulders. I said nothing as she guided me to bed.

Eve had stayed the entire night, quietly sitting next to me. I wasn't sure if she quite understood just how little sleep found me most nights or if there was something else that drove her to take care of me the way she did. Her generosity and kindness had been as devastating as it was sweet. I knew her days were full of tasks given to her by the king, yet she spent whatever free time she was allowed with *me*. I had been slow to trust my handmaiden, but now the very reason for that hesitance is also etched into my own palm. A scar to show that I too am bound to the king in yet another way.

Eve slipped into my room every night afterward, sometimes bringing food for us to share and books or stories of her day in the castle. And it was sweet—had been sweet—for her to continue to do it despite the lack of conversation I offered in return. But tonight, I told her not to come. Begged, really. For tomorrow brings another meeting with the sirens, the king having informed me during our dinner. He had not forced me to drink wine tonight, likely due to that meeting, and so I stay awake and stare at the night sky. Wishing, shamefully, that I had the haze of wine to coat my mind so I could not feel all the things that continuously threaten to pull me under.

And beneath the pitter patter of the rain falling, I ask myself that quiet question, one that I know there is no answer to. *Where are you?*

❧ ☙

"You are growing weaker," Queen Amari chides as she looks at me, the ice in her voice making my shoulders lift. King Dolian's hand flexes on the small of my back, my balance having gone unsteady after the last siren I poured my magic into. Her dark eyes flick from me to him before narrowing as she drums her fingers along her golden trident. "Why is that?"

The king tips his head to the side as if in thought. "We have been busy preparing for our wedding," he says, fingers pressing more firmly against me. "The excitement has likely just made her tired."

Queen Amari smirks as she returns that terrifying gaze to me. "Is that so?"

While beautiful, the siren queen's features do not hide just how deadly a predator she is. Her lethality is present in the muscles of her arms and her toned legs, how her eyes watch both the king and I *and* the guards that stand behind us. With the exception of Xander, who flanks my other side. The sun plays off the deep purple scales that line her hips and breasts, some glinting on her arms and the sides of her torso. Her voice is as regal as the king's, but her tone hits with more lush notes.

"No," she answers in my silence, lifting a finger that a black talon now protrudes from and dragging it down my cheek as she leans in closer. "I don't think that's it at all. Tell me, *Rhea*, what has drained you so? Where else have you been using that wonderful magic?"

My gaze widens at the rush of power that infiltrates my mind, powerful currents of it drag me deeper and deeper, making any command given by the king look weak in comparison. "Healing the king's army."

Her smile sharpens, dark eyes gleaming as she turns her attention to the king. He doesn't cower beneath that menacing glare, though his hand continues to push down on my back like he's hoping to make an imprint of it through the fabric of my dark blue dress.

"This can't come as that big of a shock," he says coolly. "I must make sure my kingdom is as adequately protected as yours is."

"It isn't a shock. I'd be disappointed if you hadn't done so." Pulling away from me, Queen Amari looks back over her shoulder at her waiting sirens. Each of them stand at attention, waiting for whatever command their queen will give them. "But I would be remiss if I did not remind you that I don't appreciate being deceived." The shift in her tone is immediate, as is the way Xander's hand grips the hilt of his sword in response.

"These are delicate times, Your Majesty. Despite our working arrangement, I was not sure if you would *appreciate* knowing my army is as free moving as yours."

Queen Amari laughs, brushing the long strands of her black curls off her shoulder, revealing one half of her bare chest completely to us. "When is the joyous occasion?"

"Three weeks' time," he answers, somewhat reluctantly. It's the first time I am hearing just how close we are to being married, and yet the information doesn't pull terror or anger from me. It doesn't make me bristle or curl my fingers towards my palms. Instead, my vision glazes over as a dull sound that might be something as benign as the wind or as damning as the screams of the men I had killed plays in my ear.

"Excellent. You may add myself and my daughters to the guest list. We'll arrive the evening before for Rhea to heal us and another batch of my legion."

Three weeks. That hardly seems like any time at all to escape. I have already been here in the Mortal Kingdom for at least double that amount—or was it more? I don't quite know. If I look at the passage of time as told by the seasons, the warm autumnal evenings have given way to bitterly cold nights, and my once favorite golden, red, and orange-hued leaves on the trees have all transformed into brittle, brown clumps on the ground, ice clinging to them in the mornings.

"Think this through, Queen Amari," King Dolian says, a sharp edge to his voice. "By coming, you're revealing that you have the power to cross through the Spell. Right now, that knowledge is known only to us."

"I do not fear anyone finding out that my people can now access the very land they were promised. Let it serve as either a reminder or a threat that we are *very* much a part of this continent and the time of keeping us stuffed beneath the sea is *over*."

After those ominous words, the queen and her sirens retreat, and when they have all disappeared beneath the surface, the king turns to me, his hazel eyes burning bright. "Starting tomorrow, you will heal battalions at a time. No more small groups." His hand moves to cup the side of my face, surprise crossing his own when I don't attempt to lean away. "Your magic is powerful," he continues, thumb brushing the apple of my cheek. "And you will help prepare us for *any* threat that might attempt to separate us."

I don't bother telling him that I don't think I can manage healing more than I already am. It won't matter, not as magic suffocates me like my head has been pushed beneath water. He forces me to look at him, my eyes taking in every minute detail of his face against my will. I watch his eyes soften, even as the corner of his mouth kicks up in silent victory. *Yes*, I want to say, *you've won*. Maybe I do speak it because then he is leaning in, not with command but as if he's testing my crumpled resolve. That discordant sound in my ears grows louder, my vision doubling when he presses his lips to mine. I can't feel if they are soft or rough, can't detect the coarseness of his beard scraping against my cheek. There is nothing as he lingers there, kissing me but not. I'm an imposter in my own body, watching from the outside. A shell of a woman.

Only when Xander begins to address his guards to head to the carriages does King Dolian pull back, that smirk framed within his beard deepening. "I love you," he says. *Love*. As if he could ever understand what it is to love. To be in love. I don't respond, but he doesn't seem to care as he turns and places one of my hands in the crook of his bent arm, leading us off the beach.

My head aches the entire way, but I settle into the pain as I stare out of the carriage window, watching the landscape pass by in a blur. This is not the story I wanted for myself, to become an unwilling main character in a tragedy that was supposed to be a fairytale. How much longer will I endure hoping for a future that might never come? How much am I *willing* to let those in power use me until I become someone unrecognizable? Until I became the villain of my own story?

Chapter Eighty-Two

BAHIRA

"**I**SN'T THERE SOME SORT of rule about taking a member of royalty's blood? Like death by beheading or something?"

I pause, my gaze moving from the glass slide in front of me to the little girl with brown curls currently holding a small vial filled with said crimson liquid up to the light in front of her. "Not that I'm aware of."

"You should probably double check," she murmurs, as if I'm a fool for not having done so already. "What if this is illegal?"

I snort, refocusing on the single bead of red that sits perfectly center on the slide. "Then I suppose you'll be considered my accomplice if we're caught." I clutch the small dropper tightly, forcing a steady hand as I bring it over the slide. Starla starts to respond, but I tune her out as I slide my thumb over the plunger at the top of the dropper. Once I'm sure it's aligned, I push the plunger, and another bead of blood falls to join the one on the slide.

"—and besides, everyone will think you forced me to help."

Standing up tall, I lay the dropper on the table and stretch out my back, my muscles sore from being hunched over. "What are you talking about?"

Starla heaves out a sigh as I grab the glass slide and bring it over to my magnifier, setting it in place. "If we're caught with the royal blood and they threaten to kill us."

Clicking the first glass disc into its slot, I look up at my grim partner. "First, no one is going to kill us because we have the prince—*the king's*—blood. I'm not sure if you are aware, but I happen to have a pretty good relationship with him." Even if he's currently falling apart.

Leaning forward, I close one eye and peer down the scope of the magnifier. What I don't tell Starla is that if we are going to get in trouble for *anything*, it's going to be the fact that I'm experimenting with blood so I can find how it interacts with magic. This small test is the first step in determining where to go next, if I can get Nox to cooperate with me.

It takes another two dials clicked into place before I can see the cells of the blood drops.

"Are you ready to take notes?" I call, my mouth quirking when she lets out another signature sigh.

"Of course."

"Red blood cells look healthy. Round in shape with a small dark blue nucleus. Indicative of mage blood. The same as they looked before merging." Adding another glass disc to the magnification, I adjust the knobs at the side to enhance the enlarged image. "Magnification up to three discs." The sound of Starla's scribbling fills the otherwise quiet atmosphere of my workshop.

Walking in this morning had partially untangled the knot of stress wound tightly in my chest. Between prepping Cass, Daje, and Elora's mission to the Fae Kingdom and the absolute havoc caused by the council for my family, this is the first time in weeks I've been able to come here, as Starla berated me for when I stopped by the orphanage on the way over.

Blinking, I lean back from the scope of the magnifier and slide the next disc into place. This had been the setting when I looked at the shifter blood samples. When I saw something *light up* in Kai's.

"At final magnification," I tell Starla, stretching my neck before leaning back in. It takes a moment for me to clarify the image, and when I do, a small gasp parts my lips.

"What?" Starla asks, footsteps sounding as she moves closer.

"There is *light* in their blood," I say quietly, my hands planted on the tabletop to keep them from shaking. "Just like the shifter king's, but there is *more* of it."

"Light? In blood?" Her incredulous voice mimics my own surprise. What I had seen in Kai's blood had been no larger than the point of a pin. A barely there flash of light winking in and out. But now, looking at the sample of Nox and Cass's blood, there aren't just flashing dots of light but *streaks* of them. Brilliant white flares, passing not just between the blood cells but *through* them. Not something foreign but a part of the viscous liquid on a molecular level. The sheer amount of sparkling lights is nearly comparable to the number of blood cells present.

My mind sorts through different theories, but there is really only one answer I keep coming back to. This is magic. Magic present in the blood, a physical manifestation of the power roiling through Nox and Cass's veins. It explains why I've never seen such a thing in my own blood, why my own didn't affect the plants I tested on. But why was it present in Kai's? Why had there been none in Tua's?

In Jahlee's? While Kai's sister didn't have the power to shift, was that the cause for the absence of light in her blood? Or was it merely coincidence? *Would I ever again get the chance to talk with her about it?*

Groaning, I sit back in my chair and rub my eyes.

"What is it?" Starla asks, coming to stand at my side.

"I think the light is magic present in our blood." Dropping my hands to my lap, I amend, "In mage blood." Blood and magic experimentation is forbidden because of the warnings ancient mages had written in long since locked away tomes—ones I hope to find on my next trip to the archives. But by finding proof of magic in the blood, then there is no denying that, as mages, we are *born* with it. It may not manifest until around the age of eight, but the capability for that power has always been there.

Just as it has always been *absent* for me.

Starla's brows furrow as she taps her pen against her chin. "So if our magic is in our blood, is this why the plants we tested on before grew?"

"Yes," I nod, staring absentmindedly at the magnifier. "And it explains why my previous experiments with using expelled magic didn't work in the same way. When using magic to, let's say, make a plant grow, there is intention behind it. A mage isn't so much *growing* a new flower by using magic to make it bigger or altering it in any way when spelling it to stay bloomed in perpetuity. But when blood is involved, the magic becomes something that the plant cells *feed* off of. Consuming the magic differently."

I quickly stand and walk towards the desk, ignoring the pang of sadness-laced rage that guts me when I spy some of Haylee's papers. Pushing them out of the way, I grab my personal journal and flip to the page where I described what I had seen in the leaves that I later realized included Haylee's blood.

My finger drags beneath the neatly written text, and Starla, once more at my side, begins to read it out loud. "The cell walls are plump and bright green, the healthy chloroplasts moving within. Some decaying cells found among them. Attached to the healthy cells are red org— organ—"

"Organelle," I supply.

"—organelles, of which the origin is unknown."

I tap my finger on the page. The origin *is* known now. It had been the blood cells feeding the cells of the plant not with blood but with the magic that was woven within it. Leaning a hip against the desk, I fold my arms over my chest and ruminate on how this information might help Nox. His blood is compatible with Cass's at least, neither of their cells reacting negatively to the other. Could I infuse his blood with Nox's via a cut? Similarly to how Kai had done with the toucan back in the Shifter Kingdom? I pinch my lips together as I think of that moment in the forest, the elated and *proud* look on Kai's face when my suggestion had worked. Then there was the disappointment that followed closely after when the same experiment—this time on a shifter woman stuck in her animal form—hadn't worked. But the magic in Cass and Nox's blood far exceeds what I had seen in Kai's. If these flaring lights are supposed to be markers of the raw, wild magic of mages, then what the *hell* is it doing in the blood of a shifter? Except, hadn't Tua said that Kai's father tested fate with magic and blood? Icy awareness travels down my spine as I glance back at my notes. How the *fuck* had Noa known about a blood and magic connection? And how had *he* used it to alter Kai?

"It's weird," Starla says into the silence that's lingered while I've been lost in my thoughts, and I jerk my head in surprise towards her, thinking I've spoken one of them out loud.

"What is?"

She looks down at the notes that she's taken from today, the journal brand new. "The color of the magic in the blood. You would think it would be the same color as the magic they wield. Like King Nox's magic is dark purple and black. Why isn't the magic in the blood that same color?"

"Perhaps the addition of color is only *because* it is being wielded by an individual," I muse, tilting my head. "Maybe the magic we are seeing in the blood is what it looks like at its core. Its purest form."

"Well, that's still weird."

I snort, leaning away from the desk to begin cleaning up my experiment. "Why is it still weird?"

"What happens if someone's magic doesn't have a different color? If the magic they wield is white?"

"In theory, if my other assumptions are correct, then it would mean that they are wielding magic without any kind of filter. Which would make it the strongest magic at their disposal." I'm not sure that the magic changing colors has anything to do with it being altered from its supposed natural state, but I don't have any information that *disproves* that theory either.

"Ha!" Starla barks out, earning a curious look from me as she shuts the journal. "That is even *more* ridiculous because the person I saw whose magic was white could barely wield it at *all* during our training."

I pause as I look over at her. "Who did you see wielding magic that was white?"

"The king's new girlfriend," she answers with a roll of her eyes and a wave of her hand. "Or, I guess, old girlfriend? Lady Margaret said he is now marrying your friend. Helena."

"Haylee," I murmur, to which she shrugs her shoulders. "You're sure Rhea's magic was white?"

"Yep. I saw it lots when Dilan made me train with her."

"And you've never seen that color from a mage before, right?"

She pauses cleaning up her own small table to look at me over her shoulder and drawl, "No."

I dig back in my memories to what Nox had told me about Rhea's magic. But other than the revelation that her flame had turned blue in the Cauldron of Vires, marking her as the next Void queen, he hadn't shared anything else. I purse my lips together. With so much unknown about Void Magic, it's impossible to even *begin* to predict all that she might be capable of. And, I realize as a chill moves over me, all that she could be forced to do while in the clutches of King Dolian.

A stilted eeriness has settled over the palace, one that whispers from the corners that something here is very *wrong*. Between Nox disappearing every night, the council's secretive nature, and the lack of *any* correspondence from Daje, Cass, and Elora, I feel on edge. Constantly waiting for the rug to be pulled from beneath me once more. It is selfish to complain about the status of my life when, relatively speaking, the upheaval isn't as serious as, say, being kidnapped by a sadistic uncle intent on marrying me. It doesn't make it any less jarring, however. Add in the fact that Nox's last spoken words to me have been needling my brain like some kind of foreign *worm*, and it's no wonder I can't focus on the ancient manuscript on the bed in front of me.

Nox isn't my only distraction, however.

I assumed that, with time, thoughts of Kai might dwindle until they fizzled out altogether, like a lingering sunset finally giving way to night. There is nothing here to remind me of him, no reason for memories of our time together to keep playing on repeat in my head. But despite all of that, they do. His touch on my life had been brief, yet it still haunts me as if we had spent lifetimes together.

One night, while in the thrall of those memories, I drafted a letter. I rationalized it by saying I was only sticking to the things I had promised to tell him but had been unable to because of the broken Mirror. But as I wrote, each sentence grew longer until the paragraphs morphed from information about Rhea to the truths of my heart. The longing I feel, and even the bits of anger and sadness and guilt that surround it, have been unavoidable verities for the entirety of my time home. I pushed them aside to focus on other important things, ones that I thought I might have *some* control over. But doing so didn't lessen them, and they certainly didn't go away. The letter sits hidden in a drawer, unsent to the only person who might want to hear those words, to the only male who's ever deserved them, yet I do not believe that *I* deserve to say them to him.

Sighing, I turn my attention back to the manuscript and the cursive writing of its author. Three quarters through this book, and I'm finding that it is part factual text and part personal opinion and, overall, has yielded very little information besides the mention of blood mingling. My eyelids grow heavy as the night progresses, and I go from sitting up to laying on my side, lazily reading through a new section entitled *The Gods We Worship* when a noise outside my door draws my focus.

I already know whose heavy steps traverse the room on the other side of the hallway, and I move quickly to try and catch him before he disappears into his bedroom. But when I reach his sitting room, his door closes and locks, and my chest deflates. Whatever Nox has been doing, whatever is pulling him away each night, it can't be good. Certainly not when he comes back smelling of ale, his eyes full of secrets. Returning to my room, I climb back in bed, grabbing the manuscript and preparing to close it when the word *Void* leaps off the page at me.

Blinking the exhaustion from my eyes, I squint to better focus and follow the sentence.

Void Magic, while precious and holy, is also volatile. With the sheer magnitude of what the queen holds in her, it is hard for this author not to ponder if, perhaps, there is more godly work at play. After all, who else but a god could be capable of both restoring vitality and draining life? And while we have so far been blessed by benevolent queens, one day, we might not be so lucky. So it is important that we ask, when a new queen rises who does not have the best interest of her people at heart, who will be there to stop her?

I swallow roughly as I close the book, my heart pounding heavily in my chest. It's time that I have a true conversation with my brother about what, exactly, Rhea has the power to do as the holder of Void Magic.

Chapter Eighty-Three

ARIA

M Y FATE IS TO be decided today by Queen Amari.

The throne room is plunged into darkness, the cloudy sky above and the lack of crystals within making it feel no better than a jail cell. Perhaps that is an omen of things to come. Allegra has just finished presenting the information she received from Nia, telling my mother of my cave of treasures and that I had been in communication with the seamount sirens since their escape from the Queen's Legion. Allegra's dark blue eyes sparkle with her usual level of animosity towards me, contrasting the way her belly is softly swollen with life. Where my closest sister is gentle in her movements, Allegra's body moves as if she is on the hunt. She is abrupt and curt, behaving so on edge that it coaxes the feeling alive in me. I have already swapped out my old mantra for Myla's, and as my mother's gaze pores over me from where she sits on her throne, all I can think about—all I can focus on—are those six words: *Who am I willing to become?*

Sirens eagerly wait behind me to see what my fate will be, Allegra ensuring all knew that I was to be investigated by the queen today. I feel their attention on my back as harshly as I feel the queen's at my front, but I already know that if my mother is to condemn me for these supposed crimes, I will fight it. I will fight for Lyre. For Mashaka. I will fight for myself. For all the times I didn't before. And though our *alliance* is still tentative and new, I will fight for Sade and her secret crusade against our mother. Another person enters my mind—one with dark hair and even darker eyes. One whose ruthlessness is only outdone by the intensity of her stare. I find myself continuously letting my mind wander to her, even in the most unlikely of circumstances. But if our last interaction had been any indication, Myla prefers to keep her distance from me.

My mother pounds her trident on the stone at the base of that rotten throne and the room falls silent. "Allegra, you bring serious accusations against one of your own," she says, her voice resonant as it fills the throne room. "A princess's duty is to her queendom and queen. To her people. One found to be acting against those priorities should be punished in a manner that befits the severity of the crime."

"I agree," Allegra chimes in, her eyes meeting mine as she snarls.

"Sade, General of my legion and second eldest daughter, what has your investigation of Aria revealed?" My sister swims forward from her place in line above me. We had already discussed what she would say and how she would have to act so both our mother and Allegra would not become suspicious. While Sade has the queen's trust, my sister reminded me that all it takes is one slip up, one moment where our mother might not believe we are loyal to her, and everything will fall apart.

"Your Majesty, I followed up with the information Allegra was given by the banished Nia Adanna. She *was* correct in saying that there is a hidden cave among the rocks."

The females gathered behind me hiss in disapproval, bubbles swirling from their frenzied movements. Allegra's smile is a vicious thing, as if she can already taste the bloodshed that is dancing around in her mind. When I look at the queen, there is an emotion I'm not sure I've ever seen from her before. It isn't quite shock or disappointment or anger but some mild mixture of the three.

"However," Sade continues, her voice loud enough to be heard over the chattering sirens, "when I entered the cave, I did not find the items and correspondences that Nia claimed would be there. It was empty. No sign that anyone had kept anything there."

"Impossible," Allegra growls, darting to Sade and stopping right in front of her face. "That is a *lie!*"

Sade's expression remains bored, one hand holding her trident while the other lays lax at her side. "By all means, Allegra, go check for yourself. Ask the queen for permission to prove that I'm wrong. Surely, you, someone who has not left the palace in months, must have proof that what I'm saying is incorrect."

"Don't insult me, Little Sister," Allegra snaps, her talons growing from her fingers. "We both know that Aria is sympathetic to those traitors. That she is the weakest of us all. To suggest that there is nothing when we were told there would be *many* things there to prove Aria's pathetic bleeding heart is to suggest your own compliance to her treason."

Sade leans into Allegra's space, towering over our eldest sister in a way I had never noticed before. Because Allegra has been bound to the palace, her muscles have grown smaller, her curves more voluptuous. But Sade is sculpted, her body a testament to her training. There was a time I believed Allegra was the fiercest of us all, but as Sade forces her to back up with nothing more than a low-pitched growl, I recognize that I was wrong.

"To suggest that my intentions—that my heart and soul and blood—are not fully devoted to this queendom is to show your stupidity, Sister. Perhaps the better question is why Nia would come to *you* of all sirens with this information." She turns to look at our mother. "My Queen, I am nothing if not your humble servant. Ask me to take you to the cave, and I will. I have no love for those who aim to hurt us, and I do not believe Aria is one of them. Is she aloof? An annoyance? Someone I wouldn't trust as a member of the Queen's Legion? Absolutely." Despite knowing the words were coming, I still lift my shoulders with a cringe.

"You have always shown your loyalty to me, My Daughter," Queen Amari says, making Allegra tense at her side. "It is not *your* devotion I question but hers." She nods to me with her chin, her face now perfectly masked with indifference. "Princess Aria, you are accused of treason in the highest order for helping those I've banished and working with them while they avoid prosecution. You're also accused of direct violations of our laws regarding those we kill for our benefit by attempting to honor their lives after death with a collection of treasures and trinkets found that belonged to them. Have you anything to say before I give my final judgement?"

"Your Majesty, I am innocent of these accusations. To believe I am guilty of them is to assume that I have not only secretly been helping an entire group of sirens underneath the noses of Sade and Allegra but under *yours* as well. As my sisters have pointed out, and as I know *you* believe, I am not the kind of siren capable of such sleuthing. I may have shown empathy to the youngest of the sirens when they lived in the seamounts, but I would like to remind some of you here that I was gone when they escaped. It would be impossible for me to have contacted them when I wasn't even here. Nia Adanna is a vengeful siren, and it would not surprise me if her reaching out to Allegra is less about painting *me* as a traitor and more about weakening the queendom by tearing our family apart." I practiced my answer to this question in the mirror on repeat last night, Sade helping me perfect it. The shake infused in my voice is real enough, as is the slight tremble in my hands. I had never stood up to my mother before, never once defended myself. But I am not alone in this, and too much is at stake to risk failing now.

My mother's gaze is uncompromising as she stares down at me, and my stomach churns at not being able to even guess which way she is leaning towards. "We will vote on your fate, then," she says, looking down the line at my sisters. There are only three as Dyanna had been given permission to sit this hearing out in favor of her pursuit of whatever knowledge my mother wants her to find. Lyre is the first to speak.

"I find Princess Aria Malika not guilty," she says, her voice steady and calm. I swallow, my gaze falling to Sade.

"I find Princess Aria Malika not guilty." The sirens behind me feign shock at this, apparently sure they were going to witness me being punished today. There is still a chance of it. Regardless of how my sisters vote, the final decision is the queen's. Allegra's vote is, predictably, one finding me guilty.

All the attention turns towards my mother. Her eyes haven't strayed from their position on me, her gaze piercing as if she is hoping to see the truth by looking hard enough. A part of me wonders if she is waiting for the right opportunity to finally strike me down. Not that she needs one. As each second ticks past, the knot in my stomach grows larger. Sade has already vowed to help me escape should this take a turn for the worse, but leaving is not something I *want*. Not unless Lyre is at my side.

The queen's trident meets stone three times again, and in the silence that follows, she announces her decision. "Based on the information presented and the votes of my daughters, I find Princess Aria *not guilty*." Brief chaos erupts, siren voices riding the current of the water as the queen rises and leaves the room, Allegra close on her tail. It isn't until Lyre joins me at the bottom of the dais that I let my mother's decision wash over me.

"This is good news," Lyre says, her hand coming to my shoulder.

All I can do is nod. It *is* good news, and for reasons I don't quite know how to verbalize, that scares me even more.

Chapter Eighty-Four

ARIA

D AYS LATER, I STILL question why Queen Amari didn't take the opportunity to rid herself of me when she had it.

She and Dyanna returned to the Mortal Kingdom, and this time, I was not invited. Guilt surged at the instant relief that hit me.

It is late in the evening when I meet Sade and Lyre in the latter's room. Sade had confirmed that the weapons and memorabilia from the cave had made it to Eersten with Cali and Althea. Izel would make sure that the sirens were kept hidden and that Nia would stay pacified. With Allegra forced out of whatever command she might have had over the legion, and our mother more concerned with her business with King Dolian, Sade's hope is that she can divert attention away from Eersten. At least for a time.

Silence had blanketed the space between my sisters and I, but it didn't last long as Sade brought up my magic. "When did you realize it was different?" she asks, swimming restlessly at the front of the room.

"A few weeks ago before I went on the mission to the Northern Island. I knew my magic didn't work on males at that point, but that day, I was forced to sing and nearly drew a female on a shifter ship into the water."

"Prior to that, I would always go on hunts with Aria. To make sure that no one could tell her song wasn't luring males in," Lyre adds. She leans back on her bed, head lolled to the side and resting on her shoulder. Dark circles hug the skin beneath her eyes.

"So you discovered that you can draw females in," Sade muses quietly. "And then what? Did you try to use it after that?"

"Of course not." I'd be happy to never use the magic again.

"Why?"

"Because the purpose of our magic is to procreate. I cannot do that with a female, so why would I subject one to suffer death at my hands? Especially another siren?"

"Practice," Sade says, shrugging her shoulders when Lyre shoots her a scowl. "You will not be able to wield a power you have not practiced with."

"Again, I cannot *mate* with—"

"I'm not talking about who you fuck, Aria." The sharpness of her voice silences my own and causes Lyre to sit up a little straighter. "What Queen Amari is preparing for on the surface is unprecedented. Despite how she views mortals as weaker, they *will* fight back if she tries to overthrow them. Our songs are not just tools to aid us in getting pregnant. They are *weapons*." Her orange eyes gleam as they look at me. "Even yours. *Especially* yours."

"Why especially mine?"

"Because. You might be the only one able to stop our mother," Lyre says, her smile tight.

I shake my head, eyes wide. "That's impossible."

"Is it?" Sade asks, swimming until she's right in front of me. "There is a reason you have this magic, beyond whatever sad excuse you've tried to tell yourself." Her eyebrows arch as mine lower. "Practice feeling it in your throat. Calling it quickly. You don't have to lure anyone, but you *need* to ensure that it's at your disposal when you do want to use it."

Her gaze is hard until I relent with a nod, and since there isn't much I can say after that, I bid them both a good night and swim towards my room. *Surely*, they don't actually believe *I* could control my mother. What I had done in that cave *must* have been a fluke, but even as I think the words, another voice within whispers that it wasn't. I had *felt* my magic in my throat. I felt it when I screamed at them to stop. *My magic can control sirens.* I hadn't let myself think about it, let alone *acknowledge* it, since that day.

I continue down the dim hallway, my thoughts racing. Maybe Sade has a point. My experience with Myla when we were hiding from the dragon is evidence of my need to practice. I had thought I was only pulling on enough power to keep her alive. Then something had shifted within her. Her hands had gripped me harder, and the kiss changed into something... *more*.

But no. That wasn't a conscious choice made by her, and the distance she is insisting stay between us is evident of that. Even so, I can't deny that I'm excited at the thought of seeing her again. Of continuing my training. It feels *nice* to have something to actually look forward to. I don't notice the smile tugging on my lips until it falls when I come to an abrupt stop, my eyes connecting with a familiar pair of yellow ones, her matching braids floating around her head.

"Aria," Lore says, her voice deceptively soft from where she is waiting in front of my bedroom door. "Where have you been?"

Panic thrums beneath my skin, kicking my heart rate up to a sprint as she approaches. "What are you doing here?"

She laughs, but the sound is edged with something dark. I move to slide against the wall, Lore at my front as she reaches out to tug at a handful of my braids. "What a silly thing to ask," she says, her hand sliding down to the bare skin of my shoulder. "I'm here to see you."

"I don't—" I push away the knot of fear that threatens to make my voice tremble as I pull away from her touch. "I don't want to see you."

"Aria, don't be ridiculous." Moving in again, she pins me against my door with her body, one hand pressing into the glass by my head. "It's been a long while since we've had some time together. You've been so *busy* lately." She leans in closer, smirking at the way I draw back while her gaze traces over my face. "Don't you remember how well we fit? How hard I can make you come?"

Heat rises to my cheeks with her words, but whatever embarrassment I feel from them is not enough to let her use me again. "Lore." With a hand pressed to her chest, I push her back. "*No.* I do not want you to come near me again."

"Is that right?" she grits out between her clenched teeth, canines gleaming beneath the light of the crystals on the walls as her shock morphs into something bitter. Maybe it's the newfound defiance that Lore sees in my eyes or simply that I'm putting up a fight at all, but with a roll of her shoulders back, she nods. "Fine. Have it your way."

I waste no time making my exit, turning to open my door into the darkness of my room. Except, I should have known that Lore wouldn't give up so easily. She shoves me hard from behind, propelling me forward as her hands close around the outsides of my arms, talons pricking the skin.

"You think you can just *leave* me, Aria? That you can cut me from your life?"

I jerk against her hold, spinning us around so I'm facing the open door.

"Let me *go*," I growl, bending my arm and sending my elbow back until it connects with her gut. She lets out a grunt at the impact, and I dart towards the door, moving fast enough to pull one arm free of her grasp. The other isn't so lucky. Her talons slice through my skin, the tearing of my flesh making me scream as she yanks me back towards her.

"You are *mine*, Aria." Dark blue blood taints the water as I snap my tail furiously against her tight hold. "Your *body* is mine." I gnash my teeth at her, tears beading at my eyes as I retract my own talons and form a fist with my free hand. "Everything about you belongs to *me!*"

"No!" My cry vibrates along my chest, calling my magic to pool at my throat. It's instinct—or newly formed muscle memory, maybe—when I turn and crash my fist into her jaw. The drag of the water weakens the impact, but the surprise that I've attacked her at all is more than enough to get her to release me. I lift my arms up in front of me, bending at the elbows as Myla's voice screams in my head. *Keep your guard up!* My magic pools at the base of my throat, making it tingle despite how I try to swallow it down. I'll be damned if I give Lore any more of me than she already has.

Her eyes are wide as she takes me in, the question written on her face before they leave her mouth. "How did you—"

But I don't give her time to ask it before I lunge again. She dodges my first hit, my fist brushing across the tip of her nose, as the daze of her shock fades quickly. Lore is well-trained—even if she isn't officially in the Queen's Legion, her mother has ensured she can fight like them—but her growing anger fuels her movements. There is no finesse to her attack, just feral swings and swipes until she grows tired of the way I elude them. With a furious growl, she wraps her arms around my torso, pinning my own to my body as she begins to swim backwards, dragging me towards my bed.

"Stop fighting me!"

My bravado in this fight falters as terror pierces my chest. How can I get the advantage when she has me so easily in her grasp? *Who are you willing to become?* Gods, *anything*. Fucking *anything*. I transform my lower half to legs, bending one at the knee as I lift it in front of me and then send it crashing back into her. Skin meets scales, and she growls at the impact, her hold on me slipping. So I do it again and again, our bodies propelled by my momentum away from my bed. Bubbles surround us from the flips of her tail and kicks of my own legs, and then her arms loosen, just enough for me to move one of my own.

I claw at her scales, sliding my hand up as high as I can to reach the soft skin of her belly. She bellows as my talons puncture her, pushing me away as her hand clutches her gut. I return to my full siren form and dart to the bag laying by my bed, quickly pulling the dragon bone dagger free and spinning to face her. Our chest both heave from our efforts, a veil of dark blue clouding the water between us.

"Go, Lore," I manage to say, every muscle tense in anticipation. "Before I tell the queen you attacked her daughter." We both know my mother holds no love for me, but then again, she *had* spared me from death a few days ago. And Lore knows that too.

She studies me with her lips peeled back over her teeth, her fingers still curled in an attack position. Her eyes linger on the dagger before they travel over my body, not in the same lewd way as before but like she is searching for an explanation as to *who* this version of me is in front of her. But then she winces, blood leaking beneath the hand covering her stomach. "This isn't over," she snarls before swimming for the door.

The moment she is in the hall fully, I close the door and lock it, my bottom lip trembling as I float in the water, momentarily bewildered by what just happened. For a long while, I don't move, sure she'll attempt to come barging back in. But when enough time passes that the muscles in my shoulders begin to ache, and the gashes at my arm stings in discomfort, I finally swim towards my bathroom, and search for something to wrap it with.

"Gods above," I whisper while reaching for some gauze. I had fought off Lore *and won. I* had done it. Without help. *Me.*

A hysterical laugh bubbles up my throat. I defended myself, and as a pair of fathomless dark eyes flash in my mind, I realize that there is only one person in this world that I can't wait to tell.

Chapter Eighty-Five

NOX

GALEN'S FACE IS STERN where he stands across from me, the old mage's eyebrows furrowed. "Prince—ah, *King* Nox—it is imperative that you continue the treatment as we have laid out. Skipping a dose will only put you back."

"The medicine isn't strong enough. It's doing nothing but numbing my aches temporarily. Then the pain returns tenfold," I grit out, my hand cradling the side of my head. "I'm not getting better, just going in circles. There has to be something else."

Galen shuffles closer, the vial of pink medicine clutched in his grasp. "Your Majesty, sometimes in order to get to something better, we must trudge through the uncomfortable. The magic in your veins will be yours again—of that, I have no doubt. But for now, we must help you along." He extends his hand, and my stomach hollows out. "If nothing else, trust that I have been caring for your family since before you were even born."

My hesitation lingers, even as my head throbs harder. Eventually, the thought of even temporary relief wins out, and I grab the vial, uncorking it and forcing the medicine down my throat.

"Do you have the other item I requested?" Walking over to the sink, I open the cupboard above it and grab a glass, filling it with enough water to rinse out the taste in my mouth. Within seconds of the medicine hitting my stomach, a numbing sensation curls outward, coating me in a hazy lightness that leaves me slightly dizzy.

"The sleeping tincture?" Galen's voice ebbs in and out, and the anger and anxiousness that has made a home in my chest softens into something less urgent.

"Yes. I've been having difficulty sleeping at night."

"To be expected, given your current condition."

Taking a gulp, I set the glass down before turning, leaning heavily against the counter's edge. Galen digs through a different cupboard across from me, glass bottles clinking against each other as he searches for the tincture. I press a hand to my chest, Rhea's engagement ring warm against my skin from where it hangs on a chain, and I use its presence as a way to feel closer to her. A temporary reprieve in the aching of my soul without her near to me. When Galen signals he's found the tincture, I exhale the breath I was holding in relief. *One step closer.*

"This should do the trick, Your Majesty. Though I should warn you, don't drink it until you are already in bed for the night." He lumbers over to me, dropping a vial filled with a dark blue liquid into my hand. "The lavendaris plant works quickly and will have you peacefully asleep within a minute."

I snort as I hold it up to the light, my vision doubling before I blink it back into focus. "Hard to believe something so innocuous looking could be so potent."

"It's the way of plants. They are a magic all their own."

Thanking Galen, I pocket the sleeping tincture and exit the medical room, heading to what will no doubt be another day filled with Kallin's incessant droning. Since my official coronation, the council has shown no mercy in testing the limits of what I will agree to in exchange for allowing our family to stay on the throne. I have bent the knee on nearly everything they've asked of me.

All except for one.

I slip my hand into my pocket, fingers brushing against the cool glass of the sleeping tincture. It had taken me a while to find more information on Stephan, though my position as king has certainly aided in getting what I needed. I've learned that he floats from post to post, filling in wherever he might be needed. It makes his absences when he returns to the Mortal Kingdom all the more unnoticeable. Unfortunately for him, his shifts this week are in the dungeons, which makes what I have to do much easier.

The council room is cold as I step inside, greeting the faces of the nine members seated around the long table. The chandeliers above burn brightly, and you'd never know that I had nearly brought this place down to the foundation weeks ago. *Weeks.* A mockery of power stirs in my gut at the thought, but it's easier to ignore as I sink into my chair at the head of the table, Borris on my right and Kallin on my left.

"Your Majesty," the latter says, lacing his fingers together in front of him. "We've heard word from the party sent to the Fae Kingdom."

My eyes slide to his as I lean forward, elbows resting on the table. Cass and I had agreed that all communication should be limited, considering we still don't know who the moles are. If he sent a message, it must be worth the risk of it being read by someone else. Which, as Kallin slides the missive to me, I can see was a worthwhile worry.

Something like irritation heats me from within as I slide my finger beneath the already broken seal but it's dulled, pressed behind an invisible shield to be dealt with at another time. Though the words on the paper blur in and out, I manage to read that they have been delayed in crossing over the Fae Kingdom's border. Cass adds that they are safe and will continue on, but it will mean they will be home later than they thought. I fold the letter, pocketing it despite how Kallin holds his hand out for me to return it. "Let's hope that they can find what they are looking for without interference," I tell him instead. "What else do we have to discuss today?"

Kallin gives me a small grin before he and the rest of the council launch into their agenda for the day. Their voices are quiet beneath the murkiness created by the tincture, but though it makes it hard to follow what they are saying, I'm grateful for the way my muscles are relaxed. For the absence of that ever-present pain that's taken residence in my body. Galen believes it is due to my lack of magic. That with only a ghost of its normally brimming presence, my body is suffering. It seems as good as any theory I can come up with, I only wish he could tell me *why* my power is still so distant. Why, sometimes, I can sense the full capacity of it only for it to fade again by my next breath.

When the meeting adjourns, Kallin asks me to stay behind, leaving just the two of us in the room. I don't bother asking him why, preferring to sit in the silence that stretches wide between us before he is the one to finally break it. Joining his hands together behind him, he tilts his head to the side while slowly pacing the long side of the table opposite me. "How are you feeling?"

I fold my arms over my chest, leaning a hip against the edge of the table. "You'll need to be more specific."

"Let's start with your transition to king." He pauses behind one of the chairs, his hands coming to rest on its back.

"It was time," I answer, keeping my words measured.

Kallin smiles. "And how is your strength? Are you taking the medicine?"

"As prescribed, yes."

"Your magic?" he asks, continuing around the table until he stops only a few seats away from me. "Is it still eluding you?"

Something about his tone catches my attention. "You speak as if it's purposefully hiding from me."

"Well you've given us *very* little information about your magic since this madness began."

"You know more about my magic than nearly anyone else. You oversaw my childhood to ensure it."

Kallin smirks. "Is that bitterness I hear? It's misplaced if so. Everything I have done, both then and now, has been in service of my home. I will continue to protect her, no matter the cost, Your Majesty."

I mimic his smile, even as I struggle to latch on to the anger that I know is simmering within me. "As will I."

❧❧❧❧❧❧ ❧❧❧❧❧❧

The air is thick with the scent of must and mildew, each lungful a battle not to cough it right back out. Even with the fabric of the scarf covering my face, the smell of the dungeons is one that can't be dampened. In the cracks between the stone that surrounds me, water drips, the rhythmic sound of it hitting the ground matching the pace of my steps.

Carrying a small white bag in one hand, I sink the other into my pocket, playing with the now empty glass vial as I whistle a tune to announce my arrival to the two guards posted at the end of the tunnel. It's a stupid fucking plan, but it is the only one that doesn't necessitate involving other people. If I am going to go against every oath I took as king, then I damn well better make sure no one else can be an accomplice to my crimes. Sweat beads at my temples, my heart pounding at my ribcage as I follow the tunnel and turn right, revealing a guarded metal gate.

"Who goes there?" one of the guards shouts, hand going to the sword strapped at his hip. The lights of the spelled flames on either wall reflect amber over his leather armor, his partner also reaching for his weapon as they watch me come closer.

"I've come bearing gifts!" I shout, lifting the hand holding the white bag in front of me. The guards take in the armor I wear—stolen from Cass's room—and my half-covered face before looking at each other.

"What's that?" the younger of the two asks, shaking his head to move the red curls dangling over his forehead off to the side.

"A gift from His Majesty." I toss him the bag, his partner's eyes fixed on me as I stop in front of them. His fingers flex against the hilt of his sword for another moment, and I arch my brow in response.

"The king has never sent us anything before," he says, allowing his hand to finally fall as he steps back next to his partner. "What's in there, Damien?"

I watch as the younger man opens the bag and reaches in. He pulls out the iced lemon bar before handing off the bag to the man at his side. "There's a new king now," I say.

The other man snorts, palming a lemon bar for himself. "Unsurprising. His Majesty seems like the type to try to win you over with something simple like sweets." He lifts it up, inspecting the icing on top. "Gods, did lightning strike the person who was trying to ice these? It's a mess."

My brows lower, but I keep my mouth shut as he bites into the dessert.

"If he wants to send us dessert every day in order to get our support, he'll hear no complaints from me. Especially when it's about time for us to go home,"

493

Damien counters, biting into his own bar before pulling the bag from his friend. "Did you want one?"

I shake my head, taking a step back. "Already enjoyed one with the others upstairs. Just wanted to make sure you guys got some as well." As I speak, I count the seconds that pass. Galen said that lavendaris worked quickly, I can only hope that adding it to food doesn't lessen the effects.

A few moments later, that proves to not be the case. Damien's eyelids begin to droop as he mumbles something about sitting. His partner watches him stumble to the ground before slowly moving his gaze to me, realization hitting just a few seconds too late. Another handful of seconds pass as he tries to fight it, and then he too goes down in a heap.

I pull the scarf down and draw in a steady breath, the cold air of the underground tunnel sticking to my sweat laden brow. Kneeling at the side of the second guard, I unhook the keyring from his belt, sifting through the keys until I find the one I need. Sliding it into the lock of the gate, I turn it as a click rings out and the gate lifts. Behind it are rows of cells in a grid-like pattern. They should all be empty, as it is rare to keep someone down here for long periods of time. It's a cruelty that my father never enjoyed employing, and I only knew of one in his entire reign as king who was sentenced to years of solitude here before he was granted the mercy of death.

Flipping the keys on the ring, I find the master key for the cell doors and open the closest one to the gate before dragging Damien and his companion in.

For days, I had tracked the movements of the dungeon guards, learning about shift changes under the guise of needing the information as the incoming king. It was an abuse of power for my own personal gain, and I didn't fucking care. My timing had to be damn near perfect, as I am unsure how long the effects of the lavendaris will last. Locking the door to the cell, I move to a pillar framing the gate into the dungeon and tuck myself behind it while I wait for Stephan. When his steps finally sound in the hall, I slip two daggers from their sheaths at my belt just as I hear his steps halt and draw his own weapon.

I hold my breath, clammy hands gripping my hilts as I wait for him to make his next move. This entire plan hinges on the fact that if I have deduced *anything* about Stephan, it is that he believes himself to be infallible. After all, he had taken me down without any fight—regardless of the fact that I'm at my weakest. I had seen the way his eyes gleamed in utter satisfaction, his power over me as he dragged me through the woods unquestionably boosting his ego.

I nearly sigh in relief when his profile comes into view as he crosses the threshold of the open gate, his sword lifted in front of him.

"What the fuck?" Spotting Damien and his companion, Stephan's steps slow as he looks down the row of cells. I stay tucked back within the shadows, letting him pass me on his way to the cell holding the guards. He shifts his weapon into one hand as he reaches back with the other to his belt, where his keyring hangs.

I lunge at him then, the element of surprise helping to close the gap between my current shortcomings and his advantage over me. He turns, eyes wide and mouth agape, just as the hilt of one of my daggers smashes into his temple. Stephan crumples, the clang of his sword hitting the stone beneath us loud as he collapses.

My chest heaves, and my fingers tremble around my blades, but I relish in the small feeling of victory that warms me from within. *Finally,* something goes right. Once I'm sure he's out and the other two guards are still asleep, I sheathe my weapons and kick Stephan's away from him, stripping him of his remaining blades. I drag him through the maze of cells into the center of the dungeon, sparsely spread out spelled flames the only source of light. Placing him inside a cell, I lean against the metal bars of the door and tip my head back in exhaustion.

I picture Rhea as I close my eyes, the ever-present headache between my temples throbbing harder. This dungeon is supposed to just be a temporary holding spot for those who dare to betray their fellow mages or their king. But in my presence, it will become something darker. Something harsher. For her, I will be the most monstrous thing this dungeon has ever seen. For her, I'll do *anything*.

Chapter Eighty-Six

NOX

I KICK THE BOTTOM of Stephan's boot, his entire body jolting with the movement. "Wake up."

It has only been a few minutes since I knocked him out, but the adrenaline coursing through me is begging me to act. To bring my weapon to his throat and demand he tell me everything he fucking knows. And I will resort to that, if necessary. For now, I'm trying to let logic and rationality—no matter how miniscule those feel within me—win out.

Stephan groans as his head lolls to the side, his body partially slumped over where I propped him up against the damp stone wall. Pressing my hand against the leather armor on my chest, the imprint of Rhea's ring pushes against my skin, grounding me. I watch as Stephan's eyes flicker open, taking a few seconds to focus. A laugh barrels out of him as he looks around the cell before turning his gaze to me.

"Well done, Your Majesty," he says, heaving his body a little more upright as a breath hisses from between his teeth. "I knew there had to be more to you than a pretty face. How did you incapacitate those two guards?"

"I took a page out of your book."

He groans as his fingers prod the swollen red mark at this temple. "Trick Galen into giving you something? He's always had a soft spot for you."

"I want the names of those who helped turn Rhea over to King Dolian."

"At least woo me first, pretty boy. After all, *I'm* the one with all the information you need." He leans his head back against the stone, laying his hands on top of his thighs.

"You're the one at the mercy of a man willing to do *whatever it takes* to get that information." I straighten and walk towards him, towering a few feet away as I clench my fists at my sides. "You may have had the upper hand before, but do not mistake that as a sign of weakness from me."

Stephan chuckles, the sound scraping along the cell walls as it echoes. "I quite like you like this. *Feral* for her. Willing to risk it all." Biting his lower lip, he tilts his head to the side as he stares up at me. "Love is a funny thing, isn't it? It has the potential to make people tip over into either a better version of themselves or"—he gestures to me with his hand—"something worse. It can bring families closer together or brutally rip them apart." His eyes narrow, deviant delight dancing on his lips. "It can force kings to risk everything just for a fucking *taste* of it."

My chest heaves as a muscle at my neck thrums, and though I lift my lip in a snarl, Stephan's taunting is undeterred.

"She looked *so* concerned that night. It wasn't hard, really, to convince them both that you were waiting for them. Poor Daje looked like he thought something was wrong, but Rhea—"

"Don't say her fucking name," I growl, breath trapped in my throat.

"She convinced him to go. The way you have her wrapped around your finger... Or, I guess, *had— Ah!*" My boot comes down on the top of his shin, his shout of pain stirring my magic inside of me. Faint as it is, I'm satisfied at the feel of it curling over my spine, eager and vengeful.

"*Who* did you work with?"

"She cried out for you," he grunts out between panting breaths, and I stomp my foot down harder. "*Fuck!*" Stephan's hand attempts to wrap around my ankle, but I kick it away, the edges of my vision blurring.

"Give me *fucking* names!"

"Luring her away from the safety of your room was entirely too easy. Her eagerness to get to *you* was her downfall." He laughs, his upper body twitching from the pain in his leg. "I watched them hold her down as she begged for you to come. And as her blood painted her hair and they pulled her ring from her finger, she kept fighting against them. All until they knocked her out. Then it was a frenzy. Each mage there wanted to carry her to the beach, but one was more adamant than the others. He made sure to keep hold of her *nice and tight* before handing her off to the siren bitches."

I plant my boot into his chest *hard*, making his head ricochet off the wall. Crouching down in front of him with my hands on his chest plate, there is no kernel of rationality that I am entertaining now. They had fucking hurt her, and he had bore witness to it. Had lured her to danger. "Tell me what I want to know, or I'll start hurting you in earnest."

Stephan splays his hands on the ground by his hips to steady himself as he blinks slowly. "Even with names, there is nothing you can do, *My King*. It doesn't change the fact that your magic is weakened—as is your body. It doesn't save *her* from enduring the king's touch—"

The shout that rends from me is primal, a noise I can't stop just as I can't help the fist I send crashing into his jaw. Stephan's head snaps to the side, blood trickling from the corner of his mouth as it lifts in a jarring, macabre smile. *Kill him.* I hear the command in my head, but the voice isn't mine. It's something deeper, darker. Something that lures me like a siren call into that shadowy monster I've tried so hard to tame. *Kill him*, it whispers again, and I reach back for one of my blades. Stephan moves quickly, something clicking before pain lances across my wrist and warmth spills down my forearm. He swings at me again, this time something cutting into my shoulder.

"It's okay, Your Majesty," he growls, shoving me off of him. I lose my balance and fall to my knees, my heartbeat loud in my ears. "You couldn't have known I have blades hidden in my vambraces." Lifting his hand up, he shows off the crimson-stained tip of a blade hidden at the sleeve of his armor as he struggles to his feet.

Heaving a breath, I force myself to stand, my fingers scraping at the hilt of one of my daggers. Air stirs, but I'm too fucking slow to avoid Stephan's fist, white exploding behind my eyes as it connects with my cheek. A metallic taste fills my mouth and drips into the back of my throat as a second hit comes directly into my side. "You're a pathetic excuse of a king, just like your father before you. You'll never be able to turn back the events that have already been set in motion. It's been *decades* in the making, and while I think it is valiant that you are trying your damnedest to get Rhea back, the truth is that you will never see her again."

My neck flexes as I grit my teeth, calling on my scraps of magic to begin healing my cuts as I barrel into Stephan, sending us both crashing onto the ground. We scuffle, metal hitting stone as I lose one of my blades. My muscles strain, the persistent throbbing in my head drowning me as he wraps a leg around my hip and flips us so my back collides with the ground and his knee digs into my chest. The air squeezes from my lungs as he leans in close, his hands framing my head.

"Well, maybe that's not true. Your friends are on a quest to repair the Mirror, right?" I slide my hand back to the other blade strapped to my belt. "Perhaps you *will* see her again, though I imagine she'll be on King Dolian's arm like the pretty little fucking trophy she is."

He licks his lips and pushes his knee harder into my chest, forcing a strangled groan to rise up my throat. I grasp at the dagger's hilt, moving it up out of its sheath an inch before my fingers slip from the blood coating my hand. Black splotches begin to cover Stephan's face, my throat constricting with the attempts to draw enough air in. *Fuck.* I shoot my other hand out to grasp at his neck, clawing into the skin there.

He growls as I draw blood, easing off of my chest just enough for me to get a quick breath before the pressure is once more crushing my sternum. Pain radiates out from my back, every muscle coiled tight, as Stephan brings the arm with the hidden blade right up to my neck, pressing into the skin. "I know the council has you on a tight leash, Your Majesty, and your laughably feeble attempt to overpower me has only made me angry. So, in return for not killing you, you will grant me a favor. I want my own room within the palace. I'll keep quiet about this, both to save you embarrassment and because I can't *imagine* what Kallin will do if he knows. They've already got an eye on your sister, don't they? Accusing her of treason and sleeping with a foreign king."

What surges through me is too raw to be called *only* anger. Planting my feet on the ground, I press into my heels and thrust my hips up in an attempt to throw him off balance. But, *fucking gods,* I'm too weak, and all it does it make him laugh as the blade nicks my throat.

"It's pathetic, really, what you're willing to risk for her. Especially when she's been... *tainted.*"

"Shut the *fuck*—"

"He touched her. *Claimed* her. Right in front of everyone. And she let him. Though, what could she even do against him? Not when her magic is blocked and—" At the widening of my eyes, Stephan chuckles, and the sound shreds me apart. "That's right. King Dolian somehow figured out how to make her magic *his* to control."

No. That is *impossible.* "You're lying." But even as I drop the accusation, my mind spins with the horrific scenario he's laid out. *Rhea at King Dolian's mercy, her magic unable to protect her in the way it had in the past. Unable to heal her while she sleeps or comfort her while she's alone.* Each thought builds upon the previous one until I'm suffocating beneath their weight, cut off at the knees and forced to bear the consequences of my failures. They live within me, within my very blood, coating my veins in an icy culpability that leaves me numb to the small voice inside that is urging me to stop. To calm down. To wait for the *right* moment to strike.

But I am fucking done with waiting. I stretch my fingers out again, the tips of them brushing the edge of my dagger's hilt.

"You don't have to take my word for it. I imagine, with the way he was touching her, that he's already ravaged her in all of the depraved ways he's wanted to. In fact, perhaps when the Mirror is fixed, you'll see her swollen with the king's heir—"

Holding the dagger firmly, I slip it from its sheath and plunge it into his side, right in the gap of his armor. His howl echoes out in the dungeon, my free hand pushing at his shoulder until his own blade is away from my neck. With my hand coated in my blood, I rip the dagger free and drag it across his neck, splitting it open. Blood sprays from the wound, his hands frantically trying to stop the flow. I jerk us to the side and crawl out from underneath him, shoving him onto his back as I kneel at his side. Blinded by the rage that floods my body, my vision is haloed in shadows as I unbuckle his leather armor at his chest and discard it to the side. His magic works to try and heal him, flaring red at his neck as gurgling sounds in his throat. But even if I had intended to leave him to his own devices, he's not strong enough to save himself.

With his dying gaze meeting mine, my arms swing down, the feel of the blade cutting through skin and muscle before scraping against bone sending a terrifying thrill through me. Yanking the dagger out, I don't care that he's already stopped breathing when I plunge it in again. And again. And again. *He's already ravaged her in all of the depraved ways he's wanted to.* Crimson splatters my face and neck, and still, I get lost in the motions, wishing they'd drive out the voice that repeats his words in my head. Everything around me fades into the background until there is only the blade and my anger, the two inexplicably intertwined as they meet Stephan's body over and over and over again.

Chapter Eighty-Seven

BAHIRA

I HAVE CHECKED ALMOST everywhere in this godsdamn palace for my brother. The moment I realized he hadn't been accounted for in hours, I began my search, left uneasy by the fact that he's been so reclusive and withdrawn.

His stubbornness is only matched by own, and it's that same obstinacy that has brought me to the lowest levels of the palace, the entrance to the dungeons currently blocked by an annoyingly familiar face.

"Well, well, well. It's about time you finally came to me." Max's deep voice skates along my skin, but where it once caused desire to simmer low and deep, now it simply makes me arch an eyebrow in question. He folds his arms, the leather armor covering him stretched to the absolute limit. He really is massive for a mage.

"And what is it you think I've come to you for, Max?"

He mimics my brow lift, uncrossing an arm to gesture over his body. I can't help but snort, rolling my eyes as I shake my head. "Listen, I'm not above being objectified. Especially by a beautiful woman such as yourself."

"I'm afraid I'm only here on business. I need to get into the dungeons."

The playful attitude shifts into something more serious, Max dropping his hands to his sides. "And why is that?"

Chewing my lip, I grimace. "I can't tell you why. Only that I need a few uninterrupted minutes to look around." Nox is more likely to be at a tavern in Galdr getting absolutely drunk off his ass than in the dungeons, but it is the only place in the palace I haven't checked yet. The part of my brain interested in solving the *where is Nox* puzzle is insisting that I make sure no rock goes unturned—or dungeon goes unexplored, as it were.

"Listen, I know, given our history, I should you give you special treatment—"

"We have no history, and certainly none that would equate to you treating me differently."

"—but I can't let you down there without a reason, Bahira."

I sigh, my hands coming to my hips as I tip my head back in frustration. "I appreciate your dedication to the job, Max. Especially given how tumultuous things have been around here lately." I watch his expression, gauging his reaction to my words. When he merely gives me a curious look, I continue, hoping that trusting him with a little of the truth won't backfire in the end. "I'm looking for my brother."

A line forms between his brows. "The king is missing?" he barks.

I shush him, turning to look over my shoulder before shooting him a frustrated glance. "No, but I can't find him."

"I'm not a smart man, but I'm fairly confident that is the definition of missing."

"Stars above," I groan. Stepping in closer, I ignore the way his breath stutters in response to my proximity. "He's just not where I expected him to be, so I'm searching in *unexpected* places." When it looks like another retort about the definition of the word "missing" might make its way past his lips, I hold a finger up to them. "Max, please," I say softly. "I'm only asking for a few minutes. In and out."

His dark eyes bounce between mine, and when his shoulders eventually round in defeat, I smile as I exhale roughly.

"Thank you."

"Yeah, yeah," he retorts, reaching for his keyring. "Just be quick. And maybe if you *do* find your brother down there, ask him why the earlier shift got treats from the kitchens but I have yet to have one delivered to me in his name."

What? "Okay... I will do that."

Max unlocks the gate that leads into the dungeon, the metal blocking the threshold lifting out of the way. "Just a few minutes," he warns, and I nod, stepping past him. "Also, any time you want to revisit that rule of yours, just know I'm ready. *Any time*." He drops his voice even deeper, the timbre making the hair rise on the back of my neck. Not because it's his, but because it reminds me of another.

Clearing my throat, I toss him a smile over my shoulder. "Should I ever decide to break the rule, I will find you." Only a little bit of guilt flickers. It's not like he will ever cross paths with Kai. Shaking my head, I force all thoughts regarding the shifter king out of my mind as the gate closes behind me and I begin my descent into the dungeons below.

My fingernails press into my palms as I stare at the open gate, wishing instead that I was holding my spear. I might take joy in being right on the hunch to come down to the dungeons if it weren't for the fact that it's ominously unguarded. Reaching for the dagger I have hidden in my boot, I clutch it tightly before continuing forward, passing under the gate and into the darker section holding the cells.

I move slowly down the first aisle, nearly misstepping when I spot two guards slumped over in one of the cells. I lean in closer as I scan the surrounding area, battling the rapid beating of my heart into submission as I listen for a sign of life. But when I hear their heavy breathing, I relax a fraction and decide to continue deeper into the bowels of the dungeon. I have only ever explored this area once, years ago after my father all but forbade me from coming here without a guard. I was morbidly curious, so I snuck in, charming one of the guards to give me a tour. But the cells had been empty and the air so thick with stagnant water that it made it hard to breathe. I never returned until now, and as I force myself deeper into the heavy darkness, its shadowy depths only broken up by the occasional spelled flame, anxiousness coils itself around my spine with every step.

Rounding a corner cell, I squint into the darkness and peer down another row, my back pressed to the cold metal bars. I make it past another handful of rows, the maze of the cells making me dizzy with worry that I won't be able to find my way out again when a noise forces me to stop. Goosebumps roll over my body at the squelching sound, and I hold my breath in my chest when it's followed by a deep growl. *Fucking gods, I better not get attacked by some creature down here.* Gripping my dagger tightly, I hold it out in front of me and resume my careful steps. There is a rhythmic pattern to the odd sound that spills out into the space and as I reach another corner cell, I prepare for something to leap out and snap at me.

But instead, there is only the movement of shadow. I press further, my breaths coming so quickly I'm sure whoever or *whatever* is down the corridor will hear me. Wetness splatters out onto the ground in front of me, catching just enough of the sparse light to reveal its color. *Red.* My stomach hollows as I swallow down my fear, sweat beading at my neck.

My boots are silent against the stone while sweat beads at my neck, the edges of the cell where the noises are coming from nearing. Spelled flames highlight more blood pooling inside, originating from where a male is kneeling, his upper body heaving with labored breaths. I watch silently as he raises his hands, a blade glinting in his grasp before he plunges it back down, a sickening wet sound skating over me.

His back expands with a deep breath, and though I shouldn't announce myself yet, I suspect I already know whose eyes I meet when he turns around. "Hey!"

My fears are confirmed when he startles and twists his body to look at me, his gaze overtaken by whatever rage has propelled him to this moment. I take in his blood-splattered face, the way I can't see the color of it on his clothes but can tell he is *painted* in it by the way it glistens beneath the firelight. And it *guts* me when recognition flashes in his gaze, clearing the bitter darkness that clouds them.

I take a step closer, avoiding looking at the mess that's heaped in front of him as I instead hold his gaze. "Nox?"

"Stop."

His command is given roughly, his voice a shred of itself. But I ignore it and chance another step towards him. "Nox, what happened?"

He shakes his head, working his jaw as he drops his gaze from mine. "I failed her," he grits out, his shoulders tensing as he drags in a quick breath. "He's torturing her, *touching* her, and I can't do a godsdamn thing about it." I get close enough to see the faint tears now gathering on his lower lashes, and gods, he's never looked so broken. So completely *shattered*. "She's suffering, and I'll *never* be able to forgive myself for that."

"It's okay." I force the tears that threaten to spill from my own eyes away, stuffing my rising sadness down with them as I close the remaining distance between us, sliding my blade back into its hidden spot in my boot. "Nox, give me the dagger."

"I've failed her," he says again, this time not softly or with anger. But with utter devastation. "And *he* was the only one who had information and I—" The dagger shakes in his trembling hands, and though I can't sense magic, though I know his is currently too weak to be felt regardless, I swear the air thickens with *something* as it causes the hair at the back of my neck to rise.

"There is nothing we can do about that now." I keep my tone light and my words gentle as I hold my hand out. "But we can figure out what to do next *together*, Nox."

"You shouldn't be here, Bahira. I never wanted you to be dragged into this mess. To suffer from my own failures."

I blink back my surprise at his words, even though they break my heart. I *know* my brother has been suffering, but taking in the scene around me—the way Nox can't quite seem to let the rage that led to this go—I'm ashamed to admit that it's worse than I imagined.

I kneel at his side, watching as utter turmoil lays claim to every inch of his face. "The dagger, Brother," I say again, still reaching a hand out. Hoping he knows it symbolizes more than just relieving him of the weapon. But Nox is lost, his gaze distant. He doesn't fight me when I reach out and pry it from his hand, tossing it out of reach before helping him up to stand. Uncertainty fills the space between us and I do the only thing I can think of to try and pull my brother from the darkness threatening to drown him: I wrap my arms around his torso. His body is stiff at first in my hold, but then he embraces me back, his fingers digging into my sides.

"It's going to be alright." It's the only reassurance I can offer, even if it doesn't quite feel like the truth. I wish there was anything else I could do to unburden him of his anguish, but instead, I hold him, letting him grip me like he might descend back into the chaos I found him in if he lets go. "We'll get her back," I whisper, swallowing when he stays silent. "She's strong, Nox, you told me yourself."

"Bahira! You promised only a few minutes, and it's been a lot more than that!"

Fuck. My brother pulls away and looks for his discarded dagger, but I shake my head as I release him fully. "Don't worry. He won't be a problem." At least, I hope that's the fucking truth. Nox looks as unconvinced as I probably sound but doesn't protest when I order him to stay put. Stepping back out into the aisle, I walk forward as I call Max's name out.

"Bahira..." Max nearly gasps when he sees me, lowering his sword. "What are you doing down here? I thought you said—" He abruptly stops when he takes me in, not even the darkness of the dungeons can hide what stains my body from hugging Nox. "Is that *blood*?" He lifts his sword again, eyes darting side to side. "Did someone hurt you?"

"No." My hands come out in front of me, pressing at his chest when he tries to walk past me. "I'm completely uninjured."

"But..." He looks down at me again, brows furrowed deeply. "Then whose blood is that?"

I sigh as I drop my hands. "I need to ask for your help again. But I can't tell you why—not because I don't want you to know, but because it could be dangerous for *you*." Pressing my lips together, I weigh my next words carefully. "There's been an incident, and I need you to help me cover it up."

Trusting someone has *never* come easily to me, and with Haylee's betrayal fresh on my mind, the *last* thing I want to do is make the wrong choice here. But Nox... I will not be another person that lets him down. And if Max doesn't want to help him, then I will do whatever I must to ensure my brother remains safe.

Tense moments pass between Max and I as we stare at each other. I certainly would not blame him if he told me to *fuck off* and attempted to strike me down. But the behemoth of a man just groans, as if I've asked him for the hundredth time to pick his shirt up from the floor. Resheathing his sword, he pins me with a look that I'm fairly certain is meant to be menacing but just comes off as petulant. "What do you need me to do?"

Chapter Eighty-Eight

BAHIRA

I WANTED TO LINGER beneath the hot water of the shower for the entire night, as if the steam would hide me from the truths that were waiting beyond the bathroom door. But while the idea was tempting, I had done enough avoiding of my reality lately. And when it came down to it, I was unwilling to let Nox handle whatever had happened this evening alone.

Max did everything I asked him to without question, managing to quell his questions and shock when I showed him the remains of the man Nox had killed. He disposed of the body, citing an incinerator that was attached to the dungeons. It too was guarded, but Max said he would handle getting past them, and he did.

While he took care of cleaning up and staging the scene so the two sleeping guards—I had learned that Nox drugged them with lavendaris—would appear to have just fallen asleep on the job, I worked on bringing Nox up to his rooms. A job that, unfortunately, required the help of both of our parents. While my father could have chosen to leave the palace for a quiet life away from the very politics that had turned against him, he instead requested to be one of the instructors that oversees the training of the Mage Kingdom's army. This put him in a prime position to ensure that guards within the palace would be limited, leaving points for us to pass through undetected on our way to the third floor. My mother took care of the palace aides, enlisting Sarai to help conceal and destroy our bloodied clothing. It was an unfortunate family affair but one that ensured no one saw or suspected anything.

I wait in Nox's sitting room now, having heard his own shower turn off a while ago. He had been silent on our way up, leaving me to answer any questions our parents had. But my information was limited to what I had seen with my own eyes, and after they both assured me they would tell the council that Nox was not feeling well and resting in his room, I decided that today would be the day that we revealed everything we had been keeping from each other. Admittedly, the list of secrets is likely longer for him, but I am holding on to one that I haven't found the right time to bring up. I suppose that time will have to be now.

When he finally exits his room, dressed in a black shirt and matching trousers, he doesn't look at me as he all but collapses on the sofa across from me, kicking his feet up onto the coffee table and causing the small pile of black stones there to shake. Leaning over, I pick one up and examine it. "Did you get into rock collecting while I was gone?" I ask, my thumb running along the smooth edges. "Is this dragon stone?"

"They're Rhea's. She used them to practice imbuing her magic."

Turning the egg-shaped stone over in my hand, I make out the faint glow of gray at its center. Goosebumps break out over my arm, and my scalp prickles before I place the stone back down on the table with the others, and fold my arms over my chest. "It's time to tell me what is going on."

"You know most of it."

"But not all."

Tilting his chin down, Nox focuses his gaze on me "No, not all." Shaking his head, he runs a hand through his wet hair, holding the longer strands back from his face. "I don't know where to start."

"How about from the beginning?" When that option doesn't seem to appeal to him, I kick my feet up on the coffee table too and sink deeper into the couch. "There is nowhere else I have to be, Brother. Nowhere else I *want* to be. I offered help before, and I'm offering it again. Don't shut me out."

Releasing his hair, his hand falls to his lap, and then he begins.

He starts with a place called the Middle and the woman named Selene who resides there. He tells me of the pain he's been in, how the medicine from Galen only numbs him for a short while before everything floods back in. He recounts everything Stephan did to him when he ambushed him on his way to get to Rhea, and then of his nights spent in Colter until he found him. I learn of the plan he concocted to catch Stephan in the dungeon and how the cruel words of the bastard had pushed Nox past the line of anger he was teetering against. When my brother's voice grows lethally quiet, goosebumps bloom over my skin.

"He was there. The night she was taken," he answers, the air stilling in the room at his words. "He was the one who lured Daje and Rhea out. He followed and watched as the other mages knocked them both out and then when they handed her off." His dark gray eyes hold mine, the silver flecks in them practically gone. "To the *sirens*."

My blood chills, my head snapping back in surprise. "The sirens? They are involved?"

"I don't know how deeply, and I feel fucking *foolish* for assuming King Dolian could have orchestrated this all on his own. I'm also inclined to believe that if Stephan was there to draw Daje and Rhea out of the room, then he likely had to make sure the hallway was empty so there wouldn't be any questions asked."

It takes me a moment to catch his meaning, but when I do, my eyes close in devastation. "Barron."

"Stephan didn't confess to it, but it's the only thing that makes sense. I'm going to send a few guards to search his property, just in case Barron's body is there." Gods, our parents will be distraught by this. And Barron's partner... I swallow against the tightness in my throat.

"Anything else?" I ask.

Nox's brows draw low, his face pinched in thought. "Stephan had gone to the Mortal Kingdom. That is how he found me. And when I asked a barmaid in the tavern where I spotted him, she said he would often disappear for long periods of time."

"It makes sense, doesn't it? If he was conspiring with King Dolian, they would have to be communicating somehow."

"Yes, but"—he places his feet on the floor and leans his elbows on his knees with a wince—"I've been thinking about how Stephan was able to just *leave* whenever he needed to return to the Mortal Kingdom with information. Even with his position as a guard who just fills in where needed, someone in his chain of command had to have noticed that he would be gone for days to a week at a time. Someone with a high enough clearance to approve his leave—and not worry about anyone questioning it."

"How high?"

He cradles his head in his hands, wincing as his fingers massage his temples. "When Arin was kicked out of the guard, the decision came from the council."

"Fuck," I whisper, feeling a headache of my own beginning to bloom.

"No protest at that?" he asks, his lips pulling up in a ghost of a smirk. "I expected at least *some* bite back about how our council couldn't possibly be behind this."

I give him a dry look but take my time formulating my thoughts. "I might have desperately wanted to believe that these people chosen to support our father as king were doing so with genuine, good-natured, and sound advice before. But the more that I've learned, the more I've seen with my own eyes and heard with my own ears, the more I've come to realize that at some point, things shifted. The council views our family as a threat, and they only needed the right set of circumstances to prove that threat to themselves. To our people." I pause, letting out an incredulous breath. "Now I only wonder what else they might be plotting in order to get what they want. Elora was right to suspect them."

Nox's gaze softens, just slightly, as he lifts his head from his hands. "So now what? Our only source of information is dead. Cass, Daje, and Elora—" He interrupts himself with a deep breath, patting at the pockets of his pants before he stands and walks to his bedroom, leaving me to stare at the now empty space on the couch in front of me.

"Good point," I grumble, leaning my head back against the couch as I contemplate that very question. *What next?*

Nox returns and stands at the edge of the coffee table, a letter with a broken seal in his hands. "They got it," he says, tired eyes landing on mine. "They found the dragon glass."

"What?" Leaping from the couch, I stand next to him as he lifts the letter up in the air, angling it so that a small flare of sunlight from a nearby window bleeds over the page. "I don't—"

"Look in the spaces between the lines," he cuts in. "Right where the sun is shining."

I follow his commands, my eyes adjusting as I focus them on the parts of the paper that appear blank at first glance. But when I lean in a little more closely, the faint swooping of letters becomes visible in the light. "Is that magic *ink*?"

"It is. Imbued to activate by the sun's light. It's how Cass and I have spoken in coded messages while I was in the Mortal Kingdom."

"What does it say?"

"It took them a day of searching, but they found a small collection of what we've been calling dragon glass. Cass isn't sure if it will be enough, but Daje is eager to begin the journey back to our side of the border."

I nod, an invisible weight lifting from my chest. Retrieving the dragon glass is only the first step in repairing the Mirror, but just knowing that at least they found *some* sparks hope. "How long do you think it took a raven to fly the letter here?"

"A week?" he states, though it sounds more like a question. "Hard to say without knowing the exact distance it had to cross. But this is good news." Then, in a teasing voice that almost sounds foreign after so much time watching my brother in anguish, he adds, "And soon, you'll be able to talk with King Kai."

I snort. "I'm sure he's dying to hear from me after two months of silence." Though the words come out recklessly, the silence that follows is sobering. *Two months.* It's hard to believe it's been that long since I sailed away from Jahlee and Kai. Since his voice played in my ear and his hands caressed my body. My stomach flutters at the thought of seeing him again. Of explaining why I haven't reached out to him. That it had nothing to do with *not* wanting to talk to him. Yet I wonder, even if the Mirror had never broken, if I would have hesitated. If my cowardice still would have manifested in pretending that I didn't miss him. That I didn't think about him every single day and wonder, somewhat pathetically, if I didn't also still occupy his thoughts. Or maybe I just simply hope that *if* he thinks of me, it isn't tainted with the betrayal of my lies.

"Bahira."

Nox's voice permeates my thoughts, and I blink them away as I focus back on my brother. "There's something I need to tell you."

"If it's anything about the shifter king and that doe-eyed look you just had, I think I'm good."

"Asshole," I mutter, turning to face him as my heart pounds in my chest. "The reason I came home from the Shifter Kingdom early was because when I tried to reach out through the Mirror, no one answered."

Nox gives me a confused look. "*Right*, because Father and I had been summoned by the council to go to Palatos. Though the council never said anything about King Kai attempting to reach us when we returned."

Gods, that is another thing the council must have done purposefully. "The reason I reached out through the Mirror in the first place was because of a shifter who showed up on the island. Her name is Siyala." I wait for any kind of recognition to pass over his face, but he only furrows his brow. "She is the cousin of the king and had been missing for four years. When she showed up that day, she revealed that she had been trapped in the Mortal Kingdom."

He cocks his head in question. "How? That's impossible."

"It should be, and she didn't have an answer for that, but her main concern wasn't that she had somehow survived crossing over the Spell or that she had just returned home. She was most worried about the woman she lived with while in the Mortal Kingdom. One who she said was now in the Mage Kingdom." I swallow, my eyes holding his as my heart beats harshly. "Nox, she knew Rhea."

"No. Rhea lived completely isolated. There's no way—" His mouth snaps shut as his eyes widen, a hand brushing through his hair. "She is a shifter?" he clarifies.

I nod slowly, my gaze searching his. "Yes."

"Fucking gods above," he murmurs, a small smile beginning to grow. "She's alive. Bella is *alive*."

Chapter Eighty-Nine

DAJE

I T WAS ABOUT THREE days into our journey that I came to the conclusion that I wasn't meant for traveling. I wasn't meant for spending long days riding on a horse only to then sleep in a shitty inn for a few hours at night. I wasn't made for quick meals of dried meat, fruit, and nuts while the only warm food came from equally shitty taverns. And I *certainly* wasn't made for close quarters with a man who drove me up a fucking wall and a woman who I couldn't ever tell if she was teasing or flirting with me.

But here I am, getting ready to end our fourth day of nearly nonstop riding with yet another stay at an inn where I'd likely have to share a bed with Cass and his cover-hogging tendencies. I never thought I could miss something as simple as a soft towel. Or a meal that wasn't a questionable stew. Or, *fuck*, peace and *quiet*.

"At least it isn't raining today," Elora says, and for a moment, I worry I've spoken my grievances out loud. My gaze tracks over her braided red hair where it hangs down her back, some strands having come loose from the plait. My magic coils beneath my skin like it's on the alert, perked up by Elora's signature in a way that won't let me forget just how close she is to me.

"Let's hope that streak continues once we cross over the border," Cass replies from our left, his horse choosing that moment to whinny as if in agreement.

True enough, the rain had been a constant companion the closer we grew to the north. It is expected in the late autumn season, but its predictability didn't change the fact that traveling in the rain is also another thing I wasn't meant for.

We continue on, riding in a silence that is all at once comfortable and *not*. Adapting to not speaking for long periods of time didn't come naturally to either Cass or Elora, though at least the latter didn't send covert, suggestive glances my way. My conversation with the prick back at the first inn had played on repeat in my mind until I was begging any gods that might hear my pleas to have mercy on me.

It isn't necessarily that I don't *want* Elora's attention, nor is it that I find her anything other than lovely. It's that, frustratingly, I know Cass is right. She doesn't deserve someone only capable of being partially invested in whatever might be blossoming between us. Bahira still occupies a portion of my mind that is tangled up in the space between oldest friend and longest yearning. Though she and I had never truly aligned on when those feelings blurred between the two, a part of me had hoped—for far too long—that, eventually, we would find common ground. That there was enough of myself embedded in that steel chest of hers that she might one day see me in the same way I saw her: magnificent. Stunning. She was the chaos of a wild hurricane, and I was the eye of the storm, able to withstand her strength.

In theory, us falling together should have been inevitable. In actuality, it was anything but.

I had thought cutting her out of my life like a frayed thread on a tapestry would be for the best. But the problem, I have found, is that the thread I snipped was merely a portion of the one deeply woven within me. And what remains isn't something so easily ignored. Even if I am starting to view it differently than I had before.

I love Bahira, yet that love can mean many things. Something that I foolishly have taken much too long to finally accept.

"Finally." Elora's sigh of relief as she spots our stop for the evening makes a small grin tug on my lips. "I swear on all the gods, dead and alive, that I will never again travel outside of my small bubble."

"Is swearing on dead gods going to do anything?" I ask, enjoying her snort as her head bobbles from side to side.

"Probably not, but it certainly doesn't hurt to include them."

"That's the sort of legacy I want," Cass chimes in, tightening his hold on the reins as he urges his horse to slow. "Someone to find me so powerful that swearing on me, even in death, is good luck."

"I'm afraid the road to being elevated to feared deity is quite difficult. Especially if you aren't born into it," Elora teases, and I huff a breath, mentally scowling at the retort I know Cass is going to supply.

"Quite a few people have likened me to a god, though the context was a *little* different."

Elora tilts her head back to laugh, brushing against my chest with the movement. Her scent—cinnamon and vanilla—laces my next inhale. Once again, my stupid body reacts before I tell it to, and my fingers curl into her hip. But if it bothers Elora, she doesn't show it. Instead, she looks over her shoulder at me, a smirk tugging on her pink lips.

We reach the small structure indicated on the map given to us by Sadryn. There had been a note added in the margin stating that while this place seemed unassuming, its proximity to the border had made the residents of this settlement more wary of new faces. Though it is true only mages can cross through the Spell, the uptick in missing people from border towns had made everyone jumpy. As we traveled along the fae border, Elora insisting the northern beaches would be the best place to look for dragon glass, places had not grown friendlier. Stares grew longer as the people sussed out whether our intentions were well-meaning or not. It gave us no choice really *but* to only stay for a few hours' rest. Cass had been given enough coin by the council to more than compensate for our stays, and he made sure to tip generously to hopefully avoid anyone giving us trouble. So far, curious glares were all we had received.

The Inn, appropriately and simply named, is built entirely from dragon stone, its rectangular structure shining beneath the faint moonlight coming from above. Smaller buildings made from the same stone line the main road on either side, their insides glowing with amber light.

"I'll see about getting the horses in the stable," Cass says as we come to a halt. The hairs on my arms rise as the sensation of being watched washes over me, even though no one else is walking the dark road.

"Maybe you shouldn't go alone." My eyes scan the fronts of the businesses. An apothecary is next to the inn followed by what appears to be a weapons shop. A few unmarked buildings line the rest of the way, the sound of voices coming from them not the comfort it should be.

"Aw, worried about me?" Bringing his horse to a stop, Cass dismounts and walks over to take the reins of my own horse. I hesitate but relent when Elora pats the top of my hand.

"Let's go secure our rooms so we can eat and get some rest before we're back at it tomorrow." Sighing, I release the reins and slide off of the horse, reaching up to help Elora down. Her hands plant on my shoulders as she swings her leg around and then dismounts, stumbling just slightly when both feet touch the ground. "By the time I'm able to get off of a horse without any help, we'll already be home."

I chuckle as my hands remain near her hips, making sure she is steady before letting go. "I don't mind helping you."

Her light gray eyes meet mine, and even in the cover of night, I can make out the pink that flushes her cheeks beneath her freckles. "I suppose it's not the *worst* thing to be in need of your assistance."

How else can I be of assistance to you? The thought comes on so abruptly, the tenor of the voice in my head so surprisingly deep, that I suck in a breath as I jerk back a step, leaving Elora to wobble for a moment. *Fuck.* "I'm sorry," I rush out, moving back in to do... *something*. Anything. Elora just smiles as she pushes her glasses up the bridge of her nose before turning to reach for her pack. I slam my eyes shut and silently berate myself.

Cass plants a hand on my shoulder, shaking me once and forcing me to look at him. His face, annoyingly, mimics my internal sentiments.

Elora and I watch Cass as he heads down a grassy side path to the back of the inn to look for the stables. He hums a tune and quietly sings about our "glass adventure," prompting me to shake my head as I whisper to Elora, "Let's keep the chatter to a minimum once we go in." I reach over to take her pack. She doesn't immediately hand it over, but when I arch a brow in question, she sighs and allows me to grab it. Her posture immediately straightens without the weight of all her books.

"You say that as if I can't *help* but to chatter." At my responding silence, she glances over at me and then slaps her hand against my arm in response to my expression.

I snort while we climb the wooden steps to the tavern's front door. Pausing before it, I mentally recap where my weapons are—a dagger strapped to my belt and one slipped down into my boot. Another in my bag and, finally, one given to Elora. Dilan would have trained her to use it, but I know it's been a while since she's actually practiced with one. Still, I lean down to speak close to her ear. "Should things go south quickly, for whatever reason, do not hesitate to protect yourself with blade or magic." Once she gives me a nod of confirmation, I take a deep breath and open the door.

While the inns we have stayed at thus far have all been fairly similar in their layouts, immediately upon entering, I can tell that this place isn't going to be in line with the others. Where a quiet reception area with a desk had been the status quo before, here, we walk directly into a lounge of sorts. People are draped across the furniture as if they've been there all day, too content or perhaps too drunk to move. The air is thick with smoke and just a hint of magic, and a quick whiff of it makes me think it's some kind of tobacco, except that it smells too sweet.

"Come on." With a jerk of my head, I lead Elora through the lounge, drawing more heavily lidded gazes in our direction as we pass. My skin crawls with the attention, and by the time we reach the desk to request our rooms, my anxiousness has manifested into a twitch of my right eye. The man behind the desk observes us as we near, his gaze moving over me in an assessing manner. His focus then goes to the pack that's slung over one shoulder before it lands on Elora. And stays there. "We need three rooms," I tell him, reaching into my pocket for the small stash of money.

"Are you travelers?" he asks, a hand coming up to massage his long blond beard.

"Just passing through on our way home."

He lifts a brow, eyes still pinned to Elora who shifts her weight. "And where is home?"

"Brago," she answers before I can, earning the man's smile.

Brago is the kingdom's northernmost city and a place where a high number of mages have gone missing. Sadryn had been planning a trip to visit the city before the events after the Autumnal Ball. It's not a place I *want* to visit, but in this case, Elora isn't lying. Tomorrow, we'll hit Brago, and soon after, if we're lucky, we'll find ourselves on the dangerous side of the Spell.

"Seems more and more people are leaving Brago, not returning to it."

I shrug, hoping my face conveys the same nonchalance. "We have family there."

He grunts before opening one of the desk drawers and pulling out three keys.

"Can we have supper brought to our rooms?"

"No," he answers, his expression pained as he tosses the keys onto the counter just as Cass walks up. "Dinner is available in the dining room, through that hallway over there." He gestures with his chin across the lounge, where I can barely make out an arched hallway through the smoky haze. "We don't allow food in the rooms. It draws the rats upstairs. But I can have your bags brought up while you eat." Before I can decline his offer, the man calls out to someone, his voice booming.

"Perhaps we should skip eating and just go to bed," I whisper to Cass and Elora.

"Tomorrow's journey will be longer than today's by a few hours. It wouldn't hurt to try and get a good meal in now," Cass says, throwing an arm around my shoulders. "Well, maybe not a good one, given the rats comment, but a warm one hopefully."

I open my mouth to protest, ready to argue that getting sick from the food sounds like the *last* thing that we need, but Elora nods her head in agreement. "He's right. Let them bring our things upstairs so that we don't draw unwanted attention."

Stuck between their gazes, I begrudgingly slide my pack off. A lanky man, his hair the same shade of blond as the one behind the desk, comes to stand at our side, his hands already reaching for our belongings. "You will be in rooms twenty-one through twenty-three, near the back." He points to a different hallway at our left.

"Thank you, good sir," Cass says, swiping the keys from the desktop. Elora gives a small wave, making the man's eyes glitter lasciviously before we turn and reenter the vapors in the lounge. "Don't breathe too much of this stuff in. Even just getting exposed to it like this can make you susceptible to some of the effects."

"What is it?" Elora asks, side stepping a couple who are far too comfortable with exploring each other's mouths in a public setting.

"Dimania."

Elora gasps at Cass's answer, her eyes widening.

"What? What is that?"

"Dimania is a flower that grows in the richest soil at the base of our northern mountains. It's crushed into a powder and mixed in with smoking tobacco and is known for its *aphrodisiac* effects."

Gods above. I take another cursory glance around the room as we near the other side, noting that while there still are quite a large number of people simply laying wherever, a few *are* engaged in activities of a more sensitive nature. Mostly at the edges of the space, where the shadows can hide their movements. But certainly not all.

"You look so horrified right now," Cass teases as he claps my shoulder. "Don't worry, I don't think we were exposed to much. And even if we were, we are all sleeping in separate rooms anyway." *And thank the gods for that.*

We finally reach the dining room, the space small and filled with only a handful of tables and a mismatched collection of chairs. The three of us take a seat in the farthest corner and order food. It's predictably a stew but one that's at least full of recognizable vegetables and void of any questionable meat.

"Do you think we should reach out to Nox? Let him know where we are?" Elora asks once we finish eating.

"I told him that we'd limit communication to only what is necessary," Cass says from where he's reclined in his chair, his arms folded over his chest. "Let's wait until we have good news to report."

I try to ignore the way my anxious thoughts swirl inside of me, my stomach queasy. It isn't that I don't believe we *might* find dragon glass. It's that I can't be sure we'll find it without being spotted by a fae or, worse, a dragon. I had never seen one of the beasts beyond a description on a page, but that alone was enough to spook me into believing that this trip was just a single stroke of bad luck away from becoming a suicide mission.

"Well, my reading hasn't revealed anything yet on how to actually *repair* the Mirror once we acquire the dragon glass. I'm hoping that Nox's magic will be fixed by the time we get back because if it isn't..." She shakes her head, tossing her braid over her shoulder.

"It will," Cass says confidently.

"If he's even there *when* we get back," I add, stacking my arms on the table.

The quiet that stretches between us is charged with thoughts of Nox and Rhea, the latter the type that shows up in my quiet moments when I am alone. Everything had happened so quickly the night she was taken; one moment, I was talking with her, her panic evident on her face, and the next, I was waking up alone in a small pool of my own blood. Her jewelry broken on the stone pathway next to me. Realizing that she was gone—that I would then have to tell Nox—was one of the worst moments of my life.

"He'll get her back," Elora says softly, her eyes lifting from where her hands flex nervously on the table.

"He will," Cass agrees. "And if we have to wait until—"

I don't hear his words as pain, bright and *hot*, bursts to life at my shoulder.

"Daje!" Elora screams at my side, her face draining of color as she tentatively reaches a hand towards me. I follow her line of sight, my breath choking off in my throat before reaching my lungs, as I look down and see the *dagger* sticking out of the front of my shoulder.

Chapter Ninety

DAJE

"Godsdamn it!" Cass shouts, standing and kicking his chair behind him, two blades already in his hands. "Are you okay?"

"Fuck." I stand from my chair as I scan the room. My vision goes double, each breath choking off in a groan as I struggle to draw air in.

Reaching for Elora, I attempt to tug her towards me, but she resists, her face drained of color. "You have a—"

"Protect yourself!" I tell her, my anger stirring at the very familiar hilt of my own *fucking* dagger sticking out of my shoulder. Blood trickles down my chest, and I move to reach for the blade when I'm shoved from the side, sending me careening towards the ground, my shoulder screaming at the impact.

"Fae sympathizers! You're working with them!" I look over my shoulder as the man who hit me lunges again, his dark eyes gleaming with malice while his fingers curl towards his palm and he begins to wind his hand back. Keeping my gaze on him, I quickly reach for the dagger and yank it out. More screams fill the room, my vision flashing black, and for a single moment in time, everything goes quiet. There is no chaos unfolding in the dining room of this inn. There are no entangled feelings of love and lust and friendship. There's no domineering, perpetually disappointed father with a penchant for being cruel. There is nothing but the sound of my breath rattling in my chest. My heartbeat pounding in my skull. And then, all at once, it comes rushing back in. My vision flashes back at the exact moment the man charging for me falls to the ground. Cass's shout of warning rends the air right as Elora's scream sounds. Perhaps it's instinct—something that's been there as part of me being mage or male or some combination of the two—but I react before I think as I launch to my feet.

Spinning the bloodied blade, I toss it up in the air, watching as it goes tip-over-hilt before I catch it and then fling it towards the man at Elora's back. She blinks, spinning with her own dagger drawn in one hand and her pink magic flaring in the other just in time to watch the man fall, the blade now embedded between his eyes.

"Are you alright?" Rushing towards her, my hands grip her shoulders before I cringe at the blood I've gotten on her blouse.

"Am I—" She cuts herself off, shaking her head. "Are *you* okay? You were stabbed, and I—" Her chest rises with a heaving breath, her mouth opening and closing quickly though no more sound comes out. I take stock of her shaking hands, the one holding the dagger covered in blood. Once I'm sure it isn't hers, I lean in close, getting on her eye level.

"I'm fine. I'll live, but I need you to protect yourself so that I can help Cass. Can you do that?"

She nods as a tear escapes and trails down her cheek. I don't have time to comfort her the way I'm called to, not when my friend is shouting for my help. "Follow me."

We turn back to watch as Cass blocks a man with a godsdamn sword, crossing his own longer-bladed daggers in front of him. But before I can navigate through the overturned chairs and tables to get to him, another man rushes into the dining room. His eyes search the space until they connect with mine, and I reach for the dagger strapped at my belt before he takes his next step. Pain flares over my shoulder, and I quickly pull my magic to it, cringing as the muscles work to stitch back together.

"Fae sympathizer!" he bellows, barreling towards us. I raise my hand and send a blast of my yellow magic towards him, hitting him square in the chest and sending him flying back into the wall.

"Cass!" Elora's shriek cuts through my concentration, pulling my attention towards my friend.

Cass deflects each swing of his opponent's sword, even as the man pushes him back towards a wall. Fuck, he's about to be cornered. Elora releases her magic with a grunt, the stream of pink lighting up the room as it goes right towards her intended target. The man throws up a translucent shield made of dark blue, deflecting her magic but not without a cost. Cass is quick, and his dagger is in the man's chest before he can draw in his next breath.

"Stars above, *thank you*," Cass says, making his way towards us. We eye the bodies in the room, counting four dead so far.

"Why did they call us fae sympathizers?" Elora asks, her fingertips brushing at her cheeks, wiping away tears. My own fingers flex at my sides, but I stay equidistant between her and Cass, my gaze locked on the open door to the dining room. Shadows stir outside, and I grab my second blade from my boot, ignoring how sticky my shirt is as another handful of mages enter. They're led by the man who gave us the keys to our room. He holds a sword in one hand, the item in his other hand making Elora gasp as she takes a step towards him.

"Hey! That is *mine!*" She takes another step before I wrap an arm around her waist, tugging her back with me. Her eyes, angry and sad, meet mine. "He has one of my books!"

"You admit it! You're working with the fae!"

"It's a *book*, not a damn manifesto!" Cass shouts back. Sweat gleams over his forehead, his white-blond hair sticking to it as he attempts to swat it out of his face. "She's reading about the Fae Kingdom! There is nothing illegal about that."

The man laughs, encouraging the others to join in on some bizarre display of dominance or incredulity. I'm not yet sure which. "Do you think we are idiots?" he asks, holding the book up as if to emphasize his point.

Cass opens his mouth, and I quickly kick the side of his foot to tell him to shut up.

"It's a simple misunderstanding," I tell them, holding my hands up in front of me. "We aren't working with the fae. We have no intentions of doing such a thing. We'll leave now if that will make you feel better."

"So you can run and spill our secrets to the fae? I don't think so." The man closest to the door kicks it shut before brandishing a dagger of his own. The others pull out varying weapons, and I make note of the fact that none reach for their magic. In fact, I can *barely* sense their signatures.

I step in front of Elora, Cass joining me at my side. "Keep your blade out and be ready to call on your magic the moment anyone gets past us," I whisper to her. My mouth is already forming words in response to her protest, but Elora doesn't give one. She simply nods and stays a step behind, readying her position.

The two men at the end of the formation lunge towards us first, and Cass and I both hit them with a burst of our magic, holding them back as we dart forward. I slice at the man closest to me, his forearm coming up to take the brunt of the hit. Orange magic glows at his fingertips, and I spin out of the way and kick my leg out low, swiping him right off his feet. My boot is the next thing to come down, connecting with his jaw and knocking him out. It feels like only a single breath of time passes before someone else is upon me, my dagger lifting up to block the weapon swung my way. My wound protests the movement and sweat rolls down my back as I fight mage after mage, the anger in their eyes only obstructed by the fear I see there too. My knuckles sting in pain at the punch I send to a man who looks not much older than I am, and before I can watch him hit the ground, another takes his place, hands clutching a rudimentary wooden club. Muscles aching, I duck and spin out of his first few swings of it, but don't move fast enough to avoid the next. The club hits the back of my shoulder, and I drop to a knee as air rushes from me.

A pair of dark eyes appears above me, club already raised over his head as he growls. Swirls of yellow wrap around his arms holding him in place as I drag my blade across his stomach, his bellow ringing in my ears. Blood spills down the front of his body, and as I pull my magic back, he drops the club and falls to the ground, his hands pressed into his gut. I watch as his magic flares there, but its light is much smaller than it needs to be for such a deep injury.

"You good?" Cass asks, hauling me up, Elora at his side. None of the other men remain, and as I watch Elora's chest rise and fall in quick succession, more blood staining her blouse than before, my stomach sinks at the thought that she had to step in and fight too.

"I'm fine. We need to get out of here before they do anything to our horses."

Cass nods, jogging in the direction of one of the windows. Grabbing one of the dining chairs, he wastes no time heaving it at the glass. Elora's eyes squeeze shut, her dagger held so tightly in her hand that her knuckles are flooded with white, noticeable even against her pale skin.

"That'll work," Cass says, just as voices sound outside of the closed door. "Come on. Prepare to run once we hit the ground. The stables are behind the building." He slides a second chair in front of the window before climbing onto it, jumping down to the other side.

"My books," Elora whispers, pleading eyes meeting mine.

"We don't have time to go looking for them," I answer softly, guiding her forward. "I'm sorry."

With a sigh, she follows Cass outside. I pause, looking around for the man who greeted us when we first arrived.

"Come on, Daje!" Cass calls, his voice already farther away.

"I'm coming!" A moment later, I'm at the window, jumping out and sprinting towards the stables.

A mob had formed near the inn, and while they spot us as we run towards the stables, I am relieved to find that at least the horses have been left alone. Once we mount, we race out on a dirt road that follows a small stream, the scarce moonlight flooding in through the trees guiding us as we put as much distance as possible between us and them.

The sun is beginning to rise when we finally slow the horses hours later, leading them to the spring to drink and then to a small meadow to graze. Intent with removing as much blood as possible from my person, I return to the stream, my movements slow. The balance of using my magic during the fight means that it needs time to recover now, a process that annoys me nearly as much as the exhaustion that feels heavy in my bones.

I spot Elora farther down and kneeling in front of the water, and I announce my presence once I'm a few feet behind her. "Wanting to clean up too?"

"Trying to," she says, a little breathless as she looks at me over her shoulder.

"Do you mind if I...?" I pause and tug at my top.

"Nope. Go ahead." I wait until she turns back towards the water before pulling it off, grimacing. We'll be able to buy all new supplies and clothing when we reach Bragos. All except for the books Elora had brought. Unfortunately, those were priceless. She had remained utterly silent as we rode away, her body stiff as a board. Even now, her movements are jerky as she scrubs at her hands beneath the water.

"You know what's funny?" she says as I kneel next to her, dipping my shirt into the water.

"What?"

"We are trained for most of our childhood and into adulthood to fight. To defend ourselves. We choose a weapon as our specialty. We have mock battles and sparring sessions with our peers. In theory, we are taught how to take a life without ever assuming that we'll actually need to."

I tilt my head to the side, cleaning my shirt as I ponder that. "I suppose that is true enough, though—"

"But what we *really* should have been training for is what happens *after* the fight." She sucks in a breath, a desperate laugh coming from her as I glance her way. "All this time spent on preparing for the action. On besting your opponent, and yet *no* one tells you that after you do *just that*, you feel different." My eyes move to where she is scrubbing at her hands in the water, the skin on the backs of them bright red. "Isn't that funny? Someone tried to kill me, tried to kill my friends, yet *I'm* the one who is left to feel bad. *I'm* the one who is wondering if this has changed who I am fundamentally as a person. If I'm now like *them* and have no regard for someone else's life and—"

"Elora." My hands close around hers, jolting her out of her spiral and forcing her eyes to meet mine. They're rimmed in red, a sheen to them suggesting that she's either been crying or trying her very best not to. Her bottom lip trembles as her breaths flit in and out of her, a blush rising to stain her cheeks.

Swallowing, I look down at our hands in the water. My darker ones cradling her fair ones as I stroke my thumbs over the raw red marks left by her nails. Carefully, I lift them from the water before resting one hand on her thigh and inspecting the other.

"The fact that you're asking these questions proves you are nothing like them. That your compassion is still very much intact." I keep my gaze on her delicate fingers, rubbing my thumb over each one as I check to see if there is any blood remaining. "What we had to do back at the inn was a matter of life or death. You did what you had to in order to protect not only yourself but Cass and I. And you did. You protected us." Laying her hand down, I gently pick up the other one, beginning my examination of it. "Feeling conflicted about ending another's life just means that you value it. But those men did give us a choice: kill or be killed.

And while I hope we don't have to experience anything else like that again for the rest of our days, I can say confidently that you made the right choice." I hold her hand longer than I need to, longer than necessary as my gaze rises to meet hers. She stares at me through her glasses, the cadence of her breaths softer now. "Your hands are clean," I tell her, gently laying the other one down.

"Thank you," she whispers, the words just barely audible as they pass her lips. Her hand lifts, cold fingertips brushing near the angry purple skin at the front of my shoulder. "This must have hurt." I watch as her gaze travels down my exposed skin slowly, nerve endings that have nothing to do with the bruise there burning brightly at the way she is looking at me. Something fragile and heated stretches taut between us when our eyes meet again, my throat working with a swallow as she bites down on her bottom lip.

"Friends, you're lucky I'm fabulous at everything I do! First time hunting, and I've caught us a worthy meal!" Cass's voice snaps us out of the moment, Elora blinking quickly and adjusting her glasses before pushing herself up to stand.

"Thanks for—"

"Of course." I give her a small smile and return to scrubbing my shirt, listening as Cass excitedly recounts his hunting tale to Elora. I force myself to focus on the next task at hand—getting to Bragos. From there, we'll be within a few hours of the northern fae beaches and be able to cross the Spell. The events of earlier are only a stark reminder that I need to keep my head—and emotions—in check.

At any moment, death could be lingering around a corner waiting for the perfect opportunity to strike. I can't afford any distractions; none of us can.

Chapter Ninety-One

DAJE

IT IS EARLY MORNING when we finally reach our desired crossing point into the Fae Kingdom. Cass keeps his weapons within easy access as he goes through the Spell first, followed quickly by Elora and myself.

We had replaced our clothing and replenished our supplies with new packs in Bragos the day before, dropping the horses off at a stable until we returned to get them. Then we traveled on foot late into the night, only stopping for a few hours of rest in a secluded part of the forest where the branches hung low enough to shield us from passersby. Still, I doubt I am the only one who hadn't managed to fall asleep for longer than a few minutes before my eyes would snap open and I'd survey our surroundings looking for a threat.

We continue northward without trouble, but as the new day bleeds into night again and we set up camp to catch a few hours of rest, the sense that we are anything but safe has embedded itself deep in my mind. We keep our fire small, just enough to give off a small amount of heat as we lie around it. Wrapped in a brand-new, thick wool cloak, I lie with an arm beneath my head and stare up at the small break in the trees to the starlit sky above. Elora has fallen asleep first, and her normally chatty nature still hasn't quite made its return since our battle.

Stirring from where he's lying by my feet, Cass turns onto his side, propping himself up on an elbow. "Can't sleep either?"

"No." Even with how exhausted I am, I can't quite seem to let my guard down.

"Me neither." Sighing, he pushes up to sit cross-legged before pulling out the map Sadryn gave him. His finger taps against it, and I quietly sit up so as not to disturb Elora where she lies a few feet away. "According to this, the first part of the beach for us to explore should only be another half day's journey."

My gaze tracks the lines of the rivers, roads, and markers of what lies in the Fae Kingdom. Our information is over two hundred years old, the last mage to have been welcomed here would have been before the war. But though some things could have been added in that time, it isn't like the landscape is capable of changing too drastically. That thought brings me only a modicum of comfort.

"What are the odds we'll stumble onto the beach and find what we are looking for right away?" he asks, and I can't help but snort.

"Basically zero."

"Ah, come on, Daje. Have a little optimism. We've managed to get this far on our dragon quest! That can't be for nothing." Though a smile graces his face, I see the doubt etched into his expression.

"Optimism should be reserved for things that have no bearing on whether we live or die," I counter, leaning back on my hands. "Things like choosing a new meal to eat at a tavern or investing in a new piece of furniture."

"I don't know. I've *definitely* seen my life flash before my eyes while enjoying a certain kind of meal on furniture."

I roll my eyes and send him a glare. "Is fucking all you know how to talk about?"

Cass mocks offense, a hand going to his chest. "I can also sword fight—"

"Enough." I recline again, the top of my head near Elora's softly breathing body, her dark purple cloak wrapped around her like a cocoon.

"You did good back there." The sincerity in Cass's voice draws me back up onto one elbow, my brow lifted in question. "I should have told you before, and I didn't. I'm making sure you know now. For all the shit I like to give you, I trust you with my life. And so does she. You haven't let either of us down, and I guess I wanted to make sure you knew that."

I smile as my chin drops to my chest. "Thank you, Cass."

He salutes me before folding the map back up and tucking it into his pocket. "Tomorrow, we'll get this dragon glass, and then we'll head home." I lie down again, my eyes fluttering closed. "And then I'll return to my sword fighting activities, and you can go stare into a dark corner or do whatever it is you enjoy doing."

I don't bother letting out the retort that surges up my throat, instead keeping my grin plastered on my face as sleep finally creeps in on the edges of my mind.

❦

"Damn it!" Elora's shout into the wind makes my shoulders hike up towards my ears, my feet sinking more deeply into the sand as I spin to check our surroundings. Though I doubt I'd miss a fucking *dragon* if one were to show up, my heart races as fear creeps up my spine that one is hiding nearby. Watching us. "It *has* to be here!"

"Maybe we should keep our voices down—" The look she shoots in my direction snaps my mouth shut, and I raise my hands in surrender before turning to look at Cass. "Any luck?"

"Oh, I've found a bunch of dragon glass. I just figured I wouldn't say anything." He lifts his head to narrow his eyes at me, the wind blowing strands of his hair loose from the bun that holds half of it up.

Blowing out a breath, I turn my attention to a part of the beach we haven't combed through yet, the sound of waves crashing behind me drowning out more of Elora's curses. I understand her frustration. In theory, the creation of dragon glass makes sense. After all the millennia of dragons living in this kingdom, surely somewhere in that time, a dragon had used its fire here on the beach. Had melted the sand only for the cool ocean water to then immortalize it as glass. It made sense, and yet to not have it recorded in any of the books Elora had read? To not have it mentioned as frequently as dragon stone is? That only leads me into further believing that it only exists in our imaginations.

"I'm going to check farther in, by the caves," Elora says as she passes, her brow furrowed in a scowl. I watch as she makes her way through the sand to where the base of the onyx mountains meets the beach. Another gust of wind carries with it the hint of something hot and foul, not quite decay but close. Just as quickly as I pick up the scent, it's gone, leaving me to wonder if my exhaustion is playing tricks on me. My magic stirs in my chest, the urge to call on it making my fingers flex. Instead, I turn and follow her, the looming mountains ahead casting a long shadow over the beach. She spins to face me as she begins to walk backwards. "Every second we spend here is putting us in danger, and if it's all for *nothing*, I'm going to scream."

"Cass and I chose to come with you," I counter, slowing my steps as my eyes catch on the opening of one of the caves carved into the mountains behind Elora. Only a small sliver of sunlight illuminates the first foot or so, leaving the rest in total darkness. "And Bahira and Nox agreed with the plan. You didn't make this choice alone."

"I know," she says, her hands coming up to play with her braided hair. "I just thought we might get lucky. That we'd arrive at the beach and see it gleaming in the sand like little beacons of hope."

I huff out a laugh. "If only it were that simple. At least we have this view today," I say, eyes lingering on her before I gesture to the dark peaks behind her.

"Ah, yes. The notorious fae mountains. Known for their majestic one note color and their— *Ah!*" Elora trips, sprawling in the sand as her glasses go flying from her face. The back of my hand moves to cover my mouth, attempting to hide the chuckle that breaks out anyway. "Asshole!" she shouts through her own laughter, sitting up as she reaches for her glasses. "You know, I thought you were this sweet and attentive man, and you're just—"

When she doesn't continue, I cock my head, my hands bracing my hips. "I'm just *what?*"

"Dragon glass."

My eyebrows fly towards my hairline. "Can't say I've been compared to *that* before—"

"No, you idiot. *Look.*" Moving onto her hands and knees, Elora leans over something glistening in the sand. I close the distance between us, squatting down on the balls of my feet.

"Cass! You might want to get over here!" I shout, excitement bubbling up inside of me. Our fingers grip the smooth edges of the glass, lifting it up to reveal its full expanse. I'm surprised to find it's an oval shape, twice as long as it is wide. Its weight is considerable, and at about a half inch thick, it is sturdy enough to not easily break.

Sand flies as Cass comes to an abrupt stop in front of us, his eyes wide. "How did you find it?"

"I fell on it!" Elora's excitement makes him smile, and he kneels and brings part of the glass over his knees. "How are we supposed to transport a piece this big?" she asks, looking to me.

At least a few feet long, the glass would be impossible to carry easily, especially while on horseback. "We'll have to break it." It's something that would have to happen regardless, as the Mirror's frame is at least six feet tall. In order to cast glass for something that height, we'll need to see if we can find a few more pieces. I move to voice as much when Cass lifts his hand over the glass, calling his blue magic to his palm. "What are you doing?"

"The whole point of getting the glass was so that we would have something that will work as dragon stone does. Something that can hold magic when broken and still allow a reflection. Before we go about collecting the glass we find, we need to make sure it has those properties."

"It makes sense," Elora chimes in, her fingers dragging over the glass's smooth surface. "Try it."

Cass looks to me, and I nod, watching as he turns his hand over so it is hovering above the glass. "Here goes nothing." His magic floods the glass, the center of it glowing blue as it begins to work its way out towards the edges.

"Not too much. We don't know if having your magic in it will inhibit Nox from being able to get the Mirror working again."

Cass nods at Elora before he lets his magic fade away, the air thick with the feel of his magical signature. My own churns within me, and a quick glance at Elora—her skin covered with goosebumps—tells me hers is likely doing the same. We watch as the magic stabilizes within the glass, and once a few minutes pass, we are confident that it's been imbued, much to Elora's delight.

"Let's take it over to those rocks." We stand at Cass's suggestion, lifting the glass and carrying it to a collection of jagged rocks at the entrance of a cave. "We'll drop it here and see if it holds the magic within it. That should at least confirm if it is worth bringing home."

I guide my magic out like a shield around my body, Elora and Cass following suit to protect themselves from any shards that might break away. Centering the piece over the rocks, we count to three and release it, watching through the yellow haze of my magic as the glass hits the rocks and immediately breaks, thankfully creating bigger chunks and only a few smaller shards.

Blue still glows within the broken pieces, prompting Cass to smile wide as he pumps his arms in the air. "We did it! We—"

A shadow drifts over the beach ahead of us, wide enough to leave no doubt as to what is casting it. Cass is the first to move, ushering us into the cave as the sound of beating wings cuts through the air, the deep rumble accompanying making my blood chill. Our boots are slick against the black stone as we climb, the scent of rot thick in the air.

"It's going to land," Elora whispers, her shoulder pressing tightly into mine from where we've lined up against the cave wall, Cass on my other side. The sound of my heartbeat races in my ears, and I don't allow myself to overthink the movement when I reach out to hold her fingers with my own.

Cass slides his largest blades from their sheaths at his thighs, angling his body so that he is shielding both of ours.

"What are you—"

"Shh!" His command echoes in the cave just as another growl dances above the sound of the ocean waves, making my stomach clench tight with dread. The leathery snap of the dragon's wings slowing its descent is louder than I could have imagined, but the creature still sends clumps of damp sand flying into the air when it lands. Dark green scales shimmer beneath the sunlight as it looks around, tucking its wings in tightly to its side.

"It's alone," Elora says, her voice shaking as she squeezes my hand.

I nod as I watch over Cass's shoulder, the dragon sniffing the air before its head snaps in our direction, the three of us stiffening. Its tail, tipped in two spikes longer than I am tall, thumps against the ground, and my magic pushes at my chest at the threat in front of us. But none of us possess enough magic to protect us from a *dragon*.

I search it's back for a rider, but find none, and as the dragon prowls slowly closer, I begin to wonder if my father would mourn my death. Or if he would be as callous about it as he was about my mother's.

The dragon passes over the glass multiple times with mild interest, sniffing at the spot we broke the large piece before moving on. Then, finally, it lowers onto its haunches before leaping into the air, its massive wings flaring out wide as they pump to bring the beast higher. We wait until its shadow disappears, then wait some more to ensure it won't come back.

I'm the first to break the silence. "We spend a few minutes searching for more glass, and then we get the fuck back into the forest." I'm grateful when neither Elora nor Cass push back. We bolt from the cave—Cass stopping to carefully load the broken dragon glass into a satchel, while Elora and I return to the spot where she found the piece.

Our movements are frantic, our hands swishing sand out of the way in every direction as we look. Elora finds the next piece, this one about half the size of the first. She rushes off to hand it to Cass, while I move a few more feet to my left, my breath seizing in my chest when my hand brushes against something smooth beneath a layer of sand. It's even smaller than Elora's newest piece, only about a foot in length, but I bring it to Cass, Elora already back to searching again.

"I'm going to let Nox know we found some," Cass says, bringing two fingers to his mouth as he lets out a pattern of high-pitched whistles in short succession. Seconds pass, but eventually, a small black raven that followed us from Galdr flies from the treeline near the beach, landing on a small rock near Cass. "Here, take the bag." He hands me the satchel filled with dragon glass, the pieces clinking together as I haul it over my shoulder. Cass pulls a piece of parchment out of his personal pack as well as a spelled pen and begins to draft his letter before I turn and rejoin Elora.

Together, she and I find enough glass to fill up the satchel, and all I can do is hope that it will be enough to repair the Mirror, as I'm ready to leave the beach *now*.

Cass whistles three times, and the raven takes off, now with the parchment tied around its leg. I watch it fly high in the sky, passing over the trees before disappearing altogether.

"Let's go," I command, Elora stepping up to my side as Cass tucks his pen back into his pack.

A deep, harrowing growl cuts our steps short, Elora stumbling at my side as her eyes grow wide. My gaze immediately turns skyward, heart leaping into my throat as I expect to see the outstretched wings of a dragon. But then the ground beneath my boots rumbles, and when that low, throaty snarl sounds again, there is no mistaking the direction it comes from.

We all turn to face the cave, Cass in front of Elora and I, his chest heaving as he retrieves his blades. Past him, two yellow eyes wink to life against the darkness of the space we had been hiding in, and a dragon—larger than the one that had landed earlier—prowls from the cave's mouth. Fear unlike any I've ever felt before paralyzes my limbs, my magic pressing against my skin as the black dragon lowers its head, revealing the fae sitting on its back, a silver sword grasped in his hand.

"Well, what have we here?" His onyx hair rests at his shoulders, pointed ears poking through the strands as he glares down at us, his dragon pulling its lips back to reveal a collection of sharp teeth. "It seems we have trespassers amongst us."

Chapter Ninety-Two

RHEA

M Y KNEES HIT DEW-COVERED grass as I collapse to the ground, cold moisture seeping in through the thick wool of my skirt and biting into my skin. My head swims in the wake of the severed tether to my magic, leaving my ears ringing as my heart beats slowly in my chest. *A battalion.* That's what I've been commanded to heal daily, and though I knew in theory just how many men that could include, the concept was lost on me until I came to their training grounds and stood before them for the first time.

Up to a thousand men fill each battalion, and the Mortal Kingdom's army has *dozens* of battalions. I've lost count of both the days that have passed and the number of battalions I've healed since King Dolian's demand that I do so.

"That's enough," Xander says, kneeling at my side.

I can't help the raw, crazed laugh that scrapes up my throat. "You don't get to decide that." Only the magic does, once it feels I have hit the quota decided for me by my uncle.

Xander sighs, his hand reaching out as if to help me up but stopping short. His care has been constant through all of this, his presence always quiet and steady even if the tension between us is still tender and rough. Though, if I am being honest with myself, a lot of the anger that brewed within me when I thought of the commander has become dulled beneath the repetitive schedule the king keeps me on. Everything feels that way, as if I myself have become muted.

"Rhea." The concern in his voice washes over me, his breath wasted on it.

Pushing myself up to stand, and I wonder what sort of expression I'd meet if I lifted my gaze to his. If it'd match the worry in his voice or if he'd be exasperated with me. If he'd ask me again what he can do to help or if he'd try to get me to come with him to a meeting with his resistance. But I don't contemplate long on those thoughts before they dissipate, the urge to speak with him lost to the way I just wish I could lie down.

Then again, sleeping sounds wonderful in the way that all things that once brought me comfort do. Maybe that's why my body tenses when I close my eyes. Or attempt to lift the corners of my mouth. Or when Nox pops into my mind without warning. It isn't that I don't want those things; it's just that they serve as bitter reminders of how everything has changed. Still, sleep is an escape. Even if it's only moving me from one nightmare to another.

"We need to get you back inside," Xander says, silently guiding me with a gentle hand on my elbow. My steps are shaky as I force myself forward, the allure of crawling into bed strong enough to move my feet.

Moving these sessions from the garden alcove to the heart of the training grounds had meant abandoning any modicum of privacy in favor of reaching King Dolian's goal faster. A goal that I have no idea how close I am to accomplishing. But to combat the open display of my magic, the king had ordered the castle wing facing the training grounds off limits under the guise that it was now *mine*. This had apparently stirred some discontent with the noblemen and noblewomen, and instead of directing their anger to the man who had put the rule in place, they turned it on me. Though I hardly went anywhere besides my chambers, the dining hall, and the training yard, snide whispers and hard glares followed me regardless. The realization that there were *also* women in this castle angry over the fact that the king wanted me as his wife over them or their daughters left me torn between wanting to laugh at the absurdity and wanting to cry because of the same. *I don't want him. I don't want to be queen. If you only knew who I was. If you only knew what I've been through...*

But what I think and feel doesn't matter. Not to them and not to the king.

"Wait." Xander slows his steps to a stop as we walk beneath a large tree, its branches arching over the walkway and providing a semblance of seclusion. "We need to talk."

An unbidden groan slips from me, and I prop a shoulder against the tree, my head swimming. "Xander, I just want to go—"

"It's about Nox."

My protest dies on my tongue as warring emotions fight to surface within me. How long had it been since the last update? "What is it? Is he alright?"

"We received a new missive from Stephan this morning," he starts, his voice low as his eyes survey our surroundings. "King Sadryn has stepped down."

A breath catches in my throat. *What?* Of course, Nox had told me that his father would abdicate the throne eventually, but that wasn't until one of his children was ready to ascend in his place. Nox was the one assumed for that role, but... "Who is the king now?"

Xander's gaze meets mine, and the look requires no verbal confirmation. "His coronation ceremony was recent," he says instead, remorse balanced on his tongue. But I *know* Nox, and I'm sure that whatever events led to this were unavoidable. That *this* was the best he could do with the choices. *Right?* "There is something else, and before I tell you, I want you to know that I haven't yet heard from my other sources on *any* of this. While I don't believe Stephan has ever *lied* in a letter before, that doesn't mean that he's being completely—"

"Tell me." Pushing away from the tree, I ignore the way my balance falters as I watch Xander's expression.

He clears his throat, his face settling into a mask of indifference, but his eyes... They tell a different story, and whatever glimmer of hope might have surfaced within me immediately fizzles out. "Stephan wrote that, in addition to the announcement that Nox has become king, it was also shared that he is betrothed to someone new. Someone familiar and approved by the council."

"No. No, that isn't—" I gasp, drawing in a shaky breath as I stumble back a step. Xander is there, his hand gently pressing against my shoulder to keep me steady.

"Rhea—"

"He wouldn't do that." My eyes lift to his. At the pity I see in them, I say it again. "He *wouldn't* do *that*." But even to my own ears, my voice lacks conviction. Xander's gaze darts behind me, his face hardening before he juts his chin out.

"We have to go."

I follow his attention to where a few guards are now heading our way. But my feet are rooted in place, the weight of what he's just told me rendering me incapable of moving forward. Of thinking straight.

"Rhea..." His posture stiffens as he takes a few steps ahead of me and intercepts the guards.

Though he engages in conversation, I don't hear it, my mind somewhere else completely.

He is betrothed to someone new.

There is only one woman the council has *ever* approved for Nox, and didn't I say I could picture them together? He and I had always been some strange anomaly that shouldn't work: princess and guard. Prince and common woman. Incredible person worthy of every good and perfect thing and someone comprised of broken pieces trying to pretend she is anything but. Yet Nox and Haylee? They embody every bit of the regal image the council wanted for the future king and queen.

And, gods, this would explain why no one was answering the summons through the Mirror. Both the king's and mine. King Dolian had posed the idea that their lack of communication was intentional, and I had brushed it off as one of his tools of manipulation, but what if he was right? Perhaps, when it came down to it and Nox was actually faced with that impossible choice, he *had* chosen his kingdom over me. Maybe he saw that overvaluing the life of one person truly wasn't worth the risk to many. And could I blame him for that? For ensuring that his home was safe? Especially knowing that every single day, I make it a little more *unsafe* when I heal mortals and sirens alike?

Haylee's voice plays in my ear. Her offer to marry Nox for show. Her sincerity tugging at my chest. *Had* she been sincere?

"Lady Nele, are you ready to return to your rooms?" I jolt when Xander steps into view, keeping a few feet between us as he stares down at me, calling me by my fake name.

"What?" I rasp, the word hardly audible.

"Your rooms," he repeats, gaze imploring. "You must return to them."

Only by pure muscle memory do I react, moving my body forward and following him through the newly fallen darkness. The chill of the damp fabric at my knees and the cold evening air fades as I retreat into myself, hiding behind a numbness that has once more become familiar. Once more become *welcome*.

He is betrothed to someone new.

My memories run rampant—images of Nox's hands on my body, in my hair, touching me in a way no one else ever has. Would he do that with Haylee? Had they already? I swallow back the nausea that rises at the thought.

"Lady R— Lady Nele," a soft, feminine voice calls. *Eve.*

He is betrothed to someone new.

"What's wrong?"

"We need to get her out of the main halls," Xander says from in front of me. "She needs some time to herself, and I'd rather the king not be reminded that he hasn't seen her in a few days."

"I'll help her." She wraps her arm around my waist to draw me in close. "I'll make sure she gets to her room."

I don't notice Xander leave.

He is betrothed to someone new.

My hand flies to my chest, my nails digging into the flesh as if I can claw it open and free my heart from where it's trapped in this jagged cage.

"We have to climb the stairs now." Eve speaks gently, her fingers flexing at my side as we begin our ascent. "It's going to be okay."

I want to tell her that nothing has been okay for a long, long while. That I doubt it will be ever again. Instead, the words die before they even make it up my throat.

"Lady Nele, what are you doing?"

It takes me a moment to find the source of the question, but when my eyes clash with his dark gray ones, everything snaps back into place. Reminding me who and what I am now. Betrothed to the king. Cut off from my magic. Nothing but a vessel to be filled and emptied whenever it is deemed appropriate by someone else. Nothing without *him*. Rhea Maxwell is *gone,* and has been for a while now.

Simon's attention rests solely on me, his hands clasped behind his back. "What, dare I ask, is the meaning of this?"

I look down over myself, noting the grass stains on my lavender gown and the dirt lining the hem. Eve's pale fingers drape over my side, right above the brand on my hip—as if she's remembered it's there and is trying to avoid it. Leaning into her body, I force my head back up, sorting through my thoughts until I'm able to verbalize something coherent. "I just finished healing a battalion."

The king's advisor cocks his head to the side, gaze then sliding to Eve. "And you think it's *appropriate* to be seen in such a way with the castle help?"

"The lady was having trouble walking," she responds, a slight tremble to her voice. "I am merely ensuring—"

"I don't need assurances from a rat, nor do I prefer it. *I* will make sure Lady Nele makes it to her room safely, perhaps with a bit more of her dignity intact."

"No." The word is out before I can stop it, as if someone else has spoken it for me. And when Simon's gaze narrows on Eve, I realize that it's because *she* did. Eve urges me forward, but Simon steps directly into our path.

"A warning, handmaiden, that the king punishes those who step out of line without remorse," he snarls.

"I know," she responds, her grip on my waist tightening as we move forward again. A white door with a golden rose creaks open and then we are in my sitting room, walking towards my bedroom. Air stirs and my body moves and all the while imagined scenarios of Nox flash through my mind.

He is betrothed to someone new.

I'm a bystander to it all, removed from everything but the desperate feeling of despair that rattles in my chest.

"Do you want to talk about what happened?" Eve asks tentatively from where she sits next to me on the bed. I blink, looking down at the silk pink fabric of my chemise, unaware I had even changed. I run my fingers over the fabric, the weight of my exhaustion heavy enough to round my shoulders. "You do not have to say a word, but, I have found, that sometimes holding our worries and fears in is far worse than speaking them out loud."

She nudges my shoulder gently, and I lift my eyes to meet hers. "Do you believe in fate?"

Eve looks taken aback by the question for all of a few seconds before answering. "Yes and no. Do I believe that our life is laid out before us without choice? No. But do I think that there are outside forces that might guide us in a certain direction?" I turn to look at her, her shoulder lifting with a small shrug. "Sometimes. I've seen the magic of that happen—both when I followed that intuition and when I didn't." Her eyes fall to her lap, her brow creased in thought. "What do you believe?"

"I don't know," I answer honestly. "But I do not think it is my fate to make it out of here alive."

Her intake of breath is sharp before her hand wraps around both of mine. "Xander is working hard to figure out a way to release you. If anyone can do it, it's him and his people. You are Rhea Maxwell. You have a home. You have friends who have become family, ones that love you. You have people waiting for your return."

Every word she spoke is true, yet it does nothing to that aching pit inside of me. And how selfish is that? To know that even though there are people wanting me to return, if Nox isn't one of them—if he truly *has* moved on—then I don't care.

Ashamed, I turn my gaze back to the night sky. *The moon may have the stars, but at least I have you.* What a fool I had been to think that phrase could ever be true.

Chapter Ninety-Three

RHEA

THE IRONY I FEEL at having magic that I can't control still isn't lost on me. Day after day, I feel its presence as I heal thousands of the king's army, yet I can't use it to help myself or those around me. Where its warmth had once felt like a comfort, now it slips through my fingers, taking a little more of myself with it as it does.

Both Xander and Eve still try to help, the former still encouraging me to not give up hope while the latter spends her evenings in my company, despite the fact that I'm hardly present. So little of myself remains in this flesh and bone body. It is easier for me to pretend I'm not a monster if I let my mind wander, if I let myself feel nothing over my surroundings. But, despite my desire to be numb, Xander and Eve keep trying to break through to me, even though my existence only makes their lives harder.

So one night after Eve leaves another one-sided conversation with me, I gather enough of myself to try and form a plan. One that will benefit her now and hopefully Xander in the future. One that will solidify the knowledge within me that *this* version of Rhea Maxwell is one that only a monster could love.

And so, here I sit facing King Dolian, tea set between us and his hazel eyes locked on my own. "I must admit, I'm not sure what to make of this," he says, arms resting on the table.

I put my tea cup back down on the saucer, the noise it makes ringing out loudly in the small room. Despite Eve's tutelage, I haven't quite mastered the grace one is expected to have while consuming the beverage. "There is nothing to make of it. I simply asked to have tea with you."

His brow arches, and he leans in closer, the gold thread on his vest catching the sunlight. "And *that* is why I find this so hard to believe, my darling. Not once in our many weeks together have you *ever* initiated contact with me." His smile is razor thin, and it jabs between my ribs and straight to my broken heart. "Don't mistake my curiosity for disappointment. It is always a pleasure to see the sun shining down on your beautiful face."

I force myself to smile. "It seems time has done what you hoped it might."

King Dolian tilts his head as doubt etches itself over his brow. "And what is it that you think I hoped for?"

"For me to bend to your will," I answer, keeping my lips upturned. "For a pliant fiancée."

He chuckles before taking a drink, his tongue darting out to lick his lips after. "*Pliant.* Is that what you think I want? Better yet, is that *truly* what you think I'll believe?"

I knew he would *never* presume I've suddenly had a change of heart, but I also know that despite the king's bravado and the way he presents himself to the world, his ego has been damaged by the fact that I still love Nox. That I have never uttered those three words to him. I decide to use that to my advantage, sacrificing whatever remains of myself in the process. "I know you have heard about the mage prince becoming king and getting engaged."

He traces his finger slowly over the rim of his cup. "You see now that I was right about his intentions with you. His supposed *devotion.*"

I give a rueful nod. "Yes."

"So, what? You come to me now that you can't have him?"

His defensiveness surprises me, but then again, everything between us has always been a game to him. This act is nothing more than getting what he wants from me—total submission. The admission that he was right and I was woefully wrong. "I come to you now in understanding," I lie, grateful for my voice coming out steady. For the fact that I can hide within layers of myself even if I can still acutely feel his gaze moving over me like malicious strokes of a paint brush. "I come as *your* future queen."

He laughs, leaning back in his chair as his fingers drag over his lips. "Clever woman." His amusement quickly shifts into something darker—something *cruel.* "Tell me you no longer love him."

The lie I spew next is one of the worst I've ever told, and it rots me from within. "I don't love him."

"Ah, ah, darling," he says, pushing his chair back to stand before rounding the small table. I push my chair out as well, but he orders me to stay put, instead spinning the chair around so that I'm facing him with his fingers gripping the armrests. "Let's see if you speak the truth."

"I am—"

"Do you still love Prince Nox?"

My fear spikes as the magic forces me to give the answer both the king and I know to be true between gasps. "Ye-yes."

I brace for his anger and the physical punishment it will dole out on my body. But it never comes. Instead, the king lifts a hand and cups the side of my face, his eyes blazing with something between lust and possession. "I understand now," he whispers, leaning in until I can feel the scratch of his beard at my cheek. I close my eyes, every sense overwhelmed by his proximity. "You *want* to forget him."

My heart thunders in my chest, shame a dizzying wave that leaves my palms clammy and stomach churning. "Yes. I want to forget."

"I can help." His mouth is warm at my neck, and though my shredded resolve protests at the touch, at the wrongness of it, I arch my neck to give him better access. He growls in approval, his teeth scraping and tongue lashing while I imagine myself in a pool of darkness, water surrounding me on all sides until I'm submerged. His voice sounds distant when he speaks next. "Do you know that they didn't fight me when I told them I wanted you back? Their council had written to me, telling me they intercepted my letter to the king, but that they would be willing to negotiate. Though I'm sure my threat of using my army against their small border towns likely helped with that. I told them it would all go away if they just returned what was taken from me. And they didn't fight it. The king's council agreed to hand you over as if you were as insignificant to them as their *prince* is to me."

My eyes open, one single word making it through my numbed fog. *Council.* The council had been in contact with King Dolian? "How..." I trail off, unsure of what to even ask.

"How did they know it was you? How did they agree to give in to another king's demands?" I feel him shrug against me, a hand trailing down my arm. "I told them to return the woman with golden hair and green eyes. The one who arrived with a male named Flynn. Apparently, those details alone were enough to identify you. And, as you have seen, my army has no match. Spell in place or not, healed guards or not, we are a formidable force compared to those who are losing their magic. Even as we lose some to the Cruel Death."

I nearly ask how he knows about the dwindling magic in the Mage Kingdom, but of course he knows. He has a *spy* there, after all.

"So, you see, that is why they don't answer my summons now. That is why no one has come for you. They recognize the truth in what I've always told you, Rhea. You *belong* here, with me. You always have, and you always will." King Dolian leans back just enough so I can see his face, his lips swollen from his assault at my neck. "Do you finally see it now?"

There is no magic behind the question, so I only nod. When lust overtakes the distrust in his gaze, I know I've done what I needed to. His face hovers over mine, but before he can crash his lips down on my own, I say, "There is one favor I would like to ask of you."

He tangles a hand in my hair, gripping the strands tightly enough that my eyes water. "I am not a man of favors, Rhea."

"I know," I respond quickly, wincing when he tugs my head back. "But this is small and easily within your power as my king to do."

He lets out a slow exhale, drawing so near to me that I can smell his cologne, the scent stinging my nostrils. "Humor me, then, darling."

"Eve," I whisper, licking my lips and sinking back down into myself when his gaze tracks the movement. "I would like for you to let her return home to her family for a short time."

"Eve," he repeats, eyes bouncing between mine. "You don't want her here for the wedding?"

"She misses her family, and there are plenty of other servants available to help me." It is a small thing, but Eve deserves time with her family after being forced away from them for so long. Even if only for a week or two, it surely wouldn't be enough to disrupt the daily happenings at the castle. But beyond that, I simply want the opportunity to do *one* good thing while I can. Before the chance is taken from me fully. "She has worked hard, and deserves the time off."

Just one good thing.

My next inhale is stopped short when King Dolian's lips invade mine, and I feel myself drowning as I press my fingers into his shoulders. I usher in an icy numbness to combat the knowledge of his tongue pressing at the seam of my mouth, of the way his hands roam over my body. Deeper and deeper I sink until I'm chilled to the bone, the last embers of the fire within me plunged into darkness.

I don't know how much time passes, only that, when he's done, he agrees to give Eve the time off. Helping me stand, he kisses my cheek before sauntering out of the room, passing Xander as he does.

"Make sure she heals at least half a battalion today. We've had a bit of a late start."

Xander nods, his eyes going to me as soon as the king is out of sight. "Rhea—"

"I'm fine."

"That's not the godsdamn truth, and you know it." My eyes shut as he blocks the doorway, keeping me trapped in this room. "I'm going to keep asking every single day until you say yes. Let me take you to meet the resistance. We're *so close* to finalizing a plan to get you out, Rhea. To freeing you."

I pry my eyes open again, exhaustion a lingering companion. "Don't you realize how dangerous that is? That if the king at *all* suspected you, suspected me of having *anything* to do with you, he could simply command that I tell him? You want your whole operation put at risk like that?" His stare is hard, that cold exterior he prefers unwavering. And I just... I don't have it in me to argue anymore. "Perhaps it's time that you come to accept what I have. There is nothing to be done."

His head jerks back in shock, but I don't wait for him to respond before I'm pushing past him. When I'm done healing the men of the guard, it's Brisk and not Xander who returns me to my room, my steps wobbling to the point that I have to lean against the wall for most of the walk back.

Changed and unable to sleep, my thumb prods at the pearl on my ring finger, spinning it around my finger over and over again. Time is lost as I think of nothing, of no one, until knocks on my door pull me from the bed.

"Lady Nele, it's Brisk," the guard shouts through the door when I don't immediately answer. Upon hearing his voice, I put on a robe and open the door. His brow is creased with worry, his lips drawn down at the corners.

"What is it?"

"King Dolian has demanded that you be brought to his rooms."

❧❧❧❧❧ ❧❧❧❧❧

Two of the king's Trusted are waiting outside his chambers when Brisk and I arrive, and the larger of the two glares down at me as he opens the door and gestures for me to enter.

The scent of the king's cologne coats the room, and I lay a hand over my stomach as if that will stop the nausea from churning up my throat. When I'm a few steps past the door, it shuts behind me, and I'm plunged fully into the king's private space *alone*. My eyes pass over the bookshelves that line the walls and the armchairs gathered around a table as the room flashes bright, lightning from a storm rolling in shining in through a large window to my right. I startle at the thunder that follows, my breaths quickening at the anxiousness that roils through me.

The day I had been forced to kill Sterling and his wife, the king had said he was done waiting to have me in his bed. I had been so ravaged by the guilt that coated me as thickly as my victims' blood that I hadn't given his words a second thought. But being here now, I wonder if he's finally making good on the threat.

It's between the flashes of lightning and rumbles of thunder that I hear a whimper. Straining my ears, I listen for it again, another muffled sound traveling down the hall that feeds into this room. My breath catches in my throat at the unmistakably female sound, and it draws me forward and down the hall lit by flame gems, bringing me to an open doorway where the foot of a bed comes into view.

The wooden footboard is carved with a swirling pattern, the shiny red fabric of the bed sheets bunching towards the bed's center. I force myself to move closer, just as a male *grunt* echoes out. The next step I take brings the rest of the bed into view, and my lips part at the sight before me.

The king stands with his back to me, his deep blue shirt untucked. The ends of his belt slap against his thighs as he moves rhythmically in an undeniable motion, his hands gripping the upper arms of a woman. She's completely bare, her hair unbound and draped over her back and shoulders, shielding her face from view. Heat rises up my neck, and I cover my mouth to stop the horrified sound that threatens to slip out when my eyes catch the clothing dotting the floor. A gray dress lays in a perfect pile, as if its owner slipped it down her body and simply stepped out of it. Next to it is a white apron, its straps tangled, and a pair of black flats.

"*You are mine,*" King Dolian growls, releasing one of the woman's arms to fist the strands of her blonde hair, tugging roughly until her neck is arched at an uncomfortable angle. "You have *always* been mine." He thrusts his hips forward harshly, and the woman cries out, her hands trying—and failing—to find some sort of leverage.

"Yes, My King," she says, and it's the broken tone of her voice that propels me the rest of the way forward, my hands already held out in front of me.

"Stop!" My shriek startles the king, but his glazed eyes hold mine as his fingers tighten their hold on the maid.

"Darling," he drawls, his cheeks flushed. "What perfect timing." A deep groan from him threatens to make me collapse where I stand, but I force myself to stay focused, my mind scrambling to find something to say that will get him to stop. He yanks the maid's hair until she's forced to turn her head, my gaze clashing with hers. Time halts, suspending between us with shock as I stare into her soft blue eyes.

"Eve?" I whisper.

Chapter Ninety-Four

RHEA

"**I** CAN EXPLAIN." HER throat works with a rough swallow, the movement exaggerated by the king's tight hold on her hair.

"Yes," he says, leaning over her naked body to grip her chin between his thumb and fingers. "Explain to my dear fiancée *exactly* what is going on here. What *has* been going on since before she returned to me."

Tears trail down Eve's cheeks, her bottom lip quivering. But words fail her as her chest and neck blush, her quiet sobs making her shoulders rise and fall. Betrayal is a bitter taste on my tongue for all of a few seconds before my rationality takes hold. I didn't need to be privy to this entire moment to know that Eve has no love for the king. To know that her avoidance whenever I asked what jobs the king was forcing her to do in the evenings wasn't because she was lying to me for the sake of lying but because she was *ashamed*. I recognize the emotion on her face as if it were my own.

Eve's heart is a soft one—one that bleeds for her sister back home. For Edwin, the man she loves but now, I realize with a sickening jolt, feels she is undeserving of.

"Too afraid to speak?" he says, roughly releasing Eve and forcing her face back to the bed. He rights himself, his head turning towards me. "Let me tell the tale, then." He jerks his hips forward so harshly that the entire bed shakes. Heat burns me from within, my anger pushing me another step forward before magic halts me. My fingers press in at my temples, the sound of a roaring wave deafening as my murderous intentions activate the king's command that I not hurt him. Eve cries out, stretching her arms out in front of her as her fingers claw at the comforter. "You see, when you left, Rhea, you unleashed a monster in your absence. Getting

543

you back was all I could think about—all I could focus on. And when Eve was brought to my rooms by Simon as a way to *distract* me... Well, her likeness to you was hard to ignore."

Gods, had he been forcing his way into her every night for *months*?

"And she has been a sweet reprieve while I wait for *you*."

I watch as sweat beads along his brow, my feet rooted in place both by my magic and by my remorse. I want to run as much as I want to help her.

"Had you obeyed me from the very beginning, I never would have sought her out." He thrusts again.

"Stop," I rasp, the word dejected as it leaves my tongue.

"Had you never left, Eve would have remained untouched." The sound of Eve's knees hitting the bedframe rings in my ears, my entire body trembling against the magic holding me back.

"*Please!*"

"Had"—*thrust*—"you"—*thrust*—"stopped defying me every fucking step of the way, *this* would never have happened." A silent sob wracks through me when he groans a final time, and then he's buckling his pants again, his movements blurred before he's in front of me, hand at my neck as he orders Eve to dress in the bathroom. "When you replay this moment in your head later, as I know you will, I want you to remember one thing. Everything your handmaiden is feeling right now—the pain and humiliation—is because of *you*."

When Eve comes out, she refuses to meet my eyes, and sorrow claws at my heart as she halts in front of the king.

"Rhea has requested that you be given time off so that you may see your family," he says, causing Eve to jerk her head up to look at him. "Your leave is effective immediately, and when you return in two weeks' time, you will resume your role as handmaiden to the new queen." Only then does her gaze flick to mine, her bloodshot eyes filled with fresh tears.

I offer her a small smile, trying to let her know that I'm not angry at her. That I could never blame her for what the king's forced her to do. For any of it. And silently screaming at her to never come back here. To find a way to live outside of this place, if the blood oath will allow it. She looks poised to argue with me, a new track of tears staining her cheeks as she realizes that this is a goodbye. Now that she will be out of the castle, I have no intentions of making it to my wedding with the king. Maybe she understands that too, and if so, the heartbreak that shatters her face finally forces the tears in my eyes to fall. "Let me heal her," I say abruptly, facing the king who now stands at my side. "Please."

His eyes dart back and forth between mine, a hand coming up to smooth back strands of hair from my face. I stand perfectly still, hardly letting my chest rise with my breaths. "No."

Air rushes from me, my voice cracking as I beg. "*Please*! I—"

"Leave us," he interrupts, tugging me into his body. Eve hesitates, but with a pointed glance from King Dolian, she rushes out of the room. "Did you enjoy watching?" he asks, hands sliding down my back and over the curve of my backside. When I don't answer, he clicks his tongue in disapproval. "Oh, come now, Rhea. You do know that our marriage consummation will have to be witnessed to be official. Watching—*being* watched—is something you shouldn't shy away from." His face presses into the spot my neck meets my shoulder, hot breath skating along my skin. "Every time, I pictured you. *Every* single time. Feeling you around me will be the single greatest achievement of my life, Rhea. It will be the moment things are officially made right. The moment you officially become mine. Nothing and no one will *ever* take that from me again."

Horrifically sated for the evening, King Dolian brushes another kiss against my skin before he lets me stumble away, the scent of him following me past the doorway and into the hall. Past the Trusted guards who murmur something I don't hear as my steps bring me farther away from his chambers. I pass people in the hall who snicker—perhaps at my appearance—but their condemnation falls upon deaf ears, my mind focused on doing one thing. On getting to one place.

It takes me a moment to find the side entrance that will take me there, but none of the guards I pass attempt to stop me. When I walk through a large door encased in bronze, the bitterly cold night air scraping at my cheeks, two guards finally *do* step in front of me, their eyes shifting between each other and me as I come to a stop in front of them. The storm has lightened to a drizzle, and it soaks through the fabric of my robe as I push past their subdued attempts to stop me and onto the pathway of the stone bridge. Staying in the castle after what I had just seen and learned, occupying the same *vicinity* as the man who has taken so much from others, *from me*, is an impossible task. I don't think the kingdom is large enough to feel like I'm far enough away from him, but since I'm limited by magic on where I can go, I test the boundaries by returning to the one place I never thought I'd see again.

When the magic permits me to keep going, I lower my head and rush down the length of the bridge, only lifting my eyes again when I've reached the other side. Straining against the wind and the darkened sky, I stare at the tower, memories flitting in and out as my body protests the very idea of entering again.

I had finally escaped this prison, yet impossibly, I am worse off for it.

Though dread winds its way up my chest, the feel of it is muted. Like it too is sunken in that pool within me, floating in the numbing waters separate from my body.

My fingers curl around the door handle and then I'm back inside the tower, climbing the steps that will take me to the top. It's a slow and arduous process with the way my damp robe sticks to me, and the entire way, all I can think about is how I had been *so* very positive I would never return here. I certainly never believed I'd come back willingly.

They say time can heal all things, but can it also alter memories? Can it reframe moments and reshape emotions? Do I even want it to?

By the time I reach the top, my knees ache and my lungs burn with the exertion. Even as my body shivers, sweat coats my back and neck, fire building in the muscles of my thighs and causing them to twitch. But then I'm here, on a platform barely lit by a small stream of moonlight through a cut-out window.

I stand in the same spot Nox did when he brought games for us to play. I picture it—him and I, a board game between us. His gentle eyes and quirking lips, something playful and beautiful and devious all rolled up into the way he looked at me. How he watched me calculate my next moves. How I stared at him, unsure and nervous as my hands clutched at the fabric of my gown. We had both the simplest and most complicated beginning, but it was one I would always cherish. One that would never be tainted, no matter how many of my memories were infiltrated by the king and all of the pain he inflicted on me. Because here—at the top of a tower in the middle of a wildflower field, within the borders of a kingdom that was both my own and not—I had fallen in love for the first, and only, time. And that precious love had been worth every moment that came before it. Every one that transpired after. So very, very worth it.

The next door opens easily, as if this place is eager to see me step foot in it again.

It's hard to explain the scent that hits me. It's familiar in all the ways I expect: hints of lily and of paper and books. Warm spices come next, like that of the Continent during autumn. Like the scent of a man whose neck I loved burying my face into. But woven between all of those are unexpected notes: the pungent cedar of King Dolian. The rich tang of iron mixed with must and mold.

The worn wooden planks beneath my feet creak as I take in the small black couch against one wall, Alexi's green arm chair across from it. The space in the middle is bare, the white tea table that had once filled it shattered by my body when the king threw me against it. As if spurred by the memory, the brand on my hip begins to throb, and I place my hand over the now healed mark to quell it. Spinning in place, I turn my attention to the loft where I slept. So many nights I had cuddled up with Bella—my only source of comfort—and stared out the window, hoping that one day, I might know what it felt like to be loved. To have a home and a soft place to land.

Exhaling slowly, my gaze drops to the arched doorway of the library beneath the loft. Stepping into that part of the tower is a homecoming all its own. In this room, I had escaped into new worlds and characters, pretending to be anyone other than who I was in places anywhere other than here. It had been a reprieve in the best of ways, and though I have since spent time in many different libraries, there is something so uniquely *special* about this one.

My feet pad across the room to the first bookcase, tracing the leather spines with the tips of my fingers as I look for the one book I'd like to see again. I don't need light pouring into the room to find it, its place within the shelves one I've memorized. Yet, when I stop in front of the space where it should be, I'm disappointed to find its spot empty. Dust now collects in the gap where *The Little Sun* had always lived. On the chance that I've remembered wrong, I search the shelves above and below, moving to the next bookcase and the next, only further let down by its obvious absence.

Moving back to the center of the room, my fingers intertwine as I look over at the window seat, the outskirts of Vitour just showing in the distance behind it. In my mind, I hear Nox's voice as he reads to me. The way the sunlight hit him in all the right ways, highlighting how stunningly perfect he was—he *is*. I see Bella curled up on the floor in front of us, napping quietly. Completely content and relaxed. Maybe it's the way it's easier to reflect back on the past when you're no longer stuck in it, or maybe it's the fact that I know this is goodbye, but I smile at the memories. At the emotions they evoke. There had been a fair share of utter hell captured within these walls, but there had also been rare moments of happiness. Of light. *Of love.*

With a final glance over the room, I retreat back into the living area and walk to the glass doors that lead out to the balcony. Pausing, I slip my flats off before opening the door and stepping onto the bitterly cold stone. A shocked breath hisses out of me, as does another when my palms rest over the railing and I look out at the lake in the distance. With the storm now fading, a peaceful—if restless—sort of quiet takes over, and I allow myself a few moments to bask in it. The wind stirs my hair around my shoulders, making goosebumps break out over my arms and legs. But I watch as the surface of the lake ripples, as water laps at the shoreline. I draw my eyes over the wildflower field, the time of year meaning that they aren't bloomed, and yet, dotting the otherwise dead winter grass, spots of life appear.

My throat tightens the longer I look, tracing the meadow back until I reach the treeline and the forest that looms beyond it. I had left this place—as Alexi had wanted me to. As I had wanted to do for myself. Though my story didn't quite have the ending that I wanted, I had at least *tried,* which was far more than the woman from my past would have ever thought possible. Fear had been a powerful manipulator then, but the fear that molds me now isn't one composed of wondering what might happen *to* me. It's one that poses the question: What will *I* do to others? Without the control of my magic... Without my free will and autonomy... *Without Nox...* There is nothing left for me to become *but* a weapon. If there is *anything* I have learned, if there is *anything* I've come to regret, it's that there were moments I should have done more. That I should have stood up for the people I loved. For myself. The time for mourning my previous inaction has passed, but now... *now* there is something I can do. There is a choice I can make.

A small voice inside of me tries clawing her way to the surface, begging me to reconsider. I don't snuff her down, don't try to hide her in those darkest corners of my mind or trap her inside an invisible box because it's too painful to deal with. Instead, I reach out to her. Holding her hand. And I tell her, I tell *myself*, that just because a choice is *hard* doesn't mean it is the wrong one. That, just because it threatens to shatter the already fragile pieces of my heart, doesn't mean it might not also have the capability to heal me in a different way.

I have always been a mosaic of sorts—never quite a being made of smooth edges and well-fitting parts. But I see now that there has always been beauty in it. That there has always been strength in it, too. I, Rhea Maxwell, have been a victim of circumstance for far too long, and now it's time that I do something about it.

My heartbeat is steady in my chest, even when it dips as I grip the balcony railing a little more tightly. Because of the railing's height, it takes a moment for me to heave myself onto it. When I do, I turn until my legs are dangling over the edge, my face aglow in moonlight as I stare out over that deep blue lake. Nails digging into the rough surface of the stone, I allow more tears to fall. No longer feeling the need to keep them bottled up, but simply surrendering to the sadness that begins to uncoil itself within me.

"I love you," I whisper to the moon, closing my eyes. A tortured sob plays out into the night, the overwhelming feeling of loss laying rough hands around my neck. *It will hurt,* I think to myself, *but only for a moment.*

I slide myself closer, the corner of the banister digging into my upper thigh. A gust of wind softly caresses my skin, carrying with it the scent of jasmine, as I suck in a breath, my fingers dangling off of the edge now. The wind rushes against my ears, drowning out any sound but that of my own breathing and heartbeat. I lean forward, my palms sliding off the railing as my stomach bottoms out and—

Abruptly, I'm yanked backwards, falling into someone as we both land on the balcony. Air is forced out of me with a rough *humph*, and my eyes shoot open as I scramble off the hard body beneath me and onto my hands and knees. Only to meet Xander's dark eyes.

"*What*," he huffs, his chest heaving and eyes wild, "the *fuck* are you doing?"

Chapter Ninety-Five

RHEA

XANDER SITS UP, HIS elbow resting on his knee as he catches his breath, an uncomfortable tension brewing between us. I'm the first to break it when I drop my gaze to the ground. "How did you know I was here?"

"I didn't until— No, *you* don't get to ask questions until you explain to me what you were doing." He shakes his head, raking a hand through his already mussed black hair. "Because it almost looked like you were about to jump from the balcony. And I *know* that can't be right when..." His words trail off as I lift my head to look at him, bleak realization flattening his mouth. "*Fuck*," he whispers, his shoulders going slack.

"It's more dangerous for me to be alive than it is for me... *not* to be."

Xander exhales sharply, emitting a noise caught somewhere between an incredulous laugh and a menacing *growl*. "How long have you been contemplating this?"

"Long enough to understand all that it means."

"Rhea." He drags his hand down his face, his mouth opening and closing as words catch in his throat.

"I know," I cut in, moving to stand. My legs wobble beneath me, adrenaline and nerves crashing tumultuously together. "But, Xander, I'm *dangerous* because of *what* I am. And so many have been hurt in my name. So many lives taken because of *me*. When does it stop?"

"When we get the ring off of you."

The laugh that tumbles out of me is despondent. "And do *you* think King Dolian will be taking it off me anytime soon? I have tried *everything*, Xander!

Even attempting to cut my own finger off. But nothing has worked. *Nothing* has come close!"

Xander stands, his hands bracketing his hips. "And what if you had succeeded just now?" he asks, his voice poignantly soft yet still demanding my attention. My heart races until my vision begins to blur. Or maybe it's the tears gathering there. But Xander presses on. "What about Nox? What do you think he would do when he found out?"

"You know the reports from the Mage Kingdom," I offer lamely. "He is too preoccupied with his own kingdom and family to..." To what. *Care*? Even in my current state, I know that would never be true. And so does the man standing across from me. He frowns, his disappointment something that pricks at the shame bubbling inside of me. "I'm tired of people getting hurt. Of them dying. Alexi, Immie, Tienne, Bella—"

"She's alive," he interrupts, his gaze boring into mine.

"I— What? Who is alive?"

"Bella."

I let out a croaked noise of confusion, sure I've misheard him. "What are you talking about? King Dolian *told* me she was dead. I asked you, and—"

"You didn't ask. You accused," he says, taking a step towards me. "And I could have corrected you then, but you weren't ready to hear it. I'm not entirely sure that you are now, but I'll say *anything* if it means you won't give up on yourself. Bella is alive, and her name—her true name—is Siyala." Slowly, as if afraid he'll frighten me if the movement is too sudden, he turns and extends his hand out to me. "And if you promise to get off of this balcony and come inside with me, I'll tell you everything I know about her."

I search his gaze, looking for a hint of deception or manipulation. Xander lets me, his hand staying extended as he drops all pretense of a mask, leaving himself bare and vulnerable in front of me for the first time ever. "Please," he says again into the darkness between us, and I wonder if he has ever uttered that word to anyone before.

Bella is alive.

My chest cracks at the revelation, my heart torn between *wanting* to believe him, and knowing that every moment I'm left to the king's whims could mean more lives put at risk. Despite not having tipped over the balcony, I still feel as if I'm in a free fall, the shattered pieces of myself scattered as I struggle to reach for them. I'm mid-scream, unmoored in a way I never have been before, but...

Xander takes another step towards me.

Bella is alive.

With trembling fingers, I slip my hand into his.

Xander finds some towels in the bathroom of the loft and brings them down for me to dry off, my teeth chattering from more than just the cold.

"It's the adrenaline," he says without prompting, letting me choose where to sit first. I sink down into Alexi's chair, and Xander takes the couch, his elbows resting on his knees. "It'll be coursing through you for a while, so don't be surprised if you find it difficult to sleep tonight."

"It already is," I say under my breath, setting the towel on the ground before leaning back, hugging my knees to my chest. Emotions I haven't let surface in weeks press at my chest and behind my eyes, but instead I focus my attention on Bella. On *Siyala*. "Tell me about her."

Xander does. He launches into the tale of how she was captured by the guards at the Mage Kingdom border, shot but not dead. The pain of the arrow had forced her to shift, a surprise to everyone including her. "It took a while for her to talk to me, to *want* to talk to me," he says, his gaze forward as he recalls his time with her—with Siyala.

"What made her talk?"

"I didn't torture her. I didn't lay a finger on her," he says quickly, likely hearing the accusation in my tone. "I got her to open up to me by telling her about *myself*." He lets out an embarrassed laugh, the tops of his cheeks turning a light shade of pink. "I groveled, for lack of a better word, and apologized for my inaction when the king came to the tower. I explained the resistance and who the king was to me. I assumed she wouldn't give a shit about any of it, but Siyala proved me wrong. She is strong. Fierce. A force to be reckoned with, and I figured that the only way I could gain her trust was to give her something she could use against me if she needed to."

"And did she? Need to, I mean?"

He shakes his head, tucking the dark strands at his temple behind his ear. "No. Siyala and I became friends. Of a sort."

My eyebrow arches at the added definition.

"We talked a lot about her life in the tower. What she remembered from back home. And about you."

Heat creeps my own cheeks when I ask, "What did she say about me?"

"She didn't dive into anything personal when it came to you, not for my lack of trying. I didn't know anything about you—besides the fact that you are the true heir to the throne and that the king is obsessed with you. I had no idea what sort of danger you might pose or what kind of obstacle you'd be. All I knew of you is that you ran away with a guard who I later found out was a prince and that you had magic. Beyond that"—he shrugs, the right corner of his mouth lifting a fraction—"it wasn't until I spoke to Siyala that I learned enough about you to know that you were—*are*—a good person. And if she was willing to endure whatever torment King Dolian might inflict on her, while snarling in his face that she'd kill him, then you must be someone worth protecting. You must be someone *of* worth to her."

My chin falls to my chest as I bite down on my lower lip. I don't deserve that sort of praise and certainly not from her. She had been trapped, just as much a prisoner as I was. "And yet she endured more suffering because of me. Because of who I am to the king."

"You can't hold yourself accountable for other people's choices, Rhea," he counters, flexing his hands where they rest between his knees. "You didn't order the guards to shoot her. You didn't demand that they bring her back to the dungeon for the king to question. And if you want to argue that she was only in the forest *because* of you, then you also need to acknowledge that at *any* moment, Siyala could have chosen to leave you. She had the mental awareness to run away from you and Nox and try to find her way back to the Shifter Kingdom on her own. But she *chose* you. She made that choice not out of command by you but because she *wanted* to."

My chest rises with a ragged breath.

"Take it from someone who has had to learn how to navigate around their own guilt. There is no amount of self-imposed penance that can ever fix someone else's choice."

"And what sort of things might you blame yourself for?"

"The death of my mother. Of my friends. Of Alexi and countless others." He looks down at his hands, turning his palms to face up. "I know what it is to feel like everyone who comes into contact with you is now in danger. I *know* because it's something I live with too."

"I'm sorry," I rasp, shaking my head. "For those losses. For the way I treated you when I first got here."

Xander gives a quick nod, looking about as uncomfortable as I've ever seen him—earlier talk of Siyala included—before stoicism once more masks his features. The ease with which he can let his guard down and put it back up again is impressive. I ask more about Siyala, and he explains her time in captivity and how he helped her escape.

"She is back home in the Shifter Kingdom?"

"I made sure of it," he answers. Then, more quietly and with a gentle fondness, he adds, "Much to her chagrin."

I smile as a fraction of the tension caught in my chest eases knowing that Siyala is now safe. And I'm *honored* to know her true name, even if I might never have the opportunity to call her by it. My shivers begin to subside as quiet once more trickles in, Xander and I watching each other until he lets loose a long sigh and leans back against the couch.

"So."

"So," I mimic, sweat beading along the back of my neck. I expect him to berate me for my actions, and I prepare whatever meager defense I can in preparation.

But Xander catches me off guard when he says, "Come with me to meet the members of the resistance."

"I— Xander, it's too risky. If the king—"

"Look, I understand, probably as well as you do, what the risks are. The dangers. I've lived my entire life pretending to be something I'm not in order to build this movement. I'm going to tell you what I told the men who wanted you dead because of the risk you pose to it all: If *I* am willing to bring you in, knowing that at any moment you could betray us, that the king could force you to tell him everything, then that should be enough reasoning for anyone else. Please, Rhea, I think it will be beneficial for us all if you go."

My throat constricts around a single word. "Why?"

"Because my people need to see that you aren't a threat. They need to look at you with their own eyes in an environment not controlled by the king. My word, as much as they all trust it, will only get them so far. But beyond that, you need to be there when we finalize our plans."

"Plans? Plans for what?"

"Your escape."

I fight back a chagrinned look as I lean back in Alexi's chair. "How, Xander? With the ring on my finger, I don't think I *can* escape."

"Let's leave the details for when you meet the people who will be helping."

I laugh around a frustrated breath. "I'm not sure I hold the same conviction you do."

He shrugs before standing, taking a step towards me as he once again extends his hand out for mine. "I don't blame you for having a healthy dose of skepticism, but I trust you enough to expose everything I've spent my life working towards." He swallows roughly. "Can you trust me to help you?"

I look out to the balcony, noticing the way the clouds from the previous storm have parted and now reveal a night sparkling with stars. And though the weight of everything I have done and seen and learned feels impossible to bear, when Xander softly says my name again, wiggling his fingers to get my attention, I decide that in this moment, I can make another choice. That perhaps his timing had been more than luck. He and I have the kind of history that isn't so easily forgotten, but I have seen him try his best to help me. I do trust *him*, even if I doubt that he can actually help me escape.

I stand and slip my hands into his, our handshake tentative when something he said earlier snags my attention. "What did you mean when you said you explained to Siyala who the king is to you?"

He sighs again, dropping my hand to rub at the back of his neck. "In the spirit of honesty, there's probably *one* more thing you should know about me."

My eyes narrow, arms crossing over my chest. "And what is that?"

"King Dolian is my father."

Chapter Ninety-Six

ARIA

Lore's attack had left a fairly deep gash on my arm, one that required Lyre's assistance to wrap as the injury worked to heal itself. Visiting her early this morning before I depart for my meeting with Myla, she keeps her lips pinched in a tight line as she tends to me. She had already asked me several times who was responsible for the attack, and I had managed to dodge the question, much to her frustration. Worry shines bright in her lavender eyes as she ties off the gauze and then draws me in for a hug.

"Be careful," she whispers.

"I will."

Her words haunt me the entire swim out of Lumen. As does the memory of the fight with Lore.

My fingers trail along the faint bruise that remains on my jaw as I exit the water beneath the cover of the cavern. I had relished in the idea that I actually overpowered her, but with every day that has passed, I can't help but wonder if all I'd done was prolong the inevitable instead. If my victory was less about me fighting back and more about Lore choosing not to continue pursuing me. A shiver works over me as I walk through the soft sand, water dripping from my curls and down my hips making goosebumps lift on my skin.

I search the sky above through the holes in the rock, listening for the sound of leathery wings. It's a habit now to check after our run-in with the dragon and its rider. Climbing the large rocks that lead to the platform, my stomach dips when I find Myla already waiting. She leans against one of the side walls, one foot crossed over the other as she twirls a small dagger in her hand.

"Hello." I turn so that my injured arm is hidden from her view by my hair, carefully taking my bag off and setting it on the ground.

"Your tunic is over there." She points to the opposite corner, where a cream top is laying over a large rock.

She remains silent as I slip the tunic over me, her gaze appearing lost in thought when I turn back to face her. The rhythmic flipping of her dagger is smooth and practiced, and as she stares at an indistinct point to my left, I let myself study her. Just like every time I lay eyes on her, I can't help but marvel at the long elegant lines of her face. From her slightly pointed chin to the gentle arch of her ears, everything about her is perfectly placed. As if carved from the smoothest marble by the most talented hand. Those long lines continue down her body, the tight fit of her clothing betraying her strength.

"It's rude to stare," she says, her voice flat as she slides the blade back into its sheath at her ribs.

Heat creeps up my neck to my cheeks, but I clear my throat and ask, "What are we working on today?"

Myla tilts her head, still avoiding looking at me. "We'll continue practicing different methods of attack, both with and without the dagger you call yours."

"Because it is mine," I counter, taking a step towards her. A stream of sunlight from one of the cracks above cascades over Myla, highlighting her high cheek-bones and slender nose. It makes the shadows beneath her eyes stand out in contrast. Had I ever seen Myla anything other than angry? Frustrated? Exhaustion never crossed my mind as something she *could* feel, yet the more I look at her, the more she seems as if she could plop down at any moment and fall asleep.

Her eyes flick to me then, and I mentally double check that I didn't say *any* of those thoughts out loud.

"It belongs to my father."

"So you say." In truth, I don't believe Myla to be lying about that. Her reaction to the dagger had been swift, hard to fake if she didn't actually care. But if Myla has taught me anything in our lessons, it's that pitying her would be a mistake and showing weakness would be even worse. She may want that dagger, but she will honor the fact that I took it from her fairly because anything else will make her look *weak*.

"Start warming up." The command is given in her usual curtness, but I don't find it as cold as I once did. There is a strange sort of comfort in these meetings between us. I am holding on to so many secrets below the surface of the water, it is... *nice* to know that where Myla is concerned, ire will always be close at hand.

I move through warming up, surprised when she pushes away from the wall and joins me. Where my intent is to get through them as fast as possible so we can move on to the actual lesson, Myla's movements are calculated. Precise. It's less a person going through motions that they've done hundreds of times before and more like she's *embodying* them. Feeling what it is to be in each stance before moving on to the next.

As her muscles flex beneath her black leathers, I find myself utterly transfixed by her strength. By the way she moves. Her presence has always pulled from me feelings of not quite *jealousy* but a wish that *I* could be looked upon with the same reverence that I was sure others gave her. Because to look at Myla is to recognize that beauty and power can be combined in a way that is more alluring than any siren song.

Refocusing myself, I get through the rest of the warm-ups with my gaze on the ground, and then Myla instructs me to grab my dagger.

The bone hilt is cool in my hand, and I remember what she had said about this weapon. How her father had been given it as a gift from the mage queen who put up the Spell. That it had then been lost with her brother, a male who had been dragged into the sea by one of my kind. It makes sense why she loathes the sirens as strongly as she does.

My mother's tales of her experience during that time always focus on what others had done to her and what she lost as a result. But I know that she sifts through details like one lets sand trickle between their fingers. What actually happened to start The War of Five Kingdoms might only ever be known to those who were there, but as my mother prepares to infiltrate the Mortal Kingdom using her control over King Dolian and the magic at Rhea's fingertips, I can't help but wonder if we are about to learn the truths of war all over again.

"Your mind is elsewhere." Myla's voice cleaves through my thoughts.

"Sorry. It was a long night." I pull my guard up in front of my body, my dagger held in my right hand.

"Have you had much experience fighting someone larger than you?" she asks as she looks over my form.

"I don't have much experience fighting anyone at all." Lore had been the true test of that, and I had almost failed. If not for the element of surprise on my side, I would have. Lore would have had her way with me, and I would have been—

"Aria."

I blink and give Myla my attention again. She arches a dark brow, but I ignore her unasked question. She doesn't *care* why my mind keeps wandering off other than the fact that it interrupts our lessons.

"For opponents bigger than you, you're going to have to leverage their size against them. I'm not sure how the dynamic will work beneath the water, but you have to force them to get closer to you, and then you need to be quick and precise with your own attacks." She tells me how to angle my stance and then fakes an attack at me, her movements slow as she talks through them.

I don't want to move through these lessons in slow hypotheticals anymore. I need real world application, and Myla is the perfect teacher for that because she won't think like a siren. The benefit to her teaching me is that her moves are unexpected. They might not translate perfectly under the water, but I will take *any* advantage that I can.

"I want you to attack me for real," I blurt out in the middle of Myla speaking.

She snaps her mouth closed and draws back the arm fake-swinging a dagger in my direction. "Why?"

It's my turn to send her an arch look. "I would have thought you'd be jumping for joy at the opportunity to attack me. The magic won't hold you at fault for injuring me if I'm the one who asked for it, right?" I turn around so that she is at my back, my heart pounding against my chest. "Attack me."

Myla chuckles, the noise skating over my skin. "I don't think you want that."

"I do," I rasp, lifting my dagger out in front of me. "I need to learn how to handle the element of surprise, or this will never work."

Silence ticks by for a few heartbeats before she drawls, "This being?"

I open my mouth to answer, but all that comes out is a *whoosh* of breath when my back is pulled into Myla's front, her dagger pointed at my throat. *Fuck.*

"Is this what you wanted?" she taunts, breath stirring the strands of hair by my ear. The arm not holding the blade is banded around my front, reaching over one shoulder and stretching across and down my body so her fingers press into the tunic near my hip.

I'm not fully restrained, not even without the use of my arms, but the panic of being confined still surges within me. With my chest heaving, I stand there motionless. Frozen. The heat at my back is not that of the fae trying to teach me but the siren trying to *own* me.

"You have to fight back, Aria," she says, but her voice is distorted. Muffled as the past clashes with the present in my head.

Come on, Aria, you and I both know that this is what you want. That was what Lore had said to me the last time I had let her into my room. The last time I had given her access to my body without so much as a word of protest.

A sound caught between a whimper and a growl erupts from me as I bring the dagger up, attempting to slash at Myla's arm. But she quickly abandons her hold on me to catch my wrist, pressing her thumb into the tendon there and forcing my hand open. The metal echoes loudly as the dagger falls to the ground, and in my panic, I send my elbow back to collide with Myla's torso. Just as I had done with Lore.

Except I meet nothing but air.

Myla sidesteps, avoiding my hit, while keeping the tip of her blade hovering over my neck. Unable to spin to either side to escape her grasp completely, I try the second move I can think of and lift my leg, driving my heel into her shin. Myla laughs as she sends a kick of her own to my calf, forcing the leg to bend and sending my knee crashing into the stone below.

The anger that rises within me is potent—*bitter*. Growing my talons from my fingertips, I twist into the dagger and slash at her knee, forcing Myla to either let the blade cut me or take the hit to her leg. She chooses the latter, cursing as the dagger disappears and she jumps back. Even with the extra move, she still manages to get a surface-level scrape, just enough to cut through the fabric of her pants. I breathe through gritted teeth as I grab the dagger again and stand. Myla takes one look at me and readies herself, but I'm already lunging in her direction. There is no encouragement, no feedback, nothing at all as Myla blocks each swipe of my blade.

My song builds at the base of my throat, a scream of frustration tainted with it. Myla's eyes widen, and perhaps it's the fear that I'll use my magic on her again that quickens her movements because between one breath and the next, I'm no longer attacking her. Faster than I can comprehend, my back is against the wall and the hand holding the dagger is pinned above my head. I yelp at the pain that tugs on the gashes in my arm, Myla immediately stepping back.

"Did I hurt you?" she asks, and gods, I must be hallucinating because I swear I hear *concern* in her voice.

"No," I say between gasps of breath, my magic still tingling as it waits for my command. I swallow it down, willing it to dissipate as I try to focus on the gray stone beneath my feet. The cool temperature in the air. Anything to ground me *here*.

"Someone did." It's spoken quietly, but there is nothing soft about the words. I tilt my head up to look at her, finding her gaze locked on my arm. "You're bleeding."

Looking down, I gasp at the blood seeping past the gauze, the dark blue color now staining the tunic. Myla closes the distance between us again, and I straighten as her smoky vanilla scent invades my next inhale. My shoulders press back against the wall as Myla reaches for the collar of the tunic. "What are—"

She pulls until the fabric rips, just enough for it to expose my shoulder and then the bandages that cover my upper arm. They've loosened from our training, revealing the jagged skin of the gashes between each strip.

Her chest rises with a deep inhale before her eyes snap to mine, and the look there freezes me in place. "Aria," she says, her voice tinged with a rage I don't quite understand. "Who did this to you?"

Chapter Ninety-Seven

ARIA

S HE SAYS MY NAME again, letting go of the tunic to wrap her fingers gently around my arm beneath the gashes. Her touch is gentle, opposite to the way her tone could cut glass. "Who hurt you?"

"Just another siren," I answer, air growing thin under the scrutiny of her stare. "I'm fine."

"Fine," she repeats slowly, eyes narrowing when I slip away from her.

She lets me go easily but pivots to follow as I make my way to the other side of the cavern to sit on one of the larger rocks. Pulling my injured arm out through the ripped collar, I begin to carefully unwrap the gauze. While my quicker healing abilities have stitched the smaller stretches of separated skin back together already, the thicker parts where Lore's claws dug into me have reopened enough for blood to slowly ooze out. But before I can dab at it, the old gauze is ripped from my hand as Myla squats down in front of me.

"You should have told me you were injured." Reaching into an inner pocket of her vest, she pulls out a white piece of cloth that's folded neatly into a small square.

"I didn't think you would care." I watch as she shakes the cloth out to make it larger before ripping it into two long strips. "What are you doing?"

"Do sirens normally attack each other like this?" she asks, ignoring both my statement and question. "Hold your arm out." When I hesitate, her eyes meet mine. There is always a small bit of fear that rises when I have Myla's full attention on me, but it's usually because she regards me with either utter fury or disdain. As we stare at each other in the shadowed sunlight of the cavern, the look she gives me is different from any other I've seen before. It isn't exactly soft, as I don't think I could ever call any part of Myla that, but it toes the line of being... *tender.* "Look, if you don't want me to touch you, that is fine. But you should staunch the bleeding with clean cloths so that we can continue with our lessons."

Right. Maybe she is concerned, but it has nothing to do with *me.* It is concern that our deal might be affected if she doesn't help. I lift my arm abruptly and immediately regret it, a breath hissing out between clenched teeth. Myla's stare lingers as she watches me, her mouth opening like she might say something before she thinks better of it and looks at the marks on my arm.

The silence that stretches between us is stifling, and to keep my stare from wandering over her features like earlier, I answer her previous question while picking at the fabric of my tunic with my free hand. "Sirens can be vicious creatures—as you've repeatedly pointed out. Like any other being, there can be disagreements that lead to fights."

"And what was the cause of your fight?" she asks, laying one of the strips of cloth over my thigh and wrapping the other around the gashes.

I sigh, unsure of how to word what happened with Lore. "The female that attacked me wanted something that was no longer hers to have, and she got mad when I told her 'no.'"

Myla's fingers suspend in the air between us at my words, but only for a moment before she continues wrapping the cloth around my arm. Her closeness, the way she doesn't respond with more than a slight furrow of her brows, leaves me unsettled. I begin to ramble.

"She wouldn't have gone far enough to kill me, if that's what you're worried about. Lore is possessive about the things she believes she owns, and I've always given in to what she wants. So this was just..." I trail off, unsure of what to say. Lore had never *attacked* me like that before, but I had never given her a reason to think she wasn't in control. I had never tested the boundaries of that possession before. How can I say with any bit of confidence that I know how she would react?

I'm so lost in my own back and forth in my head that I don't realize Myla has stopped until she resumes moving again. Glancing at her from the corner of my eye, I take in her tight expression. Any emotion I thought I might have seen earlier is hidden behind her familiar mask of contempt, and I can't help the way a pit opens inside of my stomach because of it.

She reaches for the second piece of cloth but hesitates, her gaze stuck on where it lays on my thigh. "In my kingdom, the balance of power leans starkly to one side. While females of all stations and nobility are treated as *less than* compared to their male counterparts, it is even more drastic in the capital. They are brutalized there." She picks up the second strip and begins to bind it around my arm, her movements slow. "The word 'no' has no meaning to those in power, and even if it did, it is weightless when said by a female. There are those who believe they have the right to claim someone else's autonomy. That it is theirs to do whatever they please with. And there is no justice given to the ones they harm."

My stomach churns, a chord striking too close to home. Myla is royalty, but she speaks as if she understands intimately what it is to have free will stripped from her. I have always viewed her as someone impenetrable, untouchable. Even with the bits of information Navin had given me about her, I never believed Myla was anything other than a force to be reckoned with. But what if I was wrong? What if the anger—the toughness and that willful darkness that simmers beneath the surface—wasn't hers because she chose them but because she was forced to *become* them? What had she said to me before? Just because what is inside of us is dark doesn't mean that it holds less value than something light. I hadn't known what she meant at the time, hadn't truly understood it. Was she saying that to me because she wanted to comfort me as I told her about my life in the Siren Queendom? Or were they words she wished someone would've said to her? My fingers slowly brush against her forearm, her gaze snapping to the contact.

"Is there anyone who can help them?"

"There is a vigilante known as the Shadow," she answers, a roughness to her voice. She ties the ends of the cloth off, letting her fingers linger as one of them brushes gently over the curls gathered at my shoulder. "They hunt down those who harm others and do so without mercy. To be caught by the Shadow is to be tormented. It is a fate worse than death. Worse than being burned alive by dragons." She pinches the ruby-red strands between her forefinger and thumb, dragging the latter over them as she tilts her head to the side and smirks. "Those in power are frightened by the Shadow. By what they represent."

My heart flutters beneath my ribs. "And what do they represent?"

"A threat to the status quo." Her eyes meet mine then, the look sending a shiver down my spine. "The Shadow reminds them that they are not infallible. The king and nobles only thrive when everyone else believes that they cannot fight back, when they are hopeless. I think the Shadow represents a kink in that power, and sometimes, that's all it takes for people to make a stand of their own."

I had once thought that a single person wasn't enough to enact change. That their actions would be only a single drop in the current. I realize now that my way of thinking was a crutch. If I tried to stand up to my mother, to Allegra, to Nia and Lore, I could fail. By accepting their cruelty over me, by not acting at all in defiance of them, I wasn't risking anything. But I wasn't living either. So much of my life has been wasted in the shadows of my own fear instead of being spent doing something that *matters*.

Fingers wrap around my chin, warm and gentle, as Myla draws the gaze I had let drop back up to her. "Your 'no' should have been enough."

A shaky breath passes from my parted lips, my stomach dipping when her eyes focus on them. "If only there was a vigilante to protect me," I tease.

I'm rewarded with a flicker of a smile before she stands, walking back to the center of the platform. I mourn the warmth she takes with her. "You don't need someone like the Shadow to rescue you, Little Siren." Picking up my dagger, she flips it in the air and catches the blade between her fingertips, holding the hilt out in my direction. "Not when you can learn how to rescue yourself."

Whatever comfort Myla dared to offer me was immediately replaced with an even more relentless training regimen. By the time our session was over, I was coated with more sweat than when I climbed the cliff to the palace on the Northern Island. My muscles were so taxed that my knees wobbled as I walked, and I could barely lift my good arm higher than my shoulder. I was exhausted, yet I had never felt better.

In the week that followed, I only saw my mother once. She had issued banishments to sirens who were no longer able to shift into their mortal forms, deeming them dispensable now that they could no longer procreate with those captured by our song. Yet, the energy in the palace was frenzied as whispers about the siren queen being invited to the mortal king's wedding echoed down the halls. My mind immediately went to Rhea, wondering if she even wanted to marry the king and then why my mother would be invited. Not even Lyre seemed to know. She and I met every night, Sade joining us when she could. To keep those in the legion from getting suspicious—and from word traveling back to the queen—Sade stationed legionaries around Lumen with the task of helping to search for the seamount sirens. She assured me that most of those she sent out were allies, though a few that made the rotation who genuinely wanted to find and harm those they considered to be traitors. But Nia and the rest of the seamount sirens were safely tucked away in Eersten, and that was all the information Sade would give me.

She had, however, begun pairing me with one of the sirens who was aware of my sister's true loyalties.

"They need to see that you're one of us and not just our mother's punching bag," she told me, before pushing me out of her office in the garrison and right into a pretty siren with teal braids and aquamarine eyes. Our interactions were friendly enough, if a bit stiff at first. Each day we pretend to patrol Lumen, I tried to remind myself that this would all be worth it. The more females who trusted that I was on their side, the safer I would feel when it was time for Lyre and I to leave. Which was a subject my pregnant sister had been avoiding. There was still time before she had the baby, about a month if I had to guess, but what once seemed like eager excitement at the prospect of escaping our mother's rule had now turned into wincing smiles and changing subjects. And maybe that was for the best. A strange feeling buried itself between my ribs every time I thought about running away from Lumen. When I realized it wasn't just those below the surface I'd be leaving but someone above it too. In all likelihood, I wouldn't finish the full twelve lessons with Myla before Lyre's babe was born, and something about that truth felt like trying to swim on land.

When I wasn't spending my time forced to make new friends or catching up with Lyre and Sade, I practiced the moves Myla had taught me in my room. They were different beneath the surface, of course, and I doubted that training in the water alone would be as effective as training with Myla on land. But I moved until the exhaustion hit me, and behind a locked door, I fell asleep more easily than I had in a really long time.

I had not seen Lore at all during the week, and while I wanted to believe that it was because she had taken my resistance to heart, a small voice in my head warned against letting my guard down. The thought pushed me to train a little longer. It drove me to get up earlier for my meeting with Myla, knowing that, while she wouldn't be there yet, I could get a head start on our warm-ups, leaving us with even more time to train.

The sea thrashes at my knees when I can finally transform into my mortal body. Though there are light gray clouds in the sky, they have broken apart enough to allow the early morning sun to peek between them, cascading through the holes and cracks in the cavern and illuminating our training space in golden light. It highlights the vines of green ivy that crawl up the walls and stretch across the ceiling.

Feeling energized, I begin my warm-ups while I wait for Myla to join me. I'm well into my third round of poses, sweat already gathering on my brow, when I hear the distinct beat of dragon wings. As a precaution, I inch towards the pool of water behind the platform, suppressing the memory of the last time I was in it as I crouch down to try to see better past the opening of the cavern.

Navin's dragon, Lan, lands harshly enough to send sand flying in all directions, his powerful wings flaring out as the sun filters through them, highlighting every vein and their leathery texture before they snap closed. Tilting his head to the side, the dragon's blue scales shimmer brightly as he extends his leg out in front of him, a deep rumble vibrating the air. I wait to see Myla climb down, a confusing amount of anticipation fluttering in my chest. Navin's dragon lays his head on the sand, eyes closing as the voices of his two riders carry past the rock.

"You need to let this go for your own good, Myla."

The growl that she gives is enough to cause his dragon to lift one eyelid, the yellow eye squinting against the sunlight. "The fact that you would even *suggest* that shows how absolutely asinine you're being." In a blur of black, she climbs down Lan's leg, jumping the remaining few feet to the beach below.

"This is beyond anything I've trained you for. You're good, Myla, really *fucking* good, but not even you can fight against an entire squadron of King's Riders!"

"It's insulting you think I'd be dumb enough to get caught in the first place," she seethes, walking into the cavern before turning to look over her shoulder at him. "You have *never* been able to control my actions, so I don't know why you are trying to do so now."

"Right," he shouts as he adjusts his position on the back of his dragon, grasping a leather strap. "Because trying to keep you safe is *controlling* you. Gods above, Myla, I *swear* you want to die!"

Myla stiffens as her steps come to a halt below, and I watch a quick flash of emotion cross her face before something icy and detached settles back in.

"*Fuck*, I'm sorry."

She ignores him as she tilts her head up, her brows furrowing as she inhales deeply. I'm assuming that she is smelling the jasmine too until her gaze snaps right to where I'm standing, the glittering darkness in her eyes making heat bloom deep inside me. I swallow as I stand to my full height and offer a stupid wave of my hand.

"I'll see you in a few hours," Myla shouts, continuing forward and climbing up to the platform until she's standing right before me—all menace and ire and *her*. "Spying are we, Little Siren?"

Chapter Ninety-Eight

MYLA

I TAKE IN THE way Aria's skin gleams, her scent strong as I take another step towards her. My eyes disobey any sort of logic as they travel of their own volition down the length of her curly hair to the very ends, where it brushes against her hips. The slight shimmer of her scales changes color there, moving from the same garnet of her hair to something that resembles sunrise—golden and orange-hued.

"I've been told I'm a terrible spy," she retorts, drawing my gaze back up. A stream of sunlight coming in from one of the cracks above splits the distance between us, making their hazel color glow.

"I find that unsurprising."

She frowns as I hand her a new tunic, this one black. I watch as she pinches the fabric between her finger and thumb, feeling the soft cotton as she steps back to slip it on, and I turn to give her privacy. I had noticed that whenever I brought her one of Navin's training tunics, she would tug at it, as if she didn't like the way it felt against her skin. I dismissed it as her not being used to wearing clothing until I accidentally grabbed one of my brother's nicer tops that went beneath his formal uniform for events. The fabric was of richer quality and a softer material, and not once had Aria fidgeted with its collar or sleeves as if she couldn't wait to peel it off of her the moment we were done. If she wasn't messing with the top, she was more focused on our training. The reasoning was sound, and that was enough for me to disregard any other thoughts for why I might give a shit about whether or not she was comfortable.

"I got here early so that I could get warm-ups out of the way," she says, her steps quiet against the stone. That explains why her scent is fucking *everywhere* in this damn place. "I'm ready to get right to our lessons."

"Then let's start with the hand-to-hand combat. After, we'll move to wielding your dagger." She doesn't bat an eye at the way I don't acknowledge her arriving early, and though it doesn't make sense, I find myself *annoyed* by that.

I've been on edge for what feels like *weeks* now, ever since guards were sent to scuttle around Khargis like an infestation of rats. Shen's been unable to give me anything new about the handful of males I had been watching, all of the information she'd usually glean at her bar snuffed out by the presence of silver armor and longswords. According to Navin, more guards will be added each week that the Shadow isn't caught, pressuring both the people in the poorest sections and the miserable guards who have nothing better to do than be cruel as they patrol the streets.

Shen's hands had shook with anger as she recounted hearing of assaults by the added males, and though she wouldn't say the words out loud, I could see the pleading in her eyes: *Do something.* Of course, I wanted to apprehend each and every guard and bring them to the basement of my warehouse. I could collect a handful of them at a time to hang from the rafters on metal hooks while I questioned them, torturing them with the edge of my blade.

But I haven't made it this far by being impulsive, something Shen knows.

"Are you alright?" Aria asks from where she waits across from me, lowering her guard.

I lift a brow as I tug the sleeves of my black top up to my elbows, Aria tracking the movement. "Put your arms back up," I command, stretching my neck from side to side. "And I'm fine." I give her the time to fix her guard before sending my right fist in her direction, pleased when she blocks it with her forearm, her brows settling low over her eyes.

"That's good," she says.

"Is it?" I counter, delivering a quick combo of punches that force her to utilize both arms to block. But she's clearly been practicing because her reaction time is the quickest it's ever been.

"Why wouldn't it be?"

The corners of my lips wiggle a fraction. "Don't forget that you can attack me too."

She smiles, sidestepping and forcing me to counter. I had been intrigued when Aria came injured to our last meeting, and that curiosity had turned to outright fury when she tried to be covert about how she had gotten hurt. But I had spent the past five years skinning the flesh from those who harmed others because they wanted to take what was never theirs to begin with. And while I never interacted with the victims, Shen did. I wanted her to be the good they saw, while I was the monster in the dark. But she told me, sometimes, when we'd meet up for a briefing, what the victims had said. What they felt. How, in some cases, they would downplay their abuse with an "at least it wasn't worse" statement.

Aria swings her right fist towards me, and I lean back to dodge it, straightening just in time to catch her guard a little too high, punching the space beneath her ribs on her side. She hisses out a breath, adjusting her guard as she keeps her feet moving. Where fear once rattled her every time I so much as *breathed* in her direction, determination now blankets her soft features.

I had thought a lot about what she said and how I responded in the days since our last meeting. Aria is a siren, a being I have hated since I learned about The War Of Five Kingdoms. But she is also a female subjected to the same cruelty of rulers, a victim to those who take what they want without asking. Something had pulled at me from within, warning that if I did not show her that she had the ability to protect herself from whatever dangers might come her way, I would not be fulfilling the bargain between us. In the same breath, however, something else whispered that it was more. That the urge to *care* for her had nothing to do with whatever was magically binding us together. But that voice was easy enough to silence, especially when I could distract myself with what my father was doing with the guards, the dragons, and the abduction of mages.

Fuck, things are really going to shit around me.

Aria and I continue our sparring until even *my* arms begin to burn and sweat drips down my back. It works to relieve some of the unspent energy humming beneath my skin. If *I'm* feeling this way, she must be completely fatigued, but she doesn't complain. Not once. Using my forearm, I swipe at my forehead and tuck my hair behind my ears to get it out of my face. Aria's eyes go straight to them, and I watch her reaction for signs of disgust. Or some other lingering prejudice against the fae that might have become ingrained by her queen. I'm met with only open interest. She stares at them like one would look upon a full moon. I'm reluctant to call it awe, yet that's the only word that comes to me. When she realizes I've caught her looking, she drops her gaze to the ground, her hands bracing her hips. Even wearing the baggier tunic, the silhouette of her body is unmistakable beneath it, and a jolt of desire shocks me from where it pools low in my gut.

I grind my teeth together and palm the dagger at my thigh, content to ram it through my leg to stop whatever is happening to me. "Go grab your blade—"

"Actually," she interrupts, her head snapping up so her eyes can meet mine, "I was wondering if we could revisit how we sparred last time."

I tilt my head, releasing the hilt of my dagger. "What do you mean?"

Aria purses her lips, thinking her words over as she reaches up to play with a few strands of her curly hair. I had been unable to stop myself from touching it as I bandaged her arm in our last meeting, an annoying curiosity overtaking me as I reached up to see if the strands were as soft as they looked. It had been a lapse of judgement, a momentary and fleeting response to having her so close and unguarded. "I froze last week. When you attacked me from behind. It's because when she—when Lore—came at me, that's how she did it. And I froze then too, only able to eventually fend her off because I had the element of surprise." I work hard not to show a reaction, despite how tension rides my shoulders. Aria offers a small smile in response, as if she can somehow tell what I'm feeling. "I just want to make sure I can defend myself from anything. As much as I can with the limited lessons we have left."

The reminder that we are on the tail end of our time together should give me a feeling of elation, but paired with the image of someone holding Aria against her will, all it does is sour my stomach. Weeks are all we have left, and that isn't enough time to teach Aria everything she needs to know to defend herself. Fuck, it had taken me *years* of dedicated training before I could best Navin. Then again, what are the odds that Aria is fighting a trained warrior? Is *Lore* someone who has years of training over Aria? But despite how the question attempts to slip free, I keep it locked behind my lips. *It isn't any of my business.*

Stepping close enough to her to count the freckles on her cheeks, I say, "Show me how she restrained you."

She spins until her back is to me, holding her arms out to the side. When she feels me at her back, she tentatively reaches for my wrist, delicate fingers wrapping around it, and positions my arm around her torso. "One arm was like this while *this* arm"—she reaches for my other limb, tugging that one so that it's banded across her chest—"was like this. And we were—"

I tighten my hold, her back becoming flush with my chest. Her breath stutters at the movement, heart fluttering fast beneath her ribs as I take in a deep lungful of air that is tainted with something sweet. Like honey, but not quite.

"Like that," she rasps, bringing her arms down to her sides. Our height difference makes it so that my chin ends where her forehead begins, and as I assess our positioning, my mind briefly makes note of the way she *fits* in my arms. With an internal growl, I push the thought away. Someone had fucking *attacked* her like this. My muscles flex as if meaning to tighten my hold on her, as if that will somehow protect her from what has already been done. "Now what do I do?"

"Normally, I would tell you to go limp in their arms. That alone would force them to try to regain control so that they don't drop you. But under water, that technique isn't going to work." I narrow my eyes as I cycle through different poses in my head, each one tailored to fighting on land. To counterattack, Aria will need to focus on different points of contact. Elbows. Hands. *Claws.* I lift the arm crossing over her chest to grab at her wrist, my fingers splaying over the back of her hand. "Instead of one fluid movement to take an opponent down, you will have to do a series of quick ones with the intention of not besting them but getting away."

Her hand twitches in my hold. "What if I don't want to just get away? What if I want to hurt them?"

The words are spoken softly, but the intention behind them—the *gravitas*—has my own throat working to swallow roughly. "So violent," I murmur, my breath disturbing the strands of hair near her ear.

Aria huffs an unsteady laugh. "In the Siren Queendom, if someone is attacking you, more often than not, it is with the intention to kill." She shakes her head, her soft curls brushing at my jaw. "I can't bet on simply escaping. I need to know what to do once I'm free to ensure that they can't harm me—or anyone else."

The addition at the end of her statement reminds me of the reasoning she gave me weeks ago about why she wanted to learn how to fight. It was to protect someone close to her. Someone she cares about deeply. I lean back until inches separate us again. "The first thing you need to do is think about how to create space with your attacker. You'll start by arching your back and sending this elbow"—I mimic the movement slowly with her arm—"behind you, aiming for the space between their ribs."

"How am I supposed to know where that is?"

"You'll know when you hit bone because it will hurt, but you'll be sure you've hit the space between when you hear the air squeeze out of their lungs." I position her arm back at her side, my hand sliding away before banding my arm around her front again. "Try it." Aria attempts to wiggle enough to give her arm some leeway. It works, and she is able to send a relatively gentle hit into my ribs. "Good." I can't see her face from my spot behind her, but I watch the top of her cheek lift in a smile at my praise. "Next, you want to use your hands and those menacing little talons that decorate them."

"Menacing?" she questions, growing them out from the tips of her fingers.

"To anyone attacking you? They should be."

She hums, the vibration of it skating over my chest. Stars above, I am overdue for a kill. Or a fuck. Or some other carnal form of physical movement because I've never been so innately aware of someone else without being engaged in either of those two things.

"You need to force one of my arms away so that you can spin and face me. To do that, you're going to drive the heel of your left palm into my right forearm." She does the move slowly, testing that she's hitting the right spot. "Now spin in the same direction." Again, she follows my instructions until we're face to face, my left arm now wrapped around her back. She lifts her hands between us but hesitates laying them on my chest, her gaze lifting to search mine.

"Now what?"

"Now you'll go in for the kill." Using my right hand, I push her own forward until her talons are scraping along the skin at my neck. Aria doesn't breathe, and my own inhale is trapped in my chest as I draw the sharpened tips of her claws down the space beneath my ear, mimicking the motion she would use if she were truly attacking me. "There is an artery here, at least for the fae," I say, and Aria nods. I search her neck for her gills, having only just barely seen them when we were hiding from one of the King's Riders and his dragon. In her mortal form, they are nothing but the faintest outline, only visible from just the right angle. "I imagine shredding a siren's gills would be just as devastating?"

"Yes." Her eyes bounce back and forth between mine.

"Then that's what you go for. No hesitation. No remorse." My fingers tighten around her hand. "It is *your* life versus theirs, and the person who is victorious is the one who is willing to do whatever it takes."

"Who am I willing to become?" she whispers. I nod in acknowledgement, and her hand relaxes in my hold, talons retreating until her fingers close around mine.

Tension suspends between us, the heat of our bodies kindling that feels just an inch away from igniting. Yet that thought does nothing to stop the way my eyes trace the outline of her face. Of her round eyes and the dark freckles dotting the skin beneath them. Her supple lips and how they are just barely parted. I tilt my head down a fraction just as Aria angles hers, our lips perfectly in alignment. All I'd have to do is weave my hand through her hair, draw her in half an inch and— My stomach pitches, a strange sensation taking root that knocks me from my stupor and forces me to release her and take a step back. Aria's hands remain in the air in front of her for another moment before she lowers them, her gaze dropping to the ground while her brows furrow. *Do you feel it too?* I want to ask. *That annoying draw?*

Instead, I command us to run through the exercise again.

Part Six

Sympathy is an emotion I've long since discarded. Now there is only venomous *anger*.

Chapter Ninety-Nine

MYLA

'M FRESHLY SHOWERED AND just barely dressed when Leesi enters my room. "Father Yamin has requested your attendance in the temple."

My slippered steps are soft against the polished stone as I follow two guards through the palace to the temple's entrance, the sight of the dark door tightening my chest. Dressed in light yellow, I curse the way the beads on my veil are just long enough to fall over the tops of my eyes, obscuring my sight in a way that leaves me feeling too vulnerable. I have no doubt that I could pull a sword from the scabbard on one of these assholes' backs and drive it through their gut if it came down to it, but all the violent thoughts dancing around in my head are just that—*thoughts*. Acting on them would be pointless, *stupid and reckless*, without a dragon to back me up.

Cold air rushes from the temple doors as the guards push them open, stirring the sheer fabric of my dress. I keep my spine straight, my hands clasped in front of me as I walk past them and into the empty temple where the appointed Divine Father stands right next to the pole I was tied to the last time I was here.

He takes note of the way I hold myself tall and not in supplication like he expects. "Defiance has never been a good look on you, Myla," he chides, forgoing my royal title as he steps towards me. In his usual black robes with his hands pulled behind his back, the picture he tries to paint of an imposing figure might scare most. It *used* to frighten me. But I take a sadistic sort of pleasure in knowing that—while I may pretend to bend the knee to his will, the will of the gods he represents—there is only one being powerful enough to end a life in this temple. And it *isn't* him. "Show respect to Khaos and Solana," he snaps, his voice echoing through the otherwise empty space. "*Now.*"

I take my time lowering onto my knees, facing not the thrones I did last time where my father, my mother, and Navin sat but to their right, where statues of the god Khaos and goddess Solana are etched into shiny white marble. The former is depicted in layers of fabric that gather over one shoulder and drape down his back like a cape. Next to him stands his daughter, her hands held in front of her, palms turned up. She wears a dress, the fabric split down the middle with a carved line in the stone. In one palm rests a flaring sun, and in the other a crescent moon.

"They watch over us with sadness in their hearts," he continues, and I flatten my lips. "To have created us in their image, only for so many of us to spit back in their faces. But a reckoning is coming for those who are no longer pious. For those who are not... *pure* of heart." Father Yamin moves behind me, the sound of his robes shuffling is followed by another noise I'm familiar with. I keep myself exceptionally still, even as my veins ice over at the clinking metal of a chain unrolling from a wooden baton. "Tell me, Myla, have you begged for forgiveness in prayer?"

I could lie and pretend to be someone good. Someone eager to please him. But it won't make a difference; it never has. I'd rather take his abuse than give him an *ounce* of satisfaction. "No."

"That is what I feared. Now, you know what must be done." The air stirs as he pulls his arm back, and I can picture the silver chain swinging from where it is lifted high above him. "Our kingdom will know mercy from the gods soon, *Princess*, and one can only hope that they will strike those they know are unworthy from this land. That they will purify it with dragon fire until only those who deserve to know their light remain. Something big is coming. The gods have whispered so."

I grit my teeth together as the first hit of the chain streaks across my upper back, jolting me forward from the impact until my hands plant on the ground in front of me. I quickly straighten, but Father Yamin shoves me back down.

"Only in the bowing of our heads can we find the guidance of the gods," he says, repeating a prayer.

I close my eyes as the next hit comes. The father continues his rambling nonsense, but I tune it out as I draw on years of slipping out of the present to focus on something else. I think of Shen and the victims I'm failing by not being able to hunt my targets. Of Sunis and our bond that's yet to form. Without trying, I think of Aria. White flashes behind my lids as another whip of the chain ignites the skin across my back, the permanent tenderness of the flesh there throbbing in time to my heartbeats. I bury myself in those memories, ignoring the realization that something within me has shifted when it comes to the siren. That of all my mind has conjured up, getting lost in thoughts of her is by far the easiest to do. As the strikes continue and Father Yamin angrily speaks, over and over again, I think of Aria.

The shingles creak beneath my weight as I crouch lower, my eyes squinting against the darkness of night and the cold wind that scrapes against the side of my face. Across the street, a tavern is lit from within, the curtained window showing silhouettes of its patrons as they dance or play cards. Palace guards and King's Riders are among them, some surveying the space as if the Shadow would openly drink in a tavern. *Fucking idiots*. Others partake in the drinks offered, though even through the shrouded glass, I watch as they make demands of things *not* offered.

Shen had been busy in her own tavern when I arrived, but in the note hidden in her apartment, she told me that she was handling the guards' presence well enough. It was affecting her ability to gather information, but she hadn't been harassed or encountered a situation in which she felt she was endangered. I had trained Shen in the same way I was doing with Aria, enough so that if she could lure a male to her apartment, there were enough weapons hidden within reach to easily kill him. She knew I would dispose of the body, no questions asked.

But, even with the task made more difficult, Shen had still come through with enough evidence on a newer target.

Kaito was his name, and Shen had only been made aware of him a week ago when a female so battered and mutilated that it took three separate baths to clean all of the blood off of her was found in the street just a few blocks away from the group home. The females who ran the charity reached out discreetly to Shen, believing that she used the profits from her bar to help supply them with whatever items they might need. My fingers had itched for my blades as I read what Shen said the victim experienced, everything from having the tips of her ears sliced off to being branded in multiple spots by an iron. It was horrific, and though there were so many foul *beasts* that needed my particular expertise, Shen had been able to learn where Kaito was going to be *tonight*.

And after *weeks* of being idle, of having my blades be all but *useless*, I desperately needed to watch the blood drain from an opened vein.

I observe the tavern most of the night, noting the guards as they leave and enter in batches, never once emptying the place entirely or leaving the street bare of their presence. Kaito doesn't leave either, and my frustration grows as the moon does above me, until it's resting at its highest point and I find my muscles aching from holding my position for so long. Tonight won't be the night I give Kaito the justice he deserves, and the thought that he'll have more time to terrorize another victim nearly has me leaping off this roof and storming into the bar, guards and consequences be damned.

That reckless line of thinking is my signal that it's time to go. My leg muscles shake as I slowly stand, checking the streets and alleyways that surround the structure to ensure no guards can see me. My back is still tender from Father Yamin's discipline, but the pain is a reminder of my purpose. Of that bigger goal.

Like the one I'm standing on, the neighboring roof is built with its highest point at the center, the tiles angling down on either side. Backing up, I eye the distance in the silver moonlight and, with a deep breath, launch into a sprint, covering the roof quickly and leaping a few inches from the edge. My arms windmill as I soar over the empty space between the structures and then land, tucking into a roll to minimize the sound of my weight colliding with the tiles. The hood of my cloak falls, and I quickly tug it back up before crouching and listening for any shouting or voices to indicate I've been spotted. When the streets retain the same low hum of noise, I stand back up and prepare to jump again.

Leaping from rooftop to rooftop, I'm not heading in the direction of the palace but towards my warehouse. It's become habit to check in on it now that so many of my father's men occupy Khargis. The space is *mine*, and finding another that can accommodate all the things I need it to would be a pain in my ass that I simply don't have time or patience for. Though guards patrol here as well, it's more thinned out as there is nothing but the façade of broken-down buildings and abandoned businesses. One day, this place might know glory under a different ruler, but for now, even in its current state, I'm grateful for the darker purpose it serves.

Climbing down to the ground, I creep to the edge of a dilapidated building, curling my fingers around the corner of the jagged stone and leaning forward to make sure the street is clear when voices halt me—one male and one female. I palm my curved blade as I duck behind the corner and wait, keeping my eyes peeled on the street.

"*Shut up!*" the male shouts, a whimper following in response.

"Please. *Please* let me go. I didn't know—" A loud *slap* silences the female, and my blood heats as my fingers tighten painfully around the hilt of my dagger. Leaning forward again, I watch as they come into view. A guard, tall and broad, his dark hair shorn close to his scalp and stark against the shine of the silver armor he wears, grasps a female by her arm, tugging her behind him while she cradles the side of her face.

"Stop talking, or I'll make it even *worse* for you."

My blood thrums beneath my skin. This isn't Kaito or any of the other targets I've been trying to get my hands on for weeks now, but surely, it isn't coincidence that a prime example of the filth I like to hunt appears *right* in front of my warehouse? A hedonistic smile breaks free beneath my mask as I begin to formulate my plan. Whether *divinely* placed in my path or not, it doesn't matter. Tonight, I'll *finally* scratch an itch that has spent far too long being ignored.

I had questioned my morality in the past when it comes to what I do, to the joy I take in it. Now, a certain pair of orange-hazel eyes annoyingly flickers to the forefront of my mind and brings with them the question of what *she* would think about this. Stupid considering that once our time is done, I will never see her again.

"Isn't this the part where you threaten me?" the guard asks from where he hangs when he finally wakes. I had knocked him out and then given the female information for the group home before dragging him, armor and all, into the warehouse. Stripped of it now, he watches me as I tilt my head, my fingers dancing along the outside of my thigh.

"Is that what they tell you the Shadow does?" I counter, adopting a male voice. The light of a nearby flame gem cascades over his face, revealing him to be a rather handsome male.

"You'd be surprised what the king knows about you," he says, and I scoff. That prompts a laugh from him, the chain he's hanging from rattling in a way that briefly pulls me back to the temple with Father Yamin. I yank my dagger free, if only to let the cool dragon stone hilt tether me back to the present. "That's what he's counting on. You underestimating him. Underestimating *us*."

"You cannot underestimate that which is not a threat to begin with. After all, it was fairly easy to catch you, wasn't it?" He says nothing, only closing his eyes as the corners of his mouth draw up.

"So go on, then. Do whatever it is you need to do to try and get information from me. It will be pointless, just so you know," he drawls, opening his eyes when he hears my footsteps. "I'm afraid I'm just a lowly grunt without the clearance to know anything of value."

I click my tongue as I walk behind him, dragging the tip of my blade against his back, only a thin undershirt preventing the cold metal from splitting his skin. My own arms break out in goosebumps at the thought, and I keep walking until I'm at his side, his head turning to look down at me. "I could do all of those things if I wanted to, but I'm guessing the king didn't let you in on this *one* little fact about *me*."

"And what is that?" My blood heats at the mirth still in his voice. Just like Sir Dae, there's a defiance in him that I ache to snuff out.

Reaching up, I undo the mask covering the lower half of my face before pulling down my hood. The guard's eyes widen as he takes me in, his gaze running down the length of my body twice while his mouth works to pull words from his brain. Only stuttering noises come out.

I drop my voice modification. "Sometimes, I don't capture and torture fae for information." He heaves a shuddering breath when I twist the tip of my blade into the soft spot between his ribs. Smiling up at him, I revel in the way fear finally alights in his eyes. "Sometimes, I do it just for fun."

Chapter One Hundred

MYLA

I BREATHE EASIER AS I walk through the forest towards the dragon fields, the trees having shed most of their leaves in preparation for the impending winter. They crunch beneath my boots despite the lighter steps I take as I reach the edge of the treeline, and the expanse of the mountain base and the field next to it come into view.

I had taken my time in the basement of my warehouse, finally releasing that invisible weight that had been slowly crushing me the past few weeks. Despite the cocky way in which he promised he knew nothing, I *had* learned something new from the guard. There is to be a celebration in the coming weeks that will call some of the guards out of Khargis and back to the palace. He didn't know *why* or *what* the celebration was in name of, and unless my father created a new holiday, I can't think of anything before the winter solstice that would merit both festivity and an increased guard presence. Then again, perhaps that wasn't so out of the ordinary. I had recently learned that not only was my father kidnapping *mages*, he was trying to repair broken bonds with dragons. Or form new ones with Bali and likely Sunis. He had increased patrols of our borders in what Navin and I could only assume was a desperate attempt to find more mages.

Walking across the loose gravel that leads to Sunis and Bali's cave, my gaze skims over the dragon fields. They are dark, the mist hanging lower than usual as it partially obscures my view. But even with what I *can* see, something notable is missing from the grassy area: burning remains. It isn't until I've reached the mouth of the cave that I realize there is also an *unnatural* stillness in the air, making the hair at the back of my neck lift. Palming my dagger, I prowl closer, narrowing my eyes to help them adjust to the darkness as I peer inside.

"Bali!" I shout, my voice bouncing off the cave walls in a way that sends my heart galloping in my chest.

No resounding growl or adjusting of leathery wings answers, just more of that unnerving silence. It isn't completely unusual that they are both gone, as occasionally they've gone out together to hunt or simply stretch their wings. But there's a sinking feeling in my gut that I can't explain, one that propels me away from the cave and onto the dragon fields. I don't have to walk far before the scent of rotting meat hits my nose. Reaching into my pocket, I pull out my small flame gem from its pouch, its light dimmer than usual but enough to see about a foot ahead of me, where the scattered and half-charred bodies of goats and sheep lay.

"Shit," I whisper, inching closer and looking for any sign of the belladragis. My stomach reacts, attempting to purge itself at the rotten smell of the meat, but I get close and sniff the air anyway, searching for that pungent floral, acrid scent among the decay. Squatting lower in front of one of the goats, I close my eyes and focus on my next inhale, and there, layered between the ever-present brimstone scent and that of putrefaction, is just a hint of the belladragis. I look at the carcasses that dot the darkened field, my stomach sinking. It can't be coincidence that there are no burning remains mixed among the tainted meat.

Standing I pocket my flame gem, anger forcing my nails to bite into my palms. My father had taken them. Was likely trying to *bond* them, and I have no fucking clue where they could—

Spinning on my heel, I run back towards the forest, fury pushing my legs faster. *I* may not know where the dragons have been taken, but I am sure there is someone who does.

❧❧❧❧❧ ❧❧❧❧❧

"Let me get this straight," my brother says as he paces blindly in front of the couch in our sitting room, his hands pressed over his eyes. "You think that Bali and Sunis were taken by our father to the same place they are doing the experiments with the mages—"

"That is what I said."

"Don't interrupt," he growls, still pacing. Still covering his face. "And you want to sneak into where they are doing said experiments to try and *rescue* Sunis because even though you haven't bonded, you consider her to be your dragon?"

"She *is* my dragon," I say sharply, looking up at him from where I'm sitting on the couch.

Navin drops the hands over his eyes, letting his arms turn into dead weight as they hit his sides and he turns to face me. Not wearing a tunic, I can see the scars he's collected over the many decades breaking up the colorful tattoos that otherwise cover his upper body. The two most prominent are that of a blue dragon, its wingspan wide over one half of his chest as if mid-flight while the tail trails down and wraps around his torso, and the goddess Solana over the other half, her hands outstretched much like they had been on the statue depicting her in the temple. I have given up asking him to explain why, of all things he wanted permanently inked on his skin, he would choose one of the deities Father Yamin weaponized against us. Against *me*. Navin had never given me a straight answer, and I suppose for all the secrets I both asked him to keep and kept from him, I shouldn't be annoyed that he would have one of his own.

Beneath the goddess, however, is something new. Not a tattoo, but a wound. White gauze starts on the front of his stomach and wraps around his side, the large piece held in place by tape that winds around the width of his torso. "What happened?" I ask, jutting my chin out towards it.

He looks down, long raven locks spilling past his shoulder as he does. Shaking his head, he mumbles, "Training," and then strides to the armchair where a dark top is laid across the back. I don't miss the way he grimaces as he tugs it on, and though I know my brother can handle himself, my teeth still grit together in anger. "Myla, you aren't asking me to help you traipse into a secret room in the palace. This is *different*."

"Technically, I'm not asking you to help me at all."

"Yeah," he huffs, folding his arms over his chest. "You're just asking me to tell you where the dragons are and then to pretend I don't know you are going to rush there and get yourself killed."

I give him a deadpan stare. "Tell me where they are."

"No. No, I'm not going to."

Standing from the couch, I prowl towards him, my lips in a grim line.

"Is that supposed to intimidate me, Little Sister?" he asks, though I don't miss the way he adjusts his stance closer to where his weapons are on the table to his right. "Don't forget, I trained you."

"I'm a hundred years old. Calling me 'little sister' is an insult to us both. And you may have trained me, but it's been a long time since you've seen me fight." I stop a foot in front of him, fingers tapping along the hilt of my dagger. The one I stole from our father. Navin's gaze drops to it, and despite the seriousness of our discussion, the left side of his mouth curves up.

"You don't outgrow being a little sister—"

"*Navin*." He doesn't shrink from me, he never has, but he hardens his own shields. While I may have taunted him with my dagger, he knows my tongue can cut sharper than any blade. Guilt and shame slam into me, reminding me that I've made the only person who has ever cared about me enough to risk his life build a shield to protect himself from my ire. But I've already accepted the fact that I'm a lost cause when it comes to being decent. Navin deserves better, and the only way I can pay him back for all he's done for me is to give him the freedom I know he wants.

And I need my fucking dragon to do that.

"Glare at me all you want. Curse me out and tell me you wish I were dead. It's not going to matter." His chest heaves, and my withered heart clenches at the way his face contorts into something tortured. "You may have a death wish, but I care about your life enough for the both of us. So you can fuck right off."

I blink at his brashness, momentarily stunned as I watch him run a hand through his hair.

"Was that too much?" he finally asks, breaking the stilted silence.

"No," I answer, tilting my head back as I blow out a breath. "Though I *appreciate* what you've said, Navin, I have to go."

"*Why?*" It's a question that comes out as a plea. "Why can't you let this go?"

Maybe it's the exhaustion that lingers over me like the faint mists that coat our kingdom, but I don't want to have this fight. Not when each second that ticks by could be Sunis's last as an unbonded dragon. Leveling my gaze again with his, I drop my own shields.

"Not everyone has someone like *you* to rescue them," I begin. Navin's eyes widen, his body stilling as he doesn't even dare to breathe too loudly. "For most in Khargis, there is no one to help them. No one to force them to greet each day with a new sense of purpose after they were sure there was nothing left to live for. When Daiya—" I trip over my own words, my brain used to shutting all thoughts of her down. But I force them out. For Navin's sake. For Sunis's. "When she lied about us being in love after we were caught—when she so easily convinced everyone that I forced her to be with me—it began a chain of events that would leave me angry that I woke up each morning to face an existence where I was so sure *no one* wanted me. I felt ashamed. Unworthy. *Unclean* in my own body. In my own *head*. If you had not recognized that I was sinking beneath the surface, I would have drowned. In Khargis, so many get put through *horrific* things, and they have no one else to help them but the Shadow."

"What you see as me running towards my death is actually me saving myself from it. This is my purpose, and without it, I have *nothing*. But I can enact more change if I become the true heir. If I bond a dragon, the first female ever to do so, and show our father the impossible. After all, his precious gods *surely* wouldn't allow a bond to happen unless it was supposed to." The last statement is given with sarcastic flair, and Navin smiles. "And I get to free you from being trapped in a position you did not ask for."

His gaze softens as he reaches out a hand to awkwardly pat my shoulder. "You don't have to do anything for me. I'm happy to be in this role if it helps keep you safe."

I lay my hand over his, squeezing it once before letting it go. "But this isn't just about me, Navin. Or you. It's so much bigger than that."

He nods, bringing his hand to his face as he covers his mouth in contemplation. "Well, fuck," he curses, shaking his head. "I suppose I can't argue with any of that."

For the first time since my last meeting with Aria, the corner of my mouth quirks. Navin eyes it, a victorious look settling over him. *Idiot.*

"I'm not going to tell you where it is." Anger immediately floods my veins, and I lift my upper lip in a snarl as I take a step towards him, my fist raised. "Because," he drawls, walking over to the desk in the corner and sliding a piece of paper and pen over. "I'm going to *show* you."

I open my mouth in protest, but it snaps shut at the serious look he sends me.

"I'm going with you. That's the deal. We do this together." Seeing the conflict in my eyes, he amends his statement. "We do *just* this together. I'm not asking to interfere with your vigilante enterprise. But you *are* my little sister, and regardless of how fearsome I know you are, I'm using my leverage as your brother to bully you into this."

I grit my teeth but relent, giving him a curt nod. "*Fine.* How do you even know about where he is keeping them?"

Navin shrugs, far too casually. "When I found out about the mages, he offered to show me where it was happening." Something bitter rises up my throat before I can stop it at the notion that Navin didn't even need to *ask* for information. That our father viewed him as valuable enough to tell him outright. He claps his hands together once before waving me over as he begins to draw a map. "Now, let's discuss how to break into one of our kingdom's best kept secrets."

Chapter One Hundred and One

MYLA

KING KAMON RYUU, RULER of the fae, has a fucking *compound* northeast of the palace, hidden within a mountain range where the mist coats the peaks in near perpetuity. And even if it didn't, King's Riders patrol the air in shifts so it's never left unguarded. It's impenetrable. Or it would be, if not for Navin.

"I don't like this plan," he says for what has to be the fifth time as we walk down the corridor towards our rooms after having early evening tea with our mother. The idea was mine, to ensure that people saw both of our faces today before we left for the remainder of the evening. Navin had told our mother that I would be entering a night of prayer not at the temple attached to the palace but at one located on the *holy grounds*. A place that, allegedly, had been the very spot where the Fae Kingdom was born into existence by the touch of Khaos. The brethren had built a temple over the land and required yearly visits for all royalty and nobility. Everyone else was banned from even setting foot in the area. But Navin had promised our mother that he would take me there and ensure I spent the proper time in the reverent place. It is utter shit, but she bought the lie easily.

Now, preparing to leave, I ask him questions about the compound, including if he knows how many mages are being kept with the dragons there. He shrugs his shoulders sheepishly, offering me a crooked grin. "I haven't needed to know."

"I'm not asking because I'm going to judge you. I'm simply trying to learn information." I'm not there to free the mages or interfere with whatever they were doing with the dragons and their bonds—not yet anyway. My main objective is to get Sunis out, Bali as well if she is there.

We enter the corridor to our wing, rounding a final corner and immediately coming to a halt. The beads of my veil hit each other with a tinkling sound, and through them, I stare at where Father Yamin stands in the center of the hallway.

"Divine Father," Navin says, lowering into a bow that I do not duplicate. "How are you today?"

"Ah, Prince Navin, I am basking in yet another lovely day that our beloved Khaos has given us." His smile is reedy as he shifts his gaze to me. "And Princess Myla. Where are the two of you being called to?" My name is said with disdain, and I smirk beneath my veil and mask at the way he looks like he wants to repent after being so *cordial* towards me. I wait for Navin to answer for us.

"Actually, Princess Myla and I are off to the holy grounds to pray. We haven't gone yet this year, and it seems like the perfect time to ensure we stay connected with our gods."

The father has a good enough straight face to hide his initial reaction, except for his fingers flexing where they hold a scroll of parchment paper, making it crinkle. "That is wonderful to hear. Though, perhaps, it might be best for me to join the princess." His robe flutters as he walks closer, the soft soles of his leather slippers whispering against the tile. I keep myself still as he rakes his gaze over me, like he is sure if he just ripped off the teal dress I am wearing, he'd see all my secrets spread out on my body beneath. Ironic, considering the only story my body conveys is the one *he* beat into my flesh.

"I know you and the king have much planned for today, and I would not want to draw attention from His Majesty's most important business. I'm happy to take my sister. Happy that she wants to try redeeming herself in the eyes of the gods." I have to give my brother credit, he can sound convincing when he needs to.

"Then I hope it is a worthwhile visit for you both." With a final glare shot at me, he pushes between us, continuing down the hall and out of sight.

"Asshole," Navin whispers. I say nothing as we resume walking, entering our sitting room. "You have ten minutes."

"I only need five." Shutting the door to my bedroom, I take down my veil, tossing the garment to the floor. The dress comes off next followed by the chemise until I'm standing in only my undergarments and staring at a fresh pair of leathers and a matching cloak. The unease Father Yamin conjured with his presence calms the further dressed I get. By the time my hood is over my head, the dragon insignia on my shoulder clasped to my leather vest, my thoughts are clearer. Securing my blades, I let out a contented sigh before exiting.

I find Navin in the final stages of strapping his swords to his back, his own cloak flowing down from his shoulders in the same onyx shade as my own. Glancing up at me, he smiles as he draws a hand down his front. "Not to brag, but I think I look better."

"Not to brag, but I think I look scarier."

He barks out a laugh and nods. "That you do. Do you have your weapons?"

I tap the sides of my vest and the blade at my thigh.

"Then let's go." Navin opens the glass slider, allowing me to pass before he shuts it behind him. The sun is low, the sky a deep blue shade blended with lavender. "I locked the door to the sitting room, so if Leesi or anyone else gets curious while we're gone, they shouldn't be able to get in right away. Hopefully, they'll think we locked it on our way out to the temple." He climbs over the balcony railing first, edging around it until the landing platform on the side of the mountain comes into view. His leap to it is fluid, and I follow suit, landing next to him a moment later. "I *definitely* looked better."

I send my fist into his arm, earning a chuckle that draws a small smirk of my own beneath my mask. Navin lets out a series of high-pitched whistles, the call to Lan paired with pushing his intentions down the bond. Lan's claws dig into the platform as he lands a few minutes later, his weight causing it to shake a little as it creaks. Without a word, we climb onto his blue-scaled back, and I clutch the leather strap tightly as he soars into the air. "The guards on the southern end will find themselves preoccupied with a distraction at their shift change. There will be a marginally small window where we should be able to land, and then you can hide, while I make sure we won't be caught."

I tap his arm in acknowledgement before leaning back and looking out over the side of Lan as he flies in the layer of mist that rises above the mountains. Small black peaks jut out within it, but Lan expertly navigates so that we don't come anywhere close to hitting them.

After thirty minutes, Lan dips through the mist, right on the southern edge of the compound. Navin tenses in front of me, eyes scanning the sky in either direction. Though two riders on a dragon is rare, it isn't completely unheard of, particularly with dragon bonds fading. With my hood and mask, I might not get questioned as to why I'm riding with Navin when I'm in the same leathers he is. But though my physique bares the evidence of nearly a decade of training, I'm nowhere near as thick as most of the males in the guard and King's Riders. If someone looked close enough, they'd figure out I was female.

Hovering forward to fight against the pull of gravity as we dive, I squint my eyes against the rush of cold air until we level out, Lan's wings catching as they expand wide and we move into a glide. Right into empty air space. Navin's exhale is loud, even against the gusts of wind surrounding us.

When Lan tips to the side to find an inconspicuous spot to land, I get a good look at the compound in the last dredges of sunset. Large buildings are built both into and away from the mountainside, guards and their dragons meandering in the outdoor spaces between them. Keeping to the outskirts, Navin guides Lan down between two of the structures, its width only *just* large enough for us to fit. The landing is jarring, my entire body rattling with the movement as my brother leans over and whispers something to his dragon. The beast rumbles low in his throat in response.

We wait in silence to see if we've been spotted, my hand going to the blade at my thigh on instinct. It smells strongly of sulfur, but there is something else mixed with it. I sniff again at the air, picking up the metallic scent just as Navin leans back and says, "It's all the magic here. It has a unique smell."

"Mage magic?" I clarify, to which he nods.

"In my scoping of this place last week, I learned that this structure to the left holds the dragons that have just arrived. And this one to the right is where the mages are held."

"How are they transporting the knocked-out dragons?"

"They attach harnesses and have a team of dragons fly them out. The King's Riders ensure the space is clear for them once they've captured one." Navin stands, holding out a hand that I ignore as I join him. Lan wiggles his body slightly as he turns to look over his shoulder at me. My eyes narrow when he does it again, and I swear the fucking dragon looks on the edge of laughing as I throw my arms out to balance myself.

"*Rat*," I hiss out through my teeth.

"Enough, children," Navin says, sending Lan a disapproving look. The dragon chuffs and returns his gaze to the landscape in front of us. "A mighty beast and a feared vigilante fighting as if they are toddlers."

"Where is *my* dragon?" I ask, changing the subject.

"I don't know. I haven't been here in nearly a week." He reaches behind him and slides one of the two swords that cross over his back free, the blade slender and gleaming silver. "Here. Just in case. Do you remember how to use it?"

I rotate the sword in my hand, its light weight perfectly tailored for precision. "It's been a while since I've held a blade like this." Daggers are easier to transport, less cumbersome to move with. "But you don't have to worry about me, Brother." Moving to slide down Lan, I'm stopped by Navin with a hand on my arm.

"Remember the plan, Myla. Find a spot to hide in the enclosure holding the dragons and *wait* for me. Once I'm sure the area is secure enough for us to search for Sunis without getting caught, I will join you, and we will look for your dragon together." His eyes bore into mine, their shade infused with more gray than black as we wills me to agree. I nod, and his shoulders relax. "I'll be back soon." He waits for me to climb down, and I feel his gaze on my back as I edge along the black dragon stone building, its exterior smooth beneath my free hand. When I finally reach the front, I hear Lan take off and watch as they rise into the sky before disappearing to the other side of the compound.

Gripping tightly to the sword, I eye the front of the building as I cautiously walk towards its entrance. Calling it such feels like a misnomer, considering the *entrance* is just a fucking hole in the facade large enough to fit a dragon Bali's size through. With the sun gone, I stick close to the edges of the structure, a shadow blending into the onyx.

Rounding the very edge of the enclosure's opening, I slip in without issue, my eyes taking a moment to adjust to the dim lighting. The air is warmer here and thick with a myriad of smells, all of them unpleasant. Edging against the inner wall, I take in every detail I can see beneath the sparsely lit torches. The inside is round and carved *deeply* into the mountain in a feat that must have taken *decades* to accomplish. My steps falter when I realize that the dark heaps set between more standing torches at the center of the enclosure are fucking *dragons*. The hum of their snoring vibrates the air, and an uneasy feeling slithers down my spine as I get close enough to take in the first one.

A metal cuff is attached to each foot that I can see, chains thicker than my forearm looping together and connecting to a stake as thick as a tree trunk into the stone floor. A muzzle made of metal and stone is strapped to the dragon's snout, preventing it from breathing fire with any sort of efficiency. I take a step closer to the dragon—its green color indicating it's predominantly from the Hiravar line, though striations of black flow on its side—and I'm hit with the pungent smell of belladragis. It makes saliva gather at the back of my throat. An empty metal basin sits to the dragon's right, the opening wide enough that it can dip its entire caged mouth in to get a drink of what was likely the tainted water.

I push forward to the next dragon and then the next, the color of their scales indicating they aren't Sunis. But the scene is the same for every beast I visit; dragons are chained and drugged, awaiting whatever methods my father has mapped out for the mages to use. The scent of the paralytic plant grows stronger the deeper I traverse into the cavern, completely abandoning Navin's commands to *stay put*.

I had never done well at following instructions anyway.

Despite the cargo this enclosure holds, I only spot a handful of guards. The king has no reason to worry that this place will be infiltrated. It's a fucking suicide mission to even try.

Metal scrapes against stone, and I duck behind a water basin set between two knocked-out dragons as a guard leisurely walks up to the one closest to me. "Hey!" he shouts, his voice booming as it echoes out. "Look at this!"

Without waiting for his companion to answer, he begins to climb the sleeping dragon's side. I slink deeper into the shadow cast by the basin, holding my sword at an angle in front of my body to try and keep it hidden. Dragons have always been treated with the utmost respect because they were supposed to be gifts from the gods specifically to the fae. It's why no other kingdom commands them. Why no other being can bond with them.

Laughing rings out, another male voice taunting the guard now pumping his arms over his head as he begins to jump on the slumbering dragon. "It's the only way you'll ever ride one of the beasts."

"Fuck you. I'll get a dragon soon. Especially after the king is done messing with them." He squats down, fingers scraping down the dragon's scales. "There's that young black dragon we just got in. Bali's offspring. Maybe I'll take that one."

To make this male bleed would be a *gift*, and I consider leaping up and sliding my blade across his throat before I calm myself. While it would satiate the need to shut him up, it would also alert the others to my presence. I was already breaking my word to Navin by venturing in here without him. I suppose I should at least *try* to keep the casualties low until I get to my dragon.

"I think the king wants her for something else." The second voice grows closer, and steady my breathing as my fingers flex around the sword's hilt.

"Well what can he do if I bond her first?" The male jumps off of the blue dragon's back, his armor clanging together when he lands. "We've got another mage test to get ready for—there's a fresh batch of them, I hear—but after that? I'm bonding that fucking dragon, even if I have to keep her drugged in order to do it." Laughing, they carry on with whatever it is they are supposed to be doing.

Once they move out of earshot, I slink deeper into the cavern until I'm so far back that I can no longer see the monstrous opening at the front. I pause when I finally spot Sunis, relief sweeping through me until I catch sight of the muzzle and chains. Then my eyes move to the right, and I grit my teeth together *hard*.

Sunis is here, and she isn't alone.

Chapter One Hundred and Two

MYLA

SUNIS BUCKS AT HER chains, her roars smothered by the restraint clamped around her snout as she tries to back away from the guards surrounding her. My blood roars in my ears as I watch them close in, every instinct within me *screaming* to go to her. But two things grab hold of the rationality that now feels volatile within me: Sunis might be injured, and until I assess that she is okay to fly out of here, I will have to be strategic about how I kill these males since I have no clue when Navin will join me. And the other is the fact that Bali lies next to her, completely motionless.

Sunis is old enough to not need her mother, but the two have remained close, challenging the knowledge I had read about when it came to parent and offspring relationships between dragons. If Bali is critically injured, I do not believe my dragon will leave her behind.

Inching closer, I hide behind a cart filled with medical supplies as I count ten guards surrounding her, not including the males I had passed on my way back here. My hand runs over the two blades tucked into their slots on my vest, a matching pair on the other side. If I can manage to draw a guard or two into the dark corner behind Bali, I can kill them quickly there without drawing attention right away.

"Can't we give her some more belladragis?" one shouts, swinging his blade in Sunis's direction when she attempts to lunge for him, the chains clanging loudly at her ankles.

"The king says the dragons need to be awake when the mage comes again," another responds, his voice deep as he steps in front of the others gathered. I take note of the insignia stamped on the front of his armor, near his right shoulder, that signifies he is a commander of the King's Riders. "She'll tire out eventually, and maybe this time, the mage magic will work to bond her." My jaw clenches as I slip out from behind the cart and dart towards Bali, all the guards' attention on Sunis in front of me. Steps light, I reach Bali's side and take in her slumbering form. Her breaths are labored, her chest rising and falling slowly as the scent of belladragis sits heavily in the air. My boot scuffs against a handful of broken stone pieces on the ground as I crouch low. *The perfect distraction.* Scooping a few up, I wait until the guards have quieted their conversations and toss them against the wall behind me.

The guard closest to Bali, his long black hair braided down his back, turns, eyes narrowing in my direction. "What was that?"

"What was what?" his companion asks, a male with a missing ear.

"I thought I heard a noise."

The commander steps between them, his own raven locks cut short with a few strands hanging over his forehead. "Do a patrol and ensure the space is empty," he says, eyes narrowing. "Last thing we need is an escaped mage hiding back here." The two nod, placing both hands on their swords as they begin to prowl in Bali's—in *my*—direction.

"What do we do if we find one?" the guard with the missing ear asks.

The commander smirks, lifting his own sword. "Keep them alive, but show them what happens when they disobey." The commander turns and joins the other seven guards who have backed away from a still aggravated Sunis.

Staying low, I watch as the guards split, one going towards Bali's tail while the other goes towards her head. I follow the first, tossing another chunk of stone so that it bounces on the ground and draws the male's attention in the opposite direction. Launching into a sprint, I leap over Bali's tail and land behind the guard, weapon already swinging around his front. He doesn't have time to do more than quickly inhale before my sword is slicing across his throat.

His shock keeps him held in place even as his knees wobble beneath him. Wrapping my free arm around his torso, I slowly lower him to the ground just as he releases his sword, the clang of metal hitting the stone making me wince. But Sunis rattles her own chains in a moment of serendipitous luck, drowning out the alert that the guard is dead.

Searching for the other guard, I catch a glint of his silver armor near Bali's head and crouch back down, pulling a short dagger from its place at my vest. I have never been perfectly precise with throwing blades as I've always preferred an up close and personal kill. But my luck with not being spotted will run out soon enough, so I wait until the guard with the missing ear is close enough that the margin of error should be fairly low, then stand and send the blade sailing through the air.

Unfortunately, it doesn't embed itself in his neck like I'm aiming for but in his *eye*. "Fuck," I growl, boots pounding against the stone as I run, Navin's crimson tipped sword held firm in my grasp. It takes a moment for him to realize what's happened, his hand reaching up to pat at his face and the blood now streaming down it. His mouth opens to scream, the first note of his panic filling the distance between us before I'm there, metal slicing through his throat without resistance. He cuts off with a gurgle of blood as he falls to his knees, my arms reaching out to catch him before laying him down.

Heart pounding in my chest, I move closer to Bali and watch as two guards break from the group, mumbling something about the king. With six remaining, I plan out my route of attack, edging to the water basin next to one of the stakes holding Bali's chains. The sound of fabric rustling plays to my left, and I spin with my blade lifted on instinct only to see the same blade held up across a broad chest mirrored back at me.

"*I told you to fucking wait.*" *Navin.* I take in the blood already painting his sword and the small flecks of it that dot the front of his chest as he tugs his mask down. "Gods above, Myla, what are you doing?" he whisper-yells, guiding us down into a crouch.

I pull down my mask so he can hear my whisper. "They are going to attempt to make Sunis bond. I need to get her out before they bring in more mages."

"Father is already in the next compound picking out mages to come," he says, shaking his head as his gaze moves to the guards spread out in front of Sunis. His eyes narrow. "Fuck, that is Commander Anya. He's one of the more *brutal* of the King's Riders—"

"Do not worry about him," I cut in, angling my body so I can see them all more clearly. "There are these eight plus another few at the front—"

"I took care of them."

My brows rise at the challenging look he sends me. "I took care of two over there," I say, tossing a thumb over my shoulder. "We need to kill them and unlock Sunis's chains."

"Anya likely has the keys as the one in command, but he's not going to be easy to best." Tense silence passes as we observe the guards. I'm fully prepared for Navin to warn that this is too much of a risk, and begin to form my own plan on how to take the guards down. Instead, he says, "You attack from the right, and I'll come in from the left. Kill quickly to get to the commander but keep him alive."

I smile as I tug my mask back up, my nerve endings alight with the anticipation of the kill. "I can handle all of them alone if need be."

He moves his own mask into place. "I was able to sneak up on you."

"That's different," I murmur, annoyed. "You trained me."

He lets out a quiet snort. "Sunis, huh?" *Fuck.* I hadn't realized I let her name slip with him. When I don't answer, he gives another quiet laugh. "It's a cute name. Don't die."

With that, we separate, Navin darting left as I take a path to the right, my steps quick. Rotating my blade, I lift my arm high as I make my way to the guard closest to me, the unsuspecting male only able to glance over his shoulder before I drive my sword in the gap between his front and back armor pieces. It doesn't kill him right away, and his shout plunges the room into chaos as my presence is made known.

Drawing the sword out, I slide it against his neck, the sight of blood spurting from the wound all I see before I'm moving on. The next guard has a dark beard that frames his jaw, and he rushes at me with fervor, raising his arms over his head as he prepares to strike. I duck and spin, kicking him in his chest before he has a chance to bring the sword down. Another guard appears, his eyes feral as shouts sound a few feet away, announcing Navin's arrival on the other side.

I tug a dagger from my vest and launch it in the direction of the newest male coming for me, elation soaring when the blade hits him directly in the throat. He falls, and I turn and lift my sword above me, blocking the swing of the guard I had kicked. "You're no mage," he says, gritting his teeth as he dances back, sliding a hand down to where a short sword is strapped to his belt.

I stop him with a flick of my third dagger, the blade implanting itself at his wrist with a wet thud. His screams echo out as I spin, adjusting my hold on the hilt so that the sword is angled straight down. Then I drive the blade right into his torso at his shoulder, watching his eyes widen in fear before his lids fall and he goes limp. Kicking him away as I draw my blade out, my chest heaves with exertion as I turn and find Navin engaged in a battle with Commander Anya.

My brother is as quick as I am, his movements graceful and fluid. A male with a gift for killing who wants to avoid it at all costs. But the commander is a worthy foe, and when his blade catches the outside of Navin's arm, I run towards them to help.

Sunis lets out a wailing sort of growl, one higher pitched as it rattles the cavern around us. But I don't spare her a look, not as I watch the commander send his fist into Navin's jaw, tugging his mask down while silver arcs the air. I remind myself that Navin wants him alive, but as my brother stumbles backwards, I find that I'd rather see a commander my father loves *dead*. I don't need him to be alive to take the keys to Sunis's chains.

I'm sure I've got him as I run towards his exposed back, but then he turns sharply and blocks my incoming attack, his strength evident in the return swing of his sword. I leap back and then charge forward again, engaging in a dance with him that causes metal to sing as our blades meet. Navin enters the fray again, his cloak snapping at his heels as we work in tandem to bring him down.

"Does the king know his son is a traitor?" Anya grunts, breaths labored.

"He won't ever find out," Navin answers, driving his sword forward. Anya dodges it, dropping and sending a kick my way before silver flashes and Navin arches back to avoid being sliced open. I find my balance again, sweat dripping down my spine as I lunge forward, only for my blade to slide against Anya's armor.

"It won't stop what is coming. You know this." The last part is said to Navin. My brother growls as he dances forward, his brow gleaming as shorter strands of hair stick to it. I pivot and reach for the remaining blade in my vest, ready to draw this asshole's blood. "The gods are finally showing us that we have reached their good graces again. The stain of your sister will no longer be something we suffer for."

Navin shouts as he swings his blade, and before I can get my dagger flipped and ready to throw, he is backing the commander up, fury etched in his expression in a way I so rarely see from him. "Fuck you, and fuck what you think about *her*." His movements are quick, and then his sword is painted in the blood of Commander Anya, the male standing for only a few seconds before he tips over and collapses to the ground.

Navin shuts his eyes as he exhales roughly, running a blood-stained hand through his hair. But I'm already kneeling at the commander's body, searching for the keys. I finally find them tucked into the pockets of his trousers. Together, Navin and I run towards Sunis, knowing that I have no way to communicate with her efficiently without the bond. That knowledge doesn't stop me from yelling her name, and her eyes immediately fall to mine, narrowing into slits as she growls beneath her metal muzzle.

Though she still pulls at the chains, she lets me get near enough to get a good look at the first cuff. The iron bands around the width of her ankle completely, locking in place by way of four latches. I go to reach for the first one and Sunis growls low in her throat, prompting my gaze back to hers. "I'm going to free you," I tell her, presuming it yet again pointless but surprised when she doesn't move her foot away from me. There are four keys on the ring, and only by pure luck do I happen to guess the right one. It slides easily into the first lock, the click ringing out as it pops open.

I move down the line of latches, and once I unlock the last one, I unclasp them and begin to pull on the cuff before Sunis realizes that leg has been freed and shakes it the rest of the way off, nearly hitting me in the process.

When she sets her foot back down, it's a tentative movement but my search doesn't show any injury. I make quick work of the cuff on her other front leg before moving to the ones in the back until all that remains is the cage over her snout. As if understanding this is the last barrier to her freedom, Sunis's head lowers to a height I can reach just as a flurry of new voices infiltrate the enclosure.

Chapter One Hundred and Three

MYLA

I QUICKLY SHOVE A key into one of the latches of the muzzle, but it jams, not pushing far enough in to unlock it.

Sunis's wings flare as she stomps her feet, a muffled roar blasting heat past me. I tug at the stuck key with a frustrated growl, my adrenaline making my muscles shake and focus blur.

"They're coming," Navin says unhelpfully.

Sunis jerks against the restraint, tugging the stuck key from me and nearly knocking me down in the process. Behind us, dragons begin to stir, the sound of their claws lazily scraping against stone only making Sunis more restless. Her head snaps to the side, her gaze locking on where her mother still lies motionless, in a sleep somehow deeper than the others. Did the mages already get to her? Force her to bond with someone new after two hundred years?

"Sunis, come here," I coax, my voice harsh enough to draw her gaze back down to me. "Let me get it off of you." The keys dangle on the key ring as she swings her head side to side, the movement slowing until she finally lowers back down. My fingers wrap around the cold metal at the base of the key, and I brace a foot against the muzzle as I tug as hard as I can. It finally budges, sending me stumbling backwards, and right into Navin's steady hand at my shoulder. Reaching for the next key on the ring, I quickly slide it into the lock. The click that rings out is satisfying, but I don't get the chance to celebrate it. The voices behind us grow louder as I slip the key into the second latch, and then the third.

"Fuck, Myla—"

"We can do it."

The fourth and final latch pops open, and I drop the keys to the ground as Navin and I pull the two halves apart, creating enough space for Sunis to shake her head. The muzzle crashes to the stone as it falls from her, her answering mighty roar reverberating through the air. The jostling of chains and dragon chuffs join the cacophony, and when I turn around, I spot the owners of the voices we heard moving directly towards us. The guards and King's Riders are far enough away still that their faces are nondescript, but that won't be the case soon enough.

"Let's go." I look over at Bali, but the black dragon must have been given a massive dose of belladragis, because despite everything that's transpired, she's still asleep. I tamp down the urge to unlock her chains. I can't do anything to help her right now, but I *can* get Sunis out. "Come on—"

"Myla—"

"What?" I snap, bracing myself as I reach for my discarded sword, eyeing the blades I threw but deciding to leave them embedded in the bodies they felled. Navin gestures for me to look back, and when I do, I find Sunis with her head lowered and her eyes *glowing*. Not with the normal yellow hue that all dragons have a variation of but with *white*. Pure, glittering white illuminates the entirety of her eyes, the gleam so bright I have to squint. "What is happening?"

"It's the bond," Navin whispers, awe and disbelief heavy in his voice. "She wants to initiate the bond." My stomach flips, my fingers trembling as I let his words settle within me.

"Halt! By order of the king!"

Shit. I stare at Sunis, my hand aching to reach out and touch her, and I lift it about halfway before I take stock of the chaos around us. Spinning, I grab Navin and push him at Sunis. "You need to get on her and hide. Pull your mask up."

"I can't touch her when she's ready to bond. It could sever it completely." He shakes his head, tugging on his mask to show me that the fabric was shredded in his fight with Anya before reaching for a long dagger strapped to his belt. "Fuck, this is going to hurt." My eyes flare wide, but he moves too quickly for me to intercept, plunging the dagger into the side of his torso, letting out a yelp as he falls to his knees. "Go," he huffs out between labored breaths. His hand cups around the blade, putting pressure there. But it still leaks crimson, the sight inducing an unfamiliar amount of panic within me. "Myla, *go!*"

The footsteps of the running guards are right behind us now, and before I can second guess or allow myself to feel bad, I kick Navin at his shoulder, sending him sprawling backwards. If we're faking an attack, it needs to look fucking believable. Then I reach out for Sunis, my intent to climb up her leg and onto her back. But the moment I touch her, my entire world tilts. Black veils me on all sides, only peripheral white flashing as my stomach hollows to the sensation that I'm falling. Air rushes past me, the sound of it like when I'm flying on Lan's back as my hair stirs around a phantom wind, and then all at once, it stills, and there is nothing but darkness.

⁂

"Welcome, Myla Ryuu, Princess of the Fae, Shadow of Khargis, and the First Bonded."

A female's voice—soft and lilting—trickles in my ears. It carries with it a soft caress of fingers against my cheek and the scent of something light and floral—jasmine. Am I asleep in the cavern that Aria and I meet in? No. I had been in a different hollowed out space—the enclosure with Navin. Attempting to rescue Sunis.

"Open your eyes, Dragon Queen," the female says with another brush of gentle fingers. My mind is slow to catch up with what is happening. The voice and the touch. The fact that my eyes are even fucking closed. The information trickles to me one piece at a time. "Open," she coaxes again, just as something brushes over me, tickling my arms and legs.

Someone is touching me. *The thought wrenches my eyes open as I lurch up to sit, my curved blade already in my hand. My arm trembles with the anticipation of incapacitating someone, except I'm only met with an expanse of darkness. Darkness dotted with flecks of silver and white that glow as brilliantly as Sunis's eyes did and flicker as if they are breathing in the distance. It's a night sky, except I've never seen so many stars glow like this before.*

I twist my head, taking in more of the same scenery. Miles and miles of an unending night sky. It is beautiful and completely unnerving because I have no clue where the fuck *I am.*

"Hello, Myla."

A shiver races down my spine as I lift my blade in front of me, trying to stand but finding that my legs feel too heavy to move. The jasmine scent thickens, and when someone clears their throat behind me, I turn on my knees towards them, coming face to face with a pair of bright green eyes. "Who the fuck are you?" I ask on a breath as I take her in. Her fair skin is stark against the black satin dress she wears, the fabric reaching down to the tops of her feet. Golden hair frames her face, its soft waves cascading past her shoulders to her mid back. She stands perfectly straight, her expression somewhat serene as she looks at me. Pain throbs at my temples, my eyes narrowing as my palms begin to grow clammy. "I said, who the fuck—"

"I cannot answer, and we don't have time," she interrupts, taking a step towards me that I try—and fail—to move away from. The woman lifts her hand, and I'm pulled into a standing position, though nothing is visibly holding me up. "I have a message for you."

"A message?" My eyes scan past her to more of that same night sky in the distance. It's ethereal in its beauty, unlike anything I've ever seen in the Fae Kingdom.

Everything about this place is, including the female in front of me. "Oh, fuck,*" I whisper, realization hitting me as bluntly as a hilt to the temple. "I'm dead. I died while trying to bond with Sunis." Anger surges as I drop the hand holding the blade to my side, blowing out a frustrated breath. I would fucking* die *because of the bond. This place is my purgatory, an endless expanse of boring* nothingness *for me to suffer for eternity in.*

"You're not dead," she says, cutting into my thoughts, her tone amused. "And if it will help us move this conversation on more quickly, I will tell you that this place is a pocket of space between worlds."

I blink, my brows drawing low as I repeat her words in my head, somehow more confused than before. "Did you bring me here?"

"No. And yes." She lowers her hand just as I flip the dagger in my own. "You should know that you can't kill me here—" The dagger sings through the air as it flips tip over hilt, sailing through *the woman. She stares at me with less amusement than a moment ago, her lips pinched in a straight line. I look at the spot the dagger passed through her body, not so much as a scratch or hint of the blade cutting her.*

"Are you a goddess?" The question slips out, leaving room for fear to replace it within me. I did not believe in them, but wouldn't it be just my luck to fucking meet one upon death?

"Again, you are not dead, and we do not have time." She lowers her arm as her hands clasp in front of her, her fingers nervously flexing around each other. "When you bonded Sunis, the magic that forged that bond temporarily brought you out of Olymazi and to this place where I linger. But I am no goddess."

Questions rapidly fire off in my mind, and as if she can hear them all, the woman in front of me flinches. Wind begins to blow, coming from both nowhere and everywhere as it weaves through my hair and brushes over my face.

"We do not have a lot of time," she repeats softly, something aching within her tone.

"Then tell me this message of yours so I can go back home." Despite there being a weightlessness to my body, something heavy weighs on my chest and prickles the back of my head.

The woman slowly steps closer, her feet bare beneath her dress as she walks on nothing but air. "When she tells you to take her to the one named Rhea Maxwell, do not hesitate."

I shake my head, my vision blurring as a throaty growl rumbles around me. It isn't from a dragon, though it rattles my bones just the same.

The female's eyes are imploring as she repeats what she's said, though fear colors her words when a second voice—deeper and wholly male—barks at her to stop. My stomach pitches upwards again with the sensation of falling, only this time I actually am. I thrash my hands out in front of me, reaching for anything to stop myself as I tumble head over heels. My head grows dizzy and my temples pound, my bones weighing me down in a way I worry might make them pass through my skin. The stars blur until they turn back into those streaks of white light, darkness once more blanketing me while the sound of arguing voices murmur around me.

Then, as if I've been cut from a tether, there is nothing.

My eyes open with a start as I gasp, the lingering words from the woman playing in my ear as I try to blink away the night that surrounds me. Sweat makes the leathers I'm wearing stick to my skin, the oppressive heat coating every inch of me prompting me to sit up faster than I should. The world spins and my vision blurs, my temple throbbing in time with my heart. I suppress the urge to groan out at the way my entire body aches, as if I've spent sunup to sundown engaged in battle.

Battle.

I suck in a sharp breath at the word, reaching for the blade at my thigh as I remember where I was. What I was doing. *Navin.* I had left him in the cavern, left him to the guards coming because I had bonded—

Safe.

The word comes to me unbidden, a collection of emotion that centers in my mind as if someone carved out space and plopped it there. My eyes fall closed and I go to lean back, intending to get myself under control when my hands press against a smooth surface. One that *moves.* Turning to look over my shoulder, I see nothing but black against black. And feel nothing but that overwhelming heat that scrapes against me. Remembering the flame gem in my pocket—one I still hadn't charged—I retrieve it quickly as I shift onto my knees. When the dim light erupts from it, it reflects off of diamond-shaped scales, their onyx color shimmering iridescent. "Sunis," I rasp.

I take in the way her body is curled around mine, her tail stretching behind her before it wraps around behind me. Following the line of her large body, I pause when I meet the gaze of her yellow eye, only one visible with how she is laying her head. *Safe.* The emotion pummels me, forced through the chaotic push and pull of my thoughts. *This* is the bond, I realize, and something within me snaps. A long-held chain bound around my soul finally releasing as I close my eyes, tears leaking from their corners.

Sunis makes a soft noise as she adjusts her head until I can feel the heat of her breaths pressing on me. *Sad.* There's almost a question to the emotion, and I shake my head as if Sunis can understand that answer. Despite waiting *years* for this moment, communicating with my dragon is something that I couldn't have studied for. Preparation had been nothing more than words I happened to hear from males with loud mouths and Navin insisting that it wasn't something explainable. That it had to be *felt,* and I had been so fucking frustrated by that answer that I had promptly left the conversation. Now I wish I had asked him to explain it further. Because how could I tell Sunis that I'm not sad but *relieved* that we are now bonded.

Relieved. The word is echoed back to me, warmth suffusing my chest as if a weight has finally been lifted off of it. Is that all it takes? Just *thinking* about a feeling or a word? I open my eyes and turn until I can see most of Sunis's face. *Sunis,* I think, and her head tips in my direction, yellow gaze burning bright with acknowledgement. "Stars above," I whisper, walking forward until my hand can lay on the edge of her snout.

But as elated as I feel, as *right* as this all is, it has come at a cost. I had left Navin to deal with the consequences of our infiltration.

And then there is that strange visit with the woman amongst the stars. She claimed to not be a goddess, but what other being could *exist* where she did? Could behave as she did? The memory of my blade twirling through her makes an uncomfortable shiver work its way down my spine. Her message plays again in my ear as if carried on a phantom wind: *When she tells you to take her to the one named Rhea Maxwell, do not hesitate.* The name means nothing to me and is, at this moment anyway, the least of my concerns.

I tug at my mask and lift it to cover my mouth and nose, checking that my blade is actually still at my thigh and not at that *pocket between worlds* where I had thrown it. Feeling the cool press of the hilt against my palm, I look at Sunis. The last thing I want to do is leave her, but I have to return to the palace first and see if Navin is there. See if our alibi has been completely ruined with him being discovered. "I will return," I tell her, drawing my hand over her smooth scales. "Rest until I come for you and do *not* eat meat you haven't caught yourself."

She chuffs, and I take that as acceptance of my demand. Something wraps around my heart as I turn to exit the cave, a thorny vine pulling more taut with every step I take away from Sunis. *This is the bond,* I tell myself as I break into a run, the night air cooling my heated skin. *I have finally done it.* My heartbeats quicken as I force myself to move faster, replaying the night's events in my mind. The woman's voice once more returns to me, but her message isn't the only thing I hear in between each breath that fills me.

It's what she called me, the last title she spoke as if it wasn't some honorary appellation thrown out on a whim but an undeniable truth. One that came with a crown and subjects and beasts of flame and fury.

Dragon Queen.

Chapter One Hundred and Four

KAI

MOLSI IS BUSTLING DESPITE the chill in the air, shifters filling restaurants and taverns and spilling from shops as they meander about beneath the dwindling sunset. Leaning against the stone façade at the back of an apothecary, I watch my cousin work his charm on a female running a clothing store across the street, her guard completely lowered if the blush on her cheeks is any indication. Kane's flirting is intentional, and I can only hope it draws out the information we need without being too obvious.

Though direct attacks in Molsi have dwindled, skirmishes keep popping up in surrounding towns and with them, a single message has become abundantly clear: The rebels are still active, and someone is still leading them in Tua's place.

When Kane laughs riotously at something she says, I snort and divert my attention elsewhere.

It's been weeks since the night I found him in the fighting pits, and in that time, Kane has changed in subtle ways. He's more present during meetings, more engaged in topics when he previously wasn't. He still teases Jahlee, my sister all too eager to taunt him back, but there is a certain kind of fondness that glimmers between their jabs at each other now. My sister and I had come to view Kane as the enemy for so many years. It is *nice* to simply see him as my cousin now.

A high-pitched laugh draws my attention back to Kane just as he bows and kisses the shop owner's hand before gently dropping it and sauntering away. I push away from the wall and round its nearest corner, losing the remaining sunlight to the shadows of an alley.

"You know you're too big of an oaf to hide properly," Kane says when he joins me, taking a stance across from me and folding his arms over his chest. "Everyone knows it's you just on your height alone."

My lips flatten as I stare at him. "What did the shop owner say?"

He arches a brow but answers quickly. "Nothing beyond what we already assumed. She hasn't seen Malin in weeks, and he wouldn't tell her where he was going before he just disappeared."

Malin is a presumed rebel, the male spotted at several attacks of small businesses. I tilt my head as I eye him. "All that flirting, and that's as far as you got?"

"My flirting skills aren't the problem here. The rebels know we are looking for them, and they assume the former Tua sympathizers in our dungeons are feeding us information. They just decided to act and make that information no longer relevant." Kane shrugs. "Besides, a little flirting could do *you* some good. When was the last time you even *talked* with a female who wasn't working for you?" When I don't answer, his gaze finds mine again. "Please tell me you have at least *fucked* someone since Bahira left."

"I'm not having this conversation with you," I grumble, turning on my heel to begin heading back to the palace.

"Holy gods above, Kai. *No* one since her? Not even your cute little assistant, Inessa?"

I grind my teeth together, brushing past a crowd of shifters that pile out of a tavern, their steps sloppy. "Inessa is a valuable member of my council—"

"Yeah, yeah, and she is fucking gorgeous too. Unsurprising considering who her mother is." He smacks his lips together before looking over at me. "I don't know how you can spend so much time in her proximity and *not* think of fucking her."

My brows lower, the stares of a few shifters drawn our way by Kane's crude speech. "Just because you can't manage not involving your dick in every thought doesn't mean it's hard for everyone else," I say quietly, earning a deep chuckle from my cousin.

"Fair enough. Still, it's been *months*, Kai."

I don't need the reminder. I had utilized the Mirror plenty every week, calling out to *her* kingdom with no response. I have so much I want to say to Bahira, yet I am still being denied the opportunity to do so. It goes against everything I thought we had together. Every moment where I felt like we had found something similar in one another. I *knew* Bahira. Beyond how she felt in my hands and on my lips. I knew she valued being praised for her intelligence more than she ever would for her looks. That she wanted to help because it gave her purpose and because she hadn't received that same feeling from home. I memorized the way her eyes warmed when I put my trust in her. How they then dimmed when I told her it had been broken. "You don't just move on from a woman like Bahira," I finally say as we reach the center of Molsi, a few females lingering their gazes on my cousin and I. Beyond them, three males dip their heads in greeting while even more offer small smiles. A far cry from how my people treated me mere months ago, and it can be traced back to the stories of Bahira and what she learned while shackled with Kane.

"What are you going to do? Just mope around for another three months and hope that she eventually reaches out to you?" When silence again answers him, Kane shakes his head. "Why don't you just *go* to the Mage Kingdom? Call it a diplomatic visit or something."

"Because Bahira has already been given trouble from a letter Jahlee sent. The last thing she needs is to be the subject of even more whispers of treason just because I can't get her out of fucking head."

Kane rubs a hand at the back of his neck as we walk, his voice dropping lower. "I'm sorry, Kai. I didn't mean—"

"Kai Vaea, you are a fucking *liar*!" I stumble over my feet at the voice that comes from directly behind me, Jahlee taking up the entirety of my vision when I spin around to face her. Her finger immediately jabs at my chest, and I hiss as her nail digs into the skin. "You never told me you had heard from Bahira!"

"I didn't," I say, my eyes scanning the faces of the curious shifters that pass us.

"Stop lying! I just heard you say—"

"Were you following us?" Kane interrupts, eyeing the bright red wool coat slung over Jahlee's shoulders, and the scarf wrapped around her head.

"Yes, I was following you," she growls, rolling her eyes. "I could tell you've been hiding something from me."

"Jahlee." The rumble of my voice does nothing to ease the rage in her eyes, so I guide us all to an alley between a tavern and a bakery for a semblance of privacy. "If you had questions, you should have just come to me."

"Oh, sure. Like you would have answered anything involving Bahira. Like you haven't avoided talking about her since the moment she left." She narrows her gaze at me, making Kane laugh. He quiets when we both turn to glare at him, prompting him to lift his arms in mock surrender. Jahlee's voice cracks when her eyes flit to mine again. "What is going on? And please, don't lie to me. I can tell when you are, and it's embarrassing for us both because you are so bad at it."

I consider lying, but Jahlee is nothing if not persistent, and I know my sister well enough to understand that I've already lost this battle. "I did not receive correspondence from Bahira or anyone in the Mage Kingdom."

She groans, throwing her arms out to her sides. "Kai, I *swear* to the gods above—"

"King Dolian reached me through the Mirror and told me that Bahira was being accused of treason."

Jahlee's mouth drops open, her arms falling limply as Kane whistles and rocks back on his heels. "What? Because of the letter I sent?"

I keep my voice low as I tell her about my interaction with the mortal king, and his questions about my time with Bahira. But in my hurry to explain, I slip and accidentally insinuate the king was not alone when I spoke with him.

"Who was with him?" she asks, her light brown eyes brimming with emotion. Jahlee has always felt many things all at once, and I often wondered if it was a hindrance to be so open in that way. I had been raised to live behind a mask, to always hide so that my weaknesses were not exploited. I look to Kane for help, but my stupid cousin gestures with his hand for me to continue, apparently just as invested in the story as Jahlee is.

"It doesn't matter who was with him—"

"Oh, yes it does," she says, laying her hands at her hips and cocking them to the side. "Why avoid answering otherwise?"

"I'm not avoiding," I lie, and she gives me a look as if to say, *see*? I do curse under my breath this time. "Fucking gods, *fine*. But you cannot say anything about what I tell you. *Neither* of you can."

Jahlee sucks in a sharp breath, one of her hands flying to her mouth. She mumbles something unintelligible beneath her palm, her eyes growing wide enough that I see the whites all around them.

"What the fuck did she just say?" Kane asks, annoyance carving a line between his brows. She sends him another withering look.

"It was Rhea, wasn't it?" she asks after lowering her hand. "Rhea was with him in the Mirror."

I nod as I answer. "Yes."

Kane steps closer. "Who is Rhea?"

"None of your business, idiot. Kai, you need to tell Siyala."

"Absolutely not," I counter, folding my arms over my chest. "She has already tried sneaking off this island three times to go to the Mage Kingdom. I will not risk Siyala getting hurt. Not after she just returned home."

"But is she even *here* when her mind is so preoccupied with whether or not Rhea is okay? This information will be hard for her to hear, but it will also at least give her the truth. There is freedom in that."

I exhale roughly, drawing a hand down my face as the memory of King Dolian and Rhea pushes to the forefront of my mind. "This is not a truth that I think will help. It will only hurt her."

"Kai." She says my name as if it's both a question and the answer. "If you could know the truth about what is happening with Bahira right now, and you found out someone you thought you could trust was withholding that information from you, how would that make you feel?"

The air feels too heavy to breathe in as I look at her, my chest clenching at the thought.

"She's right," Kane says softly at my side. "I don't know the context—"

"Because you don't need to," Jahlee draws, rolling her eyes again.

Kane ignores it. "But I do know that when faced with being honest or not, honesty is always the best way to go."

Godsdamn it, of all the times for Kane to suddenly agree with Jahlee, this certainly isn't the moment I would have picked. "Fine," I say, my voice sharp. "We tell Siyala the truth."

Siyala heeds my call for her to join me in the throne room, Jahlee and Kane also present. We had spoken on the walk to the palace about the scenarios that might play out once Siyala learns that Rhea is in the king's clutches again, and they all pointed to one conclusion. One that I will need Kane's help with in order to execute.

The door hinges creak as they open, and Siyala enters. Her hair is windswept, and the normally golden skin at her cheeks is stained red from the chilled air outside. She eyes the three of us warily, her gaze lingering on Kane the longest. "What's going on?"

I swallow as I take a step towards her, my hands clasped behind me like it will somehow bolster me and make this conversation any easier. "We need to talk." With a deep breath, I tell her about how I had seen Rhea with King Dolian in the Mirror—what she looked like and how little she spoke. The longer I speak, the more I watch Siyala's shock morph into something keener, something more jagged, until rage carves lines between her brows.

"You knew," she breathes out quietly, her voice dangerously rough, "this whole *fucking* time that she was with him?"

"I did."

She takes a step towards me, rings of gold now glowing in her eyes. "You *knew*, yet you lied and told me you didn't."

"I did," I repeat, expecting her anger to manifest physically. But Siyala works her jaw twice before she swallows all her emotions down, instead lifting her chin in unbridled defiance.

"I'm going to the Mortal Kingdom."

"No." I hold my hands out in front of me when she lifts her upper lip in a snarl. The veins at her neck bulge with her unrestrained fury, and though her temptation to shift is visible, now is not the time to do it. I need her calm and rational if we are going to attempt what I suggest next. "*We* are going to the Mage Kingdom."

She scoffs. "To see your pathetic and worthless girlfriend? I don't *think* so."

The rumble that builds in my chest and travels up my throat bounces off of the stone that surrounds us, a reaction I hadn't meant to let slip. But the slight against Bahira isn't one I will ever tolerate, no matter who it comes from. "We are going to the Mage Kingdom because *you* may be able to pass through the Spell, but the rest of us cannot. You will need help to go after Rhea. I will not have your mother suffer any more than she already has over the thought of you being dead."

Siyala drops her gaze to the floor, drawing in a deep breath.

"He is right, Siyala," Jahlee says, laying a hand gently on her shoulder. "If you want to help Rhea, this is the only way."

I watch as Siyala runs through the options in her head, but she is smart enough to know that this is the best one. Alone, she might not get very far. But with my help? Her odds are better. *Rhea's* odds are better. "If this is the way it must be, then fine." She tugs her shoulder from Jahlee's grasp, her gold-threaded eyes lifting to meet mine. "But let it be known here and now that I will *never* forgive you for keeping this from me. No matter what you try to do to atone for it."

I nod even as Jahlee sucks in a quick breath. "Pack your things and meet us back here in two hours. Then we set sail for the Mage Kingdom."

Chapter One Hundred and Five

BAHIRA

MY FATHER HAD FOUND pieces of Barron's armor in Stephan's home—the man Nox killed in the dungeons and who had also spied for King Dolian. Though guards that work in the palace all have the same uniform, Barron's was made special with an engraving that celebrated his tenure. As my brother suspected after Stephan admitted he had lured Daje and Rhea out the night of the Autumnal Ball, there was the evidence that Barron had met his end at the hands of a traitor.

When my father returned from Stephan's house—sadness coating him after speaking with Barron's partner—he, my mother, Nox, and I planned how we would bring this revelation to the council. The problem was, we knew that *we* couldn't be the ones to tell them. We suspected Kallin had a rather large role in the betrayal of our family, of Rhea and Nox specifically, but none of us could say with certainty just how deep that betrayal went. And who else on the council might be involved. We sent in an anonymous tip detailing that Barron's partner should be informed that his armor had been found and an investigation needed to be launched into a guard named Stephan.

I wondered if we were being too forward, if the council would recognize the trap before they had fallen into it. And at first, it seemed like they were going to disregard it. Kallin did not bring it to Nox during their daily meetings, and as my father and mother began spying on other members of the council—enlisting the help of friends they swore we could trust like Sarai and Cass's father, Otto—it became apparent that they were not going to act. So we leaked the information.

Well, technically Sarai and Max had done most of the *whispering*. The latter was more than delighted to be further involved in the secret chaotic mess my life had devolved into. But it worked. As the information spread, so did the public outcry. Kallin wasn't the only asshole who could weaponize their opinion.

They sent guards to Stephan's home, and the rest unraveled from there. As expected, the council was careful about how they framed Barron's murder and Stephan's disappearance. On our nearly nightly convergences, not once had my parents or Nox gotten the impression that anyone on the council might be aware of what actually happened. There was relief in that, just as there was suspicion.

There were nine members of the council—Lady Moira's absence something my mother was investigating in secret—and the only person we could assume as innocent was Hadrik. Who all was involved in this scheme with the mortal king? And to what end? For all their preaching about keeping our kingdom safe, they had given away the Mage Kingdom's biggest weapon and their best shield in Rhea.

"You should eat, Bahira," my father says from where he sits across the table a few days later, eyeing my untouched plate of food. "And so should you," he adds, using his fork to point at Nox.

"Terrible manners for a king to use his utensil in that way," Nox snarks, earning a snort from my mother.

"Then it's a good thing I'm no longer king." The mood in the dining room grows glum in the silence that follows.

"You should still be king." Nox leans his elbows on the table, his fingers interlacing beneath his jaw. "You're certainly better suited to it than I am."

"I don't know if you realize you insult me *and* your mother with statements like that," he counters, narrowing his eyes playfully. "After all, have we not prepared you—*both* of you—to take the mantle? Are you saying we did a terrible job?"

I pinch my lips to hold back a laugh as I look at my brother, noting the way the corner of his own mouth twitches. "Sorry to humble you both," he says, earning a chuckle from everyone.

When the laughter eases, I manage to get a few bites in, forcing my appetite to cooperate. Nox taps his fingers on his thigh, drawing my attention. His hair has grown longer, the waves curling around the nape of his neck and touching the tops of his eyebrows. A dusting of hair covers his jaw, and I realize then that I have never seen Nox with even the semblance of a beard before. He looks wan and drained, acts as if even holding the conversation is enough to fatigue him. It has worsened in the weeks following his return from trying to save Rhea, and though his attitude about getting her back is still as determined as it was the moment he woke up from his deep sleep, there is a defeat in him that slips out when he's too tired to hide it. It's as if he's at war with himself—his heart desperate to reunite with Rhea, while his brain tells him that he can't leave now. He could crawl to her, yes, and I have no doubts that he's considered doing just that, but what would that do except get him killed? How would that help *her*?

I don't need to know the intimate details of how King Dolian's cruel mind works to understand that if he captured Nox, his death would be long and drawn out. Likely used as a punishment for Rhea. And yet, the fear that Nox will leave still simmers beneath my skin, a silent threat that sits unspoken between us all. I wish I could get him to see that his value is more than just who or what he can be to Rhea.

"If you keep staring at me, I'm going to assume I have food on my face," he says, turning to look at me, his chin resting on his hands. His dark green tunic is unbuttoned down to his clavicle, and from the opened space hangs a chain holding a gold ring, its gems glimmering when it catches the light of the spelled flames. His hand wraps around it, and when I lift my gaze to his, the faintest smile curls his lips. "It's hers," he says, full of reverence. "And I'll return it to her when I see her again."

"I have no doubt."

His dark eyes roam mine, the silver I'm so used to seeing in them hardly visible when he nods and turns to look at our parents. "It's time I tell you something about Rhea," he says slowly, leaning against the back of the chair and wincing.

"And what is that?" our mother asks, lifting her chalice of water to her mouth. My own brows draw together until I remember that there is a fairly large secret that Nox and I know that our parents do not.

"Rhea did her Flame Ceremony before the ball, and her flame—"

"Was blue?" my father interrupts, a dark brow lifted in question. And knowing.

My eyes widen as they dance back and forth between my brother and our parents, their amusement only confusing me more.

"You knew?" Nox asks.

My father nods, wrapping his hand over our mother's where it's resting on the table. "We suspected when we first felt her signature, when the entire palace did while she was in her deep sleep after your arrival."

"We knew it for sure when you joined us for that first meal and we gave her the dragon stone necklace," my mother adds, her head tilted to the side while her curls—twin to my own—drape over her shoulder.

"Why didn't you say anything?" I ask, seeing Nox's nod at my question from the corner of my eye.

My father looks to my mother, his smile soft as he signals for her to answer. She lets out a small puff of air, tracing her finger over the rim of her chalice as she answers. "Two hundred years is a long time for information to get distorted. For history to be reshaped." Nox and I glance at each other, our shared looks of concern making our father chuckle. "But though those in power might want certain facts altered, or erased all together, there is something that none of their machinations can take away—personal experience. As you both know, my father's business was in perfumery, and there was a particular farm to the north of Galdr where he liked to get his florals from. He touted them as the best of the best, the flowers so beautifully pungent that you could often catch a whiff of them from miles away if the wind was blowing just right." Her eyes grow unfocused as she talks, as if she is more present in the memories than she is here with us. "Occasionally, my mother and I would tag along on his trips to the farm, as my mother had befriended the farmer's wife. They had a little girl who was the same age as me, and she and I would play while the adults talked business.

"They lived on a beautiful property, the space lush with banya and pirang trees, their trunks so wonderfully tangled together that in some parts, it was impossible to pass through. For hours, she and I would play. Climbing trees and pretending to be adventurers." She smiles, and my father squeezes her hand. "I saw her every year. As we grew older, our conversations switched from that of make-believe to more fun topics like love and boys and how our fathers were both so strict." Nox huffs out a laugh, my own grin wide. "But on the last year that I saw her, she had been withdrawn. Sullen. Normally, our conversations picked up right where they had left off, as if no time had gone by, but this year... This year, she did not have the same light in her eyes that I had come to know. I pleaded with her to tell me what was wrong, a friend beseeching another to trust and let her in. But she said she couldn't, that she had promised her parents she would not speak a word of what was going on. So I did what any idiot teenager does when turned away: I stormed off, muttering curses under my breath."

My mother swallows, her gaze refocusing as she drops it back to us. To Nox.

"That was the last time I ever saw her. Shortly after, she disappeared. I tell you both this, but you especially, Nox, because I remembered something about my friend the first time I ever saw Rhea." Nox adjusts in his seat, his eyes locked on hers. "On one visit, she and I were talking about anything and everything, as children do, and I made a comment about the color of her eyes. They were a lovely shade, one I had never seen another mage have. She told me that her mama had them but not her grandmother. That, in her family, sometimes, the women have eyes like hers. Sometimes, they have a certain color of hair. Sometimes, they get both, and it was because of the special magic they had. It was then she told me that she was scared to do her Flame Ceremony. That a man named Kallin from the king's council had come to their house to inquire why she hadn't done it yet."

I think back to the few glimpses I had ever seen of Rhea and compare the memory of her to the details I had been given by Siyala. Green eyes certainly weren't a common trait among mages. I chance a glance at Nox, and I'm not sure he is breathing as he leans forward, a look on his face I can't exactly pinpoint. "What was her name?" he rasps.

"Stellaluna to most. Occasionally, her mother also called her by her middle name, and to some, she was simply Luna."

"Fucking gods above," Nox swears, pushing away from the table as he stands, his hands resting on his head as he begins to pace.

"What?" I ask, standing along with him.

He turns to look at our mother, his gaze hard. "You knew Rhea's mother." A statement, not a question. My eyes widen as I swing my head to look at her.

She nods, remorse drawing her mouth down. "It had been so long since I had seen Stellaluna, since I had heard her name spoken, that I forgot. I knew someone named Luna had been made queen in the Mortal Kingdom, but I knew my friend as her true name, so I did not put the pieces together. But the moment Rhea came into this very room with you, it all came rushing back." She stands and lets go of my father's hand to walk around the table. "I did not tell you because I did not know *how* to. Or if it would matter at all."

"It would have," Nox snaps, closing his eyes and blowing out a breath. More calmly, he adds, "It would have mattered to Rhea."

"Then it will be my top priority to tell her everything I know when she returns." The promise does very little to appease Nox's scowl.

"Wait," I say slowly, holding my hand out in front of me as I organize my thoughts. "You said Kallin knew that they hadn't done Stellaluna's Flame Ceremony?" At my mother's nod, I continue. "Does that mean that Kallin might have recognized Rhea too?" If she looked like Stellaluna, then it stands to reason my mother wasn't the only one who saw the resemblance. But if he suspected her to come from a Void queen line, why would he get rid of her? Besides his preference to have Haylee in her place.

"It's possible," she answers solemnly, and Nox curses again.

"That fucking *bastard*. I'm going to *kill* him."

I can tell protests begin to form on my mother's tongue, on my father's, stars above, even on my own, but they don't get the chance to fall before the door to the dining room swings open, and Max, of all people, is standing there.

"Highnesses, Sarai sent me," he says, his chest heaving as sweat gleams over his brow.

"What is it, Max?" I ask, drawing nearer to him.

He gulps in a few more breaths, wiping his forehead with the back of his hand before looking to me. "They're back." At the silence that follows, our confused glares boring into his, Max clarifies, "Your friends are back from the Fae Kingdom."

"They snuck in a side entrance and found Sarai in the seamstress quarters. She brought them up to the medical wing," Max says from ahead of us, sharp breaths bisecting each word. While he hadn't been brought up to speed regarding the mission to the Fae Kingdom, his willingness to help clean up and hide evidence of what Nox had done to Stephan—and his silence after—was proof enough that he could be trusted. Sarai must have felt the same if she sent him to retrieve us.

"Are they injured?" Nox asks, breathless where he runs beside me, our parents just behind us.

"They are, but I'm not sure to what extent. I haven't actually seen them. I just got the order from Sarai when she came to my post."

My heart pounds in my ears in anticipation of seeing my friends as Max rounds a corner and slows to a stop in front of one of the doors lining the left side. A cautious elation fills me at the chance to try to repair the Mirror and, selfishly, all that may come after that if we are successful.

But those thoughts are expelled from my head the moment Max knocks on the door and Sarai opens it with a look of devastation that makes it hard to swallow. Stepping out of the way, I let Nox in first, following behind him and coming to a stop as I take in the two beds and the two figures that lay in them.

Only the two figures.

"Where is he?" Nox asks, confusion tilting his brows down as he searches the room again, as if his friend is hiding. At the impossible silence that answers, Nox asks again, "Where is Cass?"

Chapter One Hundred and Six

BAHIRA

IT'S ELORA WHO ANSWERS, her face contorted into a grimace as she cradles her left arm, white bandages wrapped around it from her wrist to her elbow. "It happened while we were collecting the glass. They came from inside the caves and hidden tunnels within their dark mountains."

"The fae?" my mother asks from where she is sitting on the edge of Daje's bed. I take in the white gauze wrapped carefully around his head, stark against his dark brown hair, and swallow roughly.

"And their dragons."

Air squeezes from my lungs as I shut my eyes, my chin falling to my chest. *This can't be happening.*

"I don't understand," Nox protests from where he stands centered in the room, his hands flexing at his sides. "We received Cass's letter. I *know* he wrote it."

"It was right after he sent it," Daje says, voice raw and eyes weary. Then he relays the story of the dragon riding fae who had descended upon them, each detail more horrifying than the last. As he speaks, Elora softly cries, the hand of her good arm covering her mouth as her pale skin grows pink. "We fought them off, but they were faster. Stronger. Our magic only held them back long enough for us to catch a breath, and then we were back to fighting simply to block their blows. We were nearly surrounded, the fae at our fronts and their dragons behind them. The forest at our back was our only escape, but we knew that if we turned, if we ran straight for it, the dragon fire would blast us before we ever got to the safety of the tree.

"I could feel Cass's signature building in the air, but he refused to look at me. All he said was that when he gave the signal, I'd better make damn sure Elora started running. The fae advanced, and we retreated. The dragons roared, and then Cass's magic glowed at his hands. He caught them off guard as he sent it barreling into the fae, a wall of glowing blue that knocked them all to the ground. I knew it was the signal, and still, I hesitated, calling my magic to the surface. But Cass, he—" Daje shakes his head as he stares down at his blood-splattered trousers, bottom lip trembling. Pressure builds behind my eyes as my father's hands land on Nox's shoulders to steady him. "With one hand outstretched towards the fae, the other reached in our direction. Blue surrounded us as he used his magic to carry us to the treeline, his power giving out right before we reached it. But it was enough. Enough for us to close the rest of the distance as the magic holding the fae flickered out. Enough so that, when we turned around, we saw him gutted by dragon claws, his body collapsing before flames engulfed the beach. I tried..." Daje clears his throat, the back of his hand wiping his eyes.

"He tried to go to him," Elora adds, her gaze locked on Daje. "But I stopped him. Selfishly, I stopped him because I didn't want to make the journey home alone. I didn't want to watch two friends die."

"It is not selfish," my mother says, shaking her head. "Cass's choice was his and his alone."

"I'm sorry, Nox." Daje's voice wavers, and his shoulders rock with silent sobs, my mother scooting higher on the bed to wrap him in her embrace.

Numbly, I sit down on the edge of Elora's bed, staring at the tears that line her cheeks as she whispers, "I'm sorry your friend did not make it home."

Her words, so filled with grief, sit thick and heavy in the room. Nox spins on his heel, breaking free of our father's hold as he barrels towards the exit. The door bangs shut behind him, and Elora's shoulders round in defeat.

"I'll go after him—"

"No," my father interrupts me, his red-rimmed eyes meeting mine. My heart cracks at the devastation within them, at how his chest heaves as if each breath is a struggle. "Let me."

The quiet that blooms in the air when he leaves is suffocating. No one moves, as if we all recognize that doing so will settle us into this new reality. One where Cass is gone.

I will never again hear one of his taunting jokes. I will never again watch in awe as he wields his blades, his skills growing masterful over the years. I pinch my lips to hold back the mournful howl that tries to break free at the thought that the orphanage, a place so near and dear to him, will never again be lit up by his presence. His is a loss that this world does not deserve, one that *Nox* does not deserve, yet fate was cruel enough to deal such a horrific hand.

Eventually, my mother stands from Daje's bed, wiping the remaining tears from beneath her eyes before brushing her hands over her skirt. "Tonight, we feel everything this tragedy warrants without abandon." Her gaze turns towards Daje and Elora. "We rest after a hard-fought journey." Then she looks to me. "And then tomorrow, we ensure that his sacrifice was not in vain."

Nox acts surprised when he sees my setup upon returning to his rooms later that night, my pillow and blanket spread out on one of the couches. I sit up, massaging one of the dragon stones imbued with Rhea's magic in my hand. There is no way I am going to let him spend the evening alone, and I let him know as much. Though his sigh is resigned, he doesn't protest my demand that he grab his own pillow and blanket and take the couch across from me. Lying in the darkness of the room, only the light of a half moon shining through the windows, I expect the silence to remain between us as I continue rolling the smooth dark stone in my hand, the feel of it warm.

"After Father and I talked, I went to Galen," he says quietly, the words tumbling out slowly as if they are a secret he still isn't sure he wants shared.

"Are you feeling alright?" A stupid fucking question, given the circumstances, but Nox understands what I mean.

"I feel like a stranger. My body thrums like it's on fire half the time and aches like it's struggling to contain my missing magic the other half. It's like I'm being split in two, and after learning what we did, I just— I don't have the energy to fight against it."

"You asked Galen for more of your tinctures?" I guess.

Nox's pause is significant, and then his voice comes out rough, a blade scraped over stone. "I asked for enough to put me asleep for days."

"Are you going to take it?" I ask, reserving judgement because I *would* understand if he did. If he needs to escape for a while, even if I know him to be stronger than that.

"No. But isn't it pathetic that I considered it? That, for a moment, I was weak enough to think I deserved to just... *pretend* none of this is happening?" I turn my head in his direction, unable to see more than a faint outline of his profile. "I've failed so many times lately, and a part of me just wanted to exist somewhere other than my failures."

"Do you believe me to be the smartest person you know?" I ask, the abrupt perceived change in conversation choking a broken laugh out of him.

"I do."

"Good. Then perhaps you'll heed the weight of my words when I tell you that none of this is your fault, Nox. Not Rhea being taken. Not Cass's d-death." I stumble over the word as my throat tightens. "*None* of it. These are not *your* failures but the failures of the people around us. Of the people we should have been able to trust implicitly." Nox doesn't respond, but his quick breaths tell me that maybe he's trying to hold himself together too. "And, in some cases, there is nothing and no one to blame other than bad luck," I add quietly, squeezing my eyes shut.

"I owe you so many apologies. You're a much better sister than I am a brother."

"This is true." His soft chuckle joins mine before the room grows quiet again. "It will be okay, Nox. I promise."

"You have no business promising things you can't prove. Doesn't that go against all your logical rules?"

"It does," I agree, setting the stone down on the table with the pile of others and laying my hands on my belly as I picture my last interaction with Cass in my head. "And yet I promise it anyway."

⁂

Early morning comes quickly, and it brings with it an overcast winter sky that matches my sullen mood. Sarai wakes Nox and I with gentle knocks on his door before the sun has fully risen, explaining that Elora and Daje are already waiting for us at the secret location we had agreed upon prior to them leaving. I see the same hesitancy in Nox's gaze that I feel in my chest as we set off, trying to navigate plans we had put in motion amongst unfathomable grief. But my mother's words ring true in my head. The loss of Cass would *not* be in vain.

Dressed to combat the cold, we sneak out of Nox's room to avoid the guards posted beyond the door. I keep my attention on my brother the entire time we scale down the side of the palace, timing our escape to when there is a gap in the patrol of the grounds. I can tell when we finally hit the bottom he is frustrated by my watchful eyes, but I merely shrug as I brush past him. He can be annoyed by me all he wants, but I will *always* do my best to ensure he is safe.

Hidden within the forest, we make our way to the place where we hope we can make a new Mirror. The forge we chose is only used when there is an overflow of work for the palace blacksmith, but our father encouraged us to work quickly just in case. Yet that is the catch—I'm not sure if we can. Can the fire of a forge get hot enough to melt what has been created by dragon fire? None of us know, and the unknown feels just as scary as getting caught working on the Mirror without telling the council.

Made of stone and covered in crawling ivy, the forge looks fairly unassuming from the outside. Smoke already billows out of its short chimney, but it's the man standing outside the front door, hand resting comfortably on the black hilt of his sword, that slows my steps as Nox and I near.

"Max?"

"Good morning, Bahira. Your Majesty," he says, lowering into a deep bow.

"Just Nox is fine, thank you, Max. And none of... *that*." Nox gestures to Max's frame.

The guard smiles as he straightens, letting his hand fall away from his weapon.

"Bit conspicuous to have you out here, isn't it?" I ask, arms folding over my chest as I scan the forest around us. But it's still early morning, and the forge's location is away from the main paths in and out of Galdr.

Max chuckles as he steps away from the door. "I thought the same, but those two insisted I stay out. Said they didn't trust me enough to talk about the Mirror in their presence, so I was banished to stand in the cold." Though his voice is lighthearted, Max's next words are solemn. "I am sorry for the loss of your friend. I didn't know Cass well beyond the occasional passing, but he always seemed happy." I watch my brother take in Max's words with a dip of his chin, pushing waves of hair away from his forehead. They just flop back into place.

"Thank you. Shall we enter?" He reaches for the door and opens it, and I smile at Max as we pass, jerking my head for him to follow.

When he hesitates, I roll my eyes. "Stay out here and freeze to death if you want. But you know enough about both of us to get us locked in the dungeons if not executed on the spot. This," I say pointing to space just past the door, "is nothing compared to all of that." His steps are lighter as he follows, his smile as unrestrained as Starla's is when I let her use the magnifier. I don't know whether to snort or roll my eyes.

Warmth immediately embraces us as we enter, the scent of metal and earth mixing and clinging heavily in the air. At the front stand Daje and Elora, the former's eyes narrowing when he spots Max, but Nox lifts his hand to quell the argument. "He's one of us."

"I told you," Elora teases Daje, her arm cradled in a sling. She looks marginally better than yesterday, her magic healing most of the smaller cuts and scrapes. Though it does nothing to the fatigue evident in her eyes, her lids swollen and the skin beneath them stained the color of bruises.

I half expect Daje to send her a glare or a scoff in return, but to my surprise, he just grins, lifting a single shoulder in a shrug. Where yesterday his head was wrapped in gauze, only a bandage covers his temple now. "I won't apologize for being cautious." I could smirk at how familiar the response feels, but Elora just smiles, a moment of time suspended between them as they look at each other. Daje is the first to look away, clearing his throat as he turns to gesture to the three packs on a nearby wooden table. "It's all in there."

"Do you think it will be enough?" Nox asks, leaning a hip on the edge of the table. Max meanders to the opposite side of the room, crossing one ankle over the other and folding his arms over his chest, his leather armor creaking with the movement.

"I hope so," Elora answers, and the lack of surety in her voice makes us all bristle. She holds a hand out in front of her. "There is no text I've found that tells us how to repair the Mirror, how to make it magical again, and I suspect that, even if such a text existed, it would likely be obsolete." She tucks a loose strand of her fiery red hair behind her ear. "As we all know, raw magic can be a fickle, sentient thing. Our intent is what wields it, but that doesn't always *control* it."

I nod at Elora, grateful that she hadn't censored the way she spoke about magic around me. It is a subtle thing, but after so many years of many others acting as if even *talking* about their magic around me would cause me to fall apart, I appreciate the small gesture by her. Even if it was unintentional.

"What is the plan?" Nox asks, his hand bracing the table. "We melt the glass and then what?"

"We'll likely need magic to help grow the flame into something hot enough to match dragon fire," Daje answers, turning to look at the open flame of the forge. "We will have to move quickly once we melt the glass and can pour it into a frame." At that, he points to the where the previous frame that held the Mirror is leaning against a wall. It seems that it wasn't destroyed by Nox's outburst. "And then we hope that it can be imbued with magic before it cools completely." His next words are said tentatively. "Is your magic—"

"No," Nox answers swiftly, his curtness not going unnoticed.

A deep line forms between Elora's brows. "Still?" she says, inspecting him like one of her books.

"Still. But we'll use what I can muster and hope that it is enough."

"And if it isn't?" Daje asks.

"Then Cass's life was forfeit, and I'll be to blame."

Chapter One Hundred and Seven

BAHIRA

NOX AND I GATHER ceramic crucibles and place them over the flame to begin heating up, while Max, Daje, and Elora use their magic to move the frame onto a steel table set nearby. Its height is well past Nox's own, perhaps even reaching Kai's. I nearly sigh at the thought of the shifter king, the memory of him always flashing at the most inconvenient of times.

"In a few hours, I will have to return to the palace so the council does not get suspicious," Nox says, now leaning back fully against the wall next to Max, looking unsteady. *Is it possible he looks even worse than last night?* "And I have a meeting with Haylee *and* Kallin to attend."

At the sound of her name, I clench my jaw, my reaction visible enough to draw Daje's attention. His gaze bounces from me to Nox and even to Max before returning to mine, his brows drawn together. "What is it?"

"At Nox's coronation, your father announced that Haylee and Nox were engaged."

Daje's mouth drops open, then closes, then drops open again. "*What*?" he asks at the same time Elora shouts, "That *bitch*!" Max's deep chuckle reverberates out.

"It's not worth discussing, as there will be no marriage. Your father knows this, but I suspect he thinks if he harasses me enough, I will eventually give in." I think of my brother's confession last night, of the exhaustion that lingers around him like a fog. His dulled gray eyes meet mine as he gives a slight shake of his head, uncompromising resolve hardening his expression. "There are many battles I've grown weary of, but that will *never* be one of them. Getting Rhea home and upon her rightful throne is something I will continuously strive to do. Even if it kills me."

"I assume there has been no update on her?" Elora asks, her voice trembling.

"Nothing beyond what we already can assume." The admission is a sword plunged into the room's beating heart, silencing it as the five of us look at each other.

It's Max who pushes us past it. "I think the crucibles are ready."

And with that, we move into a semblance of order as we form an assembly line to begin melting the dragon glass. I run my fingers against one of the smooth pieces, its iridescence reminding me of the Spell. My curiosity wants to know how they found the glass and if the shape of it before they broke it down for transport was something unique or uniform. But I keep my questions behind my teeth, the knowledge that Cass had sacrificed himself to get the glass enough to keep my focus on the present. Elora, Max, and I sort the pieces by size, while Nox uses a handheld shovel to bring them to the crucibles. Daje carefully sends a slow but steady flow of his magic into the flames. It tints the fire unnaturally golden, his yellow blending with the oranges and reds. As we work in tandem, in a silence that grows more and more tense with each minute that passes, I run through everything I know about the Mirror.

Its magic was ancient, likely the same raw power that flows all over Olymazi. Nox said he couldn't remember if he saw magic leave the Mirror when it broke, but I wonder if its color might be like that of the Spell. Like that of the magic I saw in blood. Like Rhea's magic.

"The first crucible is nearly melted," Daje says, his voice strained.

I turn to find sweat already beading on his brow, his hand shaking from the continued use of his magic. *Fuck*, we still have so much glass to melt to fill the frame. "Perhaps you should go help him," I tell Max, halting his sorting of the glass. "The two of you can sustain the flame longer than just him alone."

But Elora stops Max from going, her dark eyes darting from me to Daje while something soft flashes in them. "He doesn't want anyone to help," she whispers, the corners of her mouth turning down. "Rhea's abduction, Cass's death... He feels responsible for them both and is desperate to prove that he can fix this. That he can be more help than burden."

"Is that what he thinks? That he is a burden?" I ask her under my breath as Max goes back to silently sorting.

"He tried, Bahira. He tried *so hard* to go back for Cass. He nearly hurt me trying to get to him, but I—" She swallows, hand trembling from where it rests on the table. "I couldn't watch him die too. But this... this is almost worse. This is a slow death. One orchestrated by him. One, I'm afraid, we won't be able to stop if repairing the Mirror doesn't work. If Rhea doesn't come home."

I think over her words as Max waves Nox over, the both of them bringing the next round of filled crucibles over to the flame.

"Daje's always wanted to be the one to save those he loves," I murmur, grabbing two new containers for us to fill. "He deserves someone showing him that he is worth saving, too."

"Someone like you?" she asks, faint vulnerability coloring her tone.

"No," I smile, feeling her eyes scouring my face. "I was never supposed to be the one to do that."

Time passes slowly, Elora and I sorting through all of the glass, and Nox and Max adding crucible after crucible to the flame so that it can all be melted at once. Only when Daje wobbles on his feet does he finally give in and allow Max to take over, his blue magic hugging the flame as he keeps the temperature steady.

Nox paces restlessly, looking out of one of the forge's high windows as he denotes the faint trickle of sunlight showing through it means he will have to leave soon.

"We can wait for the glass to harden before you try imbuing it," Elora suggests, her cheeks pink from the warmth emanating into the room.

"I disagree." Though dirt covers the stone beneath us, his steps still echo as he comes to stand next to the empty frame. "We need to test it now to see if my magic will do anything at all or if this has just been a massive waste of time. Is all of the glass melted?"

Daje checks over the crucibles and nods. "The last one finally melted."

"Thank gods," Max breathes, his magic beginning to flicker. "Can I stop now?"

"Yes, but we have to move quickly."

There's a flurry of movement as all but Elora leap to grab a pair of large iron tongs. One by one, we remove the crucibles from the flame, the hot glass meeting the cold steel releasing a high-pitched hiss. Elora uses a wooden block soaked in water to smooth the glass into one even layer, and when the last crucible is poured, we stare at the iridescent glass. It glimmers like the Spell, pressing into the edges of the frame as it begins to cool.

"I'm ready," Nox says, his magic already glowing in his palm. It's just a small ball of dark purple laced with a single wisp of black, and as my gaze lifts to meet those of Max, Elora, and Daje, their faces express my own concern. *It isn't enough.*

In silence, we all watch as Nox feeds what little magic he can summon into the Mirror. Eventually, it changes the entire surface to that same deep purple, black wavy lines interspersed throughout. Within minutes, Nox's heavy breathing fills the space. Another few pass, and he's forced to lean his other hand on the table to steady himself. I lay my hand on his shoulder in silent warning, but he ignores it as he continues to send scraps of his power out. It's when he nearly faceplants into the hot glass that I finally pull him back, his magic sputtering out like a candle flame.

"Enough," I whisper, panic rising at how deeply he leans into me.

"It isn't. It never will be. Not until—" He doesn't finish before his eyes roll to the back of his head and he becomes dead weight in my arms.

"Fuck! Max, come help me!" He rushes over, and together, we lay Nox gently on the ground, his sweaty, pale face gilded in the warm light from the flame. I press a hand to his cheek, calling his name as I stare down at him.

"Has he ever passed out from using his magic?" Max asks from where he kneels at Nox's other side. Daje and Elora stand behind him, the latter leaning into Daje with his hand resting on her hip.

"Never," I answer, glancing back up at the table holding the Mirror. "Is the glass still holding his power?"

As one, Elora and Daje move to inspect the Mirror. "The glass is hazy, but it appears his magic is holding." She looks at me just as Nox begins to stir. "Do you think that means it will work?"

"Perhaps," I answer, my fingers curled in towards my palms to hide their trembling. "We might need Nox to imbue it with his blood all over again." This time not as crown prince but as the new king.

"What happened?" Nox groans as Max helps him to sit, sweat gliding down his temple.

"Your magic infused the Mirror, but we don't know yet if it's enough to make it work."

He attempts to push himself up to stand and falters, needing help from Max and I to get up fully. "I'll try—"

"Nox, you just passed out from using your magic. I don't think you should try again."

"I can do it," he says, tired eyes framed in desperation. Without waiting for me to respond, he steps up to the side of the table. Max and I join him, Daje and Elora across from us as Nox calls out, "King Kai Vaea of the Shifter Kingdom." My heart pounds against my ribs at Kai's name.

There is always a moment while in the thrall of experimentation when time seems to halt. It happens when I'm peering down the scope of the magnifier, clarifying the image to discover what lies beyond what can be seen with the naked eye. It happens when my mind latches on to a new theory or hypothesis, and all I can think about is how I might test it and prove it true. And it happens now, as I watch the Mirror begin to ripple, Nox's command a pebble tossed into an otherwise calm lake. Breath halts in my chest, and blood slips past my ears in time to the thrum of my heartbeat. I don't dare blink, don't dare take my focus off of the Mirror as those tiny ripples travel down the length of it. And then disappear. Leaving the Mirror as it was before Nox spoke.

All at once, the sounds of the room return, and with it, so does the heaving of my frustrated breath. "Damn it."

"Did it not work?" Max asks, leaning over to look at his reflection in the Mirror.

"No," Nox sighs as he braces his hands on the table. "I'll try again—"

"Tomorrow," I interrupt, arching a brow at Nox's scowl.

"I'm *fine*—"

"And you're due back at the palace." A muscle flexes in my brother's jaw. "This battle is multifaceted, Nox. I promised we would figure this out, and we will. But we can do *nothing* if you're not well enough to help."

He looks to Daje and then Elora for help, but when he only meets their pleading gazes, he reluctantly yields. Together, we sneak back to the palace, but I don't see Nox for the rest of the day, the duties forced upon him by Kallin and the council keeping him behind closed doors. I spend time sifting through the journals taken from the archives, but the Mirror and Nox's failed attempt keep my attention muddled, and when I meet my brother the next morning as we sneak back out under the cover of dawn, the anxiousness at trying again is an incessant hum beneath my skin.

We enter the forge to find Daje and Elora already there, sharing a pot of tea between them.

"No Max?" Elora asks, her hair pulled back into a ponytail that sits high on her head. She still wears a sling, but her color looks better, as if she actually got a good night of rest. Daje is faring better too, but I see the cautious way he watches my brother, concern tugging his mouth into a straight line.

"I figured I'd give him the day off from holding more of our secrets," Nox says, running a hand through his hair. My lips quirk, but the moment is sobered quickly when Nox approaches where the Mirror still lies on the table. "It's still holding my magic."

"Cass's is in there too," Elora says, and Nox stiffens. Her cheeks grow pink as she swallows, Daje reaching over to rest his hand at her back. "We had to test that it would hold magic before collecting the pieces. Cass volunteered."

My throat prickles with sadness, but it's the way Nox seems to brush Elora's comment off that makes it tighten further. "Let's try again," he says, voice uncharacteristically cold. "And I think I should give my blood and a drop of Bahira's as well."

In the stilted silence that follows, Daje finds a clean blade and pricks my finger and Nox's, both of us giving a drop of blood that the Mirror seems to *absorb*. Once it's back to that same purple and black smoky state, Nox feeds even more magic into it, this time pulling back before he collapses. The glass darkens and then ripples when Nox calls out for Kai again. For a moment, I think that it's going to work. That Kai's face will appear on the other side. But, like it hits a wall or runs out of magic, the rippling stops.

Nox and I return to the palace, and when I try to speak with him, he waves me off, citing more meetings.

On the morning of the third day, I meet my brother in his sitting room, his hair disheveled and eyes wild, as if he's been up all night pacing. The frazzled energy fills the room, and I lay a hand on his shoulder to stop him when he tries to walk towards the balcony.

"Let's forget the forge today," I say, squeezing my fingers to keep him in my hold when he tries to walk forward again.

"Bahira, we *can't*—"

"We can," I interrupt, guiding him towards the door that will lead out into the hall.

His brows draw together in confusion as he looks at me from over his shoulder. "What about the guards?"

"I told you, we aren't going to the forge today." Pulling the door open, we step past the guards posted outside his room, their gray eyes watching us with curiosity. I let go of Nox to walk to my own door.

"Then where are we going?"

"I'm going to beat your ass at the training grounds."

Chapter One Hundred and Eight

BAHIRA

WATCHING NOX FIGHT HAS always been a worthy spectacle. For as tall and broad as he is, he moves with the same grace and ease that I do. I hadn't realized just how much I've missed sparring with him until we get to the training grounds and begin to warm up, Nox ordering the guards who followed back to the edge of the field.

"The Mage Kingdom's most fierce warrior is with me," he had said, rotating the long sword we swiped from the palace in his hand. "I do not think anyone will be dumb enough to attack." Though I rolled my eyes at the compliment, pride had bloomed in my chest.

We take our time warming up, our movements slower than usual as our muscles fight against the cold temperature. Eventually, we slide into a rhythm, one that is nearly what it was like before I had left for the Shifter Kingdom. Before Nox's body had become somehow trapped within itself. For all I thought that he was the one who needed the distraction of physical movement, I find it's my steps that are lighter, *my* spirits that are lifted by the time we're half an hour in.

I spin my spear over my head as Nox and I circle each other, the training grounds fairly empty because of the chilly early hour. No one save the two of us and a handful of other mages that are likely preparing for their first fighting test under Dilan's tutelage, their magic volleying back and forth from the obstacle course in the distance that they train on.

His chest heaves and sweat already stains the back of his tunic, but I forgo teasing him about it. He'll return to his full strength again. He has to. I decide to move first, arcing my spear through the air and straight towards him, my arms reverberating with the clash of metal. He counters quickly, pushing his sword against the body of my staff as he charges. I jerk my spear away, spinning to the right and swinging it out towards his torso. He lifts his sword just a fraction of a second too late, his weakened state making him slower than usual. I pull back my hit at the last minute but still cringe at the grunt he lets out when the body of my spear collides with his ribs.

"Shit." He laughs, and the sound warms me as I flip my spear and jab the tip into the ground to hold it in place. "You've gotten stronger."

I shrug, sending a smile his way. "Couldn't let you continuously be referred to as the strongest in our kingdom, now could I?"

He laughs again, and the familiarity eases that invisible tightness in my chest. "Should we head ba—"

"Hey! Daxel!"

Nox's eyes shut as his shoulders tense, and though I recognize the voice, I peek around him to confirm my suspicions. *Arin.* He marches over a small hill towards us, a longsword already gripped in one hand, the other clenched into a fist. And at his side, her gaze shrewd as she glares at me, is Haylee.

"Well, it seems *His Highness* can crawl out of hiding every once in a while," the asshole says as he comes to a stop a few feet away from us, ignoring me entirely while he stares at Nox. His eyebrows dance up his forehead, a cruel smile tilting his lips. "You look like shit."

"Arin," Haylee snaps, jutting her hip out as she folds her arms over her chest. "He is your *king*."

"Right, yes." He mocks a bow, the sun reflecting over the short strands of his blond hair. "Excuse me, I tend to forget to show respect to those I find weaker than myself."

Nox laughs, his head cocking to the side. "How many hours of practicing in the mirror did it take you to come up with that one?"

Arin growls as he takes a step towards Nox, only to find the end of my spear now blocking his path. He finally notices me, his gaze flicking my way with utter disdain. I send him a wink. "Get your fucking weapon out of my face."

"Or what?" I taunt.

"Bahira, don't egg him on," Haylee chides, her hands wrapping around Arin's arm as she tries to tug him back.

"If you have *any* self-preservation skills, you'll be mindful to not speak another fucking *word* around me," I seethe. While Haylee's reaction is a subtle jerk of her head, Arin's is much more aggressive. Wrapping his hand around my spear beneath the dark metal tip, he yanks it towards him. I go with it, sending the heel of my boot down on the top of his foot when I'm close enough. He howls and drops my spear, both hands clamping the hilt of his sword as he raises it above his head. My blood ignites at the idea of fighting him, of sending the tip of my spear through his gut until blood paints the end of it. I've never been a fan of his, but for Haylee's sake, I had always been cordial.

There would be no more of that. No more dancing around how much he annoys me with his petty jealousy of Nox and his need to feel like *he* is at the top of the proverbial food chain. He grits his teeth as he stares down at me, eyes flaring wide with feral rage before he swings his sword down directly over me. "Don't ever speak to her that way again!"

I laugh as I block, planting my feet and pushing against the momentum he created. I lean in closer, enough to see my own reflection in his sword. "How noble of you to stand up for a woman who doesn't even want you."

"Guess you would know a thing or two about that, wouldn't you?"

Fuck. I walked right into that.

"Enough!" Nox's raised voice draws the guards' attention but he waves them off. I use the distraction to slide my spear down the length of Arin's sword before snapping the body into his torso. It won't break skin, but it will at the very least knock the wind out of him. His breath hisses out between clenched teeth, and satisfaction surges through me as I step back, meeting Nox's exasperated gaze. "That is enough. Arin, go the fuck home and take Haylee with you. Bahira, come on."

"I want my rematch!" His voice bellows over the training grounds, but neither Nox nor I stop as we give Haylee and Arin our backs. I should have known that the following silence would be a precursor to nothing good. "Did Rhea tell you she danced with me?"

Nox comes to a stop, every line of his body going rigid.

"It's true," Arin continues when I glance at him over my shoulder, his feral gaze even more twisted with delight. "Gods, she looked beautiful that night, didn't she? That dress fit her so perfectly, showing off every single curve. No wonder you protected her so fiercely. I would too if her pussy was any bit as lovely as her face." *Fucking gods.*

"Nox—" But he ignores me as he turns slowly to face Arin again, and my stomach sours when Arin gives us a look that screams, *I win.*

"I can see by your face you're surprised, but of course she didn't tell you that I held her close enough to catch her scent. Lilies, right?"

My brother takes a step towards him, rotating the sword in his hand. Godsdamn it, Arin is goading Nox, and it's *working*.

"Her body in my hands felt so... *right*—as did the parting of her lips when I leaned in close. Do you want to know what I saw in those gorgeous green eyes, Daxel?"

"Are you going to shut him up?" I ask Haylee, drawing an impressive frown from her. "Or does the humiliation kink go both ways?"

"Oh, fuck you, Bahira!"

"It was *fear*," Arin proclaims, dropping his voice on the last word. "You weren't there for her, and something dangerous found her." He traces his lower lip with his tongue, shaking Haylee off when she tries to guide him away. I might feel bad for her, for the way hurt flashes across her face, if it weren't for the fact that all I've pictured since she confessed to using me is punching her square in the jaw.

"Nox, he's trying to rile you up. Don't let him." But one look at my brother tells me that he isn't listening, and so I hold my spear more tightly and angle the sharp tip in Arin's direction.

"Where is she now, *Your Majesty*? Did something dangerous find her again?" His brows lower, the sound of Nox's heavy breathing bisecting the thick tension in the air.

"I am warning you, Arin, *shut up!*" I growl.

He widens his stance, his sword held out in front of him as his knees bend. "You failed her twice that night, didn't you? And now you're *both* getting what you deserve."

The movement is quick, a flash of black and silver from the corner of my eye as Nox lunges towards Arin, sword raised and anger radiating off of him. Arin is knocked back as Nox attacks, their movements parrying each other. But Nox isn't his normal self, and we've already spent time sparring this morning. When the adrenaline fueled by his anger begins to wane, Arin capitalizes, sending a punch right into Nox's ribs.

My brother lets out a grunt, gasping for air as Arin kicks out, hitting Nox square in the chest. I rush over, spear aimed directly at the asshole, but Nox holds his hand out, my feet skidding to a stop. "Don't" is all he says before he pushes himself back up, and he and Arin begin fighting once more.

Haylee stands opposite me, her stance readied to step in, but I can't imagine who she'd rescue first. Perhaps she can't either, because when Nox finally lands a decent punch on Arin, sending him stumbling towards the ground, her fists twitch at her sides, but she stays put.

Nox brings his sword down hard, the guards at the edge of the training grounds edging closer as they watch the two duel. I'm torn between letting this play out—letting Nox show Arin that even weakened as he is, he's still a better opponent than Arin will *ever* be—and remembering that the council will likely use this against Nox when they hear of it.

"You need to end this," I yell, wincing when Arin's hips buck and he throws Nox off of him, my brother's back slamming into the ground. He loses the grip on his sword, and Arin kicks it away before he can grab it again.

Nox growls as he rolls to his side, but it isn't fast enough to avoid the tip of Arin's boot, the kick landing near his hip. Arin tosses his own sword before he drops to his knees, forcing Nox onto his back with one hand while the other begins to rain punches down.

"You're such a fucking prick!" he shouts, accentuating each word with well-aimed hits. Nox is only quick enough to block some of them, his arms too sluggish to keep up. "All that power, and what has it gotten you?" Chest heaving, Arin sends another punch towards Nox's head. And another. And another. "You're nothing without it now!"

My gaze lifts to Haylee's, her eyes blown wide and her cheeks growing red as she bears the brunt of my ire. "You fucking *told* him?"

"I—I didn't." She gives a curt shake of her head, as if chastising herself for the way she stumbles over her words. "I didn't *have* to tell him. Anyone watching Nox close enough can see the difference. Can—can *feel* it." I snarl at her, but the moment is short lived when Nox screams at something Arin says. The fine hairs at the back of my neck rises, and Haylee's lips part in shock as she looks at me. "Arin's magic—"

The crack of bone colliding with bone sounds, and Arin's head snaps to the side brutally. Nox rolls, taking Arin with him as they flip positions. He doesn't bother throwing punches. Instead, he wraps his hands around Arin's neck. Haylee and I both take a step closer, Nox's shoulders tensing as he hears us near.

"Nox," I murmur, mindful of the guards and the small crowd of people beginning to head our way, led by Dilan.

But he persists, his arms shaking as Arin claws at his forearms, his entire face flushing red.

"Brother, not like this."

As the moments pass and Nox doesn't relent, I fear I will have to intervene. Especially as Arin's magic begins to glow around him, dark green crawling up Nox's arms like vines in a last-ditch effort to get my brother off of him. But then Nox leans forward, his voice soft but not gentle. "Don't *ever* fucking speak of her like that again, or I will *kill* you."

He releases Arin unceremoniously, standing up and stepping over his body like he's no better than a wayward piece of garbage. Bending over, he picks his sword up before righting himself, his expression grim as malice gleams in his eyes. He looks crazed, driven to this point by his love for Rhea and the guilt that I know is destroying him from within. Behind him, Haylee works to help Arin up.

"Well, fuck," I say on a sigh, looking Nox over to ensure he wasn't seriously hurt. "This is going to be fun explaining to the council."

He doesn't answer or follow me when I step forward, instead wobbling on his feet as his eyes flash to mine. "Are you o—"

Green light pours over Nox, rooting him in place. Arin barely draws his arm back as he swings it towards Nox, the glint of silver flashing beneath the sunlight forcing me to gasp. I reach for Nox, gripping his forearm as I yank him towards me. But it isn't fast enough. His body arches, his mouth wrenching open with a shout before the magic disappears, and he stumbles into me. I look to where Arin stands, Haylee tugging on his tunic harshly, her eyes wide with fear. But it's what Arin holds in his hand that makes me lose all composure, white-hot *rage* blinding me at the dagger covered in Nox's blood.

Arin takes a single step towards us before two guards are on him, tackling him to the ground and pinning him there. With him apprehended, I return my focus to Nox, my hands trembling as I grip onto his forearms.

"I'm going to kill him," I snarl, watching Nox wince in pain, his skin growing pale. "It's not a threat but a fucking *promise*."

"You'll have to get in line," Nox retorts through gritted teeth, his chest heaving. Dilan reaches us, my old instructor glancing from Nox to me in shock.

"How can I help?" he asks, gesturing with his hand to Nox's back.

I force my brother to turn around, my heart beating a discordant rhythm as I lift his shirt. The cut from Arin's dagger is long, spanning the entire width of his back. It's deepest to the left of his spine, blood seeping more heavily from there. "Fuck," I whisper, pulling his tunic up higher. "It's bad, but—" My gasp cuts off my words, my eyes widening as I stare at the space just beneath my hand, at the expanse of exposed skin there.

"Fucking hell," Dilan blurts, his hand framing his jaw.

"What?" Nox asks, turning to look over his shoulder at me.

But I can't quite find the right words. Instead, I push his shirt all the way up his back until it's bunched at his shoulders, and my blood runs cold. Black lines stretch over his upper and middle back, like the sickly roots of a tree. The skin around them is more pale than the rest of him, and when I lean in to get a closer look, another breath gets caught in my throat. "Gods above," I whisper, turning to meet Nox's concerned gaze. "You've got something *living* in your back."

Chapter One Hundred and Nine

BAHIRA

"**Y**OU'RE GOING TO HAVE to repeat yourself," Nox says slowly, his words almost slurred. "Because I *think* you've just said I've got something living in my fucking back."

"I did," I respond, temporarily abandoning my concern for the injury in favor of what looks like a tattoo spiderwebbing its way across his upper back. But it's what those dark lines do that makes my mouth dry and my pulse race. They *writhe*, moving slowly between layers of skin like ink come to life. "When was the last time you saw your back?"

"It's not something I'm looking at frequently, Bahira." But his eyebrows furrow as he shakes his head. "I've been in pain since the moment I woke up from the Middle."

I trace the black lines with my eyes, their jagged shape reminding me of lightning arcing across the sky. As I study them, I notice that the closer they get to his left shoulder, the thicker they are. But as they move away, stretching towards his right side, they grow thinner.

The commotion of voices reminds me we aren't alone, so I tug Nox's tunic back down and force his arm across my shoulder before directing Dilan to his other side. Arin fights against the guards' hold on him, gnashing his teeth like a rabid dog, while Haylee stands with a hand covering her mouth, the traitor having the audacity to look mortified. I give them both one last glare, one that I hope denotes the promise of vengeance.

Turning back around, I lead us off the training grounds. "Let's get you to Galen."

Despite how much pain he must be in, Nox's steps are steady. Though when we finally reach the healers' wing in the palace and I order Dilan to fetch Galen, he all but collapses on the edge of the bed.

"Take your tunic off," I command, ignoring his mumble of protest as I move around the room, searching for some fresh gauze and antiseptic soap to begin cleaning out the wound while we wait for the healer. Setting the gathered supplies down, Nox leans his elbows on his knees, his head hanging between his shoulders as I get to work cleaning him up. "You'd think they'd rush a little more considering *His Majesty* is the fucking patient." Nox's back tenses as he hisses a breath out through clenched teeth. "Sorry," I mumble, gently wiping away the soap from the edges of his cut. "The bleeding is already slowing down."

"That's good."

I lay fresh gauze over the deepest parts of the cut, pressing down on them firmly as my eyes travel back up Nox's back and to the webbing of black lines there. "You truly haven't seen your back?"

"No. Why, what's there?"

"It's hard to describe." With one hand, I trace one of the lines from the middle of back to his left shoulder, my brow furrowing as the line *reacts* to my touch. Nox's grip on the edge of the bed tightens, his knuckles growing white. "Does this hurt?"

"Extremely. But every part of me does now."

My heart drops at the agony in his voice, but I force my emotions back down and try my best to describe to him what I see. "It looks like someone has filled your veins with black ink, just below the surface of your skin. It starts here," I pause to press the tip of my finger to the back of his right shoulder. "This line starts here and stretches all the way across your back to the other side." My finger drags to the other side, stopping where the line is thickest. Then I start over with a new line that zigzags its way from his lower back up to that same point, again growing thicker as it nears his shoulder. "It seems to be originating here." I press down at the center spot, the skin more pallid than the rest of him now that I'm looking more closely, and instead of feeling the push back of muscle and tissue, the tip of my finger presses against something *hard*.

"Fuck!" Nox yells, jerking away from me. Sweat beads at his temples, his chest rising and falling quickly as we look at each other. "Gods above, that fucking *burns*."

The door to the room opens, and Galen finally walks in, his steps shuffling as he enters. "I'm so sorry about the delay!" he says, shutting the door and rounding the bed to the side I'm on. "What has happened here?"

"What is this?" I ask him.

"I'd say it looks like a pretty decent cut from a very sharp blade."

"I mean this," I point out, my tone exasperated because *obviously* I mean the very out of place black markings on his skin.

"Oh, those are just a side effect from the tinctures," he says, his gaze down as he moves towards a cabinet along the wall. "In fact, it has been a few days since you've had a dose, hasn't it, Your Majesty?"

"It has. They seem to be losing their potency. Not lasting for as long."

"To be expected. Sometimes finding the right dose takes time." But Galen has been treating Nox for months, and he hasn't yet improved. If anything, he's getting *worse*. "Here you are, Your Majesty. This will ease your pain, and then I can begin healing your laceration." He gives the vial of pink liquid to Nox.

I wrap my hand around Nox's arm and gently squeeze before he brings the vial to his mouth. "Those are from the medicines?" I ask, drawing Galen's eyes towards me.

He takes his time answering as he rounds the table to Nox's back. "It is. Sometimes the ingredients can have unintended reactions."

A line forms between my brows as I give Nox another squeeze of his arm before letting go. "But there is something *inside* of him, and this spot—" I go to touch where the lines seem to originate from when Galen snaps his hand out.

"Don't touch it!" he barks, startling both Nox and I as I jerk my wrist out of his grasp.

My eyes lock on the side of the healer's face, a muscle throbbing to the quick beat of his heart. "Galen? What's wrong."

"Nothing. It's nothing." He waves me off, beginning to heal the cut on Nox's back. But his reaction gives me pause, and as I look back at those disturbing lines, unease simmering in my gut.

"How long have those been there?".

"A few weeks."

"Why haven't you said anything? To Nox? To our parents?"

"What is there to tell when it is merely a side effect?" he answers, sweat beading at his brow.

"Is that really all it is?" I ask as Nox sighs in relief. But he has been so secretive, hiding so much of his pain—of *himself*—from his family prior to Stephan's death. There have only been two versions of him I've seen in the weeks since Rhea was taken: angry and exhausted. And as time has passed, the former has given way slightly to the latter.

"What is this tincture made from?"

"Oh, a collection of plants. Lavendaris. Gelsemium."

Wait... "Isn't gelsemium known for its paralytic qualities?" It has been a while since I've studied plant properties, but gelsemium is one I've always remembered because of how utterly terrifying it sounds. Ingest just a little of the crushed petals, and you'll be left completely aware of your surroundings but unable to move.

"It is, but there is not enough in the medicine to cause paralysis. Just enough to numb His Majesty to the pain he's been feeling." But it isn't just numbing his pain; it's numbing *him*. Thinking back over my time being home, Nox's steadfast assuredness that he was going to get Rhea was ever present at the beginning. But when he was dragged back to the Mage Kingdom by Stephan, paralyzed in a way that sounded a lot like a side effect of gelsemium, that ever-present determination began to weaken. I had seen glimpses of it, particularly when something angered him enough to protect Rhea's honor or name, but even those had been fewer and farther between.

"Galen, how often does Nox get this tincture?"

"Every few days." It's Nox who answers, his head turning to look at me, eyes narrowed.

"If it has been a few days since he had his last dose, shouldn't these lines be more faded? Not as stark?" I shake my head, something not quite adding up. "If they were truly related to the medicine—"

"Enough, Princess Bahira." Galen lifts his hands away from Nox and turns to face me, gaze boring into mine. "*I* know healing best. You focus on what *you* know best and leave the care of your brother to me."

He brushes past me, leaving me in a stupor as he says something to draw Nox's attention to him.

I return to staring at the horrific map of secrets covering my brother's back. What Galen suggested they are could be true, yet why wouldn't he have brought it up to Nox? On the off chance that my brother—or someone else—might have seen them? Like when Nox removed his shirt to spar or— But I *just* sparred with him, and he didn't remove his shirt. With how he is feeling, it isn't like he's sparring regularly. And he's certainly not inviting anyone to his bed, but could Galen have banked on those facts?

I pinch my lips together, making a gut decision as I reach for the blade I keep tucked in my boot. I'll apologize to Nox for not giving him a heads up after I prove my theory right. *Or* wrong. Clicking the blade out of its hilt, I take a step towards Nox and place my hand on his back where the dark lines gather, pressing against that hard clump beneath his skin. But before I can make contact with the blade, green ropes wrap around my wrists, my hands firmly tugged away from Nox and suspended in the air with Galen's magic.

"Galen, release me!" I snap, in partial awe that he dared to use his magic against me.

Nox shifts on the bed to look at me, his eyes flaring wide. "Do as she says, Galen."

"This is for your own good, Your Majesty."

"Release Bahira. *Now.*"

He shakes his head, hands shaking where he holds them out in front of him. "This is the only way. He said so. You're still too dangerous."

"Who said so?" I ask, struggling against the magical restraints and finding that they are already starting to give.

"Everything we did was to protect you, Your Majesty. To ensure that you'd be ready to *protect us* when the time came. But, Princess Bahira, you cannot interfere. You've already drawn too much attention to yourself." His lip trembles, spittle flying as he talks. "You must leave this be. You must let the plan roll out accordingly for the good of our people."

Dread lands like a rock in my stomach. "Those lines—the markings on his back—aren't from the medicine, are they?" His grip on his magic falters. "Is it?" I shout.

"Leave it be—"

"We both know your magic is going to fail any moment now, and then you'll be stuck in this room with two curious individuals—one with nothing to lose, and one who may show you mercy if you answer our questions," I implore, my arms flexing as I fight against his hold. "Whose pl—"

His magic gives out, and he falls to the floor, hands planting to catch himself just in time. I move to help him, but Nox stops me. "Who, Galen?"

"Kallin's!" he answers, his head hanging between his shoulders. "He promised it was only temporary, that until the damage the girl had done to you was reversed, we had to do it this way."

"Girl?"

Galen lifts his head, the gray of his eyes lost behind unshed tears. "Rhea," he breathes, and Nox lets loose a low growl. "Kallin knew about her. Knew that you weren't being truthful about who she was and where she came from. After I examined her for the first time, he asked for a full report. I told him the truth, that she felt stronger than even you, King Nox, and that you tried to hide her signature from me."

"Why would you break a lifetime of trust with your king and queen for *Kallin*?" I ask, my eyes searching his.

"Because even though I have always respected your father, Kallin saw how much he put the wants of his family over the needs of his own kingdom."

The accusation stings, and I point my blade at Galen as I sneer, "You know *nothing* of how much my father *loves* his people if that is what you think. A king can only be made better by his dedication to his family."

"I have made sacrifices in the name of the kingdom that your father never could," Galen says, righting himself enough to sit back on his heels. "Do you know what it is like to turn in a family member because you've found out they are *hurting* the kingdom?"

"Do you?" Nox asks, far too quietly.

"Yes. Years ago, my sister's beloved husband, Simon, a renowned anatomist, was found to be *killing* mages in order to experiment on their dead bodies. It was *I* who led the guards to his house when I discovered what he was doing. *I* who helped raise his son as if he was my own. Though Simon managed to disappear before he could be held accountable for his crimes, the fact remains that I took a husband away from my sister and a father away from my nephew in the name of doing what was right. *You*"—his gaze leaves mine to look at Nox—"could not make that choice. Neither could your father."

"Are you comparing the woman I love to a murderer?"

"While the intent may be different, Your Majesty, the crime against the kingdom remains the same. Kallin understood this, and that is why he did what he did."

"And what is that?" I ask, battling the urge to throw my knife at his head.

He sighs, the sound exaggerated. "When word came that King Dolian threatened to attack our border towns if the girl was not returned, Kallin knew he had to act. I do not know the details of the exchange, but in return for getting her back—for righting the wrong *you* brought on our people when you stole her from the Mortal Kingdom—the king promised to leave our most vulnerable towns *alone*."

"And you believed him?" Nox asks, his voice raising with the question. "You returned one of your own back to a monster!"

"But she wasn't one of our own!" he volleys back in a rare show of anger. "She had never stepped *foot* in this kingdom until you. That is not someone *worthy*—"

"Worthy? *Worthy*? She is ten fucking times more worthy than anyone in this kingdom!"

"Galen, when you treated her, felt her magical signature, did you *know* that you were looking at the next Void queen?" I ask, pathetically hoping that his answer at least buys him a small amount of grace. Kallin has been convincing in his campaign against every perceived threat against our people, enough so that I could almost understand Galen's betrayal.

Unfortunately, he all but guarantees that there is no coming back from this with his answer.

"I suspected," he says slowly, no remorse showing on his face. "And I will tell you what Kallin told me when I brought my suspicions to him. Who is more dangerous: the enemy who proudly proclaims themselves as such or the one who hides behind pretty lies and manipulation, waiting for the right moment to strike?"

Nox growls as he leans forward, preparing to jump off the table, but I stop him with a hand at his arm.

"I believe you genuinely cared about her, Your Majesty. And I think that it blinded you to what the rest of us saw. She is not a queen of our people. Only a threat to the Crown."

I shut my eyes as I squeeze Nox's bicep, willing him not to act on the murderous thoughts I know must be dancing in his head. "What is actually on Nox's back?" I ask, once again pointing my blade at him when he looks ready to protest. "The truth, Galen. It is your only saving grace now."

"It is a lock," he answers hesitantly, twisting his hands in front of him. "How do you control the man with the single strongest source of power besides the Continent itself? You smother their access to said power, and then you make it so that they don't care that they've lost it."

The shock of his confession is enough to draw a curse from me. Galen says nothing more, ushering in a silence that feels like a fuse waiting to be lit. *Gods above*, this hasn't been about Nox healing. They've purposefully been blocking him from his magic this entire time. *And then you make it so that they don't care.* The medicine—it really had been numbing his mind. His emotions and feelings.

"Bahira."

The plea in Nox's voice as he says my name *guts* me. I nod as he stiffly turns back around, and I press my hand to his back while I angle the blade over that rough bump beneath his skin, right at the center of those dark lines. All this time. *All this fucking time.*

"If you do this, there is no going back," Galen rasps, sadness and fear mingling in the threat. "The council will see to it that you will never remain king. They will turn our people against you."

With the tip of my blade against Nox's skin, I cut into it.

"Then so be it," Nox responds, body tensing as the light gray skin over the hard mass splits beneath my knife, blood dripping as I cut through layers of skin and even muscle to reveal something *black*. Carefully, with my brother's labored breaths filling the room, I tilt the knife back, forcing the item to the surface where I grab it with my other hand.

And then Nox begins to scream.

Chapter One Hundred and Ten

NOX

MY BACK BURNS AS Bahira digs into it with her small blade, but I keep my eyes pinned on the man I thought was a friend. Who I exposed Rhea to because I assumed he could be trusted. Galen had betrayed more than just my trust; he betrayed everything he ever promised to our family as our chosen healer. And despite his poor attempts at excusing his behavior, there is nothing that can change the fact that he had a hand in throwing Rhea back into a cage.

It's an unforgivable act.

"I'm sorry," Bahira whispers, my jaw clenching tightly as she pushes the blade in deeper, the pressure building until whatever is inside of me—this *lock* as Galen called it—begins to move. The pain morphs into something all-consuming, an unbearable force that explodes throughout my body, radiating into my muscles and bones and blood until I'm knocked off-kilter, falling into a familiar place as black rolls in along the edges of my vision.

***

My chest rises with the heave of a strained breath, and I find myself standing in the Middle.

Goosebumps break out over my arms, a phantom wind carrying glittering stardust winds along my skin and weaving into my hair. Lifting my hands in front of me, I stare at the deep purple that pulses within me, changing me from a man to something more *again. Magic rushes from that deep well, a lid blown off after weeks and weeks of suffocation. And as it fills me with everything I've been missing, everything I've yearned to have again, it also wipes away the pain I've been shackled to. I'm stripped bare of it, and in a brief flash of panic, I forget what it is to be without that pain. What it is to be me.*

"Prince of Stars." Selene's voice is unmistakable, but so is the terror that rattles it. "You must hurry now."

"To her?" I ask, flicking my gaze back up to the stars and galaxies that surround me, the scent of jasmine wrapping around me.

"Hurry" is Selene's only response before the stardust begins to spin around me, faster and faster until it's all I see. Bright light flashes as my stomach lurches, my power thrumming beneath my skin to the beat of my heart until I am not surrounded by the stars anymore but made *of them. This space between worlds cannot contain all that I am, all that I'm capable of becoming. I don't fall but soar past the markers of other worlds, past even the gods rumored among them. Past everything that has been holding me back for fucking months, and I vow that all this power returning to me will be used for only two things: bringing Rhea home and punishing those who sent her away in the first place.*

That purpose fills me as my eyes open, as Selene's voice reverberates in my ears. *Hurry.* A veil of purple covers my eyes when they open, my sister's concerned face consuming my vision before she jolts back at what she sees looking back at her.

"Nox?" she breathes, one hand shaking my shoulder while the other clutches something, blood dripping between her knuckles. She swallows, tension bracketing her parted lips as her gray eyes bounce between mine. "You're glowing." To prove it, she lifts my arm in front of me, deep purple indeed flaring over my skin. Or shining *through* it.

I sit up, blinking until the purple haze over my vision clears. When Bahira cautions me to move carefully, I can't help but smile.

She frowns. "What?"

I direct my magic to grab at the shadows in the corners, drawing them nearer until they hover behind Bahira like an ominous cloud.

"Show off," she mumbles, stepping back as I stand and stretch my neck, calling my magic to settle.

"What was in my back?"

"A dragon stone shard." Holding her hand out, she shows me the jagged chunk of dragon stone coated in my blood, its center glowing with an array of contrasting colors. "While you were passed out, Galen told me that some of the members of the council imbued their magic into the shard." She closes her fingers around it before tilting her gaze up to mine. "When the guards found you on the beach, they brought you to Galen who then put the shard in you to cut off access to your magic. That, combined with the tinctures, didn't just weaken you, it dulled your emotions. Made you not *want* to care." She shakes her head, hands bracketing her hips. "I should have fucking known there was more to this then just you being ill, Nox. I'm sorry."

"No," I say harshly, giving her shoulders a gentle shake. "You don't get to take the weight of that burden, Bahira. He does." We both turn our attention to where Galen is still kneeling, and I direct the shadows at our back to coil around his body like thick ropes, pinning his arms to his sides. The healer shouts when I force his body up into the air, the shadow ropes binding his legs together and wrapping around his neck, coming to an end over his mouth.

Gesturing for Bahira to give me the shard, I drop it to the floor before smashing it with the heel of my boot, releasing all of the magic that's tied to it. Galen whimpers at the sound, and I tighten the restraints around him as I take a step forward. Though I no longer glow with my magic, I use it to call more shadows forward, allowing them to cloak me as wisps of darkness dance around my shoulders. "Let me tell you how this is going to go, Galen. I'm going to uncover your mouth, and you are going to tell me who in the council took part in abducting Rhea."

Tears trickle down his cheeks as he attempts to struggle against his bindings. When I send him a warning look—willing the shadows surrounding me to grow larger—his shoulders sag.

When I uncover his mouth, he draws in a deep breath. "It won't matter if you go after her," he rasps, looking to Bahira. "The council will never allow the two of them to be together."

A noise rumbles at the back of my throat while my magic pulses in my chest. Covering his mouth again, I grasp a shadow and harden it to stone, shaping it into a baton while the cold of it bites into my hand. I ignore the way my sister tenses as I swing it into Galen's leg, shattering his kneecap instantly.

"Nox—"

"If you don't want to be here for this, Bahira, I will not think less of you for leaving." I move to Galen's other side, drawing my arm back in preparation. "Tell me who in the council is responsible. Who did Kallin work with?"

Free of the restraint on his mouth again, he answers, "You s-said earlier that if I t-told the truth, you would show me mercy." His eyes move to my sister's, the plea in them clear.

"Bahira might have promised you grace, but I offered no such thing. You are going to die for what you did to Rhea. For how you prevented me from going to her." Stepping close, I return the baton in my hand to its shadow form and release it back into the room. "But you can make your death mean more than how you've chosen to live the past few months. Tell me what I want to know."

I give Galen the time to cry and plead and beg for his life, but only so that Bahira can decide if she wants to stay or leave. She should go, but of course my resilient sister stays, gaze hard as she stares at the man who betrayed us.

Galen finally calms, seemingly accepting his fate. "When you are done doing whatever it is you have planned, might I ask for a single favor?" he asks.

"You're not exactly in a place to ask for *anything*," I counter.

"I know, Your Majesty, but it is only a small thing. Please, tell my nephew that I am proud of him. That I know it hurt him to learn I had turned his father in, but that I tried to teach him all that I could in his father's place. Please."

At my answering silence, Bahira steps in. "How do we find him?"

"Oh, thank you. Thank you! He's in the guard, though I'm not sure where they have him stationed currently. I'm afraid we've lost touch over the years—"

I lift a hand wreathed in magic up in front of me. "Get to the point, Galen."

"Stephan. His name is Stephan."

The shadows around me pause, Bahira's sharp inhale mimicking my own shock.

"It can't be," she says, tilting her head. "What are the fucking odds?"

"You're the scientist," I counter, earning an incredulous look from her. But the odds don't so much matter to me as the poetic justice does. He hurt someone I love, and maybe it's the rush of magic talking, or maybe I simply have become the monster they feared I might with Rhea at my side, but I find myself enjoying the fact that I'll get to return the hurt that he's caused.

"It seems fate has a funny sense of humor," I muse as I draw him nearer, the tips of his toes dragging along the floor. I direct magic to my eyes, hoping that his low, pathetic cry is because he recognizes that he's no longer looking upon his king but his executioner. "Your nephew's a little shorter than me, right? With shoulder-length black hair and a cruel little smirk? He knows how to make gelsemium tinctures, which I suppose makes sense considering who he's had as a father. Well, father *figure*." Galen's eyebrows race towards his hairline. "Yes, Stephan and I have met, and I'm afraid, I'm not going to be able to give him that message after all."

"W—why?" he asks, complexion turning red as the ropes around him tighten.

"Because I watched Stephan die," I murmur, my lip lifted in a snarl. "When I killed him myself."

Galen's reaction is short lived, his distress at what I've said and the life being squeezed out of him lasting for only a few minutes. He fights to breathe through the shadow tightening its hold on his neck, and I watch as the life slowly leaves his eyes, second by second until they gloss over and fall closed. When I let his body brusquely drop, sending the shadows back to where they came from, I release a breath and tip my head back. There is relief in Galen's death, but there is also something insidious that peeks from behind a corner in my mind. A reminder that every action taken since I woke up from the Middle has been one that has taken me farther away from Rhea.

"You good?" Bahira asks, prompting me to nod.

"I will be, but there is something I need to do," I tell her, reaching to grab my tunic. It is cut up and soaked in blood, but I slip it on anyway, remembering the jealousy that filled a certain pair of green eyes when I had come in from sparring with Cass bare-chested. The thought of my best friend, of my brother, stops me in my tracks, a knot of emotion I've tried to keep buried struggling to make its way back to the surface. But now is not the time to acknowledge the devastation I feel.

Stepping over Galen's body, I reach for the door, Bahira following behind me. "Are we just going to leave him here?"

"For now. I'll use the shadows to lock the door from the inside to buy some time for me to gather the council without suspicion. Will you relay everything Galen shared with us to Mother and Father?"

"Of course, but this doesn't end with the council, Nox."

A dark wisp of a shadow slides beneath the door at my command, a few seconds passing before we hear the lock of the door click. The shadow returns to where I grabbed it from.

"Gods, it's been a while since I've seen your magic at work."

I smirk as I guide us out of the healer's wing, heading in the direction of the main foyer. "I'm not staying a moment longer than I have to, Bahira. It's been... *fuck*, it's been far too long that Rhea's been in King Dolian's hands. I have to go."

"And you will, but first, I have an idea about the Mirror." We continue down the hallway, passing only one other healer who averts their gaze. "The stones that Rhea practiced imbuing with her magic, are they still in your room?"

My brows furrow, our steps loud as we climb stairs to the first floor. "Yes, why?"

"Because I think that is the missing link. I'll explain once we finish whatever it is you're planning with the council."

"You can leave, if you want to," I say as we enter the final corridor. "You've already helped more than necessary."

She lets out a short laugh, glancing at me from the corner of her eye. "If you think I'm going to let you take all the credit for bringing those guilty on the council to justice, you're sorely mistaken."

I shake my head as a grin tugs at my mouth, the door to the council room finally coming into view. "It won't take long," I tell her as our steps slow. But they come to halt completely when the sound of blended voices rises not from the council room, but from the main foyer.

"Is there something happening today that I forgot?" I ask in a low voice, my magic humming beneath my skin.

Bahira leads the way, fingers flexing at her side. I realize she isn't holding her spear, likely having left it on the training grounds. "Not that I'm aware of." We step out of the hallway and into the massive room at the front of the palace and find the council, our parents, guards, and some of the palace court staring at us as if they were waiting for our arrival. I push more of my power to right beneath the surface, expanding my signature so that everyone can feel its presence. A few people gasp, some guards even lay their hands over the hilt of their swords, their brows lifted high. I meet my father's gaze, his relief instant as he forces a smile to his face. And then I drag my eyes to Kallin. He's always been a guarded man, never one to show much emotion outside of his calculating stoicism. But I watch as he takes the two of us in, as he realizes his plans to keep me chained like a dog have failed.

"Your Majesty," he says, pulling his hands behind his back as he takes a step forward, his black boots clicking against the stone floors. "We heard you might have been injured on the training grounds today. I'm pleased to see that you are... *well* now."

"I'm sure you are." I lift my chin as Kallin examines me, and I only just now realize how I must look. Hair disheveled because it's grown too long. Clothes dirtied from fighting with Arin. Tunic ripped and tainted with blood. I look down at my hand, the one I used to pummel Arin, and find flecks of his dried blood in the grooves of my knuckles. I smile as I look back up to the councilman and call my magic into my palm, letting the purple glow and wisps of black dance around my hand. "To be honest, I haven't felt this good in a long, *long* time."

"No doubt in thanks to Galen," he says slowly, pacing in front of councilmen Osiris, Arav, and Borris. Hadrik stands next to my parents, his lips tilted to the right in a victorious smirk. Councilwoman Naji's dark eyes scour Bahira and I, her arms folded over her chest in clear disappointment. The rest of the council is spread out, some looking at me with the same uneasy ire as Kallin, while others keep their expressions more reserved. More cautious. Unfortunately for everyone outside of Hadrik, they are going to find that my own wrath burns hotter, and it demands justice. "I've gathered everyone here because I had a feeling you might want to see just how many people support you, Your Majesty, through this new transition into king." He walks closer to me, lowering his head in a mock bow as he speaks only loud enough for me to hear. "Be mindful of what you do in front of all of these people. Public perception is as fragile as it is damning, and forgiveness will not easily be given. No matter what you proclaim." Then, even more quietly, "Or what *she* does."

He lifts his head, offering me a grin colored with the victory he's so sure he's earned.

I lean close as well, my voice a weapon all its own. "A well-played move, Councilman. But you have forgotten one crucial thing."

"I highly doubt that, but humor me, Your Majesty."

I tug on my magic, forcing it to fill my body until Kallin's eyes widen at how my own are haloed in purple and black. "That there is only one person in the whole of Olymazi whose opinion I give a shit about."

A retort sharpens on his tongue but doesn't get the chance to be spoken before the screams and shouts of those around us begin to slice through the air. Shadows peel off the walls and lift from the floors, following my command as I guide them to each councilman and woman, catching a few off guard while snatching others who have attempted to run away. To his credit, Kallin doesn't fight as the first rope of darkness bands around him, swirling over his legs and up his torso. The guards disperse, a clear divide between those who are working for Kallin and those who aren't with the former drawing their weapons. Bahira runs to our parents, and I surround them with a magical barrier before clearing my throat.

"The council has betrayed the Crown and everything they are supposed to stand for. They have participated in secret machinations to not only weaken the royal family but harm the rightful heir to the throne." I choose my words carefully because even though this kingdom and all its subjects belong to Rhea, until she claims them for herself, it is not my place to share that she is the queen of Void Magic. Panicked eyes meet mine, but the guards don't advance any farther. They stay in place, marveling at my magic.

Or trembling before it.

"They will be held accountable, and in the interim, my father will once more bear the crown of the Mage Kingdom until this is all sorted out." Murmurs of surprise volley around the foyer, but I ignore them, instead looking to my family, my father nodding in approval. When the guards put their swords away, I drop the shield of my magic. When there are no attempts to harm them, and focus again on the eight council members I've captured.

"You cannot do this!" Borris howls, red staining his cheeks. "We deserve respect for what we have done for the kingdom! For the Crown!"

"Please continue to shout about what you deserve, Borris," I begin, lining the council up before dragging them behind me as I begin my walk to the lowest level of the palace. "I'm sure you'll find the walls of the dungeons to be an amenable audience."

Chapter One Hundred and Eleven

NOX

RETURNING TO THE DUNGEONS is more anticlimactic than I thought it might be. I'm not a stranger to killing men. I had happily slain mortal guards without a second thought as Rhea and I escaped, had vowed to kill anyone who got in our way. But what occurred in this damned place was something I had never done before. A kill had never been so... *personal*. So inefficient. So bloodthirsty. As I pounded Stephan's body to a pulp for the way he spoke of Rhea—for what he insinuated—killing him had been all of those things.

I don't have regrets about what I did, but I can't help but wonder what Rhea will say when she finds out. Her words from the tower, the day of her failed attempt to leave, come rushing back to me. *I don't want you to kill for me. I just want you.* I can't even blame killing Stephan on a way to get closer to bringing her home. I had pulverized him before he could have even given me anything useful. No, what I had done was cruel. In those moments, I had fallen prey to my anger in a way that was so fucking unworthy of the type of man Rhea deserves to have at her side, yet the thought of anyone else getting to experience life with her sends my heart beating against my chest in a painful and riotous manner. I will not keep what I've done from her. Once she is safe again, I will tell her everything and hope that, despite how my mind has tried to distort our last moments together, her love for me is how I actually remember it. Tender. All-encompassing. *Just for me.*

"What is your plan, Son?" my father asks at my side, the members of the council in individual cells surrounding us. Arin is here as well, having been brought directly from the training yard by my guards. The asshole whines about his false imprisonment despite his charges of attempted regicide.

"They will all stay here where they will be interrogated by you and anyone you trust until I return from the Mortal Kingdom. I want to know every single person that was involved with the abduction of Rhea, the collaboration with King Dolian, and the underhanded treachery that took place in order to get you removed from the throne." As I speak, I pace in front of the cells, meeting each council member's gaze.

"Let us not forget how they poisoned you with magic and herbs," my father adds, earning some comments of confusion from a few of the councilmen.

But it's impossible yet to know who was truly aware of what Kallin was plotting, and who, if any, didn't realize just how corrupt his plans had become. "Whoever is found guilty will be killed."

"You can't be serious!" Councilwoman Naji shouts, her fingers curling around the iron bars. "You cannot expect us to simply *wait* here while you go on a suicide mission to save a woman who does not need saving!" Her chest heaves while her tears catch the light of a spelled flame. "This is madness, Prince Nox!"

"No, this is the *consequence* of the madness you created." Pausing in the center of the aisle, I lift my arms out at my sides. "You tried to force me into submission, to create some twisted fantasy world where we can just keep to ourselves and pretend that no one outside of this border is worthy of worrying about. That line of thinking might have worked a long time ago, but it no longer rings true."

"Your Majesty, I understand your need to punish those of us who you believe wronged you," Councilman Arav says calmly as he sits at the back of his cell, twirling his magic over his knuckles. "But do know that some of us were fed lies by Kallin about Lady Rhea."

Borris scoffs, banging his closed fists against the bars. "You were all too eager to believe those supposed lies, Arav."

"Because I was told it was for the betterment of the kingdom! That she *lied* about being from Santor. That the Daxel family lost their way." He runs a hand down his face, his magic dissipating. "I should have seen it for the farce that it was. What was your plan, Kallin? To eventually take the crown for yourself?"

"I don't care about your bickering," I interrupt, turning to look back at my father. "They do not leave these cells while I'm gone."

"I will only have those I trust guarding them."

"Thank you."

My father smiles as he places a hand on my shoulder, his grip firm. "I'm sorry, My Son, that I did not do better as your king. That I could not have predicted how my own failures would fall to you." I hold his gaze as I return his gesture, my opposite hand squeezing his shoulder. I can't find it in me to refute his claims, not yet. He seems to recognize that in my gaze and offers a sad smile in return. "But I am proud of the man you have become, Nox."

I nod in thanks, though I don't know if I feel worthy of the sentiment. I doubt he'll feel the same about me when he discovers Galen.

"Go on. I'll keep things handled here until you are back. Until you *both* are." He draws me in for a hug, and then I head towards the dungeon exit.

"You're fucking *pathetic*, Daxel," Arin seethes as I near his cell. "I hope when you find her, those pretty green eyes are lifeless." Magic writhes along my bones, spelled flames flickering as shadows peel away from the walls. "I held her after we knocked her out."

My eyes meet his, feral rage wrapping a fist on the air in my lungs and trapping it there. I hear my father's voice but it's muffled beneath the way my power rises within me.

"It was *me* who carried her to the beach, my fingers gripping her body tight enough to feel her curves. To feel the heat of her skin through that incredible dress." He licks his lips before quirking them to the side. "Do you want to know why I'm telling you this? Of course, you do. It's because I know that you won't do anything, not when you've got a moral line to hide behind. No—"

It's effortless, the way I command the shadows to turn into something sharp. Slicing through his neck and watching his face show the horror of what I've done for a split second before he tumbles forward is easier than taking my next breath. As shouts and screams filter through the chaotic haze of bloodlust that coats me, I drink it in. *This is what you made me*, I think to myself, but even that feels like giving them too much credit. No, I've always had the capacity to become *this*, I just hoped that Rhea would never have to see it.

My voice is calm as I say, "He stays here to remind the council to talk."

❧✦✦✦✦ ✦✦✦✦❧

Bahira is waiting for me in the foyer when I make my way back up from the dungeons, wearing her pack and idly twirling her spear as she glares at Haylee, who stands across from her. Glad to see she has her weapon again.

"I just need a few minutes to wash up and change," I tell her, gesturing to the stairs that lead up to my rooms.

"Your Majesty, Nox, please. Can I speak with you?" Haylee asks, as she steps in front of me, laying a hand on my forearm.

"No." I move to brush past her, but her fingers tighten along my skin. My reaction is swift as I pull my arm back, sending her a warning glare. "What do you want, Haylee?"

"It's not about what *I* want," she says, earning a scoff from Bahira. Haylee ignores her as her eyes implore mine. "Nox, I know that the way the council has gone about things wasn't right, but all that matters is that our people are safe. That they feel supported by the Crown. That they *trust* them. If you go to retrieve

Rhea, you will return to a weakened system where the people are split on trusting you or condemning you. But it doesn't have to be that way. Together, we can earn their trust again." She moves in closer, reaching back out to touch me before my narrowing eyes freeze her hand mid-air. "You are powerful, Nox, but not even you can withstand losing the peoples' faith."

"There is only one person I need to have faith in me, Haylee. Together, she and I will deal with whatever happens next."

Her head jerks back in indignation. "You'd leave something as precious—as powerful and important—as public approval to chance so that you can, what? Follow your heart? Love is for the weak, Nox. Any fool can fall in love, but only the rarest man can be king. This moment does not have to be another failure on your family's name. You can fix this—*we* can fix this!"

"You're so fucking *pathetic*," Bahira snaps.

I trace my gaze over Haylee's face and note the genuine concern there. It's in the sheen covering her eyes and the lines denting her forehead. But it's the hunger that lingers beneath that gives her away. Even if she were not someone who has been in my life for nearly as long as Bahira has been alive, I would recognize the thirst for power, because I had seen it so many times from King Dolian. Leaning in close, I don't bother keeping my voice low.

"Whatever you think it is that you are owed by me or this kingdom is not rooted in anything remotely factual or concrete. You will *never* wear a crown. You will *never* share my bed or my name or my duty to this kingdom. And if I find out that you were involved with Rhea's abduction in any capacity, I will not hesitate to show you just how *easily* my power can be wielded without the support of the people."

I leave Haylee with a stunned look of defeat on her face and climb the stairs to my rooms. Once there, I quickly undress and get in the shower, the warm water a welcome reprieve as I close my eyes and drag my hands down my face. I check in with my magic again, prodding at the source of my power to make sure that I can still feel it. That I can still wield it. It was that spelled shard of dragon stone that the council had Galen put in me that was holding my magic back, not my own body. It was the fake medicines—tinctures the old bastard fed me—that numbed me to what was happening, not my own mind. But the fear that I might lose myself again before I can get to Rhea remains present, and it makes my movements jittery and my thoughts chaotic.

How can I in one breath tell Rhea that Bella is *alive*. That despite how we've come to understand the laws of magic and the rules of the Spell, she was able to live with Rhea in the tower, and then she returned home to the Shifter Kingdom. That her name is Siyala, and that Bahira had met her. And then in the very next breath, tell her that Cass is gone. That me breaking the Mirror set off a chain of events that led directly to his death. Gods, how am I supposed to look into her perfect eyes and tell her that I killed for her. That I *happily* sacrificed my reputation and crown and title for her, but that I was too weak to rescue her sooner. That I had been tricked so fucking easily by men I thought I could trust and she had paid the price for it?

Pushing away from the wall, I quickly finish my shower and dress, heading back down to the foyer where Bahira waits, a second pack in her hands. "This is for you," she says, handing it to me as we cut through the gathered guards and nobility still lingering. Their gazes are heavy on us as we pass, but we keep our steps quick as we exit, descending the white stone steps before heading into the forest, and to the forge.

"You'll be alright?" Bahira asks when we are nearly there, breaking the silence that has been weighed down with my thoughts. "I can go with you—"

"No," I interrupt, shaking my head. "Thank you, but no. You are needed here, both to support our parents and because I know you are eager to speak with Kai."

Bahira makes a strange noise at the shifter king's name, clearing her throat immediately as if that will disguise how we both heard it. But I give her mercy as the forge comes into view, a familiar figure pacing in front of it.

At the sound of our steps, his head snaps up, his dark blue eyes widening in both relief and slight annoyance. "*Finally*!" Daje groans, opening the door to the forge and running in, leaving it open behind him.

"Rude," Bahira mumbles as she follows. I'm the last one to step in, the scent of the burning coals powering it overwhelming.

Elora's expression falters when we enter, doing a double take as she looks at me. "Oh gods, you're okay! We heard you had been attacked and—" Her mouth hangs open, brows drawing in as she takes a step towards me. "Your—your magic. I can feel it again."

I nod, pushing my hand through my hair to draw back the damp strands that lay over my forehead. "It's back."

Her cheeks lift with a smile, eyes bright when she asks, "Does this mean that you're back to being *you*? That you can go get Rhea now?"

"Yes. As soon as we try one last attempt at fixing the Mirror."

Elora claps, turning her joy to Daje as he comes to stand next to her. "Let's not waste any time, then."

"My thoughts exactly," Bahira agrees, taking her pack off and setting it on the ground, laying her spear next to it. "Now, this is nothing more than a hunch. I don't know for sure that it will work, but I think with Nox's magic fully returned, it's worth a try." Undoing the buckles, she reaches in and, to my surprise, pulls out one of the dragon stones that Rhea imbued, my magic immediately perking up at the sight of it.

"Why do you have this?" I ask her, Daje and Elora drawing nearer to look at the stone.

She pulls out stone after stone, piling them on the floor until it's obvious she grabbed every single one that was littered throughout my rooms. "In order to explain why, you're going to have to tell them the truth."

I pause as I look at our friends, an emotion I can't fully identify sitting heavy on my chest. It isn't that I don't trust them, or even that I think Rhea would mind if they knew. It's that she isn't here to tell them herself. That I hadn't told Cass, and now he would never know that her flame turned blue or that she is the rightful mage queen. This is such an intimate part of who Rhea is, and with all of my missteps, I hate to add yet *another* to the list.

But if Bahira thinks it will work, then I have to push aside my own urge to keep everything regarding Rhea guarded as if it will do anything to help her *now*. "Rhea is the queen of Void Magic."

Daje's brows climb high on his forehead, his mouth falling open then closing again before he asks, "How do you know?"

"Of *course* she is!" Elora says, her smile beaming.

"We did a Flame Ceremony before the ball. Her blood produced a cobalt blue flame."

"No one else knows except for the people in this room," Bahira adds, her serious tone relaying that it will *stay* that way. "Well, and our parents."

"We won't say anything," Elora says, her fingers resting over Daje's wrist.

He glances down at the contact, a small smile flickering. "What can we do to help?"

I defer to Bahira, who has us gather the stones and lay them on the table next to the Mirror. Once they are piled on the steel surface, Bahira picks one up, showing us how Rhea's magic glows at the center. "What we know of Void Magic is that it is something chosen and given by the gods, right?" she begins, earning nods from the three of us. "And what we *assume* of the magic in the Mirror is that it is as ancient, as gods-given as the magic of Olymazi. What if those magics are the same? What if there is *no* difference between Void Magic and the magic that is in the land except for how it is wielded?"

Elora cocks her head to the side, the hair piled high on her head shifting with it. "You're saying that you think that Rhea's magic as Void queen is the same raw magic that we manipulate? That runs through Olymazi?"

"Yes," Bahira answers, but then shakes her head. "And no. When I looked at the blood of those with magic under the magnifier, there were magic particles mixed within the blood cells, and they were *white* in color. Just like the Spell, and just like—"

"Rhea's magic," Elora cuts in, her expression relaying just how quickly her mind is turning over everything Bahira has said.

"Exactly. There's still some testing I have to do, but if her magic is the same as that which flows through Olymazi, then it can be reasoned that her magic should power the Mirror. But until she returns, all we have is the magic imbued in these stones." My sister points to me. "If we can break these open, do you think you can direct her magic into the Mirror?"

Fuck. "I don't know," I answer. Theoretically, one of our magics should cancel the other out. *Except...* Rhea's magic had always acted differently with mine. One didn't overpower the other; instead, they blended together. Drawn to each other in a way I had never seen before. At least, that was the case with her healing magic. Still, I had never attempted to manipulate her magic other than trying to shield myself from it before. Then again, I wasn't going against the full brunt of her power. "I can try." I hold my hand out for the stone, Bahira placing it on my palm as I lift my other hand out above it.

"Because it is imbued dragon stone, the moment it breaks, it should release her power, and then all you have to do is..."

Her words trail off as she watches my magic begin to coat all sides of the stone. It takes a moment for me to find the threads of Rhea's magic past the layers they are locked behind, but when I do, the warmth of it immediately caresses my fingertips. Pulling gently, like threading a sewing needle, I begin to coax the small bit of Rhea's magic past the stone. It doesn't resist, instead latching on to my own power easily until there is a glowing ball of white hovering at the center of deep purple and black.

"That works," Bahira says, her voice coated in awe. "Now just direct it towards the Mirror." I do as she says, guiding both magics into the dragon glass. We watch as the glass *ripples*, white light flaring before eventually sinking in and disappearing. "Great. Let's do it again."

The process of extracting Rhea's magic moves quickly, and soon, I'm down to the last stone, retrieving the magic within it and directing it into the glass. My pulse beats at my temples, my anxiousness to leave beginning to gnaw at me, but I force myself to stay still until we can at least see if this attempt worked.

"Let's stand it up," Daje suggests, moving as if to grip the frame's edge. But I call my magic out again, letting it surround the Mirror before lifting it from the table to stand at the center of the room.

Bahira snorts, standing in front of the Mirror and meeting my gaze in the glass. I smile at her and join her on her right, Elora and Daje flanking her left. "This is a good sign," she says when we step closer and the Mirror begins to ripple and grow cloudy, changing its appearance just as the old one did.

"It definitely didn't do that before," Elora breathes.

Bahira shifts her weight from one foot to the other, her quick breaths the only tell of her nerves.

Lifting my chin, I call out for the shifter king like I had before. The four of us watch the Mirror with bated breath, holding it tightly in our chests as the echo of my command rings out over the room. Each second that passes is weighted, and as they drag on and the shifter king does not answer, Bahira's shoulders begin to slump.

We try again, even Bahira calling out since her blood is also keyed to work. But the result doesn't change. There is no answer. Putting a hand on Bahira's shoulder, I squeeze it gently as I apologize. "I'm sorry, but I have to go."

"I know," she answers quickly. Curtly. Not in anger at me, but frustration at the Mirror. "It's alright. I'll keep trying." I draw her in for a hug, her arms squeezing my torso tightly. "Please be careful. I'd really hate to have to travel to the Mortal Kingdom to rescue you."

I laugh quietly as I kiss the top of her head. "Be careful here. We still don't know who has sided with the council's lies and who remains loyal to our family. Treat everyone with caution." My goodbye with Elora is quick, her demanding that I hurry as if that was not already my intent. But when my hand reaches to shake Daje's in parting, he shakes his head, instead straightening his posture and pushing his shoulders back.

"I want to come with you."

I look to Elora, expecting a bit of protest considering she and Daje have appeared to grow closer, but she nods her head, her gaze just as determined as his, even if worry seeps in at the edges of her smile.

"Please," Daje continues, his fingers closing into fists at his sides. "It was *my* fault that Rhea and I were lured out, that she was taken. I promised you I would watch over her, and I *failed*. I couldn't do anything to protect her or to protect Cass." I look away, my teeth gritting together as a shaky breath passes his lips. "Please, let me help make this right. It's the least I can do. The *only* thing I can do."

Elora's hand reaches out for him, her fingers threading with his before squeezing them tightly.

"We'll be on horseback to get there as fast as possible. It will not be an easy journey, and I have no idea what will be waiting for us. But if you come, your sole mission is to ensure that Rhea gets home. No matter the cost. No matter who stands in our way." I look back at him, my magic thrashing deep within me. "Do you understand what that means?" I have no doubts that King Dolian has ensured that Rhea is well protected and likely behind multitudes of safeguards. Daje will have to kill, and he will have to do it without hesitation or moral objection.

His gaze hardens as he gives me a short nod. "I understand. I will not fail you. I will not fail *her*. Not again."

"Then say your goodbyes," I tell him, turning towards the door. "Because we're leaving right fucking now."

Chapter One Hundred and Twelve

ARIA

T HE SUN HAD NOT yet risen when Sade knocked on my door, drawing me from a sleep filled with dreams of fighting the Queen's Legion. Spears had been thrown, hitting their mark in the ones I cared about most. Lyre. Sade. Even the sirens of the seamounts and the ones creating their own rebellion in Eersten. And, though it did not make any sense, Myla had been in the dream too. Her figure was cloaked in black, her long cloak trailing on a gusting wind as she watched from the edge of the beach. I've never given much credence to dreams, but having Myla there felt like a premonition of sorts.

Or maybe I am just nervous about our meeting today.

Rushing to my door, my movements sloppy from having just awoken, I open it to reveal Sade. She roams her sunset eyes over me, amusement creeping into the right corner of her mouth as it rises. "Good morning, Aria."

I grumble something out, brushing my braids away from my face as I blink quickly to clear my vision of the last remaining haze of sleep. "What's going on?"

"I wanted to speak with you and Lyre before you left for the day."

Still trying to rouse myself, I don't realize what Sade's words mean, nor do I censor my response to them until the last moment. "This couldn't have waited until I returned from my meeting with—" My eyes widen as I slap a hand over my mouth. *Gods, Aria.*

Sade snorts, swimming backwards to make room for me in the hall. "Fear not, Baby Sister. I'm used to holding the weight of secrets. I won't falter under yours."

I shut the door behind me as I follow her, my hands nervously fidgeting in front of me.

"Do you know—"

"Where you go? No," she interrupts smoothly, tucking back in a loose braid from the knot she's tied at the base of her neck. "But I don't need to."

I bite on my lower lip, working it between my teeth before asking, "Aren't you worried about what I'm doing? That I might mess it up?"

Sade glances at me, that small smirk still firmly in place. "No." I must look unconvinced as we continue down the crystal lit hallway to Lyre's room because she adds, "You risked the queen knowing that you were helping the seamount sirens. You held on to a secret cave of trinkets because, I'm assuming anyway, you wanted to honor the lives that have been lost under the sea." It's scary how spot on she is with that despite me having never told her the reason for my cave. "I have seen enough of the actions you've taken in private to know the workings of your heart, Aria. I do not have to question anything because you've already shown me who you are. And I'm hoping the queen is too preoccupied with what is happening on the surface to pay too much attention to what you're doing beneath it."

My chin falls to my chest as I feel a blush creep up my cheeks. Part of me wants to deny—to amend and say that I'm not anywhere near where I need to be to earn such praise, but that small flame within me that has been stoked to life beneath Myla's tutelage and my love for Lyre banish the rebuttal before it ever leaves my mouth.

We come to Lyre's door, an amethyst embedded at its front, and Sade gently knocks.

Lyre's command for us to enter is muffled, Sade and I looking at each other before she turns the handle and pushes the door open, our eyes falling to where Lyre is laying on her bed. Her hands cradle her stomach, a grimace pinching her features while her back arches in an uncomfortable looking position. I rush over to her, panic lancing through me as I look for an injury or another reason why she appears to be in so much pain.

But it's Sade's calm voice that draws me away from the edge of fear. "It's just her body prepping for labor. She's alright." Sitting on the edge of Lyre's bed, Sade draws a hand down Lyre's arm, the tender touch one I never imagined seeing from the domineering general of the legion.

"She's right," Lyre grits out between her teeth. "It'll be over in just a minute." The minute comes and goes, then Lyre's face grows more relaxed, the tautness of her body smoothing until she's lying on her back, her lavender eyes bouncing between Sade and I. "To what do I owe this ungodly early visit?"

The amusement of Sade's expression fades to something more serious. "I have news."

Lyre and I look at each other as I help prop her up into a sitting position. She transforms her tail into legs, crossing them as she leans back against the wall, her arms wrapped around her belly. "Go on, then. How is our mother ruining our lives now?

"As you know, she's been keeping her plans regarding the mortal king and Rhea close. She has Dyanna searching for the magical limitations of mages but isn't telling her *why*."

"Can we trust that Dyanna is telling the truth?" I ask.

Sade nods, folding her toned arms. She is bare of any armor today, though a bag is strapped across her chest. "Dyanna's loyalties lie on the path of least resistance. She'll do as our mother commands, but even she has a line she isn't willing to cross." Sade arches a brow. "It's usually only when her books are compromised, but still. I don't think she is lying about that. In any case, Queen Amari is planning another visit to the Mortal Kingdom, and this time, she is demanding that Dyanna, myself, and Aria come with her."

I tense as my fingers flex against the scales on my tail. "When do we leave?"

"Tomorrow morning. She's bringing some legionaries with her on the journey, but they are ones that have already been healed by Rhea's magic."

"Wait, didn't you say that the last time you attended a meeting with King Dolian, our mother asked when his wedding was?" Lyre asks, her gaze latching on to mine. I nod, dread already knotting my stomach. "Has she already had Rhea heal her to pass through the Spell?"

I look to Sade, who shakes her head. "She wanted to wait and see if there were any adverse side effects to Rhea's magic. All the sirens passed through the Spell as a test after they were healed. It's been weeks, and they all still live."

Lyre purses her lips, concern settling on her shoulders and making them round. "She's going to have you healed so that you can pass through the Spell with her."

Sade groans in frustration, tilting her head back to look up at the ceiling. "I wish I knew exactly what she is planning. With both Rhea and King Dolian beneath the control of the siren rings, she has the potential to do exactly what she promised she would."

"But to what end? She might be able to control their actions, but it is not like that puts her in control of the king's army," I say, only to receive damning silence in return. "Gods above, you think she is trying to get their army too?"

"I think our mother is power hungry and willing to do whatever it takes to grasp as much of it as she can. We know Rhea has been healing the mortal army to pass through the Spell as well. If our mother controls them both, she'll have more than enough man and siren power to march into the Mage and Fae Kingdoms," Sade says, her tone grim.

I look at Lyre but direct my next question towards Sade. "What do we do?"

"We have to get the ring off of the king's finger," she says, already lost in thought as she formulates a plan. "And, ideally, off of Rhea's too."

"How are you going to manage that while our mother is there?" Lyre asks, and again, that damning silence answers.

"It might be something we plan out *after* we already have access to the Mortal Kingdom's land," Sade finally says, wincing slightly. "Unfortunately." No one else says anything, and it isn't until Lyre yawns that I'm reminded I need to leave if I am to meet Myla on time.

"I need to go," I say, rising from the bed and swimming towards the door. But Sade stops me with a hand on my arm.

"This is for you." Reaching into her bag, she pulls out a sheathed dagger, its opalescent hilt reflecting the small crystals in Lyre's room. When I'm reluctant to take it, confused why Sade is giving it to me, she grumbles something under her breath and forces my fingers to wrap around the hilt. "Every siren should have a blade of their own to defend themselves. This one is made in the same style of weapons before the war. Keep it close at hand and practice with it."

Gripping the handle, I slide the thin silver blade free of its covering, marveling over how light it feels in my hand. So different from the fae dagger I had found and claimed as mine. The timing of this gift could not be more perfect, and I tightly swallow the pressure that threatens to release as I look at her.

"Thank you."

She shrugs with nonchalance, but I don't miss the way her lips quirk. "Now, go off to your secret meeting and, for the love of all the gods, please make sure you aren't being followed."

⚜ ⚜

Hours later, I arrive at the cavern, rising out of the sea only to shiver against the bitter cold air.

I spent the entire swim here replaying what I am going to say to Myla in my head. This will be our eighth meeting—ten weeks having passed since we made the life debt—and somehow, I'm more nervous about this meeting than I was for our first. Trudging onto the sand, I squeeze the excess water from my hair before draping it over my shoulders to cover my chest when a deep rumbling sound halts my steps, my head snapping up to the opposite end of the cavern where a pair of yellow glowing eyes surrounded by black scales are peering through the opening. My heart lodges in my throat, a sound crossed between a whimper and a scream joining it as I stumble backwards.

"She is not going to hurt you." Myla's smooth voice echoes against the stone, and I scan the cavern as a cold sweat drips down my back.

"Does *she* know that?"

Myla chuckles and finally steps into the open beside the dragon's head, the pair making quite the menacing duo with the all black they both wear. "I've let her know that you are... *not* a snack." The corners of her mouth curl, and it does nothing to temper the odd beating of my heart. "At least, not yet."

"Comforting," I rasp, resuming my steps towards the center of the cavern where I wait for Myla to meet me. "Is she *your* dragon?"

Myla stops a few feet away from me, looking over her shoulder at the beast who waits just beyond the large archway. "She is." When she turns back, any follow-up questions I have about dragons and why she has one vanish at the look on her face. She's... *smiling*. And not a smile tainted in cruelty or mockery. It's a genuine one. One that lifts her cheeks and makes her eyes squint. I'm acutely aware that I'm staring at her, that I'm sure there is a stunned look on my face, yet I can't force myself to look away. Myla meets my fascination with an arched brow, her smile slowly falling until her lips are a flat line. "Little Siren," she says, warning laced in her low tone.

I catch the tunic she tosses my way but don't put it on, instead reaching a hand into the bag strapped across my chest. "I have something for you," I tell her, forcing my breaths to come in evenly as I grip the smooth hilt of the dragon bone dagger. Pulling it out, I lift my head to find Myla watching me curiously, her hand pressed into the side of her thigh where her curved blade is strapped. "This," I say, taking a step towards her with the dagger resting in the palm of my outstretched hand, "belongs to you."

Myla stares at my hand for a long moment before her eyes narrow. "As I recall, you won the ownership of that dagger in a rather ruthless display if I do say so myself."

A soft laugh tumbles from me, but I again take another step towards her. "I did. But this blade is yours. Or, at the very least, your father's. It should be wielded by fae alone. So take it."

When she again makes no effort to grab the weapon, looking at me like she's trying to figure out the trap in my words, I exhale sharply and throw my other hand in the air. "This isn't some kind of weird exchange or bargain, Myla. Take the dagger!"

"Why aren't you keeping it for yourself?"

"Why are you not taking it when I know you want it?" I counter.

She smiles again, though this one is all jagged edges. "Let's fight for it—"

"Oh my *gods. No!*" Marching towards her, I reach for her hand, like Sade had done to me, only for her to latch on to my wrist and twist my arm until I'm forced to spin and give her my back. Then she tugs me close, her scent overwhelming me as the heat of her body radiates over the bare skin at my back. "What are you doing?"

Her cheek brushes mine as she lowers her head. "Fight me," she says, the caress of her voice sending a shiver down my spine. I send the elbow of my free arm back into her torso, just as she taught me last week. Only she dodges it, because *of course* she does, and then has the audacity to laugh in my ear. "Why are you trying to give me the dagger?"

"Because it is *yours*!" I grit out, lifting my leg and kicking it back towards her shin. My bare foot slides against the outside of her leg, and the growl that leaves me is nearly animalistic.

"You were *so* adamant that it was yours only a few weeks ago, Aria. What changed your mind?"

"Does it matter?" *Damn fae and her need to turn everything into some sort of exchange!*

"It shouldn't matter," she says like a confession, her tone making me pause. "And yet..." Myla's hold on me relaxes slightly, as if she's just realized our proximity to each other. Or the fact that I haven't dressed in the tunic she gave me, leaving me naked in her hands. I hear her throat work with a swallow, her next inhale painfully slow. "Yet it does. I want to know *why*, Aria, and I find that fact entirely too infuriating to examine closely. Do you understand what it is like to have someone show up in your head despite your best efforts to push them out?"

Yes, I want to say. *I do. With you.* But instead, I finally remember how to get out of the hold she has me in. I go limp, turning into dead weight and dragging us both down. Myla curses, using her quick reflexes to turn us at the last second so her back hits the ground first and I land on top of her. Facing her, I brace my weight on my knees as they bracket her hips, keeping space between our bodies as I angle the edge of the dagger over her throat. "Will you take the dagger now?" I ask through heaving breaths, her closeness making my skin tingle with awareness.

"Tell me why."

I groan in frustration, moving to push away from her when she grabs my wrist more gently than before. Her eyes search mine, something desperate and edged staring back at me from their dark depths.

"Tell me." This time, it comes out as a plea.

"Myla—"

"*Why*, Aria?"

"Because I'm freeing you from the life debt!" I shout, my voice scraping over the stone and stirring Myla's dragon from where she rests just outside. She releases a low rumble, and I look out the opening and meet those luminous eyes again, the dragon's top lip peeled back a fraction and showing just a hint of the large teeth that wait behind it.

A soft grip on my chin guides me until I'm looking once more at Myla, at the confusion that forms a line between her brows. "Say that again."

"I am freeing you from our life debt early. You have met the terms we set when we made our bargain." I gesture for her to take the dagger again. But she doesn't move, held in stillness by a rare show of emotion. With a soft exhale, I keep my eyes on hers as I reach back to the empty sheath I know is at her upper thigh, finding the open spot with my fingers before guiding the dagger into it, the sound of it sliding in making Myla's eyes shutter. I plant my now free hand near her shoulder, letting my eyes trace the sharp edges of her face. "You taught me how to fight in every aspect. I wanted to learn how to protect those I love, but I *needed* to learn how to protect myself too, and no matter how you feel about me or how much you loathed to do it, I need you to know that you helped me. You gave me a choice in my life that I never had before, so I want to try and return that to you. You have fulfilled the debt. You're free."

I had made the decision after our last lesson. It makes sense, given the fact that Lyre will be having her babe soon. It is coincidental that Sade thinks our mother is going to have Rhea heal me to pass through the Spell, which likely means that I won't so easily be able to return to our meetings anyway. But beyond those things, I don't need to know every facet of Myla's life to know that she is a female who understands what it is to survive in oppression. Where I had spent so many of my years *failing* to do anything but feel sorry for myself, Myla had taken action. She became something to be feared. I knew as she told the story of the Shadow, she was talking about herself. I knew as she carefully bandaged my arm and told me that "no" should have been enough, she was speaking from experience. Myla is a complicated fae, but I have seen enough glimpses beneath her hardened exterior to know that complicated can also be generous. Protective. *Beautiful.* I should tell her those things, but I'm afraid I've already said too much and her silence is because she's convinced herself that I'm lying.

"Say something," I whisper, only to gasp as she surges from the ground, sitting up and forcing me into her lap fully. I try to brace my weight onto my knees, *very* aware of the fact that I'm still nude. But the warmth of her hand settles on my hip, and though her touch is light, I heed to her command not to move.

"You've fucked everything up," she rasps, releasing my wrist and moving her hand as if to cradle my face or weave it into my hair, only to hesitate. My eyes widen at her words, hurt slicing into my chest as she exhales roughly. "I should be elated by this. I should feel *freed* by it, and yet"—her voice drops lower, a seductive song all its own as she studies me—"tell me why all I can feel is disappointment?"

She stares at me like I might actually hold the answer to her question, and what could I even say in response? The truth? That I am disappointed too? That when I think of my future, the silhouette of her is always there, haunting me from the shadows because there is no way in this world that the two of us could ever be anything more than *this* and even that has a time limit. And yet, as I watch her study me, her face full of vulnerability for the first time *ever*, I decide that maybe *I'm* the one that needs to be braver. The one to show her that she's worth the risk. "This doesn't have to end," I say softly, laying my hands on her shoulders, my fingers brushing against the delicate skin at her neck. "We just get to *choose* whether or not it continues."

"And is that what you want?" she asks, head tilting to the side, her mouth perfectly lined up with mine.

My pulse races as I lean in slowly, giving Myla ample opportunity to stop me. But she doesn't move as my hands travel up to cup the sides of her face gently, bright hazel eyes meeting dark onyx ones. "It is *one* of the things I want. And before I show you the other, I want you to know one more thing. I know you are the Shadow." Surprise flares as she watches me, her eyes dipping to my mouth and back up again, like she can't decide what part of me she wants to look at most. "I know who you are, Myla, and your darkness does not scare me." And then I crash my lips onto hers.

Chapter One Hundred and Thirteen

MYLA

The last time my lips had met Aria's had been because of survival. I needed oxygen, and she knew how to give it to me. That same drowning panic claws its way to the surface now, my body stiff beneath hers as all the reasons why I shouldn't touch her cycle through my mind. But even those protests are lost to the gentle way she coaxes our kiss to deepen, to the way her soft body arches into mine, warm and tender and sweet. Her quick intake of breath when my tongue meets hers ignites the heat already spreading through me, desire pulling my muscles tight as my fingers curl around her hip. My awareness narrows down to her taste on my tongue as I map out the shape of her, the space between us eaten up inch by inch as she draws my face even closer.

And because I can't help myself, because it's been so long since I've felt this way, my mind tortures me with memories of the past. Suddenly, it's not Aria's lush lips that move against my own but Daiya's thinner ones. It's not Aria's soft moan but Daiya's deeper one as we hid in a palace corridor, hands questing and tongues exploring. I tense, Daiya's voice playing in my ear just like the day we were discovered. *She forced me to do it! I never wanted this—I never wanted her!* There had been a power imbalance between Daiya and I, just as there is with Aria.

Our kiss breaks when I jerk myself back, my gaze roaming over Aria's expression as I search for proof of what my mind believes—she doesn't want this. Doesn't want *me*. I take in her parted, swollen lips, her hazel eyes fogged by lust as she studies me through lowered lashes, and I think that she's never looked so perfect. That she's never looked so open and unguarded and *raw*. For as much as it makes me want to draw her back in, to claim her as mine in a way that makes my core ache and my stomach clench, it also *terrifies* me. Because she may know that I'm the Shadow, but does she understand just exactly who, and *what*, I am?

"Myla," she whispers, her thumbs gently brushing over my cheekbones.

I release my hold on her hips to wrap my hands around her wrists, pulling her touch from my face. "You don't want this," I say, horrified by the uncertainty in my voice. By the sympathetic expression it pulls from Aria. I realize *that* is the thing I have feared most. Not giving in to this tension between us. Not being vulnerable or even falling for a being whose kind was responsible for my brother's death. It's that look—that *pitying* look—that screams, *here is this broken thing, how can I fix her?*

I drop her hands, about to silently command Sunis through the bond to burn this entire cavern down when Aria says my name again. Not with pity, but with desperation. It halts my movements enough to meet her gaze again, finding them alight with something like conviction.

"So rarely have I had the opportunity to look at someone and tell them that I want their touch. That I *crave* it. And so rarely have I *ever* gotten what I wanted." She drags her bottom lip in between her teeth. "But, if you'll allow it, I'd like to see how you taste beneath your ire and malice. I'd like to feel your heart race in your chest as it's pressed against mine." The stupid organ hiding behind my ribs responds, skipping to a pace that makes my breath come faster. "I'd like for you to *touch* me like I'm not something you hate, but—" Her inhale is stilted as she drops her gaze to her lap.

Fuck that. Wrapping an arm around her back, I pull her flush to me and roll, gently letting her back hit the ground before sliding my arm out and bracing my weight on it.

"Like what, then, Little Siren?" I ask, tracing her bottom lip with my thumb. Her knees press into either side of my hips, eyes flaring wide as her hands leave a scorching trail up my arms. "You don't get to be shy now that you started this."

"Like you think about me as much as I do you," she whispers.

The admission halts my thumb as I stare down at her, something dangerously soft threatening to take root within me. "Do you want to know if I think about you?" I ask, dropping my hips lower but still not making contact with her bare skin.

"Yes."

Tilting my head, my lips brush against the corner of her mouth, our breaths mingling in the tight space between us. "I think about you when I'm angry," I whisper, smirking when her brows lift. "That's how it always starts. I'm always angry when you first enter my mind, and then I picture you standing across from me on this fucking platform, your eyes glowing with newfound determination. With bravery. And strength." I graze my fingers down her neck and between her breasts, trailing them over her stomach. Goosebumps flare over her skin, her breath catching when I force my touch to linger in the space between her hips, higher than we both want.

"Myla," she rasps, her throat working with a swallow as her hands move from my arms to brace my hips.

"Look at you," I murmur, my lips finding her jaw and then lower, taking advantage when she arches her neck to taste her with my teeth and tongue. "If I were to slide my fingers between your legs, would I find you wet for me, Aria?" She whimpers, the sound skating over me like a soft wind. The threads of my tightly woven control begin to fray as I toy with her, my fingers just barely brushing right above her clit, each taunting swipe making her writhe and buck her hips towards me.

"I want you to touch me," she moans, eyes glazed in the heat of that want, and maybe I'm no better than the males who act on their base level desires because my fingers inch lower, the anticipation of sinking them deep inside of her—of watching her come around them—snaps those tethers that restrain me. She reaches up to capture my mouth with hers and I let my hips sink lower, let the tips of my fingers brush over the swell of her clit as my throat constricts with the ache of wanting to drag my tongue over every inch of her.

My own body hums at the way she feels beneath me, the slickness of her desire coating my fingers as I press them at her entrance, rewarded when it makes her moan softly in response. I grit my teeth together at the sound, something dark stirring within the heat of what should be pleasure as forbidden to me as *she* is when the word *mine* stabs into my mind. I latch onto it, so lost in working her higher, in drawing my fingers in and out at a pace that is torturous for us both, that I almost miss the single thought that bursts through the fog of my own yearning. *Leave.*

Fucking dragon. *No*, I send back, nipping at Aria's lip. But before I can go any further, Sunis's intention is sent again down our bond, forcing me to rip my mouth away from Aria's to send a withering look to my dragon.

"What is it?" she asks from beneath me, chest rising quickly as her hands draw up my sides.

"My damn dragon—"

Leave, it interrupts, and my eyes close my forehead coming to rest over hers. The interruption seems to remind us both of where we are, though covered by rock, we're still exposed to anyone who might come by and get past Sunis. As much as I want to watch her unravel, I'd prefer not to do it with the threat of being caught. When my gaze meets hers again, she seems to have the same thought as a small smile curls her lips.

For a moment, neither of us says anything, only the sound of her breathing and my steady heartbeat filling in the gaps in the silence. It's in that quiet I remember the last time I felt this way. The last time I let myself get lost in another to the point that I didn't want there to be an ending to me and a beginning of them. I just wanted there to be a joining of *us*.

Maybe Aria somehow knows that there is an old wound threatening to split, and that's why she reaches up to kiss me softly and without urgency, as if the only goal is to remind us what it feels like. Or maybe I'm rationalizing with myself like an idiot.

Pulling away with a groan, I help Aria to stand and look her over, something new stretched thin and raw between us.

"I will be here next week," Aria finally says, tucking her curls behind her ears. Her round eyes hold mine as she looks up at me, and a feeling I can't explain constricts my throat. "You are free from our bargain and free to choose whether you will be here too." After letting herself linger a moment, Aria grabs her bag from the ground and climbs down to the sandy beach, returning to the sea and leaving me wondering if, when it comes to her, there had ever really been a choice to begin with.

⁘⁘⁘⁘⁘⁘ ⁘⁘⁘⁘⁘⁘

I linger in the cavern for longer than necessary, staring at the ocean as I work to remind myself just how fucking dangerous that entire interaction was. For my own safety, I've always made it a point to keep myself in control of my emotions and urges until I'm in the safety of my warehouse, a male hanging before me. But Aria had expertly chipped away at that control with each flick of her tongue and soft press of her body against mine. It leaves me feeling exposed, a nerve left open to the world when I need to be hidden behind shadows instead.

Breathing in the salty air, I wait until it has replaced the warm and sultry scent of *her* in my lungs before returning to Sunis, climbing her front leg and settling on her back. *Leave*, she sends again down the bond, and I lean down over her as I prepare for her to take off.

Go, I send back, and then we are launching into the air, Sunis's wings beating powerfully as we begin our ascent towards the mist-covered sky.

While flying is a natural instinct for Sunis, having me on her back and feeding her instructions through our bond has proven to require practice. I had snuck out of the palace often in the first few days after our bonding, finding her on the dragon fields pacing as if she waited for me to arrive. Our flights had been chaotic at first, both testing exactly how to properly communicate while she figured out how to fly gracefully with my weight between her wings.

Soaring over the onyx mountaintops, I keep my eyes peeled for any other dragons and their riders. Despite my wishes to go to my father as soon as possible with proof of bonding a dragon, Navin *graciously* pointed out that our bond needed time to strengthen. "There is no substitute for time, Myla," he had said, stripping himself of his armor and the tunic beneath to reveal his stitched-up self-inflicted injury in our sitting room the night we rescued Sunis. "If Father and his dragon challenge you both to a fight, you and Sunis will lose."

The logic made sense, yet it did nothing to quell the disquiet within me that wanted to go to my father immediately. But Navin had fucking stabbed himself so Sunis and I could get away, selling a story to the guards that the Shadow had come for a dragon and killed to get one. There were no witnesses to refute his tale, no reason to believe he was lying. My relief was immense when he came through the door that night, and then my guilt had flooded in right behind it. Especially when he explained that his delay coming home had been less about getting his wound looked at and more about withstanding our father's disappointed rant.

The fae king is nothing if not consistently dissatisfied with his children.

Home. The word slips into my mind as Sunis spreads her wings out wide, blocking my view on either of the landscape below as she slows her speed to a glide and we start to descend. The mist is cold against my cheeks, the high altitude penetrating my leathers.

When we finally break through to clear skies, Sunis turns, giving me a quick glimpse of the break in the forest below and the small black dots that mar the grass. Dragons prowl through the area away from the mountains that house Sunis and Bali's cave, and she guides us in that direction, flapping her wings to slow herself before she lands in a crouch, jostling my body with the movement and making my teeth clack together.

"We have to work on your landing," I tell her, not for the first time, fighting off a smirk when she growls low in response.

Letting go of the leather strap, I tug my hood back over my head and stand, climbing down as Sunis shakes her wings before tucking them safely into her side. The harness that keeps me on her back will stay on her to help her get used to the feel of it, though I hope eventually we can fly without it. My breath clouds in front of me as I survey the fields, spotting green and blue dragons in the distance. Being bonded should protect me from their ire should they see me out here without Sunis, but I stay close to her side, following her towards the cave just in case.

But as we near, a growl deep and low rumbles its way out, the ground shaking beneath the dragon's steps. Out of habit, I reach for my curved blade, only to remember the new weight on the other side. Aria had freed me from my debt early and then given me a dagger that was more powerful than she ever could have known. Fingers dancing over its hilt, I brace myself for what is going to emerge from the cave, when Sunis releases a deep chittering noise. Lowering her head, she watches as Bali walks out into the sunlight, moving slowly as if she's unsteady on her feet.

Navin had been giving me updates on Bali from where they still held her in the compound when he could, but our father had tightened his hold on his secrets, and Navin didn't think he could ask without the king getting suspicious.

My shoulders relax as I watch Bali nuzzle against Sunis's head, the two finally reunited again.

When Bali's attention shifts to me, I stand tall, looking over the massive black dragon. Her head drops low, my eyes widening as she gently nudges her nose into me, and the word *safe* shimmers down the bond from Sunis. My stomach hollows as I place a hand over one of her hard scales, her show of appreciation an endearing move I hadn't expected from a dragon.

I understand now why Sunis wanted to leave the beach. She somehow knew her mother had returned. When they walk into the safety of their cave again, I begin my trek back to my own home. But a persistent thought nags at me the entire journey back. If Bali was freed from my father's enclosure, does that mean she is now bonded to someone new? Or had the mages been unsuccessful? Unease curls and claws at me again, but I snuff it out in favor of focusing on what matters most *now*.

I have Sunis, and soon, I will demand a meeting with the king to show him exactly how much his cursed daughter has just become an even bigger thorn in his side.

Chapter One Hundred and Fourteen

MYLA

The next morning, I'm forced to attend a service in the temple, watching as Father Yamin paces while talking of the gods' mercy over our kingdom. Sitting in a pale blue satin dress and matching veil, opalescent crystals dangle over my forehead from my headdress as I track the father with my eyes.

He had glared at me with unfaltering steadiness when I entered the temple behind Navin and our parents, meeting my eyes through the gaps in the fabrics covering my face. I didn't shy away from his leery gaze, and though I knew he couldn't see it, neither did I stop the smirk that lifted one half of my mouth as I passed him. I felt the press of his attention on my back and over my scars as I walked past the king, queen, and crown prince's seats. My place was not with my family but on the benches across from them, where the rest of the nobles sat to look upon fae royalty with the deference they were owed. Per usual, I was not included in that honor.

As Father Yamin prattles on and on about what a blessing this winter solstice will be for the kingdom, I let my mind wander to thoughts of the spelled dagger I now have in my possession. It had been a gift to my father from the last Void queen. History says that by giving an offering of blood, it will allow temporary passage into another kingdom without the usual repercussion of death. As far as I understand, the bigger the sacrifice of blood, the longer one can withstand the Spell's effect. It is a weapon I can't imagine having to use myself, but one I don't want to give to my father or anyone he might associate with. So, for now, it will remain at my side and be used in other *ritualistic* offerings. I smile at the thought.

"We will have a celebration in five days' time here at the palace," the father says, coming to a halt beside the pole I was tied to. Where I was whipped. My stomach churns, but I keep myself still as I listen. "It will be a momentous time, a showcasing of the miracles granted by the gods." The father's onyx eyes scan over the crowd, their excitement over his words palpable in the air. "For the first time since the end of the war, we have finally been given a positive omen. Proof that our gods are beginning to favor us once more." The voices around me grow louder, and Father Yamin basks in the chaos he's created, holding his arms out wide. I look to Navin, finding his gaze already on me, and lift a brow in question. He gives me a subtle shrug of his shoulders, the fae around us clapping and cheering. I turn my focus on the king, his stoic expression made more so by his hardened gaze. A crown of onyx dragon stone sits centered on his head, shining in the dancing flames of the torches lit throughout the temple. Despite the rousing speech from the Divine Father, the fae king looks no more motivated by it than he ever has. Next to him, my mother stares at the leader of the brethren, her gaze lost in his movements while she clutches my father's hand tightly.

Though they have never deserved it, I once looked upon my parents with a sympathetic eye. To lose a son in war is no easy thing. To then be preyed upon in that grief by vultures claiming to have the words of gods in their ears is sickening. And yet they so callously tossed a daughter of their own flesh and blood away to earn favor of the very gods who had taken Shah. If such beings existed, where was the righteous rage at them for allowing the heir to be killed? If their influence was so vast and so powerful, why didn't they step in? Why hadn't they *ever* stepped in? No, sympathy is an emotion I've long since discarded when thinking of my parents. Now there is only venomous *anger* remaining as I stare at them seated on their thrones.

The service ends, and Navin finds me immediately, walking at my side as we return to our rooms. "You don't know what any of that was about?" I ask once we're secluded behind the closed door, taking my veil off.

"Not at all," he answers, unbuckling his King's Rider armor and piling it on the ground. "All Father told me was to not be late for the celebration." He tugs on the tie securing his long hair back. "And Father Yamin hasn't bothered me at all this week."

"Is that strange?"

Navin all but collapses onto the couch, throwing an arm over his eyes. "Yes. I usually am forced to pray in his presence at least once a week. And I thought for *sure* after the debacle last week that he would want to berate me with all kinds of nosy fucking questions." Navin sighs, the sound relaying his exhaustion. "But it is almost as if there is some sort of secret that I'm not in on."

"Feeling left out of the gossip, princess?"

Navin snorts and arches his neck as he lifts his head to look at me. "I'm tired of being forced to keep secrets I don't want to keep and kept out of the ones I actually *need* to know."

"Fair," I deadpan, earning a collection of curses. "I can't imagine there is anything more important than knowing that our father is abducting mages and using them to test repairing the bonds with dragons. Anything beyond that is entering the realm of impossible."

"I know," he says, sitting up and running a hand through his hair. "But it's just... *strange* that father is keeping things from me. Knowing his plans was keeping myself safe as well. If he's suddenly *not* telling me things..." He swallows and leans back against the couch.

"Then there is a reason."

"Exactly."

Walking over to him, I kick his boot with the side of my foot. "I do appreciate you holding my secrets for me."

His eyes widen, and he brings a hand to his mouth in mock shock as he shakes his head. "Is my rough and mean sister *actually* showing appreciation for the brother who so selflessly trained her? Who has tried his best to keep her safe *despite* her inclination to draw herself into danger?" He gasps, sitting up tall as his hands cradle his head. "This is the good omen Father Yamin was talking about, isn't it?" I stare at him, contemplating a way to cut his tongue out of his mouth without killing him. My intent must be written on my face because he laughs in earnest, earning a harder kick on me as I turn and head for my room, his laughter trailing behind me.

My own lips curl at the sound.

Though the number of guards in Khargis has begun to thin, I avoid going to see Shen. Her tavern has become one of the main stops for my father's men to sit and drink, and I don't need a drunk idiot spotting me heading into her apartment and either accusing her of helping the Shadow or attempting to apprehend me and causing damage to her business.

Instead, I go to check on my warehouse, nervous that the previously larger presence of guards might have led to the space being searched. The deeper into Khargis I go, trading in buildings in moderate condition for ones that are dilapidated, the less frequently I spot the guards. By the time I arrive at my destination, the street is all but empty, save for a few drunkards. Still, I keep my ears open and eyes peeled for any sudden movement or unwelcome sound.

The door to my warehouse is at the back, hidden amongst overgrown ivy and blended into the wall by the ancient brick somehow still keeping this place together. Pressing it open, I slide a blade from my thigh and step inside, keeping my breaths shallow as I look around. The apprehension is part of my routine. With the windows mostly boarded up on the outside, only a scant amount of light trickles in. I fish a flame gem from my pocket and toss it to the center of the room, closing the door behind me and taking a deep breath of the stale air.

Silence greets me, the room void of any life and, from what I can see from my quick inspection, any damage. Resheathing my dagger, I walk to the trap door that leads to the basement, grabbing my flame gem as I go and descending the stairs into the room where I plan to bring my next target. I check the chain and hook hanging from the ceiling, ensuring that they are ready before grabbing the wooden box I use to help me hoist the males up and setting it into place.

My fingers skim over the blades tucked into my vest and then down my sides to the two strapped at my legs. I drum them over the hilts, rolling my shoulders back and running through my plans for the evening. Kaito would once again be my target for the evening, and I can stake out the tavern like last time, getting a good view of not only the establishment but also the street below. Once Kaito leaves, I'll follow him from the rooftops until he's away from prying eyes.

With my plan locked in place, I tug my hood over my head and slip my mask on, pocketing the flame gem before turning towards the stairs. Darkness greets me at the top, but I only make it a few steps past the landing when I halt at the sight of the open door in front of me. My hands immediately go to the blades at my thighs, pulling them both free as I slowly spin and eye the room. As if on cue, guards step out from the shadowy corners and away from the walls, at least a dozen of them drawing their swords and angling them towards me. *Fuck.*

"Shadow of Khargis, you are to be detained on orders of the king," one of the males shouts as he takes a step forward, the others following him. I don't respond, keeping my blades high as I back towards the exit, glancing at it from the corner of my eye. Surely, there are guards waiting for me right outside the door, but I'll take my chances out in the open rather than trapped in here with them. Spinning on my heel, I bolt towards the door, only to be pushed back as two guards step in front of the doorway.

I kick at the chest of one of the guards and send him stumbling backwards. Voices shout, and creaking metal rends the air behind me, every nerve ending alight with rage as I rush the second male. His sword is already drawn, and he wastes no time jabbing it in my direction, forcing me to jump out of the way. I shiver with the knowledge that there are more guards behind me as I drop to my knees and slide my blade over the guard's heel, severing the tendon. But I time his fall poorly, the metal armor of his shoulder colliding with mine as I push myself up to stand. I grunt at the impact, stars bursting over my eyes before I push his body into the fray behind me and dart past the door.

Cold winter air stings my eyes, and through the tears that form, my breath once more clouding the air in front of me, I come face to face with another dozen guards. Spinning on my heel, I rush down the side of the building, resheathing my curved blade to grab the smaller ones in my vest. I ready the first one and release it as I run, the stumbling of the guard's steps at my side telling me I've struck true. I grab another and aim for a male behind me, throwing the blade only to watch it whiz by the guard's head. *Shit.* I grab another and throw it at an angle in front of me, that one sinking into the flesh at his throat. But as I push myself to move faster, the silver sea surrounding me begins to close in.

I pump my arms harder, the hood of my cloak slipping off of my head as I finally see the dark alleyway that separates my warehouse and the building next to it. If I can get there, I can lose them in the shadows. And I nearly do. Retrieving the daggers at my thighs again, I slash at a guard who attempts to reach me from the side, leaping over his body and landing roughly on my feet. I'm ten steps away, air scraping along my cheeks as I breathe heavily through my mask. The darkness ahead reaches out to cradle me in its arms, and I'm almost there, just another few steps—

Except, when I finally break past the corner of my warehouse and step onto the loose gravel of the alley, I don't account for the guard already waiting in the shadows. His fist connects with my jaw before I have time to react, my feet getting swept from underneath me as the sound of bone on bone rings out and my shoulder slams into the ground, knocking both daggers from me as my head ricochets from the impact.

I try to roll onto my hands and knees, my head swimming and vision blurry, but before I can make it up, the other guards are there. One wrenches one arm behind me, while another grips my hair and yanks my head back, forcing me into a backbend to stare up at his hungry eyes. "We've finally caught you!" he shouts. My wrists are tied behind me as my chest heaves, the guards collecting my weapons while I'm hauled to my feet and spun around to face the male who pulled my hair. "Now, let's see what this fearsome Shadow looks like."

He tugs my mask down, revealing my full features to him and the rest of the guards. A few let out dramatic gasps of surprise, while others leer, licking their lips like the pathetic dogs they are as they drag their gazes down my body.

"Who are you?" the guard before me asks, leaning forward so that his nose nearly touches mine. "There is no way that a *bitch* is the Shadow."

I tilt my head, my tongue dragging over the front of my teeth and the blood that stains them. "Why not? It looks like they allow bitches to be guards."

He snarls, winding his hand back so slowly that I'm able to laugh before he lands the punch to my cheek. It snaps my head to the side, both sides of my face now equally throbbing with pain. "Take her to the dungeon and inform the king that the Shadow's associate was caught."

Perhaps it's because of the fucking day I've had, or maybe it's because I know that I likely won't live to see sunrise, but the fact that this *idiot* doesn't believe that *I* am the Shadow pisses me off more than it should. I wait until he turns around, then send the bottom of my boot directly into the soft spot at the back of his knee, smiling as he crumples to the ground. There is more shouting, more creaking of armor, and then another explosion of pain before everything goes black.

Chapter One Hundred and Fifteen

XANDER

CRADLING MY HEAD WHERE I sit on the edge of my bed, I try to banish the thoughts that have plagued me for the past few days to no avail. Every time I close my eyes, every moment I have alone where I'm not actively working on my plan to help her escape, I see Rhea leaning over the edge of the tower balcony. I feel the rush of panic that propelled my feet to move faster, that silvery voice that had roused me from sleep screaming in my head to *hurry*. It had all happened so fast, though I still can't explain how the *fuck* I knew to go to the tower when I did.

Three gentle knocks ring out on my door. "I'll be out in a minute," I shout.

"Better hurry. The king's meeting with the council is finishing up," Anderson answers back.

Groaning, I stand and grip the towel around my waist, running a hand through my damp hair as I push the strands back from my face. My room at the barracks is the same as every other guard's, despite the fact that they call me their commander. But even if my father hadn't forced me to stay here from the moment I joined as his guard, I still would have chosen it. I may have been the commander, but to the majority of the men here, I am just Xander. And when they think I'm just like them, they are more willing to talk in my presence. Or, at the very least, not mince words when I'm near.

Heading to my closet, I grab my clothes and begin to dress, mapping out my day based on what I know about the king's. He has been conversing a lot with his council lately and entertaining Queen Amari's calls through the Mirror. I had thought it strange that he was so willing to talk with her when he had already gotten Rhea under his thumb. The ring Rhea wears puts her at the mercy of not only the king but the siren queen as well, and in our brief conversation as I escorted her back to her rooms from the tower, she explained that King Dolian can *also* be controlled by Queen Amari. Admittedly, I had begun to suspect that was the case and had intended to ask Rhea about it, but her decline over the past month had motivated her to keep me at arm's length. After learning about King Nox's supposed betrothal to another woman, after bargaining for Eve to have time at home, after *everything* my cousin has been through, I can't exactly blame her for not wanting to speak to *anyone* about... well, *anything.*

I reach for my armor where it's resting on a stand, buckling the cuirass on first before moving on to the pauldrons. My movements are ingrained in my head, automatic after years of repetition. Strapping my sword to my hip comes last, and then I step into the bathroom to look in the mirror, checking that everything is in place. I run my gaze over the horrible golden armor, hopeful for the day when King Dolian is finally dead and we can move on from the gaudy color. It may have been a Maxwell tradition, but if my father taught me *anything* in my twenty-four years of life, it is that I have no interest in carrying on any tradition bearing his name.

I exhale roughly as I look at my reflection, almost all of the physical attributes of my face coming from my mother with the exception of the shape of my eyes and jaw. When I notice those, all I see is him. Unable to stop myself, I squat and tug on the bottom drawer of the vanity, lifting the small towel that is folded there to reveal the picture and book I've hidden. The picture is of my mother, a small portrait she had painted shortly before she died. I was only a boy then, unable to understand exactly what my mother was going through. What she was shielding me from, but it fucking hurts like hell to know that, even as she was sure her life was soon going to end, she thought of me. The tip of my finger caresses her long black hair, her smile soft as it stares back at me. Kissing the photo, I set it to the side as I eye the book. *The Little Sun.* Immediately, my mind flashes back to that cramped space in the dungeons and the white-haired female who made me question everything about myself. Whose wit and charm was only outdone by her steadfast loyalty. It was at her request that I grabbed this book from the tower, as it had been one of Rhea's favorites. I had forgotten to grab it when preparing for her to leave, but selfishly, I am happy to have it with me now. To have the reminder of Siyala, even if a part of me aches to see it. To know that this is all I will have of her ever again.

Those three knocks sound on the door again, and I bite back the urge to rage at Anderson and instead slide the picture of my mother back over the book, laying the towel on top, and closing the drawer.

"You good?" he asks when I enter the hall, shutting the door behind me.

"Fine. Have you heard from Brisk?"

"He stopped by a little bit ago. Lady Rhea is in a fitting for her wedding dress," he answers, voice low as he avoids using the fake moniker for Rhea created by the king.

I fight off the urge to shudder. If luck is on our side, Rhea will be free from King Dolian within a few days. It's a plan that has taken weeks to formulate properly. To make sure that every angle we can control is covered. There can be no slip-ups, no mistakes. I am going to get Rhea out of here, and then, when my father is distracted by his rage at losing her *again*, the resistance will strike. In less than a week, everything I have spent the majority of my life working towards will finally come to fruition.

"What is on the king's schedule for today?"

"He wants you to meet him outside the council chambers, and I haven't been able to find the reason why." Gods, there could be a myriad of reasons why he would want to see me, none of them good. "From there, you've got to look over the last battalion that Lady Rhea healed and ensure everyone is still..."

"Alive?" I supply, watching as he bristles.

"Essentially."

It is no secret that, while Anderson may believe that Rhea is someone we can trust, he's convinced himself that Rhea's magic is going to slowly kill all of those who have been touched by it, and as such, he has conveniently left himself out of the battalions she's healed so far. "I may not understand Rhea's magic, but I believe that her intent is not to hurt anyone with it."

"Then why haven't you had her *heal* you?"

It's a fair question, but the answer isn't some secret. "I have no intention of leaving the kingdom and, therefore, no need to be able to do so."

"Glad to see that is still the case because there are some—"

"I know," I cut in, lowering my voice as the council chamber doors come into view, one of my men standing guard next to them.

Ever since learning that Rhea is not what my father had described—a reclusive woman debilitated by her own grief who abdicated the throne to him—she has been viewed as a threat to the resistance. That is, until I got to know her. While most have come around to the belief that Rhea does not want to be queen of the Mortal Realm, a few still think of her as a package deal with King Dolian. Despite what I've told them, they only see how she is forced to act in public. How she's docile, submissive, *whatever the king wants her to be*. It's why I'm desperate to have her meet those who will help her escape not because they want to but because they are putting their trust in me. It's an honor I don't take lightly, but one I can't be careless with either.

The resistance needs to talk to Rhea face to face to know that my cousin has no secret goals but to return to her *true* home with King Nox at her side. Assuming that the rumors of him betrothed to someone else are indeed false. I clench my jaw at the thought of someone hurting Rhea, of the man I knew as

Flynn only using her until it was inconvenient for him. I want to believe that he cares about her as much as she clearly does for him, but if I'm being honest, I expected him to have come for her already. Enough time has passed for the seasons to change, and as far as I or my team know, the mage king hasn't stepped foot in the Mortal Kingdom.

The door to the chambers open, and I straighten, Anderson at my side as we clasp our hands behind us. The council members file out, their faces betraying too many emotions to even begin to decipher what the fuck happened in this meeting. The king and Simon emerge last, the latter sending his beady-eyed gaze my way.

"It is a temporary problem, My King. Our numbers far outweigh theirs. As you say, patience is our finest ally and greatest strength. Let her show her hand now so we can respond appropriately when she least expects it."

King Dolian acknowledges Simon with a nod before coming to stand in front of me, the disappointment coating the air between us nothing new. "You will visit the battalions Lady Nele healed yesterday," he says. I can't help but wonder if the fake name is less about hiding her true identity and more about making himself believe that he isn't actually attempting to marry his niece. My fingers wrap around the hilt of my sword as I dispel the nausea that rises at the thought.

"Of course, Your Majesty. Is Lady Nele scheduled to heal any more today?"

The king doesn't answer right away, not as he leads us towards the castle wing designated for a royal's betrothed. Rhea's rooms are located deeper into the castle, but the rooms that line this corridor are intended for wedding preparation. He reaches for one of the door handles, and remembering what Anderson said Rhea was doing, I clear my throat.

"Isn't this the seamstresses' room?"

King Dolian's brow lifts as he tilts his head in that menacing way that makes my skin crawl. "It is."

"It's bad luck to see the bride in her dress before the wedding." It's a shit attempt to keep him away from her, but as a line forms between his brows, I think for a moment that it might work. The chuckle that he answers with dashes that hope.

"When it comes to my betrothed and I, *luck* has never been part of the equation." Turning the handle, he pushes the door open, stepping inside as if he owns the space. I guess he fucking does.

"Y-your Majesty," one of the seamstresses stutters as she lowers into a curtsy, the older woman next to her already settled into a deep one. Rhea stands between them, draped in layers of shimmering white fabric that is pinned tightly to her body. I glance at her reflection in the mirror placed in front of her, catching her gaze for only a moment before she drops it to the floor. I don't miss the redness that lines her eyes or the tears that she quickly wipes from her cheeks.

My grip on my sword tightens, but the murderous thoughts I harbor of killing the king are just that—*thoughts*. With the mark of the crescent-shaped blood oath on my palm, I'll never be able to make the killing blow. And now Rhea bears the mark of a blood oath to the king too, one that might complicate our plans to help her escape. But that will be something she and I can work out when I take her to meet the rest of the resistance.

"Leave us," King Dolian says to the room, startling the seamstresses as Rhea looks up to find him watching her through the mirror. Where before she would have shot him a glare or at the very least tightened her expression, now she stares listlessly, a gauntness to her complexion that has only worsened over the past two weeks.

"Your Majesty, perhaps we should discuss the plan for Lady Nele to heal another rou—"

"There is nothing that needs to be discussed at the moment. My *fiancée* and I will enjoy some time alone before the chaos of the wedding." The two women rush out of the room, but my feet stay planted, my mind too slow to come up with a fucking reason not to leave her behind. King Dolian circles Rhea like a predator, his fingers trailing along her waist and stopping when he reaches her side. Then his gaze snaps to mine, his brows dropping low.

"Is there a reason you are lingering?" he asks slowly, his eyes darting from me to Rhea. My heart doubles its beats, my grip so tight on my sword that the skin covering my knuckles feels like it might split before I force it to relax. "Is there something I should know about?"

Rhea's shoulders stiffen, her eyes losing focus for a split second as the magic of the ring washes over her. *Fuck. Fuck. Fuck.* Her lips part, and though I know I can't hurt the king, I prepare to draw my sword anyway, cursing internally when the magic of my oath begins to burn at my palm.

"I do not like my dress," she says, her green eyes wide and showing off the whites as she exhales loudly. "You should know that I do not like it."

The king's body relaxes, and after a dramatic sigh, he releases her hip and takes a step back, turning to face me. "You *will* wait outside the door while I talk to Lady Nele, and then you will escort her to her room so she can rest. We've many important things coming up in these next few days. I don't need to worry about your loyalty, do I?"

"No, Your Majesty." I swallow when he focuses back on Rhea, her eyes meeting mine in the mirror. The plea in them is clear—leave now before she's forced to say something about me. About the resistance. Gritting my teeth, I lower into a bow and head towards the door, fucking *hating* myself for doing so.

King Dolian emerges from the room first, one hand shoved into his pocket and an expression I don't dare look at too closely plastered over his face. "Take her back to her room," he commands, not waiting for my response before he's already striding down the hall. Rhea comes out a few minutes after that, having changed into a light yellow gown with long sleeves and a gold chain belt wrapped around her waist.

"I'm fine," she says, an automatic response to a question I haven't asked yet. Flicking her honey-blonde hair over her shoulders, she keeps her gaze on the wall across from us as she waits for me to lead her back to her room.

But that's not fucking happening.

"Rhea, w—"

"I don't want to talk about it." It's the quiver in her voice that silences me, her eyes growing watery despite the way I know she is fighting not to let any emotion show. I step in front of her so that she is forced to look at me, her head tilting up just enough to meet my gaze.

"We don't have to talk about anything you don't want to, but I'm not letting you be alone right now."

"Xander—"

"Do you trust me?" I ask, the words soft but the question sharp. Rhea's mouth snaps closed as she swallows roughly, her arms folding over her chest.

"I do," she finally says, the words whispered.

I check down the length of the hallway to confirm we are alone and then reach my hand out for hers. "Come on. It's time that you meet the resistance." When she hesitates, I stretch my hand out farther. "There are people who are kind, Rhea. They will not judge you. And we have a plan that you need to hear." My relief is immediate when she finally slips her hand into mine. I hold hers tightly, hoping she remembers our conversation in the tower. That there are people who want her home. Want her safe.

We go undetected as we make our way to her rooms, Brisk greeting us at his post outside her door. "I'll say that she's sleeping and is to be undisturbed should anyone come," he says, his gaze soft when he looks at Rhea. She nods in thanks, offering a sad smile, and then we slip into her room and right to the door that leads to the tunnels. And what I hope is the first official step towards her freedom.

Chapter One Hundred and Sixteen

RHEA

X ANDER SAID THE PEOPLE he was taking me to meet wouldn't judge me based on who I was—*am*. On who they perceive me to be because of my relation to the king. Both as his niece and his betrothed. But standing in a room beneath the castle, the gazes of the small group gathered don't seem short of condemnation. Yes, some look at me with pity. Or maybe sympathy or some other emotion I don't care to decipher that doesn't come across as malicious. But others observe me like a suspected thief. I can't say that I blame them, and as they cast those multilayered glances towards Xander, I wish I could tell them that I am just as confused as they are why Xander believes I need to be here.

To his credit, Xander looks more than put off by the lackluster reception to my presence. He sighs as he folds his arms, having ditched his golden armor for the evening. Just as Nox had worn for so many of our meetings. My gaze drops to the floor as memories try to pierce through the fogginess of my mind and fail. With each day that passes, thinking of him becomes more and more difficult, my recollection of our time together murky with the way I am drowning. With how tired I am.

"Rhea." Xander's voice—strong but soft—plays in my ear, and I lift my head to once more meet the gazes of those gathered before us. Though torches are lit on opposite walls, what provides the most light is the large flame gem at the center of the room. I look to him, realizing that the room has lapsed into an awkward silence while I've been stuck in my own head. "These are my closest confidants and the men and women who keep the resistance running outside of the palace

679

walls. With their help, and the help of the men I trust in the guard, we think we have a way to get you away from the king." He gestures with his chin to my hand, where the pearl ring rests. "The goal is to get the king to release you from the magic of the ring quickly, but if we fail, then it will be to get you as far away as possible so that he cannot command you. Home and in the safety of the Mage Kingdom, hopefully they can help you remove the ring."

I swallow as my thumb presses into the pearl, twisting the cold jewelry around my finger. *There is nowhere safe anymore*, I want to say. *I don't know that I have a home anymore.*

"I'm sorry, Xander, I know you have faith that she has no intentions for the throne after being freed, but I'm just not buying it," a man says, crossing his arms over his broad frame. He looks to me then, his eyes as weary as they are damning. "Why should we risk everything we have worked *years* for on someone like *you*?"

"Remi," Xander growls at my side, his voice bouncing off of the thick stone surrounding us.

"It's alright," I supply, giving Xander what I hope is a reassuring smile. "They should know, at the very least, what is at risk if they *don't* free me."

His dark brows lower, and for a split second, I see the resemblance to the king. I blink and look away, a knot forming in my throat.

"I can try to assure you that all I want is to be free of the king. That I hate him as much as you do. Perhaps even *more*." Though I try to ignore it, the scoffs at that statement bury their way into me. They could never understand what it has been like, but I don't need them to. I just need them to be more afraid of me than they are of him. "But none of that matters. The truth is, I *am* dangerous to your cause. Just not in the way you think." I turn to Xander. "Do they know about my magic? About how I've been forced to use it?"

He inhales slowly, taking a long while to answer, his expression somewhat sheepish. "Yes. Not everyone, but most in this room. I wanted them awar—"

"I'm not upset that you told them," I interrupt. "It makes what I have to say even easier with context." I scan those in front of me, skipping from one pair of eyes to another. "The king will not stop until his entire army is able to pass through the Spell. The number of men I've used my magic on already is..." I shake my head. I have no idea just how many I've healed. How many sirens. "This gives him access to other kingdoms, inviting conflict into spaces that have previously known only peace. If the king marches into the Mage Kingdom and the Fae Kingdom, they will be able to retaliate."

"Can the fae cross the Spell without repercussion too? Like the mages?" a woman near the back asks.

"No, but they have dragons," Xander answers, following my line of thought. "And animals are immune to the Spell."

"And you've healed sirens as well?" Remi asks. I nod, and he curses. "So, really, we're fucked if the king attacks anyone but the shifters."

"King Dolian and Queen Amari seem to have a tentative alliance," Xander says, his fingers caressing his jaw.

"My magic is something not seen since the war. I don't think the king realizes just how powerful I am, but it is not something I want him to find out." The words are given solemnly, not from any place of pride but from the utter fear that coils in my stomach. "And he's not the only one who can control me. With this ring on," I say, pausing to hold my hand up, "the siren queen also has the ability to command me, and I have to follow through. Where the king lacks the understanding of my capability, Queen Amari seems more cunning, more... *sure*. But she isn't *just* controlling me. She has power over the king as well."

Their voices buzz in my ear as everyone begins talking in hushed voices, their hands gesturing as they glance my way. But Xander quiets them quickly as he steels his spine, taking a step closer to me. "This doesn't change our plans, only ensures that we cannot fail in two days."

Two days. The day before the king expects me to walk down the aisle. It's an arbitrary number at this point. Whether it is two days or twenty or two hundred, time passes all the same. I lay a hand over my hip, right above the brand—that permanent reminder. It's healed on the surface, the skin a white array of lines and curves in the arrangement of the king's sigil, yet the ache of it still haunts me. It's persistent, following me no matter what corner of my mind I try to retreat to.

"I do not want to cause any more harm. I do not want anyone else hurt or *dead* in my name." The words come out thick, the effort to push them out heavy on my soul. Some of those in front of me might soften their gazes, or maybe that is only what I wish to see. "Freeing me is risky, yes, but keeping me here is even more so." Swallowing hard, I return my attention to Xander, who is already watching me, likely seeing more on my face than I mean to show him.

He dips his chin. "Then let's go over the plan."

We move to a large table surrounded by chairs, Xander offering me one before he takes his own. On the table are wooden figurines, string, and fabrics of blue and green. Xander begins moving things on the table until it resembles what our meeting on the beach with the sirens will look like, with the dark blue fabric representing the water and the string the Spell in the sand. Figurines stand on both sides of the string, representative of the king, myself, and an array of guards.

"Every guard will be in full armor, including helmets, to help conceal the identities of the men and women here," he says, gesturing to those who sit around the table.

"Are you all guards?" I ask.

"No. Most of us work in Vitour," Remi answers, his expression still guarded. He looks at me as if I am both the solution and the cause for his problems, and he can't decide which one he believes is more true. "We haven't been forced to take a blood oath of any kind."

"They will be closest to the king. Closest to you," Xander adds, his dark eyes boring into mine. "I will walk with you and the king into position on the beach. Unfortunately, we will need the distraction of you healing the sirens to get everyone else into the correct positions." He waits for me to react, but I simply swallow and nod for him to continue. What is another handful of sirens to the hundreds I've healed already? "I will drop back to the other side of the Spell to stand with the king's Trusted. The moment you're done healing the sirens, Remi and the others will apprehend the king and force him to free you from the magical ring."

I look from Xander to Remi again, then the others who watch me eagerly before clearing my throat. "It's not going to work."

"I can send one of my men with you if you really think—"

"No, I mean, you'll never get the king to say that he frees me from the ring."

Remi arches a brow in challenge, leaning his elbows on the table. "A knife against the throat will get anyone to talk, especially a prick like the king."

"You're right, and the worst thing you can do is let King Dolian have his voice when he knows all he has to do is command me to kill you, and I will obey."

"Is that really how the magic works?" the woman next to Remi asks, her short dark hair swaying above her shoulders as she tilts her head to observe me. "He just gives you a command, and you *have* to obey?"

"*Yes*. If he says the words, I can and *will* kill every single person on that beach." My heart ricochets at the thought, my bottom lip trembling until I bite down on it hard enough to get it to stop. "If your plan hinges on him freeing me that way, it's not going to work."

"Can King Dolian just *take* the ring off of you?" Xander asks, tucking his hair behind his ear.

"I don't know," I answer honestly. "He is the one who put it on, so I would *assume* he can take it off, but he's never tried, and I obviously can't take it off on my own."

Xander nods, beginning to work a new idea out in his head. Remi looks like he might be sick. "Okay," Xander says after the silent tension in the room has grown thick. "Remi and the others will still subdue King Dolian, but he'll cover his mouth the *moment* he catches him so he cannot command Rhea to do anything. They will command with whatever brute force necessary that he *takes* the ring off of your finger. If he fails to do so, then the goal will be to create as much distance between you and him as possible." He reaches out to the table and grabs the figurine that I think is supposed to represent me. It's carved into what looks like a small sun. "You'll run to the carriages on the other side of the spell. There, a pack with supplies and one of my men will be waiting. They can get you to the edge of Vitour, maybe a little farther, before they will have to leave you to complete the journey to the Mage Kingdom on your own. It's the only way I can ensure they won't be caught."

My heart beats in protest at the plan, something about it not quite feeling *right*. Then again, nothing has in a long time. "And the king?" I end up asking.

"Once the Trusted are dead, I will join Remi as he kills him." Xander's expression is cold, reminding more of the man I saw in the tower.

"Just like that?" I ask as I stare at him.

He shrugs before leaning forward. "The blood oath makes it so that I can't be the one to make the killing blow. But I want to be there as the light fades in his eyes. I want my face to be the last thing he sees before he goes wherever people like him go when they die."

I pinch my lips together but say nothing, drawing Xander's curiosity.

With the small revision now sorted, they move on to how they will handle the sirens if they interfere.

"We'll have clay in our ears," Xander says to the table. "All the men will. Which means communicating with each other once everything is in motion is going to be difficult. Stick to your jobs. Do not deviate unless King Dolian is able to break out of Remi's hold *or* a Trusted gets past the Spell and to the king. It's not worth the risk to your life then, so abandon the beach and run like hell to the trees." He points to a small circle of green fabric on the table. "Here, you can travel to the castle undetected and get to a tunnel entrance. Don't linger. Don't hesitate. We get Rhea out *first* and foremost. Whether it's after the king takes the ring off of her or instead of."

While there is still a measure of distrust in the air, everyone surrounding the table acknowledges Xander with a look or gesture of agreement. I wish I could say that their confidence bolsters my own hope, but instead, all I feel is the phantom ache of the brand. The caress of hands I never wanted along my body. A press of lips and an invasion of more against my mouth. It all lingers over me, and when I try to sink deeper into myself to shy away from it, those things only feel harsher. More painful. More *real*.

"Any questions?"

Silence passes for a few beats, and then I ask, "Who will take over the Mortal Kingdom?"

Xander shifts back in his chair, his gaze on the table for a few short moments before he quietly answers, "I will." He says it like it's an admission he isn't quite sure he wants known. But another glance around the table informs me that everyone not only *knows* but seems to approve. There isn't a *hint* of reservation at the thought of Xander ruling over them.

Which means Xander's own hesitation is because of me. I wait until the meeting adjourns—last minute details solidified —and we're once more in the tunnels to say, "It explains a lot."

Xander walks ahead of me, the small torch he holds lighting the way for us. "What does?"

"Why you were so cruel to me in the tower." His shoulders tense but he doesn't stop. Doesn't look over his shoulder at me. "You wanted to be king."

"It was more than that. You posed a very real threat to *everything*. Especially when I realized just how much the king had lied about you." He laughs mirthlessly. "I *never* trusted him about *anything*, yet I didn't question that you were there against your will until the first time I saw him beat you."

I press a hand against the cold stone to steady myself.

"When you captured me as I was attempting to leave the tower, was your plan to tell the king what I had done?"

"No," he answers quickly. "When I caught you, I meant what I said. I was surprised that you had attempted to escape, but I was stuck. I couldn't get you out of the tower without invoking the blood oath. I needed time to think and to handle *Flynn*." His name is said with a hint of something spiteful. "But when I descended the stairs of the tower, he was there and attacked me." The torch light flickers, and we turn a final corner that leads to my rooms.

"He wanted to kill you," I confess. Maybe because I want to, or maybe because I need Xander to know that at *any* point, Nox could have killed him. With his fists or with his magic. And maybe Xander knows that because he sighs and runs a hand through his hair.

"Yeah, he was rightfully pissed, and I deserved to be stuck at the base of the tower for as long as I was. I deserved a lot more than that, if we're both being honest."

"Maybe," I respond as we reach the end of the tunnel, Xander leaning his ear against the door panel as he listens for any movement inside of my room. He reaches behind him for a dagger, pulling it free before opening the door. Cold air from my bedroom rushes at us, but nothing follows. The space is empty, so I wait for Xander to extinguish the torch and step through, turning to extend a hand to me. "So, king, huh?"

Xander walks across the room to a covered flame gem. I sit on the edge of the bed as golden light floods over me, and he turns to face me. "Yeah." His eyes search mine as he exhales roughly. "I know that it probably seems like I hid that tidbit from you—"

"It's fine."

"And like I'm claiming something that isn't mine—"

"You aren't."

"But—" He pauses and drags a hand over his face. "Rhea, I don't know what to say in this situation."

I drop my gaze to my lap, my thumb brushing over the pearl on my ring. "You don't have to explain anything. While I was locked in that tower, you were putting in the work to build something better. You saw the king treat his people poorly and found a solution."

"One that might lead us into a revolution, that might cause more anguish before it brings peace. And it doesn't even begin to address the Cruel Death and its ramifications. And, yes, I know you can heal people from that too, but I promise you right now, I will never ask you to do that."

It had been weeks—a month?—since King Dolian tested that theory. Of course, healing the sick would have been a worthy use of my magic. But I understand what Xander is trying to say, he wouldn't be another person to exploit it.

"What if this isn't the right thing to do?" Xander asks into the silence I've let linger. Beneath the light of the flame gem, he looks younger. More unsure than I've ever seen him.

"It is," I answer, forcing my mouth to remember what the shape of a smile feels like as I offer him one. "And you are the right person. You know the people of Vitour—more intimately than the king. Than me or anyone else. And your claim to the throne is legitimate." At his snort, I amend, "*Mostly* legitimate."

He brings both hands to his hips as he levels me with a serious gaze. "So is yours."

My smile falls, that ever-present exhaustion beginning to dig its claws into me, pulling me beneath the surface again. "But I do not want a throne."

"What about the Mage Kingdom?"

I chew on my lower lip, shrugging a single shoulder. "It belongs to *him*."

Chapter One Hundred and Seventeen

RHEA

"**A**RE YOU NERVOUS?" THE question comes from Erica, her hands gentle as she brushes my hair. With Eve gone, Erica has been tasked with helping me dress when the king wants to show me off. Yesterday had been tea with the ladies of the court, their judgmental sneers and thinly veiled gibes rolling off of me easily. After all, what could words hope to accomplish against someone who is tired of fighting anyway?

"I'm nervous that people will get hurt," I answer, watching her face in the reflection of the vanity mirror. Avoiding my own eyes.

"They know the risks." Erica, of course, knew about Xander and his resistance. Was a part of it, and would be instrumental in helping to get men and women inside the castle after the king's death to help them overthrow the council and the guards loyal to King Dolian. "No one is being forced to do this."

"I know."

"In just a few hours, you will be gone from here," she muses, setting the brush down on the vanity and lightly placing her hands on my shoulders. I had been given a corseted maroon gown to wear, the skirt flowing to my feet in a fabric too thin for winter. My shoulders are exposed beneath tiny straps, while long sleeves flutter down my arms. Were it any other time, were I in any other situation, I would love this dress. But, today, it feels more like an omen. A reminder of a different gown I had been forced into. Erica has no way of knowing that my plans have changed. That instead of chasing something that no longer exists, I've decided that the best thing I can do is disappear.

686

Distantly, the last reverb of an echo whispers that I'm wrong. That home is a pair of star-flecked eyes and strong hands, and that he's waiting for me to return. But then it is silenced, and I'm turning to thank Erica for her help.

"I'm sorry I could not do more, Lady Rhea," she says, her voice heavy with regret. She reaches out to gently grasp one of my hands. "If I could sneak you out of here myself, I would."

My voice sounds raw, unused, when I respond, "You and Tienne helped me more than you could ever realize after Alexi was killed. Your kindness..." I swallow down the emotion that dares to sit heavy in my throat. "It was the first time anyone besides him had ever offered it to me." Tears crest her eyes as she nods her head, saying that Xander will be up to retrieve me within the hour.

Closing the door behind her, I walk to the bathroom and open the cupboard below the sink, sifting through the folded towels until I find the hidden diary. When Xander had given me Alexi's journal, I had been insatiable reading the entries. It was lovely, getting to know my former guard in a way that I hadn't yet seen. That he hadn't been able to show me. He was a complicated man, but he also was the most selfless. The most endearing. A father to me when I had known none before.

My thumb caresses the worn leather as I take a seat on the bed, flipping through the pages until I reach the final entry. I had hoped that I could read it when I was back in the Mage Kingdom. I envisioned myself wrapped in Nox's arms, his voice gentle as he gave life to the last words Alexi had written in this journal, the date only a month before he died. Closing my eyes, I let my shoulders slump at the vision. Gods, in another lifetime we could have been so very happy together. I had once thought that the love I felt for him was more than one existence should allow, and maybe that was a truer statement than I ever realized. But if this was all we would get together, then it would have to be enough. I would have to learn to let it *feel* like enough.

A tear drips down onto the cover of the journal, and I brush it away before flipping to the last page, taking in his handwriting for the final time. At first, the entry details how it has been nearly two weeks since he last saw me, the ache in his chest similar to when he goes too long without visiting Alanna's tombstone. He talks of the Cruel Death taking his friend, and his hatred once more for the king. But it's what he's written at the end of the entry that disrupts my heart, a breath lodging in my throat.

Perhaps now is as good a time as any to give this to Rhea, yet I still do not know if it will harm or hinder. Would she long for them more by having this portrait? Or would it soothe a part of her to be able to look upon them whenever she wants? I hope I can figure it out by her birthday.

I turn the page to read more, finding only one sentence remaining and a detached, thick piece of paper, the edges bent and ragged.

She is the best thing to happen to me outside of Alanna.

My fingers tremble as they reach for the paper, and when I turn it over, a crestfallen whimper—one forged in my loneliness and shaped by my desolation—tumbles from me as I stare down at a perfectly painted, highly detailed portrait of a couple standing side by side, crowns sparkling on their heads and fine clothes tailored to their bodies. His hair is medium brown and cut short, a few errant strands dangling over his forehead in a way that defies what I've come to believe about mortal royalty. He doesn't smile; instead, a far too serious look is depicted, as if to combat the aforementioned rebelling of his hair. Next to him, the woman stands tall, her hands crossed in front of her. But where the king's expression is regal, a slight smile shapes hers. Bright green eyes glow, even just on paper, and her hair—that familiar honeyed golden blonde—is left loose to drape down her back in soft waves.

Beneath their portraits, written in cursive script, are their names: King Conrad Maxwell and Queen Luna Maxwell. My parents.

❧❧❧❧❧ ❧❧❧❧❧

The knock on the door comes far too soon, and I quickly hide Alexi's journal again, hopeful that in the chaotic aftermath of what is about to happen, I'll be able to retrieve it once again. The portrait, however, I tuck into a layer of my bralette, ripping a seam and slipping the picture between the lace and the fabric it covers. Righting my dress, I open the door, reviewing Xander's plan in my mind, only for everything to halt when it's Simon and not my cousin standing in the hallway. The king's advisor has his hands clasped behind him, his dark gaze running over the length of me in that assessing manner that draws me right back to those nights beneath his blade, reality blending with the horror of my mind.

Simon grins, a cruel thing, as if he is reliving the torture too. "Lady Rhea, I have come to escort you to the carriage."

"What of Xander?" I ask, my stomach sinking when I don't see any other guard waiting in the hall.

Simon's brow arches, his head tilting in calculation. "Careful, Lady, asking for a specific guard might give the impression that you two have grown *fond*."

"The commander is always the one to escort me," I answer, begging my voice to stay steady. "I am only asking for clarity. Nothing more."

Simon purses his lips as if he can taste my lie. Stepping back, he gestures for me to exit, and I have no choice but to move.

"Do you want to know why I haven't paid you a visit in some time, Lady Rhea?" His voice is low, but the fact that he has the audacity to ask such a question in a public place has my eyes darting to see if anyone is nearby. Unfortunately for me, this floor is empty of everything except the sound of our steps. When I don't answer him, he hums, as if my response is expected. "It is because I *know* that you are hiding something. Secrets have a tendency to grow over time, and I have a feeling the ones inside of you are just *bursting* at the seams." Fear creeps down my spine and over my limbs until I'm nearly paralyzed with it. "You, Lady Rhea, may have everyone fooled that you are submitting to the king, but I've *seen* the defiance in you. I've watched it spill out of you like a crimson wave, begging to be studied. To be *dissected*." We descend the stairs, my heart racing as my hands grow clammy.

"I *will* find out what you're hiding, and when I've got the information I need, I will go to the king and watch as he makes you tell him *everything*. Together, we'll finally strip that last layer of armor you try to hide behind." Another flash of that wicked smile and then, "Maybe the mage king can even help us."

My eyes widen and though I don't speak a word, Simon reads the question on my face anyway.

"Oh, pathetic *girl*. I know Xander has given you information on the Mage Kingdom. He is, of course, the one who receives Stephan's letters. At least, *some* of them."

"I don't kn—"

"Spare me the lies, Lady Rhea. The commander believes himself to be impervious to my observational skills, but he, like all others, will eventually crack with time. Did he tell you that King Nox tried to come for you? That he was thwarted?" We reach the bottom of the steps, my legs moving on muscle memory alone as my ears ring. "Stephan is exceptionally skilled in the use of plants to subdue. He knows how much of each to give to make someone *just* a little bit numb, both to their surroundings and their predicaments." The palace doors come into view ahead of us when Simon chuckles, as if in on a joke I'm unaware of. "But greatness is to be expected from any son of mine."

I'm not sure I'm breathing, the ramifications of what Simon's just said hitting me harshly enough to rob me of air.

"You want to know why the mage king has not come for you again? How I know he will not come for you? It's because he has no *desire* to. And when my son returns with yet another update for me, you and I will have another of our meetings to discuss it all. Would knowing that King Nox has wed Lady Haylee get you to spill your secrets?" His words deliver the punch they're meant to, my hand coming to rest on my stomach as if I've just been punched there. "After your wedding to His Majesty, I suppose we'll find out."

Xander waits outside near the carriage, not bothering to hide his glare for the king's advisor.

"I'll see you when you return," Simon says, perfectly aware of the snare he's just laid in my chest as he heads back towards the castle.

"What did he say?" Xander asks, his voice hushed. I think about telling him. About asking him if what Simon said is true. If Nox is really married to Haylee. But, in the end, knowing the answers to those questions won't change anything.

Xander and his resistance will still enact their plan on the beach today. I will get away—either freed of the ring or not—and I will leave, not with the intention of being found by the man who will forever hold my heart but with the intention of getting lost. Of disappearing.

"Later," I murmur to him, just as King Dolian approaches.

Soon, we are in route to meet with the sirens, the king at my side. "Are you okay, darling?" he asks, dragging the back of his knuckles down my cheek. There is no magic behind the question, so I nod without looking at him. "Good. We'll heal the sirens and then get you back for dinner with the court. By this time tomorrow..." His fingers curl around my chin to turn me towards him. But even as he looks at me, he isn't really *seeing* me, so he doesn't recognize the anxiousness I know is showing. He doesn't see anything but a framework that he can build upon. That he can ruin. "I will finally be wed to you, and we can forget anything that came before. We can start anew as husband and wife. King and queen."

"Uncle and niece," I add on. Sunlight pours through the window at our side, making the hazel color of his eyes glow nearly orange. "Mustn't forget that one."

King Dolian tightens his grip for a breath, rage rising in his gaze before it suddenly banks and he releases me, sitting back as he looks straight ahead, his hands clasped in his lap. "Yes, that *will* likely affect how we have children, but I suppose it is a good thing I had the foresight to find women who look like you to fuck when the desire that *you* cause becomes too much to bear." I stare at him, my fingers gripping the fabric of my dress tightly. "Oh, don't worry. I will fuck you and have my fill, but considering our *relation*, getting you pregnant is too risky. As such, we will have surrogates, and you will raise the children as ours. Eve is the closest physical match to you, so I think I'll start with her."

The carriage slows to a stop, and the king smiles at me, perfectly regal and without any hint of the monster that lies within. And in this moment, with the threat to Eve made *clear*, I decide that today *must* go to plan. That the king *must* die.

He exits the carriage first, turning to extend his hand. I take it, playing meekness as my eyes meet Xander's through the gaps in his helmet.

"Let's get this over with," King Dolian says, leading the way.

Chapter One Hundred and Eighteen

RHEA

THE SIRENS ARE ALREADY waiting for us, the queen standing tall with her trident in hand and a crown of diamonds and seashells stark against her dark hair. At her immediate left is a female with bright orange hair, the trident in her hand similar except that it is smaller and made purely of gold. I can't remember if she has accompanied the queen on past visits, but I know the siren next to her has. Her pink hair glows against her dark skin, curls cropped to her shoulders. The final siren stands on the other side of the queen. I recognize her from past visits as well, her round eyes even more so as she meets my gaze head on.

"Queen Amari, it is a pleasure as always to see you," King Dolian says. I feel Xander's presence at my back and watch as the siren queen tracks the movement of the other guards behind me.

"I should hope so, considering everything I have done for you."

King Dolian bristles but quickly hides it with a tight smile. "The first wedding attended by a siren in over two hundred years. That's quite a thing to celebrate," he says, a hand sliding into his pocket. "Though I do wonder if it is wise for you to attend."

"Why wouldn't it be? We are *allies*, are we not?" she asks, taking a step forward. Glints of golden armor shine in my peripheral vision, the cold winter breeze brushing more harshly against my back now.

My uncle meets the queen's stern expression with a glower of his own, and it makes a corner of her mouth lift. "We are, bu—"

"Because I seem to remember that you are in my debt not once but *twice*," she interjects. "Of course, you know that." The darkness in her eyes expands as she takes in the full extent of the king, dragging her gaze from the crown resting upon his head down to his pristine boots. "It was only, what, twenty-two years ago that you first came to me on this very beach? Dressed very much like you are now, except for the crown." Her fingers curl around her trident, claws scraping against metal. I shiver at the noise. "I remember the night so *clearly*. For it's not every day that I get to both *fuck* a king and create one."

Twenty-two years ago...

"Does your fiancée know?" she continues, turning her attention to me. "How it is that you became king? What you *sacrificed* that night?"

She smiles broadly at his silence, but my own mind is stuck on her words. *Twenty-two years ago...*

"It wasn't the mages," I murmur, brows furrowing. "Was it?" The queen outright laughs, the sirens at her sides looking just as confused as I feel as their eyes bounce between the three of us.

"Is that what you told her? Told your people?" Queen Amari clicks her tongue as she shakes her head, a melodic hum slipping from her. "All these years, and they don't know just how connected our two realms are."

"Queen Amari, this is hardly the time or place to divulge this information. That night, we made a bargain—one I intend to honor to the full extent," King Dolian growls, lifting his chin as he rolls his shoulders back and gestures with an idle hand towards me. "But it has no bearing on what we will be doing *today*."

"Oh, but it does, and you know that." She bites her lip and then releases it, and though we are out in the open, air feels scarce as I try to draw more of it in. "When you called on me to help with your *problem*, I told you I would do it under one condition. Do you remember what that was?

"Rhea, heal the queen," the king says—*commands*—my magic rushing up from behind that invisible wall. I inhale sharply as it floods my body, warmth tingling down my arms to my fingertips, where glittering white flares from my palms.

The queen's laugh is beautiful and ominous, and as my magic streams over her body, its bright light in stark contrast to her dark braids and even darker eyes, she makes a demand of the king. "Tell her, as she heals me with power from the very kingdom you claim killed your *brother*, the truth of that night, mortal king."

Though King Dolian attempts to fight against the magic, it's to no avail. He turns stiffly to face me fully, the words prying his lips open before he's ready to. "The night you were born," he begins with difficulty, each word shoved out against his will, "my brother gave me an ultimatum. He had found out that I had fathered a child with a woman from Vitour because she had come to the castle asking for help raising the boy. Conrad had never been someone overly affectionate or tender growing up. He had been cruel to a fault, just like our father, until he and Luna became *involved*." He spits the last word out like he can't bear to call what they had love. "I guess becoming a father exacerbated those weaknesses, because he abruptly began giving a shit about me. About what I was doing with *my* life. He threatened to have my royal title stripped. To have me removed from the Maxwell line as if he could simply erase who I fucking *am*."

The queen sighs, and my magic begins to retreat within me, a waterfall of warmth returning back to its source. "Your magic is a lovely feeling," she muses, speaking slowly. "Dyanna, come here." The pink-haired siren moves from her place at the end of the line to right in front of me. "You'll heal my daughters next, starting with Dyanna." *Daughters*. Magic surges from my hand again, the queen's command washing over me as King Dolian starts talking again.

"He had taken *everything* from me, and it made him feel invincible. As a king. As a man. A husband. *A father*. I *hated* him for it. He constantly underestimated me, and in the end, that was his true downfall."

"What did you do?" I breathe, the sensation of my magic lost to the focus I give him. "What did you do to my father?"

"Father?" the queen questions, clear surprise in her voice.

"I asked him to go for a walk with me. Preyed on that newfound gentleness of his as I told him how I had made a mistake but wanted to make it right. As I *lied* to him." Though his chest heaves, there is no remorse for what he's done. "We walked to the beach, a little farther east. It was night, the water blending into the dark sky, no moon in sight. Which made it impossible to see the siren queen as she rose from its depths."

The flow of my magic begins to slow, but in its place within me a new invisible weight sits. "You led him to his death?"

"No," he says, reaching out to cup my face. "I created our beginning."

My magic trickles to a halt as I stare at him, the salt in the air stinging my wide eyes. I hadn't believed he was being truthful when he told me of my parents' deaths before, but stupidly, pathetically, *naively*, I never imagined that he could do *this*.

"Sade," Queen Amari barks, directing the siren with orange hair and the smaller trident to stand in front of me. My magic already knows what to do, and within a few seconds, it is filling her, streaks of white magic glowing beneath her skin.

"And my mother?" I ask, utterly terrified of the answer and, yet, still needing it anyway.

"An unfortunate sacrifice," he grinds out, and my heart stops. I think of the picture of my parents I had just found and how young they looked. Three lives impacted forever because of *him*.

"You look upset, Rhea," the queen drawls, her outline blurry from the tears that have gathered in my eyes. "But you did not just *lose* family that day; you gained a new one too." I blink, warmth trickling down my cheeks as I direct my gaze to hers. "The deal I offered *your uncle* that night was simple: I would lure his brother into the water, thus handing him the crown he so desperately wanted, and in return, if an offspring were to come from the *pairing*, she would be recognized as royalty in the Mortal Kingdom."

King Dolian inhales sharply, and my mouth parts on a shocked gasp as the queen turns her gaze not to Dyanna or Sade but to the siren with ruby-red hair.

"Princess Aria is the product of that night. A siren born from both queen *and* king." Her chin lowers, her eyes narrowing on her daughter. "Officially mortal royalty."

The siren—*Aria*—turns her hazel gaze from her mother's to me. To the king's. Her color is brighter, as if lit from behind with a candle, but knowing who her father is—*was*—there is no denying that she got her eyes from him. My shock is mirrored by her horror. I have a *sister*, one born of the same violence I had been raised in. One that is a siren. We continue to stare at each other, my pulse so loud in my ears that I almost don't hear the sliding of the swords from their scabbards.

My magic is still being fed into Sade when the guards surround us, the king standing so close to me that I am caught in the fray. He shouts for them to stop, or at least, I think he does until I feel the tether to my magic sever, and Sade falls to her knees. I don't have time to question the loophole as King Dolian is yanked back from me, a guard tackling him to the ground and knocking the crown from his head. It rolls to a stop near my feet, only to get kicked away when another guard rushes past me to the king, restraining one of his arms.

But, despite appearances, the king knows how to fight, and he catches the two on either side of him off guard as he shoves a shoulder into the breast plate of the one on his left. He raises his head, eyes scouring the beach until they meet mine, his mouth opening. And I should move—I know that I *need* to move—but fear and sadness and anger keep me rooted in place. I want this godsdamn ring off of me. I want the fear that it induces every time I rub my thumb over it to go away. I want even the illusion of freedom from this monster. I want it, and I want to watch him *die* so that I can have it.

"Rhea! Ki—" Even with his command cut short, I feel my magic rise, peeking above its confines for a single moment before it's yanked back down again. Remi is there, one large hand planted firmly over King Dolian's mouth while the other is pressing a dagger just beneath his chin.

I finally manage to take a step forward, only to crash into an incoming guard, sending us both off balance as we crash into the sand. My head spins and my ears ring as I look back up to where the king is struggling against the guards, blood dripping down his neck from small nicks of Remi's knife. Remi screams, the hand covering the king's mouth gone as he shakes it out in front of him, grimacing in pain.

The chaos around me is overwhelming as the sounds of swords clashing and men yelling fill the open air, yet I know that I will hear whatever the king says.

That I will be forced to heed his command. And he will not hesitate to have me kill everyone here. *Neither will the queen.* The truth in those thoughts propels me to my feet, my arms and legs moving faster than my body can keep up with, making me nearly stumble.

I watch the king inhale deeply, watch as the first syllable makes it past his lips, only to end there. Remi covers his mouth again, silencing the command as both look at me with different levels of desperation.

"Run!" Remi shouts, gritting his teeth before he screams again, and I realize with no short amount of terror that King Dolian is *biting* his hand. "Run *now!*"

The panic in his voice finally breaks through and spurs me into motion. I turn and run. Past Queen Amari and Sade and Dyanna, their mouths opened wide as their voices blend together and their song blankets the beach. Past Aria, who stands motionless, her hands curled into fists at her sides as those round eyes take in the havoc. Sand kicks up behind me, the air freezing as it races across my skin, and I run. Away from the king's command and Xander's stoic but steady presence and Erica's tender care. Away from Eve's sweet friendship and Brisk's gentle eyes and all the other men and women fighting to help get me away.

Pushing myself faster, I nearly sigh when the carriages come into view through the small distortion of the Spell ahead of me. But as I pivot to follow the path, only a few feet away from crossing, something *slithers* across the sand, black and wispy like dark smoke from a fire, and my steps halt. I watch as it moves over the tops of my feet—the feel of it like silk and colder than ice. *You know this.* The thought scratches at my mind. The tendrils get darker as they move across the beach to where the guards and the king are fighting. *You know this.* My heart flips and leaps to my throat because I *do* know what these tendrils are, and it is not smoke.

Even though I can't feel my own magic and I shouldn't be able to feel any other, something tugs at my heart—at my soul—as if to say, *look at me, look at me.* It overpowers the manic fear that rises and the rational thoughts that scream, *it's been too long,* and forces me to look back towards the Spell.

Right into a pair of star-flecked eyes.

Suddenly, he is there, right on the other side of the Spell, and I can't breathe or speak or think. There is just him against the gray-blue sky and those eyes that I know so well. That I've dreamed about, even when it was painful. Him, dressed in black with stubble that shadows his cheeks and jaw and waves of onyx that curl over his forehead and ears, a menacing tableau of death manifested.

I try to say his name, my mouth shaping the word uselessly until only a broken whimper is tossed into the space between us. But that sound motivates him, because in two steps, he is right in front of me. Consuming the entirety of my vision. Consuming *me.*

"Hello, Sunshine," he rasps, and I think it might be the most beautiful thing I've ever heard.

Chapter One Hundred and Nineteen

RHEA

"**Y**OU CAME," I SAY, the words carried on a broken breath. Blurted out without thinking of the repercussions of them. Nox's face shatters, too many emotions to identify flickering through his gaze as he stares down at me. I reach out to touch him, desperate for any evidence that this isn't some cruel trick, and whimper again when his hand closes around mine.

Nox's eyes soften as they somehow begin to decipher the battle in my own. He's always been able to read me, always able to pluck out that which I could not give voice to. "What have I always told you, Rhea? You are *mine*." A sob pushes past my lips as he gently draws me to him, autumn woods and salt and *him* dominating my next inhale. He's here. *He's here. He's here.* "I'm sorry it took so long," he adds, his voice low and raw. "I'm so fucking *sorry*."

I don't know how else to respond, afraid I might say something that will hurt him again. Afraid that the illusion will fracture.

"I have so much to tell you," he whispers against the top of my head. *So do I.* I watch as Nox's magic directs the shadows to keep moving away from us, and I remember that we aren't alone. "So much has happened." I don't hear the sirens singing anymore, only the shouts of the guards. "But first, I'm taking you away from here. Away from *him*."

There is a single pause between what Nox says and what happens next as I squeeze him more tightly to me. As I drag in another deep breath of his scent and allow myself to sink more deeply into his hold. That single pause is all I'm allowed before something stirs within me. Ancient and familiar. I stiffen, choking on the

696

gasp that travels up my throat. The ominous presence blooms in my chest, a cover sliding off the well of my magic. It's an awakening of that dark power, and as Nox leans back, his brows drawing together in confusion, I remember the command and the vow I then promised in blood. *Vow to me that you will obliterate anyone that says they will take you away from me. Away from the Mortal Kingdom.*

My eyes widen as that icy feeling seeps up my torso and spreads over my chest. "No!" I scream, pushing at Nox's chest as I back away, my steps clumsy in the sand.

"Rhea, wha—"

"Run!" I shout as my arms lift in front of me, the motion automatic. Nox takes in the glittering black magic pooling at the center of my palms, and instead of running, instead of raising his own magic to shield, he reaches out for me. Just as he's always done.

I try to back away, but the building magic rushes through every vein, every muscle and limb and then to my head, shadows clouding my mind until my vision is veiled in black. I know there is no stopping what happens next. Just as I know by the look in his eyes that Nox won't leave me here. That, even if the cost is himself, he'll stay.

I thought I knew what ruination was as I watched Alexi die. As I watched Bella collapse before the Spell. I thought I had experienced the worst this life could offer me beneath the cruel ministrations of an evil man as he tortured me. As someone of my own blood branded and abused me. But as that last imaginary string holding my power is cut and the dark magic at my palms bursts in Nox's direction, all of those moments pale in comparison to this. To knowing I'm going to hurt Nox. That I am capable of doing so much more than just inflicting pain. My wail is lost to the wind, hidden behind the glittering onyx that partially overtakes my view of him.

I *feel* the moment my magic hits him, the shock of his parted lips barely visible through the power that flows out of me. It takes him far too long to call his own magic up to block mine, a shield of dark purple and black shooting into the air. I'm pulled farther down into the tide of the command, pushing more and more magic from within as my throat grows raw from my screams. My fingers flex painfully, anguish coating me in sweat as I repeatedly try and fail to regain some control. *Any* control. Bright yellow flares in front of Nox's magic, a second person stepping up next to him, the silver sword in their hand painted in blood. Sapphire-blue eyes find mine through the congestion of magic, and I think he screams my name as he looks from me to Nox. But there is no responding to him, there is *nothing* but the darkness of death as it's drawn from me.

Leaning into the shield created by his magic, Nox grits his teeth, his eyes never leaving my face as he forces one step, then two, his boots sinking into the sand. But any progress he makes is undone by the brunt of my power, and I watch in utter horror as he falls to his knees, the strain turning his face red. Daje moves to stand behind him, but his magic is already flickering.

"Go! Now!" Nox shouts, and my magic pulses stronger.

"I'm not leaving y—"

"Go, Daje!" His face falls as he stares at me, and I don't miss the betrayal in his eyes. The confusion laced within it. He stays another few heartbeats, but then his magic gives out fully, and he's forced to stumble away, collapsing into the sand. Terror pulses through me when my magic begins to creep out to the edges of Nox's barrier. He notices it too and surrounds himself in a dome of dark purple as my shadows encase it completely, until there is only writhing and impossible *black*.

"Rhea!"

The magic forces me to move closer to him, tears stinging my eyes and coating my cheeks as my lips part on another horrified scream.

"It's okay," he shouts as I get closer, my shoulders shaking from my sobs. But this—this isn't okay. I cannot survive this. I *cannot* survive knowing that he's gone because of me. "I love you. Do you hear me, Rhea? *I love you!*" My shoulders shake with my sobs, and my magic continues to surround his, a raging storm pummeling at a glass house.

And it is only a matter of time before it cracks.

Chapter One Hundred and Twenty

ARIA

ONE MOMENT, RHEA IS healing Sade, her magic glowing inside my sister's body in streaks of white, and the next, the king's own guards rush and apprehend him. In a stilted moment of confusion, all I can do is watch as the king is wrestled to his knees, a large man holding a knife to his throat and covering his face. On the other side of the Spell, swords are drawn and clashing together, the golden guards attacking *each other*. And then there is a flash of maroon, blonde hair whipping behind her as Rhea runs as fast as she can in the opposite direction.

"Your Majesty, you need to go back in the water," Sade shouts over the chaos, standing in front of our mother, trident angled out.

"No! We cannot let anything happen to the king. He's still needed for my plans. Sing and get the guards to *stop*!" Sade nods and opens her mouth, magic coating the air as she, Dyanna, and my mother sing. I try to join them, to at least *feign* that my magic will work, but I'm still reeling over what was just exposed. As sirens, it is our destiny to never know who we were sired from. It is something my mother has drilled into us. Males are for fucking to get pregnant and nothing more. Rearing offspring—taking care of them and raising them to be just as vicious as their elders—is the siren's lot in life. And yet... Queen Amari held on to the knowledge that I am not just a siren princess but also a *mortal* one for my entire life.

My gaze flicks to Rhea's back as she continues to run. *Sister.* I have a sister who is not a siren, our blood shared by the father neither ever knew. Another life affected by the cruelty of my kind.

"Something is wrong," Dyanna says as she stops singing, pointing with her chin to the guards around the king. "They aren't affected by our song."

"Are they female?" my mother asks, stepping between her two daughters as her talons scrape against the metal of her trident. But even I can see that at least *some* of the guards are indeed male, their size and the shapes of their jaws giving them away.

"They plotted this," Sade guesses, watching the fighting in an assessing manner. "They must have something blocking their ears from our song. What do you want us to do?"

"What is *that*?" Dyanna asks before our mother can answer, pointing a taloned finger in the direction Rhea is running, at the dark *shadows* billowing towards us.

"Magic," my mother hisses. She raises her trident, as if she can fend off the clouds of darkness that coat the sand like a sinister mist before she lowers it with a growl and looks once more to the king.

"A coup?" Dyanna asks, to which our mother nods.

"How *very* inconvenient." The magic grows thicker, and it reminds me of the feel of Rhea's. Except this doesn't glitter like hers, and it moves with more fluid and grace, like black water gliding in from the tide. "Where did Rhea go?" Queen Amari scans the beach in the direction Rhea went, but with the magic writhing in front of us, so thick in the air we can't see through, it's impossible to figure out just how far away she got. "Go retrieve her," she commands, trident pointing to Dyanna. "Your magic, as royalty, will work on the ring. Infuse your voice with your power and command her to return."

"Your Majesty, send me," Sade says, stepping in front of Dyanna.

"No. We do not know if Rhea's magic fully healed you before the attack. You will help me protect the king." Her dark eyes flick to me. "Get in the water and wait until Rhea is back and can heal you as well. You're useless to me as you are." Sade catches my eye behind our mother's back as Dyanna takes off in the direction Rhea went. *Go*, she mouths, chin jutting towards the water. I watch as she and our mother raise their tridents as they approach the guards holding the king before I retreat partially into the water.

Just off the shore, the Queen's Legion awaits my mother's word to attack and though I can't see them from where I stand, I can feel their gazes pushing at my back. The icy ocean laps at my knees as I drag my gaze to the direction Dyanna ran after Rhea, entering the shadowy magic that grows thicker. What the queen has done to Rhea weighs heavily on my mind as I stand there, the scared siren I've always been begging me to retreat to where it's relatively safe. To obey my mother's command because, after all, what difference could *I* make?

But I have been forged into something different these past few months. Still scared—as is evident by the quick beating of my heart—still terrified of making the wrong choice, but there is now a spark within me that wasn't before. One born of the need to take care of those I love and made stronger by the lessons from a certain fae. Yes, I could run. I could hide and be the same female everyone around me expects. Or I can choose to do something *more*. *Be* someone more. *Who am I willing to become?* No, a different question stirs in my head, one more pointed. *Who have I become?*

I begin to run after my sister—*sisters*, my hair tickling my back and toes squishing in the wet sand. I only glance back once, just to make sure my mother isn't following me. That a legionary isn't. I push farther onto dryer land when I confirm I'm alone, just as the dark magic begins to retreat. It's a slow progression, the movement jerky where it was once smooth. Then shadows *scatter* as if someone has snipped the string holding them, leaving me with a crystal-clear view of what is in front of me. And I'm not entirely sure what I'm looking at.

Dyanna has already come to a halt, her chest heaving as she looks at a ball of glittering shadows with hints of dark purple, Rhea standing just a few feet away, torment contorting her face. "What's happening?"

My voice causes Dyanna to startle, her bright pink eyes wide as she looks at me. "I don't know. I heard her screaming." Another rends the air, Rhea's voice a ragged plea as tears streak over cheeks. I move a step closer, Dyanna's fingers closing around my wrist. "This is powerful magic," she says quietly, her voice serious.

"Is... is she following a command?"

Dyanna nods. "Nothing can stop her until it's been fulfilled."

I hear my sister, but I'm too focused on the movement within all the whirling magic. Narrowing my eyes against the bright sun, I see the outline of a man on his knees, his shoulder leaning against the purple magic as his jaw clenches in pain. Rhea takes a single step forward, and the glittering shadows I know to be hers double in size, rolling in on themselves like a tumultuous wave. The keening sound she releases pierces me straight to the heart, and I watch as she struggles against her own body, screams that end in sobs repeating over and over again. The man at the center of it all grunts, his eyes flashing wide as the dark purple magic he leans against *shudders* under the power of Rhea's. But even as he fights to protect himself, his eyes stay on hers. "I love you," he says, and Rhea's answering scream could shatter worlds.

"She's killing him."

"And there is nothing we can do." Despite the gravity of her words, Dyanna speaks them as if she is reading from a book. As it is an undeniable fact. I wonder if her lack of empathy is real or if it's an act. If this is truly who Dyanna has always been or if it is something she's forced to *pretend* to be.

Looking back at Rhea, I find that I don't have the same question about myself. I *know* who I am now, better than I ever have before. "You're wrong," I whisper, shaking my arm out of her hold. "There is something I can do." Dyanna doesn't protest as I step forward before breaking into a run.

As a siren, I have always been able to feel siren magic in the air around me, but this is the first time I've sensed another being's so strongly. Even when Rhea used her magic to kill the guards behind the Spell or when she healed the sirens in my presence, it hadn't quite felt like *this*.

Pushing my curls out of my face, I feel my skin pebble at how much magic vibrates in the air, a shiver working through me as I stop behind Rhea. Fear robs me of my next breath, her magic much more terrifying up close. Her chest heaves with her sobs as she stares at the trapped man, his body completely hidden now by the shadows. *What the fuck am I doing?* I don't even know if *my* magic will work, despite being royalty, because my siren powers have never been the same as everyone else around me. But maybe there is a reason why. Rhea cries out in pain, the sound agonizing as black veins begin to appear beneath her skin, her eyes glazed over in a smoky gray shade. If she notices me standing so close to her, she doesn't show it, and again, that fear slips down my spine and urges me to run away.

But what was a life worth living if I didn't ever do what was right when I had the chance? If I *never* took a stand? Lyre is doing it as she vows to keep her daughter safe and give her a life away from the cruelty of our mother. Sade is doing it as she risks herself daily to try and build hope with sirens who are tired of being oppressed. And Myla... Myla lives in a cloak of shadows and secrets, convincing herself she is a monster while risking discovery that she is the vigilante helping her city's most vulnerable. I don't need to be a determined mother or commander of a legion or vigilante, dragon-flying fae. I just need to be *me* and believe that is enough.

I lay my hand on Rhea's shoulder, gasping when her nearly black gaze jumps to mine. "I'm going to help you," I tell her, tugging on the magic that is already pooling at the base of my throat. Rhea breathes harshly through clenched teeth, but I keep my hold on her just in case that is needed for my magic to work. Pulling in a deep breath, I lean in close enough to whisper in her ear. "I command you to *stop*." My magic tingles in my throat and over my tongue, and I swear I feel it even on the tips of my fingers. "*Stop*," I say again, my voice melodic and smooth as it coasts from my mouth to her ear.

And she does. That glittering magic dissipates like smoke from a blown-out candle as Rhea drags in a heaving breath.

"Aria, we need to leave." Dyanna's voice comes from behind me, and when I look up, I see two Mortal Kingdom guards heading our way from the other side of the Spell.

"Take the ring off," I command quickly, holding my other hand out as I watch Rhea's eyes gloss over from my words. Her motions are automatic and rigid, but she manages to take the ring off with trembling hands and place it in my outstretched palm.

"Now!" Dyanna shouts.

Just like the first time I held the ring, its magic makes me feel uneasy, but I close my fingers around it and watch as the onyx recedes in Rhea's eyes, spots of bright green peeking through the haze. I release her and step back, and like it's snapped something inside of her awake, Rhea whips her head around to look where the kneeling man should be. I look too, but he is only a heap of black on the sand—another male I hadn't seen because of the shadows lying close by—and when I turn to follow Dyanna into the water, there is only the sound of Rhea's sorrowful cries.

Chapter One Hundred and Twenty-One

RHEA

MY STEPS STUMBLE AS my body sways, the echo of the word "no" reverberating in my head, in the air around me. A quiet wrongness coats me when I fall to my knees and grip Nox, pulling his shoulders onto my lap. "Nox," I think I rasp—or scream, my throat suddenly aching with the raw sting of his name passing my lips. My heart suspends in my chest, tethered to my ribs as I stare down at his lifeless body. At his pale face and the too-still eyes behind his closed lids.

Magic thrums through me, a new pulse that beats to a different rhythm, one that should be matching his. Except when it stretches out, an animal finally freed from its cage, there's nothing for it to latch on to. Because Nox's magical signature isn't—

"Nox," I plead, one of those tethers holding my heart snapping when I shake his shoulders again and his head lolls to the side. It exposes his cheek, the flesh there *missing* in spots. Black pockmarks dot his skin, exposing the white gleam of bone underneath. I do a quick scan of the rest of him, finding the same rotted flesh at his hands and his collarbone, beneath a golden chain glimmering in the sun.

And I know that my magic did this, that it *hurt* him. That I felt the moment his shield faltered as assuredly as I felt the moment that he fell. But this is Nox, and our magics are not enemies but two halves of the same whole, and he *will* be okay, because just as my magic can destroy, it can also heal.

I *will* heal him.

With my intention strong and my power unbound, it floods my hands quickly. I stretch one down over his chest, waiting for the vibration of his heartbeat to pulse beneath my trembling hand as my magic begins to fill his body.

"Rhea—" Another's voice calls my name, the air stirring before a man kneels down next to me. "Fucking gods." I meet his dark, familiar eyes, and there is something shadowed in them that I don't like. Something sad and tortured and pitying as they stare at me, as they flick down to Nox and then shut, Xander's lips forming a frown.

Another tether snaps.

"He's just knocked out," I find myself saying. Begging. "My magic will heal him." The alternative is not allowed. White flares in my vision, and I think it must be due to my magic, but then Xander's hand is on my shoulder and he's telling me to slow my breathing down. To calm down. But Nox—he is still so pale, and his eyes won't open, and he's just *laying* here. I can't tell if his heart is beating because my hand is shaking so much, and *why can't I feel his magic?*

Another tether snaps, and it takes a rush of air with it as I feel my chest caving in.

"Xander, the king—" Another voice, softer than Xander's, says.

"I know. Give her another minute."

Just another minute. As if healing Nox could have a time limit. As if I wouldn't stay here for one hundred minutes, one thousand, for a lifetime if it meant that he would be okay. Yet it was just earlier that I had thought of time as this arbitrary thing. What was the ticking of another hour when I was still stuck in this place? Now that minute feels like both too much and not enough, and I can't *calm down* as I watch my magic fill him. As it begins to seep past the edges of his skin, forming an outline of white around his body as if to say, *all done.*

That minute passes, and Nox doesn't so much as flutter his lashes. An ugly word rattles in my head, one that denotes a finite end, a line drawn in the sand, and I *refuse* to let it be true. I move both hands to his face, cradling it as I will him to look at me. To smirk. To run a hand through those errant waves. To undo this horrible thing that *I've* done. Because there is no *me* without *him.* "Nox, please. Please don't leave me. I can't—" My voice breaks. My *world* does. "I can't do this without you." How selfish and stupid I was to think I could live in a world without him. I had intended to run away, to get so lost in the world that I became lost even to myself, yet now all I want is to be here with him at my side because he came. *Nox came for me,* and I punished him for it.

The final tether snaps, and I feel the moment my heart shatters. Feel the way my blood freezes and that precious time stops. The world around me eddies and sways, distorting into nothing more than the shape of his face and the sound of a dying heart. The taste of salt coats my lips as tears drip down my face and fall onto Nox's cheek. I let myself slip away because he's already gone, so what is the point in holding on? His name still echoes in the chasm I sink into, but it's nothing more than a vow broken. A promise unkept. *Nox, stay with me. Nox, I can't do this without you. Nox, come back,* I cry.

But all that answers is a deafening silence.

I had once thought that taking a life felt too easy, especially when it came to the scope of my magic. I've always seen the value in life, never once sought out violence for the sake of it. I hated the notion that the magic I carried inside of me was something that, at its core, could be used for destruction. Nox had told me that this Void Magic had been given to me because I was seen as *worthy*. Because I was chosen to receive it like one might pluck a pretty flower from a garden to be set into a vase. It didn't make me feel special then, and I didn't think the choice was right, but I was willing to accept it, to do my best even though I was scared. I was willing to be that pretty flower placed upon a pedestal because who was I to disagree with the powers that be?

Except I had forgotten that the moment a flower is cut, it begins to die.

Receiving this magic has been nothing but a slow withering of everything that I am. I only wish I realized it sooner. Maybe I could have saved *him* in the process.

My awakening back into this world is a twisting blend of the shouts of the men and women somewhere outside of the room I'm in and curling in on myself in a pit of jagged darkness, barbed reminders of what I've done surrounding me so I can't move without feeling their sting.

And I deserve to feel every ounce of pain that scores my flesh and writhes in my marrow. But before I can succumb to it fully, there is something I have to do.

Shadows cloak me as I pad quietly out of the room, my magic curling up from that well within me—both warm and cold. The feel of it nearly makes me stumble, my hand reaching out to press against a gray stone wall. Stone like the tower. Stone like the palace. Impenetrable and suffocating. At the contact, a sharp prickling draws my gaze down. Right to my palm, one now bare of the crescent scar.

"She needs to know—"

"—needs to rest, and *then* we'll tell her. There's no point—"

I push away from the voices and my thoughts, past a room where people are gathered, my fingers sliding along the wall as I search for a way out. I know I am with Xander's resistance, here in a space hidden from the king. I know that they have sacrificed *everything* to help me escape, yet all it resulted in is King Dolian now knowing that there are guards working against him. Everything Xander has worked for, everything these men and women have endured and fought for, is gone.

"—sirens have infiltrated—"

I finally catch a break in the stone, tracing the perfect line as it travels up and to the right. The outline of a door.

"—know we can trust you? *You* were knocked—"

I push at the corner, and the door gives, my steps quick as I enter the hidden tunnel and shut it behind me. I call just enough magic up to light my way, forgoing the discarded torch on the ground. In the quiet of the tunnel, there is only the sound of my shuffling steps and the swish of my dress against the ground. The sluggish beating of my heart in my chest. But those things don't hold back the thoughts that crowd my mind as effectively as the voices of the resistance did, and the farther into the tunnel that I travel, the more insistent each memory becomes.

Him and me in his bedroom in the Mage Kingdom, his body beneath mine as I straddled his hips, knees digging into the bed. "You are my universe. You are my infinite sun and my endless sea."

My jaw clenches, the hand not flaring with magic twitching along the wall next to me. I push back at the memory, as if I can shove it off a cliff never to be seen again. But I suppose that is both the blessing and the curse with recollections—they are meant to serve as reminders and are not so easily ignored.

I round the corner and follow the blue markings on the wall, and yet, despite how I try to focus on what must be done, my mind drags me back to what was. *Sunlight gilds his onyx hair and plays off the silver in his eyes, his smile brimming with victory despite how it was supposed to be worn by me. "Why did you stop, Rhea? It was just starting to get interesting." My eyes narrow, and his smile grows as a blush creeps up my neck to my cheeks—*

"Stop it!" I shout, as if there is someone else in control. But there isn't, the curator of my torment is me and me alone. Pausing my steps, I close my eyes and *shove* at the thoughts that haunt me. I stuff them back, back, back into the darkest corners of my mind. Into the pit of that grief and despair while I call my magic up, the cold and ancient half, and command it to smother them. To decay the memories until there is nothing remaining but black ash.

For a moment, I think it works. My magic rises, bitter and insistent, and it spreads over my body and coats me in an icy numbness. Not to cleanse me of the pain that rises but to keep me frozen within it. But that is the other thing about memories—they endure. Especially the good ones. They rise past the magic and right back to the center of my mind. Like flipping the pages of a picture book, I'm trapped as an unwilling participant, reliving every tender moment with Nox.

My lungs seize around a stilted breath, the hollow beats of my heart punctuating the fact that I'm still alive. That I shouldn't be—*I shouldn't be*—the one still here. But I am, and he isn't. I want to scream. I want to pull myself up from the depths of my rage and shout that it isn't fair. That I've endured so much and that *he* was the one good thing. *Just one good thing*. But, of course, it won't matter if I do, so I don't. Instead, I focus on the task I've deemed more important than telling

Xander I've woken. More important than apologizing to him and his resistance for messing everything up.

Flaring my light brighter, I force my pace to quicken until, *finally*, a new door comes into view. I call my magic back and reach for a small handle fastened to the door's façade, the click of it separating from the wall making me pause. When only silence answers, I open it the rest of the way, amber light from the flame gem fixed to the opposite wall painting over me as I lean past the frame and peer down the hallway.

It's empty, and I should find myself more relieved by that fact. Yet as I step out of the tunnel and onto the dark rug that lines the floor, quickly closing the door behind me, I wish the king would appear. That his affinity for materializing in my life, despite my attempts to rid myself of him, would manifest in this moment so that I do not have to ponder on what I'm going to do. So that I can finally end this, *end him.*

My magic stirs again, and this time, I let it wreathe my hands, a stream of glittering black coiling around my wrists and up my forearms. I'm reminded of my time in the Middle, when I escaped there after learning Nox had been tied to Alexi's fate. My magic had burst from me, inky daggers forming in my hands, and the image had been so viscerally terrifying that I had thought it an omen. A warning of what could happen if I dared to try controlling that half of my magic.

Holding my hands out in front of me, no sooner do I see those daggers in my mind than they form, shadows made tangible and sharpened into blades that I know will draw blood. Maybe it's due to the lack of warmth in the now hollow space in my chest, or maybe it's that my dark magic is encouraging me forward, but I clutch those daggers more tightly as I ready myself to kill the king, the light from the flame gems adorning the hallways distorting when I pass.

I try to orient myself within the castle, a pair of double doors punctuating the corridor I walk, and beyond it, the noise of other people. I allow myself one moment of pause, one moment to see if humanity pushes past the darkness and whispers in my ear to stop. To leave before I do something I might come to regret. But no such voice rises, no internal protests come, and as I command a shadow to turn the gold handle of the door, I wonder if the morality I thought I lived by was just as much an illusion as the idea of being free. Of having hope for something better for myself.

I recognize the small atrium as I step past the door's threshold and into what seems to be a small gathering of noblemen and women. Perhaps I should have considered how it might look to see a woman in a wrinkled, dirty dress wielding daggers made of black magic emerge abruptly into the space, because all it takes is a single noblewoman noticing me, her eyes widening as her bright red lips part and she screams *monster* at the top of her lungs, to send everyone running. I suppose the name is fitting, for only a monster could have killed the one they love.

"Where is King Dolian?" I ask, calling more magic to my hands when the two guards make their way past the fleeing crowd and draw their swords. I'm convinced they aren't Xander's men, not with how they stare at me maliciously, their blades firmly raised in front of them. "Do you know who I am?" I'm proud that my voice doesn't waver.

"Yes," one of them answers, his long blond hair tied away from his face as he glares at me. "You're the king's betrothed. Our *supposed* future queen; though after what we've heard took place on that beach, I'd be surprised if you make it to morning without being hung."

If they only knew.

"If you know who I am, then you know what I can do." I command more magic to my hands before spilling it out into the room, tendrils of black beginning to snake their way towards every corner.

"You killed our men at the beach," the other guard snarls, his hair a shocking shade of red that borders on orange.

I nod, my power rising as if noticing it's being talked about. "I did. And make no mistake, doing so was easier than *breathing*. But I have no qualms with you, I only wish to speak with the king. Tell me where he is."

"Our oaths are to keep His Majesty safe," the first guard says, his fingers tightening along his sword's hilt. Their golden armor and blades reflect the light of the flame gems on the walls surrounding us, the flares running over my face. "If you intend to harm him, you'll have to get through us."

"You do not know my intent, only that I wish to speak with him." I choose my words carefully, not wanting to activate the blood oaths these men took. Despite how much time this is wasting. "I do not want to hurt you."

The blond one laughs, even as the friend at his side looks unsure. "We are under orders not to let you escape, but there is nothing stopping me from marking up that pretty face." My stomach drops, and the shadows writhing around me pause.

"If you attack me, I will defend myself by any means necessary," I warn, looking directly at the man with the red hair. "You can go, and no one will think poorly of it."

"We aren't *fucking*—" But he doesn't even get his statement out before his friend pivots on his heel and bolts for a hallway on the other end of the room. "Coward!" he shouts before returning his attention to me, ire burning brightly in his gaze.

"Don't." I try to be severe in my delivery, but it comes out more like a plea. One that falls on deaf ears. The guard sprints towards me, a growl erupting up his throat as he lifts his sword to prepare to strike me.

The shadow dagger in one hand dissolves as I focus on surrounding him with my magic. A tendril wraps around one of his arms while another weaves between his feet and tightens, tripping him. He goes tumbling to the ground, still gripping his sword. I don't want to kill him, and I don't *have* to. I just need to make sure he can't come after me. I send the intent of my thoughts out, and the magic responds instantly, swirling down his arm to his wrist and squeezing tightly. The snap rings out a second before his scream does, his hand falling limp as he is forced to release his sword.

"You broke my wrist, you *bitch*!"

Walking towards him, I call my magic back to my hand, re-forming the dagger there and holding it to his neck when he tries to lunge towards me. He, wisely, pauses before contact is made. "Be grateful for us both that is all I did."

I leave the guard, chest heaving and cradling his arm, and exit the atrium, continuing my search.

Chapter One Hundred and Twenty-Two

RHEA

THE SCREAMS THAT FOLLOW in my wake bounce harmlessly off of me, my magic cocooning me from the nobles' judgment. Though this half of my magic is cold and lifeless, I wrap it around me like a cloak, knowing that I need to find the king before the castle is overwhelmed with guards. Wisps of black shiver around me at the thought, something eager taking root in the fissure that has split me in two. The daggers in my hands pulse in time to the beat of my heart, that icy numbness spreading like a winter's chill as I near a new corridor, and the king's name comes tumbling from someone's mouth.

"—Dolian knows. He *knows* about everything," a male says, his tone giving away his panic. I slow my steps, pushing my shadows back as I press myself up against the wall, my ears perked.

"Xander's going to be fucking pissed," a deeper, raspier voice responds. "And keep your voice down."

The two men drop their conversation to just above a whisper, and I get as close as I can to the corner to hear it.

"—he'll kill them all."

"If he ever manages to leave his rooms. The prick has been hiding in there since his return—"

The king is in his rooms. I step out into the juncture of the hallway, ignoring the men, and instead, turning left. Though my exploration of the castle has been minimal, I know that I need to find the main entranceway. If I can make it

711

there, I can figure out how to get to the third floor, which not only holds my rooms—what *were* my rooms—but the king's as well.

As I walk, aware there are screams of terror that surround me as people cling to walls or run in the other direction, I think about what it will be like to finally threaten the king to his face. To perhaps pull on the rage that had been born of Alexi, Immie, and Tienne's deaths and use that as an anchor within me to power me through it. I do not think the king will beg for his life. In fact, a sick part of me wonders if he will enjoy a death at my hands if only because I'll be touching him willingly. But as the stairs that I've climbed a hundred times finally show themselves, I find that everything surrounding the king's impending demise feels oddly anticlimactic.

King Dolian has been such a large presence in my life—an unshakable sickness that has slowly rotted me piece by piece until I've turned into the very thing I once feared, yet he is also just a man. No magic of his own. Nothing but his guards and a deal with a siren queen that seems more beneficial to her than him.

I climb the first handful of steps as I focus on drawing just enough breath that I don't pass out, my head still fuzzy and the shadows still surrounding me, when my name is called out from below.

"Rhea!"

Looking over my shoulder, I meet a set of blue eyes that give a temporary resurrection of my broken heart, fear and joy mingling together as I take her in. She stands in the open door that leads to this main foyer, the night sky a dark backdrop behind her. "Eve," I breathe, my magic drawing in a fraction as we stare at each other.

"Lady Rhea." Her hands work nervously in front of her, a small thing, but it makes me more aware of how I must look than any reactions from the nobles and guards did, though they all seem to be hiding now.

"What are you doing here?" I ask as I turn around.

Eve takes in the way my magic surrounds and clings to me, a dress made of darkness for a woman barren of light, yet her expression shows no disgust. No judgement of any kind. Instead, she quirks her lips, which can't be right because why would she smile at a monster?

"Did you really think I was just going to *leave* during your most important moment?"

I descend a single step, my fingers twitching around the daggers' hilts. "I'm not going to marry the king," I say, my voice wrong to my own ears. Eve notices the change in it too, and a look that I might have called proud gives way to concern.

"Of course, you aren't. I was talking about your *escape*."

Her lavender tunic shines beneath the flames of the chandeliers above, and the magic that flares for the briefest second isn't frigid or numbing but... *warm*. Just a flicker of it—no bigger than a candle flame—but I feel it come to life as our gazes hold, and I realize just how much I have missed her presence. "You are supposed to be visiting your family."

"And I was," she counters, pushing away from the door. "But I didn't feel right leaving you after..." She trails off, and I know we're both back in King Dolian's room at the moment I realized just what he was doing to her. What he *had* been doing to her.

"I'm sorry, Eve. I'm *so* sorry." The words are not nearly enough, as if *anything* I say could make up for her suffering.

Her gaze softens, and it's worse than when the king laid his hands on me because I don't deserve her kindness. "There is *nothing* for yo—"

Eve's body jerks forward abruptly, the motion strange and her accompanying gasp just as unnatural in its sound. I'm so busy scanning her face—her expression twisted into outright *horror*—that it takes me a moment to recognize the metal that glints in front of her. To absorb that it's the bloodied tip of a sword protruding from her chest. Her eyes only grow wide for a breath—a single blink where her body reacts to the invasion of the weapon. The blade retreats, and she collapses, the scene all too familiar in a way that pushes a fractured sob past my lips. My vision flashes, replacing Eve's body with Alexi's, the pooling of their blood merging together in my mind's eye as I rush down the stairs. I reach for the warmth of my healing magic, fanning that small flame as I call it to my hands, the daggers melting away until only white glows.

But someone else is standing over her body, his eyes glaring at me and a savage smirk already painted on his face. Simon takes a step closer, holding a guard's sword out in front of him as he stares down at the blood—*Eve's* blood—spreading away from her body and towards his shoes.

No. No, this isn't happening. Not again. Not with Eve. Eve, who had endured the king's vile attention and unwanted touch. Who took in my somber attitude and judgement of her blood oath and *still* tried to befriend me. Who showed me the tunnels and a way to the library because she knew I needed a place to escape, even if it was still within these stone walls. *Eve*, who isn't supposed to fucking *be* here! *She isn't supposed to be here!*

I had tried—*gods*, how I had *tried*—to be someone worthy of this life. Of the magic in my veins and the responsibility needed to wield it. But there is no hesitation, no stopping the way I send the shadows out like whips, wanting him to suffer, my scream burning a savage path up my throat until I'm sure the whole world will hear it.

Simon's stance shifts before the first onyx rope strikes him, as if he means to avoid it. But my magic is faster, and it lashes at his chest with a brutality that can't be explained, only felt. I don't watch him fall as I rush to Eve, kneeling and pretending I don't feel her blood soaking through the fabric of my dress.

"You can't save her," Simon taunts with a pained laugh, turning to watch as I scoop her into my arms, my magic already filling her body. I don't lift a hand as shadows lash at him again, my intention to hurt him but not yet kill him. His pained scream is nothing but an echo as I keep my focus on my friend, sure that I can save her. That this time is different because how could it *not* be? I am *right* here— But this close, I can see her wound more clearly. It isn't at the center of her chest, where there are no fewer vital things, but slightly off to the right. Directly through her heart. Intentionally placed for instant death, and that knowledge slithers through me like poison.

Eve's lips turn blue, and though her body feels warm beneath my touch, it is artificial. I don't blink away any tears because there are none left in me to shed. There is just this void, empty and fathomless and eternal as it beckons me deeper into it.

Simon's laugh is cruel, even as it wheezes from his chest. "You'll never fucking escape him. You will *never* be queen of the Mage Kingdom, and I hope you remember what it is to fail like this *over and over again.*"

My hands are steady as I gently lay Eve down, her hands crossing her stomach as I commit her sweet face to memory. *Another failure. Another life.* I lay my forehead against hers, and for all the sadness and rage that I know brews within me like a storm somewhere in the distance, when I rise, blood clinging to my skin and heavy in the fabric of my dress, I feel nothing but that ancient magic. That knowing feeling. That brutal urge to *end* and *decay* and *rot.*

When I look at Simon again, he is attempting to crawl towards an open door just past the stairs. My shadows gather at my silent command, black cords wrapping around him until he's spun and then lifted in the air. His tattered tunic reveals decaying flesh on his chest, and I cock my head to the side when I meet his gaze. Goosebumps mottle my skin and hair tickles the side of my face as my vision flashes, color seeping out with each blink until only shades of gray remain. Without hesitation, and with the kind of numb apathy that can only be nurtured in the absence of anything *good*, I let my magic attack Simon in all the ways I wish I could have attacked everyone who hurt me. Who took something from me without my permission. Who abused and *killed* others in my name. I'm tethered to every way my magic cuts into his body, and I hate that it's come to this. That it's always *me* who has to concede a part of myself. *Me* who has to be the sacrificial lamb when all I've ever wanted is to be *free.*

Wetness splatters against the surrounding surfaces as the king's advisor lets out a guttural scream. I move forward, the floor gone beneath my feet, until I'm right in front of him, *feeling* the sluggish way his heart beats as if it were in my own chest.

There's a pause in my magic—the skip of a different pulse as more shadows writhe around the room. It nearly draws my attention away from Simon, nearly makes me question what I'm doing. But then my vision darkens and that icy feeling creeps along my spine and over my ribs, and there is no stopping what comes next. It takes no effort at all to will my magic to drain his remaining life, and it should scare me—all of this should *scare* me—but as I watch his body wither until there is only the macabre pile of ash in bloodstained clothing, all I feel is *relief.*

Rhea. I press the heels of my palms into my eyes at the sound of Nox's voice, power surging into every limb. How *dare* my mind conjure him now. He would *hate* to see what I've become. Hate to—

Sunshine, look at me.

My eyes open at the closeness of his voice. I expect to see the graphic mess I've left in the foyer or hear guards marching down the halls ready to execute me at the king's command, but instead, Nox stands in front of me, a beautifully cruel deception of reality. Color is leeched from him, his skin swathed in a shade of gray that reminds me of what he looked like when I last held him in my arms. When he *died.* The memory forces me a step back, the room lost to the shadows pulsing and gray light seeping in around the edges of my vision.

We need to go.

"You aren't real," I whisper as I shake my head, hoping it will dispel the illusion. "I killed you."

But Nox's ghost follows me, closing the distance between us with a single stride. Dark magic curls around his shoulders and tumbles down his arms, the wisps stretching out towards me as if to link us by any means possible. *You didn't, Rhea. I'm here.*

"Stop."

I'm here, and we need to go—

"Stop!" My scream scatters the shadows, revealing the gore of what I did to Simon. Chest heaving, I spin away from it, only to face where Eve is laying, as if she is merely asleep. My fingers dig into my hair as I curl over myself, everything that I've been holding in and pushing back rushing to escape in the form of a terrible sob. "Please, don't do this," I beg, blinking hard against the tears in my eyes, the weight of what I've done pressing down on my chest as it slowly suffocates me. "*Please*, don't taunt me with your memory. It isn't fair to live in a world that you aren't in. It isn't *fair* that you're gone and I'm still here, and it's my *fault*—"

Warm hands—the feeling so *real*—gently grip the sides of my face, tilting it up until Nox is all I see. "Do you honestly think there is a *single* force on Olymazi or in the universes that surround us that could keep me from you?" His eyes bore into mine as he draws me closer, letting go of one side of my face to gently grab my wrist and guide my hand to his chest. Where a steady heartbeat hums beneath his ribs. "Don't you remember what I told you back home?"

Of course I do. But the agreement won't move past my lips, and my mind is *so full* of my own grief and sadness and anger—so much *anger*—that I can't make sense of how Nox is standing in front of me. Of why my mind won't just let him *go.*

"I'm sorry that it took me so long," he whispers, his forehead pressing against mine. When I don't respond—when I *can't*, still sure he's nothing more than a figment of my imagination—he leans back until his eyes meet mine, the silver in them bright. The skin at my cheek grows cold when he lifts his other hand, longing tugging at my heart from the loss of contact. But he moves to grab something underneath the collar of his black tunic. My brows furrow as I hold my breath, Nox's heartbeat quickening beneath my hand. He pulls out a golden chain, and that breath releases with a loud gasp. My engagement ring, the one that was yanked from my finger the night Daje and I were attacked, dangles from it, flashing pink for a quick second before the gray takes over again. My finger brushes against the metal, warm from where it rested against Nox's chest. When my eyes find his again, tears limn them and his throat works with a rough swallow.

"Nox," I whisper, trembling hands reaching up to cup the sides of his face, returning his gesture from earlier.

"I'm here," he says, tucking the chain back beneath his tunic as he pulls me close, his arms banding so tightly around me that he is all I feel. Despite his hold on me, my inhale has never been deeper, and I want to stay here, in this moment where it's just him and me and the realization that he's alive even if logic tells me he shouldn't be. But heavy bootsteps pound on the floor, growing closer and closer. Nox attempts to guide us towards the door, but I stop him with a hand at his chest. He follows my gaze to where Eve lays and though it's with reluctance, he lets me go, throwing up a wall of gathered shadows to form a barrier around us.

Walking to her, I kneel and rest my hand over Eve's cheek, the tears I couldn't form before falling heavily. "I'm sorry," I tell her, lip trembling as shouts sound beyond us, metal clashing with stone. "It will not be in vain."

I stand and look to Nox, the menacing wall of his magic sinuous in its movements behind him. But he reaches his hand out for mine, and I don't hesitate to grab it, following as he leads me to the door, the chill of the outside air stinging when it hits me.

I don't question how he knows where to guide me or stop him when he urges me into a sprint. We cross the gardens and stone pathways into an open grassy area where three horses and three men stand waiting, dark silhouettes against an even darker night. "They are with us," he says at my side when I tense. But it isn't until we are close that I see their faces and allow myself to believe they aren't a threat. Brisk and Xander stand together, heads bowed as they talk. But it's who stands off to the side that nearly halts my steps, my chest heaving and eyes blinking through the still present shades of gray as my magic coils deeply in my gut. *Daje.* His eyes scan me intensely, and I can't say I blame him for the way he stiffens as we near.

"The guards are coming," Nox says with a panting breath as we come to a stop. But they all ignore him in favor of staring at my bloody dress.

"Is it yours?" Xander asks, stepping forward and sending Nox a disgruntled look.

"No," I say with a shake of my head. Through a strangled breath, I add, "It's Eve's." His eyes widen, lips parting in shock, while Brisk curses under his breath and runs a hand over his head. There isn't time for more of a reaction as our attention is drawn in the direction we've just come from, the guards pouring out of the palace in numbers that make my stomach churn.

"Go," Xander says, handing the reins of a beautiful black horse to Nox. Daje mounts a brown one with a stripe on his face, which leaves one horse remaining. "That one is for you." He points to the beautiful horse whose white coat looks silver under the moonlight.

"Xander—"

"No. I'm *not* leaving," he snaps, cutting Brisk short.

"You were identified by Dolian. By the Trusted," his friend says, clasping his shoulder. Neither wear their armor, instead cloaked in black similar to Nox and Daje. My shoulders fall at the news. Everything that Xander has worked for is *ruined* now. "We need to lay low while the king figures out how he is going to respond. We can't lose anyone else, *especially* not you." Xander looks poised to protest, but Brisk shakes him gently.

"Come on, Sunshine," Nox says gently, chin jutting to the black horse. "Let them sort it out while we get ready." My feet are slow to move as the urge to use my magic chokes me from within. But I let Nox direct me to his horse. "Can I help you up?" he asks. I might have thought I couldn't possibly have more tears to cry, and yet, at the question, more spring to my eyes, the pressure building as I nod my head. To give permission to touch me feels foreign now after so many months, but to have *Nox* ask? A man who knows my body—knows *me*—better than I know myself? It feels... *wrong*. Maybe because so much has changed since the last time we were together.

Questions I'm not sure I want the answers to press at the back of my teeth. But as Nox lifts me gently onto the horse, making sure I'm comfortable before launching himself up behind me, I keep them trapped there. He's here, and that should be enough, shouldn't it?

"We're going." Nox's voice is a battle ax that drops right at Xander's feet. It causes my cousin to glance his way, neither man wearing a congenial expression. "Come or don't, but we leave now." Nox slowly wraps an arm around my torso, giving me time to protest the movement. Instead, I force myself to lean back against him, my gaze catching on the glinting armor of the guards heading in our direction and, beyond them, the looming castle. I want to call it a monster for the way that place took so much from me. So much *of* me. The monster, however, is not made of stone.

"Go," Brisk urges. Xander pulls him into a one-armed hug, and it's the last thing I see before Nox guides the horse around and sends him into a gallop, Daje and his horse keeping pace behind us as we move through the palace courtyard and out an unguarded side entrance to the road.

It isn't long before I hear the hooves of another horse and exhale a relieved breath, but it's short-lived knowing Xander is leaving behind everything he's ever known.

The trees blur from gray to night-cloaked green as we pass, and though the siren ring is gone, I find myself jerking in fear that the king's commands will suddenly be activated and I won't be able to leave. But as we put more miles between us and the castle, quickly losing the clamoring of armor to that distance, I succumb to the gnawing exhaustion that overtakes even my terror. And when Nox whispers that it's alright for me to close my eyes, that he's got me and he's never letting go, I don't fight the sleep that comes for me.

Even if I know, deep down and hidden within those dark corners inside of me, that safety—like hope—is a fickle thing.

Part Seven

There are men who believe in the gods and others who worship magic itself. I find my divine holiness in you. *You* are the only thing worth believing in.

Chapter One Hundred and Twenty-Three

ARIA

I PACE THE LENGTH of the platform inside our cavern, my ears trained to hear the telltale sound of dragon wings. It is still early in the morning, but sleep the night before had been futile, and so when there was enough light in the pale sky that it could no longer be considered night, I checked in on Lyre—who was peacefully asleep—and began my journey to meet a fae who, despite the events of the last two days, has been a consistent thought on my mind.

She'll be here. The affirmation swirls around in my head, my own voice echoing as I fold my arms over my chest, holding back a shiver from the winter air. Myla isn't the only thing to blame for my anxiousness. Dyanna had not spoken a word to me the entire way to Lumen from the Mortal Kingdom. When we arrived last night, Sade and I met with Lyre, and I told them both of what I had done for Rhea. How I had helped her. Lyre's look of surprise had at least been punctuated with a soft smile after her shock wore off, but Sade's brows had lowered as she pursed her lips.

"This could either be nothing or turn into something that will get you killed." At the terrified look that must have crossed my face, she added, "Dyanna may appear loyal to our mother, but as I've said before, I think at her core she serves herself first. Though"—she paused, casting me a concerned glance—"I have known her to cause chaos for the sake of chaos."

I don't want to think about how Dyanna could now hold this over my head or the fact that she might tell our mother just for *fun*, but the alternative is to pace a groove into the black stone, wondering if Myla has thought about our kiss just

720

as frequently as I have. If it is something she might want to do again or if our time apart has made her believe it was a mistake.

She'll be here. Not because of a life debt or because she's bound to come, but because she wants to. Because we both do.

The sentiments give me only a few minutes of reprieve before the doubt creeps in again, especially as more time passes without her arrival. When I get bored of looking at the same vine-covered walls, I climb down from the platform and walk to the edge of the cavern, making sure to stay beneath the covered portion as I look out one of the openings to the clear skies and, in the nearby distance, the Spell. Eventually, the sun rises high enough to indicate a passing of time that makes my heart sink.

It shouldn't hurt so much that Myla isn't here, that she took the opportunity to not return. After all, I had given her a choice for a reason. No one deserved to be held against their will, least of all someone like her. But I suppose I thought that she felt something for me. That, despite our rocky beginning, there had been a new bond forming between us that had nothing to do with magic or owing the other something.

I wait a little longer. Just in case. But when morning officially gives way to afternoon, I turn and face the inside of the cavern for the last time, wondering if it is ridiculous to be sentimental about a place. Myla's smoky-sweet scent still taints the salty air, and though tears sting my eyes I don't allow them to fall as I say goodbye, and walk back into the ocean.

Sinking farther into the water, my eyes close as I pass through the layer of the Spell, the light feel of it tingling over my skin. Strangely, my magic rushes up my throat and pools there, drawing my hand to lay at my neck in confusion. But as I open my eyes and begin to swim, I only make it only a few lengths before I startle backwards, my heart careening in my chest at the siren who waits just in front of me.

"Well, Aria," my mother starts, her trident held in one hand and a blue eelgrass sack in the other, her dark eyes piercing. "What are we going to do about this?" She moves the bag as she talks, and dark blue leaks from it in small wafts. It doesn't take long for the scent of blood to hit me, panic trickling down my throat and into my chest. At the look on my face, she clicks her tongue and shakes her head. "Before I show you what I've brought for you today, I must tell you a story." I say nothing though my talons lengthen in response. "I must admit, Daughter, that I might have underestimated you. When *she* came to me right before we left for the Mortal Kingdom and told me of your treachery, I thought *surely* she must be lying. Aria? Going to meet with a *fae*? It seemed... *improbable* at best."

I swallow as Queen Amari begins to circle me, forcing me to turn in place as I follow her. "Who?"

She pauses, a smile born of savagery curling her lips. "Why Lore, of course."

"L-Lore?" How in all of the Five Realms does *Lore* know about Myla?

"You look confused, but here's the thing about a siren scorned, Aria: There is *no* depth to the fury that we let build inside of us when we are slighted. For Lore, I imagine her fury began when you rejected her."

"How do you know about that?" Our fights had been private, no one spotting either of us. My mother just chuckles as she resumes circling me slowly.

"Just a hunch," she says, all too calmly. "She followed you out here before we left for the Mortal Kingdom." My fingers curl in towards my palms. *Godsdamn it.* "Is it true, then? Have you met with a fae?"

"No," I answer quickly. "I just use this spot to transform into my mortal form safely for a bit. I don't know what Lore is talking about."

Whatever mirth my mother was playing with drops immediately as her eyes grow darker. "It's a pity I didn't teach you how to lie better. You're pathetic at it."

Indignation—and maybe that deep-seated rage for my mother—forces the next words from my mouth. "No, you were too busy being cruel to teach me anything of value."

"*Cruel*? Aria, cruelty is merely an adjective the weak use to describe those more powerful than themselves. It is not *cruel* to demand power in places where they would give us none. It is not *cruel* to take what we are owed from those who stole it in the first place." She darts closer to me, and my magic blooms so harshly in my throat I have to pinch my lips closed to keep from singing. I won't show her that part of me unless absolutely necessary. "You have been a disappointment since the moment you came of age to hunt."

"Then why keep me alive?" I snarl, satisfied when her eyes flash briefly with surprise. "We both know how fond you are of making examples of those who displease you. So why bother constantly having such a *disappointment* attached to your good name?"

"It is easy to overlook your failures when I know what you are capable of achieving is far greater." I blink, jerking my head back. "You are a product of two royal lines, and I knew it would only be a matter of time before we would once again have our chance at the Mortal Kingdom throne. Though, I couldn't have predicted that there would be a rightful mage queen who could heal beings of Olymazi to pass through the Spell. I assumed that it would fall before then, but it was imperative that I have you at the ready as a way to convince the current king that we had a claim to the throne."

Of course. She was going to use me to further her own insane ambition. "I'm not going to the Mortal Kingdom," I tell her, shaking my head as magic tingles over my tongue.

"But you *will*, Aria." Coming to a stop in front of me, she floats in place, swishing her tail languidly and reminding me of the strength that is hidden within her body. She's as formidable as Sade, even at her age—and with centuries more experience than myself. "Do you want to know how I know?" My pulse flutters rapidly at my neck, and though I'm not breathing with my lungs, my chest still constricts at her question. "Because I warned you what would happen if you didn't listen." My eyes drop to the bag she is holding again, dread seeping down my spine. "There is nothing and *no one* who will distract me from my mission to reclaim what was stolen from us. Let this serve as a reminder that blood means *nothing* in the face of power."

As if its contents are no more important than trash, she turns the bag over and empties it. I recoil in horror, swimming back with a few flicks of my tail as amethyst braids come into view. My heart stills as a ringing in my ears takes over, terror swelling in my belly. Even with the evidence in front of me—the stillness of her wide-open eyes and the blood still leaking from her exposed neck—I shake my head in denial. "No."

"You'll come home with me where I will announce your intention to take your place as siren royalty within the Mortal Kingdom's court."

"No." That ember within me that had started as defiance ignites, my song *clawing* at my throat to be released.

"But first, I have Lore held in our prison. You will kill her for her discretion against you and *then—*"

"*No!*" I shout, unable to keep my magic contained anymore as I watch Lyre's head sink towards the ocean floor, a trail of dark blue following behind it. I flick my gaze back to the queen's, my anger a living, *breathing* thing inside of me. "I will *never* do anything you command of me again."

The queen's black braids float around her like venomous snakes posing to strike as she tilts her head, letting the now empty bag drop from her grasp. She holds her trident firmly, angling it in my direction. "You will. I *know* you will because you've proven time and time again that when it comes down to it, you would rather kneel under the weight of my wrath than stand tall at the challenge of your convictions. You're weak, Daughter! You always have been!" Her sharpened canines flash in a devious smile. "But I have use for you yet." She moves quickly, swinging her trident out an angle that months ago I would not have been able to deflect.

Even now, as I watch it swinging towards me, I know that what I've learned with Myla isn't enough to fight her off. Not yet. But physicality isn't my only weapon, and it certainly isn't my *greatest* one. Opening my mouth, I finally release the full weight of my song on a harmonious wave. It *hurts* to sing like this, to expose my magic to *her* when I no longer view it as a defect but as something *precious.* Just as Lyre was. As her unborn babe was. I duck to avoid my mother's trident, bubbles swishing in the water right above my head as the faintest line of confusion settles between her brows. My magic is slow to grip on to her, maybe her age or strength to blame. She laughs, the sound relaying how pathetic she finds me as she closes the distance between us in two easy flicks of her tail. But just as she is poised to strike me again, I push my voice louder and *finally* start to see the hint of my power leaking into her. It begins with her eyes, their dark edges growing hazy. She jabs at me with her trident again, but her movements are slower, more inaccurate.

Perhaps there is a monster within me that's been created in her likeness after all because I smile at the panic that widens her eyes as my magic freezes her body and she begins to sink towards the ocean floor. I let my song fade as my eyes lock on hers, the emotion visible past the haze of my song bolstering the confession I've longed to give her.

"I *hate* you," I whisper through clenched teeth, my vision blurring with brief tears before they are swept into the ocean. "For what you did to Lyre. For what you did to *me*." I curl my fingers, my talons sharp and gleaming as I position them at her neck, nails pressing into skin. "You will *never* hurt another being again, and when you are dead, when you aren't around to ensure that your *legacy* is one of power and fear, I will make sure everyone knows you for what you really are. A wicked female no better than the creatures that belong in Tula's pit." I try to ignore how my heart beats out of rhythm as I glance down at the soft flesh of her neck. Myla would not hesitate to kill someone like my mother, and yet, despite how I know her death is *earned*, I have to gather enough confidence to do it. Or maybe it's bravery. Either way, I know that the moment my hands end her life, my own will never be the same.

Gritting my teeth together, I press the tips of my talons into her, a strange feeling surging when I see the first trickles of her blood. Something jagged takes root next to that ember of resilience within me at the sight, and I'm so mesmerized by it that I make a fatal mistake. I don't realize I'm in danger until her hand wraps around my arm, holding me in place when I try to jerk away. Queen Amari's face takes up the entirety of my vision as she blinks away the last remnants of my magic. My song rushes up my throat, my lips parting as the first note enters the water, only to be cut off. Pain explodes at my midsection, radiating up my chest and down my arms and forcing my voice into a guttural scream instead. The queen drives me backwards on the end of her trident, her expression nothing short of feral as I try to claw at her with my free arm. The first few swipes miss, but then the next one lands, the ends of my talons digging into her cheek and splitting the skin as I drag them down. Her responding growl is petrifying, her dark eyes alighting with vicious revenge as she moves her grip farther down the trident so that she is now out of my reach.

She swims quickly, and I'm forced to abandon trying to hurt her in favor of getting myself free of the trident. But I'm skewered, those jagged diamond dips more than halfway into my body, and I can't draw enough oxygen through my gills to try using my song. "The thing is, Aria, I welcome being called a monster. For it is only a monster who can do what needs to be done to reclaim what is hers."

White flares in my vision as she jostles the trident, the sharp prongs digging deeper into my flesh. Panic seizes my chest while my tail snaps in the water as I try to slow her down, a trail of too much dark blue mixing with the water in front of me. But she continues driving me backwards, until we are in the layer of the Spell and then our heads are popping above the surface. She pushes me to the shore before she pulls the trident from my body, changing to her mortal form as I try to do the same. The process is excruciating, and the first breath I take through my mouth burns as it fills my lungs, but it isn't deep enough to satisfy the need for more. My hands try to cover the three holes her weapon has left in my body as I roll over, water splashing up against my shoulders and face.

At first, I think my mother will leave me here to bleed out on the beach, but then she is at my side, gathering my curls in her hand. I scream as she tugs on my hair, my hands reaching up to grip her own as she begins to drag me the rest of the way out of the water. My heels try to catch in the sand, to slow her down, but she yanks me forward, strands of hair snapping as streaks of blue stain our path. "I hope you weren't planning on living after revealing just how much of an abomination you are." I wasn't expecting to, but if the price was also *her* life, it would have been worth it. "I was disappointed when I learned Rhea had escaped, considering she still had you and more of my legionaries to heal. But now I think it might have been fate, *Daughter*. Because your betrayal is one that can only be dealt with in the most painful of manners."

Dizziness sweeps in and blurs my vision, my attempts to hit at her arm and to kick my feet growing sluggish. I try again to call up my song, needing just a few seconds to get her back under my sway, but I can't hold it long enough before I start coughing and the salty metal taste of blood fills my mouth.

This is it. This is how I'm going to die.

Planting her trident in the sand, she finally releases my hair, and I whimper at the prickling sensation that floods my scalp. But any hope that my torture will end here is temporary when my gaze lifts and I find the iridescent wall of the Spell in front of me, the shadow cast by my mother painting the sand. Without hesitation, she pierces my shoulders with her talons as she grips my body and heaves it off the ground. My vision flashes black as my head rolls to the side, the sound of water dripping onto the sand matching the slow beat of my heart.

Not water, I think. *Blood*.

Between one drowsy breath and the next, she tosses me through the Spell and into the Fae Kingdom.

My body slams onto the beach, sand flying at the impact, but the pain is drowned beneath the pressure that blooms at my chest. As if something is trying to break free from behind my ribs, gripping the bones with uncompromising strength as it attempts to pry them apart. Queen Amari sends a kick into my back, pushing me the rest of the way through the Spell and dooming me to a brutal death.

"Goodbye, Aria."

Through misty eyes, I watch her retreat back to the ocean as I writhe in pain, my screams deafened by the heavy thumping of my heart, each inhale shorter than the one before it. My grip on consciousness slips fully through my grasp, dragging me into darkness.

There is agony, unrelenting and unequivocal *agony*, and then there is nothing.

Chapter One Hundred and Twenty-Four

MYLA

SITTING ON THE COLD, damp ground encased by black stone and a wall of iron bars, I cross one ankle over the other and try to figure out just how many days I've been trapped in the dungeons. I had awoken to the sound of other prisoners in the surrounding cells, one of the male guards bringing me a meager plate of stale bread and questionable meat while I still blinked the bleariness from my eyes. I didn't eat then, sure that it was only going to be a short wait before the king arrived to see the female who called herself the Shadow. The excitement of watching his eyes widen with realization, of staring at the daughter he felt was an abomination, had provided me with sustenance that food couldn't touch.

Hours passed, and I thought it odd that, as guards came and gathered those in the cells around me to be brought to the dragon fields, the king had still not come. When a new plate of food arrived from a new guard, I paced my small cell, sure it wouldn't be much longer before I would be rewarded with the shock I so desperately wanted to see spread across my father's face. But then more prisoners arrived and more were taken out—guards changed and more plates of food came—time becoming something I could no longer measure the passing of other than the fact that it must have been *days*. Yet no one deigned to visit the fucking Shadow in the dungeon.

I tilt my head back and fold my arms over my chest, looking up at the black stone and imagining I can see through it to the palace overhead. Where life is continuing on as normal *despite* my absence. Then again, with the exception of Navin, would anyone even notice that I'm gone? *At least Sunis has.* Though I

727

don't know if that is such a good thing. With our bond so new, I am still learning how to decipher her thoughts and feelings and how to send her an accurate representation of my own. When I said I was trapped, I felt her fear unravel over me. It took quite a while to calm her down, so I decided to treat our conversations delicately until I could figure out how to get the fuck out of the dungeons.

Something that has eluded me thus far.

My body aches from sleeping on the stone floor, and I would kill the next person within arm's reach if it meant I could shower with even the iciest of waters. A long bout of time passes, long enough that my eyelids grow heavy and my head lolls to the side as sleep once more wraps her arms around me, when the echo of footsteps travels down the hallway separating the cells. I jerk my head back up, my hands reaching for the sheaths at my thighs out of instinct, only to be reminded that I've been stripped of my weapons. My legs shake as I force myself up, keeping my back against the wall.

The light of a single torch down the hall casts the incoming figure in amber light, and I narrow my eyes against the surrounding darkness as I try to make out their features. But they are cloaked, their face obscured by dark fabric as their boots beat against the stone. The firelight dances on a bronze dragon insignia at their shoulder, and despite my circumstances, anger crackles low in my gut at the sight. *They're fucking dressed like me.*

"Fucking gods above, *finally*." Even without seeing his face, the sarcastic lilt to his voice is one I would recognize anywhere. Navin steps in front of my cell, metal jingling in his hands as he searches for the right key. "Do you know how long I've been trying to figure out where you were?"

"At least a couple of days," I guess, peeling myself away from the wall to walk towards him.

"Try *five*. I didn't realize you were missing until like a day in"—he slides a key into the lock, only to curse when it doesn't turn—"which I know sounds terrible, but you can't blame me when you disappear for long hours in the night to go to Khargis."

"I definitely can blame you and plan to." Folding my arms over my chest, I watch him fumble with a new key. Only for it to not work either. "Navin, hurry up."

"Helpful, Myla." Mumbling something else under his breath, he tries another key, and this time, we both sag with relief when it turns and clicks, and the door holding the iron bars slides open. "Anyways, I thought you had likely died in Khargis, so I began searching the streets until I overheard one of the guards say they caught a female who called herself the Shadow."

I pause midway out of the cell. "You *assumed* I was dead?"

"Well, *yes*. Don't act like there wasn't an equal chance of you being dead as there was of you being captured." At his exasperated look, I smirk instead of arguing with him. "Anyway, we need to hurry before anyone realizes you've escaped." He takes the cloak he's wearing off and hands it to me before we head down the darkened corridor.

"Is there anyone else here?" I hadn't heard a single noise made by another fae for a while.

"No. All the prisoners prior to your capture were brought to where they are doing the testing with the mages." He turns right, more cells lining the walkway on either side. The scent of mold and wet earth is heavy with each breath, and I nearly cry out in relief when I spot a staircase ahead, ready to breathe fresh air. "It's where Father has been this whole week, which is likely why no one came down to visit you. They are all prepping for the big celebration."

"The celebration..." I pause, stopping part way up the steps as I stare at my brother's back. "How many days did you say I was down here?"

Navin looks over his shoulder. "Five." His brow lifts. "Why?"

Five days... "Fuck!" I growl, running up the steps until I pass him.

"What is it?"

"Aria," I answer, an uncomfortable thread pulling taut in my chest. "I was supposed to meet her today. It's been a week."

We reach the top of the stairs, and I lurch for the handle, but Navin stops me with a hand at my shoulder. "Listen first." My impatience scratches at my skin, and a feeling I haven't acknowledged since Daiya left me to bear the consequences of our relationship *alone* burns acidic in my stomach.

Navin lays his ear against the door, its wood rough and likely as ancient as the rest of the surrounding rock. When he confirms we are good to move forward, I open the door and bolt through it, annoyed to find more stairs.

"How far down are we?" I ask as I take two steps at a time, Navin following my lead.

"Do you not remember the trek down?"

"They knocked me out when they captured me outside of my warehouse. They must have been watching it ahead of time." Shaking my head, I clench my jaw at my failure. I should have *known* I wasn't alone that night.

"Did your informant tell them?"

"No," I bite out quickly. "She wouldn't. It's my fault. I got careless, and instead of killing one of the targets I've been watching for weeks, I went for the easier prey."

We reach another door, pause another moment to ensure we are alone, and then continue up another flight, that rage within me growing with every step. "Let me guess? A guard?"

"An asshole." I press my hand along the grimy stone wall as we climb, dizziness making my knees buckle beneath me. "So same thing."

Navin snorts as we reach the landing at the top and a set of double doors this time. He presses his ear to one of them, eyes closing as he listens to the sounds beyond.

"Is it normal for there to be *zero* guard presence up here?" I ask, pulling the mask of the hood up until my lower face is covered.

"Everyone is at the celebration," he answers, signaling for me to back up as he pulls one door open. "There is a big announcement Father has been teasing behind closed doors."

We step out of the dungeon and into the first floor of the palace, golden light flooding my eyes and making me squint as sunlight pours in from the large windows across the room. I send a message to Sunis down the bond to meet me as fast as she can at the landing post outside of my room. We've only practiced landing there once, since the risk of getting caught is much higher, but I hope to capitalize on the distraction of my father's gathering.

"Is Sunis coming for you?"

"Yes. I need to go up to our rooms." Navin nods and alters his direction to lead us there. Already, I can hear Father Yamin's voice from where he speaks in the palace courtyard, a wide expanse of space only accessible to those the king invites. "Do you know what he's going to announce?" At my brother's lingering silence, I glance his way and find his face contorted into a grimace. We reach the twisting staircase that will take us up to our wing of the palace, and as my thigh muscles protest the climb, I vow to kill *every* guard who locked me up in that dungeon. "Navin."

He sighs, running a hand over his hair, the locks braided down his back. "No. Well, I have a hunch, but"—he lets out an incredulous laugh—"it's impossible."

My brows knit as I study him, Navin purposefully keeping his gaze ahead to avoid mine. Father Yamin's voice is somehow louder on the second floor, carrying through the glass windows and sliders with ease. That irritating impatience returns as his words press into my ears, his topic of choice once more a supposed *miracle* bestowed upon us by the gods.

"And so, without further ado, I give you that which can only be explained by a benevolent god. One who has finally reconciled all of our misgivings and wrongdoings, all in thanks to our king! A male who has led his people back into the light! You cannot question the cost of a pious and virtuous society, not when the reward is a fallen prince brought back from the dead!"

Both Navin and I falter in our next steps, our eyes meeting over a chasm of confusion before we rush to one of the nearby glass sliders, opening it and stepping out onto a small balcony. The air is brisk despite the afternoon hour, and though unimpeded sunlight casts the courtyard below in a buttery glow, shadows lurk at the corners. Guards, dozens deep, line the space in every direction, their silver armor gleaming. My father sits upon his throne at the top of the stone dais, his black spire crown making him look even larger. Next to him, my mother wears a gown of dark plum, her headdress beaded with gold and pearls. In front of them both is Father Yamin, *His Holiness* in his traditional black robe with his hand outstretched to the right, as if waiting for someone to join him.

And then someone does.

Walking out from a line of guards is a fae male. He's tall, towering over the father and the brethren that flank him. He moves with just the slightest limp, and his hands stay fisted at his side as if ready to throw a punch at any moment. My mother is already standing when he gets close, her outstretched for him. I lean in closer, noting the *tears* that play down her cheeks, a show of emotion I've never seen from her before. As if they've all just realized who the male is, a gasp rolls over the crowd in a wave, fae standing from stone benches as they grip the arm of the person next to them or clasp their hand over their mouth.

"What the fuck?" I whisper, tensing when the male comes to stand in front of my father after hugging my mother. For a long moment, no one moves, but then the king of the fae stands and wraps his arms around the man, their conversation muted by the cheering and hollering of the crowd surrounding them.

"Who is that?" I ask, unable to look away. Unable to fucking *fathom* my father caring enough about *any* fae to hug them like that in public. Not once had I seen him show that level of caring towards Navin—and certainly not towards me.

Again, Navin lets silence answer, so I look at him, a line carved between my brows.

"Navin, *who is that*?"

His hands squeeze the white stone railing as his breaths grow shallow. Swallowing, he keeps his gaze pinned on the king still hugging the male below. "*That* is the true heir to the Fae Kingdom. King Kamon Ryuu's first born."

"What?" I hiss, my gaze bouncing from Navin to the commotion down below. "That's impossible."

"I recognize him, Myla. I *remember* what he looked like." His voice cracks. "That's Shah."

⁕⁑⁂ ⁂⁑⁕

Shah is alive. I hunch low over Sunis as she flies us to the beach, that phrase on a loop in my head. Fucking stars above, how in the *hell* is he alive? My father had seen him dragged away by the sirens, had lamented about his death for *centuries*, yet the bastard had been... what? Hiding away? Tucked into some cave or hidden amongst a small town, while the rest of us were forced to endure a kingdom under the rule of a broken king and a zealous fanatic?

Calm. The word forms over the pathway in my mind, and I blow out a breath at the dragon's command.

I just found out that the rider bonded to your mother is alive, I respond, testing Sunis's ability to understand more than just a quick word. I'm surprised when her body jerks as she processes the information, a blend of emotions returning to me.

I detect confusion and longing but also happiness and relief. Could this be why Bali never bonded again? Not because she didn't want to because she somehow knew that Shah was alive? I grit my teeth as the Spell and the shoreline beyond become visible over Sunis's head. Or was the real reason my father wanted Bali so that he could force her to bond with someone *pretending* to be Shah?

Sunis begins to descend, flying us through the thin layers of mist that hover over the mountain peaks. When we break through the final layer, a wave of shock travels abruptly down the bond and Sunis angles her wings to dive towards the ground.

"What is it?" I call out.

My blood ices over when she replies. *Dying.*

I look her over from what I can see at this vantage point. I hadn't noticed any wounds on her when she picked me up at the palace, but maybe I missed something in my own confusion about the news with Shah. *I don't see anything!*

Sunis doesn't respond, instead letting gravity do its work as we head towards the ground at neck-breaking speed. A scream lodges itself in my throat, but at the last minute, Sunis flattens her wings, leveling as we approach the Spell. *Pain*, she says, flooding my system with the feel of it. Again, I look her over, my own unease rising when I still spot nothing. Sunis turns at an angle, and I let my gaze trace down the long line of her wing and then beyond it, to a shade of ruby waiting on the beach. A riotous sensation travels from my stomach up to my chest at the sight of Aria, the siren having occupied my thoughts often since our last meeting. Yet, as we get closer, that excitement is quickly replaced with fear as I realize something is horribly wrong.

We land seconds later, and I quickly unseat myself to run to Sunis's front leg, sliding down the smooth scales before leaping the last few feet onto the sand. My arms pump furiously at my sides as I rationalize the fact that Aria is on the fae side of the fucking Spell. "Aria!" Sliding on my knees, I gently turn her over, her eyes fluttering as they struggle to meet mine. "Aria, what happened?"

She groans and flexes her hand where it's laying on her stomach, and when I move it, my eyes widen at the grisly sight. She's been *gutted*. Three large holes pierce her stomach, leaking dark blue blood onto the sand. I hadn't seen it with the way her body was curled up, but up close now, I can *smell* it. The air is tainted with the scent of iron, signifying just how much she's lost. And she's on *this* fucking side of the Spell!

"Fuck!" I shout, laying my hands over her abdomen to slow the bleeding. Sunis's panicked emotions flood my mind and mix with my own, making it difficult to think clearly. Aria groans again, her eyes rolling back in her head. "No, stay with me." I abandon her gouges to cradle her face, my bloodstained hands leaving their mark on her. "Aria, stay awake."

"I'm s-sorry," she rasps, coughing and speckling my arms with her blood. Not once, in all the years I have flayed others open and spilled their blood, have I ever been sick at the sight of it. But as I look at how it glistens against my leathers, I find myself ill at the knowledge that it's hers. That someone hurt her *here*—just feet from our cavern, where she had been waiting for *me*.

"How can I help you?" I ask, frenzied. *Terrified* by the proof that she is dying. "Aria, tell me how—"

"It's alright. Y-you already have."

"No, *fuck that*. No!" Taking my cloak off, I lay it next to me before carefully scooping her into my arms. "Aria, wake up!"

The bark of my voice makes her eyelids lift again, the bright color of her irises dimmed as if shadows have bled behind them. Her skin is too cold, her body too limp, and as I lay her down on the cloak, pulling the fabric tightly around her, I think this might be worse than any whipping, any punishment I've endured. Watching Aria die had once been something I craved, and now that it is happening? I can't imagine a worse fate. For her. For *me*.

I pick her back up and take her to Sunis, my dragon letting out a high-pitched sound that I've never heard her make before as we near. She does her best to help me mount by extending her front leg, and within a few moments, Aria and I are strapped to her back, my siren tucked into my arms. "I can take you to a healer," I think out loud, my fingers gripping her tightly. But that would only address her most pressing injuries and not the fact that she went through the Spell. That's assuming they don't kill her once they realize she's a siren. Looking down at her, I watch as she blinks and stares back up at me. "Please tell me what to do," I whisper, anger and sadness a toxic blend within me.

Aria's hand moves beneath the cloak, and I carefully peel the fabric back so that she has full range of motion. She reaches up in jerky movements, like the effort is too much. But when her fingers find the side of my face, when she attempts to smile through blood-crusted lips, something decidedly breaks within me. There has to be something that can help, that can stop the effects of the Spell—

I inhale sharply, tracing the tips of my fingers down Aria's cheek. *The dagger.* The one given to my father by Queen Lucia. It's meant to be used before crossing the Spell, but maybe—

Aria's lips part on a breath, her gaze latching on to mine. "Rhea M-Maxwell," she says, her eyelids fluttering closed. "Mage Kingdom."

Chapter One Hundred and Twenty-Five

RHEA

THOUGH EXHAUSTION HAD EASILY dragged me under its dark wing at first, escaping the king and the horrors I had both experienced and inflicted did nothing to keep me there. I sleep fitfully, jerking awake with a gasp lingering on my lips and sweat beading over my brow despite the bite of the winter air. Eve's death paints the back of eyelids every time I close my eyes. Simon's voice whispers in my ear that I will never escape all the things I have done, that my value will always be less than what I can do or be for the king. My mind takes me back to the balcony of my tower again. I see myself standing there, feel the wind caressing my cheek as I lean over its edge—only this time, there is no Xander to stop my fall. I plummet downwards, my scream echoing as the earth rushes towards me until there is a hand at my hip and a deep voice in my ear, catching me in the darkness before I ever hit the ground.

Except everything has become so *muddled* in my mind that I don't know where I am or if I am really escaping. If *this* is my reality or only another dream. So when Nox wraps his arm around me, it isn't *him* that I feel but King Dolian. It isn't his lips at my temple but my uncle's. I jerk away, startling both him and the horse we ride. When I look over my shoulder at him, his face highlighted by the silver moonlight, I see a flash of hurt before he hides it beneath a tight smile. Nox has never been the one to hide his emotions, *always* letting them play openly on his face for me to see. But I watch as he throws a shield down over himself, as he carefully keeps his touch light and only what is needed to ensure I don't fall off of the horse.

And I hate it. Hate that I've caused him to do that. I hate myself.

In these broken hours between sleeping and awake, I contemplate this all while *also* knowing that, somehow, I have to tell Nox *everything* I have gone through. The fear of doing so plagues me relentlessly, forcing uneven breaths into my tight chest as my clammy hands hold on to the pommel of the saddle. I feel sick with the knowledge of it all sitting on my shoulders and, eventually, give up on sleeping altogether so that I might be distracted by the ride itself. Nox has slowed our horse down to traverse the dark terrain carefully, Daje and Xander somewhere close enough to hear their horses' hooves behind us. But no one speaks a word, the silence both aiding in our awareness of the guards' proximity and pressing invisible walls into me from all sides.

We continue riding at a slow but steady pace through the night and into the next day, finally stopping in the afternoon to let the horses eat and drink from the nearby Vida River. Nox asks if I want privacy to wash, but the thought of being vulnerably naked out in the open sends my heart ricocheting against my ribs. I don't want to be still caked in Eve's blood, but I don't know how close the guards are. If the king is with them this time. If Queen Amari is. These worries hold me prisoner on the edge of the river, nervously chewing on my bottom lip as I stare down at Nox's boots.

"I can surround you with shadows," he offers, so quietly and softly that all it does is stir up the feeling that I don't deserve him. His gentleness and steadfastness. I don't deserve it when, in our time apart, I had believed he had faltered. Had chosen something else—*someone* else—over me.

I take him up on his offer, if only to not subject us both to riding the rest of the way with the reminder of what had happened in the palace. He leaves a pack that had been attached to our horse's saddle at the water's edge, and then I am surrounded by thick darkness on all sides but above, sunlight shining in on me as if I am in a shallow well. Sinking into the icy waters, I welcome the numbness it ushers in. I don't linger, quickly running my hands over the areas that are sticky with old blood, watching as the rust color seeps into the water. Despite how hard I scrub, Eve's death still clings to me when I exit the river.

Now changed into simple black pants and a white shirt, a wool cloak clasped at my neck, I join Nox, Xander, and Daje around a fire, its heat doing nothing against the chill that has taken residence in my veins. I, naively, thought I might be the only one who had both too much and not enough to say, but as I look at each of the men's faces, I recognize the same conflict in them too.

"So," Xander says first, his voice raspy as if it is on the verge of going out, "what happens next?" Had his been one of the shouts I heard? When Remi told me to run? Before the shadows traveled over the sand. Before I had killed—

"Rhea." Nox's voice snaps me out of my spiral, and I look up from where my gaze had settled on the fire to find Daje staring at me and Xander staring at where Nox sits at my side.

"I'm sorry." I turn to look at Nox, finding his hand hovering in the space between us, as if he meant to reach out and touch me only to stop himself. He lowers it quickly to his knee, and I pretend the action doesn't shatter me further, "What was the question?"

"The guard asked you what happens next?" Nox answers, no short amount of malice in his tone as his eyes slide to Xander. My cousin narrows his in return.

"Oh. Why are you asking me?" Of everyone here, I am the least qualified to make any sort of decision on what comes next.

"Well, considering it is sort of up to you whether or not I stay in the Mortal Kingdom, I figured you'd be the best one to direct the question to," Xander says. Nox stretches his legs out in front of him, his arms crossing over his chest as he watches our exchange. The air thickens with his magical signature, both halves of my own power rising as it presses against my skin to meet his.

"In what world is that *my* choice?"

Xander frowns. "The one where you can *heal* people to cross through the Spell."

Daje's eyebrows rise high on his head. "You can do that?"

At the feel of their stares on me, I twine my fingers together in front of me. I suppose there is no avoiding this conversation—and all it will lead to.

"I tried telling you both earlier," Xander cuts in, fingers reaching towards the fire. "But you wouldn't listen."

Daje scoffs as he tilts his head. "We had just woken up disoriented in a foreign place, and Nox had almost *died*. You can't exactly blame us for not being the most receptive to new information."

Xander and Daje go back and forth arguing, their voices muffled when my eyes catch on my blood-flecked fingers. Eve's blue eyes flash in my mind, cracking my chest open just as easily as the sword had slid through hers. I blink, and my fingers are clean again. Turning my gaze towards Nox, I find no reprieve as his form flickers to closed eyes and decaying skin before I blink and he is whole again. But the memories have already left their mark as I hug my knees to my chest, as if that might hold *me* together. How many times could I be pulled apart? Forced to break over and over again before I'm nothing but that sickly black ash my magic makes of others.

Movement in front of me makes me stiffen on instinct, Nox's concerned face coming into view as he squats down in front of me, blocking out Xander and Daje. Making himself the only thing I can focus on. "Are you alright?" he asks, and gods, I wish that question didn't feel so impossible to answer.

"I— Yes." I swallow, twisting my fingers together again. Nox notices the nervous movement, and with a slowness that I know is only because of what happened earlier, he gently reaches out and clasps both of my hands in his, brushing his thumbs over the tops of them. Our eyes hold, grief balancing precariously between us. Mine *and* his. "I thought I killed you."

"You didn't kill me. You—"

"—still doesn't explain how she healed them!" Daje's raised voice cuts between us, drawing Nox's gaze over his shoulder.

"I didn't know that I could do that," I tell them. Lay it at their feet like a barbed confession. The woods around us fall silent, and I imagine the shadows of the trees growing towards me, as if even they are leaning in to listen to my failures. Nox moves so that he's sitting at my side again, close enough that I feel his warmth even through the cloak. "Not until the siren queen forced me to try on her legion."

"Forced you?" Nox asks, a muscle in his jaw ticking.

I nod. "It was because of the ring the king put on my finger. It was controlled by the siren queen's magic—" I pause at the image that flashes in my mind. *Nox buckling under my magic. The feel of his own shield faltering, my shadows overpowering him. A gentle hand on my shoulder and a lyrical voice in my ear. Ruby-red hair and glowing hazel eyes.* Nox squeezes my hand again, and though I push the memories down, my body is not so easily swayed into forgetting what I did. My fingers curl in towards my palms, as if trying to stop the magic from leaving me. The act pulls my hand from his before I even realize what I'm doing, and though Nox gives me a tender smile, it's the same guarded one as before. Desperation floods me, the urge to keep him from *literally* slipping through my grasp pushing words I'm not ready to acknowledge past my lips. "One of the siren princesses is my sister."

Nox blinks, his lips parting as if to speak only for him to pinch them shut again. But where words fail him, they find Daje just fine.

"I'm sorry, did you just say one of the sirens is your *sister*?"

I meet Daje's wide eyes, his brow crinkled as he leans forward. "Princess Aria and I share the same father."

A collection of choked sounds tumble from him, a question jumbled in there that I don't know how to answer without starting down a new path of misery over the fact that my uncle had been the one to murder my parents.

"King Dolian sought a deal with the siren queen," Xander says into the silence I let linger. "In exchange for killing Conrad so that he could become king, he agreed that any child—any *offspring*—sired between the coupling of his brother and the queen would be recognized as mortal royalty." Nox's chin draws down to his chest as he shakes his head, and Daje runs a hand over his own. "It should *also* be noted that King Dolian wears a ring controlled by Queen Amari," Xander adds, which doesn't seem to help Nox's mood, the silver in his eyes glowing brightly when I look over at him. "So not only do we now have a siren legion *and* mortal army that can pass through the Spell, but the siren queen has the ability to control them both."

"Wait," Daje says, rubbing his temple with one hand. "I need more context. What ring? Why can the mortals and sirens *also* pass through the Spell?"

This time, Xander gives me a look that relays *I* should be the one to answer those things. So, for what feels like the hundredth time, I cleave myself into two parts. One part holds my grief and regret behind a shield of my own making, attempting to hide it from the other part who launches into an abridged version of my time spent in the Mortal Kingdom. I leave out certain things, like how I was branded and Simon's torture, how the king touched me. The murder of Sterling and his wife. The moment in the tower. But I tell them how I was forced to use my magic through the power of the ring. How I had healed battalions of the king's army and the queen's legionaries, which leads to the admission that King Dolian had forced me to heal him too, something Xander did not even know.

My shield falters as the memory spills out, as I tell them I had been trying on my wedding dress when the king came in and commanded me to use my magic. I stumble over my words, hot tears gathering in my eyes, but Nox effortlessly steps in. Maybe he does it to save me from myself, or maybe it is because he can't stomach hearing that I was preparing to wed the king, but he begins his own retelling of his experiences in the Mage Kingdom.

I listen intently as he talks about waking from a deep sleep after I was taken. Of how he had been weakened and left without magic. He recounts his attempt to rescue me, and how he had been thwarted by Stephan. I use the moment to tell him all I had learned about the traitor and how he was related to King Dolian's advisor. Then he speaks about the council, about Kallin's treachery and Galen's betrayal. How a magical shard in his back had hindered him, blocking his magic, and how he was poisoned. I can tell he is censoring himself just as I'm sure he knows I did the same, but something insidious in me grows roots when he doesn't mention Haylee at all. Still, we trade stories long enough for the sun to sink low in the west, and in the aftermath of it all, a heavy quiet lingers, the tension thick as honey.

Daje is the first to speak when he asks how many battalions and legionaries I've healed as the firelight gleams off of his tawny skin.

"I don't know," I answer, looking to Xander. "Towards the end, I just didn't..." *Care.* But I can't say that, so instead, I let him answer. I feel Nox's magic rise, my eyes going to where his knuckles have turned white from the tight fists he holds.

"If my count is correct, you healed a large legion of sirens, and close to fifteen battalions," Xander says, and I don't miss the dread in his voice.

"And how many are in a battalion?" Nox asks.

"On average? About eight hundred men, give or take."

Gods above. I exhale and again look to Nox. But his focus is entirely on Xander now.

"How could you allow that to happen?" Goosebumps break out over my skin at the flare in Nox's power. Even Daje's eyes widen at the feel of it. "Did you even *try* to help her? Or did you just stand by, ever the king's lackey?"

"Nox—"

"Really?" Xander interrupts, throwing a hand out in Nox's direction. "You heard *everything* she said. I was bound by my oaths just as terribly as she was by the ring's magic."

Nox's voice drops to something dangerous and low, and shadows begin to creep towards us over the dead leaves scattered on the forest floor. "You could have done *more*," he growls, the power thrumming from him drawing my own.

Xander laughs, running a hand through his hair. "You have no fucking clue what you're talking about, *Your Majesty*. Because you weren't there." My voice catches in my throat as both men stand. "I did *everything* that I could to help her within the bounds of my blood oath *and* the oath I made to my people."

"And that is where you fucked up. Because Rhea is worth *more* than every person in that kingdom combined."

"Stop it," I rasp, moving into the space between them.

"Oh, it's easy to say that," Xander mocks, pushing his sleeves up to his elbows before curling his hands into fists. He's only an inch or so shorter than Nox, but they're built similarly, years and years of physical training honing their bodies into weapons. Even so, Nox has magic, and there is no amount of training or skill that can beat that. "Not so easy to act on, though. *Is it?*"

I gasp as shame crosses over Nox's face, there and gone in a blink, before he takes a single menacing step towards Xander. I send a silent plea to Daje for help, but he looks just as stricken as I do.

"You can blame me for thinking I didn't do enough, but *you* weren't the one who had to watch her suffer every single day as the king attempted to destroy her piece by piece. *You* didn't watch the light leave her eyes—"

"Xander," I warn, my voice shaking as my heart pounds against my ribs. Nox's eyes meet mine briefly, the devastation in them squeezing the rest of the breath from my lungs.

Xander composes himself enough to say one last thing. "I *may* have been able to help her more, but *you* weren't there for her *at all*."

The shadows Nox has pulled halt their movement, as if suspended in time. He stands utterly still, jaw clenched as he glares at Xander. I try to string together enough words to form a sentence in protest, to remind them *both* that things beyond their control were at play, but gods, I can't think straight.

"Guys, I think I hear something," Daje says as he finally lurches up from his seat, looking out into the forest just barely lit with waning sunlight, just beyond where our horses are tied to the trees. They whinny in what feels like warning, and my throat tightens as the distinct sound of swords being unsheathed breaks up the slight crackling of our fire.

"You're surrounded!" A voice calls out, male but higher pitched. "Return the king's betrothed, and the rest of you go free."

Xander frees the sword strapped at his hip, palming it confidently as Daje steps up to his other side. Nox moves close to me, arm brushing against my shoulder. "Not going to happen," Xander shouts back.

"Commander, such a disappointment to find you mixed up in this."

"I'm afraid I'm all kinds of disappointing."

Daje snorts.

"You know, the king didn't say we *had* to let *you* live. Only that *she* had to be brought back alive." Xander steps ahead of me, his sword angled out, while Daje's yellow magic flares from one hand, a dagger held in his other.

The backs of my fingers brush against Nox's, and he turns his hand over in invitation for me to take it. I do, wishing I could spend time mapping out all the places our palms meet. That my mind could be empty of everything but *him*.

My guilt festers within me at the thought.

"We should get to the horses," Daje whispers as his magic flares brighter.

"They'll kill us before we can take another step," Xander answers. "We need to draw them out and see how man—" A scream sounds, then another, the blood-curdling noises echoing off the trees as the bellowing of men reverberates around us. Magic pulses beneath my skin and pools in my free hand within seconds, Nox gripping me more tightly as I lift a shield of glittering white in place around us. Xander's sword lowers a fraction as he inspects my magic. "This is helpful."

I don't respond as I scan the woods ahead of us, searching frantically for the threat. Though I know my finger is bare of the king's ring, the ghost of the cold metal still stings the skin there. I send more magic into the shield just as something moves between two of the tree trunks—a flash of gold that makes my pulse race.

Another scream rends the air just as something hits my shield directly in front of Nox. My heart leaps into my throat as Daje curses and Xander adjusts his stance. But Nox remains calm, looking down at me with eyes that pulse bright silver. The panic that something could harm him claws at the back of my mind. *What if I'm made to hurt him again? What about the vow the king forced me to make in blood?* I try to warn Nox that maybe it isn't safe for me to be here, my feet already backing up so that the three of them might escape before I'm forced to use my magic on them. My throat closes as my tongue presses behind my teeth, Nox's name impossible to push out.

I make the mistake of looking down, and then all I see are my bloodied flats on the fallen leaves blanketing the forest floor. *Alexi's blood. Nox's. Eve's.* They had all bled because of me.

"Something is attacking them," Xander says. "Maybe we should try to leave." More leaves crunch, the cadence quicker, as if someone is sprinting directly towards us. The sound intensifies, one pair of steps morphing into more until I'm sure we must be surrounded by at least a dozen men hidden within the trees.

"I'm almost done," Nox replies calmly, his fingers twitching around mine.

I scream when a man leaps out from behind a particularly thick tree trunk, his golden sword aimed for Xander, who lifts his own to block despite being behind my shield. But the man doesn't make it more than a foot before he's abruptly yanked back and slammed into the ground. My ears ring with the reverberation, and I don't realize I'm shaking until Nox draws me in, one hand cradling the back of my head as the other stays firmly gripped around my own.

"Don't watch this," he murmurs above me. But I do—*of course*, I do. With an ear against Nox's chest, I watch as a shadow curls around the hilt of the fallen guard's sword, yanking it out of his hand and spinning it until it's angled at the soft spot between his helmet and chest plate. There is no hesitation as the shadow—as *Nox*—plunges the guard's own weapon into his neck, his whimper cut off before it's more than a single note.

Nox continues, effortlessly extinguishing the guards that we can see, manipulating shadow and steel, and mercilessly killing the ones we can't, their terrified screams alerting us through the trees. Both of us command our magic without so much as lifting a hand, even as arrows fired in rapid succession hit my shield. The guards' screams eventually dwindle beyond us, but I hear them still in my mind, feel myself go stiff in Nox's arms when he suggests dropping the shield. As if my magic now bends to his will, the shield retreats despite my fears, and the woods return to the silence from mere moments before.

"Now can we go?" Daje asks, using his magic to extinguish our fire.

"I have something I need to do first," Nox says, earning a frustrated word from his friend. He kisses my forehead and begins to pull away before registering that I'm gripping his tunic, my fear-stricken eyes flicking up to his. He gently cups both sides of my face, and I want to scream that I can't let him out of my sight. That even as terror begged me to run and leave him behind moments ago, now it has my feet rooted into the earth and is demanding that I keep him here with me. "I'll be back in a few minutes," he whispers, his face unguarded and open. His touch on me is warm and firm. "I promise, Rhea."

Reluctantly, I force my fingers to uncurl and release him, watching as he walks towards the guards, pulling shadows from the ground as he passes by. He uses them to *gather* the dead bodies, lifting them a few feet in the air to trail behind him.

"What the fuck," Xander says under his breath, more statement than question.

We wait until Nox disappears behind the trees before we gather the horses and lead them to the road we've been traveling on. There, I pace as I wait for Nox to return, stopping short every time I hear a twig crack. It isn't long before he emerges again; though, by then, the night has fully cloaked us in darkness only softened by a crescent moon.

Unable to help myself, I run my gaze over his body, confirming he is unharmed. Still, I ask, "Are you alright?"

At that, his serious demeanor fades, and he steps closer, gentle hands featherlight at my waist. "With you at my side? Always." Then he lifts me onto the horse and mounts behind me, Xander and Daje mounting their own.

We ride out of the thickest part of the forest to a natural break in the trees, picking up our pace while staying off any roads that might get us spotted. But as we ride, I keep glancing over my shoulder, paranoid that we're being followed and also extremely curious as to what Nox did with the guards' bodies. "You know you can just ask me," he says the fifth time I look behind us, and I pinch my lips together as I look up at him.

"I wasn't sure if you wanted to share."

"I want to share everything with you, even the things I'm afraid will shake your love for me. Because we promised each other honesty, didn't we?"

My breaths are uneven as I stare into his darkened eyes. "We did."

He nods, fingers flexing where they drape over my hip. Thankfully, not the one with the brand. "I left King Dolian a message with the bodies. He can come for us, for *you*, but this time, there will be no hesitation in our response. There will be no holding back to spare those *just* following orders or because of my fear it will throw his kingdom in chaos if he is murdered." The resolve in his voice is absolute as he adds, "I will slaughter his men as easily as I breathe, and I will do it over and over again to keep you safe."

Words escape me at his declaration, but I slide my fingers over his, interlacing them as I force myself to relax against his chest. In the silence, with only the crunching of dead leaves beneath the horses' hooves, I replay what he's said in my mind. And I wonder if safety will always be an illusion, an elusive idea that we are always running towards but never quite reaching.

Chapter One Hundred and Twenty-Six

RHEA

"**S**AVILLE IS A SMALL town about three hours to the south of Celatum," Nox explains as we slow the horses to a trot when we spot the first home on the town's edge, its walls built with white stone and roof thatched with straw. "I figured it would be better to go somewhere where I'm still anonymous," he adds on quietly. I draw my fingers closer to his, the only solace I can offer as the reminder of what King Dolian had done to Immie plays briefly in my head. She likely wasn't the only one who knew Nox was mage, but even if she was, the town of Celatum had been searched because the king was looking for a guard named Flynn who had stolen the princess from the tower. It would be foolish to return and risk being spotted, but my heart still ached over the way Nox spoke as if he was ashamed.

"What happened there wasn't your fault."

He sighs softly. "Neither was it yours." The following silence gives away what we both feel: We may not be *fully* responsible, but neither are we completely blameless. Another tally for King Dolian hurting others in our names.

A wide road opens up for us to follow into the town, and Xander and Daje flank us as buildings begin to take shape in the darkness ahead. More of the same one-story stone homes dot the landscape, the grass tall enough that it brushes against the horses' legs. The air is fragrant with a sweet smell, and my stomach eagerly reminds me that I haven't eaten since... I'm not sure when.

"We'll make sure to get some food at the inn," Nox says in near my ear in response to the sound.

"I can't even remember the last time I was hungry." It's meant to be an innocuous statement, but I don't realize just how careless it is until Nox tenses behind me, the sensation of his magic crackling in the air like the beginnings of a summer storm. Though I've avoided looking at myself in the mirror for a long while, I know that my body bears the evidence of my time apart from him in more ways than one. How different do I look to Nox? Can he still see the woman that he loves in this new version of me? Or has the emaciation of my body—of my mind and soul—changed me too much?

Daje spots a sign that directs us to the stables behind an apothecary shop and down a small hill. We drop the horses off after gathering the bags and then make our way back up to the main road until the largest building comes into view. Our reflections in the windows as we pass keep my breaths quick, fear that the guards are already hiding in one of them forcing my magic to coil together in my chest. Nox and I follow behind Daje, Xander walking behind us as we step onto a creaking wooden deck and into a noticeably warmer space.

"Welcome to the Saville Inn," a man says from behind a dark wooden counter. "How many rooms, travelers?"

Daje looks back at us, his pointer finger raised. "Just one?" he asks slowly, his gaze bouncing between Nox and I.

I look up at Nox to find him already staring down at me, his face serious but otherwise unreadable. "Would you like your own room?"

"No," I answer, my brows pulling in. "Do *you* want your own room?"

At that, the corners of his mouth lift just a fraction, and I see *him* again. "I want to be wherever you are. Always. For as long as you'll have me."

I reach out for his hand as our gazes hold. My fingers twitch with the urge to trace the stubble at his jaw and that small smile on his lips, to run my hands through the longer strands of his hair as a way to anchor myself to a time before... just *before*.

"Okay, then," Daje drawls, turning back to answer the man.

Xander brushes past us, close enough for his shoulder to graze Nox's. "I need to speak with you."

Nox keeps his eyes on me, the silver in them shining brighter as he answers. "No, thanks."

My cousin grumbles under his breath as he continues forward to stand next to Daje.

"You should speak with him," I say softly, squeezing his hand. "We can trust him."

"Can we?" he asks, and I'm surprised to find the question is genuine. At my nod, a strange look crosses his face, one that I'm sure I'm reading wrong because—

"I had bad luck the last time I stayed at an inn," Daje interrupts as he turns around to hand us the key to our room. "Let's hope that doesn't repeat here." His eyes gleam beneath the light of candles spaced throughout the inn, but he doesn't clarify any further as we all climb wooden stairs to the second floor, the art on the walls passing by in a blur as I force my mind to focus on the feel of my hand in Nox's.

Daje and Xander quickly go over our plans—rest for a few hours and then leave just before the sun rises—and then we are each in our rooms, Nox setting our bags down before stretching his arms overhead. I clasp my own hands together, my gaze roaming over the room as Nox walks past me to the bathroom, light spilling out a few seconds later from the candles he's lit within. When he comes back out, a nervous energy thrums between us as we stare at each other. It's filled with all the words that are not so easily spoken but that are written so clearly on both of our faces.

But maybe that is for the best.

There was so much that happened, so many memories that I selfishly do not want to dwell on that keep trying to pull me back in. It isn't that I think avoiding them will do any good—I had learned my lesson regarding that—it has just been *so* damn long since I have held Nox. Been held by him. So many weeks of harboring a loneliness that bled from my heart and into my veins until I thought I could die from it.

Until I almost *did*.

And I just... *I want him*. Even if I don't deserve him anymore, even if the relief he brings me is only temporary.

"There are clean clothes and toiletries in the bag," he says, his voice low. "I can grab us some food while you shower."

He takes a single step towards the door, and I feel something tug me in his direction. My magic or maybe something more, but I don't waste time questioning it. "Or you could join me," I suggest, voice shaking as I flatten my palms over the wool cloak at my thighs.

His swallow is rough, as is the silence that crashes down on me when he doesn't respond. I retreat, again *keenly* aware of the fact that I've changed. Months under the abuse of King Dolian had left me gaunt with regret and guilt, and I can't exactly blame Nox if that is too much for him.

"It's okay," I rush out, already backtracking towards the bathroom. "I'll just—"

"Rhea." He takes tentative steps towards me until the heat of his body permeates my clothing, stoking a different kind of heat to life at the base of my spine. His hands frame my face, thumbs brushing tenderly over my cheeks. For a long while, he doesn't say anything, just holds me like I'm precious. Like he can't believe we are both here. But then he inhales deeply, and his forehead drops against mine. "I'm worried about you," he confesses, the words rough with emotion. "You're here—tangible and real in my hands—but your mind is so far away. And I don't know how to reach you. I can't—" My eyes close at the crack in his voice, at the stuttered breath that follows, as I grip onto his wrists. "I failed you. I *failed* you, Rhea. And all I keep thinking about is how Xander was right. You needed me, and *I wasn't there*." He leans his head back, thumbs brushing away my fallen tears. "I wasn't there for you, and you suffered. You deserve—"

"Do you love me?" I interject, sliding my hands from his wrists to either side of his face. Keeping him close.

"Yes," he answers without hesitation, without any consideration, even if the question looks as if it's caught him off guard. "But what I've done—what I *will* do—in the name of that love should terrify you, Rhea."

"What if it doesn't?" I ask him, the pounding of my heart heavy in my ears. "What if I love you just as much? What if I'm already the monster you're so afraid you're turning into?" I remembered what he said, back in his room on the night I had told him about my nightmares. About all King Dolian had done to me then. He wanted to choke the world in his shadows to keep me safe. I had already seen a glimpse of what he would do on the other side of that promise. I had been taken from him, and I had been hurt. Yet the version of Nox who stands before me, retribution flaring in his eyes, doesn't frighten me. Nothing about him does because I know that he does *everything* for me.

But what had *I* done? There were lines crossed—moral ones. Intimate ones. The king hadn't managed to fuck me, but did it matter when he had touched me? When I *let* him kiss me? When *I* had given up on Nox? My hands fall from his face because, *gods*, what right do I have to act like we could just have a single moment together after everything?

"Hey," he whispers, catching my hands and resisting when I try to pull them away. "Please, talk to me, Sunshine. Let me in." Though he stands tall, he might as well be on his knees for the way he begs me.

I shake my head, chewing on my lower lip as I battle to corral my anger and grief and guilt. But Nox's affect on me has always been something stronger than I could fight and this is no exception. "I know about Haylee," I start, forcing myself to look at him, even as his eyes widen like he's just had a secret exposed. "And I wish I could say that the moment I learned of the betrothal, I knew it was fake. Or that I thought the information was wrong. I wish I could say that there wasn't a small part of me that always thought the two of you go well together." My eyes bounce between his as his outline blurs. But he deserves the truth. He should know every way *I* had failed him too. "But I can't. I doubted you—I doubted *us*—and those doubts led me down a path that can never be undone. And it wasn't because I don't love you, Nox, because I do. Stars above, do I *love* you. It was because I hated the thought that you could love someone else. That I would have to exist in a world where you aren't *mine* anymore. And I wasn't strong enough to keep fighting, and I—"

My own tears choke me as the taste of salt stains my lips. And Nox... He looks at me as if I've utterly destroyed him. Like I've dismantled him piece by piece until he, like me, is only a collection of broken parts.

"I'm sorry," I breathe through a fractured sob, the words sawing from that hollow place within me. "I'm so sorry I couldn't be better for you."

"Gods above, Sunshine, I did *not* get betrothed to Haylee. The council tried; they even announced it at my coronation, but there was nothing official between us. I *never* touched her. I do not, *could not*, want her. *Ever.* There is *only* you. There will only *ever* be you, and if you think there is *anything* you can say that would change my mind, I'm telling you right now that you're wrong." I know his words should bring me comfort, but they only amplify the fact that I had done so much worse.

"King Dolian kissed me," I say, barely louder than a whisper. "I *let* him do it because I needed something from him. A favor."

"Rhea, don't take on guilt for something you had no control over." His voice is so gentle, eyes so full of that regret for me—*me*—that something within me snaps.

"You're not listening!" I bark, forcing myself away from him as magic presses at the space between my ribs. "I *let* him! I let him touch me. I let him fill my head with poisonous thoughts about you. About *love*." I undo the clasp of the cloak and throw it to the ground before pulling off my shirt. Standing in the faint candlelight, I undo the laces of my pants, tugging them down just far enough to show Nox the one thing that could never be hidden from him. "He changed me forever, and he *knows* it." And now Nox knows it too.

There is a pause, a moment frozen in time, in which Nox inhales sharply at the sight of my scarred hip. I watch the shadows of the room creep towards him, his jaw clenched so tightly that I can see his pulse ticking along it. And then everything explodes. Between one blink and the next, darkness is *splattered* against the walls and the ceiling, as if Nox threw paint instead of shadows. He claims the distance I created and I hold myself still, preparing for his wrath. It won't be the same as the king's, and that knowledge somehow makes it worse because I know Nox's anger won't come in the form of barbed words or pounding fists. It'll come as soft heartbreak. As a declaration that our love is no longer enough.

But, though anger carves deep lines into the center of his forehead, his voice is steady when he says, "*You* didn't make those choices because they were never really choices to begin with. *He* caged you. *He* laid his hands on you. *He* manipulated you because he knew that it was the only way to break you." My shoulders rock as I cry, the safety of Nox forcing my walls down. "But he didn't, love. He didn't break you. Because you're *here* now, and whatever you did, whatever you *had* to do to survive that torment, I would never hold against you." Two fingers gently press beneath my chin, making my eyes meet his. "There is nothing that you could tell me that would erase the way I feel about you, Rhea. Don't you see? I'm infinitely yours. In this life and every other."

Breaths rush past my lips, and though I am raw—sliced open and exposed—it's not nearly as suffocating as it once was. It still hurts, and the memories still linger just beyond the edges of my mind, but in *this* moment, there is just Nox and his devotion to me.

"Hear me when I say that, while there are men who believe in the gods and others who worship magic itself, I find my divine holiness in you. *You* are the only thing worth believing in."

Chapter One Hundred and Twenty-Seven

RHEA

OUR NEXT MOVEMENTS ARE slow, like the untangling of snarled threads, as Nox's words wrap around me. "Tell me what you want," he says. *Pleads.* "Grant me the permission to be what you need now so that I can worship you in the way you deserve, Rhea." He brushes a loose strand of my hair away from my face, fingertips trailing down my cheek. "Let me atone for every way I've failed you. *Please.*"

I want to tell him that it's ironic he feels that way. That after *everything* I just revealed, he isn't the one who should carry that guilt, yet I had shown him my biggest fear. I had confessed my darkest shame, and Nox had stared at those ugly, thorny pieces and declared me a flower worth wanting. Had pricked his fingers as he reached for me, jagged edges and all, and it had not turned him away. I wanted to do the same. I wanted to have him.

For the first time in so long, I simply *wanted.*

But I can't make the words scrape up my throat, can't pull them from the pit that's still very much inside of me. So I gently grip his tunic instead. Giving the consent he wants as I lightly tug him with me into the bathroom. And Nox, as he has always done, understands what I can't say as he reaches over and turns the shower on, his gaze never leaving mine. Another unhurried dance begins between us—one where we take turns removing clothing as if there are no guards hunting us down or kings and queens desperate to keep us apart. As if I'm not still coated in the imaginary blood of those I killed and Nox isn't bound by the way his kingdom is turning against him. Because, of course, we are and I am and he is.

Bare in the golden light of the pillar candles lit around us, I fight the urge to cover myself. To hide the space between my hip bones that is more concave. The ribs I can easily count beneath my skin. And the brand...

"You are so beautiful," Nox murmurs, and if I thought it might be a poor attempt at making me feel better, one glance at him tells me that he's not just plying me with sweet words. With his lids half closed and his eyes glazed over, Nox doesn't just *look* at me. He studies me, venerates me with the way his entire body leans in my direction as if he's caught in some invisible orbit. His fingers twitch at his sides as steam begins to curl out from the shower, tendrils of it stretching in our direction, yet all is lost to him except for me. It's silly to feel myself warm beneath his observation. To have my magic rising to meet his, and yet I had been so sure he wouldn't be able to stomach the mark and, by extension, me. I had felt so lonely, and now—

Drawing in a deep breath, I reach my hand out, and together, we step beneath the hot water. It's darker in here, shadows that aren't controlled by Nox or made by me cradling us as the water hits the tops of our heads and travels down our backs. I watch as rivulets drip from the longer strands of Nox's hair, creating pathways over his forehead and down his nose. Over the curve of his lips, a sight I linger a few breaths longer on. Heat, both foreign and familiar, sparks to life low in my stomach—so abruptly that it nearly makes me gasp as I flick my eyes up to Nox's. Finding him already looking at me. Patiently meeting me where I'm at as he's always done.

In truth, that feeling—the longing and attraction and love—that stirs within me is frightening. Does feeling that, here and now, mean I'm trying to absolve myself of everything that came before? Is it *selfish* to want to just have this moment with him? To find that buried beneath the cold and bitter darkness, there is warmth brimming? That there is a yearning for him that perhaps was never snuffed out as I had thought but only masked?

Is it unforgivable that I want to surrender to it?

"Do you trust me?" The question knocks me from my own head as I blink away water that has gathered on my lashes. The skin at Nox's chest has taken a slightly pink hue from the hot water, evidence of just how much time he must have been waiting for me to do or say *anything* while I had been trying to figure out if I deserved to be temporarily absolved from my sins.

Though the answer to the question is pressing at my lips before I even take my next breath, I still force myself to say it slowly. To make sure Nox knows that my hesitations are not because of *him*. "I trust you with my life. With my magic." I swallow roughly. "With my body and with my heart. There is no part of me that is not yours, Nox."

For better or worse, I am his.

Reassured by my answer, he nods and reaches past me to grab the new bar of soap resting at the tub's edge and a clean washcloth next to it.

"When we were separated, I had the hardest time doing things alone that we had once done together," he admits, giving me the first soapy cloth before grabbing one for himself. My throat constricts as I watch him run his cloth up his arm. "Eating. Sleeping. Training. Even showering. Everything reminded me of you, and doing them alone was admitting you weren't there. It was admitting that my heart was missing half of itself. And sometimes—" He drags the cloth across his chest—over the ring he had given me when he asked me to marry him—and down the other arm. My grip on my own washcloth tightens, my hands suspended in the air. "Sometimes, I would let my mind wander to dark places. Ones where voices whispered that I wasn't going to see you again. That my weaknesses had led to you being taken. That they were the cause for your suffering. And something as simple as a shower would turn into me hating myself. First, because you weren't there. And then, because I was replacing the memory of us doing it together with this new, horrible one."

I draw my washcloth closer as I turn over what he's said, startled at the fact that he felt similar to how I did in our time apart. "I was assigned a handmaiden," I begin, dropping my attention to where the wash cloth meets my forearm. "Her name was Eve, and I'm ashamed to admit I did not like her at first. The king ordered her to bathe me, and I hated the idea that her hands, even as benign as the touch was, would replace yours on my skin. Hated that anyone else would see me undressed and vulnerable because those were things I only wanted to be with you. But she was bound by a blood oath to obey the king, and I was stuck under his influence because of the ring."

I don't look back up at Nox, but I see his movements still, the cloth's path halted over his defined stomach, the muscles perhaps showing a little more easily than before.

"She was persistent in her attempts to befriend me and relaxed at her job as she tended to me, and towards the end, when everything felt hopeless, she was the only bit of brightness that remained. But when I found out what the king was doing..." My voice breaks on a too sharp breath, so I focus on moving the cloth over my other arm and then my chest, waiting for the tightness there to ease before continuing. "When I found out how he was hurting her, I knew that I would do anything to get her away from him. To try to protect her so that no one else would be hurt by him in my name. That is why I let him kiss me. Why I invited it."

"And that act is not one that deserves punishment, Rhea," he reminds me gently, waiting until I finally look at him. My heart aches at the tenderness in his gaze, at the softness of his expression. I love him. Gods above and below, I *love* him. "Certainly not from me."

I shake my head as I stare at him. "I don't deserve you," I confess, the words bitter on my tongue.

But Nox lifts the corner of his mouth, just a fraction, as he shifts his body closer to mine. "Funny, I was about to say the same thing to you." I can't quite laugh, the gesture too unfamiliar now, but that small blossoming warmth within me grows. And I find myself eager to latch on to it. To let it give me hope that we might be okay. That, one day, *I* might.

Lifting my cloth from my body, I reach it out towards Nox, a fluttering in my stomach signaling my nerves. And as I watch his expression shift from that slight playful edge to something more reverent, I decide that surrendering to our love could never be a bad thing. He takes the cloth from me, and I turn around, my breath caught in my chest.

I feel him come up behind me, close enough that the heat of his body battles against that of the shower but still not touching me. In the small pause that lingers, I feel the question that he hasn't asked. I had given my consent earlier, but this is another step further. This isn't just permission to see me naked but to touch me. Even if it is just something as banal as washing me and nothing more, Nox needs me to say that I want it, and I need him to know that I trust him.

I look over my shoulder at him, taking in the way his hair is plastered to the sides of his face. The slight stubble that shadows his jaw and the way my ring is nestled right over his heart. "I want you to touch me, Nox," I say, eyes moving up to his. Infusing my voice with the love I have for him, I add, "I give you permission to touch me however you want." Turning back, I let my eyes close and force my fingers to relax, even as my heart races.

The first touch comes at my shoulders, his fingers draping over one side while the wash cloth glides over the other, the lavender scent of the soap mixing with the steam around us. And though I let my imagination run rampant at the idea of what Nox might do, how he might touch me, he keeps the press of his fingers light and the graze of the washcloth rhythmic down the length of my back. As the minutes pass, the tension seeps from my muscles until my head is lolling to the side and my chest rises and falls to the even pace of my breathing. And that calm, so tentative and sweet, stays when Nox lowers, the cloth dragging over my backside and down the backs of my legs. It remains when he moves to my front, dropping to a knee as he drags it up my thighs and to my hips. It's only interrupted when he pauses as the cloth moves over the scarred skin in the shape of a roaring lion.

Looking up at me through wet lashes, he moves his hands to brace my hips and then, slowly enough that I can stop him, leans in until his lips brush against the brand. My hands reach for his shoulders, breath caught as I watch him kiss me there just as affectionately as he does the skin around the brand. My fingers dig into his muscles, half to hold myself as my knees threaten to buckle and half because I'm suddenly terrified this is nothing more than a dream. But then Nox whispers something low against my skin, and my magic curls around my spine as goosebumps flare over my body. And suddenly, I'm not thinking about the brand or the nightmare that followed it, but instead, I'm overwhelmed with the softness of Nox's lips. With how his grip tightens just a fraction against me. How heat and sensation and *desire* flood the apex of my thighs.

Nox keeps his eyes on me as his lips travel to my other hip, his kisses feather-light, and yet I feel them *everywhere*. I cradle the back of his neck as he moves higher, his mouth traveling in the valley between my breasts as he coaxes me out of my head completely and into this moment.

Standing at his full height, he looks down at me, and the small smirk returns. "My turn," he says, seeming to ignore the way my skin has flushed pink in spite of the water, which has now begun to cool. I reach for his cloth, adding more soap to it before positioning him so that his back is to me.

Nox tilts his head back as I begin to drag the cloth over his shoulders, a trail of white bubbles following in its wake. When his entire back is covered with soap, I let my free hand make designs in the suds, watching as his muscles uncoil. My hand sweeps over his right shoulder and then to his left, but as I move lower, something rough catches my attention. And I might have ignored it were it not for the fact that Nox's hands clench at his sides. Using the cloth, I wipe until his tanned skin peeks through the soap and the barest dance of light from a nearby candle shows the jagged line of a scar.

"What is this?" I ask him, tracing over it with the tip of my finger, my healing magic warming my chest.

"That's where the shard of dragon stone was," he answers, lifting his head. "Bahira cut it out, and even though my magic returned to its full capabilities, I guess the mark will always be there." My throat tightens at the reminder that he had been magically bound, his body caged and his mind poisoned. And he, like me, bore a permanent tribute to how much we had endured in our time apart.

"I'm sorry." I curl my fingers over the outsides of his arms and lean in, pressing my lips to the scar. Just as he had done for me. "I'm sorry that you suffered."

He lays one of his hands over mine, squeezing it softly before I resume running the cloth over his backside and down his legs. I move to his front, my mind stuck on the realization that this man had given up so much in the name of our love. Had willingly sacrificed *everything* because it all became so easily worthless if I wasn't at his side for it. And I try, I really do, to make this moment last longer. To return the reverence with which he tended to me and force my gaze to only stay on the more *decent* parts of him as I work my way up his body. But all it takes is a single glance, and that heat is coiled at my core again, the faintest memory of us together making my lips part on a rushed breath.

I let go of the cloth as I stand and press my hands to his chest, feeling the way his heart beats in a faster cadence. "Do you remember the day you proposed?" I ask, lifting the ring that hangs from a golden chain and cradling it in my hand. "Do you remember what you said?"

"I do," he answers, his hands coming to rest on my hips. "But humor me and be more specific."

My lips quirk. "You said that our love was not a beginning or an end—"

"But an infinite constant," he interrupts.

"Yes." I lay the ring back down and reach up to brush the soaked strands from his forehead before resting my hand on his cheek. "Forever would be a wish for most people, yet that does not feel like enough time for us, does it?" I ask, pressing myself closer to him.

"No." His eyes dip to my lips as I rise onto my toes, anchoring myself to him. "It doesn't."

"I want forever with you," I breathe, my thumb gliding over his lips. "I want every second of every day to be spent with you from now until this life ends—and even beyond. This love is more than just that. It is destiny. It is *fate*, and all I want is to surrender to it."

The admission flows easily from me. His chest rises with a quick breath as he weaves a hand through my hair.

"I surrender everything that I am to you, Nox. Every version of me is yours." And because I want it, because I want him, I let everything else fall to the wayside as I close the distance between us and kiss him.

One Hundred and Twenty-Eight

RHEA

I HAVE KISSED NOX innumerable times, but as his lips open to mine, as passion drives our tongues to glide against each other, an exploration of feel and touch and taste, this time feels different. *Momentous*. Our mouths move together in the way that only two people who know what the other likes can, but there is a tentative softness present. A tether that loops around and around and reminds me to slow myself down. To spend time refamiliarizing myself with every part of him.

To remember that this moment almost didn't happen.

The morbid thought nearly stops me in my tracks, but then Nox is closing the distance that threatens to separate us, chasing after me as he presses his hand into the divot of my waist, his other holding the back of my head. One of my arms stays looped around his neck while the hand of the other spears into his hair, fingers rustling through the wet strands in all the ways I imagined doing when we were apart.

"I need more of you," I say between the pressing of our lips, despite how there isn't a single inch of space between us. But, of course, he understands what I want better than I do as he turns the water off, lifting my slick body against his as if it is the easiest thing in the world and stepping out of the shower. All while keeping his mouth on me. His tongue dancing with mine.

Cold air caresses my back for a handful of steps, and then he's gently laying me down, a gasp escaping me as my heated skin hits the cool blanket. Nox crawls over me, and I shamelessly take in the sight of him, my gaze scouring every divot of muscle and inch of naked skin. He braces his weight with one arm, and then his lips are on mine again, and I'm lost. Adrift in a starlit sea not made of sadness or loneliness but of *us*, and how easy it is to let myself drown in it. In his love.

My legs fall apart, and he sinks his hips deeper into the space created, his cock already hard as every single drop of awareness hones in on the silky heat of him teasing my core. "Fuck," he rasps, moving to kiss my jaw. Teeth and tongue working the skin there before he draws lower. I arch my neck to give him access to everything. Anything. It's all his to do whatever he pleases with. "I want to be patient with you, but I fucking *need* you," he says desperately, his lips paying homage to that need as he slides farther down until his mouth is hovering over one of my breasts, his heated eyes lifting to meet mine. "So you have to tell me what you want me to do. Command it of me, Rhea."

Gods, how am I supposed to function with him looking at me like that? When the hunger in his gaze is matched by the desire that burns low in my belly? But I know what he means, because that same ardent need feels fragile within me. It forces me to toggle between asking him to take his time and *begging* him to fuck me. My magic ignites, both halves alive and writhing until I'm sure glittering light will spill from my palms.

Unable to form words, I lace my fingers through his hair again and press his head down until his mouth closes over my peaked nipple, and then his tongue is swirling around it and every thought eddies as the world beyond him fades. *Yes, this.* I moan quietly, my hands gripping any part of him that I can reach. My only reprieve from the dizzying desire he coaxes comes when he kisses across my chest, his tongue then toying with my other side.

"Nox," I whisper. *Scream.* A noise somewhere in between as my hips buck beneath him, evidence of my wanting him undeniable as it slickens the skin between my thighs. There is only this, only *him*, as I swallow down a sound that I'm not wholly positive won't come out as a sob. Soon enough, he's hovering over me again, lips swollen and eyes glazed. I expect him to keep devouring me, the feral acuteness with which he stares at my own lips like a cursory warning, but I watch as he reins himself in. As his fingers trail over the side of my face and down to the now sensitive skin at my neck. Not in question or hesitation, but in that worshipful awe that leaves me breathless.

"There is no part of you that I don't revere with everything that I am," he says, exhaling slowly. "But we don't have to do anything you aren't ready for. We could stop here and now, and that would be enough, Rhea."

My chest aches as I look at him, as I take his face into my hands and draw him in for another intoxicating kiss. He lowers his body until his weight is just enough to blanket me in his warmth—his scent. Despite our history, my stomach flutters as if this is our first time together. But I meant what I said. I want to surrender myself to him. I want to fall apart with the safety of knowing he'll be here still when I resurface. I want to claim him as mine because for a moment...

For a moment, I wasn't sure that he would be. And as if I need to make us both aware, make any gods listening sure of the way I feel, I give voice to that vow. "You are mine," I promise, my lips ghosting over his while my power flares again.

"And you are mine," he counters, those four words uncompromising, my body shivering under the magical pull of them.

"Show me," I whisper, utter need pulsing through me as I take his hand and press a kiss to his palm before laying it over my chest. My ring dangles from that golden chain around his neck in the space between our hearts, and my throat tightens at the sight of it before I move his hand over my breast and then lower, the calloused evidence of his training scraping my soft skin until he's right where I'm aching for him. Bare and open and unrestrained, I implore him. "Show me that I'm yours."

Though I trust him implicitly, for a brief moment as his fingers graze that sensitive bundle of nerves between my legs, panic flares. The flash of a still opened wound in my mind makes my muscles tense, and I berate myself for the reaction. The king had never touched me *there*, had gotten close, yes, but—

"Sunshine." Nox's mouth hovers over mine, his hand frozen in place as he waits for me to open my eyes. I hadn't realized they were pinched shut. "It's just you and me," he swears, dark gray eyes spotted brilliantly with glowing silver drawing me in. "Just us."

I nod, bringing my hands to his shoulders. His back. His hair. Letting his body be the pillar I moor myself to. He must sense me relax—sees it, perhaps—because his fingers are moving again, a gentle exploration that makes us both groan. I let myself get lost in the sensation that rises as he dips his head into the crook of my neck, hot kisses painting my skin as my body surrenders to his ministrations. My breaths grow labored, a wave building within me and guided by every torturously languid stroke he makes. My toes curl against the blanket, knees squeezing his hips, and I must moan his name because he's begging me to say it again. "Nox, I—" My words are cut short as my release barrels towards me with an intensity that knocks air from my lungs.

"I know," he says, mouth moving against mine before his tongue dips in and matches the movement of his finger. "Let go, Rhea. Come for me."

I can't deny him. I've never been able to. So my body obeys his command, my back arching as the sweetest pleasure rolls in, taking every ounce of uncertainty that might have remained hidden within secret corners of my body—my mind—and replacing it with the euphoric high that washes over me. My nails dig into his skin unbidden, but Nox only groans as if my pleasure is all he needs to receive his, and then he's panting over me, his cock hard on my thigh as he rests his forehead against mine.

"I love watching you like this," he says between deep breaths, his hand shifting so that it rests at my hip, opposite of the brand.

It takes a minute for me to regain feeling in my body; so many weeks deprived of his touch leaves me overexposed with awareness in the wake of it. But when my vision focuses back on him and I replay his words in my head, I realize that I might want to watch him unravel too. That maybe his pleading for me to command him is only partially to put power back in my hands. Maybe it's also because he's craving the safety of surrendering to *me* too.

"What is it?" he asks, hand coming to cradle the side of my face as he studies me.

"Nothing, I just—" I rise onto my elbows, capturing his mouth again before guiding him to lie back, his hands reaching for my waist as my knees brace his hips. Leaning forward, my hair curtains us, and I take my time tracing the outline of his face. His jaw and lips. Those eyes—the most beautiful eyes I've ever seen. "I missed you, Nox. Every moment of every day." One hand plants on his chest while the other reaches between us, a thrill rising when he groans as I wrap my fingers around his cock, beginning to stroke him.

"Fuck, Rhea—" His neck arches, head tilting back as his jaw flexes and the speed of my hand increases. I had wanted this moment to arrive faster, had wanted to finally fill that void within me with everything made of him. But this, watching him begin to unravel slowly, is worth the wait. Worth the self-imposed torment. "Gods, you have no idea," he pants, lips peeled back as his heart races beneath my palm. I pause pumping my hand to roll my hips over him, his cock glistening with my desire, before I resume the motion again, a smile tugging at my lips at the satisfied sound he releases.

He snaps his head back up to look at me, and even beneath the darkness of the room, the golden light of the candles scant here, his eyes glow with unbridled longing. And for a small eternity, he just watches me with ragged breaths, that reverential expression tugging at my heart. The muscles in his stomach clench, his fingers tightening on my hips, but he drinks in the way I become flustered at the mounting craving that braids its way through me. Then he's sitting up, one hand bracing his weight behind him while the other weaves back into my hair.

"I missed you too," he finally says, tilting my head to the side so that my lips slant over his. "I missed you so *fucking* much." He kisses me hard, making up for that lost time. As if we have more than enough of it now.

But I know that we don't and that reality is waiting just beyond this door. That waiting is a luxury we do not have. So I lift higher on my knees, my inner muscles clenching in preparation as I position the tip of his cock right at my entrance. My thighs shake, and my hands tremble, and I might laugh at the nervous energy that rolls through me if I wasn't so utterly lost in the way Nox looks at me. How he's always looked at me. As if I'm a goddess walking amongst mortals. As if I'm more than the flesh and bone that makes me. More than the magic that fills me.

The first inch he consumes shocks me, air stilted in my chest as my lips part and my fingers curl into the hard muscles of his shoulders. When my eyes try to fall closed as my body consumes another inch and then another, he calls my name on an uneven rasp. "Rhea, watch what you do to me," he begs, and what can I do but let my eyes flutter open to take in his gaze as it falls to where our bodies are joined. I sink even deeper, molding to the shape of him as he demands another inch, then even more, until I can't feel where he ends and I begin.

It's just him and me and this all-consuming, ever-present, maddening love. *Infinite. Destiny. Fate.*

Chest heaving, I breathe through the fullness of him seated to the hilt, once again torn between taking our time and wanting him to make me forget my own name. I aim for somewhere in the middle as I rock my hips, my back arching at the blinding lust that pools within me. Time becomes lost to our movements. To the sound of sawing breaths and whispered benedictions. Magic rises at our joining, mingling in the space around us, and something in me splinters at the feel of it. The easing of a fear that has sat heavily on my bones since that horrifying moment on the beach. I had always thought of our magic as two sides of the same coin, and I was afraid—so *afraid*—that something had changed in our time apart. That this integral part of us both was no longer suited for each other. But as wisps of black and glimmers of white dance around us, that fear ebbs away, and once more, I surrender to the knowledge that Nox is mine. In every way. In every form. And I am his.

He draws me to his chest as he lays back, never severing our connection but changing the angle at which he enters me. I moan at the feel of him, at how deeply he hits me, the change in position giving him leverage to pull me down onto his thrusts. I want to kiss him more than I want to breathe, so I fuse my mouth to his as he drives into me, my body softening around him. Every part of me pliant to his will, and every part of him desperate to fulfill my own.

Quicker than before, release rolls in on a fast-moving tide, pulling me under and sending a spike of panic through me because I don't want this to end. But my body craves the peak that Nox and I are climbing together. "I love you," I croak, my vision flashing as need pulses through me.

The words make Nox groan as his hips fall out of any sort of rhythm, his arms banding around me to hold me close while he hits harder, *deeper*. "I love *you*," he promises. "Rhea—" He groans again as I meet his next thrust. Each of my breaths become shorter than the last as I'm finally pushed off that ledge, left freefalling as my entire world shifts. He slides a hand down to my low back and holds me in place, my muscles clenching so tightly around him that I *feel* the moment he finds his own release. His body unraveling beneath mine as shared breath caresses our lips, my hands still clutching at his shoulders.

When I claw myself out of that sated haze, Nox is there, heavy-lidded eyes staring at me. Devotion written all over his face and evident in the content smile he gives me. I force my limbs to move, reaching up to trace his lips with my fingers. "I love your smile," I tell him, heat rising to my cheeks when it widens.

"And what else?" he asks, leaning up to kiss me. Though hunger is present in the movement, it's softened as he glides his hands up and down my back softly, the featherlight touch drawing out goosebumps. I smile as I lean back, though it quivers at the feel of him still very much inside of me. We both let out a sighing moan before I carefully slip off of him and lie on my side, Nox mirroring me.

"I love your hair," I continue, smiling at the half-dried waves that tumble over his forehead messily. "Though this is new." I run my fingers over the shadow on his jaw, the stubble there pricking my skin. "I think I like it."

"Good," he chuckles, watching my hand move down to his chest and the chain now dripping onto the bed. A different sort of silence falls over us as I look at the ring, the elegant cut of the diamond glinting despite the low light. "I know a lot has happened. I know that the idea of marriage right now—or maybe *ever*—might no longer be appealing because of what that bastard did to you." His hand reaches out to tip my chin so that I'm looking once more into his eyes. "But if being married to me is still something—"

"Yes," I interrupt, chewing on my lower lip until Nox's thumb moves to gently pry it free. I lay my hand over his cheek, blinking back the pressure that builds behind my eyes. "*Yes.* I want to marry you." His answering grin is brilliant—*incandescent*—as he sits up and undoes the necklace's clasp, pulling the chain through the ring.

He gently takes my hand in his, kissing my knuckle before slowly sliding the ring on my finger. I worry that the sight of a ring at all might take my mind to a darker place, but as I stare down at the pink and green diamonds that flank the center one, all I can think about is what it felt like to put it on for the first time that day in the garden. "I thought it might have been lost forever," I say quietly, swallowing down that bitter knot at the memory of the night Daje and I were attacked. "When she commanded that they take the ring..." My voice trails off as I tug on that thread, the one that leads to the memory of the voices from that night. "Her voice..."

"Rhea? What is it?" Nox tilts his head, catching my eyes with his.

"That night, on the pathway where we were attacked, there was a woman," I rasp, my hand trembling as I stare at him. "I couldn't remember much before, nothing beyond seeing Daje lying on the path unconscious and bleeding, but there was a female, one who commanded that I take the ring off. That she *needed* it."

His jaw hardens as he curls his fingers around mine and brings them to lay on top of his leg. "Did you recognize it?"

"I didn't at first, and I could still be wrong, but..." I swallow, my stomach souring with the accusation, even if a part of me can't deny that it's *possible*. "I think it was Haylee."

Chapter One Hundred and Twenty-Nine

RHEA

I N THE WAKE OF the revelation that Haylee might have been there the night I was attacked, Nox tells me what she had done while I was gone. How she had insisted, in a way that seemed as if there was no other logical choice, that she and Nox marry. That they appease the council. Exhaustion lingers heavily around my mind, and yet, even as we agree to discuss it all in more detail once we are back in the Mage Kingdom, I cannot find rest easily. The thought that Haylee had been deceiving me, deceiving Nox and Bahira, the entire time, makes me uncomfortable with anger and thirsting for a vengeance I had only tasted once before.

I manage to doze off for a little while before the press of Nox's lips at my shoulder rouses me from sleep. We shower again before we leave, this time painted in the soft yellow glow of early morning light. Nox shampoos my hair and then lowers to his knees so that I can do the same for him. I'm desperate to hold on to one more moment of just us before we thrust ourselves back into the reality we're running from. It starts with a kiss, soft and sweet and slow. Then I'm delving my hands into his hair and wrapping my leg around his hip as he holds me to him, and together, we steal an intimate moment that is far too rushed.

The ride is just as arduous as it was the day before, stripping us of the ability to engage in conversation as we push the horses well into the night, only pausing twice briefly to let them drink and rest. Without the distraction, my mind wanders, collecting images and memories I'd rather forget as if they are trinkets to be shown off.

I already tried pretending that my hurts didn't exist, and I had learned the consequences of that action. So as we ride, I try to focus on each memory that rises. But what I don't account for is the *guilt*. It twists and contorts each image until I'm left white-knuckling the saddle, my chest heaving with fractured breaths.

When we finally stop to rest, it is well into the night, and though we aren't quite in the Mage Kingdom yet, the trees grow more thickly here. Daje starts a fire as Nox and Xander guide the horses to drink first before tying them to trees and giving them sacks of grain. Gathered around the flame, we eat a small meal of dried meat, nuts, and fruit before Xander breaks our tired silence.

"If I am to cross the border tomorrow with you, you should heal me now." I stare at my cousin over the fire as I reach my fingers towards it to warm them.

"Why now?" Nox asks, his arms folded over his chest where he sits at my side.

"While I'm sure that we have enough resources just between the two of you to fend off a decent number of men, it's in our best interest to avoid as much conflict as possible while crossing. Especially if you want to handle the delicate situation of revealing that there are now mortals who can pass through the Spell. If there is trouble, I don't want to be a distraction for her."

"Are you sure you *want* to cross?" I ask him, tugging my cloak around my shoulders more tightly as a shiver works over me.

"No," Xander answers honestly, tossing a small stick into the flames. "But Brisk was right. Staying in the Mortal Kingdom is too dangerous right now. I can figure out how to get communications going again, maybe with your help." I don't miss how he gestures to me and not Nox. Neither does Daje, whose eyes shift back and forth between them.

"I'm sorry, but what is the connection here," Daje asks, a brow lifted as he points from Xander to me. "I mean, I know you are leading the resistance, but—"

"He's my cousin," I interrupt, glancing at Nox from the corner of my eye. I had told him before we left the inn about who Xander was to me, and though I had seen a small flash of relief cross his face, Nox had been otherwise unbothered by the reveal. He had cited that being my cousin didn't absolve Xander of all he had done against me in the king's name. Considering it had taken *me* a while to trust Xander, I couldn't exactly blame him for feeling that way.

"King Dolian had children?" Daje asks, his eyes wide.

"He had *a* child," Xander answers, arms folding over his chest as he stands in front of me. He wears a cloak similar to Daje and Nox, except he has the hood pulled up over his head, his onyx hair lost in the shadow it creates. "I am, for better or worse, his single bastard heir."

"But heir enough," I reply quietly, and Xander's expression softens at my words. "Ready?"

He exhales roughly but nods, watching as I lift my already glowing hand. The magic blankets him easily, and though I keep my focus on Xander, ensuring my intention doesn't stray, I hear Daje stand and step closer, Nox doing the same. Xander's eyes eventually fall closed as my power pours into him, seeping beneath his skin until he is glowing with it. I realize that this is the first time I've healed anyone without the ring on, and just as I begin to wonder how I will know to stop, I *feel* the moment Xander is healed, and my magic starts to pull back. His veins show through the white light beneath his skin, but then that fades too. When his eyes open again, I'm sure I see white glowing behind them, but then he blinks, and all that remains are those dark irises.

"Do you feel any different?" Daje asks, eyeing Xander like he might shift into another being at any moment.

"A little. It feels *warm*." His brow furrows, a line carving between them. "And like I can take a deeper breath."

I grin at him, grateful that my magic has done something *good*.

"We should get some rest," Nox says, from behind me, his hand finding mine. "I'll put a shield over us with my magic."

We all make our way to wool blankets that are spread around the fire, Nox and I settling down on one together as his magical signature flares, and then we are encased in a deep purple dome that covers our small camp on all sides. "Can you hold it while you sleep?" I ask, looking over my shoulder at him. My heart sinks when he doesn't answer, so I turn until I'm facing him. "Nox, you can't stay up all night. Why don't we take shifts?"

"No." The word is spoken softly, but it leaves no room for negotiation. When I arch my brow at his curtness, he smirks before leaning in to kiss me. "I'm not going to exploit your magic," he says against my lips.

"It's not exploitation if I'm offering," I counter, leaning away when he tries to kiss me again. I study his face, tracing each perfect angle before returning to his gaze. "Nox, what's wrong?"

He looks to where our hands meet over the blanket. "I think that your magic, Void Magic, is wonderful, that it gives you the ability to heal people. But... Rhea, when more and more people find out what you can do, they are going to want you to do things for them. And if you refuse? They'll feel like you *owe* it to them to do so."

"Why?"

"Because if I've learned anything spying in the Mortal Kingdom and navigating the politics of my own, it's that when men find a source of power, one of two things happen: Either they find a way to twist it to their own advantage, ensuring that it's something they can wield however they want, *or* they fear it and find a way to destroy it."

I pinch my lips together, laying a hand over his chest, thinking of King Dolian and Queen Amari. "I won't let anyone use me ever again," I whisper, proud of the conviction of my own voice. "I promise."

"And I'll kill anyone before they get the chance, but I *also* worry that if there comes a time to say *no*, your heart won't let you."

I huff out a breath as the light from the fire behind me dances over his face. "I was so terrified when I learned I had the magic to kill. That I could wield shadows into something so deadly that it drained another of life. If there is a way for me to *help* people, I don't see why I should keep that to myself." It made me happy to heal those suffering from the Cruel Death, even given my circumstances. If I could still figure out a way to help them...

"I'm not saying that you should," he counters, pulling me closer. "I just want you to remember that there is a hierarchy when it comes to who you keep safe, who you protect. And *you* are at the top of that list. *Always.*"

Our conversation falls quiet after that, Nox encasing me in his warmth as I close my eyes and try to find sleep. But his words dance in my head the entire night, just as much an affirmation as an omen.

Chapter One Hundred and Thirty

BAHIRA

I T HAD BEEN FOUR days since Nox left to rescue Rhea, his magic and strength back after removing the dragon stone shard from beneath his skin, which held the magic of who knows how many councilmen. Even now, staring up at the dark ceiling of my room during another sleepless night, my teeth grind together at the thought. I don't need magic to know that being cut off from it for long periods of time could change someone. Make them go mad. And in a way, Nox *had*. Perhaps the effects were lessened by the tonic that they gave him, but my brother had never behaved like I witnessed, and I can only hope that he's able to bring Rhea back with a clear head, ready to tackle whatever this next phase of restoring our kingdom will look like.

With the council locked in the dungeon for their treachery, Elora and I, with the help of Max, had moved the Mirror back to its original place in the throne room. Since Nox left, I have spent every day using the Mirror to call out to Kai. The magic within it responded to my command, swirling and shifting like thick mist over water. But the shifter king never appeared on the other side. I had gotten pathetically desperate late one evening, debating the merits of calling out to another kingdom to make sure the Mirror *actually* works. The fae king seemed like the safest option, so I called out for him, assuming that it wouldn't work but unsure of what I would do if it did.

I nearly jumped back when he appeared on the other side, his black eyes staring at me with a malice I hadn't known one could harbor for a stranger. I made up a reason for reaching out to him on behalf of my father, something about confirming trade routes. The male didn't speak a single word before abruptly stepping away from his Mirror and ending our conversation. It was better that he did, but I still found myself cursing him under my breath as I ran a hand down my face.

The truth had become undeniable. The Mirror works—which means Kai is ignoring me.

If there is a moment when you decide you'd like to talk with me again, I will make sure someone is always guarding the Mirror.

His words are a hollow echo in my mind now. Perhaps, he's already confirmed that Rhea was taken through other means and has deemed contact with me pointless.

Be my ruin. I huff out a broken laugh.

It has been nearly three months, and it's easy to imagine him moving on with his life, *with someone else.* My mind runs rampant with thoughts of a mystery woman's hands on his body. Tracing the edges of his tattoos. My stomach twists at the imagined scenario, but what makes it worse is picturing her learning what each line and curve and shape mean. Him trusting another as he had trusted me and telling them about his mother. About Jahlee and his childhood and his fears as king. It is selfish to feel as if I have any claim to him anymore, because I know that I don't. Yet my heart still races at the thought of him falling for someone else, and perhaps, that is my penance. After all, what could be worse than finally admitting that I fell in love for the first time, only to follow it with the realization that I will never see him again.

❧❧❧❧❧ ❧❧❧❧❧

"Tell me Kallin's given you *something*," I say as I practically barge into the queen's dining room, my mother and father already sitting. Steam wafts off of the food set at the table's center, an array of seasoned chicken, warm rolls, and grilled vegetables spread out on various platters. "Because if he hasn't, I'm sure some light torture will get him to speak."

"We don't torture people here," my father answers, though amusement lightens his tone.

"Maybe we should." Pulling out a chair, I collapse into it, reaching aggressively for the platter of chicken in front of me and sliding some of the sliced meat onto my own plate. "Give me and my spear ten minutes, and I'm sure we can convince *anyone* to talk." I reach for the vegetables next, then top my plate off with a warm roll. I can feel my parents' stares on me as I roughly pierce the food with my fork, shoving it into my mouth as I angrily chew.

"Is something bothering you, my rose?" my mother asks, drawing my gaze to her.

I chew the food, stabbing another piece of chicken but pausing before bringing it to my mouth. "I ran into Haylee on the way here. Why the *fuck* is she still allowed access to the palace?" Though the chicken is delicious, its flavor is all but lost as I replay our interaction. Dressed in a gown the lightest shade of pink with her hair done in a coronet braid, she looked every bit the blushing bride-to-be as she strolled down the hallway followed by a detail of guards.

"Unfortunately, we need her while your brother is gone and the council is imprisoned."

I scoff as I meet my father's gray eyes over the table. "Why? What could we *possibly* need from *her*?" I'm adult enough to admit that I'm hurt after finding out the woman I considered one of my closest friends since childhood has actually been pretending in order to get to Nox. That it has jaded logical thought surrounding her. But fucking gods above, running into her in my own home is not a mistake I want repeated.

"Kallin was smart in the order that he did things as well as what information he chose to take public," my mother answers, her hand resting on my father's. "And Nox wasn't with the public way he removed the council." She pinches her lips together as she thinks over her next words. "Your brother will return with Rhea and step into his role as king without the council that the people have known. It makes us look like *we're* the ones who were deceitful. Haylee, unfortunately, is a buffer. If she's still parading around the palace..."

"Then it gives credibility that Nox hasn't completely betrayed his people." She nods, and I lean back in my chair. But still, this doesn't sit right with me. "It's only been a handful of months since they started their public perception campaign against us, right? How much damage could possibly be done in that time frame?"

"Enough that we are teetering on a very thin ledge. One made more precarious with the knowledge that Kallin is still controlling some of the guards from his cell. We have an idea of a few who are truly loyal to us, but the majority..." My father blows out a breath, a finger tapping on the table. "Kallin's deception began far earlier than when he found out about Rhea. Earlier than when he made the choice to leave Hadrik and I out of the decision to keep the law regarding a future king's betrothed."

I knit my brows together, my food forgotten in front of me. "What do you mean?"

He takes a small drink from his chalice before continuing. "I've had a lot of time to wonder why a man I thought was on my side might go to such lengths to dethrone me. To tear down one child while elevating another."

"Poor Nox, always getting the short end of the stick," I joke, earning one of his grins.

"Kallin's actions are not that of a man only recently obsessed. And I *think* it has to do with our ancestors' decision after the war."

"The war?" I question.

"When Queen Lucia died putting up the Spell, she did not have a contingency in place for a successor. A Void queen doesn't just have powerful magic, she also has the gift of immortality for as long as she is queen. Until a successor is found through the Flame Ceremony." I nod my head, vaguely remembering reading this.

"Why have a plan of succession when you're all but invincible until the next Void queen comes around," I state, folding my arms over my chest.

"Precisely. So you can only imagine how it rocked the men and women left in charge. Of course, you know a member of the Daxel line was one of her closest advisors, and he was eventually named king, but it wasn't without protest, and the loudest voice came from that of the Keria line."

I let out a groan. *Fucking Kallin.*

"Because a queen of Void Magic could be long-lived between successors, they often took multiple partners through their lifespan, and one of Queen Lucia's was from the Keria line."

"Are you telling me that Kallin—that *Daje*—are part *royalty*?" I ask incredulously.

My mother laughs as she shakes her head. "Not exactly. Though Void queens all descend from a single familial line, it's not like passing the crown down through a born heir. But Kallin's ancestor tried to claim that it was. He knew that if it went to a vote among the council members, he would lose."

"Which is eventually what happened," my father supplies, taking another drink. "All that to say, I don't have proof, but there is a chance that Kallin is acting on some long-term revenge plot."

I scoff, reaching for my own drink. "Gods help us against the wills of men who believe they are owed something they aren't." At that, my parents chuckle, and the mood in the room softens.

"How are you, Bahira?" my mother asks, in a way that tells me she sees more than I want her to. I bristle because of it.

"Well enough." I drag my fork over my plate as I avoid my parents' knowing gazes. "With my discovery of the connection between blood and magic, I might have a new pathway to reversing the loss of magic. I've borrowed some journals from the archives—"

"The archives?" my father cuts in, an eyebrow raised.

Shit. I may have forgotten to let them in on that little adventure.

"Yes, and before you question it, *you* are the one who showed me where they were, and *your* best friend is the one who let me in."

My mother covers her mouth with her hand, but not before I see the smile blooming there. My father rolls his eyes in feigned annoyance, but his own grin gives him away.

"*Anyway*, though they talk of blood and magic separately, there isn't much yet in the way of what exactly happens when you *mix* them. I meant to try it on Nox when I had gathered samples of Cass's blood, but—"

I pinch my lips together and swallow roughly. When I glance up at my parents, I find their eyes glassy and red, Cass as much of a son to them as he was a brother to Nox and me. Clearing my throat, I push back the pressure that builds in my eyes.

"I hope that I can experiment some more, if the state of things will allow, but..." I pause, searching for the words. "It is strange to focus on *this* when there is so much happening externally. I've been trying for so long to uncover why our people's magic is failing—why I've been cursed to live *without* magic—that it feels selfish to keep focusing on it while Nox is trying to rescue Rhea and run a kingdom. While you both try to figure out who on the council is innocent while making sure our people don't revolt." While *I'm* trying to figure out how to move forward knowing a piece of me is still back in the Shifter Kingdom.

"You are a leader, Bahi," my father says, giving a small shrug. "You always have been. Those qualities won't just quiet themselves because other things try to grab your attention."

"But what if I'm wrong? What if I've spent all this time chasing a dead end when I could have been doing something else. Something of value. Something—" Something *worthy* of my status. My position. The privilege I've been given as princess—former princess—of the Mage Kingdom.

"There is no failure in trying something only to have it not work out. The only failure is to never have tried at all. You care for your people, for your family and loved ones. But you cannot expect to be something for them if you are not first honoring *yourself*."

I stare down at my plate as I wonder if I know how to do that anymore. However, I have a feeling there will be many nights spent stuck in my own head wondering just that, so I opt for a topic change as I return to the meal ahead of me. "So, a Void queen has returned. What are the odds that the heir to the throne would be the one she fell in love with?"

Conversation blossoms from there, the topic shifting from Rhea to Nox and his reluctance to take the throne without Rhea at his side to my father's temporary return to said throne. I ask if the power has gone to his head. He answers, saying that it never left. And though there is the persistent hum of chaos surrounding me—the Spell and the Mirror, Nox and the council, Kai—I'm able to temporarily block out the noise as I laugh and eat with my parents.

When dinner is over, we get up and say our goodnights, my father's embrace tightening around me when I try to pull away. "I am proud of you, Bahira. You haven't just been the smartest among us but the bravest. Your instincts haven't guided you wrong yet. Trust them. Trust in yourself."

I don't voice the questions that nag at me in response. Instead, I just wrap my arms around him more tightly and hope that if I never do anything else, I at least keep making my father proud.

Chapter One Hundred and Thirty-One

BAHIRA

MY WORKSHOP IS COLD when I enter it the next morning. I drop my pack and spear and rub at my arms over my thick winter coat as I shiver, looking over the samples that line the nearby wall. My heart sinks when I see the one that holds Cass's blood, but I force myself not to linger on the sadness that rises. It's not what he would want, and in truth, I'd rather honor his memory by working harder to find the answers I'm seeking than allow myself to wallow in his loss.

Moving my magnifier to the center table, I plan out what I'm looking for today. While tests for infusing the blood of one mage with another are on hold until Nox returns, something has been nagging me about the connection of blood and magic and how it all might relate to the Spell. It's a wild hypothesis, but with nothing else to do besides question the council, I figure it's as worthy a use of time as anything else.

Leaves crunch just outside the door to my shop, and I look over my shoulder at the small window set into the wood to find nothing but the pale morning light streaming through the barren branches. But just as I'm about to turn back around, something bright yellow darts past the window, too large to be a bird.

Brows drawn, I walk to the door and peer out to the forest beyond, my hand resting on the handle in front of me. It's early enough that I don't expect to see many people out, but as I stare out at the trees, something ominous presses over my shoulders, like the feeling of being watched, even though I know I'm alone. Blowing out a breath and cursing the fact that I'm exhausted from a shitty night's sleep, I drag a hand down my face as I step back. Except when my eyes open, they aren't staring out at the forest anymore. They meet the emerald gleam of another's. "Fuck!" I startle, jumping backwards as I stare at the woman. Green curls—the same color as the pillow grass in the training grounds—frame her face, her full lips peeled back in a snarl that reveals two sharp canines. I blink, sure I must be seeing incorrectly because mages don't have elongated teeth, but then her gaze drops and the doorknob to my shop turns, and any rational thought gives way to instinct as I race for my spear in the corner of the room.

Cold air rushes in behind me, the hairs on the back of my neck rising as I spin just in time to block her sharpened claws as she swipes at me, instead hitting the spelled wood and metal of my spear. Her chest rises and falls quickly as she studies me, the predatory gleam in her eyes not entirely mortal. Then again, neither is she. Completely nude, the only thing that adorns her dark brown skin is a faint set of shimmering scales the same color as her eyes and hair.

"You are not mage," I say as I grip my spear tightly in both hands, watching how she shifts her weight like she's uncomfortable with the feel of her body. And, *fuck*, she probably is.

"Afraid not," she hisses, and even in that terrifying sound, there is a note of something beautiful. Something lyrical that floats in the air between us, cascading over my skin in a way that reminds me of that moment on Kai's ship. Would that happen again if she were to start singing?

Ignoring the *how* of it all, I ask, "What are you doing here?"

Her fingers curl and flex, those long onyx talons more menacing the longer I stare at them. "We have come for Rhea Maxwell. She was stolen from the Mortal Kingdom, and our queen demands her return."

Shock widens my eyes before I can stop it, the siren's own darkening with hunger as she leans forward. "You know her." I don't respond, letting my training slip to the front of my mind as I watch her. I have fought mages with magic and shifters in both animal *and* mortal forms. Sirens are no different, only wrapped in a more beautiful package. "Tell me where she is, and I will spare your life."

I smirk, one eye on the front door as a shadow passes it. "Afraid I can't do that."

A tongue clicks. "That's unfortunate."

Her arm arcs towards me, claws gleaming, the movement fluid but likely slower than it would have been in the water. I leap back and then swing my leg out, connecting with the side of her knee and making her wobble as her arms lift to balance herself. Darting in front of her, I adjust my hold on my spear so that my hands are shoulder-width apart, and then I slam it into her chest, forcing her back to the shop wall and pinning her raised arms at her sides as she releases a frustrated growl in my face.

"How did you get past the Spell?" I ask. She kicks out, but I avoid it easily, leaning my weight into the spear. "Tell me how you got through the Spell!"

"I'll die before I tell you." She snaps her jaw at me and then opens her mouth, and between one breath and the next, her music fills the air. Panic floods my veins, and I lift and spin my spear, plunging it into her chest until her song devolves into nothing but a gurgle.

Chest heaving, I watch as her dark blue blood drips onto the floor of my workshop before yanking my spear out and prowling to the front door. Peeking just past its edge, I bite down on my tongue to keep my gasp trapped behind my teeth at the sight of *dozens* of sirens running past me on the main footpath. Some are as naked as the one I just killed, while others don what looks like armor and carry silver spears tipped in colored glass.

"What is happening?" I whisper to myself, turning back to look at the dead female slumped on the ground. If they are looking for Rhea, they are likely going towards the palace. My stomach hollows at the thought—my parents are there. I take a step in that direction like I alone can protect them. But in truth, they have magic. They have more than enough guards, and though it's been *centuries* since other beings have walked in the Mage Kingdom, they have the means to protect themselves. But there are so many things between here and the palace. The orphanage and library. The training grounds. *Fuck.* Indecision cements my feet to the ground as I watch more and more sirens flood the forest. I can't be in three places at once, but— Drawing in a deep breath, I map a route to the beach that's off the beaten path. That has to be where they are coming from, right? I can't be everywhere, but I can try to cut them off at the source and weaken them enough that those between the beach and the palace won't be overwhelmed.

Decision made, I steel my spine as I step out into the sunlight, bolting to the left, directly into the path of a siren with bright orange hair, the ends dancing along her hips. She looks at me, dismisses me, then does a double take when she notices my weapon. Her top lip peels back in a snarl, showing off those unnatural canines. We run towards each other, her arms pumping at her sides with those sharp claws poised to attack. My steps ring loudly in my ears over the crunching dead leaves on the forest floor. Cold air fills my lungs with every inhale, shocking me with its temperature and keeping me alert. She's close enough to see those glimmering scales inset on her skin, the muscles of her bare biceps bulging with how tightly her fingers are flexed. I time each step—*one, two, three*—and drop to my knees, sliding over the fallen leaves and cold ground as I duck under her attempt to swipe at me, then swing my spear out and slam it into the backs of her legs.

Hopping up, I turn just as her knees hit the ground. Using the capped end of my spear, I hit the back of her head hard and watch as she collapses to the ground. I hesitate to kill her—just for a moment—before the thought of her attacking my mother or Starla crosses my mind, and I sink the tip of my spear into her chest. I don't spare her another glance before I pivot and run into the thicker part of the forest, navigating the closely packed trees with a familiarity born from having lived here my entire life. Keeping my steps as light as possible while I run, I search for bright colors that stand out against the dormant winter landscape. They don't expect anyone to be hunting *them*, and I capitalize on that surprise as I use my spear to trip them up and send the leaf-tipped end into their chests. Or, in the cases of those in armor, into the soft spot of their necks.

Yet for every siren felled by me, there is a handful of dead men I find as I make my way closer to the beach. Most have claw marks to their upper bodies and necks, the sign of them fighting back set in the fists curled at their sides even as their skin turns blue. Others bare no mark besides a single stab wound, crimson blood pooling on the forest floor beneath them.

Those cause the most fury to rise within me because they aren't just attacking guards who are protecting their kingdom. They are attacking the vulnerable. The men whose only crimes were being genetically predispositioned to be lured by a siren's song. Which still doesn't answer how the *fuck* I was able to be put under their spell, but it seems that whatever kind of siren had called to me on Kai's ship was not one I had run into yet.

I might have pictured a siren attack to be louder, the normally tail-clad beauties using their song to lure men to their deaths far before they would ever use their mortal forms. But this—an ambush through the Spell on an otherwise unassuming morning—leaves me reeling, and as the sound of the crashing ocean waves begin to trickle towards me, I wonder if there is more to their presence than *just* getting Rhea back. Which, at the very least, means Nox was successful in rescuing her.

The crunch of footsteps draws my attention to the left, and I quickly press my back against one of the thick tree trunks as I wait for the owner to draw closer.

"They should be at the palace by now if the queen's memory of its location is correct."

"It is. She's had over two hundred years to ruminate on the events of the war; I'm sure she's mapped out every detail," another siren answers, and I steady my breath as I grip my spear more tightly.

"Bet she didn't plan on the fucking *shifters*—"

My heart stops. My breathing stops. The entire word stilling around that single word: *shifters*. The movements are automatic, my mind elsewhere as I step out from behind the tree and right into the path of two sirens, swinging my spear into them both. The one on the left, her hair a brilliant teal, takes the brunt of the hit, her body flinging backwards towards the ground. The pale pink eyes of her companion widen as the sharp silver tip cuts into her stomach when I drag my spear down diagonally. She casts her gaze to the blood pooling on her skin, an animalistic snarl rising from her throat before she launches herself at me, hands thrashing and teeth bared. With my spear parallel to the ground, I block her attacks, her claws scraping against the wood and metal, while I keep my feet moving and circle around her until both sirens are near each other.

The teal-haired one rises on shaky legs, opening her mouth to sing. I can feel her magic slide along my skin, but it doesn't pull me under its thrall. It does, however, motivate me to end them before they can draw more attention to us. Spinning around, I kick back into the stomach of the pink-haired siren, her huff of breath clouding in front of her before I twist and jab my spear forward. She pivots, but not quickly enough, and the serrated metal dives into the flesh between her ribs, her scream loud enough to make my ears ring. I push my spear in deeper, her eyes flaring before I see the light leave them, then tug my weapon back. I run towards the remaining siren before her friend collapses to the ground and slide on one leg as I thrust my spear towards her. It catches her in the space beneath her arm where it meets her shoulder, blue blood spraying me as I pass.

Growling, she moves quickly despite her injury, and before I can fully turn around, she's on top of me. Dropping my spear, I send an elbow back into her chest, her wheeze tickling my ear before I spin on my knee and send my fist into her temple. She crumples to the ground, dazed but awake.

"What did you mean by the shifters?" I ask as I climb on top of her, my knee driving into her sternum as my hands close around her throat. Her eyes widen as she blinks, nothing but venom shining in their hazy blue-green depths. "Tell me!"

She laughs, dark blue trickling from the corners of her mouth. "You can rot in Tula's pit!"

I don't understand the reference but squeeze her neck more tightly anyway, leaning in close enough for her panting breaths to hit my face. "*Where* are the shifters?"

Her fingers close around my wrists, talons pricking my skin. I dig my knee in harder, and she screams, her neck arching with the pain. "There is a *ship*," she says finally, her body growing fatigued beneath mine. I catch a glimpse of the blue blood now gathered in a pool beneath her. "You'll die today. Either by the claws of my sisters or those of the *beasts*."

Growling, I release her and stand, swiping my spear from the ground as I brush my curls away from my face. I stiffen when the wind carries with it a resonant melody that sends a shiver down my spine. The logical part of me knows that I should go back to the palace—that I should ensure my family is safe. But there is a part of me guided by my heart, and *that* idiot pushes me towards the beach.

Like the fool that I am, I listen, leaving behind a wheezing siren to die.

Chapter One Hundred and Thirty-Two

BAHIRA

WITHIN A HANDFUL OF minutes, I traverse the thickest parts of the forest and reach a more sparse area. And even if I hadn't spotted the shifter ship floating just off the coast, I would have seen the animals as they fight the sirens still emerging from the water. The scent of blood mixes with the salty air blowing in from the sea, and as I carefully make my way closer, running from tree to tree, I look for a familiar large wolf, his fur a rich dark brown with matching eyes ringed in gold. I hadn't even seen him more than twice in his wolf form, and there's a chance he could be a different animal, the result of whatever his father had done to his mother while she was pregnant with him giving him the unique ability.

Bodies litter the sand, a mix between the obvious sirens and shifters killed in their animal forms and mortal bodies indistinguishable between shifter or mage. I spot a gorilla, perhaps the same one whose toes I had stepped on my first day on the ship, holding a siren by her ankle before brutally flinging her to the ground and sending sand flying. Pausing behind a tree to catch my breath, I watch through the iridescence of the Spell as predators not already engaged in a fight prowl the shoreline, running after the sirens who exit as they bolt towards the forest.

A siren with light purple hair stands from the water, her thin braids giving way to loose curls as she makes her way forward. Wearing armor and holding a silver spear, her muscles flex as she fights against the lapping waves, her eyes set on the black bear that paces the beach in front of her. It lets out a warning growl, the rumble skating over my skin and waking up that instinct within me that tells me

I should run. Instead, I move a little closer, my palm scraping against bark while my heart beats loudly in my ears. The siren lowers her upper body as she holds her spear out, staying just within the water so that it washes up to her ankles. Hissing at the bear, she dares it to come closer, laughing when it lets out frustrated rumbles.

"Pathetic creature!" she shouts, taking a step forward while flashing white teeth. "You think you can kill *me*? Have you any idea the beasts that I've fought? Ones much larger than *you*!" The bear lowers, paws digging into the sand as its muscles flex beneath black fur. I work a swallow down, sweat beading over my spine despite the cold temperature, and wait for them to collide. I'm so enthralled by the interaction, by the loud rhythm of my quickly beating heart, that I don't notice a presence behind me until it's too late.

A twig breaks, and then I'm shoved forward, my feet tangling in the underbrush as I stumble and crash into the ground. The first kick blurs my vision as pain bursts to life in my side, but I force myself to roll, avoiding a second hit. Leaping to my feet, I immediately throw my spear up to block the swing of the siren's own weapon. She hisses at me, red eyes feral and canines gleaming as she keeps her movements quick, already withdrawing to come at me again.

Backing up, I angle the sharp tip of my spear in her direction. But she keeps her attacks quick, darting forward to jab at my chest and hips, my training forcing me to counter her moves *just* fast enough to avoid getting cut. My breaths turn labored as we move in circles on the main pathway to the palace, but the siren with short red hair keeps coming at me, her movements so fluid and graceful that I can only imagine just how much of a terror she must be beneath the surface. Still, I hold my own against her, every bit her equal as we battle back and forth to be the one to gain the upper hand. I feint left, drawing her guard before I snap my spear to the right and drag the jagged edge across the outside of her arm. She doesn't scream, barely making a noise to acknowledge the hit at all, and wastes no time countering my attack. She raises her spear and brings it down in a sweeping arc, rivulets of blood pouring from the cut on her arm. The reverberation when her spear collides with mine is strong enough to make me falter, but I recover quickly and push away from her, creating space for me to swing my own weapon.

Air stirs as I slice my spear through it, aiming for her ribs only to be blocked, metal on metal ringing out. But it isn't the red-haired siren who stops me, it's the purple-haired one I spotted earlier. I glance at the blood that coats her dark skin, then shoot a look to the beach, lips parting on a breath at the dead bear lying in the sand.

"Why, aren't you a pretty one?" Purple eyes as dark as Nox's magic meet mine, and the siren licks her lips as if she is tasting the blood of her bested opponent. *Fuck*, she probably is. "Do you know where Princess Rhea is?"

"No, but I know where you're going to die."

She smiles wide, the presence of it almost grotesque before she slides her spear down the body of my own, snapping it to the left and just barely grazing my front with its sharpened edge. A dull pain blooms over my chest, but I force myself to stay at the ready. No other words are spoken as the two sirens attack me at once, jabbing their weapons forward and then alternating their swings. I grunt with each hit my spear takes, my muscles fatigued already from how many I've fought before them. Dancing in circles, I keep us moving, but the sirens are freshly entering this fight, and I'm tired and slower than I was. The red-haired siren leaps forward, her spear nothing but a flash of silver that meets mine with a harsh *clang*. I kick out at the glint of purple that moves to my side, but she's quick to skit past my attempt as she moves behind me. *Fuck*. I shout as I push the first siren back, turning around to just barely block the downward swing of the purple one's spear.

She smiles just before she rotates her weapon too quickly and sends it cracking into my jaw. I bite my tongue from the impact as tears flood my eyes. My leg buckles beneath the weight of her next kick, dropping me to my knees. Holding my spear above my head, warmth tingles over my palms as my shoulders dip from their next power-laden blows. I spin on my knees to keep both sirens in view, working to stand, only for a burning sensation to light up my leg when a third siren shreds into my flesh.

I howl as I fight to push myself up. Dark blue eyes gleam in delight from my newest opponent, and all I can do is try to turn away from the next swipe of her claws. But they connect with my side this time as hands grip my shoulders and force my back to the ground. I raise my spear in time to stop the next swing of a weapon, but the sound they make when they collide is deafening, like lightning cracking the sky overhead. Except, as air is forced from my lungs and skin slices open on my chest, I realize it wasn't lightning at all.

My spear *broke*.

Time slows as I struggle against the blue-haired siren that keeps me pinned to the ground, the other two standing over me with their spears raised, preparing to impale me. I try to kick at their legs, but they dodge me easily, each planting a foot on one of my ankles as the siren who grips my shoulders sends her talons into the skin. I scream as they pierce muscle, my vision blurring with flares of white while my labored breaths burn in my chest. Tears leak from my eyes as I continue to struggle, a sinking realization wrapping tightly around my throat that I very well might *die* here at their hands.

When I look up at them through tear-stained eyes, there is no kindness or pity. Instead, a wild and raging glee glares down at me, all three of them smiling in utter delight at my demise. They raise their spears higher, my shoulders burning as the claws there dig deeper and I attempt to cross the two halves of my spear over my chest. A roar, mightier than I've ever heard, shakes the ground, startling us all, and I watch as sword impales the siren with red hair, splattering her blood over my face and body. The glinting metal retreats, and she collapses, dark blue pumping from the hole in her chest as her spear hits the ground next to her. The purple-haired siren stares down at her dead friend in shock, her eyes wide, and she doesn't have time to react to the small blade that appears in front of her neck, slicing across the delicate skin in a matter of seconds. Blood sprays from the wound, and I'm forced to shut my eyes as it rains down on me.

Still clutching the two halves of my spear, I scream at the pain that scorches my shoulders, but then the siren behind me disappears, and the unmistakable sound of blood gurgling forces me to roll quickly to my side in the hopes that I will avoid the same fate as these sirens. My ears ring as a shadow falls over me, and I scramble to my feet, arm already swinging towards this new opponent when I turn around and stop.

I simply *stop* at the sight of the male before me.

He holds a hand to his chest, the other gripping his blood-coated dagger so tightly his knuckles are white. But his eyes... They hold mine, and though pain pinches the harsh features of his face, his gaze only softens the longer he stares at me. I think I say his name, the word caught between a plea and a cry, but then he's collapsing, blade falling from his hand to join the sword on the ground as he bellows out in pain.

"Kai!" I cry out, taking a step before I fall to my knees, my injuries forcing me to crawl towards him. But beyond the pain, icy terror fills my veins as I watch Kai writhe on the ground. As I reconcile where he is in regards to the beach. "You *idiot*, you crossed the Spell!" I frame his face with my hands when I reach his side, his gold-ringed eyes flicking to mine in agony.

"Hello, Princess," he grunts out between jagged breaths, a grimace contracting every muscle of his face.

"Why did you do that? *Why*?" I shout, holding him close as I lean over him. He crossed the Spell. And he's *dying*.

Trembling fingers reach up to my face before touching the curls dampened with blood hanging by my cheek. Tears line his eyes, and for all the pain I know he must be feeling, for the way his body is tense with it, he just stares at me. Like he can't believe *I'm* the one that's here. That *I'm* real.

"Kai," I whisper, wetness tracking down my cheeks and past my chin, a horrified scream bubbling up my throat. *He crossed the Spell.*

"I've missed you," he says through gritted teeth, his eyes growing wide enough to see the whites surrounding them before they abruptly fall closed. Then, Kai Vaea, king of the shifters and the only male I have ever loved, falls limp in my arms.

Chapter One Hundred and Thirty-Three

RHEA

"I T FEELS *WRONG* BEING on this side of the Spell," Xander says from where he rides next to Nox and I the next day, Daje flanking our other side.

"Speak for yourself. This is *home*," Daje responds, looking more lively now than the entire rest of the trip. When we woke this morning, Nox had lowered his shield before leaving to wash up. I took the opportunity to talk with Daje. To apologize for how he had been attacked because people were trying to get to me. But though he insisted the apology wasn't necessary, he dodged most of my other questions, giving answers that felt like half-truths. When Nox returned, the two shared a quick glance that made nerves stir in my chest.

I knew that look; it was one that spoke of secrets kept. I wasn't naive enough to believe Nox had told me *everything* that had happened while I was taken, but I hated feeling like something was being withheld from me that was important enough to concern Daje. But I wouldn't push for answers right now, not when our priority was to get home first. So I brush my teeth and freshen up as best as I can, and then we all mount our horses and continue on the final stretch of our journey.

I watch as Xander takes in the closely knit trees and the way the canopies obscure the light from the sun above, and I wonder if he wishes he was seeing the Mage Kingdom for the first time under different circumstances. My fingers trail along Nox's arm from where it is wrapped around my front, and the movement catches Xander's gaze, his eyes lifting to meet mine with a quirk of his brow. "What?"

I shrug, trying to be nonchalant. "You'll have to get used to crossing through the Spell, you know."

Like he can sense the bait, Xander narrows his eyes at me, even as he asks, "Why?"

"How else will you visit Siyala?" At the mention of the fox shifter who had shared the tower with me for four years, Nox flexes his hand over my stomach. I had been restless last night, unable to sleep knowing Nox was lying awake to hold the shield that protected us, my mind too full of things that were better suited to speak about daylight. All except for one. The knowledge that Siyala was alive unburied itself, and in my desperate attempt to keep those darker memories at bay, I told Nox. I expected the same shock that flitted through me to roll over his handsome face, but instead, he just smiled and leaned in to kiss my temple before telling me that he learned that Siyala and Bahira had met in the Shifter Kingdom.

"I don't know what you mean," Xander says, though a sweet shade of pink stains his cheeks. He clears his throat. "How much longer?"

"Galdr should only be another mile or two away," Nox answers, kissing the shell of my ear. I bite down on my lip as I smile. "We'll drop the horses off the stables and go to the palace on foot since I'm unsure of what we will encounter when we get there." His words sober the moment quickly. With the council imprisoned, there is every reason to believe that our reception might be fraught with bitter tension.

"You know how to ruin a mood, I'll give you that, Daxel," Xander jokes, earning a snort from Daje. "Sorry, should I say *Your Majesty*?"

"I don't care what you call me," he drawls, causing Xander's expression to harden.

Small homes begin to trickle into view, some freestanding and others built into the trees. Again, I'm eager to watch Xander take it all in, and again, I'm caught staring at him, prompting him to frown.

"Do you guys hear that?" Daje asks, drawing my gaze to his furrowed brow as his eyes narrow down the road ahead of us, dappled sunlight creeping in through the trees.

I lean forward slightly, trying to listen past the sound of the horses' hooves against the dirt and leaves. My hair stirs with the gentle wind that brushes against me, carrying within it the sound of... *music*. No, not just music but— "It sounds like singing." A festival perhaps? Or celebration of some kind? I turn to ask Nox, only to find him rigid against my back. "Nox?" His gaze stays fixed forward as his hand leaves my hip to reach for the reins. He kicks our horse's side, and I lurch backwards as we launch into a gallop, Daje and Xander's horses following suit on either side of us. "Nox!" Reaching over my shoulder, I grasp the side of his face and force his eyes to fall to mine. But they are glazed over, nothing warm or familiar within them. I look from Xander to Daje, calling out both of their names.

But they keep their attention forward, the grip on their reins tight enough that their knuckles flare white, as if they are unable to let go. To stop. As if...

Oh gods.

This is siren magic.

I call my own power up quickly, circling it around the four of us. I don't know if my magic can even *block* sound, and that doubt makes the glittering white surrounding us flicker in and out, disrupting my concentration. "Damn it!" I shout, throwing a leg over the horse as I twist in the saddle, struggling to keep my balance. "Nox, look at me!" My voice slices through the air with razor-edged terror, but it doesn't clear Nox's gaze. He's pulled completely under their song. Looking back out to the road, I watch as the homes grow closer together and the trees begin to thin out. If the sirens are here, they must be looking for me. King Dolian and Queen Amari *must* have sent them knowing that no one would ever expect sirens to infiltrate the kingdom. But I have to do *something* before we pass those trees because there have already been too many deaths in my name, and I *refuse* to let them take Daje or Xander. Or Nox, *again*.

One hand gripping the pommel of the saddle, I stretch the other out towards the road as I call for my magic to build a wall dozens of feet ahead of us. The pull of my power is easy, and it flows from my hand in every direction, growing that wall wider and taller and thicker. My vision flashes white as my heart beats loudly in my ears, and I keep my intent on using my magic to drown out the sirens. The seconds pass slowly, but when the hooves of the horses sprinting grow louder than their song, I know that the magic is working. Holding the wall in place with my mind, I turn and look at Nox again, my hand reaching out to cup his cheek.

"Nox," I say again, my thumb brushing over the high part of his cheek. "Come back to me."

And he does. The silver flecks in his eyes grow bright as he blinks that magical film away, and he looks at me with recognition that relaxes my shoulders fully. I whimper in relief, looking to Xander and Daje and finding them in the same state.

"What the fuck was that?" Nox asks, cursing again when he takes in the speed that our horse is still running at. He tugs at the reins to slow us down, Xander and Daje following suit.

Xander shakes his head, his hand palming the dagger strapped to his thigh as his eyes find mine. "Sirens?" he asks, and I nod, dread heavy in my stomach. *It's because of me.*

"So *that's* what it feels like to hear a siren sing," Daje says sluggishly, rubbing a hand over his head. "I don't recommend it."

"Rhea, you can drop your magic," Nox says, his lips brushing my temple.

"No, their song—"

He points to his ears and the dark purple magic that now covers it. I glance at Xander, and though he frowns as if he'd rather *not* have Nox's magic touching him, I'm grateful that it covers his as well. A quick look at Daje shows his own yellow magic glowing.

I sigh in relief and reach for those threads that tether me to my magic, snipping them in one swoop as Nox once instructed.

"It's okay," Nox says, keeping his voice soft. I melt against him, my shoulder digging into his chest as I cling to him. But with the wall gone, *I* can hear the cacophony of noises that we approach, and any reprieve I had is short-lived as the road begins to curve towards the city center. My magic perks up again within me, alert to our surroundings as it floods the space between my bones, at the ready should I need it.

Movement draws my attention to the right, to a small clearing just beyond the road's edge. It's the only warning we get before the glint of metal flying through the air lodges a breath in my throat. White magic pours from me, my attempt to create a shield thwarted when gravity shifts and our horse goes down, crying out as he falls. Nox's arm wraps more tightly around me, shadows rushing in to cushion our fall just in time. Daje and Xander wrestle to control their own spooked animals, but when their horses continue to buck, they bail, letting the scared animals bolt into the forest.

When the shadows fade, my heart leaps at the sight of the three sirens in front of us and the ten guards standing in front of them. The sirens' mouths hang open in song as they walk slowly towards us, the guards under their control prowling ahead with their swords extended. Nox helps me stand, his magic still cupped around his ears as the shadows he is wielding twist and wind around our feet.

"I don't want to kill you," he shouts, his hand squeezing tightly around mine. "But I will if you come closer."

One of the sirens stops singing, her head tilting and rustling the short light blue curls that touch her shoulders. She wears the armor of the legion, though the other two sirens do not, and she carries a spear made of silver, but its unstained tip tells me she hasn't had to use it yet. "We do not want *you*; we want *her*." She points to me, and Nox growls low in his throat. "Come with us, Rhea Maxwell, and we will withdraw from this city before more blood is shed. After all," she smirks wide enough to show a single elongated canine, "you cannot protect them all." They all move closer as a unit, and Nox stands his ground, though he takes a half step in front of me. I struggle to form words, my fingers curling in towards my palms as that cold and bitter half of my magic floods my veins, begging to be used. And my indecision costs me.

One of the guards shifts, his sword lifting as if he's readying to attack, and that's all it takes for Nox to act, despite the protest that leaves my lips. His shadows are quick, as they were when we were ambushed by the King's Guardsmen. He forms them into onyx spears, and they rise as one and pierce through every guard's chest, as if the leather armor they wear is inconsequential. As if their very *lives* are. One siren with pink hair shrieks, the fear in her eyes matching my own before she turns and runs, but Nox spares no one. Within seconds, no siren remains singing and no guard remains standing. My heart beats harshly as I look over where they lay, crimson and dark blue blood seeping from their lifeless bodies.

"Rhea?" There's a different softness to Nox's tone, one that might be pleading as he steps in front of me, the shadows behind him dissipating. I signal that it isn't okay for him to drop the shield around his ears yet, but he gently tilts my chin up, his eyes scanning my face and seeing the shock there. The fear. The *guilt.* "Your life above all else." He repeats his words from last night as if he can hear my thoughts. "Always."

I nod, knowing that he is right yet wondering if taking a life will ever get easier. If I even *want* it to. Despite everything that's happened. Despite what I had once vowed to myself in the mortal castle. My humanity seems like a weakness I just can't properly shake.

It feels wrong to leave the bodies out in the open, but Nox insists that we hurry to Galdr, the terror permeating from all of us at what we might find propelling us faster as we round that final bend past the thickly spaced trees to where businesses line the forest clearing. Running between two of the free-standing structures, we finally meet the open air of the square, but what greets us isn't something we could have prepared for.

I gasp as we skid to a halt, right in front of a man lying lifeless, the skin split at his neck and rivulets of red leaking onto the ground. I stumble backwards at the sight, my eyes moving away from the gore on instinct only to be met with something worse. Bodies, *so* many bodies, litter the ground of the once bustling space. Some are siren—the colorful hair an easy giveaway—but most are mage, a lot of them without armor. Rubble from toppled fountains and statues at the center of the square is dispersed between heaps of armor-clad men, and I scan their faces, unable to look away even as Nox tugs me closer to him. The sirens' song is loud but not enough to drown out the grunts of the few remaining guards fighting against them. But the bodies... *Gods*, some of the men look young. Barely teenagers. And it isn't just men. Women also lay slain with gouges in their sides and chests, no doubt their only crime being in the wrong place at the wrong time.

"It's a massacre," Daje says hoarsely, even though I'm the only one who can hear him. "It's— *Gods.*"

I watch as, in the distance, a mage guard blocks the swiping claws of a yellow-haired siren, only to have a second female swoop in and impale him with her spear from behind. My scream echoes out, my hand covering my mouth as jewel-toned eyes flick in our direction, magic flaring within me in response.

"Fucking stars above," Xander says, his own sword held in his hand as he readies his stance. Nox lets go of me to take a step forward as a handful of the dozen or so sirens still attacking pivot in our direction from across the square. My stomach knots as he stretches his hand out, drawing shadows from the ground and shaping them into weapons. The sound of bare feet hitting the ground as the sirens run matches the discordant beating of my heart, but my gaze is stuck on Nox. On how he's prepared to take on the weight of killing the sirens, even though it isn't *his* fault they are here. I can't allow him to do that alone. Even though my stomach sours at the thought, even if I have to *force* myself to step up to his side and lift my own hand, my glittering black shadows born not from the things around us but from somewhere within me, gathering in my palm.

After all, it was *my* magic that had given them access to this place. It only makes sense that it's mine that takes it away.

I feel Nox's gaze on the side of my face, as if we have the time to talk about this. But we don't, not as I watch the magic flicker around the ears of the mage guards still fighting for their lives. Yet Nox knows me so terribly well, and my heart breaks when he quietly says, "You don't have to do this."

I shake my head just as he laces his fingers with mine, and though I know he can't hear me, I say for myself, "Yes, I do."

Our magic surges at the same time, shadows reaching out in either direction. I focus on that tether to my power, my intention guiding it around the mage guards and over the scattered dead, until it reaches the first siren. I shiver at the scream she lets loose, but she's nothing more than a pile of black ash when the sound finishes echoing out.

"What the—" Daje cuts off his own shock from where he stands behind me, but I know he's reacting to what I've just done.

Like storm clouds rolling in, my magic travels the length of the plaza, Nox's shadows more tangible beside mine where he uses them to kill the sirens just as quickly as I do, a horrific combination of falling bodies and black ash left in our wake. I squeeze Nox's hand hard as fear ratchets up my spine. Unlike when I killed the mortal guards on the beach, I am choosing to use my magic in this way. *Choosing* to end lives for the sake of saving others, but even that rationale feels flimsy in my head.

Though it can only be a matter of minutes at most, it feels longer as our shadows work until no siren is left standing. Nox is the first to release his magic, turning to face me as the dark purple surrounding his ears fades. Scanning my expression, he takes in the cold sweat coating my skin and brings a hand up to cup my face. "I love you," he says, low and just for me, thumb brushing over my cheek. "*Every* piece of you."

"I love *you*." My voice breaks, but I hold back the pressure building behind my eyes. Now is not the time, not as decimation surrounds us. Daje and Xander remain near us, but both seem to be frozen in place.

"Your Majesty," a man says from where he stands in front of a tavern, next to a half broken statue. *Your Majesty*. I had nearly forgotten that Nox is now *king*. Leaning his hands on his knees, he looks up from where his head was hanging between his shoulders. "Thank you."

"When did the attack start?" Nox asks. "And how far into the kingdom have they gotten?"

I look around at the shops and businesses on either side of us as the guard answers, taking in the broken windows and doors and the people who wait just beyond them. Women hold children in their arms or stand in front of them protectively, their wide eyes darting from me to Nox and back again, their mouths parted in wild shock. I pull my gaze away to hear Nox's next words.

"Those of you that remain, search for survivors." The guard nods, running a hand through his dark brown hair before shouting the orders to the *six* other men that are spread out amongst the bodies.

"They had no warning," I surmise, once more devastated by the sheer loss of life.

"How could they? By the time they realized what was happening, they would have been under the sirens' song." Nox flexes his jaw. "It's an effective way to kill." And they had been so *very* effective. "Daje, I need you and Xander to go to the palace. If the sirens' mission was to find Rhea, I can't imagine they wouldn't go there."

"What about you two?" Xander asks, his voice rough. "We aren't going to lea—"

"Your Majesty!" To our left, closer to the center of the square, a guard calls for Nox as he kneels next to a body, clutching his arm to his chest. We sprint at the urgency in his voice, at the way horror twists his expression.

As we approach, my gaze falls to the body he kneels beside. Blood pools around the figure, black tunic shredded and revealing the ribboned tan skin beneath. But when my eyes shift higher, when I take in the familiar wavy onyx hair that sticks to the man's temples, when I see the silhouette of his face, devastation pries my ribs apart and latches on to my somehow still beating heart.

One step ahead of me, Nox comes to an abrupt halt, his intake of air sharp as his body grows rigid.

My hand reaches for his back just as a steady *thumping* fills my ears. I think it might be my heart, the truth of who lies dead before us making it beat in a broken rhythm, but then the sound grows louder—*harsher*—and reverberates through more than just my chest as a massive shadow not made of magic cloaks the ground. My head tips back just as the sky is eclipsed by pure black, heat barreling over us as a gust of air knocks me back a step. Nox pulls me to him as we duck, the sun abruptly shining over us again as the creature's wings clip the front facades of the businesses surrounding us, sending chunks of wood and shattered glass flying. The ground rumbles as it crashes abruptly into the ground, feet tipped in claws digging in to slow its speed as it slides to a stop, right on top of the destruction left by the sirens.

"Dragon," I whisper, my stomach leaping as I clutch Nox's tunic tightly. The beast snaps its head in our direction, iridescent black scales shining over its body.

Yellow snake-like eyes glare at us, the scent of sulfur strong as heat wafts from a mouth large enough to bite clear through one of the massive trees surrounding the square. My magic flares, Nox's signature thick in the air as shadows are pulled in our direction, but I lay my hand flat over his chest in silent protest not to attack. Not yet. The dragon lowers its body to the ground, keeping its head hovering a few feet higher and its gaze narrowed directly on us.

I think Daje curses at our side, and quickened steps sound as the guards run towards the forest for cover.

But movement on top of the dragon keeps me rooted in place, as I watch a figure dressed in black and holding something wrapped in a cloak stand and sway before stumbling to the dragon's shoulder. *Gods above*, this isn't a wild dragon but a bonded one. Though my research on the creatures was limited, I've read enough to know that dragons only let those they've bonded with ride them.

"What is that?" Xander asks, the dragon growling and showing off teeth half my length as if in response to his question. I swallow as I watch the figure slide down the dragon's extended leg, hitting the ground hard and falling to their knees.

"Nox," I breathe in awe, attempting to take a step forward only for him to pull me back. The dragon rider lays what they are holding carefully onto the ground, the fabric slipping to reveal a glimpse of dark brown skin and ruby-red hair. My breath catches in my throat, heart clenching, as the dark figure lifts a shaking hand to the hood of their cloak and pushes it back.

Eyes as dark as night look out at us, hair tangled around her slightly pointed ears. *She's fae.* "Bring her—" The distinctly female voice breaks before she inhales deeply, her upper body beginning to bow over the person at her knees.

The dragon behind her growls deep in its throat as it moves its head closer.

"Bring her to Rhea Maxwell," she grits out before collapsing.

Epilogue

You will get me *that kingdom, one way or another. Even if it costs you your life in order to do it.*

My mother's words haunt me, her dark gaze reflected in my own as I stare at myself in the standing mirror. *Well, Mother, you were right in one regard. Life was lost. It just wasn't mine.* Neither of us could have predicted just what would transpire to bring sirens back into the Mortal Kingdom.

I run my hands down the teal fabric of the dress the servants helped me into, the clothing restrictive in a way that makes my talons threaten to show. The urge to shred the dress is only beaten into submission by the promise that this small inconvenience is the price in order to receive something *grander*. Still, the idea that wearing a dress makes me more *palatable* to the mortals, as their foolish king suggested, draws a deep scowl. It is as if they believe clothing will cloak their true nature. As if it will somehow *disguise* my own. But let them hide behind their chaste ideas of modesty and order. Let them look upon me and fool themselves into seeing a being more female than monster.

After all, the trick isn't to disappear. It's to hide in plain sight.

I turn before the knocks on the door arrive, startling the woman who stands on the other side when I abruptly pull it open. "Lady—"

"Ah, ah," I tut, grabbing her delicate, pale chin in my fingers, letting just enough of my talons out that they indent her skin. "I am not a lady. I am *not* one of *you*. I am a *queen*."

"Y-yes, Your Majesty. My apologies." Her light brown eyes gleam with fear, the air practically tainted with it. I breathe in deeply as I release her face, my tongue running over the tips of my canines. "King Dolian says he is ready for you. The guards here will escort you to him."

"And my daughters?"

The servant swallows, running nervous hands over the white apron of her uniform. "Being given a tour of the castle. Shall I fetch them for you?"

Stepping past her and into the hall, I make note of the two men in golden armor. Both smart enough to keep their hands away from their weapons. The trick with training pets is making sure the rules are established ahead of time. They saw what my power looked like on that beach. How *easy* it was for me to get their comrades to bend to a will not their own. I do not *need* them to willingly fear me, but it certainly makes things easier if they do.

"No," I answer the servant as we begin our walk to where the mortal king waits for me. "Leave them to explore their new home."

The sun is shining down on the king when I join him on a shiny white stone balcony. He draws his shoulders back at the sound of my footsteps, as if pretending he can handle the weight of the gold crown upon his head might make me respect him more. Might make him seem *valuable* in our little endeavor together. But I see the way his knuckles turn white as they grip the banister, the gold coral ring on his finger glinting.

I think of the other who wears a matching ring, and a smile nudges the corners of my mouth.

"Are your accommodations to your liking, Queen Amari?"

"Don't bore me with pleasantries. It is beneath us both."

He huffs out a breath but nods. "Have you figured out which of your sirens released Rhea from the ring?"

"I have my suspicions, but as I told you earlier, our charge's absence will be short. The attack on the Mage Kingdom is well under way."

"And if they are able to fight your sirens off?" he asks, finally turning his gaze to meet mine.

Annoyance filters through my veins, my eyes narrowing as my magic pools at the base of my throat.

"Worried the mage prince—I'm sorry, *king*—will touch what you think is yours? *Again?*" I taunt, grinning when his lip lifts in a snarl. "How long until he's fucking her? *Tasting* her in all the ways you wanted to."

Heat flares at his cheeks. "How dare y—"

"No," I interrupt, taking a step towards him as I let my magic flow off my tongue. "You will not argue with me, Mortal King." I watch as the magic of the ring makes him stiffen, the defiance in his hazel eyes slowly fizzling out. I hum low, dragging my claws down his arm. "You share the same eyes as your brother."

His jaw clenches, making a muscle that runs down his neck flutter. "Does it ever bother you? Looking at your daughter and knowing that her birth was the result of his death?"

"I do not mourn those whose purpose is greater in death than it was in life," I answer. Aria flashes in my mind, unease creeping over me before I remember that she's dead. I turn my attention back to the field ahead of us and the army that trains on it. *My* army.

"What is the plan now?" he asks.

I breathe in deeply as a bitterly cold wind stirs my hair, sending the curls off to one side. "We await word from the sirens in the Mage Kingdom."

The king remains silent for a long while until he finally scrapes up enough bravery to ask the question that I know lingers on his tongue. "And if they fail? If Rhea isn't returned to me?"

I lift my chin, looking out over the innumerable rows of mortal men now able to pass through the Spell. "Then we go to war."

❧❧❧❧❧ ❧❧❧❧❧

In a space between worlds...

Millennia have passed, and what was once a place I held deep fondness for has now become a prison. I had saved a dying planet, only to become tethered to its people for eternity. How ironic, to have once been the god of Time and Void only to be held frozen in both.

I had warned my daughter that, eventually, immortal beings would grow bored. She had assured me that her love for this new world we created would be everlasting. And for thousands of years, it was. But even the best of us grow weary.

She left for Eternity, and in her absence, something bitter in me grew. Time became a punishment instead of a reprieve, and the Void Magic I had so lovingly blessed upon those Solana cared for was now a curse without her here. Thousands of years have passed, and the magic continues to morph and shift, forming something more sentient than it had ever been.

And I have been left to rot, alone save for one being who tests my will at every opportunity. I thought I might use her to end this madness, that the deal she made would set in motion the events needed to finally free me. But it seems fate is more fickle a mistress than I anticipated. So now it is time to take things into my own hands. Now it is time to remind those who have forgotten just how powerful I can be.

Now it is time I usher in the beginning of the end.

Rhea, Bahira, Aria, and Myla will return in the fourth and final book of The Five Realms Series.

Acknowledgements

Friends, how did we get here? Truly, that is what I have been asking myself since the moment I finished the manuscript of this book. I said this for COSAT, and I will no doubt say this when it is time to write the acknowledgements for the final book, but Thrones was the most difficult book I've written to date. It's gritty, raw, emotional, and a technical undertaking in a way that really was experienced by trial through fire. My biggest hope is that you've fallen so in love with these characters that you don't mind the story was long or that it hurt or that it deviated from where I think a lot of third books in a series go. Rhea, Bahira, Aria, and Myla are such integral parts of my life, each of them carrying a small piece of me in a way that is personal, but they also represent what it is to be women in a world that was built to tear them down. At the core of my storytelling, I have always weaved two threads: one being that hope can arise in the least likely of places and always at the time we need it most, and the other being that strength, as witnessed by our four heroines, can look different for everyone. I can't wait to bring you the conclusion to the series, and cheers to you for surviving the mayhem of this book!

To my editor and friend, Allie, for which this book (and series) would not exist: thank you. Thank you for dedicating so much of your time to helping me hash out this world and characters. Thank you for loving them as much as I do (sometimes even more, let's be honest), and thank you for being my biggest supporter, even when I'm sure that what I'm writing is garbage. There is no Five Realms without you!

To my husband, thank you for letting me chase this dream. For being beyond supportive. I can write the best male leads because I have you for inspiration. And to my babies, Leia and Isla, I love you dearly, and everything I do is in honor of you.

To Sheila, Gretchen, and Whit, thank you for always being a safe spot to come to. For offering your advice, insight, and friendship in an industry that can sometimes feel isolating and lonely. Thank you for walking me off multiple hypothetical ledges as I struggled to bring this book to readers. I look up to you all, and am beyond grateful to have you in my life.

To Ashley, thank you for being my best friend and also joining me on this author journey. Life, and authoring, is more joyous with you in it. And thank you for bringing the Books & Banter Babes into my life. Girlies, I love you all so, so much.

To my beta readers, Reenie, Kimberly, Heather, Ash, and Katie. Thank you for willing to be the first set of eyes on my books. Your feedback and reactions helped power me through getting this book out.

Finally, thank you to *you*, the reader, for embarking on this epic journey. For your hype and your love. Nothing I achieve is possible without you!

See you for the finale!

Jenessa loves romantasy so much, she wrote her own book in the genre. The Five Realms series is an epic fantasy romance series with multiple POVs, romances, and storylines. It spans across four different fairytale retellings, and is planned as 4.5 book series. These are not interconnected standalones and must be read in publishing order. When not causing chaos for the pretend world of

Olymazi, she can be found hanging out on bookstagram or fangirling over Pedro Pascal edits.

You can follow her on Instagram and Tiktok at @jenessalikes

Make sure to subscribe to her newsletter for the latest information on her writing and books!

https://www.jenessaren.com/